Born Audrey Cooper just before the Second World War, Audrey Reimann lived in Macclesfield in Cheshire where she was educated at the Macclesfield Grammar School for Girls.

After she married she lived for many years in Southport in Lancashire before her husband's work took them to live in Scotland.

'Southport and Edinburgh are where I have spent my adult life,' she says. 'My three children are Lancastrians, my three grandchildren are Scots. I have not lived there for thirty years but my dreams are all set in Macclesfield. Macclesfield is where I belong.'

She says she is haunted by that medieval town set on an escarpment in the foothills of the Pennines; haunted by old Macclesfield legends; a barrel of treacle rolling down a steep, cobbled street; a court-jester named Maggoty Johnson and the old Saxon called Macca who tilled his field.

This is the third novel by Audrey Reimann to be published by Corgi Books.

*Also by Audrey Reimann*

THE MOSES CHILD
PRAISE FOR THE MORNING

*and published by Corgi Books*

# ALICE
# DAVENPORT

## Audrey Reimann

**CORGI BOOKS**

ALICE DAVENPORT
A CORGI BOOK 0 552 13921 1

First published in Great Britain

PRINTING HISTORY
Corgi edition published 1992
Corgi edition reprinted 1992

Set in Monotype 10/11pt Plantin by Kestrel Data, Exeter

Corgi Books are published by Transworld Publishers Ltd.,
61–63 Uxbridge Road, Ealing, London W5 5SA, in Australia by
Transworld Publishers (Australia) Pty. Ltd., 15–25 Helles
Avenue, Moorebank, NSW 2170, and in New Zealand by
Transworld Publishers (N.Z.) Ltd., 3 William Pickering Drive,
Albany, Auckland.

Printed and bound in Great Britain by
Cox & Wyman Ltd., Reading, Berks.

# Chapter One

As far back as Alice Davenport could remember people said of her, to Mama, 'Alice is the image of you, Clara.'

Alice, very young when it was first said, looked up at her mother and felt a flush of pride seeing Mama's beauty; the large grey eyes glistening in the perfect oval of her mother's face, a long straight nose, the handspan waist above a bustled skirt and the golden-blonde hair Mama wore curled and high at the back in the fashion of the 1890s.

The only difference was in the promise of height Alice showed and in the shape of her mouth. Alice had a full, soft mouth with an upper lip that curled back when she smiled, revealing square white teeth and an expanse of rosy gum.

Mama said, 'If you want a tiny rosebud mouth you must say, "Stewed prunes and prisms", twenty times a day.' And Mama would say it for her, laughing and crying in turns.

Alice Helena Davenport was little more than a child when she realized that her mother was insane.

And as far back as she could remember, because of Mama's 'being excitable' as Papa called her mother's madness, Alice had duties and responsibilities.

The fifth and last nursemaid left them when Alice was about seven years old and it was then that Papa told her, 'It's your duty to help Mama with your sister and brothers.' There were four Davenport children; Alice – then came George and Beatrice with barely a year between them – and last came Leopold who was two years younger than Beatrice.

She had always known that Mama was 'excitable' and different but Alice Helena Davenport was fourteen and almost grown up before she discovered that her father was not God.

Captain Charles Davenport, a medical officer at the military hospital in Chester, was a regular army officer who wore his best blue uniform when he took his children to church. Papa was tall and handsome with sandy-fair hair and crinkling blue eyes. And as Alice was the eldest and, in the eyes of her brothers and sister, their father's favourite, she stood on his right-hand side in church, proud of her position as Papa's right-hand girl, yet confused about her position in God's sight.

Once there had been a baptism and she had heard the words, 'A Child of God'. She had seen pictures of Jesus but not one of God though she was sure he had sandy-fair hair and blue eyes.

Prayers were said to God the Father. Hymns asked 'Heavenly Father Send Thy Blessings' so that for many years Papa and God were confused in her young child's mind. Alice was only sure of one thing – she loved Papa much more than she loved God. Like God, Papa commanded respect and instant obedience from his children without once raising his voice to them. He had never needed to.

Mama was joyful and bright, holding and cuddling her children, filling the house with her gaiety, filling Alice's head with song and rhyme and story-telling. To Alice she seemed like a beautiful fairy queen who could wave the magic wand of her presence over everything. When Mama was well nobody noticed the dusty, untidy house, the half-open drawers with their contents spilling out, the books and clothes and occasional plates of food littering the sofa and the dining table. Nobody noticed that the big, tall sideboard was heaped with hats and cups, shoes and pencils, scissors and bottles of cordial; when Mama was well.

But hunger and cold had always been a part of their lives for Mama was an improvident, erratic housekeeper who gave away to tramps, beggars and the downright feckless the money Papa gave her for food. Mama's days were filled with haphazard attempts to manage a home and family and with injunctions to her children to 'Be quiet when Papa comes home. Papa cannot make medical discoveries unless he has a tranquil house.'

When the house was tranquil Papa spent hours in his attic laboratory, making and mixing medicines. He had patented one and was working on another. And it was just as well that Papa was inventive, Alice came to know, for a captain's pay was barely enough to bring up a family of four, even though their dark and lofty town house came free. It was an army house on a main road, a mile from the military hospital and a short ride by horse-tram from the barracks and the other officers' married quarters.

Apart from the injunctions for quietness when Papa was home, Mama could never bear to chastise them and George and Leopold grew noisy and wild. Alice was always spoken of as 'the responsible, good child' and Beatrice was a pale and timid girl who cried a lot. But there had been no need for Mama to tell them to behave well when Papa was home because his homecoming was the best part of the day. When Papa returned from the army hospital he'd hold Mama in his arms and kiss her upturned face and say 'What sort of a day did you have, my darling?' and 'Have the children been good?'

Mama would reach up for a kiss. 'They are impossible, Charley!' she would laugh in his arms adding, 'I'll make something of them, in time.' Papa would smile at them and pat them on the head and tell them to remember always to be obedient to Mama. The relief when Papa came home was immediate. Their father's even-tempered strictness was the only stability his four children knew.

For Mama was given to sudden changes of mood with spells of calm between them. The calm times were the very best times; weeks, sometimes months on end, of happiness in the house when Papa went up to his attic to make his medicines. Downstairs Mama would be singing in her clear voice, 'I Dream-ed I Dwe-elt in Mar-ah-ah-ble Halls' or 'Twas the Last Ro-ose o-of Sum-mer, Le-eft Bloo-oo-ooming Alone' and reciting poetry by the hour. Mama's stories and poems could move them all to laughter or tears.

Following the calm would come wilder moods with quick nervous bouts of laughter and no bedtimes. Then Papa would see to the children when he came home; bathing them with gentle hands, feeding them and tucking them into bed. And when Mama was in one of these moods it was frightening for she went out into the city dressed strangely, humming to herself on the horse-trams, talking to strangers in the street and ordering lavishly from the shops.

New clothes would be made for them all. The table would be laden with delicacies, no attempt would be made to clean the house but Mama would put on her pretty clothes and amuse them all. There was a lot of laughter, wild laughter and relieved laughter, as well as extravagance, when Mama was in a frenzy.

These moods were shorter-lived than the calm times, no more than a week or two before they changed in an instant, without warning, from wild gaiety to black depression and, since the mood of Mama was the mood of the house, tears followed close behind the laughter; tears when Mama could not sleep, tears when Mama cried a lot and gave away their new clothes and their treasured possessions to the poor, and tears when another long-suffering domestic gave notice, saying that nobody should have to work under these conditions.

And Papa would try to comfort them. He'd gather them around him and talk about love and honour and truth and loyalty and not telling anybody about Mama's excitable state. There was always a threat somewhere that 'If they told – they might be brought in.' 'If they told' Mama would be 'certified'. The bogey-men of their nightmares were magistrates and receiving officers, for these men would put Mama into a lunatic asylum, if they told anyone.

After Papa had spoken and put them on their honour not to tell anyone about Mama's illness, Aunt Harriet would be sent for. The depression always took a few weeks, and many bottles of Papa's medicine, before it left her. And three times a day Mama had to be coaxed to take a tablespoonful of bitter, purple medicine whose formula – Pot. Brom. and Nux Vomica – Alice would remember to her dying day.

The medicine took weeks to cure Mama but eventually she began to smile again and a tonic, a pretty bright yellow with a dry pleasant taste, would be ordered for her and Mama would return to normal.

Alice realized they were poor when she was about seven or eight years old but, since Mama had no friend but Aunt Harriet and they did not mix with the other army families, their poverty was not obvious to outsiders. Being poor was never spoken of inside the family either, for Papa wanted them to keep up appearances.

His strictures were 'Never let the side down,' and 'Honour above all.' Papa often took Alice aside and spoke about honour. She would promise some little thing to him and he'd say 'Word of honour?' or 'On your honour?' and she'd give a little salute and say, 'Honour bright.' But they all knew that as well as honour, appearances were what counted. Appearances mattered to Papa. The family must appear to be comfortable.

For her own part, as well as appearing comfortable, Alice wanted to appear normal and was afraid that outsiders might see how different, how abnormal, they all were. When things were bad with Mama, Alice, secretly wondering if she were letting Papa and the side down, would look at other children's mothers and wish

Mama to be like them; quiet, ordinary women who wore sturdy shoes and brown wool coats and brown felt hats with a straight brim; women with broad chests and pursed lips. She knew just the sort of woman Papa could keep up appearances with.

In time she'd come to despise the pretence that went with keeping up appearances and would vow to herself that once she was a mama, with a home and children of her own she would never pretend, or live in hungry poverty. But that was much later and while she was still young and since it was so important to Papa that they hid their poverty from outsiders Alice learned to mend and darn at a very early age. She could do the neatest patching, with tiny secure stitching, by the time she was ten years old. Papa had taught her.

She had grown very close to Papa by the time she was ten and had begun to ask questions but never had the courage to ask the most puzzling questions of all; 'Why, when Papa was so good and handsome and strict, like God, didn't he make Mama obey the rules he imposed upon the children?' and 'Why did she, Alice, have so many duties and responsibilities and Mama have none?' and 'Why did Papa give orders to the children yet never say a stern word to Mama?'

Then at this time Papa sent her to confirmation classes and she began to understand a little. She learned her catechism and the commandments. Number five was 'Honour thy Father and thy Mother.' She learned the questions and answers and could recite in her clear, carrying voice '. . . To keep my hands from picking and stealing, and my tongue from evil-speaking, lying and slandering. To keep my body in temperance, soberness and chastity: not to covet nor desire other men's goods; but to learn and labour truly to get mine own living, and to do my duty . . .'

She was a diligent pupil and tried to understand it all. She honoured her father and mother. She supposed that washing every day kept her body in the way that she promised. One day she wanted to earn her own living. And every day she was dutiful.

By the time she was twelve, Papa had taught her to do invisible mending on the boys' jackets and trousers; pulling threads of the material from inside the seams and weaving them across the holes until the garments looked as good as new. Nobody, seeing Captain Davenport's children in the clean clothes Alice repaired, would have guessed that they lived in such wretched poverty and that their Mama was so different from all the others.

They went to a small private school where the fees and the standard of tuition were very low. And the only difference the other polite little pupils might find between themselves and the Davenports was that the Davenport children did not accept invitations.

'Never accept invitations,' Papa said to each one of them when they started school. 'Never bring friends to the house. Mama cannot have too much excitement.'

Alice dutifully refused the invitations, though she would have liked to go to a birthday party. She was not sure she would like the games but she knew without question that she would have liked the cake.

Cakes seemed to Alice to be symbolic of all that was absent in their lives: colour and richness, order and care. Cakes were miraculous; from the ordinariness of flour and sugar and butter and eggs and fruit came the astonishing perfection of a round, perfectly-risen cake. And afterwards the marvel could be hidden like a lovely secret under coatings of almond paste and sugar icing and the miracle transformed into a confection which the family could celebrate and share.

So birthday party invitations came and were refused and Alice could bake a birthday cake by the time she was eleven. And as the years went by more and more often the cry would go up, 'But Clara! I gave you the money only yesterday. What have you done with it?'

Since Mama never knew where the money went, Papa had come to rely on Alice to keep the household accounts.

By the time she was thirteen she had an old head on her shoulders and was in charge of the household shopping. It was about this time, when Alice was growing into a woman, that she realized that Mama's black moods were steadily getting worse, that the happy periods of calm between them were growing shorter.

Mama was between moods now for only days, not weeks on end. Mama would be happy on these few days, singing and story-telling, weaving her spell about them as only Mama could but these were becoming rare glimpses of the old Mama. At other times she would still be in bed at tea-time, unwashed, her hair straggling about her shoulders, wrapped in a shawl, the house strewn with the litter and the detritus of her foolish day; a book torn to pieces, a string of cut-out dancing dolls, incongruous messages written in soap on the windows. And Mama would be insulting and hateful to Alice – accusing her of picking and stealing and her tongue of evil-speaking, lying and slandering – as Alice went about the house tidying before Papa came home.

Aunt Harriet would be summoned by telegram but, before she arrived, at the end of such days Papa would talk to Alice when at last order was restored. He would find her, white-faced and occasionally in tears, sitting by the kitchen fire, saying 'I love Mama. I know I have a duty to help her, but I am finding it so hard. Why does she behave like this? Why?'

'Nobody knows.' Papa would shake his head. 'There is no cure. But she is such a wonderful woman when she is well. We must remember that.'

Once he had said sadly, 'Your Mama thinks she is the linchpin of the family. But she isn't, always.' That was as far as Papa had ever gone in making excuses for Mama, and Alice would wonder about her darling father who was kind, clever and honourable and loved by everybody - what was it he loved so much about Mama? Alice loved Mama too; they were alike after all. They were very much alike in looks. But it was hard to feel love for her in a

12

cold and dirty house when Mama was in one of her wicked moods.

'Unconventional,' Aunt Harriet used to say every time she saw the untidy mess that was home to the Davenports. 'Yours must be the only army family living in such disorder.'

Aunt Harriet, Mama's unmarried cousin, was conservative, comfortably-off and well-intentioned. She had started to visit them every few weeks, regardless of Mama's state of mind, from her house in Southport. They had never seen their aunt's house. The Davenport family never went away, or visited.

Aunt Harriet either did not see, or else she pretended not to notice, that Mama was not right in the head. 'Try to keep the place tidy,' was the most she ever said.

'What does it matter?' Mama always answered. 'Charley doesn't complain.'

'Perhaps Charles would like to entertain; to invite his fellow officers to the house, Clara,' Aunt Harriet had answered on the day Alice would remember ever afterwards as the day on which she grew up; the twelfth of October in the year of 1898, her fourteenth birthday.

Mama, in one of her happy moods, was wearing her jet beads and a beautiful scarlet dress with a small bustle. For the last few days she had been calm. 'Charley and the children are entertainment enough for me,' she answered. 'And I don't have help in the house.'

'But you should, Clara.' Aunt Harriet had two servants; a cook and a parlourmaid to help her. 'Why don't you?'

'They never stayed,' Mama answered. 'They came and went. They came in fair weather and left when I needed them most and, besides, I can't bear all that tidying up. I can never find a thing.' She gave a little smile here and added, 'We employ a washerwoman every Monday. Charley has to look right. He insists on having his linen well-laundered.'

The house was happy again in accordance with Mama's

13

mood. It was not quite as untidy as usual since Aunt Harriet brought a little order to the place. When Aunt Harriet was here there was enough to eat at supper-time. Aunt Harriet sent out for extras.

Alice, who had come in from school a few minutes earlier, flung her satchel across the room and heard it land with a thud on the pile of papers behind the battered sofa. 'I'm not going back, Mama,' she said.

'What's all this?' Aunt Harriet drew herself up to her full, impressive height. She was tall, slim and ramrod straight with a haughty air and a kind of remote, cold beauty. She was thirty-eight. Papa's age. She raised her eyebrows. 'What will your Papa say about it? You may regret tomorrow what you do in haste today . . .' She looked at Mama. 'Or something like that . . .'

'It's no good, Harriet,' Mama said. 'We don't know what gets into her but once Alice digs her heels in she won't be budged.'

Alice smiled at Mama. It was not often that she did go against the tide, in fact she had only done it once before but today something had 'got into her' as Mama called it. She'd known for certain that she would not stay on at school. All at once she didn't give a fig for school, for anything Papa might have to say or for regrets that might come tomorrow.

She said to Aunt Harriet, 'I can read and I can write. I'm very good at arithmetic. I can play the piano without music. I can't learn any more at that school. I'm going to stay home and help Mama.'

'Why don't you stay on?' Aunt Harriet asked again. 'You're a clever girl. I've told your mother that I'll pay for more education for you . . .'

'No,' Alice said firmly. Aunt Harriet must know that Papa would not allow anyone else to educate his children. She was in the act of pulling off her school raincoat and hanging it on the arm of Mama's chair when she saw the look of annoyance on her aunt's face. Placing the coat over her arm she said, 'I'll hang this up in the back of my cupboard. I won't need it again.' She looked at Mama. 'Did you buy the icing sugar?'

She had baked a birthday cake yesterday and was going to ice it before Papa came home. Yesterday Mama had promised to bring it to the table after supper when everyone would give their little gifts to her. There was to be a special gift this time Mama said. And always, on birthdays, they had a family evening with a hot supper followed by acting, singing, recitations, party-pieces and magic tricks. It was a family tradition and one of the few unvarying things in their disordered way of life. Alice had brought about the tradition. A family needed traditions.

Later, after supper, Alice knew that Aunt Harriet would give her ten shillings. She always gave them money for their birthday. Mama usually took it from them after she'd gone, saying that it was Aunt Harriet's way of giving money to herself, to Mama. If Aunt Harriet offered money directly, Mama said, it would be too embarrassing. It would imply that they needed charity.

Normally they didn't mind giving up the birthday money. What they had always hated was sitting down afterwards, taking a letter to Mama's dictation. 'Dear Aunt Harriet, Thank you for the birthday money which I spent on . . .' Then Mama would decide what it should have been. '. . . on a beautiful picture book . . . and some toy soldiers . . .'

This time Alice was going to refuse to hand the money over. Mama would waste it and Alice wanted to buy something for herself, just this once. She needed stockings and last week she had fallen madly in love with a pair of eight-and-elevenpenny boots of ice-blue kid. They were still there in a bootmaker's shop she passed on the way home from school. When a girl was fourteen, had left school and grown up she should have a little say about her own life.

'Darling!' Mama wailed. 'I forgot the icing sugar! If you run . . .'

Alice tried not to let her annoyance show. Lately she had known resentment like an irrepressible urge come boiling up in her. If it were not for the fact that Papa relied on her she could almost let herself go and tell Mama to make an effort to pull herself together.

She fought back the impulse and said quietly, 'Right. I'll go at once.'

She ran, as she did in the early mornings when Mama would rouse her from sleep, shaking her shoulder and saying, 'Run like the wind. Buy a pennyworth of oats for Papa's porridge,' and she'd get up, dress and fly, gasping for breath, to Dale's little shop a mile away, with the penny Mama had probably taken from Papa whilst he slept.

Today she ran because she didn't want to be seen by Papa who would probably have left the hospital early, knowing it was her birthday.

It was three quarters of an hour before she arrived home again, hot and breathless, to find that Mama and Aunt Harriet's conversation had not moved much further on. They were sitting at the kitchen table which for once was half clear and Aunt Harriet was launching into a mild but meant criticism of Mama. 'You should play your part, Clara.'

Aunt Harriet made Mama's name sound like Clair-ah. Papa called Mama Klara, as if it rhymed with Tara. It sounded beautiful when Papa said Klara in his deep, melodious voice.

Mama didn't reply. She went on sipping tea.

Aunt Harriet said, 'You're an officer's wife. You should call on the ladies, take afternoon tea. You'd meet some very nice people. It would be good for you, Clara.'

She put her cup down and leaned her head sharply to one side, like a parrot does. 'Have I mentioned my new friend? Did I tell you about Lady Cranston-Bartlett?'

'What's her Christian name?' said Mama. 'I might remember if I knew . . .'

'Oh. We're not on such friendly terms, dear.'

'Then you can hardly call her your new friend, can you?'

Alice wanted to laugh but made do with a little smile that Aunt Harriet would miss. Aunt Harriet courted people of a higher social standing than herself but this was certainly her best catch so far. A lady, no less!

'She is very old and lonely, Clara. She has no family,' Aunt Harriet explained. 'And you know how formal old ladies can be . . .'

'I know very little about old ladies,' Mama said, 'but I expect she's looking for a companion. She has latched on to you, Harriet. You're far too generous with your favours.'

When Mama was well, as she was today, she could be very amusing. Aunt Harriet wouldn't realize that Mama was having a bit of fun. Aunt Harriet would think she herself had put the wrong interpretation on her cousin's remark about generosity with favours. It was naughty of Mama, for she sat there with her face showing nothing but kind concern. Of course Mama used to be a very good Shakespearian actress.

Alice pressed her lips together to stop a laugh escaping, gave Mama a knowing look and excused herself. She was choking with laughter when she went into the little scullery beyond the kitchen and began to ice and decorate her cake.

When it was done she washed and dried a pretty plate, slid the cake carefully on to it and put it on the pantry sill so that the icing would dry in the cool draught of air from the open window. Then she went upstairs to change into her dress.

It was an airy bedroom. She and Beatrice kept their room tidy so that it was the one place in the house where they could sit, talk and read. Beatrice was only twelve but in some ways, Alice believed, the wiser girl. Once she had passed her early childhood Beattie had developed a manner of calm acceptance and never fretted about Mama and Papa or asked 'Why?'

Beatrice, pale and blonde like herself, was standing at the washstand in the chimney alcove, using the water.

'Leave some for me, Beattie,' Alice said. 'Papa's not home yet.'

'Don't look on the windowsill,' Beattie warned as she splashed. 'I haven't wrapped your brooch! Ooh! Forget what I said.'

Alice smiled. 'There's plenty of time. Mama's in a good mood today. She's all happy and acting the part of . . . Ooh! I don't know.'

Beattie said. 'She must have been a wonderful actress, Alice. No wonder Papa . . .'

'Yes.' Alice sat on the bed and watched Beattie. Only last night Alice had asked Mama to tell her again, how she and Papa met.

Beattie came and sat on her bed, facing Alice. She held the towel in her hands and said, 'Tell me again. Tell me how they fell in love. How Papa proposed to her.'

Alice couldn't resist the sight of Beattie's eager face. 'All right. I'll tell you.'

She settled herself and began. 'You know that Mama was left an orphan and she'd gone to live with Aunt Harriet and her family?'

'Yes.'

'You remember all about that? How Harriet's parents were very strict, but kind?'

'Yes.'

'And how determined Mama was?' Alice smiled here.

Mama, brought up by her father, was sixteen when he died, leaving her in the care of the retired greengrocers; the strict and worthy aunt and uncle whose only knowledge of the theatre came from sitting through the church pantomime every Christmas. Mama had gone against her own father's wishes and had just got her first part in her first play. And though her guardians were worried about it they were assured by Mama that Shakespeare was not low, riff-raff theatre. They were good people who understood that Mama could not break her word. But she was

18

to leave the theatre company after this one play. The only condition they could enforce on their wilful niece was to insist that their own daughter, Harriet, should accompany her everywhere, including the theatre. Harriet was to watch over Mama until her contract ended.

Harriet had proved to be a perfect chaperone, glad of the chance to escape for a few hours from the restricted life she led with her dull, circumspect parents.

'Yes,' said Beattie. 'Go on.'

Alice began to enjoy herself. 'Papa was tall and clever and very attractive to girls. He was very handsome then—'

'He's very handsome now,' Beattie said.

'Yes. Don't interrupt,' Alice warned as Beattie settled herself against her pillows.

'Papa was a young army doctor,' Alice continued. 'He was six years older than Mama and he and some other officers had been invited first to see a performance of *A Midsummer Night's Dream* which was being staged by a Cheshire theatrical company . . . and afterwards to a supper party . . .'

'Yes. I know all about that,' Beattie said quickly. 'Never mind the facts. Get on with the story.'

Alice went on, 'Papa was so smitten by Clara Walker, who played the role of Helena, that he had eyes for no other girl from the moment she walked on to the stage and into his life.'

Alice smiled at the awed expression on Beattie's round face. She loved telling Beattie this story, especially the bit that was coming.

'Mama had been placed beside him at supper and she said that for both of them it was as if nobody else in the room had any existence. It was as if the rest of the world were half-people; people with only half the awareness and wit; half the beauty and responsiveness of themselves.'

Beattie's eyes were like saucers.

'They left the party after supper. Papa escorted her and Aunt Harriet home and when he left her at her door he whispered his parting words. "Clara. I want no-one but you. But I will not share you with an audience. You must choose . . . the stage or me. Tomorrow I want your answer." '

'Ooh.' Beattie sighed. 'He wouldn't have been allowed to marry an actress – being an officer . . .'

'I don't know about that,' Alice smiled. 'But Papa told her that he didn't sleep for a second that night. He had fallen madly and hopelessly in love with her on midsummer night. It was just as if King Oberon's magic Love-in-Idleness juice had been dropped on to his own eyelids. He'd never in his life love and need anyone but his darling Clara.'

'And then . . .' Beattie asked.

Alice said, 'Papa went back to the theatre the following night. And it was at the final curtain that Mama did it.' She'd have to stand, to dramatize it.

'Papa had risen to his feet.' She slid off the bed and stood, feet apart, arms raised.

'He lifted his arms towards the stage and cried out to her, "Forsake the stage, Helena! Leap into my arms!" '

'And Mama leaped!'

'Mama leaped!'

Alice dropped down on to the bed again. Mama had made a point of saying that the leap came on the last performance and not until the cast came on stage to take the second round of applause. She assured Alice that she would not have done it otherwise

But it always seemed to Alice like a fairy-story; Mama's forsaking the stage, forsaking everything, to leap into Papa's arms.

Last night, when Mama was so easy to talk to and Mama's mood was one of her best, Alice asked 'Do you think I'll ever fall in love?' and 'How did you know?' and 'How can anyone be sure?'

And Mama had gone thoughtful and confessed, 'I can't tell you if it will happen to you. But I'm sure you'll know if it does. I knew. I knew the moment it happened.'

'I hope I marry the right man,' Alice had answered. 'If I marry at all.'

'I hope you marry your first love, Alice,' Mama said. She had looked into Alice's eager face and smiled. 'You see, I believe that if a girl and a man fall in love as your Papa and I did, in an instant, they should marry at once and their marriage will be blessed.'

'Supposing it doesn't happen to me,' Alice said. 'Or suppose it happens and I don't know it has?'

Mama said, 'You will know your own moment of glory.'

Still, Alice did not understand what it was, what love was, this great powerful feeling that could sweep a girl off her feet. It was all mixed up somewhere.

Her own reasoning had been; you fell in love, then, knowing you had fallen in love, you married. Then, when you were married, you lived as man and wife and, when you wanted a child, you did the thing that made babies. Alice knew how these things came about. Papa had told her all the mechanics of everything. Alice could not believe that everyone might fall in love; nor that everyone would want to do these things; least of all Mama and Papa whose love was all tender concern for one another's health and happiness.

Mama also said that she thought love at first sight such as hers and Papa's could only happen to the young. Then she had recited one of her favourite poems, the Lord Byron one that went:

Oh, talk not to me of a name great in story;
The days of our youth are the days of our glory;
And the myrtle and ivy of sweet two-and-twenty
Are worth all your laurels though ever so plenty.

What are garlands and crowns to the brow that is wrinkled?
'Tis but as a dead-flower with May-dew besprinkled.
Then away with all such from the head that is hoary!
What care I for wreaths that can only give glory!

Oh, Fame! if I e'er took delight in thy praises,
'Twas less for the sake of thy high-sounding phrases,
Than to see the bright eyes of the dear one discover,
She thought that I was not unworthy to love her.

There chiefly I sought thee, there only I found thee;
Her glance was the best of the rays that surround thee;
When it sparkled o'er aught that was bright in my story,
I knew it was love, and I felt it was glory.

'No wonder Mama leaped,' Beattie was saying. 'I expect Papa was irresistible.'

Alice got up from the bed and took her dress from the wardrobe, hung it over the brass rail on the end of her bed, took off her school serge skirt and her white blouse for the last time and kicked off the ankle-boots of brown leather. In the glass that hung above the washstand she could see her thin shoulders rising bony and white above her chemise and camisole. All her bones stuck out. Her petticoat hung loose over her narrow hips. She was hungry.

'What are we having for supper?' Beattie asked. 'I didn't see anything. The dining-room table's still covered in clothes and things.'

'I told Mama we'd be needing the table.' Alice tipped cold water from the jug into the china bowl and started to wash her hands and face. Now she came to think about it, when she put her cake in the pantry she had not seen the pork pie Mama was going to put in the oven. She hoped Mama hadn't forgotten to peel the potatoes and carrots, as well as forgetting the icing sugar.

She started to hurry. 'Where are George and Leopold?' she asked over her shoulder.

'Mama sent them out for something when they came in from school,' Beattie said quickly. 'Probably something she wanted for supper.'

'That's all right then,' Alice said.

The boys were dutiful these days though they had not

always been good. George, who looked so like Papa, was a year younger than Alice. George hated school. Last year he had started to play truant. Papa had lectured him for a whole hour, about decency and integrity and honour, about never going back on his word, once given, never letting the side down. George went to school after that.

But they had all agreed to hide Leopold's crimes from Papa, for Leopold, though only ten years old, always had money – and the wrong Papa would never forgive was dishonesty. Young Leopold never went to bed hungry. There was always a paper bag in Leopold's bed, full of stale buns or broken biscuits – and such things did not come free. But Leopold was generous with them and none of them asked where he got the money.

'Help me with these hooks, Beattie.' Alice stood with her back to Beatrice, pressing her hands hard against her waist so the sides of the dress would close. Soon this one would be too small and she would have to ask Papa if he could afford to pay the dressmaker again. 'Has Mama told you what my special treat is?'

'No.' Beattie fastened her hooks with quick fingers.

'What time is it?' Alice asked as she pulled the hairbrush through her long straight hair and spread it about her shoulders.

Beattie said, 'Quarter past six.'

'Are you ready?' Alice turned to look at Beattie who was wearing the pale grey dress with a lace collar that last year had been Alice's best. Beattie had straight blonde hair which she wore tonight tied with a large bow at the back of her neck. 'You look very pretty, Beattie.'

'So do you.'

Alice grinned, lifted the hem of her pink dress and slid her slim feet into Mama's old cuban-heeled shoes of black patent leather which she wore indoors. 'Are we ready, then?'

'Excited?' Beattie asked.

'Of course I am. I'm going to keep Aunt Harriet's money this time.'

'I'll bet you don't. You'll lose your nerve when Mama asks for it.'

'It will be too late,' Alice said with a confident air. 'I'm going to spend it tomorrow.'

'Come on then.'

They went down the grimy stairs, placing their feet with great care on the threadbare carpet and, to Alice's surprise, found Papa standing in the hall, in his blues - his best dress uniform as if for a night in the officer's mess.

Alice smiled and was about to ask why he was dressed up when the kitchen door opened and Mama and Aunt Harriet came into the hall.

Papa stood there for a moment, handsome and tall, blue eyes crinkling as he smiled at them all.

He went forward and kissed Mama on her upturned face, then said to Aunt Harriet, 'I didn't know you were here, Harriet.' He kissed her cheek and Aunt Harriet went brightly pink and all girlish and fluttery as she always did for Papa.

They followed Mama who led the way into the sitting room instead of the dining room. Had they conspired together behind her back? Were they going to pretend they had forgotten her birthday? Where was the big surprise?

Alice went quietly in with the others and saw that George and Leopold were already seated. They got to their feet as soon as Papa went into the room.

'Sit down,' Papa said. Then in his deep, melodious voice and smiling at Mama said, 'The colonel's lady was asking after you, Clara. "When can we hope to see Mrs Davenport at one of our ladies' charity teas?" she said.' Papa smiled indulgently at Mama as he spoke.

Mama lifted her determined little chin and said, 'I abhor ladies' charity occasions, Charley. You should just see those silly, simpering women.'

Papa was still smiling as she went on indignantly. 'They take upon themselves their husbands' rank. A

24

subaltern's young lady, for example, has to almost genuflect to the wife of a major.'

Papa was chuckling. 'But Clara . . .' he protested, as if he really meant it.

Mama was on her high horse. 'I bow to nobody. You know I don't.'

Papa, who believed in order and hierarchy, pretended to look upset for a moment then he put out his hands in a wide, open gesture to Mama. Then, to Alice's amazement, he nodded to herself and Beattie and the others to dismiss them, to send them out of the room.

And everyone obeyed. They all started to file out into the hall and make towards the dining room.

Alice hung back, sure that this was all part of a silly game. Mama had told her only yesterday that she was to have a special treat for her birthday. In a moment she was sure, Papa and Mama would say 'Happy birthday, Alice!'

What Papa said was, 'I am dining at the Grosvenor Hotel this evening Clara. A regimental dinner.' He bent to take Mama into his arms and, as he did so, saw Alice.

He straightened up, frowned in annoyance and waved a hand to send her packing. And Alice knew that he had forgotten her birthday. And before the tears of disappointment rolled down her face and before she was out of earshot she knew that they were in one another's arms for she heard Papa's voice, all low and loving saying, 'Klara! Klara! My beautiful lawless lover. Wait up for me, my darling. I need you so much.'

And, blinded with tears, she had slipped up the stairs to compose herself before she faced the family. For she understood then what it was that made all these different things come together; love and honour, the meaning of marriage and the power of passionate love. Papa and Mama were madly in love. They always would be.

She was an outsider. She had grown up.

# Chapter Two

At Christmas that year it was announced that Mama was expecting a baby and that the child would be born in June.

The waiting months were the happiest Alice had known, for Mama was well and happy. There were no storms or depressions and the manic side of her disease never surfaced. She and Alice drew much closer to one another and would sit, heedless of the domestic disarray surrounding them, reading aloud the poetry and novels Mama liked for an hour or so every day. One evening would be fixed for ever in Alice's memory.

It was May, the day before Papa's birthday and Alice had gone late in the evening to put the finishing touches to his birthday cake. Papa was out at a regimental dinner and Mama had come into the kitchen to take some barley water for the heartburn that was troubling her.

Alice smiled. The cake was done but for the bow. All that remained was for her to tie the satin ribbon on a slant across the chocolate icing that was good and dry.

'Pretty cake. It looks lovely.' Mama sat opposite her, on the kitchen chair, sipping her barley water slowly.

'You've done well, Mama. Not to get anything worse than heartburn,' Alice said. 'You've not had one of your . . .' She looked quickly at Mama in case speaking about her mania was upsetting, though Mama had spoken about it to Alice once or twice. Alice had come to believe that if Mama spoke about it, it helped keep the attacks at bay.

Mama's grey eyes were sparkling tonight. She smiled

and said, 'Your Papa thinks they have something to do with the glands. He says that since the trouble started at the menarche it will probably cease when I reach middle age.' She looked doubtful and added, 'But I don't know if he's right. It runs in my family. My mother died young.'

Alice wished she had not broached the subject. She said quickly, 'Will I suffer from the same . . . ?'

'No.' Mama sipped her barley water, smiled and assured her, 'You look like me, Alice. But you have enough of your father's strong character in you to balance my weakness.'

'Don't talk like that, Mama. It's not a weakness. You can't help yourself.' Alice made an adjustment to the ribbon on the cake and thought to change the subject.

She pulled out and flattened the bow loops. 'Why do you never go with Papa to regimental occasions, Mama?' she asked. 'I know you can't today . . .' Her voice trailed off into a fond chuckle as she thought of Mama's condition.

'I detest the army!' Mama spoke sharply and the sharpness made Alice jump and look up quickly.

'My father was an army man,' Mama was saying. 'My young life was Hell on Earth. I was treated more like a cadet than a little girl.'

Alice placed the cake on a plate carefully. 'I didn't know . . .' she said.

Mama said, 'When I was a child I was not allowed to speak unless spoken to. I had to defer and curtsey until I thought I should be bent double all my life.'

Alice wiped her hands on a damp dishcloth when the cake was safely put away on a bare shelf in the pantry, then seeing that though Mama's face was pink her expression had softened, she asked, 'Were you afraid of your father?'

'No. I wasn't afraid. My father never said a harsh word to me.' There was a hurt look in her expressive grey eyes as she added quietly, 'And he never said a kind one.'

Alice had always wanted an answer to her next question but had not asked before, 'If your father was so strict, why did you defy him and go on the stage?'

Mama's face was beautiful. Tonight she looked young and girlish as she sat there, thinking about her answer.

Alice sat at the opposite side of the table and waited for Mama to speak. When she did, she spoke in her lovely story-telling voice that was soft and intriguing.

'I was starved of colour as a child,' she said. 'I was never given pictures. I lived in a world of the imagination.' She paused for a moment then said, 'Acting is the oldest form of magic, darling. When the early huntsman went to hunt a bull, he'd draw a fine bull on the wall of his cave and show spears and arrows sticking out of it. Then he'd dress up as a bull, singing and dancing to recount his past successes. He believed that if he made the right magic, his hunting would be fruitful.'

Alice loved to hear Mama talk this way.

'When I was fifteen I was taken to the theatre, to see *The Tempest*. It changed my life. I thought, "If I were an actress I could live in the real world and in the world of the imagination at the same time." '

'So how did you . . . ?' Alice asked.

'I went back to my father and acted! I found that I could become a different person. I became bold and challenging and my father threw up his hands and said, "Do what you will." '

'But your father died . . .' Alice prompted her.

'It was a riding accident. Nothing to do with me.'

Mama looked very closely at Alice. 'We can change our very natures by acting a part, Alice. Remember that.'

The magic was gone but Mama had not finished. In a normal voice but still smiling she said, 'Before I acted I felt like a prisoner – bound and chained by rules and regulations. Never bow down before rules and regulations you don't accept, Alice. Be courageous. You are the equal of anyone. If life becomes too difficult, then you can act your way out of it.'

'Is it all the rules and regulations you hate about the army, Mama?'

Mama's smile went suddenly. Her eyes hardened. 'I can't bear the military,' she said. 'Even when there are no wars, fighting men love fighting talk. They pretend that life is one long battle with an enemy. They dress in uniforms. They wear swords and spurs. They make camps, to practise fighting. They make threatening noises . . .'

She stopped, put down her empty cup and stood up. 'Papa doesn't like me to talk like this. Your Papa is first and last a soldier, Alice. His family comes second. His career is the only thing we have ever disagreed about.'

'Did you want him to leave the army?' Alice asked.

'Yes. I wanted nothing but your father.' She managed to smile in a deprecating way, as if apologizing for her past. 'I was so much in love. I wanted him to love me more than he loved the army. I only wanted your Papa. I thought he should feel the same.'

Alice went round the table and put an arm around the tiny form in the billowing dress. 'He does feel the same, Mama,' she said. 'You know that he does. Papa loves you above all.'

That was the last time she and Mama spoke so long and intimately before everything went wrong. The easy pregnancy, the calmness had been too good to last. The black depression came back and for the last weeks before the baby was born the family was plunged into despair.

Mama lay in bed during the day and paced the floor throughout the night. Papa ordered that one of them sit with her at all times and they took it in turns to sit on the end of their mother's bed, listening to her wild ramblings, trying to stay calm under the onslaught of her anger. But it was during the night, when Papa was sleeping at her side, that Mama decided to leave the house for some tortured reason of her own.

She was found, shivering with fever, well into her

labour, sitting on the banks of the Dee in the early morning.

Papa carried her home and five hours later he delivered her of a healthy baby boy. But none of the children saw Mama alive again.

Her heart had failed. Mama was dead.

Mama, beautiful Mama was dead and Papa, after ordering Alice's duties, had thrown himself into his work.

Sometimes she believed that Papa was deserting them. He started rising even earlier than before, to join the cavalry in their early morning drills before he went on medical duty. He needed the exercise he said. He stayed late at the hospital and on at least three evenings each week went to dine in the Officers' Mess.

Alice pitied Papa. His grief must be immeasurable. She tried to understand why he spent so much time away from them. But they were stricken too. There was not enough money and her own work had increased. Papa said that the younger ones were to help. He engaged a wet-nurse and a once-a-week woman to scrub the flag-stone floors and steps. Alice had been ordered to pay their wages from the housekeeping money.

Baby Arthur had become Alice's responsibility and she had come to love her baby brother as if he were her own child. She rocked the crying infant in her arms for hours until the wet-nurse came to feed him. The wet-nurse had told Alice to 'give 'im a drop of cinder-tea if he gets the wind' and Alice dropped red-hot cinders into water, sweetened and strained it and fed the protesting infant the warm sugar-water from a spoon. She could not bear to think that the child might ever be hungry or cold as they had been.

And Papa had refused to allow Aunt Harriet to come to Chester and help out. Papa knew what was right and it was 'not done', he told Alice, for a woman to live in the house of a widower, even when that woman was Mama's cousin.

It was Alice's fifteenth birthday and there was no question this year of any kind of celebration. Upstairs, in the room that four months before had been hastily arranged as a nursery, the wet-nurse, Mrs Moss, was feeding baby Arthur whilst her own one-year-old toddler had a temper tantrum. Alice could hear it all from the kitchen where she was stirring the stewpot over the range.

She turned to Beattie who had just come in from school. 'Run to Dale's, Beattie,' she ordered. 'Ask for some Benger's Food and Fairchild's Peptogenic powders.'

'What for?' Beattie said. 'Is Arthur sick?'

'I don't think Mrs Moss has enough milk. I'm going to wean him.'

'What will Papa say?' Beattie's sweet round face wore a worried expression.

Alice banged the lid back on the pot, threw the wooden spoon into the sink and placed her hands on her hips in a defiant attitude. 'I don't care, Beattie. Papa can say what he likes! I've taken all the orders I can suffer from Papa.'

'But Papa says that mother's milk is what an infant needs . . .' Beattie began to say.

Alice would not allow her to finish. 'That baby is going to be fed on cow's milk. He is not getting enough mother's milk. If the child's stomach is full then at least he'll sleep. Which is more than any of us has done lately.' She felt as if she might burst into tears at any moment. She had been feeling like this since Mama died.

Beattie put down her schoolbag and came to put an arm across Alice's shoulders. 'All right,' she said. 'Don't cry. I'll stick up for you if Papa . . .'

Alice bit her lip to hold back the tears. 'Papa won't be angry. He's hardly ever at home these days.' She returned the pressure of Beattie's hand and made herself straighten her shoulders. 'But he's coming home early tonight. And I'm going to lay down the law.'

'You can't do that. Papa gives the orders,' Beattie said.

'Run to Dale's, there's a love.' Alice took money from inside the clock on the mantel shelf where she kept it hidden from Leopold. She handed a florin to Beattie. 'Be as quick as you can. I want Arthur fed and asleep before Papa comes home.'

When Beattie had gone, Alice sat down at the kitchen table and rested her head on her forearms in weariness. Tonight she was going to tell Papa that she could not manage the family single-handed. Papa must resign his commission. He was thirty-nine and had been in the army since he'd qualified as a doctor. And Papa had qualified as a doctor at only twenty-three; he had since done sixteen years of army service. Surely sixteen years was enough of soldiering.

She remembered, as she sat there with her head down, how Mama had felt about the army. In this very kitchen Mama had spoken about Papa's love for the army and Alice had sat on the very chair where she was sitting at this moment, thinking about Mama and asking herself, just as Mama had, whether Papa would ever leave the army and put his family first. Papa's word was never challenged and his orders were never disobeyed. As a rule Papa never listened but he must listen to her this time.

A few hours later they all dined together at the big table in the dining room. Alice did not remind anyone that it was her birthday but when they had all finished their meal and were waiting for Papa to give the signal for them to leave the table, Alice screwed up her courage and spoke.

'I want to talk to you. Alone, Papa.' She nodded to the others. 'Clear the table. Put a kettle on for the dishes on the slow plate. I'll see to them later.'

Her demand was so unexpected that every one of them, even Papa, obeyed her. George, Beatrice and Leopold pushed back their chairs and began to take the empty plates away.

Alice walked ahead of Papa into the sitting room where everything was kept tidy since Mama had died. The house was shabby, but clean and cold. Papa went to sit in a fireside armchair. He watched as she closed the door and came to sit opposite to him, then he said, 'Well, Alice?'

'I have come to the end of my tether, Papa.' She tried to make it sound like an ultimatum but the words came out in a hesitant, apologetic way and she had to swallow a lump in her throat.

Papa did not answer her for a few moments and she looked up to see his reaction to her outburst. Papa, though he looked weary, gave a fond smile and said, 'You've been my right-hand girl since Mama died, Alice. I'm proud of you.'

The tears were threatening again. She heard her own voice, thin and high saying, 'I can't do any more . . .'

Papa stood up and held out his hands to her. 'I'm afraid, my darling child, that I have to ask for more.'

She let him help her to her feet and made no attempt to stem the tears. But Papa did not comfort her. He placed a hand firmly upon her shaking shoulder until she had regained control of herself.

Papa repeated, 'I expect a lot of you, Alice. You have always been a good, dutiful daughter.'

She looked at him again and saw that Papa's face was strained and white and all at once she felt low and unworthy. 'What do you mean?'

Papa said quietly, 'On October the ninth the Boers of the Transvaal issued an ultimatum. Yesterday they invaded Natal. The first Cheshire Yeoman, Viscount Belgrave, the Duke of Westminster's heir, has offered himself as ADC to the Governor of the Cape Colony.'

Alice asked in a voice that was all at once cold with fright, 'But what has all this to do with you, Papa?'

Papa looked handsome and stern, very much a remote army officer tonight. 'Our country is at war. Cheshire county will raise and equip two volunteer companies to serve in South Africa. I am honour bound to volunteer. I am a soldier. It's my duty to go.'

Papa's shoulders were held well back. There was a proud look in his eye. It was as if he had been waiting all his life for this opportunity. And if Papa had done sixteen years of army service without once being called upon to serve, then he could not at the outbreak of war even think of resigning his commission. Alice knew this to be so. To resign his commission when his regiment was going to war would be seen as an act of cowardice.

Alice found that her voice had dropped to a mere whisper. 'What about us, Papa? What will we do?'

Papa looked down at her white face and a ghost of a smile crossed his face. 'I am making arrangements for you all to go to Southport. To your Aunt Harriet's home. You will remain there until I return.'

'But . . . Papa . . . suppose you don't . . .' A great lump of fear was tight in Alice's throat.

'It is a skirmish. We expect to see them off in a month or two.' Papa looked at the clock. 'I have to return to camp tonight, Alice,' he said. 'I'll speak to the others before I leave. You will all get your orders tomorrow.'

Then he smiled at her in the old fond way that he had always done, in the way that had always made her heart fill with love for him.

'I didn't forget your birthday, darling,' he said. 'You will find a little gift, on the hall table.'

The gift was a gold locket, containing a miniature of Mama and a tiny loop of Mama's fine blonde hair. Alice cried herself to sleep.

Within two weeks of Papa's announcement their trunks were sent ahead, the Chester house was closed and such furniture as they had was put into a repository. The four of them with baby Arthur were sent to live with their aunt in Southport.

And to Alice it was as if a part of her had been cut away. Childhood was behind her. Memories of Mama were being torn from her; gone from the home Mama had infused with her moods and her vivacity.

34

Though her tasks had become easier for Alice, easier in that she had a little time to herself, inside she was desolate. Every day she longed for Mama's bright presence and Papa's soundness. Every day she mourned Mama's departure from their life and every day she felt Papa's absence.

Every night, when she lay in the soft feather bed in Aunt Harriet's house she was filled with remorse for the times when Mama had irritated and angered her and stung her into a sharp retort. For now she saw no faults in Mama. She had forgotten the angry black moods, the bizarre ways, the carelessness that had been Mama.

At night, in this new luxury, she would wish herself back in the lumpy old bed of her old home. She would cry silent tears into her pillow for all they had lost and she would fall asleep vowing to herself that one day she would become the kind of woman Mama would have been proud of. She was like Mama. Everyone said so. And if life became too difficult, she would do as Mama had said. She would act her way out of her difficulties.

But difficulties seldom came, for ordinary life was much more pleasant in the Southport house where Aunt Harriet kept a cook and a parlourmaid and sent the washing out. The house was larger than their Chester home. This house had three rooms downstairs with a kitchen, scullery and pantry. There were four bedrooms on the first floor and two attic rooms for the servants, reached by a second, back staircase. There was an inside lavatory with a flush system as well as the outside privvy. There was both hot and cold water in the kitchen. It was a modern, convenient house. And it was Aunt Harriet's house, not theirs. Alice felt as if they were guests in it though Aunt Harriet told them to treat it as their own home.

They were not used to these high standards. Alice had to be reminded not to shout in her clear, ringing voice to her brothers and sister from one end of the house to the other. She had to be told to change into afternoon wear though she had few enough changes of dress. She was expected not to speak about anything but trivialities in front of the parlourmaid. She was constantly being corrected in the most tactful way by Aunt Harriet, about everything – her deportment, her facial expressions, her manners.

Their table manners were good but in Chester there had been barely enough food and there had been little ceremony at mealtimes. In Chester they had all gathered around the dining-room table when Papa came home and eaten the one course that was their supper. They had never expected more; Papa believed in simplicity and plain food. Papa had insisted that they eat bread, which he said was the staff of life and they had supplemented the bread with a little meat, a lot of milk and vegetables and fruit in season. They were unaccustomed to the richer fare Aunt Harriet provided and it took them some time to get used to the cream teas and cooked breakfasts and to become familiar with the assortment of cutlery and the starched white napkins that three-course meals demanded.

And things were much more difficult in other ways, for Alice had to see that none of them let Papa down. The money from Papa's patent medicine was paying for the boys' education. George and Leopold were weekly boarders at school in Liverpool. Beatrice went to a Southport girls' day school and Alice's main duties were to baby Arthur and Aunt Harriet. Appearances were to be kept up. And appearances were every bit as important to Aunt Harriet as they were to Papa.

Alice's orders from Papa were mostly to do with expenses. A sum of money had been put in the bank, the interest from which would give the family one pound ten shillings a week. Papa's orders were that she keep accurate books, accounting for every penny they spent. Aunt Harriet was not to spend any of her own money on necessities for the Davenport children, though she would be glad to do it. Alice was to contribute one pound a week to the household food and was to offer to do all the shopping. She was to give the boys and Beatrice their tiny allowances every month. The remainder was for their clothes.

When Papa returned, he said, there was to be a family conference and it was implied, though never stated outright, that Papa might leave the army and take a practice in Southport. And Beatrice had been bold enough to ask Papa if she might think about becoming a nurse when she was old enough. Papa had looked surprised and had said something about 'being prepared to do some work . . .' but he had not said 'no'.

It was two months before they saw Papa again. Christmas had come and gone without his visiting them. Aunt Harriet had put on a brave show, trying not to let them see that she too was worried about Papa's leaving. And the war news from South Africa was bad. Nothing seemed to be going right for the British forces.

Then, soon after New Year, without warning, Papa came to Southport. He took Alice aside and spoke most seriously to her about '. . . Doing your duty . . . On your honour not to let the side down . . . Do everything you can to help Aunt Harriet . . . and keep yourself pure in words, thoughts and deeds . . .'

Then he spoke to the boys and Beatrice. After supper a family evening was hastily organized by Alice. There were recitations and singing but it had not felt to Alice at all like the old days.

After it was over Papa sat for an hour, talking with Aunt Harriet in her drawing room and then came out to say his goodbyes to them all. He had been with them only four hours before he was gone from them. He returned to Chester to join the regiment which was leaving the following day.

And though he had told them they need not, unless they wished, they all, all except for baby Arthur, rose early on that winter morning to catch the early train to Liverpool to watch the parade.

It was a cold and grey January morning. They dressed in their winter clothes of serge coats and warm boots and walked to the station for a train to Liverpool where they were going to stand amongst the crowds on the Dock Road.

'Aunt Harriet!' George shouted as he rounded the corner of Chapel Street ahead of the others. 'There are hundreds of people. Come quickly.'

They turned the corner and stared in amazement. Crowds were milling about the station entrance. Hundreds of people were going to Liverpool.

'Run and buy our tickets, Leopold.' Aunt Harriet gave Leopold a sovereign from her bag. 'Run!' she said. 'First class, mind! We don't want to catch fleas.'

The four waiting trains were filling. Aunt Harriet tried to get a porter to find them a place but there were none to be seen and they had to run and fling themselves into the only empty compartment which was right at the head of the train. Aunt Harriet was as nervous as a kitten, Alice saw.

'Oh, dear. Oh, dear,' she kept repeating. 'I do hope that Charles will be safe. They won't let the doctor do anything dangerous, will they, do you think, Alice?'

Alice had never seen Aunt Harriet flustered before and here she was, eyes bright with emotion, wringing her thin hands, touching the brooch at her throat and acting as if she were some young wench whose sweetheart was setting forth.

And, as she watched her aunt, Alice saw, in a flash, that Aunt Harriet was in love with Papa. Aunt Harriet had always loved Papa. Aunt Harriet wanted Papa to come back . . . to her.

She felt a wave of affection for poor Aunt Harriet who had hidden her feelings for Papa for so long. When Papa came home he must marry her. Perhaps last evening when they were in the drawing room something had been said. They would have to wait, of course, but marriage to Aunt Harriet would be the most sensible solution to all their problems. Papa would set up in practice in Southport with Aunt Harriet at his side. Why had she not seen it before?

People were lining the streets when they arrived in Liverpool and they had to push their way through the crowds. Word had gone round that the regiment had left Chester an hour before and that the special train would soon be arriving at Alexandra Dock Station. The Cheshire Yeomanry were to join up with the Warwickshire Yeomanry and the Lancashire Hussars they were told. They were all going to parade to the dock.

'What a send-off,' Beattie said, clutching tight on to Alice's hand. 'Did you see all those people clinging on to the top of the stationary trains?'

'Yes.' Alice held tight to Beattie. 'Thousands of them. Come on, Beattie.' She started to elbow her way through the crush until they caught up with the others who had found a space nearer the dock.

A mist was coming off the Irish Sea, swirling around the dock buildings so that they could not see the far end of the long cobbled road.

But the noise of the crowd and their excitement seemed to Alice to be like a tidal current passing in waves through the arms and shoulders touching her own as they stood in the cold, waiting.

They heard the music faintly long before the parade came.

'There are four bands coming!' Leopold was jumping up and down in excitement. He was the last in the line and had started to relay all the messages and rumours that were being shouted along the road.

Aunt Harriet was pale and was still twisting her hands. 'The Cheshires. The Caernarvon Volunteer Artillery—' Leopold was shouting.

Alice clung tight on to Beattie's arm and peered into the mist at the end of the road, willing the soldiers to appear out of the silver-grey haze.

Then came the noise of cheering as the music grew

louder. At first the cheering, then the cries of 'They're coming' came faintly, but gradually they swelled into a great roar as steady, tramping feet, clattering hooves and the stirring music of the regimental bands heralded the parade.

And then they appeared – out of the mist – in such a blaze of colour and splendour that Alice was not able to see or speak for the tears and pain welling up in her throat. She pressed her hands over her mouth for fear of crying out aloud. She didn't want Papa to go.

He was there. He was behind the band and the three soldiers who carried the colours. Papa was in the last row, behind the mounted troopers, high above the heads of the watching crowd, riding a dark bay that looked as if it had been polished with a silk cloth. All of them, Aunt Harriet, Beattie and the boys, were trying to fight back the tears of pride and love for Papa who, looking straight ahead, passed them.

All at once there was a commotion next to Alice. A young woman, smaller than Alice – she could have been no taller than five feet – dressed in braided maroon velvet with grey fur trimmings at her throat and hem, with a Cossak-style hat over upswept dark hair, had pushed her way through the crowd. It seemed quite natural for the throng to make way for her; she had the air of one who was accustomed to deference. Behind her stood a uniformed nursemaid holding a baby wrapped to the eyes in white fur.

'Freddie! Freddie Blackshaw! Captain Freddie Blackshaw!' the girl cried out. She had a husky, cultured voice that was deeper than one would expect and she glanced quickly at Alice as Alice made space for her. Alice had never seen a girl with such eyes. They were long, thickly lashed, heavy-lidded and the colour a deep sea-green. They seemed to hold the onlooker spellbound. They held Alice momentarily spellbound until the girl looked back towards the parade and Alice followed the direction of the girl's eyes and saw Captain Freddie Blackshaw.

She knew the insignia of a captain. He must be the one who marched at the head of the last column.

The girl pulled a red silk handkerchief from inside her muff, waved it in the air and called again; 'Darling Freddie. Take care. Come back to us.'

Captain Freddie Blackshaw had seen the girl. Alice saw every movement of the little drama; the way he didn't smile outright but revealed in the expression on the darkly handsome face that the sound of her voice had reached him. His lively eyes sparkled under his helmet. His dark, silky moustache seemed to lift a little at the corners as if a smile were trying to break out. He appeared to hold his head even higher than before.

'Freddie . . . Darling . . . Freddie . . .' the girl called.

He was tall and broad shouldered and Alice took in every detail of him; the wide chest in the navy and scarlet jacket with its line of silver studs that went from the high neckband to the silver braided points below the waist. His long legs were encased in narrow navy-blue serge with a broad silver stripe running from the waist to the foot. On his feet were polished black boots.

'Freddie . . . Freddie . . .'

Alice, though only fifteen, knew exactly what the beautiful girl was suffering. Alice herself sensed, almost shared, the girl's love and longing for the handsome captain. To think of that poor young woman – a young wife, having to part from her husband and their baby younger than dear little Arthur. He was a glorious, dashing and handsome captain. Alice had never experienced an agony of yearning such as surged through her when first Papa and then Captain Blackshaw passed her.

They could hear the cheering farther along towards the dock but Papa had expressly forbidden them to watch the embarkation.

As soon as the parade passed the girl glanced again at Alice, gave a half-smile and spoke to the nursemaid in that unusual voice. 'Back to Hetherington, Nurse,' she said. 'We can be home before twelve.'

When the girl had disappeared into the crowd Alice turned to Aunt Harriet. 'Did you see the girl?' she asked.

'Which girl was that, Alice?' Aunt Harriet asked absent-mindedly.

'A girl. Well-dressed and beautiful. She said she was going back to Hetherington.'

'Oh. Hetherington Hall. Sir Jack Blackshaw's place.'

Aunt Harriet knew all there was to know about the titled families of Lancashire and Cheshire. It had begun to annoy Alice, this obsessive interest of Aunt Harriet's in the lives of people who would never know her.

The parade had passed and Aunt Harriet, without saying more about the girl who had so intrigued Alice, took her by the arm and began to usher her and the others in the direction of the station.

'We must be back in Southport before midday,' she said. 'Cook will have something prepared and the maid will not be able to help her, with the baby to care for. Come along.'

Alice looked at her aunt's face and her heart went out to her; Aunt Harriet would not be thinking of anything but Papa's departure and return. Aunt Harriet would not be thinking about Captain Freddie Blackshaw, Sir Jack Blackshaw or Hetherington Hall.

# Chapter Three

In the heart of Cheshire the old gentlefolk, those who remembered the ruined mansion that used to stand in a great oak forest, shook their heads over the new Hetherington Hall which exhibited an excess of money over discrimination. The very first sight of the house was enough; it was an architectural monstrosity. It was spoken of by old working men as 'The House that Jack Built' and 'Blackshaw's Folly'.

Hetherington Hall reflected to the last showy detail the loud vulgarity of Sir Jack Blackshaw. Sir Jack Blackshaw had built the Hall and enclosed the house and the fifty acres of park and gardens behind a ten-foot-high brick wall.

Hetherington Hall's red brick bulk rose monumental and tall from the Cheshire plain. It had an inner courtyard and eight pinnacled towers of sandstone and brick. The towers, with pinnacles soot-blackened from the dozens of chimneys they hid from view, soared above oak trees in the wood and the treelined walks and driveways.

On the day that her son, Captain Frederick Blackshaw, sailed for South Africa his mother was standing at a window in the East Tower. Augusta, Lady Blackshaw, drew her woollen cape tighter around her narrow shoulders and looked down the frosty avenue towards the house where she'd been born. The Dower House was an ancient, rambling house built of mellowed sandstone. Uninhabited now, it lay half a mile down the South

Avenue from Hetherington where iron gates fashioned by Italian craftsmen opened on to the old Roman road to Chester. Augusta had inherited the two thousand acre estate with its ruin, forest, village and tenanted farms when she was fourteen.

Now forty-seven years old, she had just had a sentence of death passed upon her. Two hours ago, here in this room the old family doctor had given her the verdict; the specialist who had examined her last week had diagnosed carcinoma. She had wanted to know the truth and had asked how much time she had left.

'The specialist said "a year at the most," my Lady,' her doctor had said. 'Though you know that I have always thought your trouble was caused by a stone in the bile duct . . .'

'You are kind to try to give me hope,' she'd answered. 'I thank you but I have no time to lose. Please keep the diagnosis from my husband and my family.'

Her daughters, Mary and Maggie, must not be told. Freddie, heir to the estate at her death, would have to know. But later.

Lady Blackshaw was watching for the carriage that would bring her niece with her baby son, Peter, back to the Hall. Therese and the baby had set off hours ago for Liverpool to watch Freddie leave with his regiment.

The pain was there again. It was not a pain that might bowl her over – that would come later the doctor said. This pain started in her stomach, and radiated until it reached the tip of her shoulder. It began to tighten. It would hold her in its sickening grip until she could take some milk. Then it would vanish for an hour or two; sometimes for a day.

She tugged on the bell-pull by the fire. Hot milk would be brought to her in a few minutes. She went back to the window to look for the carriage which at any moment would come into view along the Roman road. The Italian gates were closed today, probably they would be frozen. The carriage would have to travel down to the Hollin

Gate on the Knutsford road and bring her niece and the child home by the longer route.

The whole estate was visible from the top rooms in the towers and she gazed out across the white, frozen landscape in which nothing appeared to be moving.

All at once, with the pain at its height, instead of resignation to her fate – her sentence of death – Lady Augusta Blackshaw clenched her hands into tight fists and said to the empty room, 'I shall not die! No matter how much I long for death I shall not die until I see my son again. And I swear to God that today I shall get to the bottom of this ghastly business of Therese and her baby.'

She had heard the servant-gossip, knew what was being said in the village and on the farms; they whispered that her own darling Freddie had fathered Therese's child; that Therese and Freddie had spent a month together in India and that her niece had returned to Cheshire carrying Freddie's child.

It simply could not be true. If it had been true then Freddie would have demanded that they be allowed to marry.

Therese's explanation, to herself and the whole family, was that a year ago she had married in Austria and within a few weeks was widowed. Lady Blackshaw could not believe her.

Mary and Maggie accepted Therese's story. They would not hear anything bad either of Therese or Freddie. Maggie had dismissed the servant she believed was spreading vile rumours about Freddie and Therese. But Freddie would tell her nothing. Her darling son had gone to war with the secret kept from her. He had sworn to her that he knew nothing. But Freddie would protect Therese with his life. Therese had been brought up with Freddie. They had always been devoted and inseparable.

Freddie must surely know the truth. He must.

Lady Blackshaw, of medium height and slender, had been a beautiful girl in her youth but now her face was thin, almost gaunt, and ravaged with pain. Life had not been kind to her. After inheriting, she had, at fifteen, been propelled by her legal advisers into marriage with Jack Blackshaw who was heir to his father's title and fortune, in order to save the estate. He was fifteen years her senior and at the time, it later turned out, was already betrothed to Hildegard von Heilbronn, the daughter of an impoverished Austrian countess.

Jack, with his younger brother Edward, were the only sons of the renowned old Sir Thomas Blackshaw, a great and good man of Cheshire. Old Sir Thomas had made his name, earned his title and made his fortune in the cotton mills of Lancashire and Cheshire.

Thank Heaven Freddie had inherited the true and good side of the Blackshaw character, Lady Blackshaw thought. One day Freddie would restore the good name that Sir Thomas had left to his Blackshaw descendants.

A feeling of nostalgia and warmth came to her when she remembered her son's childhood. Freddie as a boy had been little more than average at his lessons but had always been popular at school because of his breathtaking skill at games. Freddie had captained the school cricket eleven as well as the football team. Her son was also a born horseman and good shot. Freddie had been a well-built, athletic boy with an easy-going nature and a son any man, any other man than Jack Blackshaw, would have been proud of.

But Jack Blackshaw had brought Freddie up to fear and detest him. He had beaten the boy on the slightest pretext, tormented and belittled him at every opportunity and – the proud smile had vanished and Augusta Blackshaw shuddered – she had never had the courage to put a stop to it.

Now, with so little time left to her, she was going to seek courage. She would begin by demanding the truth from her niece, Therese.

The carriage trundled along the Roman road under the

wall. Hetherington Hall could appear suddenly at a break in the wall; at any one of the seven gates. The ugly house was right in the centre of the park.

Inside the carriage, with her baby son, Peter, and his nurse sat Therese Blackshaw. She was a tiny, dark-haired young woman with eyes the colour of a troubled sea, a milk-white complexion, the peaked hairline and high cheekbones of the Blackshaw family and perfect, chiselled features. Today her photographic image had gone with cousin Freddie to war. These features, which would be admired by the men and officers of the Cheshire Yeomanry, appeared quiet in repose yet captivating in their variety of expression when she was animated.

Peter had fallen asleep in the nurse's arms and Therese turned from looking at her dark-haired little boy to gaze, unseeing, at the view outside the carriage. Then she leaned back a little and saw her own reflection in the little pane of glass.

Her eyes used to appear inviting, full of promise. Today they seemed to her to be cold and watchful and as she regarded herself a sudden flood of tears came to them. It was impossible always to appear self-possessed. At times she'd be overcome with fear and remorse and would lie on her bed in a paroxysm of weeping.

What was to become of her – an unmarried mother of only nineteen years of age? What did it matter that she had servants, clothes and jewels and that her child's future was assured? She had no independent existence. She was mistress of nothing. All she had was that which the cruel tyrant who ruled them all cared to allow her.

Once she had believed that she might expect to marry well, to have an establishment and position of her own. She tried, as she did every day of her life, to make sense of her past. She would like to wipe out the memory of the foolish, vain creature she had been on that bitterly cold November day just over a year ago.

It was early November in 1898 and Therese had been

47

travelling for five days: Vienna to Prague, Prague to Leipzig, Leipzig to Berlin, Berlin to Hamburg. Then had come the freezing crossing of the German Sea from Hamburg to Hull and three train journeys to the heart of Cheshire. Five long and wearying days after leaving her Viennese finishing school Therese had returned, orphaned and penniless, into the guardianship of her uncle, Sir Jack Blackshaw, her dead father's brother.

The few miles from the railway station had been put behind her as the closed carriage jerked and trundled along the old Roman road. Her glimpse of the Hall from the carriage window as they passed the first of the gates was a welcome sight to Theresa Alexandra von Heilbronn Blackshaw. She leaned back into the deep-buttoned upholstery, pushed freezing hands into the soft fur of her muff and breathed a sigh of relief as she anticipated her welcome.

The best years of her childhood had been spent here at Hetherington with darling cousin Freddie as her companion. Mother would never come to Cheshire so Therese as a young child was sent for a month every summer to Vienna, to join her mother and grandmother at her grandmother's house on Gloriettegasse.

It was not until she was sixteen that she had left Hetherington, Freddie and England, to live permanently with her grandmother. A place had been found for her at an Austrian finishing school and she was to make yearly visits to her parents in India.

In the dying light of the afternoon the coach drew up on the sweep of raked gravel in front of the house. At this, the main entrance, nine ornate stone arches bridged with a raised stone balustrade ran the length of the central three-storey house and linked two of the towers. The nine windows behind the arches were unlit and Therese knew a sudden tremor of fear that she would find the house unoccupied.

None of the family was there to greet her at the entrance hall but Leigh, the butler, was waiting for her.

Her cloak was taken and she was shown to her old room in the West Tower.

The last of the light was gone and the curtains had been drawn across the three tall windows. A fire burned in the hearth and a small wheeled table was set with tea, sandwiches and scones. A young housemaid was sent to attend her.

'What's your name?' she asked the girl. Her voice was low and slightly husky and the girl stared at her for a moment as if she had not understood. 'Your name, girl. What is it?' Therese repeated.

'Madeleine.'

'Madeleine? Madeleine what?' she asked.

The girl hesitated again. 'Madeleine . . . er . . . miss . . . er . . . ma'am,' she replied.

'Then if you are to attend me, I shall call you Maisie.' Therese shook back her dark curls and narrowed her long eyes as she looked up at the tall, auburn-haired maid. 'Madeleine is much too grand a name for a girl of your station,' she said.

The girl went red in the face. 'Yes, ma'am.'

'Help me to change, Maisie,' Therese said in the haughty manner which always achieved the effect she wanted.

The girl helped her remove her travelling clothes but Therese had washed and eaten her tea before the small reserve of optimism that was a part of her nature began to surface.

After tea she dismissed the maid and told the man-servant who carried one of her boxes to the room to inform her uncle and aunt that she was here. But, instead of the summons she expected and the apologies for their absence on her arrival, she was finally obliged to go down by herself to the long room known as the chintz drawing room where, standing with his back to the black marble chimney-piece, she found her uncle waiting.

He was a short man with dark hair merely streaked with grey although he was past his sixtieth year. He still had the handsome features his son had inherited but the father's eyes were hard and calculating and his beetling grey eyebrows bushier than Freddie's. His manner was domineering and, though he was small, he had always made any room he entered seem smaller; his very presence created an atmosphere that seemed to be charged with his own swift energy.

He had always been unpredictable. He confided in no-one yet was almost always surrounded by sycophantic and greedy men of wealth and importance. He had a roughness for all his fine clothes and possessions and his impatience and ill-temper used to frighten his family and servants.

When she looked back upon it later, she would want to kick herself for her vanity for during the last year in Vienna she had begun to be aware of the impact of her pale skin and dark, almost black hair; of her tiny, heavy-breasted figure, her fine ankles and delicate hands and feet; of the husky invitation of her voice.

Unlike the other members of the family, she had never been afraid of Uncle Jack. Facing him, after her two-year absence, she raised her eyes, glanced at him with the long slow look she had learned to use to great effect and dropped a half curtsey.

'No need for that,' he said. He had a harsh voice with a strong northern accent and this and his bombastic manner were the more obvious traits which had made him scorned by the only people he wanted to know – the landed families he tried to emulate. Unsmiling, he put out a hand.

Therese ignored the hand. The smile left her face as she straightened to the rustling sound of the hated grosgrain and taffeta mourning dress. 'Where's Aunt Augusta? Where are my cousins – Freddie? Mary and Maggie?'

'Expected a grand reception did you?'

She would not be intimidated. 'I expected you to observe the rules of good behaviour, Uncle.'

At this he dropped his hand and smiled. 'Well! You've lost none of your nerve,' he said. 'And I thought it would take more than a year to make a lady of you. You always had a high opinion of yourself.' He was smiling but his eyes seemed to be assessing her. 'How was Vienna?'

'When I left, Vienna was a city given over to the dead. Black flags were hanging from every window. The churches were full of weeping women. For the Mother Empress, of course, not for me,' she answered with the slight drawl men seemed to find amusing.

At this, the smile left his face. 'I was sorry about my brother's passing,' he said. 'And your mother's.'

'We were never a proper family.'

His concerned expression went. 'You never lived in India with them did you.'

It was a statement, not a question. She had been brought up here, at Hetherington. 'This year I spent three months in Jaipur.' She turned her head to look about the great room with four doors which opened on to the gallery and the small anterooms. Though the great house on the outside was a monument of ugliness, the inside was different. Aunt Augusta's good taste was evident everywhere in the furnishings.

Therese thought it odd that none of them had appeared. 'Where's everyone?' she asked. 'Lady Blackshaw? Mary? Maggie? And where's Freddie?'

The air of impatience had returned. He answered quickly, 'My son is with his regiment in India. The girls and their mother are in Karlsbad. Taking the cure.'

'November is late for the cures,' she said. 'Then, in the high-handed manner they had taught her in Vienna, she asked, 'Is my aunt ill?'

His brown eyes under the bushy brows were watching her closely. It was as if she were one of the many women he was reputed to keep. 'Lady Blackshaw has a wasting disease.'

His words barely registered with Therese, so concerned was she about her own reception. All she cared about at that moment was that she was cold and annoyed and that his being alone here was no excuse for his neglect of her safety and comfort. 'I'm sorry to hear that,' she said. 'I see why I was left to fend for myself.'

Again came the impatient look, the brusque words, 'What did you expect?' he said. 'A winged messenger?'

Therese felt anger flaring up in her. 'I did not expect to be told of my parents' death at school. I did not expect to be summoned to Cheshire by telegraph and told to dismiss my Austrian maid, nor did I expect my escorts to be a troupe of Bohemians.'

'You didn't find the Reinhardt family good company then?' he said. 'Johann Reinhardt is a clever man. A millwright . . . a factory engineer. One of Europe's best. He's taken a working-partnership in my Macclesfield factory.'

'I've always understood that a gentleman does not work for a living.' She was using her haughtiest manner. She began to chafe her hands together to warm them. 'Your business interests are no concern of mine.'

It was as if she'd said something significant. He said nothing for a second or two then his features relaxed a little. 'Don't pretend that money's not important,' he said. 'If my business interests were of no concern to this family . . .' At this he stopped and said, 'Nobody can live without money. And in my experience those who despise money-making are the ones who best love to spend it.'

But his attitude of challenge was melting. 'You had to have a chaperone. I couldn't let you come all this way with a servant-girl.' He smiled, evidently amused by his own excuses. 'I'll get you a lady's maid.'

Therese continued to scold him. 'You simply thought to save yourself trouble and expense by saddling me with a German *Hausfrau!*'

He began to laugh, as if the whole affair had been a huge jape.

'A German *Hausfrau* and her entire family. I had nothing in common with her daughters and the *Gnadige*

52

*Frau* – the dear madam – was intent on keeping her two sons away from me.'

He was still laughing as he explained, 'It's their way. They are more formal than we are.'

Therese carried on indignantly. 'Their two sons – Heinz and Karl Reinhardt – were never permitted even to speak to me without a third party in attendance.'

Jack Blackshaw was still amused. 'Reinhardt is a hard-working and clever man,' he said. 'His family will find our English manners more casual than their own.' He extended his hand towards the chintz-covered sofa. 'Sit down.'

As soon as she was seated he went to the bell and pulled. The butler came immediately into the room and her uncle at last turned his attention to her comfort. 'Drink?' he said. 'Would you like something to drink before dinner?'

Her affronted air went. She was still cold but her anger had gone. She said, 'I'd like something warming. After Vienna I find Hetherington extremely cold.'

He was concerned. 'You shall have an egg-nog. At once.' He spoke to Leigh, who nodded and left the room.

Before the butler could return with the drink, Uncle Jack went to a tall Chinese lacquered cabinet and took out brandy decanter and a glass. He poured a generous measure and came to her side. 'Drink this,' he ordered. 'Straight down. Quickly.'

She took the glass and, eyebrows flying in surprise at the fiery shock to her mouth, obediently swallowed the brandy in one quick draught. She had never before had anything more potent than a glass of hock.

He placed her glass on the over-mantel, came towards her again and held out his hands. 'Warm yourself at the fire.'

She stood beside him at the fireplace for a few moments until Leigh returned with the egg-nog when she again raised her eyebrows in unspoken question at the prospect

53

of taking more strong drink. Her uncle gripped her hand and led her to the sofa where, after seating her, he placed the glass on a small table at her elbow.

He was a restless man. He moved constantly – from the fire to the sofa, and back to the fireplace again. 'It will do you no harm,' he said. 'It's medicinal.'

Therese sipped quickly from a tall, foaming glass.

'What have you been doing in Vienna these last two years?' he asked when she replaced the half-empty glass on the round wine-table. 'What did they teach you at that . . . the lyceum for the daughters of kings, as your dear mother and grandmother called it?'

She settled back into the floral sofa and arranged the little tasselled cushions attractively against the black taffeta of her dress. The egg-nog was delicious. Already soft warmth was seeping through her.

'I was taught little more than I learned here with my governesses,' she answered. 'I improved my French and German and did a little drawing and music. But I am unlearned. Very ill-educated.'

Then, seeing what she took to be a look of pity on his face, she said in a manner she adopted towards social inferiors, 'I have been trained – prepared – to be a fit bride for a prince.'

What would her uncle think of such high-flown ideas? He had never spent money on 'finishing' his own daughters. He must know that her grandmother and mother wanted her to make a good marriage. Grandmother had paid for her schooling. She said, 'Mother was going to have me brought out in London next year.'

'And where is this prince to be found? Did your mother or your grandmother have any particular royal house in mind? The Habsburgs have run out of princes have they not? And I fear that the Battenburgs . . . and the Romanovs . . . ?'

'Don't tease, Uncle!' she laughed. Then prettily, she sighed. 'I am fitted for nothing else, you realize. And to be truthful there is nothing I'd prefer. I long for marriage. I could not endure spinsterhood. The sort of life your daughters lead would be death to me.'

She looked quickly at him to see if this reference to Mary's and Maggie's unmarried state had offended him but his expression had not changed. She continued, 'Is there any money coming to me? Is there anyone who could present me, when I'm out of mourning?'

'We'll talk about it over dinner.'

Leigh came back into the room to tell him that dinner was ready to serve and her uncle came towards her with outstretched arms. She allowed him to haul her to her feet and at that moment first noticed in him a slight reluctance to release her hands.

'Take my arm, Therese,' he said.

She went, arm-in-arm with him, down the stairs to the dining room where two places were set at one end of an inlaid walnut table. Silver gleamed and crystal sparkled under the light from the dozens of candles the silver candelabra held.

He was attentive. He waved away the butler between courses and filled her glasses himself with the finest of clarets and sweet white wine. And he talked to her and listened to her account of life in Vienna. They were still sitting at the table two hours later and, light-headed though she was, she was entertaining him with stories of her visits to Vienna's Burgtheater and the after-theatre suppers at Sacher's.

She had forgotten the miseries of her orphaned position. She was being flattered by an older man who must surely be entranced by her charm. His evenings were normally spent in the company of men of sophistication, men of the world of gambling, business and pleasure. She did not know that only a man of dishonourable intention would entertain or pay court to a girl who was alone. She thought herself worldly and quite irresistible.

Was it he or she who had put the idea into her mind that she herself might one day become the mistress of Hetherington? Was she intoxicated? She tried to guess his meaning. What did he mean? Mistress? She had not thought in those terms. Lady of Hetherington, perhaps, but not Mistress. Was he suggesting a marriage to Freddie? She had considered it – of course she had – in an improbable kind of way. In the Austrian royal circles, her grandmother said, it was traditional for cousins to marry. It was not unknown here. But for her cousin Freddie she had only sisterly feelings.

She became ever more elated and ever more confiding as the evening progressed. At one point she had boldly inclined her head and invited him to guess the name of the scent she wore at the nape of her neck. He would never guess, for she made it herself from a secret recipe of Grandmother's. Making preparations was her only interest and so she had asked him to touch the back of her hand and had been delighted by his amazed murmuring over the softness of her skin. She confessed again, to his evident delight, that her skin was massaged daily with a lotion she made to one of Grandmother's recipes.

Her talk had sparkled. Her eyes had shone. His face had gone red with pleasure in her talk. He had not been able to tear his eyes from her face and she had been drunk with her own powers.

At last he took her arm and steered her back, not into the drawing room but to his study which was at the far end of the Rose Gallery in the West Tower where her own room was. His study was a small room hung with red velour at the windows and furnished with a desk, a wall of books and two deep leather chairs. A fire blazed in the hearth. The door closed behind the butler who had left a silver tray laden with liqueurs, brandy and glasses on the desk.

Uncle Jack went to stand on the hearthrug and, apparently seeing that she was still in a susceptible mood, he raised his arms and said, 'Come here, you pretty little thing. Let your uncle be a comfort to you.'

She went, dizzy into his arms, with the air of an actress playing the part of courtesan. She saw desire in his eyes that belied his comforting words and still she went, flirtatious and silly, to lay her head on his shoulder and give him one of her inviting glances.

His mouth was close to her ear. 'Is my sweet little Therese breaking her heart for some young gallant?' he asked with a voice that had gone all deep and husky.

'Oh, no.' She was all at once at pains to tell him that she had never been so close to a man in her life before. But she did not pull away from his hold.

His voice was rougher than before. 'Are you unsullied? Chaste?'

She did not know what to say. She merely made a strange little coughing sound.

'Are you a virgin?' He spoke the words harshly.

She was conscious of the heat of the fire on the side of her face. Her heart felt as if it had stopped beating. Now, instead of being deliciously light-headed she could hardly think clearly.

'Are you a virgin?' he repeated. 'Tell me.'

She had never heard such a question. Could the word 'virgin' be applied to modern girls? Her mind raced. The ancient Romans had their Vestal Virgins; young adolescent girls, pious in white marble. It was a biblical term – virgin. She had never made a study of the bible. She only knew of one virgin – the Virgin Mary. What on earth was he asking? 'I . . . I really don't know . . .' she said after what seemed an eternity.

'You must know. Either you are or you are not.'

She was more troubled at not being able to answer his question than she was by his behaviour. She would have to say something; something that would not reveal her ignorance. And since the thought that she might be this virgin thing worried him she finally answered, 'No. I am not a virgin.'

'Good,' he said. Then he stopped talking and began to kiss her. And, and it was shocking later to think of it, she had encouraged him.

She had often speculated on initiation. In imagination

she had seen herself swooning with desire and falling, faint with longing, into the willing, eager arms of a crown prince. The girls at the lyceum, and especially she and her American friend, Xanthe, were wild about courts and uniforms, captains of Hussars, ribbons and decorations.

It had not felt, in imagination, either as unromantic or as wickedly exciting as what was happening to her. For Uncle Jack Blackshaw was experienced and even as she began to have her first stirrings of fear she was starting to respond to his mouth, to his hands. Her arms, it seemed of their own volition, were winding themselves around his neck and she was clinging to him as he, with practised fingers, unfastened hooks and buttons and ribbons.

She was light-headed, disembodied, hot from the fire and the wine, afraid – and very curious.

When her clothes were discarded he pushed her, quite gently, down into a kneeling position on the hearthrug whilst she watched with large, dilated eyes her own uncle removing his clothing very quickly. She remembered his hard compact body as he came to kneel in front of her, kissing her mouth, caressing and holding her heavy white breasts at one and the same time – as if he were afraid that if he stopped she might leap, outraged, to her feet.

But she could not have stopped him then for the weak feelings, dizziness, lassitude and longing, that, as much as his deep kisses and the expert manipulations of his hands, held her there, outwardly still yet with a strange inward quaking as he laid her flat upon her back, pushed her legs apart and lowered himself on top of her.

When she looked back upon it and recalled the night in all its detail she knew that she must have seemed a willing victim. She had been easy meat.

She remembered that he had been very quick that first time. He had taken her, the first time, with silent restraint. When he discovered that she was a virgin he had only kissed her more forcefully and held her down more firmly so that she would not recoil from the pain.

Her own pleasure had been swift and fleeting and, when it was over, she had been surprised to see how quickly he could return to practicalities.

When she had wanted him to hold her, to linger, to reassure her, to be told that for him it had been a momentous experience he, frowning, had straightened himself and asked her about the date of what he called her monthly function.

Then he indicated that she was to be quick in dressing herself and said in a self-satisfied voice that had no hint of concern for her feelings, 'I like my women to have a bit of class. You'll soon learn how to please.'

She could hardly believe her eyes and ears.

Then in a voice that was all but curt he said, 'Get your clothes on.'

He stood, looking down at her where she lay on the floor. 'You must keep our little secret. My wife and daughters will be home soon.'

As sober as if ice-cold water had been thrown on to her face and in a belated agony of shock and shame at what had occurred, Therese stood up and began to dress slowly with her back to him. When she had done so she gritted her teeth in her attempt to control the violence of the feelings that were sweeping over her. Then still without facing him, she went to the table and poured for herself a good measure of cognac which she drank down quickly.

'I'll send for you when I want you,' he said. 'You can come to my room after Lady Blackshaw and my daughters are asleep. Return to your own bed before morning.'

Tears came to eyes and wave after wave of pure, red anger blurred the edges of all she could see.

Then, startling even herself, she whirled around with eyes scornful and flaming. 'I'll do nothing of the kind!'

He looked at her for a full minute without speaking but she did not drop her gaze. She saw first anger and then calculation in his face.

'Did you hear me?' she repeated. 'I'll never let you do . . .'

He was daring to smile as he said, 'Then for now you can use your untried skills. Make yourself useful. Since you say you've been schooled—'

'How dare you?' She stood, rooted to the spot in fear and loathing of him, scalding tears beginning to course down her cheeks.

'Until Lady Blackshaw returns you can act as Mistress of Hetherington,' he said in his coarse voice. 'The Hall has to be managed. There will be dinners, and Christmas, to order.'

'You are vile!' She almost choked on the uprush of acid that had risen into her throat. She coughed, caught her breath as she reached for him. She would strike him across his wicked face.

'Send New Year invitations to the Reinhardt family and my business friends,' he continued as he sidestepped her leap towards him.

'I will do nothing! Nothing!' she almost screeched before she overbalanced. Finally she fell to her knees and vomited at his feet.

He helped her to stand and then silently he led her to her room where he undressed her and left her alone until morning.

And thus had begun her very short reign as Mistress of Hetherington and her even shorter one as the mistress of Jack Blackshaw. And, to her eternal shame, she had found herself unable to spurn him on the two following nights when he came to her bed. She had been shocked to discover that she was capable of passionate response to the fondling and pleasuring of a man she came to detest.

The whole sordid *affaire*, as she was later to think of it, had lasted only a week until the absence of her period had revealed her pregnant state.

First he demanded that she return to her grandmother's house in Vienna and remain there until he sent for her.

She refused.

Then he proposed that she went away to London. He spoke of adoption – of foster families – of returning to Hetherington as if nothing had happened – as if nobody need ever know.

She refused.

So he concocted the lie she had been forced to accord with; the ridiculous, cock and bull story of a brief marriage and quick widowhood, of her return to England, her return to her maiden name and the dependent plight of herself and the child she was carrying.

Only an utter fool would believe the lies. When they came home from Karlsbad her aunt, Lady Blackshaw, Mary and Maggie pretended to accept them. They had never openly questioned her. But the story had not satisfied Freddie when he came home from India. Freddie had gone to South Africa in ignorance though he had begged her to name the man.

Lady Blackshaw saw the carriage pass the Dower House and travel on towards the Hollin Gate. She had asked that Therese and Peter be brought up here as soon as she returned. Now she spoke to her daughters. 'I want to speak to Therese alone.' She looked at her elder daughter. Maggie, the older by two years, was twenty-nine years old. 'Please leave us after a few moments.'

Mary, quieter than her sister, said, 'You are not too tired, Mother?' When her mother made no reply said, 'I don't want Therese to exhaust you. Your doctor told us that you need a lot of rest, to improve.'

Augusta Blackshaw gave a wan smile. The doctor had clearly not told the girls the truth about her condition.

Within a few more minutes, Therese, with the child in her arms, was with them and Mary was holding out her arms for the infant. Both girls adored the child. It was a pity that Mary and Maggie would never marry and have children of their own. In spite of all the introductions she had been able to make for her daughters they had shown no inclination to break away from their mother.

Maggie was helping Therese take off her outdoor things and Augusta Blackshaw was struck again by the strong likeness between the three Blackshaw girl-cousins and Frederick. There was an unmistakable Blackshaw look.

'Well,' Maggie was saying to Therese. 'Did you see Frederick in the parade?'

'He looked dashing and handsome,' Therese's pretty face was animated as she told them about the parades. 'What an adventure! The Yeomen were almost knocked off their feet on the march to Chester station. The station entrance was completely blocked with people.'

'Did you travel to Liverpool?' Mary asked as she cradled the baby in her arms.

Therese laughed in her eagerness to tell. 'Yes. And do you know who was on the troop train?'

'No. Who?' Maggie asked.

'All the Grosvenors – Lady Lettice and Lady Mary – and the Duchess of Westminster . . .' Therese began.

Lady Blackshaw was tiring. She had to get this ghastly secret from Therese. She was determined not to waste any more time. She interrupted Therese and spoke firmly to Mary; her signal that she wanted to be left alone with Therese. 'Hand the child to me, Mary. If you please.'

Mary passed Peter over to her. She had removed the furs and the baby was awake, his eyes dark, wide and alert as he looked up at his great-aunt's face.

'Leave us.' Lady Blackshaw nodded to Mary and Maggie.

They obeyed her and at that same moment Augusta saw instant alarm on Therese's face. When the door had closed behind the girls, almost at once Therese said, 'What is it?'

Augusta looked intently at Peter, holding him close to her chest. Then she looked up over the warm, white bundle and knew that in her eyes was an expression of great sadness and fear.

Yet when she spoke her voice was steady. 'Not . . . This is not Freddie's child . . . Is it Therese?'

All at once it was as if Therese could pretend no longer. She stood there, a tiny white-faced figure. Only those long beautiful eyes were bright.

'I had no idea you thought that Freddie . . .' she said in a low, surprised voice. 'No, Aunt Augusta. It was not Freddie. Indeed it was not.'

Relief swept over Augusta Blackshaw. Therese was speaking the truth. Therese had never been a liar. Even as a small child she would stand, pale-faced, rooted to the spot with fear when she was caught in wrongdoing. She had never been able to lie convincingly.

The pain was back, tightening its grip on her so that her face would appear wracked with pain. She looked hard at the infant in her arms before she went across the room to give him to his mother.

It was as if she had always known. Why had she not admitted it to herself? Her husband had no morals, no scruples whatever. He had never shown a shred of decency.

When Therese had taken the baby, Augusta placed a hand on her niece's shoulder. 'This child is every inch a Blackshaw,' she said with absolute conviction. 'I know a Blackshaw child when I see one.'

Her heart was filled with pity for Therese who could not even speak. She could only stand and nod dumbly, shoulders drooping, as her tears fell on to the white lacy shawl where it turned back from the infant's face.

Augusta would not give Therese any comfort for the moment. She went quickly to stand by the fireplace and when she again looked at Therese she was filled with a quiet, dignified determination.

'We are going to move to the Dower House,' she said. 'You and the baby, Mary and Maggie and me. We cannot live under his roof a minute longer.'

The whole house seemed to have fallen silent. Therese's tears stopped in an instant. 'Because of me . . . ?'

Pity washed over her again as she said, 'No. Not because of you, Therese. This time I have the courage to do what is right. I am going to leave my husband.'

Therese interrupted her, almost shouting, 'Don't do that! I shall kill myself if you tell anyone why!'

Lady Blackshaw put a thin hand up to stop her. 'I have no intention of telling anybody why. I will keep your secret, Therese.'

Therese's voice had dropped. She could not hold back her fears any longer. She was trembling visibly. 'You . . . You won't ever tell anyone. Will you?' she whispered. 'Don't tell Mary or Maggie about . . . about what I did.'

Lady Blackshaw went to her and placed an arm about her. 'No, Therese, my little one,' she said. 'I won't tell them. I don't want Mary or Maggie to know what their father has done.'

The baby began to cry and Therese, with tears of relief streaming down her own face, held his cheek close to her own, to comfort him. 'Don't tell Freddie,' she pleaded. 'Freddie asks all the time. I can't tell him. It would break Freddie's heart. He will be fighting a war. He has the anxiety of your illness on his mind. He will have to be told about your separation. Please don't tell him the truth about me.'

Lady Blackshaw kissed the top of her head. 'I leave that to you, Therese,' she said. 'If Freddie is told – and I think he will have to be told, one day – then much better that it comes from you.'

# Chapter Four

On this part of the Lancashire coast it could rain sometimes for weeks on end but this year the weather began to change towards midsummer. The rain slackened off about noon each day. Southport steamed in the June sunshine and warm sea breezes tossed red-white-and-blue bunting to and fro where it was strung between the houses across the side streets.

The S.S. *Tintagel Castle*, bringing the regiments home, had sailed from Cape Town a month ago. Any day now the men of the Lancashire Fusiliers and the Cheshire Imperial Yeomanry would be home from two and a half years of fighting the Boers. And nowhere was a soldier's family more eager to have their father home than were Captain Charles Davenport's five children at their aunt's house in Duke Street.

Duke Street, one of the longest streets in Southport, had bunting in plenty flying at the cemetery end – the poor end where little shops lined the main street and little cottages were huddled along the back streets behind them.

At Duke Street's southern end many of Lancashire's wealthy mill-owners and merchants had built their mansion houses where Duke Street met the more famous Lord Street. The residents of Southport boasted that Lord Street was the second finest boulevard in Europe; they said that only the Champs Elysées surpassed it.

Miss Harriet Walker's house was not at the southern end. Her house was in the middle – halfway up Duke

Street. It was a substantial semi-detached house of red Accrington brick with a small square of garden in front and a long narrow garden at the back. There were shoulder-high walls of the same Accrington brick around the perimeters of the gardens and an even higher, stone-topped wall fronting on to the street, in the middle of Duke Street.

But for all that Captain Davenport's welcome would be as warm as that of any other soldier, there was no bunting flying in the middle of Duke Street.

It was six o'clock in the morning on the day before the auditions when Alice pushed open the casement window in the back bedroom she shared with Beattie and saw rain falling steadily from a low sky that seemed to merge in greyness with the rooftops opposite. A shiver of excitement ran through her.

Outside the window the leaves on the apple trees in the garden were drooping with water. The air was heavy with the smell of wet earth and she could see, between a gap in the houses, sodden bunting hanging wetly about the front of the cottages in Nelson Street.

It was a pity that Aunt Harriet had not allowed them to decorate this house. It could have looked spectacular for Papa's return. George and Leopold had offered to tie strings of flags and bunting from the chimney pots to the tall gateposts.

Aunt Harriet had refused, saying Papa might not want a fuss; asking if bunting were not rather common; saying that bunting ought to be flown only at the working-class end of the street. None of the neighbours, she declared – middle-class people living in the middle of Duke Street – went in for displays of any kind.

Alice saw that there was no convincing Aunt Harriet about the bunting but she knew also that she could never be a middle-of-the-road girl such as lived in the middle of Duke Street. The childhood years had left their mark.

All the same she knew a shiver of alarm as she wondered what Aunt Harriet's neighbours would say if they discovered that someone from their ranks might go on the stage.

Was she becoming rebellious? Did she want to break the chains of a life of duty? She didn't think so, for if she were rebellious by nature she would not be in the nervous state she was in this morning.

She knew that living here, trying to adapt to Aunt Harriet's way of life had come too late to change her. Alice would never be what she used to think of as 'normal' – a brown-coated, felt hat type of woman who wore sturdy shoes and knew her place. Being responsible and dutiful was deeply ingrained but there was another side to her nature. And this other self was like Mama – insouciant – heedless of tomorrow.

Reason told her that she could do nothing about the need to be carefree until Papa came home for she was honour bound . . . and her duty to baby Arthur was paramount . . . But Papa and Aunt Harriet would marry and then they would be Arthur's real parents . . . Beatrice had left school and was able to help . . . George was ready to go to university . . .

And she was going to be an actress, if she passed the audition.

Sometimes she wondered if she might be growing up to be like Mama, for her moods would swing from tremendous optimism - when she believed that they were all fortunate in having health and a wonderful Papa and a kind aunt to watch over them – to despair when she saw how little they had; no mother, no home of their own, no money – charity cases.

But today, the day before the auditions, was a high-hopes day. She would pray especially hard at church this morning. She would play the piano to the very best of her ability for the Sunday School children. Everything could be about to change for the better.

She looked at her reflection as she turned away from the window. She had filled out and grown since they had come to live in Southport. Tall and slim, her best features were her large grey eyes which were set in a longish face. Her nose was long too but at least, she thought, it didn't turn up at the end. She disliked one of the beauty ideals of the day – a preference for 'little, tip-tilted noses' – and was secretly rather pleased with hers.

Nor was straight blonde hair fashionable. The fashion, since Queen Victoria had died, was Edwardian; a mass of up-swept curls, a crowning-glory that looked like an enormous crown – a bird's nest of a style, held with combs and pins and topped with great wide hats with layers and layers of tulle and feathers.

Until later this morning there was nothing to be done with her hair. Her blonde hair, being naturally straight, had to be curled with tongs before it would stay pinned-up. She wore it tied back and tucked under her rain hat on the early morning walks she had been taking for the last two weeks. She pushed baby Arthur in his shiny black perambulator, a mile along Lord Street and another mile on the Promenade, rehearsing her lines as she went, mouthing them on Lord Street, speaking them out loud on the wet, deserted seafront.

She smiled at herself in the glass, saw the expanse of rosy gum under the curled-back lip and practised smiling without opening her mouth for a few tries. Then she gave up and went to sit on her bed.

She could hardly bear the excited nervousness that threatened to overcome her when she contemplated the enormity of it all. She glanced down at a postcard she'd taken from the pocket of her dressing-gown.

'Miss Alice Davenport.

'Your appointment for audition for my Liverpool Dramatic company is at two o'clock on . . .' Here followed tomorrow's date. 'At the church hall of . . .' Here followed the address and the signature of Mr Squibb.

Mr Squibb would have sent dozens of postcards out to hopeful young girls like herself. And she asked herself 'How many of us will he choose?' As she had told Beatrice, the ones who were chosen would need talent, not good looks, to be picked out. She pulled the tasselled cord of her gown tightly around her small waist and felt another shiver of excitement run through her as she recalled the way it had all come about.

Aunt Harriet, worried about Papa's long absence and the lack of any plans for Alice's future – no introductions, no parties or balls – had persuaded her to join the church's amateur dramatic society.

It had been like a blossoming – a new world had opened up for her. She had joined only last year and this spring had been given the part of Rosalind in *As You Like It*. During the last week of the play, when she could hardly bear the thought that soon it would be over and her life would become humdrum again, she told their producer – an eccentric churchwarden whom everyone knew as a crack-pot about amateur theatricals – that she had always wanted to be a real, paid actress.

That was all she had said and since then everything had gathered momentum. The churchwarden said he'd see what he could do. On the last-but-one night he'd told her about the new Liverpool company a Mr Squibb was forming. He had given her Mr Squibb's address. Then on the very last night he'd told her that someone from a Manchester Repertory Company had seen her performance and would be writing to her.

Alice had written separately to Mr Squibb.

Dear Mr Squibb,
I am seventeen years old and it is my ambition to follow in my mother's footsteps and become an actress . . .

She need not tell Mr Squibb everything. It was enough that he should take her seriously.

My last role was as Rosalind in *As You Like It* and I am currently reading and learning the parts of Ophelia and Hedda Gabler . . .

That was not a lie, not a real lie. Those just happened to be the only plays she had copies of.

But it had been the start of the secrecy. She couldn't have told Aunt Harriet, for it would have upset her aunt, who would want to please Papa. But Alice was sure that Papa would not refuse her. After all, Mama had been an actress.

As soon as the postcard came she'd started learning the parts and now – her stomach twisted into a knot once more – the day of the auditions was almost here. Papa was due home. What would happen if Papa came home today? Or tomorrow? Would she still have the courage to go?

She determined not to contemplate such a thing.

The S.S. *Tintagel Castle* had not docked yet but everything was ready. The regiments' return was even overshadowing the parties and fireworks the town was going to put on to celebrate the coronation next week. There was expectancy in the air; everyone was waiting for the carnival to begin. The papers were full of announcements – welcome-home band concerts – public gatherings – private celebrations – church services. Any day they would start.

Alice put a hand on her hollow stomach to still the agitation. How lucky she was that her audition was tomorrow she told herself. Another two or three days – and Papa would be here.

The only person who knew about her plan was Beatrice. Alice looked across to where her fifteen-year-old sister lay sleeping on the iron-framed bed that matched her own. Beattie's fair hair was spread about the pillows, a smile was on her sweet round face.

Alice could hear Aunt Harriet on the landing outside the room, heard a light footfall and the swishing of skirts as her aunt descended the stairs; heard the letter box snap to as the paper was taken from it and then came a click as the morning-room door closed.

Aunt Harriet was up early, but though she affected a

calm seriousness her aunt was just as eager as they all were for Papa's homecoming. Aunt Harriet had hardly slept since the ship had sailed from Cape Town. Papa wrote regularly to Aunt Harriet but she never told anyone what he said. There was always a look of sweet sadness on her aunt's face after she had read them, knowing Papa was so far away.

The excitement in the pit of her stomach was there again. She didn't know which was worse, waiting for the audition or telling lies to Aunt Harriet, for she had an honest nature and it didn't come easily to her, to deceive.

But yesterday she had told her aunt that they were all going for a walk in the park when she'd known that they were going to do nothing of the sort.

It had been sunny again in the afternoon and Southport had been chock-a-block with visitors who were arriving by the train load, spilling out on to Chapel Street from the Lancashire mill towns; silent men in Sunday-best suits and cloth caps, noisy children, loud-mouthed womenfolk in dark, serviceable dresses and enormous flower-laden hats. They surged along Neville Street where the gift shop windows were filled with model soldiers of men in khaki, as the new South African colour was called; buckets and spades and shrimping nets were nudging the mugs and plates of King Edward and his beautiful Queen Alexandra.

Someone had put a banner up across the front of the station. 'Welcome Home the Lancashire Fusiliers' it read. The station was ablaze with bunting as was the promenade and all the streets leading to it.

Lord Street had no bunting, but flags were flying from poles above the shops and hotels and the new electric trams had victory banners pasted on to their sides. Lord Street with its gardens and elegant shops, Hesketh Park and the Botanical Gardens were the respectable places to be seen. Aunt Harriet liked them all to keep to the good end of town, but yesterday, with her heart in her mouth and hating herself for doing it, Alice had disobeyed her aunt.

Yesterday afternoon, baby Arthur by the hand, she had been swept willingly along with the tide of day trippers towards the Promenade and Pleasure Gardens. She was going to spend the four shillings she'd saved from the housekeeping money. There was going to be a trip to the funfair for Arthur and afternoon tea for them all in Rowntree's Cafe. And Alice was going to have her fortune told.

Neither Aunt Harriet nor Papa would approve of this frivolity. Papa called fortune-tellers soothsayers and god-less charlatans and had told her that fortune-telling was against the law.

She had stopped and waited for the others who had fallen behind. The sun warmed her back through the cotton dress as she picked Arthur up and planted a kiss on his face. Arthur, looking adorable in his sailor suit, wound his arms around her neck and pressed his soft round cheek into hers.

Beattie reached them and with a worried air looked back over her shoulder. 'Alice?' she said. 'Do you think we ought to take the baby to the funfair?'

'Yes.' Alice put Arthur down and held his hand. 'I said we will.' Making declarations made her appear purpose-ful though it didn't stop the fluttering nervous feeling inside her. She smoothed down her sprigged muslin dress with a gloved hand and quickly tucked a strand of hair back under her boater. 'Where are the boys?'

Beattie said, 'They're coming.'

Alice turned her head and saw them. George was tall and handsome with thick sandy-fair hair and laughing blue eyes. He looked older than his sixteen years and he attracted looks of invitation from brazen girls; girls who looked into men's faces in the street. George was so like Papa it made Alice's heart stand still at times. He had seen her and raised a hand in carefree salute.

Leopold, thirteen and clever, had darker hair than any

of them. Leopold's hair was almost brown. He was talking earnestly to George as they came to a halt.

George put a protective arm about Alice's shoulders, making her smile as she asked him, 'You've enough money, have you? We hate fibbing to Aunt Harriet but . . .'

'But the Aerial Flight's more exciting than feeding the ducks in Hesketh Park!' George said. He grinned at Alice, 'Don't get yourself into a state about a little lie,' he said. 'You wouldn't have to lie if Aunt Harriet would unbend a little.' He pulled the last of his change from his pocket, counted it quickly and said, 'I've one and six left from my allowance. That's enough for the Aerial Flight and tobacco for me and Leopold.'

Alice gave Leopold a fierce look. Papa had told her that one of her duties was to keep a watchful eye on Leopold. 'You haven't started smoking, have you?' she asked in her most severe voice. 'You know Papa's dictum!'

Leopold reddened and fumbled in the pocket of his navy-blue jacket before looking up sheepishly. *Mens Sana In Corpore Sano. A healthy mind in a healthy body.'

Leopold's guilty expression reduced them all to laughter before he went on, after counting the coins he had taken from his pocket. 'One and twopence halfpenny. I'll pay for the tram home and Alice's fortune-teller.' Then he added with a touch of resentment, 'Father smokes. I remember he used to smoke cigars after supper.'

Beattie said quickly, 'Let's go. We're holding up the whole road.'

'Who wants to go to the fortune-teller?' asked Leopold when they had walked as far as the pier and begun to make their way towards the Aerial Flight at the Marine Lake.

'Only Alice,' Beattie said. 'And she's silly, wasting money on a gypsy-woman. It's nonsense. You can get three iced lemonades for sixpence.'

Ahead, George stopped at the point where the path divided. One path led from the lake and around the rose-beds. In the other direction lay the fortune-teller.

'If Alice takes sixpence for her fortune,' George said, 'We can have our rides, look round the funfair and then go to the cafe and wait for her. How's that?'

Alice didn't want to be selfish and deprive the others. 'I've saved enough for everyone's fortunes,' she said. 'And it's our last chance to spend it.' She was a thrifty manager. There was seldom anything left over.

George gave his deep laugh that sounded just like Papa's. 'A gypsy once told me that I would never be rich, but I was going to be happy and surrounded by children.'

'She was wrong then, wasn't she?' Beattie said. 'You're going to be a doctor.'

George gave her a mournful look. 'I'm not clever, little sister,' he said. 'I'm going to disappoint Papa. Papa has all the talents: doctor, soldier – and medicine man.'

Alice was becoming impatient with their banter. 'Medicine-man, indeed!' she corrected George. 'Papa's not a shaman.'

George grinned again, blue eyes crinkling like Papa's. 'But we know that I'm going to marry a beautiful heiress and live happily ever after.' He nudged Alice. 'And I don't need a gypsy to tell me otherwise.'

'Last night,' Leopold said seriously, 'you told me you were in love with two shopgirls, a housemaid and the matron at school. "All I want is to be loved by a thousand girls," you said.'

'He already is.' Alice shook her head in amusement and said to George, 'Stop filling Leopold's head with daft ideas, George. Give me the sixpence. You order the tea. I won't be long.'

She was bursting to know if the gypsy really could see her future for it was rumoured in the town that important people, men of rank, would only make decisions after consulting Senora Churiana; that the gypsy-woman was

74

behind the highest in the land, guiding, advising and prophesying.

But if that were true she thought as she made her way towards Scarisbrick Street, surely the gypsy would not live in such apparent poverty.

When she reached Scarisbrick Street, a crowded narrow passageway between the Promenade and Lord Street, she was pale-faced with anticipation. The house was tucked between two small shops; a mother-of-pearl shop with a window full of trinkets and on the other side of the gypsy's narrow door, a basket-maker's. The outer door was ajar. She pushed it open and tapped timidly on the glass panel of the gypsy's den.

'Enter!'

She went inside. Senora Churiana's room was tiny, hot and dark with a suffocating smell of jasmine and stale garlic. The walls were festooned with lace and painted fans. The wooden floor was dusty and unpolished. A folding screen hid half of the room. In the front half were two bentwood chairs and a rickety rattan table covered with a faded red cloth in a paisley pattern and in the centre of the table was the crystal ball.

Senora Churiana was small, Spanish and very old. Lines criss-crossed her cheeks and under heavy grey eyebrows small black eyes glittered.

'Sit,' she ordered as soon as Alice closed the door.

Alice went quickly to the table and spread her muslin skirt flat beneath her as she sat. She said, 'A sixpenny fortune please, senora.' Beneath what she hoped was an air of composure it felt as if her heart were thundering around in an empty drum. It was unnerving, being shut in this hot little room with a strange old gypsy woman whom she was sure could see into the future.

Senora Churiana's fringed and beaded headband fell forwards over her face. She leaned towards the ball and began to speak in a monotone, throaty and quick. 'I see a ship approaching. A ship that is approaching the shore carries your destiny, my fair one.'

That would be the *Tintagel Castle* and Papa.

Senora Churiana had stopped for a moment and was looking at her face. Alice felt heat begin to rise in her cheeks.

The tone of the gypsy's voice dropped. She said, 'Many changes are coming into your life. So many changes. You are going to leave this town—'

Alice's heart almost stopped beating this time. Leave Southport? Her hands were shaking. And, though she had sworn to herself not to give the gypsy any clues to her hopes and fears, she could contain herself no longer.

'Do you see me in Liverpool? Or Manchester?' she interrupted eagerly. 'Do you see where I am?'

The gypsy closed her eyes, then opened them again a few seconds later. She gazed into her crystal and, though Alice could see nothing in it but the reflection of the room, the gypsy said slowly, 'I see you again. I see a big house. I see mountains. Snow-covered mountains and a deep forest—' Here she looked up at Alice. 'Do you know where this place is?'

'No. I'm afraid I—' Alice whispered, wishing she could be more helpful.

The gypsy looked at the ball again. 'You have made a long journey over water and land. Those around you speak in many, many foreign tongues.'

Alice felt her face burning in excitement. Her mouth was dry. She bit the inside of her lower lip before asking, 'The destiny, senora? What is it?'

'It is a man. There is a tall, handsome stranger with dark hair, coming towards you from a foreign land.'

Disappointment flooded her. It could not be Papa. Papa's hair was fair. The senora was not looking at the right man in her crystal. Maybe the senora told all the girls that a tall, dark and handsome man was coming into their lives. Alice didn't want a tall handsome stranger in her life.

All the magic seemed to fall away. She could wait no longer. She stood up and demanded in her firm, clear voice, 'My future, senora. Do you see me on the stage?'

Senora Churiana appeared to lose interest in the crystal. She looked up at Alice and put out her hand. 'D'yer want me to read yer 'and?' she said in a flat voice that sounded more like a Lancashire woman's than a Spanish gypsy's. 'It costs another shillin' if yer do.'

Alice didn't have a shilling to spare and she didn't believe in the reading of palms. 'No. No thank you, senora,' she said. 'I must go.'

She left the gypsy's rooms and walked along the less crowded stretch of Lord Street towards the cafe, puzzled by the gypsy's forecast.

Normally she would have been aware of the ladies of fashion strolling the wide street under the flower-decked glass canopies. She would have pretended to be one of them, pausing here and there to look at the shops: Pidduck's the jeweller where watches, clocks and fine gold rings were displayed; the Russian Fur Shop which even in June attracted the prosperous to their showrooms – she would have admired the array of sable and chinchilla coats, arctic fox collars and winter-coat edgings of squirrel and astrakhan.

She passed by them, unseeing. So bemused was she that she was about to pass the cafe when she was pulled up with a start by a grinning George who had lifted the lace curtain and was tapping on the glass to attract her attention.

Inside, the cafe was busy. Rowntree's was the meeting place of some of Southport's richest people; well-dressed women with little to do but meet for afternoon tea after a pleasant hour or two of shopping. The cafe was full of them today, dressed in silks and fine Egyptian cotton and lace, their voices raised a little, the better to be overheard. Alice tugged at the muslin dress so that the crumpling might not show. Aunt Harriet had bought the dress and her new blue one and she was to say nothing to Papa about them.

Arthur, blond curls escaping from under his sailor

hat, was wedged between the table and a mountain of cushions and, as she approached, Alice saw Beattie nod to the waitress to bring their order. She seated herself and looked from one to the other around the table as she waited for someone to ask about her fortune.

At last Beattie said, 'What did she tell you?'

Alice leaned forward and said in a low voice that would not be overheard by any of the fashionable women at the next table, 'It all sounded so far-fetched. I'm not sure if she can see into the future.'

'She can see into your purse.' Leopold ran an awkward finger round the inside of his celluloid collar as he spoke. It was too small for him.

George gave a deep chuckle. He had all Papa's charm. George was very handsome, like Papa in looks. But whereas Papa always stood erect George had a loose-limbed, casual way of leaning when he stood about, lounging a little when he sat. The waitress was pink-faced serving them as she avoided George's eye.

Alice ignored Leopold's last remark. 'She said she saw me in a castle with snow-capped mountains all around and everyone speaking in a foreign language.'

When the tea was laid before them and the waitress had gone George said, 'The gypsy must have seen you on the stage – playing Lady Macbeth.'

'I hope you are right,' Alice answered as she began to cut and butter a tea-cake for Arthur. 'I love acting.'

A knowing smile was playing around Beattie's firm little lips. 'Every day's an act with you, Alice.'

The girl brought their teapot and hot water and for the next few minutes Alice busied herself pouring tea, buttering and cutting. She hoped that some of the others had a little money left in case the tea cost more than she had in her purse. It was an enormous, delicious spread. There were five cakes, five little iced cakes on the stand. She was also trying very hard not to think about tomorrow's audition. To take her mind off every-thing and to remind George that there were serious questions to answer she asked, 'What about the examinations? When will you get into medical school?'

George looked crestfallen at last. 'I won't pass them,' he said. 'Papa doesn't expect much of you girls but he expects us to have done well.'

'You've both done well at school, haven't you, George?' Beattie asked, a worried frown crossing her brow. 'Apart from that once, when Leopold was sent home for . . .'

'For borrowing. I was going to pay it back with my winnings.' Leopold looked round the table with defiant eyes before he added miserably, 'But we all know that Father's incorruptible. He'll never forgive me.'

Alice passed the plate of sandwiches around. 'Nobody will tell,' she assured Leopold. 'It was a misunderstanding. Aunt Harriet paid the money back. She'll say nothing to Papa.'

'Do you think the war will have changed Father?' Leopold asked as he took a fish-paste sandwich and stuffed the whole thing into his mouth.

'No,' Alice told him. 'Papa will be the same. We've changed. I hope we won't disappoint him.'

Leopold, the sandwich gone, reached for a scone. 'Father wasn't conscripted,' he mumbled through the food in his mouth. 'He couldn't have been too concerned. He could have been killed.'

Alice didn't like to hear Leopold talking that way. 'Of course Papa had to volunteer,' she said sharply to Leopold. 'It would be as bad as breaking your word, not volunteering. And we Davenports never, never break our word.'

She didn't like the way Leopold always referred to Papa as Father. It would be a good thing when Papa came home. 'Papa thought the war would be over in a few weeks,' she reminded them. 'Nobody dreamed it would go on so long.'

She poured second cups of tea all round before turning to Leopold again. 'Did you buy a *Liverpool Echo*?'

'Yes,' Leopold said. 'There's no news about the *Tintagel Castle*.'

'Just the racing results, eh?' George laughed before adding, 'We'll get word from Chester. From the regimental headquarters. They'll know exactly when the ship's due in. They'll send a telegram.'

'Aunt Harriet will be told first,' Leopold announced with absolute conviction.

Beattie sipped her tea quickly. 'Do you think that he – that Papa will—?' she began.

'Ask Aunt Harriet to marry him?' George said.

Beattie went pink and asked, 'What will become of us if they don't marry?'

They all fell silent for a moment and it seemed to Alice that they were looking to her for an answer. She felt a sudden cold chill pass through her as she realized with a shock that everything, every plan she was making for her own future depended entirely on Papa's marrying Aunt Harriet. It was unthinkable that he might not. She could not answer Beattie's question.

Leopold, who had formed a great attachment to their aunt, said, 'If they don't marry, Aunt Harriet could come and live with us, couldn't she?'

Alice said gently, 'No, Leopold. It isn't "done" for a single woman to live under the same roof as a man who is not her husband.'

Leopold said, 'He could stay on in the army.'

'He's leaving. Papa's over forty.' Alice began to collect their empty plates. Aunt Harriet said the empty plates should be left for the waitress but Alice didn't like to leave a mess behind. 'Papa will make all the decisions when he comes home,' she said. 'I'm sure he'll do the right thing.'

George looked worldly wise. 'He's said nothing in his letters to us about love and marriage.' Then he shrugged and added, 'But when you're forty-odd you can't think about marrying for love. You're too old.'

'Right we are then,' Alice said. 'Ready everyone?' And

whilst Beatrice lifted baby Arthur down she took her purse and the bill to the girl at the cash desk.

There was just enough money left for her train fare to Liverpool tomorrow. When she had paid she went out into Lord Street and found George waiting, a silly grin plastered all over his face.

He grabbed hold of her arm. 'There he is again,' he said and pointed across the street into the bustling crush opposite. 'Did you know that you've been followed all afternoon, Alice? By a Dago.' He roared with laughter.

George was being infantile. Alice glowered. 'What are you talking about?'

Beattie said, 'Ignore him, Alice. George says that a sort of Italian fellow was walking behind you earlier. I didn't see anyone.'

George could be so silly at times. Alice pulled her arm away irritably. 'Let's catch the next tram,' she said. 'Aunt Harriet will be out of her mind with worry.'

# Chapter Five

**Monday, 16 June**

At a quarter to ten every morning Karl Reinhardt saw her. Alice Davenport went by every day, pushing a baby carriage in the pouring rain, talking to herself. She was tall and slender with a clean, fresh complexion and silky blonde hair and, until now, in all his twenty-two years he had never felt like this. In fact, until he had seen her he had always known an aversion to women.

Most women outside his own family had always seemed to him to be, unlike men, dirty creatures – full of tricks. But, although it was the last thing he could have wished upon himself, he had probably fallen in love with an unsoiled, pure English girl. He was certainly obsessed by her. He watched for her every morning from his attic window of the Victoria Hotel, one of the grandest in Southport. He spent his free afternoons roaming the town looking for her. If he had known where she lived he'd have spent his evenings walking past her house instead of wasting time as he did – playing cards, gambling with the other waiters.

If he did not see her one day then he became anxious and desperate until she swam into his vision again, sailing along the promenade in navy-blue waterproofs, chattering away to herself with serious concentration, occasionally stopping to refer to a small book she kept tucked under the cover of the baby carriage.

He ran, lithe and easy, up the five flights of stairs to his attic room. He had finished his morning and luncheon duties and had every afternoon free. He closed the door and went quickly to the washstand to wash and to change out of the boiled wing-collar shirt that chafed his neck. Pouring cold water carefully into the washbowl he started to sing her name to himself, over and over as the water swirled into the big china basin – Alice Davenport – Alice Davenport.

He stripped his clothes off and began to scrub hard at his hands and fingernails. Four times last week he had seen her – Miss Alice Davenport. Yesterday he had followed her to her church. It was a Protestant church like his father's. Mother's family were Catholics though Mother had dropped out of her old beliefs and gone over to her husband's faith.

Only yesterday he had heard her name spoken in church. It was 'Meez Aleez Davenport'. He had heard the verger say, 'Will the children please follow Miss Alice Davenport to the Sunday School.' Since then he had been repeating it to himself as if by naming her he could claim her for his own. Meez Aleez Davenport – Meez Aleez Davenport.

He glanced at his face in the small mirror that hung from a nail above the washstand. It appeared to him to be a reasonably pleasant face. There were girls who would be pleased if he were to pay them court and he had never had the least inclination to do so.

But she, Miss Alice Davenport, had not even glanced his way though he had willed her to turn her head in his direction at church and on her walks along the Promenade. On Saturday he'd seen her coming out of the fortune-teller's house before he lost sight of her on Lord Street.

Once or twice he'd caught sight of her in the covered indoor market on Eastbank Street where he'd watched her making purchases. She bought well and since she bought a lot he knew she was shopping for a family. When Jamaica bananas were two for a penny she would buy a whole hand. When new-laid eggs were plentiful and cost less than a shilling for nine, she bought. A young officer

83

could take such a wife back to Prague and have every rank from the colonel down green with envy.

He sang as he splashed the cold water all over his body and scrubbed with a rough loofah at his strong arms and his long sinewy legs. Afterwards he dried himself on the rough cotton towels he liked much better than the soft fluffy cloths these English people preferred. He had not seen her this morning. She had not passed his window at the usual time.

Miss Alice Davenport was the only reason for his smiling, his singing, his new light-hearted sense of well-being. Until he had set eyes upon her his only purpose in life had been to earn enough money to get back to Prague. He had already spent more than three miserable years in England; in Cheshire, working at the hated, dirty factory work in the cotton mills of Macclesfield.

That was before he had been thrown out of his father's house.

Father was an obstinate man who would listen to no views but his own. Three and a half years ago Father had brought his family to Macclesfield, saying that it would be for five years only. The family had brought with them only a little money and Father's skills as a millwright and textile engineer. He had been recommended to Sir Jack Blackshaw who had offered Father a house and a working partnership in Blackshaw's Textile Engineering Works.

Certainly his father had worked hard. After only three and a half years in partnership his father had a big house and a motor-car. He had brought orders from abroad for his machines and had bought his way into the Blackshaw business. And Father expected gratitude and hard work from his sons. Karl detested engineering. He also detested England. He had always wanted to return home. His opportunity had come when Father decided to apply for papers of naturalization for them all; Father and Mother, himself and his brother Heinz and his three sisters, Irmgard, Renate and Anna. Karl, being over twenty-one, was being persuaded by Father to make his own application.

They were sitting in the large room at Beaufort Lodge, the house at the foot of the Pennine hills which Father had bought. Father was very proud of his property. In Prague they had lived in an apartment.

Speaking in German, Father had begun. 'We are aliens in our chosen land.'

Mother, sitting at the fireside whilst Father spoke, had nodded in agreement.

'When we have been here for five years we can apply to become British subjects.' Nobody spoke and Father went on, 'We must prove that we have the means of support.' Here he gave a little cough of satisfaction. 'I think I have proved this.' He began to pace the floor.

Mother smiled proudly at him.

'We have to be of good character.' He looked about, as if daring anyone to deny it. Mother nodded again. 'And we must have an adequate knowledge of the language.'

'*Ja!*' said Mother.

Karl at this point could take no more. He jumped to his feet. 'Why?' he almost shouted. 'You told us that we'd be here for five years only.'

'I have changed my mind. No longer do I consider myself to be Austrian.' Father spoke with that air of finality which was like a challenge to Karl. 'There are too many frontiers in Austria-Hungary. Too many nationalities, too many classes.'

'Too many classes?' Karl had protested. 'All societies have classes.'

His father said, 'Austria-Hungary has an emperor who believes in the divinity of kings. He surrounds himself with courtiers and aristocrats and is out of touch with the common people. We have the merchant and banking class, a middle class of factory owners and traders, a subversive class of clever intellectuals and revolutionaries and an underclass of peasants. Too many classes!'

Hoping to annoy his father, Karl answered quickly. 'You have forgotten the military class.'

'You spent three years at military academy.' Father's voice was rising ominously. 'All you did was learn to fight a duel. You were an arrogant braggart. We left the country just in time. Another month and you would have been an ensign, discharged from the academy, ready for the army.'

Karl remembered his disappointment. He had wanted to stay with his companions; to pass out as an Uhlan officer on the emperor's birthday with a first silver star flashing on his collar. Babushka, his Russian-born grandmother, was going to pay for his entry into the Uhlan – that fashionable and expensive arm of the service – the Lancers. He answered his father. 'It was a good life in Prague. We were not peasants. Many people have a good life in Bohemia – factory owners – engineers. You could have stayed there. We had an apartment. And there is Grandmother's house in the German Sudeten.'

'The house in Sudetan will be yours when she dies,' his father said. 'Your grandmother will leave it you. You are her eldest grandson. But what will you do with it? She is an old . . .'

Here Father looked at Mother quickly, then began to speak in English so she wouldn't understand. Father, a Protestant and clever engineer, had married his Catholic wife against the wishes of her own mother – Karl's Russian-born Babushka. 'Your grandmother – your Babushka as you call her – says she will leave all she has to you. She did not want us to leave.' He looked hard at Karl and said, 'But what has she got? Nothing!'

'My grandmother has money,' Karl answered. 'She will give me an allowance to help my army pay when I go home.'

Father's black moustache and eyebrows had almost met, so deep was his frown of disapproval. 'Your grandmother wants you to marry, to have children. And she does not have enough money to support you, and a wife,

86

and children. She has not paid the servants for years. Half of her house is unused – closed. The servants stay because it is a roof over their heads and they are sorry for her. She is living on the last of her money. What do you think you would live on?'

'I shall not need to earn money,' Karl said. 'I shall go back into the imperial army. I can live on my army pay and whatever Babushka gives me.'

'You are a fool! Worse – you are a young fool!' Father had begun to go red and to sweat a little. 'You will want to marry. And how can you hope to marry without money?'

'I shall never marry. Marriage disgusts me.' He had spoken those very words and in a disdainful, sneering manner, knowing that it worried Father, his lack of interest in girls. His only experience of them had been of the cheap girls who came to the student taverns and he'd gone upstairs with them rather than make himself a laughing stock. But everything about those experiences had been repellent to him. He had repeated to his father, 'I do not want a wife and I dislike children.'

These were the very words he had said. He had spoken them of course before he had set eyes on Alice Davenport. 'When I return I shall go back into the army,' Karl told his father again.

Father had kept his temper well up to this point but now he began to shout. 'The kaiser is building a huge army and navy. There's no solution to the Slav problem. There are too many nationalities. All want their freedom. Young men will die fighting for other men's lands. Wars are about territory not nationality. Think! Use your eyes and your ears.'

Father shouted on. 'In England all people are one. We will be one with them. We will prosper here.'

'England! England!' Karl's eyes were flashing. '*Das ist mir ganz wurst!*' Then he said with a coldness that masked the heat of his anger, 'Which, in case you have forgotten

87

your own language, Father, roughly translated means I don't give a damn about England!'

Father could lose his temper faster than any man on Earth. He made a visible effort to control it. He looked at Mother, returned to speaking in German and said in an earnest voice, 'Karl! Remember! Your mother's parents fled from Russia forty-five years ago. The Reinhardts fled from Hungary. In every generation – in both families – we have lost every penny we own, more than once.'

He looked hard again at Karl to see if his words were having any effect on his self-willed son, then he added, 'In Bohemia, people don't trust one another: Germans, Jews, Gypsies, Czechs, Slovaks, Austrians, Hungarians. All are enemies.'

Karl remained stubborn. 'Here you have the same peoples. We are here. So are other nationals.'

It was too much for Father. He could not pretend any longer. He thundered at Karl, 'They have all fled to Britain! Whoever sees British freedom and liberty wishes to be British! The peoples of Europe have never known it. They never will.'

He paused for breath, straightened his shoulders and in a deep, commanding voice said, 'From the day we become English I forbid any of you to speak German!'

Karl, as determined to retain his identity as Father was to relinquish theirs, had replied, 'And I can never be anything but Bohemian. Never will I give up my nationality.'

Father shouted, 'I wash my hands of you! If you will not take out naturalization papers then you will leave my house!'

Karl had packed his bag immediately and taken a train to Manchester. He had enough money to buy his breakfast and had then taken his wristwatch to a pawnbroker's shop and he had been given enough money for a few days' lodgings. He had returned to the station and studied the excursion board. There were cheap-day excursions to Southport. He'd been there once and liked the town. He'd try to find work and lodgings – a hotel was a possibility for that would combine the two. He'd find someone to play cards with – poker or three-card brag – and he'd save his winnings as well as his wages. When he had enough money for the fare he'd return to Bohemia.

Not for a second had he allowed for the fact that he could fall in love with a beautiful English girl whom as yet he did not even know. And he did not wish to become a *Kuemmerer* – a frustrated lover – one who loves but receives no reward.

He looked in the glass and smiled at his reflection. He was immaculate. He was ready. He would walk about the town and hope to catch sight of her. He was desperate to get to know her, desperate for someone to introduce him to her, desperate to find out where she lived, where she went.

Audition day was here. Alice had been awake half the night in a turmoil of nervous anticipation. She lay on her bed, her eyes fixed on the Alphonse Mucha print above Beattie's bed, telling herself that she was glad the day was here, at last. Aunt Harriet had gone downstairs a few moments ago and in a minute or two Alice was going to take the Shakespeare onto the half-landing and have a last little read before breakfast. Today she would not tramp the promenade in the rain.

She looked at Beattie who was still asleep. 'Beattie! Beattie!' she whispered. 'Wake up.'

'Um? What?' Beattie stirred and the high bedstead with its brass rails and knobs creaked as she rolled heavily onto her side, facing Alice's bed. She opened her eyes slowly and then closed them again.

'Sh-sh!' Alice warned. 'Will you listen for Arthur if I go onto the landing to rehearse?' Arthur slept in the adjoining bedroom.

Beatrice was wide awake. 'What time is it?'

'Seven o'clock.' Alice's stomach tightened again.

'Why are you up so early?' Beattie asked.

'You know. The auditions,' Alice whispered. 'I'm going onto the landing where I can rehearse my lines and not disturb you.'

'Have you told Aunt Harriet?'

'No.'

'Why not?' Beattie heaved herself up into a sitting position. 'Mama was an actress when she met Papa. Aunt Harriet encouraged her. She won't stop you.'

'Aunt Harriet wants to please Papa. She's hardly let me go anywhere alone.'

'Is it for a play?' Beattie whispered back.

'Mr Squibb is forming a new theatre company.'

'Who's Mr Squibb?' Beattie asked.

'Someone our producer's heard about,' Alice said. 'The producer in Southport Amateur—'

'Yes. Of course.' Beattie was sitting bolt upright with her arms wrapped around the hump of her knees. 'It's Papa who might not agree to it,' she said with the clear reason that was the mainspring of Beatrice's character.

Alice placed her hands flat on the huckaback counterpane and pushed herself backwards to lean her weight against the wall. Her bedstead creaked as well. 'If I don't get the job in Liverpool there's a chance I'll be asked to join Manchester Theatricals.'

'Is that a paid job?' Beattie asked.

'Yes. The Manchester one is a repertory company. But the new Liverpool company will pay more.' Alice put a finger to her lips here to warn Beattie not to talk too loud. 'Sh!' she said. 'Nobody but you knows about it.'

'I don't know why you haven't said,' Beattie whispered back. 'You know that Aunt Harriet likes to be told everything.' Beatrice had taken to life with Aunt Harriet as a duck to water. Beatrice liked rules and order and no fireworks.

'I'm afraid I won't be picked out. That's why,' Alice answered. 'And if I am . . . if Mr Squibb offers me a place . . . or the Manchester Repertory Company asks me to join them . . . I can say to Papa and Aunt Harriet that it is all agreed. They won't expect me to go back on my word to anyone. I might just as well wait until it's a "*fait accompli*".'

'I don't know how you dare,' said Beattie. Her eyes were wide. 'Not without asking Papa's permission first.'

Underneath, Alice thought it all very daring as well. It was as if events had taken care of themselves. She reminded Beatrice about the talk with Papa before he left. 'Papa said we'll be allowed to earn our own livings.'

Beattie said in a calm little whisper, 'What Papa said was, "If you don't marry then there will always be a roof over your heads and a meal on the table but I shall not be able to support you in great style".'

'He said—'

'—Papa says that motherhood and marriage are the highest state a girl can aspire to,' Beattie reminded her. 'He says there is no more beautiful sight than that of a mother with her baby in her arms.'

'It might be the most beautiful thing Papa's ever seen.' Alice sounded impatient. 'But I've had baby Arthur in my arms ever since Mama died. And Arthur is my brother – not my child. Arthur will have a new Mama, when Papa marries . . .'

'Aren't you happy?' Beattie asked. 'Is that why you want to leave us?'

'I'm not at all unhappy.' Alice had not thought for a moment that Beatrice would see her stage career as a desertion. 'I'll be able to come home all the time, Beattie. I'll only be going to Liverpool. Or Manchester.'

'What do you want, Alice? If you aren't unhappy you must want something more . . .'

Alice was silent for a moment. She had never even asked herself that question. After a few seconds she began to list her heart's desires, quietly, 'I don't want to be answerable to anyone. I don't want to have to say "thank you" for everything anyone gives to me or does for me. I want a life of my own.'

'When Papa marries Aunt Harriet you'll have your own life,' Beattie said. 'I'm sure Papa will let you work until you find a husband.' She smiled and added, 'Like I'm going to do.' Then, 'Are you sure you want to be an actress?' she said.

Alice sighed. It had been a waste of time explaining her longings to a young sister who was only fifteen years old. What silly questions Beattie asked. Her insides were churning with nerves about it and Beattie asked her if she wanted to be an actress. She smiled. 'You do ask daft questions!'

But even as she spoke her nervousness was dying down a little. It was impossible to talk to Beattie for long without her placid nature having its calming effect. She looked at Beattie and said, 'Do you know that in 1875 – that's twenty-seven years ago – Ellen Terry was earning forty pounds a week!' She waited to see the effect on Beattie.

Forty pounds a week was unimaginable riches to anyone. Forty pounds a week was two thousand pounds a year. Papa, as far as she could tell, earned less than four hundred pounds a year.

Beattie's eyes widened. 'I know you want to be rich . . .'

'It's got nothing to do with being "rich",' Alice told her. 'I want to be an actress because it's the only chance I'll ever have to earn money. I don't want to be kept – or have to answer or ask for everything. I'm sick of it. If I can go on the stage for a few years I can make some money.' She added, 'It's the only thing I'd be any good at. I left school at fourteen, don't forget.'

There was a second or two of silence whilst Beattie digested these statements before she smiled and whispered, 'I'll listen to you if you hand me the book.'

Beattie was an angel. It was just what she needed. Alice crossed the shiny linoleum on slim, bare feet and opened the trinket drawer of the dressing-table where the book was kept. Papa's last gift to her had been the complete works of Shakespeare; seven little, leather-bound volumes.

Beattie gave a long-drawn-out sigh. 'Give me the *Hamlet*.'

Alice opened the book and handed it over. 'Start there,' she said, pointing to the place. 'Act four, scene five. You read Laertes.'

'Papa said that if we never get married we could think about becoming schoolteachers,' said Beattie. 'Or nurses.'

'I detest nursing and a junior teacher at a board school only earns four shillings a week,' Alice replied with an impatient sigh. 'Concentrate on *Hamlet*, Beattie.' She was going to find it hard to remember the lines at all on this day of all days. Her hands began to shake when she thought about it.

'If I don't get married, I'm going to be a nurse,' said Beattie. 'Why can't you?'

'Because I couldn't bear all that lowly stuff,' Alice answered decisively. 'I couldn't bear the training Beattie. I've seen the nurses at Papa's hospital bobbing and blushing and calling him "sir".' She saw the shock in Beatrice's face and tried to explain. 'I've too much pride. It's wrong to have pride – it's a sin and all that – but having to defer to people when you're working for them for a wage seems to me like slavery. I'd feel as if I'd been bought.'

Beattie looked hurt. 'If everyone thought like that the country would be in a sorry state,' she said.

Alice had not meant to upset Beattie who looked as if she'd been told off. She said, 'I can't justify it. Maybe I'm wrong . . . But there you are . . . That's all there is to it . . . I'd make a poor subordinate.'

Beattie said, 'I don't see what's wrong with it.'

Alice looked at Beattie's round, sweet face. Then the taste of metal was in her mouth at the thought of the audition. 'Are you going to read Laertes? I want to be word perfect.'

'All right.' Beattie gave her attention to the book. 'After Ophelia's song? You won't want to sing at this time of the morning.'

'Yes.'

Beattie read, stumbling over the words, 'Laertes. "This nothing." Sorry! "This nothing's – more than matter." Now, you say—'

'Yes. I remember,' Alice came in, ' "There's rosemary, that's for remembrance; pray, love, remember: and there is pansies, that's for thoughts." '

She stopped, lay back and closed her eyes as she searched for the next line. But all at once she could not remember a single word. She felt sick with fear. She opened her eyes for a second and looked across to Beattie. 'I can't remember a thing, Beattie,' she whispered.

Beattie had put the book down and was lying back, waiting for her to continue but Alice could not. She could not go on reciting because she was remembering – but not her lines. She could not remember her lines for remembering Mama.

Beattie said, 'Do you think Mama found it easy, learning her lines?'

'Were you thinking about Mama too?' Alice asked her.

'Yes. I was thinking about how she leaped off the stage into Papa's arms,' Beattie said. 'I wonder if anyone will do that to you . . . ?'

Alice shook her head. 'Things like that don't happen to everyone.'

But lying there on the bed, Alice wondered if she could have done it had she been Mama – and was sure that she would not. No matter how handsome the suitor, even if he were as dashing as Captain Freddie Blackshaw, Alice would never do what Mama had done.

She could almost imagine what it must be like to fall in love. She knew that she had strong passions, for there were times when she ached for love and affection. But there was fear too; fear of the unknown, fear of being, as Mama must have been, out of control, overcome with a

94

passion so powerful as to make her forget everything else. Mama must not have cared a fig for anything; not thought about her good name, not given a fig for tomorrow, when she leaped into Papa's arms.

Nor would Alice ever give in to temptation, though she knew exactly what it was. Papa had spoken about it before he left. But Papa had spoken of love and temptation and honour and how a father's good name would be brought low if a daughter should stray from the paths of virtue.

'What time is it?'

Beattie's question brought her out of her reverie. She looked at the clock and her insides turned a nervous somersault again at the thought of the audition. 'Half past seven,' she said. 'Go back to sleep. I'm going to get dressed and go downstairs.'

She went to the wide mahogany wardrobe, opened the mirrored door and took out the blue ninon dress Aunt Harriet had bought for her. It was a pretty dress with a high, lace-trimmed collar and long, narrow sleeves. Ninon did not look quite like silk but it was a dress that could be worn in the daytime both outdoors or in. Blue would be the right colour for Ophelia, even if it was a little young for Hedda Gabler. But she had not a lot of choice. Beside her serviceable skirts and blouses, she had only two day dresses, the ninon blue and her muslin. She had one dress for evening occasions, a pale yellow silk; a Christmas present from Aunt Harriet which she had worn once, to a church social.

She tied the ribbons on her chemise, fastened the buttons on her petticoat and slid the blue dress over her head. She did up the hooks herself, twisting her arms behind her waist then behind her neck with an easy grace. Then she checked herself over in the mirror over the washstand.

She would look almost as Ophelia herself must have looked when her hair was curled and pinned on top of her head. She was a little too thin, but the dress with a trumpet-shaped skirt had close gathering at the back of the hips which gave her the fashionable deep-bosomed and wide-hipped look. There was no need for the hated stays Aunt Harriet liked her to wear. Stays, she thought, were for wobbly bodies. Her thin frame didn't have a scrap of spare flesh.

There was a matching hat; a blue felt threaded through with ivory ribbon. She had worn the outfit to church last Sunday.

Beattie was asleep and Alice picked up the Shakespeare without disturbing her and put it and the Ibsen in her handbag before she left the room.

She went down the wide staircase, her shoes soundless on the red Turkish carpet. The dining room was always gloomy, even on summer days, since its one narrow window overlooked the back garden and it was filled to capacity with heavy mahogany furniture; a bulbous-legged table and eight hard-stuffed dining chairs, mirror-backed sideboard and a small chiffonnier of French design which held Aunt Harriet's collection of Dresden figures.

The door was open and, although it was only a quarter to eight, she found Aunt Harriet already seated at the table. Her black poplin dress with severely cut skirt, high fully-boned neck and pintucked bodice was one of several her dressmaker had made. Aunt Harriet had worn them almost constantly since Mama had died. No sooner, she was heard to say to her friend, had she come out of mourning for her cousin Clara than Her Majesty had died.

But Aunt Harriet was beautiful in a severe kind of way; her dark blonde hair with silvery side wings was abundant and carefully dressed and she held herself well.

'Did you sleep well?' she asked. 'I thought I heard you and Beattie talking.'

'I was up early,' Alice said. 'You've not forgotten, have you?'

'Forgotten what, dear?' Aunt Harriet could be vague

and absent-minded at times. She was looking at Alice as if she were quite unaware of Alice's plans.

'That I'm going to Liverpool – to the shipping offices – to check on the regiment's arrival.' There. That was the big lie told. Alice could eat nothing but a slice of bread and butter.

Aunt Harriett said, 'It's quite unnecessary. We know the ship will be here in the next day or two. And your Papa will not expect us to be standing on the dock with the people who are waiting for the Lancashire men. Your Papa will have to go immediately to regimental headquarters at Chester.'

A proud look came over her face as she reminded Alice, 'Your Papa is not a private soldier. His duty is to see to his men's disembarkation leave before he takes his own.'

Alice said, 'But how can we be sure he's arrived safely if we don't know when the ship docks?'

'They are heading for port, Alice. It says in this morning's paper that there are going to be celebrations all over the country later in the week when the men are home . . .'

'But, Aunt Harriet . . .' Alice started to say.

'. . . It says . . .' Aunt Harriet went on, picking up the paper and starting to read aloud. 'Cathedral services are to be held in Chester and in Liverpool . . .'

Alice had to stop her. 'Aunt Harriet! I want to go!'

There was a moment's silence whilst Aunt Harriet first looked shocked at Alice's outburst, then lost the worried look and began to soften. 'Will they tell you' she said at last, 'if the ship is due in at Liverpool?'

Alice knew that her aunt's objections were crumbling. 'They left from Liverpool,' she said quietly. That much at least was the truth and she might not have to repeat the lie.

'You're not going alone?' Aune Harriet said, all at once looking severe again. 'You aren't thinking of travelling to Liverpool without a companion.'

'I must,' Alice said quickly before realizing that she

had spoken too hastily and taking a deep breath. 'I may be only seventeen, but I'm quite capable of travelling to Liverpool on a simple errand.'

Aunt Harriet did not look convinced and Alice began to gabble, rushing her words in her determination to be convincing. 'Girls do go to Liverpool, Aunt Harriet. Working girls do. Girls work as clerks and type-writers. Girls take the train every morning . . .'

'Not to Liverpool, Alice. To Birkdale perhaps or Formby but no young girl goes to the city alone. We'll go together. Tomorrow.' Aunt Harriet pulled her chair out and sat down. 'Today Lady Cranston-Bartlett comes for tea.'

Alice had forgotten that it was Lady Cranston-Bartlett's visiting day but she quickly saw that it would make her task easier. Aunt Harriet knew perfectly well that Lady Cranston-Bartlett was snobbish and condescending and that she spoke to Alice as if she were a menial.

'And I'm never at home when she calls,' she said to Aunt Harriet. 'If you remember, the first time we met she shrieked at me, "Go away! Don't touch my white gloves with your grubby little hands!" Then she took me aside and said that I was a rude girl to offer my hand and that in future I should curtsey to her and address her as Ma'am.'

'That was unfortunate,' Aunt Harriet said, 'but I do wish you'd stop that nonsense. You can't go through life thinking there are no social distinctions, no rules or conventions. There's nothing demeaning in addressing a lady properly.'

Alice said firmly, 'I think she's hateful. You know I do. Why should one person expect another to bow down?'

'You are so like your mother!' Aunt Harriet swept her hand across her sleeve in a gesture of impatience. 'We were both brought up to respect tradition. Clara never did. You are exactly the same, Alice. Lady Cranston-Bartlett asks nothing of you, except that once you have been presented to her you address her properly.'

'I "meet" people. I am not "presented" to them like – a plate of fancy cakes. And when I meet people I shake hands with them.' Heat was rising in Alice's cheeks as she heard herself answering Aunt Harriet back. It was unforgivable behaviour. 'She uses you, Aunt Harriet. She wants you all to herself. And you flatter her by paying court to her. Nobody else would!'

There was a terrible silence. Aunt Harriet had gone pale. Alice knew that she had upset her and now that she had had her say she found herself, as so often she did, wanting to retract, wishing she had not caused hurt, regretting her hasty words. She felt tears of remorse come springing to her eyes. She would not have said those things, even though they were true, had she not been so agitated.

She got up and went to put her arm around Aunt Harriet's shoulder. Aunt Harriet remained stiff and upright in her chair but Alice put her face next to her aunt's cheek and whispered in her ear, 'I'm sorry. Please don't be angry with me. It's just that – I – I can't bring myself to . . .'

'You address your father's colleagues as "Doctor". You speak to old Colonel Webster—' Aunt Harriet said defensively.

Alice tried to explain quietly, 'They worked for their titles. They deserve them. They should be recognized.' She went back to her place at the table.

Aunt Harriet sighed. Polly Gosling, the chubby, sixteen-year-old housemaid whom Aunt Harriet had engaged and Alice had befriended, had entered the room carrying a teapot.

'Gosling,' Aunt Harriet said. 'You will accompany Miss Alice to Liverpool this afternoon.'

'No!' Alice insisted. 'I'm going alone.' She looked at Polly's bewildered face and said, 'I don't need a chaperone, Polly. I refuse to take you with me.'

Polly Gosling looked from one to the other of them and then, since neither Alice nor Aunt Harriet said anything more to her, gave an embarrassed little cough as she placed the teapot on its china stand. 'Will that be all, ma'am?' she asked.

Aunt Harriet spoke. 'That's all for the moment, Gosling.'

Alice began to pour the tea when the door closed behind Polly. She passed a cup to Aunt Harriet and saw again the faraway look in Aunt Harriet's eyes. 'I'm going to Liverpool, Aunt Harriet,' she said with quiet authority. 'Today. Tomorrow will be too late.'

Aunt Harriet would drop her opposition. She was sure she would. Alice felt ashamed of herself.

'Very well, Alice.' Aunt Harriet sighed with quiet resignation. 'Go to Liverpool if you must.'

Alice felt worse. 'I wish the ship were coming in today and that we were all going to meet him,' she said softly.

'Do you remember, child?' Aunt Harriet's voice was not much more than a whisper. 'Do you remember how Charles – your Papa – looked on the day he left us all?'

Alice remembered. She remembered it as if it were a play she could recall at will and yet it was two and a half years since they had last seen Papa and watched the parade.

# Chapter Six

**Monday, 16 June**

In the small saloon on A deck of S.S. *Tintagel Castle*
officers of the Cheshire Yeomanry were celebrating.
They had reached English waters the evening before, but
at five a.m. the Cheshires had seen off the last few officers
of the Lancashire Fusiliers and there was no sign of the
party breaking up. Captain Charles Davenport, a head
taller than many of them, counted them quickly. Fourteen. They were all here.

He had a deep melodic voice which, with his height,
the head of sandy-fair hair and his natural air of authority,
drew attention to himself instantly.

'Steward!' he called to the sailor who was approaching
through the crush. 'Fourteen brandies, please.' The man
was near enough to hear above the din. 'Have my mess
bill made up will you?'

The men were in high spirits. Badges glittered on navy
dress jackets. Jackets were open, showing scarlet and
silver braided waistcoats. Shoes of black leather gleamed,
dark blue trousers with the silver stripe down the outside
leg were immaculate. Their batmen kept the officers' kit
in fine order in spite of the difficulties in the crowded
ship where a thousand troopers were cramped into the
holds.

Two and a half years of service had taken the mounted
infantry regiment over five thousand miles by foot
and rail. On board *Lake Erie* on the way out it had
been necessary to immunize the company with the new
Almeroth Wright serum against enteric fever. Charles

and a trooper-orderly had done all the inoculations. Unwisely, they had omitted to inject themselves and both had succumbed to the fever in midsummer in Drachoender. Charles recovered. The trooper died.

Recovery had been followed by the action in the Orange Free Colony – and disillusionment with this war which had seemed, at the start, to be an heroic struggle.

Charles looked at the faces around him in the mess. All these pale Anglo-Saxon skins had darkened to a warm brown with eyes lively and eager to return to their womenfolk. He wanted to be with his children, to make up to them for the years of separation.

'Hear! Hear!' Frederick Blackshaw, who had been promoted to major on the field, had just leaped on to the bar counter and all eyes were turned towards him as he announced, 'You are all invited! Nay, gentlemen – fellow officers – you are ordered!'

Here there was a loud, good natured braying from the assembled officers.

'Come off it, Blackshaw!'

'Out with it!'

Unabashed, Major Blackshaw continued, 'Be my guests – week of celebrations – at Hetherington.'

Charles would not be going to Hetherington. He no longer had a house in the city so he'd stay overnight in the officers' quarters and go to Southport to see the children as soon as he'd done the medical checks and the men had been discharged. If they docked on Wednesday morning he'd go the same day or if late Wednesday it would be Thursday before he'd be free. He would have to leave Southport on Saturday to be in Chester to prepare for the Cathedral service of Thanksgiving on Sunday morning.

What was Blackshaw going on about?

Frederick was still shouting. 'The Colonel says there will be no leave – no officers will be discharged until after the Cathedral service on Sunday. Anyone who wishes to do so – stay at the Hall – guests of my father, Sir Jack Blackshaw. Cordially invited.'

There were fourteen officers present, most of whom lived near to the Chester barracks. Most would not be affected by the order. It was a blow. No doubt about it. He'd wanted to see his family before Sunday and now – now they told them that they had to report for duty every day! He'd speak to Blackshaw about it.

Charles was fond of the young major. Blackshaw was headstrong and a bit of a daredevil yet beneath the surface, as Charles knew from the campaigns, there beat a steadfast and honourable heart.

Charles thought again about the campaigns. The battles had been fierce and confused. Command had at times been weak; mistakes had been made and they had fought in and witnessed the most awful scenes of carnage.

Both companies of Cheshire Yeomanry and the Lancashire Fusiliers had lost men in battle and from sunstroke and fevers. Officers from the Cape Mounted Police had visited the companies seeking volunteers. The offers had been accepted with alacrity and the Cheshire Yeomanry had lost forty men to the South African police service where a trooper could earn seven shillings a day against only one and fivepence army pay. These losses had had a demoralizing effect but it was the action towards the end which had been the main cause of Charles's disillusionment.

Their column had been given the task of clearing farms in the area of Senekal and Vaal Kop. Their orders were to drive out the Boer farmers' cattle, to transport women and children to camps, to burn crops. All this they had done under the pleading eyes of the poor old men who had been left to keep the land whilst the younger Boers were fighting.

Charles, for whom the sight of a mother and her children had an almost sacred significance, had been sickened. He had seen the military, the strategic, necessity for it but it had gone against every instinct in him.

He wanted nothing more of soldiering, war and cruelty for as long as he lived. His future was going to be in the practice of medicine and the preserving, not the taking, of life.

Charles looked around again. The steward had not yet appeared with the brandies but Major Blackshaw was elbowing men aside as he made his slightly tipsy way across the room. 'Will you be coming to Hetherington, Davenport?' he said.

'I didn't think I'd be able to attend your . . . what are they? A week of celebrations?'

'Yes. My father and sisters will have everything in hand. I don't know what they will entail, the celebrations. But my father has always liked to make a splash . . .'

Charles said, 'I was hoping to see the family before Sunday.'

'Send for them! You won't be able to go back and forwards from Chester to – where did you say?'

'Southport. My children are living there, with their aunt.'

'Send a message by telegraph,' Frederick said airily before going towards a group of subalterns who were loudly declaiming on the relative merits of brandy and cognac.

Charles smiled at the thought. He would not dream of inviting all his children to Hetherington. He would wait until Blackshaw sobered up before giving him an answer.

He looked around the room for the steward who should by now have arrived with the tray of drinks. The men were all laughing and talking about their homes and families and the welcome that was waiting for them. He felt out of things when soldiers spoke about their loves and he'd find that he'd become sick at heart, missing Clara. Then he'd hear them talking about their welcome home and he'd be troubled.

And again, in the few moments it took for the steward to appear, Charles was back in imagination to the time the regiment had left England.

It had been the last night before they embarked. He had gone to Southport to say farewell, give gifts to the children and issue his last instructions to his family. He'd not seen Alice for two months and had been surprised to see how she had grown. He had taken her aside and spoken very seriously to her about her duties and responsibilities.

She was very like Clara. Clara had had the sculptured features of a Grecian goddess and Alice too had her mother's looks and her mother's air of suppressed energy, the same lift of a strong chin and the same ringing clarity of the voice. Alice had even inherited one of Clara's weaknesses – a certain intemperance of speech. Both of them could be hasty and say in the heat of the moment words they would come to regret.

When he had finished speaking to Alice, they had joined Beatrice and the older boys at supper. Harriet's table had been laid with silver over a lace tablecloth; crystal sparkled and mahogany shone. For the first time since Clara's death he felt comfortable with his children around him and was beginning to believe that the pain of losing Clara was lessening.

Harriet came into the room, carrying a tureen of chicken broth. She placed it on its stand and took her place opposite him.

'Will you play the piano after supper, Harriet?' he asked. 'Alice suggests we have one of our old family nights – the ones Clara liked – the singing and the children's recitations.' He smiled fondly at Harriet as he said, 'Beatrice told me that you and she have been practising duets.'

Harriet had a quiet dignity and a complete absence of either humour or flippancy. She looked at him across the laden table with a look of devotion that alarmed him. He glanced away and spoke again to Alice.

'Help Aunt Harriet,' he said to her. 'Your aunt can't do everything herself.'

Alice leaped to her feet to pass plates to himself and

Beatrice. The embarrassment of the moment was gone so swiftly that he wondered if he had been over-imaginative.

The last few hours of his last day with them were going quickly and after supper they went to the drawing room where Beatrice and Harriet played their duet. Then Alice had them all spell-bound when she did one of her recitations and even he put his heart into playing and singing a song that he and Clara used to sing.

He asked the children to leave the room afterwards so that he could tell Harriet, without upsetting the children, about the arrangements he had made for them in the event of his death. There was a life insurance policy which he had just taken out at an exorbitant premium. And for as long as he was at war, and he did not expect the war to last more than six months, the interest on his capital would pay for the children's education and the allowance Alice was to draw and account for.

When he had told her all this he was made aware again of the turn Harriet's feelings had taken. She brought into the room a tray set with brandy decanter and glass, cigars and matches. Harriet had principled objections to drink and tobacco and he had been surprised by the relaxing of her standards. Again there was a look of devotion in her eyes as she placed the tray on a small table at his elbow where he sat at the fireside in the drawing room.

He remembered that he had felt mellow and at ease in the deep comfortable chair. What had possessed him to say the words he did?

He had turned to thank her for her attention to his comfort. He remembered his very words, 'I could not have faced a future without Clara, but for you, Harriet dear. No, I could not have managed without you.'

Harriet had replied in her unemotional yet deadly serious way, 'There is no reason why you ever should.'

But Harriet never wasted a word. She would have known what she was saying for she had looked directly at him and her meaning was clear. When a decent interval had passed he must make her his wife.

He remembered that he had, foolishly, been taken aback by what he saw as Harriet's boldness. Harriet must have known that his marriage to Clara, though fraught with fears for her mental health, had fulfilled every desire in him. For him, marriage was a holy covenant, a solemn oath to give unreservedly, minds and bodies, each to the other. Although his and Clara's decision to marry within hours of their meeting must have seemed impulsive, reckless even, it had been the most profound experience in both of their lives.

He hesitated and not wanting to shame her for making such an obvious overture said, 'Oh, my dear Harriet. Love such as I felt for Clara comes once in a lifetime. I shall never love another woman in that way.'

Her eyes were bright with hope. 'It would never be asked of you,' she had answered before she turned and left the room.

But he had seen the look in her eyes – a fervent love had been shining in her face. And he had felt his heart sink for himself and contract with pity for poor Harriet. Until that moment he'd believed that Harriet's kindness to them all over the years had been prompted by concern for her cousin.

The steward had come to his side. 'Your brandies, sir.'

'Thank you.' He dismissed the steward and announced, 'Drink, gentlemen. To the regiment!'

'The regiment!'

Charles drank the fiery liquid and left the saloon to watch the dawn break over home waters.

'The regiment!'

The men were still celebrating.

The brandy hit the back of Frederick's throat like a small explosion. He'd had enough. He'd never be a hard drinker for there came a point when another drop would floor him. He banged the glass down on the bar counter and made his way through the crush of fellows who'd still be downing the stuff when they docked.

Outside the saloon he stood for a moment or two, drawing deeply of the sobering, clean sea air before he went up on deck.

Captain Davenport, the officer he'd shared the last campaign with – the one he admired above the rest – was alone up there leaning on the rail, staring out to sea. Frederick joined him and for a moment neither spoke. They stood looking across misty water to where the English coast lay. Frederick looked at his companion, smiled and said, 'A better sight than the Orange River, eh Davenport?'

Davenport turned a sun browned face to him. 'A welcome sight, Major Blackshaw. When do you think we'll dock?'

'It depends on the tides.' He peered across the silver-misted water to where a boat was approaching. The *Tintagel*'s engines had dropped to a low murmur some time ago. Now they had stopped and the ship was rising and falling with the swell. 'We're anchored off.'

'How's the wound?' Davenport asked.

He'd been shot through the shoulder in the last action he and Davenport had seen. The pain had gone. 'All right,' he said.

'Have you made up your mind?' Davenport asked. 'Will you stay in the army or return to the land?'

'I'll see what's waiting for me at Hetherington.' He leaned over the rail, enjoying the rush of cold air that was beginning to clear his head. 'There's a lot to think about. A Hell of a lot of things have been going on there whilst I've been away.'

'But you'd rather stay in?' Davenport asked.

He nodded. 'What will you do?'

Kittiwakes, a score of them, elegant in low flight were skimming the water, their calls almost drowning the sound of their voices. Davenport seemed oblivious of them. His voice was curt. 'Look for a practice.' Then as if annoyed with himself, 'Sorry Blackshaw. What were you saying? Have you a girl waiting? Marriage in mind?'

'No.' He had not found a girl he wanted to marry. He had a picture in his mind of the kind of girl . . . tall . . . blonde . . . charming . . . burning with love and passion for him. He smiled. Every man had a vision of the perfect wife. His eyes were full of laughter as he said, 'No. No marriage plans.'

A smile started to play around Davenport's mouth, making his sandy moustache lift at the corners in merriment. 'I'm sure Major Blackshaw, that many a young Cheshire girl will hope to catch your eye. You are—' Davenport's smile became broader '—you are what is called "a catch" I suppose. Heir to a big estate.'

Frederick laughed out loud. 'Not much of a catch,' he said. 'There are bigger fish than me out there. And bigger estates.'

Most of the men on board spoke of little else but their welcome home from their womenfolk and he was no stranger to love. At Hetherington he'd had an affair with a farmer's widow on the estate, but so far he'd not found a girl who aroused in him the strong physical desire he felt for the widow and the protective feelings he'd always felt for Therese. He would need to feel both, to marry.

Therese, his cousin and childhood companion, was closer to him than anyone. He smiled and answered Davenport. 'I've only ever loved one girl. Marriage is out of the question.'

Davenport raised an eyebrow.

Frederick said, 'My cousin.'

'The girl whose photograph you carry?'

'Yes,' said Frederick. 'My father is her guardian.'

'A man may marry his cousin.' There was a trace of resignation in Davenport's voice. 'Marrying a cousin – even a deceased wife's cousin – is not one of the prohibited degrees.'

Frederick remembered that Davenport had spoken about the woman, his wife's cousin, who was looking after his children. He said, 'That's as may be, for you. My cousin has a young child.' He turned his head to look across the water at the approaching boat.

'Ah! I see,' said Davenport.

'I don't think you do,' Frederick answered quickly. 'But I can't say more. Don't ask.' He didn't know the whole story himself. But he knew they were all lying to him. The story of Therese's marriage and widowhood was a lie. She would never have done it.

'Sorry. I shouldn't have pried.' Charles gave a wry smile. 'It seems we both have troubles at home.'

Frederick felt the need to talk. They were still alone on deck. 'Davenport,' he said, 'can I ask your advice? If you decide not to stay over at Hetherington with the others we won't meet again after your discharge so I'll not be asking too much of our friendship.'

'No, I don't mind.' Davenport moved back from the rail to face him. 'I consider it a compliment – your confidence in my advice. What's the trouble?'

'My father.' Frederick gripped the rail hard. He could not speak about his father without wanting to strike something. 'He's a nasty piece of work. He's always been a philanderer. Spends a lot of money on cheap women.'

Davenport did not wear a sympathetic face and Frederick knew that he was beginning to sound like a prude. 'I sound like a puritan, don't I?' he said. 'I'm not. His excesses have given the family a bad name. Mother hates it. My father has respect for nobody; neither family nor servants. The only thing he has a genuine fondness for is money.'

The iron rail seemed to be growing warm under his hands. He spoke quickly. 'When I came back from India in '99 I found the family, the whole thing, in chaos. My mother was ill.' He fought down the knot of pain and anger that had begun to form in his throat when he thought about his mother's suffering. 'Every doctor she saw prescribed different treatment for her. She saw the last specialist before I left for South Africa.'

Davenport asked, 'What did the specialist say?'

'He believes it may be cancer.'

'Oh. Bad luck. What a shock it must have been . . .'

Frederick was silent for a moment. He remembered the next shock of his homecoming from India – finding Therese big with child. If they'd tell him who was responsible he would hunt him down. He demanded the truth and nobody would tell. It all came back; his fury, their assurances, the shame that had been brought upon Therese, the lies they tried to make him accept. He had known from the moment he looked into her eyes that she was lying. Therese couldn't tell lies. And she would never have married the kind of nonentity she couldn't even describe.

But he would not have told Davenport even had he known the truth. It was Therese's secret. He made a hard tight line of his mouth to keep the anger back. 'Soon after I left for Africa my mother, sisters and cousin left my father.'

'Why? When she knew she hadn't long to live?'

'I don't know. It was never a happy marriage. The estate is hers. I'll inherit it when she goes. Hetherington Hall was built by my father on her estate.'

'Your mother's still alive? In spite of the diagnosis.

'She's still alive. Only just, I imagine. My sisters will only refer to it as "Mother's ailment". Therese tells me that Mother is bedridden now.'

'Are they certain of the diagnosis?'

Frederick kicked at the iron upright as if it might help direct the anger. 'She's seen the best specialists. The opinions differed but she's had the best advice.'

'I see.' Davenport looked at him again.

Frederick leaned against the rail and said slowly, 'My father thinks that money should buy him anything he wants. He has always wanted position. He lost all his standing, of course, when Mother left him. You know how rumours abound in a small place – how servants talk. It split the staff – some went with my mother – others stayed with him. It's his own doing. He's brought the name of Blackshaw as low as it could be.'

Davenport said, 'Is it important to you? Social status? A good standing and all that goes with it?'

'Do I sound snobbish?'

'No. I know what it's like to keep up appearances.'

Frederick knew he'd best explain to Davenport that for himself he didn't give a damn. Snobbery annoyed him and convention bored him. 'For myself I don't care,' he explained. 'But it has been hard on my sisters.'

'And your cousin, I expect.'

At last Frederick laughed. He could not help but laugh when he remembered Therese's social ambitions – her airs and the *hauteur* she affected to cover her fearful vulnerability. Only he knew that a frightened girl lay beneath the snobbish surface. Nobody else would ever guess at it. And nobody would ever sympathize with her unless she dropped her high-handed manner.

'What have I said?' Davenport asked. 'What's so funny?'

'It was the idea that Therese – my dear cousin – would fear to lose her status as my father's niece,' Frederick said, still amused at the thought. 'Therese has always had ideas above her station. She imagines she is of a superior order to the rest of the family. Her mother and grandmother filled her head with ideas – with delusions of grandeur – with a lot of nonsense.'

Davenport was smiling as Frederick went on, 'Therese will never be seen as anything but an upstart with a suspect background by the Cheshire county set. She would never be accepted into it.' He laughed again. 'No. I can look after Therese all right.'

Then he remembered his sisters and the laugh died on the wind. 'My sisters will never marry. They can't mix socially when they have a father like ours. And though they say they have never wanted marriage I can't help thinking that it's because of him that Mary and Maggie will remain on the shelf.'

'Your father's a successful businessman,' Davenport said.

'He has untold wealth and he talks as if he's permanently on the brink of ruin.' But he was sick of talking about his father. He wondered what sort of a father Davenport was to his family. 'I know nothing about you, Davenport, except that you are a fine soldier and a good doctor,' he said. He wondered if he should say "and my honoured and trusted friend" but decided it might embarrass Davenport. Instead he said, 'I don't know what kind of a father you are, or how you've brought up your family. But I bet you've made a better job of it than mine has.'

Davenport said, 'A father can't know how he's seen by his children.'

Frederick knew that his own father could be under no illusions about his children's feelings towards him. 'Tell me about your upbringing,' he said.

'I was born into an army family,' Davenport said. 'In India. My father was posted out there after Crimea. My mother died when I was four and Father had his two sons removed from his sight. We were sent to England to be educated. I was brought up strictly. The cane was wielded very freely by the clergyman in whose care we were placed.' He stopped for a second then went on with a small smile, 'It did me no harm. I gained a healthy respect for law and order.'

'Why didn't you go to India, like your father before you?'

Davenport said, 'My father married again. I didn't care for my stepmother. I knew that my father was only going to support and educate my brother and me for as long as our education lasted. Afterwards we'd be cast adrift financially he told us.'

'So . . . Why medicine?' Frederick asked. 'How did you come to be a doctor?'

'I wanted to follow in my brother's footsteps. He'd gone to Edinburgh Medical School when he was seventeen. I went at sixteen.'

'And the army?' Frederick asked.

'Ah.' Davenport smiled. 'The army I suppose was like a family to me. I'd never known normal home-life, never was easy in women's company. Much more at ease with men. The army suited me – suited my temperament – then.'

A boat had drawn level with the *Tintagel Castle* and a sailor on deck was signalling to the bridge. Frederick watched the flags until they had ceased then, smiling, he turned to Davenport and reported the message. 'We are going to move in – a mile or two nearer the coast. We have to anchor off again – for twenty-four hours or so.'

He smiled as he said to Davenport, 'I hear you're a bit of an inventor – a businessman yourself. The medicines – what are you working on at the moment?'

Davenport's laughter was a fine sound. It seemed to resound around the mess when they were all together. Now it was carried away on the wind as the ship, engines restarted, made a course parallel with the coast.

'Not an inventor! Not much of a businessman, Blackshaw,' he laughed. 'A soldier-physician with knowledge of chemistry and pharmacology is all I am.'

Then he became serious again and said, 'I was working on a cure for ichthyosis – an unsightly skin disorder. I don't think I'll have much time for it when I go into practice.'

'It would be a pity to stop,' Frederick said. 'When you've gone so far.'

Charles had stopped laughing. He smiled as he looked at Frederick and said, 'I had to stop when Clara died. I'd come to a halt for lack of funds.'

'Clara was your wife?'

Davenport's smile had gone. 'She was my life. When Clara died I lost everything that made life worth living.'

Frederick felt a quick surge of sympathy. 'Will you marry again?' he asked.

Charles leaned an elbow on the rail. 'Marrying my wife's cousin would be a – an expedient measure as far as the children are concerned but I don't think I could marry without feeling desire for my wife. And I shall never feel the desire for any woman that I had for Clara.'

Davenport's voice had dropped. Frederick had to listen intently to catch the words against the breeze that was blowing up harder. 'What can you do?' he said.

Charles appeared to pull himself back to the present and frowned a little as he answered, 'Look for a practice. And not hope for anything else.'

The English coast could be seen clearly. The slight mist was lifting and the first rays of the sun danced across blue water ahead of the prow where it churned white and green in the ship's steady progress towards the land. Below, men were moving, voices could be heard from the lower decks.

Charles, as if he had at last come to some private decision of his own, banged his hand down on the rail. 'I don't want to talk any more about my worries, Blackshaw,' he said. 'And I'm not the man to advise you on your problems. In fact I'd prefer it if you said nothing more. Your father isn't here to defend himself and you may say something you'll regret.'

He gave a half-apologetic smile as if to take away any sting his words might have. Then he said, 'You are going to have to deal with your father in your own way. I'm going below. I'll speak to you later.'

In his cabin, the packing checked and his batman dismissed, Charles loosened the buttons of his uniform jacket, sat on the bunk and thought about his return to normal life.

There was an aspect of his return that troubled him; a difference in perspective, for he did not see his reunion with the family in the light of the return of the warrior, as they might. He had only just escaped becoming hardened and callous. He could not allow himself to be fêted and honoured after the part he had played in clearing the land at the end of this war.

And what did the family expect of him?

George was coming to an age when he would need a father's guidance. He'd missed a father's influence in his own youth and he wanted to be a better father to his children than his own father had been to him. He wanted George to follow in his footsteps and study medicine. Alice and Beatrice were almost grown up and would soon be wanting to marry. If they did not marry then he'd consider Beatrice's request to allow them to earn their livings as teachers or nurses. For himself he was trying to see ahead his settled, middle-aged future as a doctor. He was a sensible, practical man.

But sense and practical ability were one thing; love and marriage with a woman for whom one felt only pity were another matter entirely.

It was then that he made his decision. He could not make a loveless marriage with Harriet. The only basis for marriage was the sharing of the physical love he had known with Clara. Instantaneous, violent attraction only came to the young. He could never hope to experience it again.

He would take the family away from Southport. They would start again somewhere else. Alice and Beatrice would be told to look after the little one and continue keeping house for him.

Captain Charles Davenport stood, did up the hooks of his jacket and went in search of Freddie Blackshaw whom he found, still at the rail.

'Does the offer still hold?' he said as he stood at Freddie's side.

'To come to Hetherington?' Frederick looked pleased.

'Yes,' Charles answered. 'What will the "week of celebrations" entail?' He was smiling as he asked, knowing as well as Frederick did that as far as the officer's mess was concerned the celebrations had already started.

Frederick said, 'There will be all the usual sports for the men. And without doubt my sisters and the family will have a little "programme of events" laid on for us.'

'May I stay until after the Cathedral service on Sunday?' Charles asked.

'Will you send for your wife's cousin?'

'No.' Charles answered. It would not be right to give Harriet any expectations of marriage. It would be best if she knew from the outset that it had never been in his mind to ask her.

Frederick nodded his head and said with great sincerity, 'Then by all means send for your children. There's plenty of room at Hetherington. Most of the officers and their families live in Chester. But there will be houseguests. My father, sisters and cousin will have invited business friends and a few local families. Your children won't be short of company and amusement.'

Charles smiled and nodded his head quickly in agreement. 'Thank you. I can't send for them all. I'll telegraph when we reach Chester. If I think there is anything they might enjoy then I'll ask Alice and George to join the celebrations. If that's all right with you, Blackshaw.'

# Chapter Seven

Alice was about to take her seat on a plush banquette in a first-class carriage. Aunt Harriet, declaring that she would catch some dreadful disease if she travelled any other way, had finally agreed that she should go to the city only if she promised to travel first class. She would be in Liverpool in an hour.

The rain had not let up all morning but as the train pulled away from under the station's glass roof Alice could see ahead where the skies were clearing. She took off her long mackintosh and reached up to the net luggage-rack overhead.

'Allow! Pleez?'

Alice turned. A tall young man with black hair and a thin, serious face, older than herself, was holding his hands for her coat. He had risen from his place at the other end of the compartment and was standing between her and the passengers opposite: an elderly woman with a face dark with disapproval, two girls of about twenty and an old, white-bearded man.

Alice hesitated. She knew she should not speak to men until they had been introduced but she could not take exception to a misplaced gesture of chivalry.

'For you. I take. Eet!' He was standing to attention. He snapped his heels together and, despite the swaying of the train, gave a formal and very foreign bow, evidently unaware of his faux pas. 'Meez Aleez Davenport.'

Alice felt a laugh bubbling up inside. It was not the first time she had caught the attention of men. It had started last year when she first put up her hair. It always made her smile, as it seemed she attracted eccentrics. She suppressed the laugh but could not help but smile hugely at the young man's extraordinary behaviour.

She handed over the mackintosh, sat down and scrutinized him as he folded her coat carefully and placed it above the heads of the family opposite.

He was tall with sleek black hair and blue eyes and was very handsome in profile. He had a straight, longish nose, a well-cut mouth in a smooth, light-skinned face and as he looked at her again she saw he had a proud, almost arrogant look.

He was obviously foreign. His dark suit of good worsted cloth was different from those her brothers wore. Englishmen wore jackets a little longer, with wider lapels. This young man's coat was cut on high-collared military lines; it was well-fitting with flap pockets at the yoke and hips. He was a foreigner – and he knew her name.

She had better act the part of the genteel young woman Aunt Harriet would approve. She composed her face into what she hoped was a mask of formality. 'I don't believe I know you,' she said, to put him in his place.

'You not wish? Not wish to know me?'

He had not gone back to his seat but stood in front of her, engaging her eyes with his blue gaze. He said nothing for a moment or two then gave a formal sort of smile and stretched out his right hand. 'Meez Aleez Davenport.'

He had not recognized the snub. Alice felt sorry that she had given it. 'Where did you learn my name?' she asked in a friendlier tone of voice.

'I see you. I hear your name. At zee choorch. I too. I go to zee choorch.'

If he went to her church then it was her duty to take a Christian attitude. She would be gracious and forgive him his impertinence. She smiled and put out her hand to him.

Then, as if there were nobody else to see, he raised her fingers to his lips, looked her full in the face and very formally said, 'Karl Reinhardt, *Fraulein*.' He let her hand go as soon as he had spoken and returned to his seat.

Alice tried to appear nonchalant now that she was once again facing the unbending group opposite. But she knew that though he, this Karl Reinhardt who addressed her as *Fraulein*, was apparently absorbed in watching the flat townscape they were chugging through, he was aware of her every movement. It sent little shock-waves through her, knowing his eyes were upon her.

She forced herself to think of the audition. There would be no time to take the train to the Pier Head afterwards. She would buy a Liverpool newspaper before she returned home. The arrival of the regiment would be headline news. Another lie would have to be told to Aunt Harriet.

The family group opposite appeared to be a morose lot who spoke in whispers. Alice tried to concentrate on the passing scene, tried not to think of Karl Reinhardt's watching eyes though it felt as if they were burning into the back of her neck. They must be about halfway there, she decided.

The sun was shining brightly as they neared the city. She tried to act as if she were not aware of the sidelong glances of the foreigner, of Karl Reinhardt, but the train was slowing, braking for about the fifth time and he had leaped to his feet again.

The surly family was getting ready to leave the train. They were standing and the old man was reaching up for their hand-luggage when Karl Reinhardt came to their aid; once again at her end of the compartment. He was playing the gallant. She could not help but smile at his antics.

When the door closed behind the departing family, Alice, though pretending to watch the portly station-master, saw that Karl Reinhardt was hesitating about going back to his place. She felt no alarm at being left alone in the compartment with him. He was obviously at a loss, wondering how to attract her attention. She found his dilemma amusing.

Soon she would face her own ordeal – and it was made no easier knowing that it was the first time she had ever flouted Papa's strict code of conduct. It would clear her mind and calm her nerves if she passed the remainder of the journey in conversation.

She looked up and smiled.

'I sit. Here?' he asked, dropping with sudden relief on to the seat opposite her own.

'Yes,' Alice said.

'You permit? I am too bold?'

He was trying to look assured and his quaint use of English was so funny that once again Alice began to smile.

He frowned. 'I am *unterhalten*? Amusing? I not say it good?'

Alice, reminding herself of her manners, gave him a look of reassurance. 'You speak very well.'

'You go to Liverpool?'

'Yes.' She said. 'Where are you going?'

'To Liverpool.' He frowned in concentration. 'I visit my family.'

He waved his hands about as he spoke, in an unEnglish manner. Papa said it was a mannerism that intelligent people never adopted. Papa told them never to gesticulate, for he said that people who could not make themselves understood in speech ought to remain quiet. That way, their silence might be taken for intelligence. What would Papa make of Karl Reinhardt?

'What is your nationality?' she asked.

'Bohm.'

He had pronounced a rude word and had no idea that he'd done so. She simply could not keep a straight face. 'I beg your pardon?'

She saw him searching again for the words. 'Bohemian,' he said at last. 'I am Bohemian.'

Alice tried to picture a map of Europe. 'Is Bohemia a part of Germany?' she asked politely.

'Austria.' He frowned again and added, 'The Habsburgs. Emperor Franz Joseph.' He leaned forward a little. 'Bohemia.'

'Austria-Hungary?'

'Yes.' He seemed pleased with the exchange so far and began to relax against the stuffed seat as he gave another tight little smile at her. He was very handsome indeed when he smiled. He had a kind of proud elegance in his manner that was completely foreign – and creases at the side of his mouth that came and went.

'Why you go to Liverpool?' he asked.

Alice felt at ease. She would tell this Bohemian all about the audition. It would mean nothing to him and she had been keeping it secret for too long.

'I want to be an actress,' she began. 'I am going to audition . . . For a place in a theatre company . . . Liverpool . . .' She found she could not stop. The words were tumbling out. 'And if I am not offered a part with Mr Squibb . . . there's a chance I'll be invited to . . . join the Manchester Repertory Company.'

He was watching her all the time with those blue watchful eyes as she babbled on. Now and again he lifted his hands as if he knew what she meant, then he scowled. He probably had not understood more than one word in ten, she thought as she came stumbling to a halt. 'If Papa will allow it . . . When he comes home from the war . . .' she ended.

He said nothing for a few seconds before announcing in his funny, broken English, 'I think you are servant.'

Alice's eyes flew open, wide and surprised. 'I? You think I am a servant?' she said.

He was looking at her in the condescending way he had done earlier. If he were English she would think him extremely rude. He obviously did not know what he was saying.

'Yes. I see you from window,' he said, intense in his effort to be understood. 'Every day. You talk in street and push baby-carriage in the rain.'

'I was rehearsing. And where do you live that you see me every day?'

'Victoria Hotel.'

'The Victoria Hotel on Southport's Promenade?' she asked.

'I am waiter. I learn English language.' He smiled again; a strained, embarrassed smile that Alice found oddly touching.

'I see,' she said.

'You see? You see me?' He was looking puzzled.

Alice felt a laugh coming to the surface but stifled it again. 'I did not see you. I did not see you looking at me.'

'I see you. In my country servants push baby-carriage.' He looked pleased with himself.

'And you thought I was a nursemaid?' Alice asked. They were drawing up to another station in a cloud of steam but nobody approached their compartment.

'Why you do it?' Karl Reinhardt demanded. 'Why you will be actress? You are poor? You must earn money?'

Alice would excuse his impertinence since he had a poor grasp of English. 'I want to earn money. Just as you do,' she said.'

'My sisters cannot work.'

'You support them? How many sisters? How old?'

His face again took on the frowning look of concentration that amused her. His eyebrows almost met above the bridge of his long nose and his well-cut and expressive mouth was held firmly as he spoke the words that he must have rehearsed and learned text-book fashion.

'Three sisters. Irmgard. She is seventeen. Anna. She is sixteen. Renate. She is fifteen. I have brother. Heinz. He is twenty. I am two years older than Heinz. I am twenty-two.'

Alice smiled again in encouragement. 'Very good. You said that very well.'

'Why you want to work?' he asked again.

'Why not?'

'It is not custom. In Bohemia. Girls of good family do not work.' He looked pleased with himself, proud and a little condescending.

Alice was becoming nettled. Her family was every bit as good as his. 'Young men of good family here do not take work as waiters in an hotel,' she told him. 'Nor would a young man behave as you are doing,' she said. 'A gentleman here would not approach a lady unless he had been introduced.'

He had not understood. And since he seemed to have interpreted her courtesy wrongly she saw that her rebuke had been wasted. They were almost there. It was silly to take umbrage. She asked, 'Why do you want to speak English and work in an hotel?'

'Ah. I shall inherit. There is house in Sudeten. One day it will be mine. I shall make hotel. My father is engineer. I not wish to work in factory. *Mein Vater* make—' He began to wave his hands about again. 'He make with iron. Machines. We lived near to Prague. Making with iron is – it is very—' He pulled a face.

'Very dirty?'

He smiled and nodded. 'My brother. My brother Heinz. He like machines. I dislike.'

'Where does your family live? In Liverpool?'

'Macclesfield.'

'Then you're on the wrong train. You should have caught a train to Manchester,' she said. 'It is much easier to get to Macclesfield from Manchester than it is from Liverpool.'

But he was smiling to himself, unconcerned again. He had not understood, she was sure. The train was slowing and she watched him look first at his pocketwatch and then through the window. The brakes were being applied and the great engine was at last pulling to a halt at the Exchange terminus.

Then, before Alice could get to her feet, he stood, lifted down her mackintosh and umbrella, heaved upon the leather strap to lower the window and open the door and, athletic and easy in his movements, leaped down ahead of her and held out his hand for her to alight.

It was delightful to Alice, this foreign, almost flowery courtesy. She had never been treated in such a regal manner and as she stepped down on to the platform she could not help but admire Karl who looked so – just as Papa was – so superior to all the rather sensible and dour men of her acquaintance.

'You shall return today?' he said when she stood on the platform beside him.

He was very tall, almost as tall as Papa she guessed and when she looked up at him she felt for the first time ever that she was small and in need of protection.

'Later this afternoon.' All at once the coming audition made her feel shaky and not as sure of herself as she had been this morning.

People were hurrying past them towards the exit but Karl seemed in no hurry to get to his own destination since he continued to concern himself with her. He became authoritative again as his eyes went swiftly over the heads of the crowd.

'I command cab,' he said and made towards the line of Hansoms on the broad cab drive that ran through the centre of the station.

'I can do it,' Alice said, but he was striding to the head of the line and she had to walk quickly to keep up with him.

He held open the door of the first Hansom and, as he helped her inside, asked, 'Where you go?'

Alive gave him the name of the church hall where the auditions were to be held and heard him repeat it to the driver before she at last sat back against the padded seat. She turned to smile and wave at Karl when the cab moved forward and found herself disappointed that he had gone.

Half an hour later, the cab drew up in a quiet lane outside a church hall. Alice paid the driver, asked him to return for her at four o'clock and went, lightheaded with fright, up the short path towards the outer door of the low sooty building.

It felt as if her heart were beating a tattoo in her throat as she pushed open the heavy outer door and entered the musty little entrance hall. Opposite was an inner door which must lead into the hall itself. The hallway was deserted but a table laden with tracts and church notices showed her that she was in the right place. There was not a sound to be heard but the quick intake of her own breath. The palms of her hands were sticking to the inside of her white kid gloves as nervous agitation rose in her.

Should she go inside? There was a moment of indecision before the outer door through which she had just entered was thrown open and a deep, booming voice behind her said, 'Miss Davenport?'

Alice whirled round. The man who had spoken was standing with his back to the light of the open door. She could not see his face. He had on his head a big floppy hat of felt and around his shoulders a large cape was draped.

'The audition?' she asked in a small voice. There was something menacing in this man's manner. 'Mr Squibb? Have I come to right address?'

She wanted nothing so much as to push past him and dash for the open air and the safety of the street. She tried to pull herself together, to appear calm.

'Yes. Yes.' His voice was not as sonorous this time but had a smooth, oily sound.

'Come inside,' he said. He went towards the inner door, pushed it open and held it for her.

It must be all right. The churchwarden knew Mr Squibb, surely he knew him? And yet she had been under the impression that there would be others auditioning for parts. She had understood that a new company was being formed – that they were planning a series of plays – *Hamlet* – *Hedda Gabler*. Where on Earth were the other actors?

'Am I the first to arrive?' she asked as she went through

the open door into the dusty, deserted hall, glancing quickly at him as she passed. He had a florid complexion and a large, fleshy mouth with bright red, purple-blotched lips. It was a degenerate face and she felt a shudder of fear.

'I thought it best to make separate appointments, dear girl,' he said as he closed the door behind her. 'Please take a seat.'

In front of a shallow, raised platform at the far end of the hall was a row of rush-seated chairs. Alice went ahead of him and sat on the edge of the very last seat.

'Now, my dear,' the oily voice said in her ear as a large manicured hand fell upon her shoulder. 'I think we should start at once. Have you brought anything with you?'

'Oh. Yes.' Alice in her nervousness jumped to her feet but Mr Squibb had apparently not anticipated her movements for he did not move back fast enough and she found that her face was only inches from his. His breath, smelling most foully of she-knew-not-what, made her stomach turn in disgust.

'What can you do for me?' he said in a low, unpleasant voice. But he made space for her to pass and when she stood a little distance apart from him she replied, 'Ophelia. I've been studying *Hamlet*. And Ibsen's *Hedda Gabler*.'

His smile made her think of a toad. 'On to the platform,' he said.

She went to the raised platform, lifted the hem of her blue dress so as not to make it more dusty than necessary and, squaring her shoulders and taking a deep breath, went to the centre-stage position.

'Have you a copy of the play?' he called up to her in the loud voice he had first used. 'Did you bring the Shakespeare?'

'Oh. Oh yes.' Alice bent her head over the handbag she was carrying and began to fumble with the catch, her fingers numb and clumsy.

Then he leaped up beside her and took the book out of her hands roughly. 'Let your hair down!' he ordered. 'You can't read Ophelia when you look like a – like a—'

Alice found that she was shaking with fright. She could do nothing. She felt she was rooted to the spot as Mr Squibb lurched towards her, hands clawing at her hair, trying to tear out the hairpins with a large hairy hand.

It was the sound of her book dropping – her precious Shakespeare being thrown on to the dusty floor – that brought her to her senses and gave her strength from somewhere.

A wave of outrage and anger swept through her as with hair streaming out about her shoulders – and before the loose red lips could be brought down upon her own – she put her whole weight behind her right fist and brought it up from under his chin to smash into his nose with a satisfying crunch.

She felt no pain in her knuckles from the blow but, as he yelled and clapped both of his hands to his face, Alice bent down to reach for her Shakespeare and, still almost bursting with rage, she kicked him, right behind his knees and saw him fall forward on to the platform in a howling, angry heap.

Then, crying in relief and fear and before he could get to his feet and harm her, she ran headlong towards the door that led into the hallway, through it and out into the sunny, quiet street and safety.

Across the road, leaning against a high brick wall and managing to look both assured and agitated at the same time, was the now familiar and so welcome figure of Karl Reinhardt.

Alive flung herself into his arms. 'Karl!' she almost wept. 'That man! He—'

'I call him out for duel? I shall beat him! You want I beat him for you?' Karl held her close for a second then made as if to leave her there whilst he went into the church hall to attend to Mr Squibb.

'No!' Alice pulled herself together. She would not allow any brawling. Nobody should suffer for her stupidity. It was better that she collect herself; that she behave in a ladylike manner. If any of this came to Aunt Harriet's ears she would never be allowed a moment to herself again.

She tugged at Karl's sleeve to pull him back. 'It was my fault,' she said. 'I should not have gone.'

'Why?' Karl looked at her with raised, questioning eyebrows. 'Why you stop me?'

'Please, Karl.' Alice began to push her hair back under the blue hat. 'No harm has been done. Perhaps we can walk into Liverpool. We can take a tram to the Pier Head. I need to ask about the times of the ships.'

He had taken her to the Pier Head and then, evidently having decided that he would not, after all, go to Macclesfield, he accompanied her on the train back to Southport.

This time they had a compartment to themselves and were very much at ease with one another. And on this return journey Karl began to tell her about himself, his ambition to return to Bohemia, and the differences between his father and himself.

'I was at military academy,' he began. 'Near Prague.'

Alice waited for him to add something but he was silent and waiting for her reply. Alice, not used to such bald statements with the long pauses that followed them, said, 'Oh. How interesting.' Then, since that might be interpreted as a slight said, 'I'm sorry. I didn't mean to sound rude. It's just that, my Papa being a soldier . . . I know quite a bit about the army.'

'You like? The army? You like soldiers?' he said in that deep, staccato voice of his.

'No. I do not like the army. I dislike the military as much as you seem to dislike engineering.'

Alice surprised herself by the firmness of her reply. Indeed, she was not at all sure, until she said the words that she didn't like the army. It had occurred to her in a moment that she was like Mama had been. She did not like the military at all.

Karl was silent again for a moment or two. It was as if he were giving a great deal of thought to her statement. Then he said, 'I too. I dislike the army.'

'What will you do when you return to Bohemia?' Alice asked him next. He had spoken so longingly of his wish to return to his homeland.

Again there was a moment's pause before, to her utter astonishment, he said, 'What do you think I shall do? What do you want I should do?'

'Me? What have I to do with it?' she answered him.

'If you were me?' he said.

'Ah. I see.' She smiled. 'I should expect you to do as you said you'd do. Work and save money so that you could make your hotel when you inherit the house you spoke of.'

'Very good. Then that is what I shall propose.' Karl leaned back against the seat and the tight little smile, almost a smile of satisfaction, was there again.

# Chapter Eight

**Monday**

On the day that Alice Davenport in Southport was going to Liverpool for her audition, Therese in the heart of Cheshire decided to confront her uncle for the first time since the *affaire*. It was eight o'clock in the morning and she stood at her first-floor sitting-room window in the Dower House looking out on to the house and gardens of Hetherington.

Moisture clung to everything. Grass, leaves and sky were a misty sea of green and grey. Hetherington Hall seemed further distant today, shrouded and mysterious. Therese found the grey misery entirely in keeping with her mood and fitting for the ordeal she had to face this afternoon. She left the window and made her way upstairs for her visit to the nursery.

No sound came from the night nursery where Peter and his nursemaid would be. Therese pushed open the door to the day room where she found Nanny Cosgrove inspecting the child's laundry.

The girl looked up. 'Ma'am?'

Therese's lovely face was fierce. 'Cosgrove,' she said. 'Have Peter dressed and ready for me this afternoon at three. I shall drive him to the Hall in the pony trap. See that the child is rested.'

The young, trained nanny who had been in Therese's service since the baby was three months old, nodded. 'Alone, ma'am?' she said. 'You're going alone?'

Therese's eyes flashed with annoyance. 'You question me, Cosgrove?' She would not allow it from anyone, least of all a servant. Why should the nanny ask? Were the servants gossiping behind her back?

The nurse began to stammer. 'B . . . beg pardon, ma'am.'

'That is all.' Therese glanced round quickly to see that the room was clean and tidy before she left the nursery suite and descended the carved oak staircase.

She would have to be kind to Nanny later, to make up for her shortness of temper. Nanny's position, she knew, was not really that of a servant. She had been rude to Nanny because she was worked up into a fearsome state about what might happen this afternoon. And, since Nanny was the centre of her darling child's life, she had best make amends. She could spend an extra half-hour in conversation with Nanny later. She might even pretend to ask her advice.

She reached her own sitting room, closed the door behind herself and leaned against it with a sigh. Her morning wear, silk blouse and a long black skirt ruched into pleats at the back, was uncomfortably tight. Maisie had laced her stays wrongly this morning. Therese slipped a tiny hand inside the waistband and found it damp and warm.

'Dash it!' she said to herself. 'I shall have to bathe after luncheon. I need to have the upper hand this afternoon.'

She went to the fireplace and pulled on the braided cord to summon Maisie.

'Polish my bangle and brooch, will you?' she said when the girl appeared. The girl who had attended her when she had returned from Vienna had been promoted from housemaid at the hall to Therese's personal maid. Maisie was a pretty girl of around her own age with a well-proportioned figure that would probably soon become buxom. But in Therese's opinion which she voiced regularly to her cousins, Maisie was 'dense'.

The girl always hesitated for a second before replying. It gave an impression of unwillingness that Therese could not cure her of. 'Yes, ma'am,' she answered.

Therese had never taken to Maisie but then, she knew, she had never taken to women, especially pretty ones. She had no woman friend apart from a girl she corresponded with, Xanthe Madison from the Vienna days. Xanthe was rich, American and on several trips to Europe had tried, so far without success, to secure for herself an aristocratic husband. Poor Xanthe would need all the help that money could buy in Therese's opinion. Xanthe was terribly plain.

Therese simply could not trust women, seeing them all, even dear Mary and Maggie, as rivals. She knew that her suspicions were unfounded and unworthy and she was sure they were not shared by anyone who was not of a jealous nature, as she was. However, she had lived for too long at the Dower House, this hothouse of women, and she could not help her feelings. Sometimes she wished every other woman in the world dead. Mistrust of women was one of her characteristics.

'I will give you the afternoon free, Maisie,' she said, to make amends for her thoughts. 'Have you somewhere to go?'

'I come from Liverpool. There's nobody here, ma'am . . .' the girl began to say.

Therese interrupted her. 'Yes. Yes. Then I'm sure you can amuse yourself with the other servants.' She did not encourage the girl to talk about her circumstances. Maisie was paid for her services. A good employee was one who was grateful for the chance of work and wages. Maisie was well placed as her maid and need never think of her own family again.

She nodded to indicate that Maisie was to leave her and when the door closed Therese patted her hair and went down the stairs to eat.

They all took breakfast in summer in the conservatory and it was there that she found Mary and Maggie, already seated on cane and bamboo chairs which were placed around a large hexagonal table. They were neither pretty nor truly plain. To Therese they had always seemed old and staid although Mary was only five years older than Freddie and therefore seven years older than herself.

'There you are, Therese,' Mary said as she entered. 'Come in. We've sent for tea.'

Therese went to the table and kissed both girls' cheeks. Mary, sweet-natured, was the younger at twenty-nine and small and dark like herself. Maggie was thirty-one, thin, as dark as a gypsy and as much the autocrat as her sister was helpmate.

'Have you heard the news?' Mary asked in her soft voice.

'What news?' Therese sat and took a bread roll from the basket Mary offered.

Maggie said, 'The *Tintagel Castle* was sighted a couple of days off Southampton.'

'Southampton? I thought it was due in at Liverpool,' Therese said. 'They'll be home on Wednesday then?'

Mary passed the butter dish to Therese. 'Father has invited the junior officers to Hetherington for a week of celebrations.'

'And Mother wants Freddie and the men to have parties and dinners, pretty girls and dancing,' Maggie said in her forthright way as if she were ordering groceries. 'She wants it to be the biggest celebration Hetherington's ever seen.'

'Most of it is already arranged,' Mary said. 'Father has had about twenty rooms made ready. There's to be a reception and dinner on the day they arrive. Everyone's been invited. It only remains for us to write out the last place cards when Freddie sends word from Southampton.'

Maggie said, 'What about the ball? Mother wants it.'

'I don't think Freddie will want a ball,' Therese put in. 'He won't want festivities and dancing at Hetherington with his mother nearly . . . I mean, so very ill!'

'Mother insists,' Maggie said.

Mary assured Therese that it was so. 'Mother said, "I will not have my beloved son's homecoming shadowed in any way by my ill health. You are to do as I say! I order it!" '

'Can we?' Therese asked. 'In such a short time?'

'There's plenty of time,' Maggie said. 'If we have the dancing on Friday. If we send out the invitations today we'll have most of the replies by Wednesday. What is there to do?'

'Ask the regimental band to play for it,' Therese said quickly, unable to keep the eagerness out of her voice now. 'A ball would be wonderful. I'll see to the music . . .'

'I'll supervise the supper arrangements,' said Maggie.

'I'll see to the decorations as well,' Therese said. 'How many officers will be staying for the week? Does anyone know?'

Maggie was as eager as anyone else. 'We can accommodate them all. But I think about eight are sure to come.'

'Father wants the three of us at his side at the welcome-home dinner on Thursday.' Mary looked quickly at Therese.

The sisters would know that she normally avoided their father but now Therese nodded. She would attend the dinners and the ball. The officers' homecoming would be celebrated in as grand and victorious a manner as they could make it.

And it would be delightful once more to wear ball-gowns, to laugh, to be in the company of valiant young men. Therese had spent two and a half years at the Dower House in the company of women, longing for gaiety, for excitement, for the company of the young and dashing men she used to dream of marrying.

'It's such a pity that Mother won't be there,' Mary added. 'Poor Mother.'

'How is Aunt Augusta this morning?' Therese asked.

'Mother had a bad night.' Maggie rose from her chair and went to the glass door. She looked around and asked, 'You don't mind if I let a little cool air into here do you?'

She pulled back a long beaded curtain and opened the door to allow the draught waft away the intense, pelargonium- and fern-scented air.

It was one of the girls' unspoken rules that their mother's illness was never referred to within the family as anything other than an indisposition.

'Will you go in to see her today?' Mary asked as Therese reached across for the glass dish of apricots. 'She asks for you all the time.'

Therese bit her lip to conceal the nervous trembling of her chin that came whenever she thought of facing the dying woman.

'She asked that you take Peter to visit her,' Mary continued in a rush of words, as if to plead for her mother.

Maggie had returned to the table. 'I think you should go to her.'

Mary nodded her head in agreement. 'It's two weeks since she last saw you,' she said.

Therese steadied herself by pressing her hand hard against the corner of the table. 'I'll see Aunt Augusta at tea-time,' she said. 'If it's convenient. Peter and I will have returned from our drive by four o'clock.'

So many emotions were churning inside her. She had never lost her fear of Aunt Augusta and she dreaded challenging her uncle this afternoon. Both fears had to be faced today. And her coming confrontation with her uncle would be the harder one for she was going to demand money.

She had always had an allowance of five hundred pounds a year for clothes for herself and Peter. It came from the estate funds and she had no idea who had authorized it, her aunt or uncle. She had always assumed it was the interest on money left to her by her parents but her questions had gone unanswered.

Six months ago she had turned twenty-one and at last was no longer under the legal protection of the guardianship. And still nothing had been said. No official communication from any lawyer had come to inform her of her new-found rights. There had been no word of what she could expect to inherit. Whilst she was under twenty-one she had been afraid to ask.

She must be entitled to something. Her parents would not have left her destitute. Her uncle, though he had been until recently her legal guardian, had never told her anything. Today she was going to demand her rights.

No man would ever ask for her hand, not now. She could never hope to know real, romantic and passionate love. She wanted independence for herself and her son. If she were to have a home, an establishment of her own and the position that went with it, her uncle must provide it for her.

If he refused, or if he had cheated her of an inheritance, then it would be easy – and most enjoyable – persuading her darling cousin Freddie to marry her. After all, in the Austrian royal family it was expected that cousins would marry. Freddie loved her more than he loved any woman. He had told her so. He had said nothing about marriage. But it wouldn't be difficult to wring a proposal from him.

And it would be very enjoyable when, eventually, she became Lady Blackshaw. Hetherington Hall would be a different place when she was the lady of the house.

But the morning had seemed more like a week to her. She had spent an hour in the place Freddie used to call her 'Witch's Kitchen', a small, tiled room where she prepared her pot-pourri, rosewater and herbal creams and lotions. But even this, her only interest, had failed to distract her.

Before luncheon, which she intended to take alone in her private sitting room, she went to her dressing room to choose the things she would wear.

There was a dress of violet moire taffeta, with ecru lace at the wrists and neck. Wearing it, she would appear taller, older and more commanding than she actually was. If she chose to wear her matching shoes, kid skin with

French high heels, then her eyes would be only a few inches lower than her uncle's.

She was undecided about the hats. She took from its box her favourite, a violet and cream fine straw with a wide brim, placed it at a slant, pursed her lips and looked in the glass. The width and height framed her face prettily but, she decided, the long ribbon ties which fastened under her chin made her look sweet and coquettish.

It was not the effect she wanted. She replaced it and took out a felt, high-crowned affair with a narrow, turned-back brim. The ecru colour of the silk matched the lace collar perfectly. It gave her height and, she smiled to herself at the thought, the sight of the long narrow-headed hatpins she used to secure it to her hair might help convey to her uncle her determination.

It was another two hours before, bathed, dressed and prepared in her mind for whatever might follow, she found herself at the appointed time being helped into the pony trap by a groom whilst she waited for Peter.

Cosgrove had dressed Peter in a white sailor-suit. His dark curls were brushed into a halo under the ribboned hat and to his mother he looked like an angel. Cosgrove lifted him up beside her.

The sun had come out at midday; the sky was cloudless and there was no breeze. All at once, feeling with a surge of optimism that the coming interview would prove advantageous to her, Therese turned a smiling face to her son.

'Shall Mama drive you around the park, Peter?'

The sweet little face – the living image of Frederick as an infant – looked up into her own and laughed. 'Please, Mama.'

She loosened the reins. 'Walk on!' she called to the lively little Welsh cob. And they were off, trotting down the oak-lined South Avenue, turning through the Deer Park Walk and slowly, beneath overhanging branches towards the Chester Gate.

The child was bouncing around beside her, now snuggling close, now leaning over the side and squealing with delight as, ignoring the gaping stares of gardeners and estate workers, she urged the pony to a fast trot.

Her own childhood memories of summers at Hetherington came back to her as she drove the trap: long days spent in the company of Freddie. The amusement she and Freddie had given to Mary and Maggie; being driven in the painted dog-cart by the bustle-skirted girls for picnics by the Island Pool in the deer park.

'Here's where Mama used to try to swim.' She pointed out the spot where she and Freddie, clad only in cotton underpants, used to plunge and play when they had managed to dodge their nanny and the careless governess.

She smiled as she recalled telling Freddie about the water bugs she collected for her magic spells. Nowadays she gathered celandines at sunrise.

'Peter swim,' the child answered.

'You shall, my darling. Someone shall teach you.' She urged the pony to a faster trot as they turned past the Lodge at the Hollin Gate, up the North Avenue by the orangery and orchid house. 'Mama used to walk with her nanny—'

'Peter walk with Nanny.'

When they had managed to escape supervision she and Freddie used to climb trees and chase deer. They would stray behind the wall, into the forbidden territories of the cottages of the estate-workers' children and spy on adults from vantage points in the high oaks.

She drove the trap under the very oaks they had climbed in their childish searches for acorns for Freddie and the oak-apple galls for her potions.

'Mama!' Peter was bumping his little dimpled hands on the side of the trap in excitement.

The pony cart bumped and jerked, delighting the child as they wheeled around. She slowed the animal for the tricky little box-bordered pathway as they approached the parterre and finally settled into a sedate rolling rhythm as, pleased with her driving skills, she slowed the pony to a walking pace for the approach to the Garden entrance of Hetherington.

She halted and a groom came forward to take trap and pony away for her. With eyes alight after the exhilaration of the ride she adjusted her hat and ran quick fingers through the child's hair before replacing his sailor hat.

They were taken up to the small salon which overlooked the ornamental moat. Therese took Peter gently by the hand and led him to the window where they stood, waiting for Sir Jack Blackshaw.

The French clock, the only ornament on the high white mantel, under a portrait of the young and beautiful Augusta, Lady Blackshaw, ticked away the minutes until he came.

He was four minutes late but at last he came and stood before her, as combative as ever, his manicured and beringed fingers clenched into fists, brown eyes burning under heavy grey brows.

'So,' he said. 'At last!'

'What do you mean?' she asked.

'You have contrived not to be alone with me for three years,' he answered. 'Today you demand to see me. Why?'

He was not used to opposition and Therese knew that attack was her best course. 'I'm leaving the Dower House.'

'Impossible.' He showed neither surprise nor annoyance.

Her mouth tightened in disdain. 'I'm not here to plead, Jack Blackshaw,' she said. 'I'm delivering an ultimatum.'

He stared at her, anger then desire briefly flaring in his face. 'An ultimatum? Why? What are you asking for?'

'A home of my own. Servants and money.'

He looked as if he were about to dismiss her as he would a servant. 'There's nothing wrong with the way you live,' he said evenly.

'There's everything wrong with the way I live!' She

would not be intimidated. He hadn't asked her to be seated but she went, slowly and carefully to place Peter on the sofa before, with an air of supreme confidence, she settled down beside the child.

She gave a contemptuous shake of the head. 'It will not continue,' she said. 'There must be money for me. I am of age. I shall need it to set up a home.'

There was no sound but the ting-ting of the clock as it struck the quarter-hour. She had obviously surprised him, for the high colour had left his face and his mouth was a narrow line above his clenched jaw.

'I could force your hand, you know,' she said. 'If I told your daughters and Frederick that Peter is your son.'

'Why should you tell? It's not in your interest to do so.' Then he said sharply, 'You have no proof.'

'You only need look at your son.' So far she had kept her temper. She had not broken under the strain of confronting him and she had been afraid she might. She patted her son's hand and calmly looked up at Blackshaw. 'The brown eyes – he is every inch a Blackshaw – it's unmistakable, the likeness.'

'A likeness means nothing,' he said. But his voice was lower, harsher.

At the sound she began to feel the lift of her spirits that the scent of victory was bringing. 'Do you think Freddie believes your pathetic story?'

'Frederick?' He was clenching and unclenching his hands as he spoke. 'We need not concern ourselves with Frederick.'

She said, 'Frederick doesn't believe I married – that I was widowed – that I was left to bring up my son without means.'

'What does Frederick—'

'Frederick – your legitimate son,' she corrected him. 'Frederick asked me, before he went to South Africa, to give him the name of the man who disgraced me. He is going to kill him.'

Her uncle drew in his breath and strode angrily

towards the door. He opened it and peered out, suspecting perhaps that a servant might overhear, then he came back and stood before her. 'There is very little I can do,' he said. 'The estate is not mine. I cannot dispose of anything to raise the money. Otherwise I should set you up in style.'

'You will have the house for your lifetime, won't you?' Therese raised her eyelids in scorn. 'How much longer than a lifetime do you need?'

'The estate goes to Frederick on his mother's death. Not to me,' he said. 'It is you, you and the child who will suffer if the truth is told.'

He must be playing some kind of game with her. Why was he holding back the information about her inheritance?

He held out his hands as if trying to plead with her. 'Therese. Dear girl. Have a little more patience—'

'Don't you dare ask anything of me.' Angry heat flooded into her face as she took Peter's hand in hers to steady herself.

'Therese! Dearest girl—'

She would not allow him to speak like this. How dared he call her his dear girl? Leaving Peter curled into the corner of the sofa she went towards him. 'My parents must have left money,' she said. 'You are guilty of maladministration.' Her eyes blazed. 'To say nothing of rape!'

He looked away. He could not look her in the face and she fought back an urge to strike him. He went to stand at the window, his back to the room.

'I regret it,' he said. His voice was quiet. 'I don't expect you believe me. But I'm sorry.'

'How dare you!'

He turned to face her, his back to the light so that she was unable to see his expression. He held out a hand to her. 'I loved you. I told you so. I told you that I want you to live here with me.'

How could he say such things? Did he imagine he was

142

speaking to one of his silly chambermaids? Did he think she was some foolish girl whose head was stuffed with romantic poppycock?

'You say that you loved me? You dare to make excuses?' She almost shouted the words. 'I don't care a damn about your delusions. Nothing excuses your behaviour.'

'I tell you—' He stood in front of her with hands reaching out. 'I believed that you were willing. I believed that you wanted . . .'

'You detestable creature!' She had to wipe the corner of her mouth with a handkerchief before she could carry on. 'You raped your brother's child! You have ruined my life. I have no future!'

'You are a beautiful woman, Therese.'

'No decent man will have me now!' She felt the tears that had threatened this morning come to her eyes but these were tears of anger not self-pity. 'I have to fend for myself. And you! By all the Gods! You are going to pay for it.'

Peter was whimpering on the sofa and Therese turned back to the child and spoke in her softest voice. 'Come, darling. Stop crying.' She touched his cheek and saw the little eyes widen in relief. He deserved every advantage she could secure for them both. The darling boy was the only being she had ever loved so completely.

Peter, comforted by her touch, stopped crying and began to suck his thumb.

Blackshaw spoke dispassionately, as if he were conducting one of his business deals. 'There is some property I can give to you,' he said.

'What kind of property?'

'Houses. There's a family house if I remember accurately and a few dozen workers' cottages in Macclesfield.'

She would not be fobbed off with anything. She felt her lip curling in scorn. 'Macclesfield?'

'It's not too far from Hetherington.'

'I know where Macclesfield is! And what would I do with them? What do I want with houses?' she asked.

'Women of slender means,' he began, with a hard little smile before, seeing her eyebrows lift in derision, he began again. 'There are many unmarried women who live in comfort on the rents from such properties.'

The man was mad. Rents? Did he think she could live on the income from a few cottages? Live like some middle-class landlady? Contempt for him made her snap out, 'Are you out of your mind?'

'What do you suggest?'

'I don't suggest, Jack Blackshaw. I tell you. Unless you agree to give me money – at least two thousand pounds a year as well as my property – then I shall not only confess the truth to your dear daughters but I shall marry Freddie.'

That had shocked him. She saw anger leap into his eyes. 'You will what?' He lunged towards her, arm raised.

Peter began to cry.

At the sound Blackshaw appeared to pull himself together but his hands were tight fists. His face was purple with rage.

She stood perfectly still. Her eyes, as cold as the deep sea, never left his face. 'I want my inheritance. And I want an income of two thousand pounds a year. Or I marry Freddie.'

'You are talking like a fool,' he said angrily. 'Think, girl! I have to make provision for Mary, for Maggie—'

'Nevertheless,' she interrupted him, 'you will do as I say or Freddie and I will be married. And you will have to share your house – your own house – with me and Freddie and my son. And your life will be ruined.'

Blackshaw's jaw was tight. A muscle moved at the corner of his mouth. 'What makes you think that Frederick would marry you?'

'Freddie loves me. He has never found a girl to compare with me.' She saw that her words had really upset Blackshaw. At last she had struck the right note.

She smiled the smile of a woman who knows she has the upper hand. 'I only need ask him. Freddie will not refuse to make a lady of me.'

'Give me time.'

'You have exactly two days to think about it. Freddie will be here soon. And unless a document is in my lawyers' safekeeping, unless I have a guaranteed income for life, I shall ask my cousin to marry me!'

# Chapter Nine

**Tuesday, 17 June**

The day following the fiasco of the audition began like
any other. After all the weeks of rehearsing she was in
the habit of rising early, so at half past seven Alice put
on her old blue skirt and a striped blouse, tied her hair
back with a ribbon and went downstairs.

Yesterday's dreadful events had left her drained. All
the weeks of high hopes and expectation had been for
naught. She'd been foolish ever to have hoped.

On the way downstairs she heard Polly Gosling clattering about, opening and shutting the back door. Every day
started early for Polly. Alice made herself snap out of her
self-pity. Her life must appear easy and privileged to the
young housemaid who was only a year younger than
herself. Alice had made a friend of her and she went into
the gloomy kitchen to see her.

Little Polly with her rosy-apple cheeks, brown curly
hair and hazel eyes was always bright and cheerful. This
morning she was wearing a sacking apron over her grey
working dress as she raked the ash from under the range
in the darkened room. She looked up from her task
when Alice entered the kitchen, waved a dusty arm and
grinned. 'Little Polly Flinders, eh?' she said.

'Sat among the cinders,' Alice said. 'You're kneeling
among them, Polly. And you're not warming your pretty
little toes.' She crossed the tiled kitchen floor and pulled
up the Holland blind. Outside, the garden was dank. It
was raining. She opened the brass box to find papers and
sticks for Polly.

Polly returned to her noisy raking and shovelling. 'I'm startin' early today,' she said. 'I'll 'ave the fire lit before Mrs Brock gets 'ere.' Mrs Brock was the cook. Mrs Brock lived out.

Polly turned a cheery face to Alice again. 'Thanks for them books. I'm right enjoyin' *David Copperfield*.'

Alice put down the paper and sticks beside her and went to make the trolley ready for Polly, putting knives and forks, spoons and plates from the dresser on to the bottom shelf. She hated idling upstairs in bed thinking of Polly having to work so hard for her seven and sixpence a week. Polly worked cheerfully enough from morning until night and sent most of her wages home to her mother in Liverpool.

Polly replaced the fire grating and began to brush the tiled fire hearth carefully. She was obviously still thinking about the book Alice had lent to her. 'Eeh,' she said. 'What a life they had, in Dickens's day, eh?' She lifted her shoulders. 'And there's some as'll say, "Those were the days, them was!" '

' "They were," ' Alice corrected her. Polly had asked to be put right when she said anything wrong. Polly's stated ambition was to become a lady's maid.

'What?' Polly said.

' "Those were the days. They were." ' Alice told her.

'That's what I said.' Polly gave her a knowing look and shook her head. 'Thanks for 'elping me with me work. But it's not your place to.'

'It's all right.' Alice had finished the trolley. 'Shall I do the dining room while you light the fire?'

'Aye. Ta.' Polly stood up, lifted the bucket of ash and went to the back door. 'Don't you mind?'

'No. I like having something to do,' Alice answered her. Then, as she went out of the kitchen, duster in hand to do the dining room she felt again the disappointment of yesterday rise up to torment her. She would hate never to have any real work to do. If she didn't hear from the

Manchester Repertory Company then she'd have to find a job.

Aunt Harriet was in the dining room, sitting at the table, reading the newspaper. 'What are you doing?' she asked and her voice was high and sharp.

'Helping Polly.'

'You are doing Gosling's work for her? I pay Gosling to do the housework, Alice.'

'Don't be cross,' Alice said. 'I offered.'

Aunt Harriet looked as if she might puff herself up and start to lay down the law about young ladies' behaviour. Alice stalled her. 'What shall we do today?'

Aunt Harriet looked surprised for normally Alice went out with baby Arthur by herself. Alice said, 'Beattie wants to look after Arthur and take him walking now that she's left school. We could go somewhere together. You and me. If you like.' It would be a chance to talk, to forget yesterday.

Aunt Harriet's face went pink and pleased. 'What a lovely idea. Where would you like to go if the weather clears up? The Botanic Gardens? Or Hesketh Park?'

'Could we go down the pier – on the train?' Alice asked.

The Southport pier was almost fifteen hundred yards long and until last year had been boasted of as the longest in the country. It was very much in the nature of Southport's residents to boast of the town's attractions. And it was not considered infra dig to walk or ride on the pier. At the pier head, steamers left for the Isle of Man, Wales and Westmorland.

'Why not?' Aunt Harriet said. Sometimes she looked and behaved in a young and girlish manner.

'Or the Victoria Baths?' Alice said. 'I can swim.'

'I can't. I'm too old to learn and I'm frightened of water. And we'd catch our deaths of cold if we went for a hot bath in the afternoon.' Southport had a fine baths with Turkish and private hot baths as well as plunge pools.

'All right,' Alice said. 'The pier.'

So it was that after the luncheon dishes had been cleared away and washed they found themselves, at two o'clock, under a clear blue sky in a happy crowd of people, paying their entrance money for the flag-bedecked pier and buying tickets for the little steam train which would take them to the end. They had decided to walk back and afterwards Aunt Harriet was going to treat them to afternoon tea in Thom's Japanese Tea House on Lord Street.

Alice was wearing her muslin dress and the boater. Aunt Harriet wore one of her black poplin dresses and, on top of her piled-up hair, for once she wore a large white hat.

The pier was crowded and they had to queue to go through the little gate onto the wooden plank platform to the train – and wait until the people ahead were aboard. Often passengers had to wait until the train went and returned with its load, every seat full, but this time there were a few seats left when their turn came. They sat on the wooden seat in the last but one row of the open carriage. The train had just pulled away, whistling and steaming when Alice felt a tap on her shoulder.

She turned around quickly and found herself flushing with embarrassment. Behind sat Karl Reinhardt and a middle-aged couple who were obviously his mother and father. 'Hello,' she said as Aunt Harriet turned to look.

Karl Reinhardt gave one of his tight, self-conscious smiles. 'This is *mein Vater* – my father,' he said as he indicated the senior man. 'And this is *mein Mutter* – my mother.'

Alice twisted round and managed to put a gloved hand over the high back of the seat. She shook hands with Karl's parents, all the while aware of Karl's intense scrutiny of her blushing face. Now she would have to explain. She smiled and said, 'This is Karl Reinhardt.' Aunt Harriet's eyebrows shot up. 'I met him yesterday. He was introduced to me by one of your friends, Aunt Harriet – on the train to Liverpool.'

Aunt Harriet put out her hand and said, 'How d'you do?' then looked enquiringly at Alice. 'Which of my friends?'

'A lady with an old gentleman. She had two daughters.'

'Who?' said her aunt but Alice was saved from telling more lies because Karl was speaking.

'Are you going to take a boat?' he said.

'No. Oh no!' Alice said. 'Just an outing. For a little fresh air.' Then politely, 'And you? You and your parents? Are you going on an excursion?'

'No. We too. Fresh air.'

Alice looked ahead. They had passed the protection of the slatted fencing and the sea breeze, hardly ever absent on the sands, was blowing stiffly. She put her hand up to hold on to her boater. The Reinhardts behind her were talking in German. The wind was rushing past her ears.

And it was fortunate for Karl that she did not know the language for at that moment his father was berating him. 'You are a very obstinate son who disgraces the family. Hotel porter!'

'Waiter,' said Karl. 'I am a waiter, not porter.'

'Shocking!' Mother added in German. 'You let your father and sisters down. We have to tell everyone you are on holiday.'

Father went on, 'And all the time I am talking to you you are looking out of the hotel window. As soon as you see someone – this girl I expect – you drag your mother and me across the road to ride in this contraption!'

'Train,' Karl said.

'Ha!' Father turned to Mother. 'He says to the girl that we are here for fresh air.'

'Ha!' said Mother. 'We come all this way. We come to tell him to come home. What happens?'

Father turned a fierce face to Karl. 'Who is the girl?'

'*Fraulein* Davenport,' Karl answered. 'I shall marry her.'

Father said nothing for a second or two then, 'I don't

think this girl knows that you shall marry her,' he said and his thick black moustache twitched a little as if he were amused. 'She does not look like a girl who knows she is soon to be married.'

Mother nudged Karl firmly in the ribs. '*Heiraten*! Karl, *heiraten*!' she said. 'To marry! To marry! That is what we want, your father and I. We want for you – *heiraten* – to marry with good English girl.'

Then the wind took all their breath away it was blowing so strongly at the end of the pier. They had travelled high over the sands, then the brown muddy flats and pale green shallows and all the time the air was fast and brisk. At the end of the almost one-mile-long run the little train stopped and everyone made towards the wide pier head from where they could look across to their right and see the tower of Blackpool and the thin blue line of the Fylde coast.

Inky-blue water swirled below them at the pier head. Iron steps ran down from the high pier to the waters of Bog Hole. This was the deepwater channel where fishing smacks were being unloaded, rising and dropping steeply in the wind that was so strong the men were clinging to the rails as they passed up their baskets of fish.

Seagulls were wheeling and crying above their heads and Alice could hardly hear a word that was being said by Aunt Harriet who stood beside her at the rail holding on to her white hat with both hands.

'What?' Alice shouted.

'I said it's very cold out here.'

'Shall we go back?' Alice shouted to her. 'Shall we sit in the pier pavilion? We can have ice-creams.'

It was fun for her, out here in the wind. The sea and the wild free cries of the gulls made her worries melt away into insignificance.

And adding to the fun of today was the sound of the Reinhardts standing behind herself and Aunt Harriet. She kept hearing words that sounded different and exciting.

'*Heiraten! Heiraten!*' Karl's mother was saying eagerly though Alice had no idea that the translation was 'to marry'.

'*Kuemmerer! Kuemmerer!*' his father said in a jocular way as if teasing his son in some way and again Alice did not know that the father was saying in his own German dialect, 'Frustrated lover! Frustrated lover! That is all you are!'

Then she heard Karl, evidently annoyed at their teasing him, say in a deep, strong and authoritative voice, '*Das ist mir ganz wurst!*' and it sounded to Alice as if he were telling them that he couldn't care less about their opinions. The Reinhardts then fell to talking quietly, in German.

They had only been there for about five minutes, holding their hats tight in the wind when all at once Aunt Harriet turned and set off swiftly, back down the pier with the wind almost blowing her white hat off her head though she was using both hands to hold it on. Her dark blonde hair was coming loose and long strands were blowing and wrapping themselves about her neck.

'Come quickly, Alice!' she cried over her shoulder.

Alice laughed, gave a quick little nod to the Reinhardt family and ran to catch up with her aunt, holding her boater with her left hand whilst with her right she tried to keep the muslin dress held down.

They had gone half a mile down the pier before the breeze dropped and between the cracks in the planking could be seen pale yellow sand instead of the tight-ridged, wind blown waves of brown.

It was then that Aunt Harriet stopped and leaned against the painted iron railings. 'Oh, Alice! I have the most dreadful pain in my chest.'

Alice looked at her. Her aunt's dear face was as white as death and the thin hands clinging to her lapels instead of her hat were trembling violently.

Fear clutched at Alice as soon as she saw the clammy perspiration that had broken out on her aunt's forehead.

She took hold of Aunt Harriet's hand. It was ice-cold. 'Where's the pain?' she said. 'Do you feel faint?'

Aunt Harriet's breathing was fast and shallow. She could not answer for her arms, right to her shoulders, were shaking and jerking. She would collapse at any minute. Alice looked about her in desperation.

There was a seat a few yards away and nobody on it. She must try to get Aunt Harriet to the seat without harming her. People were hurrying by, looking away as if poor Aunt Harriet were drunk or something.

'Lean on me.' Alice's knees were turning to jelly in fright but she knew that for Aunt Harriet's sake she must appear to be calm and unafraid. 'Let me get you to the seat.'

Aunt Harriet, on the point of fainting Alice knew, let her weight fall against Alice and Alice with one arm fast about her aunt's waist and the other hand steadying them both by holding the iron railings, began to pray silently under her breath. 'Oh, God, please don't let anything happen to her. Please don't let her die. Please. Please God let her be all right.'

They were not moving at all. Shaking with fear herself, Alice put both her arms about Aunt Harriet who leaned against her heavily. She tried to edge her along slowly . . . slowly . . . so slowly . . . with Aunt Harriet's feet slithering across the boards at every little step . . . and desperate gulping breaths coming from her aunt's bluish lips.

'Allow! Pleez!'

Alice turned her head quickly and a wave of gratitude and relief started to spread through her. Thank God. Her prayers were being answered. It was Karl and his parents.

Karl moved her very gently out of the way, then he and his father took an elbow each and half-lifted, half-carried Aunt Harriet to the seat and placed her down slowly and carefully. Karl's father sat beside her and indicated to his wife that she was to go to the other side.

Aunt Harriet had her head down towards her lap and

as they held their arms about her the breathing began to sound less laboured and rasping.

Alice, with tears pouring down her face, stood in front and a little to the side of Aunt Harriet, to protect her from the wind and to keep a little space so that the pushing crowd of people should not notice and stand and gape at them.

Aunt Harriet's breathing was slowing. She was sitting upright, leaning against Karl's mother, eyes closed, her face pasty and damp. Karl's mother was stroking her hand and all the while in low comforting words of assurance she was saying, '*Besser* . . . *besser* . . . That is better. *Das Gute* . . . *Das Gute* . . . That is good.'

Aunt Harriet's breathing began to slow. She had opened her eyes.

Alice bent forward and saw a faint flush of colour return to her aunt's face. 'How are you?'

Aunt Harriet managed to whisper, 'I shall be . . .'

Again, the swift wash of relief. 'Don't talk,' Alice brushed the tears from her cheeks and took her aunt's hand in her own, crouched low and held on to her hand steadily though inside she was still shaken sick with fright. The trembling in Aunt Harriet's hands seemed to be dying away although they were still like blocks of ice.

Alice looked up from the hands of her aunt to glance gratefully at Karl's parents. 'Thank you,' she whispered. 'It's so good of you.'

Karl was standing close beside her. 'We help you to get home. As soon as is better enough.'

'Thank you,' Alice said. 'You are very kind.'

Alice stood and felt her own strength return a little as she released Aunt Harriet's hand. She looked thankfully at Karl. 'Thank Heaven you were here,' she said. 'How lucky that you happened to see us.' Tears of gratitude were springing behind her eyes. She sniffed and swallowed. Aunt Harriet would hate any fuss in public.

Karl put a hand firmly on her shoulder and Alice found it odd that he should do so, but comforting all the same.

British people never made any show in public. But foreign manners, she knew, were quite different from her own.

'Thank you. Thank you,' she said again. And she felt Karl tighten his grip on her shoulder and move a little closer after she thanked him.

Aunt Harriet took an arm each of Karl's father and mother and Alice and Karl walked a little way behind. They went slowly and unobtrusively as Aunt Harriet would like them to do, down the pier and out on to the hot, windless and bright Promenade.

Across from the pier was the Victoria and in a line in front of the big hotel's Promenade entrance were the hire-carriages and Hansoms. Karl raised his hand in a commanding gesture and one of the open landaus pulled away and swept round to their side of the road. Karl's mother and father helped her in and sat, one either side of her. Then Alice and Karl climbed in and they set off for Duke Street.

Once there, Karl's father handed Aunt Harriet down and Beattie and Polly took her up to her room. 'Send for doctor,' Karl's father said as soon as she was safely upstairs. 'She must see doctor.'

But when Alice went up to her room to tell Aunt Harriet that she was going to send for the doctor Aunt Harriet would have none of it. She insisted that she was recovered. It had been nothing . . . a touch of the sun and wind . . . She told Alice to leave her and go downstairs and invite Karl and his parents to tea the very next time the mother and father were in Southport.

## Wednesday, 18 June

The following morning as soon as she was awake Alice went straight to her aunt's room to see if there were ill-effects but her aunt had already risen and gone downstairs. Alice would have to tell her, later, that they had asked the doctor to call on her today.

She went back to her bedroom to dress but stopped on the half-landing to push open the stained-glass window. The air this morning was warm and balmy with a salt-laden breeze blowing off the sea. The sky above the rooftops of the houses opposite was clear blue and she could smell the laburnum tree under the window. It was in full flower and she could have touched its leaves had she reached out over the sill.

Below the window was the pathway from the back garden to the front of the house. Alice was about to leave the window but heard the noise of a bicycle rattling over the stone setts of the street. The postboy came into view, his hat awry, whistling the tune that would bring Polly Gosling running.

Polly came quickly round the side of the house before the boy reached the front door.

'I'll take them,' Polly said.

Alice listened as the maid spoke in her newly-acquired and very lofty tone of voice. At the window Alice, amused at Polly's performance, decided to watch for a few moments.

The boy lifted the bundle high out of Polly's reach and then, 'Give us a kiss for 'em,' the cheeky lad said.

Polly, apparently annoyed at his lack of respect for her new manner, forgot herself. 'I'll give yer t' back of my hand,' she replied.

'Go on then.'

'Hand 'em over or I'll tell the mistress.'

'All right.' He opened his fingers and the letters, about six of them, dropped into Polly's outstretched hands.

Alice almost laughed here but it would have given away her presence. And she was stopped in her tracks by the postboy's next remark.

'The mester – Doctor Davenport – he'll be coming back today.'

Alice's heart missed a beat. Papa? The regiment? Home today? She pushed the casement a little wider.

'The doctor?' Polly had regained her fine accent. 'How would you know?'

The lad said defensively, 'It were you as told me that you worked for Doctor Davenport.'

'Well? What if I did?' said Polly who was clearly on the defensive too.

'Yer don't. Do yer?' The boy looked at her slyly. 'Your missus is Miss Walker. You was showin' off, sayin' yer mester were a doctor.'

'Aye. Well. Temp'ry like,' Polly said. 'When the master gets back I'll be workin for 'im.'

'Who says?'

'Miss Alice says.'

Alice had read one or two of Papa's letters to Polly. Papa had spoken of 'a practice' but he would be angry if he thought his intimate thoughts were being bandied about as facts by housemaids and postboys. Alice would speak to Polly about it – but for the moment she listened.

'I said, "How do yer know?" ' Polly repeated with all her old confidence.

'Telegraph. They docked in Southampton this mornin'. Troop trains were waitin'. The doctor'll be in Chester today. He'll be 'ome tonight I reckon.'

Polly, who had never met Papa, sounded fluttery and alarmed again. 'Are you sure?'

'Don't believe me if you don't want.' The boy turned to walk back down the short path and the six steps. 'Only you'd best polish them brasses on't front door – and get them steps donkey-stoned white as snow 'afore he gets 'ere.'

Alice pulled the window shut and waited a few seconds for Polly to reach the kitchen. Then she tightened the girdle of her dressing-gown and flew down the stairs on soundless feet, her hair streaming out over her shoulders. She glanced in the big oval mirror in the cool, dark hallway as she passed on her flight towards the scullery and kitchen. Her cheeks were flushed with excitement, her eyes shining as she reached the kitchen door and stood outside for a second.

She took a deep breath to steady the uneasy feeling that Aunt Harriet's funny turn of yesterday had left behind. Then she entered the big square kitchen.

Mrs Brock was frying bacon, kidneys and sausages in an enormous iron skillet over the range. How could anyone eat hot breakfast on such a day Alice wondered, before remembering that George and Leopold were home from school and that her brothers could eat under all circumstances.

Polly was at the dresser, smiling as she stacked plates on to the trolley to lay the dining-room table.

'The letters, Polly,' Alice said. She tried to act – to appear calm and a little nonchalant. 'Did I hear the postboy?'

'Heard and saw I shouldn't wonder,' Polly answered. 'Yer father's coming home today.'

Alice acted the part of mistress of the house. She smiled imperiously and held out her hand. 'Thank you, Polly. I'll take them.'

Polly gave her one of her 'old-fashioned' looks before smiling and passing the letters to her.

Alice took the letters back into the passageway between the hall and the kitchen. There she stopped, riffled through them and instead of the letter she expected from the barracks at Chester she found one addressed to herself. With shaking fingers she opened it.

After a few seconds she ran back into the hall and stood at the foot of the stairs. 'Beattie! Beattie Davenport! Come here,' she called up in her clear, ringing voice. Beattie was probably still asleep.

Aunt Harriet appeared at the morning-room door. 'Alice. I thought you'd stopped that. Don't shout.' Then, seeing the letters in Alice's hand. 'What is it?'

'Aunt Harriet!' The words came tumbling. 'Everything – everything wonderful is happening all at once.' She waved the letter excitedly towards her aunt. 'It's for me.

It's from the Manchester Theatre – they saw me in our last play – they've offered me a part, Aunt Harriet. I don't have to go for an audition – they want me.'

Her hair was falling forward, hiding the flush of delight which had spread across her face. She pushed the hair back out of her eyes and waved the letter towards her aunt, her eyes wide with happiness and pride.

Aunt Harriet's eyebrows had almost reached her hair. There were wavy lines on her forehead, like those on a postage stamp Alice had always thought and at the moment they were deepening and growing close together as she took the letter, read it and demanded, 'What nonsense is all this?'

Alice sat down with a bump on the seat of the oak hall stand. She took a deep breath to control her excitement. 'And as if that were not enough,' she said, 'Papa's coming home today.'

She leaned back and pressed her cheek against the cool bronze arm of the figure of a blacksmith, one of a pair that stood either side of the glass inner door. The upraised arm not only held a hammer, but more often than not, as today, Alice's straw hat.

The startled, questioning air had gone. 'Today? Who said so?' There was eagerness in Aunt Harriet's voice.

Alice looked up. Her aunt was wringing her thin hands, a sure sign of agitation as Alice knew.

'They may not have docked yet,' Aunt Harriet was saying. 'We don't know how long it will take them to reach Chester and the barracks. How can you be sure that Charles—' Here she corrected herself, '—your Papa – will be home today?'

'Polly said.'

'Gosling said so?' Aunt Harriet looked affronted; as if poor Polly had presumed too much of her position in the house.

'Polly said that the postboy said that a message was telegraphed to the Southport office this morning,'

Alice told her quickly. 'The *Tintagel Castle* docked at Southampton, not Liverpool.'

Her heart was singing inside her, "I broke the rules – and yet I did it! I did it! I'm an actress!"

Aunt Harriet put her hand to her mouth. 'He may be home tonight?' She was growing pink. Aunt Harriet seldom lost her composure and yet she was starting to stammer a little. 'Go upstairs, Alice. Wake your sister and Leopold and George. We won't disturb Arthur. Arthur won't even remember your Papa. Arthur is far too – too young – to share in our excitement—'

Here Aunt Harriet seemed to pull herself up to her full height, clear her throat and make herself say with her normal calm, 'We can all talk after breakfast. We will have to think of some very particular way to welcome Charles home.'

Alice saw her go into the drawing room before she once again looked at her own letter.

Dear Miss Davenport,

I saw your excellent performance as Rosalind in *As You Like It* with the Southport amateur company. We are about to cast the play for our season of the works of Shakespeare and I understand from your producer that you would be pleased to be offered a place in the company.

The salary is seventy five pounds per annum. In our hostel a room with full board can be had for the sum of nine shillings per week. Please confirm your acceptance within seven days. Rehearsals begin on September the first. I look forward to seeing you amongst our new players.

Yours truly.

Papa was the only obstacle. He would allow her to go. Oh, surely he would? After all, Mama had been an actress.

Now, Alice realized as she ran up the stairs to dress

and wake the family, Aunt Harriet would be in a little fever of excitement that she would do her best to hide from them all. After breakfast they would talk about the preparations for Papa's return. They would have a wonderful supper prepared for him. They would all dress in their best. It was just like Papa not to send a message in advance. Papa was so – so correct and unassuming – he would not expect them to make a fuss. It would be the most marvellous reunion.

And after the family evening was over she'd ask him about the stage. No. Now that she had been offered a job, she'd tell him.

# Chapter Ten

The troop train was nearing Chester and the officers in the first-class carriage were stirring themselves after the long journey which most of them had passed in sleep. One compartment, at the end of the corridor, had been put into use as a washroom and barber's shop and it was from this place that Charles Davenport emerged, shaved, rested and bathed to stand in the corridor. He leaned against the brass rail which went the full length of the carriage, and looked out over the flat countryside of Cheshire.

Already he was noticing in himself the effects of lack of exercise. There had been no facilities on board and, as they neared their destination, he looked forward to using his muscles again. He was a natural early-riser and had always needed an hour's exercise every morning.

Major Blackshaw was the next to leave the barber's compartment and come to stand beside him.

'Are there sporting facilities at the estate, Blackshaw?' he asked. 'Do you keep a big stable? Any riding or swimming?'

Frederick Blackshaw grinned hugely and slapped Charles across the shoulder. 'Yes,' he replied. 'Everything you could want. Shooting – clay pigeon shooting all year round. There should be trout in the Dee. There are plenty of horses and it's good riding country. No hunting of course, in June.'

'I shall never hunt again. Or fish,' Charles said.

Frederick was a keen huntsman whose sporting

abilities were legendary in the regiment. He must have thought Charles was joking for he laughed out loud. 'Why not?'

Charles tried not to look too serious. He didn't want Frederick to think he'd invited a poor sport. He said, 'I've made a kind of pact with myself, not to kill anything.' He smiled at the look of surprised disbelief on the younger officer's face. 'Not even a fishing fly,' he joked before asking, 'What about swimming?'

Another officer had come to join them. Frederick edged a little to the left of Charles to make room for him before saying, 'There's a natural lake, fed by a stream, which covers about eight acres. It has a small island in the middle that's ideal for diving. Nobody goes there any more I imagine. Remind me to show it to you.' He spoke to the newcomer. 'What about you, James? Any sporting preferences?'

'An hour's riding will be enough,' the sub-lieutenant answered with a grin. 'I'm looking forward to the evening sport though.' He tapped a brown hand against the brass rail. 'I hope you've invited all the marriageable young women in Cheshire. We haven't seen pretty white girls for two years or more.'

Frederick nudged him playfully. 'Their fathers will keep them locked up, once they hear that a regiment of love-starved soldiers is about to descend on the county.' He turned again to Charles. 'Are you quite sure you don't want to send for your wife's cousin as well as the children, Davenport?' he said. 'I telephoned Hetherington. We had a telephone installed whilst I was away. My sisters said there's to be dancing on Friday. If your wife's cousin would like to join you, there's plenty of room.'

Charles drew his sun-bleached eyebrows together in a resolute frown. 'No,' he said. 'If you've no objections I'll send my telegraph message to Southport when I get to the Hall. I'll ask my two eldest children – Alice and George.'

'How old is your eldest daughter?' James asked Charles.

Frederick thumped James's arm playfully. 'Too young for you.' Then he glanced at Charles and saw the disapproval on his face.

Charles would not even allow Alice's name to be uttered by a couple of young blades like Frederick Blackshaw and James Horden. Frederick straightened up. 'Joking apart,' he said, 'send for all your children, Charles.'

Charles had relaxed a little. 'Just the two.'

'Good. Arrangements will be made to accommodate them,' Frederick said. 'What about you, James? Is there anyone you want to send a wire to?'

'No. I'm only twenty-three. I've no attachments yet.' The young sub-lieutenant smiled. 'I shall enjoy the chase.'

Then it was as if the whole train came to life at once. Men appeared from compartments and waited in line for their turns at the barber's chairs. The corridor was packed with men who, joking and laughing, pointed out to one another landmarks and features of the county that was home to their regiment.

After the train pulled in at Chester they made their way through cheering crowds who lined the road from the station to the barracks. The formalities took under an hour. Their orders were to report in every morning at nine thirty for an hour's parade rehearsal and they would be officially discharged after the parade on Sunday.

Coaches would take the men to the Knutsford station from Hetherington each morning, Frederick said. The train journey from Knutsford to Chester took less than an hour.

This last train journey now had to be made but at last they were there and found two coaches from Hetherington waiting to bring the officers who would be staying, eight of them, and their baggage to Hetherington Hall.

Frederick was seated opposite Charles. The road was straight and they covered the last miles very quickly.

'Turn in at the Hollin Gate!' Frederick called to the coachman. 'I'll give the men a conducted tour of the estate.' The horses turned at the Lodge and in at the Hollin Gate, the first entrance to Hetherington on the Knutsford road. Frederick said, 'There's the Hall. You can see the towers.' The men were craning their necks.

'We're passing the orangery on our left,' Frederick said. He pointed out the tall glasshouse and grinned across at Charles. 'My cousin – the one whose photograph I carry – and I used to be taken on sedate little walks all around here.'

Charles leaned across and indicated the water he could see as the coach rounded another bend in the road. 'What's this lake, Blackshaw?'

'The Island Pool,' Frederick answered. 'Ideal for your morning swim.'

They were approaching the west entrance where the drive was broad. It was here, beyond the ornamental moat, that they would be received. The coaches crossed the flat bridge over the water, turned and rounded the side of the house to draw up at the west-facing entrance to Hetherington where, on the wide, shallow steps, waiting to greet them was the man who must be Blackshaw's father. Charles stepped down on to the gravel and stood, waiting for the others to climb out, as Blackshaw went forward and stiffly shook hands with Sir Jack Blackshaw.

When they were all assembled and Frederick had introduced them to his father they went into this, the larger and plainer of Hetherington's two entrance halls. Servants were waiting in lines on either side of a long reception area where numerous open entrances, arched and pillared in marble, led to the apartments and reception rooms.

It was an obviously delighted staff who waited to be introduced and to welcome home the young major. It was also evident from their pink and beaming faces that his homecoming had been awaited with pleasure. There were tears in the eyes of the older servants as they took and held his hand as if they never wanted to let go.

Charles found himself suddenly wishing that he had his own family here to greet him but the feeling of envy passed as quickly as it came after he was shown to a comfortable room in the West Tower where he wrote out the telegraph message a servant would send to Southport for him.

There was to be a reception, at six, in the Green Saloon at the top of the main stairs to which officers from Chester with their womenfolk had been invited along with the friends and business acquaintances of the Blackshaw family. It seemed that all kinds of provision had been made for their amusement. Evenings were catered for with billiards. A room had been assigned for backgammon and cards. The music room would be the place for light entertainment and their days were to be filled with any sport they might fancy. No diversion would be wanting.

On Friday the dance, a victory ball Frederick had called it, would be held. The regimental ball would be held at the barracks in a few weeks time and all the top brass would be there but this Friday's dance would be much more informal and attended, not by the 'big guns', as the men called the top brass, but by the families of the lower ranks of officers from the barracks at Chester with their wives and partners, the business friends of the Blackshaws, the old soldiers of the Yeomanry with their wives, sons and daughters. It promised to be a jolly gathering.

Charles at once made up his mind to spend his time in swimming and riding and his evenings in billiards and good conversation. When the weekend was over he would take rooms somewhere and find a medical practice to buy into. There was a little money he had put aside to see the children through to maturity in the event of his being killed. That and his unused army pay could be spent. For now, he had an hour for rest.

He went to draw the curtains at the three tall windows that overlooked the South Avenue and stood for a moment, watching Frederick whose figure he could see about half a mile away. Frederick was still in uniform and appeared to be making for the house at the end of the drive near to the Italian gates. A young woman, dressed in green, with a small child by the hand was running towards him and, as Charles looked, he saw Frederick sweep both girl and child into his arms and whirl them around in a great demonstration of joyful reunion.

Charles smiled at the sight and drew the curtains across the windows, wondering if Frederick were the father of his cousin's child. If so, then they should not be prevented from marrying by worries about being related.

'Freddie. Darling.' Therese said in the husky voice he had so longed to hear. 'Put us down.'

Frederick stopped the whirling motion and let Therese and Peter down on to the sunlit drive. As soon as their feet were touching the gravel he bent at the knees, clasped their hands together in his own and kissed them, one after the other, in laughing, relieved repetition.

'Thank God you're still here, safe and well,' he said at last when he stood up and placed a strong arm around the slight shoulders of Therese.

'It is you who were in danger of not being here today,' Therese answered. 'Not ourselves.'

'Oh. You don't know how I've longed to see you,' he said as he took her hand and began to walk towards the Dower House. She looked wonderful. Her dark hair was coming loose from the pins holding it in a high-swept style that so suited her small, pointed face. He stopped and stared for a moment, holding her at arms' length, to admire her. Then he continued his walk towards the

Dower House and once again his worries surfaced. 'Mother?' he said. 'How is she?'

'Freddie . . .' Therese's face lost its vivacity. 'Don't be shocked. Your mother hasn't long to live. She's holding on to life to see you again. We really shouldn't be having this great house party – the ball and everything – not when she is so ill. But she insisted – because of you, Freddie. She said she wanted the party to go on because of you coming home.'

They went, through the little gate, towards the open front door of the Dower House where his sisters waited to greet him and, as soon as their kisses and greetings were exchanged, he said, 'Take me up to Mother, Mary.'

Mary led the way upstairs. She halted outside the bedroom door, pressed his hand hard and, when he looked down into her eyes, he saw that she was crying silently.

He brushed his lips across Mary's cool forehead as a sign that he understood, then he went in. A nurse, wearing a grey dress and long starched apron stood back as he approached the bed. Frederick indicated that she was to leave them and she did so, closing the door behind her.

Mother was lying, half-propped, asleep against an avalanche of white linen and lace which covered her pillows and bed. The air in the room was warm and still and seemed to him to hold odour upon odour – carbolic upon lavender – that could not disguise the sweet, sickly smell that rose from the bed. He was glad she was asleep and couldn't see the shock in his eyes. He had a few moments to accustom himself to the ravaged little face he had last seen in its old calm beauty.

He seated himself, awkwardly for he was so tall, on the slender bedroom chair. 'Mother,' he whispered at last, afraid suddenly that he was too late. The little figure was as still as death.

She opened her eyes and for the first minute he thought she had not recognized him. Then her face lit up with pleasure and the eyes, still the same eyes he knew, brightened with joy as her hand came out slowly to meet his own. 'Freddie—' she whispered.

It was no good trying to hold them back; tears were pouring down his face. He had not shed tears in all the years of war and fear and now, at the sight of his mother's agony, he was helpless to control them. 'Are you in pain, my darling?' he said.

She tried to pull herself up. 'I'm out of pain. The laudanum. Lift me up, Freddie.'

Crying with relief that she was not in pain, he bent and lifted her from the bed to hold her in his arms. She was so thin – weightless like a bird – that he was afraid that he would damage her but she reached up to put her arms around his neck and press her yellowed face against his cheek.

Gingerly he put her back on the bed, and delicately he covered her wasted body. Then he took out a handkerchief and blew his nose noisily, trying to smile as he did so, making her smile at him in return. 'Mother. You waited for me—'

'Freddie.' She whispered his name and crooked her finger so that he could draw closer. 'Freddie. I want you to marry.'

He patted her little hand and still smiling said, 'There is nobody I want to marry, my darling. When I find a girl who is as lovely as you . . .' He looked at her sweet face and paused. '. . . as lovely as you were when you married.'

'You – you can't marry Therese,' she said in the faint little voice.

'I don't want to marry,' he said again. Why did everyone in his family assume that one day he and Therese would marry? The servants used to talk that way before he went to South Africa. Surely they were not still doing it. It had never been an intention of his. 'I have never been sufficiently fond of any girl, not even Therese, to want to marry. And Therese is the nearest I came to loving anyone,' he told her. His crying had ceased and, as he spoke, he leaned over the high bed so that she should not have to exert herself.

'I want to see you married,' she whispered. 'I want you to be happy. Marry for love.'

'If I find someone, my darling, then I will bring her to you for your approval.' He grinned and added, 'I will even ask your approval before I ask hers.'

'Don't laugh. You will become wild, Freddie. You will never settle to life here unless you love . . .'

The effort had been too much for her. She spoke in a whisper again. 'In the desk – in the top drawer – there's a letter.' She appeared almost exhausted as her head sank back against the pillows and her eyes began to close. It was a supreme effort she was making and Freddie knew that whatever was to come, it was what she had lived to tell him.

He glanced towards the window where her little inlaid desk still stood. 'This desk? The davenport?' It had been placed there when she was a child so that she could do her lessons and look out upon the estate she had inherited.

'The key is in my jewellery box.'

Frederick brought her jewellery casket from its place on the tall chest of drawers and sat down again beside the bed. He offered it to her but she lifted her eyebrows in an unspoken signal that he was to search for the key. He found it, wrapped in tissue paper in a little velvet box. 'This?'

She nodded and he went to the desk, fitted the key into the lid and turned it. Here too everything appeared to have been left untouched for years except for the letter which lay on the little writing area of green leather. The letter was addressed to him.

He carried it back to the bedside and said very quietly, for she seemed almost to be asleep, 'Shall I read it? Now?'

Her eyes flickered open and she nodded her head.

He broke the wax seal and took out three large sheets of vellum, recognizing at once the large flowery hand that had been hers before sickness had weakened her. The letter was dated February, 1900. A month after he had sailed for Africa.

Darling boy, (he read)
Before I become weaker I must write this to you. If you do not return, the letter will be destroyed but it may be that you read it when I am dead and I shall never know if I have your forgiveness for what I am about to tell you.

There was a break here and Frederick had to turn the page to read on.

I inherited Hetherington Park estate when I was a girl of fourteen. The old mansion house was in ruins and I had always lived at the Dower House. There was no fortune and I had no means other than the income from the tenanted farms here and a few hundred pounds my father left to me.

Frederick already knew all of this. He read on.

A year after my father's death I met Jack Blackshaw, the son of Sir Thomas Blackshaw, the greatest man I ever knew. Jack was rich and clever and much older than me and was at that time engaged to marry Hildegard von Heilbronn, the daughter of an Austrian countess. It was seen as advantageous that I, landed and penniless, should marry his new title and new money.

Jack Blackshaw broke off his engagement to the countess's daughter and we married on my sixteenth birthday. We were ill-suited.

Jack Blackshaw set about rebuilding Hetherington Hall almost immediately. Perhaps he saw the new Hetherington as his natural métier for, once it was completed, he began to use the house for activities that were not centred around family life and I became unhappy with the life your sisters and I were obliged to lead.

None of this was news to him but Frederick felt the old familiar surge of anger against his father as he read on. It was here that again he had to turn the page and found that the writing on this sheet was smaller, more cramped, as if she had felt the need to press the words into a smaller space.

When Mary was four years old and Jack Blackshaw had inherited the title, Jack's younger brother, Edward, came into our lives. Edward was an army man whom I had not met before.

My darling boy, this is the most difficult thing I have ever had to write but you have to know that Edward and I embarked on a passionate love affair. He was the only love of my life.

My husband learned the truth and the affair had to end but it was too late because you, Freddie, had been conceived. I did not confess to Blackshaw that Edward was your father but I have always thought he suspected it. After this our married life ended.

The old Countess von Heilbronn was contacted and a marriage was arranged between Edward and her daughter Hildegard – Jack's old flame. Edward and his wife were despatched to India and I never saw him again. But it was agreed that, India being unsuitable, any children of their marriage should be brought up and educated here under our supervision.

Therese was their only child.

Frederick could barely take in all the implications of all he was learning. A feeling of unreality came over him as he looked quickly at his mother and turned the page over. She was lying, with closed eyes, waiting in probable trepidation he thought for his reaction. He read on.

You need never have been told any of this, Frederick, since Jack Blackshaw did not disown you. Our marriage was over but I remained at Hetherington, living a separate life, until I became ill. But I have seen the affection that you and Therese have for one another, seen it grow and prayed that it would not lead you to expect that you might one day marry her. For you share a father. Therese is your half-sister.

It was when I became ill and was seeking a cure that Therese returned to Hetherington under Jack's legal guardianship. You were in India with the regiment and Therese herself had only recently returned to Vienna from visiting her parents in Jaipur.

I came back to Cheshire from Karlsbad and found my niece, at only nineteen, with child. I was asked to believe the story of her early marriage and widowhood in Austria.

Forgive me, my darling, for suspecting the worst. I should have believed the evidence of my eyes, in Therese's bitterness towards Blackshaw.

Now, with you in South Africa, I am going to leave Jack Blackshaw. When you return I will hand the estate over to you though Jack will have the right to live for the rest of his life in the house he built. I cannot change that.

At this point the handwriting changed. It was written in his mother's hand but in a feebler, spidery scrawl and was clearly added at a later date.

Blackshaw has recently been to see me, demanding that I mortgage some property, to provide for Therese and her son. Otherwise he says, she will marry you, Frederick.

I am so sorry my darling. There can be little left for you to inherit.

You need never have been told except that you might

offer marriage to Therese. That cannot be. Marry for love. Your loving mother,
Augusta Blackshaw

Frederick found that, whilst inside he raged, one half of himself seemed to be acting like an automaton, folding the letter and replacing it in the envelope. It would have to be destroyed. He felt as if he had aged since he came into the room, yet he could not blame his mother. She had risked losing his love for her by telling him the truth. He tucked the letter into the inside pocket of his blue uniform jacket and looked gravely at her.

'The child?' She opened her eyes again. 'Therese's child? Freddie?'

'I know, Mother. I know what you thought,' he said grimly. 'Give me time to take all this in. But I promise you that I will find out who disgraced Therese.'

His mother's eyes were wide open. 'It was . . .' Under the shiny, yellowing forehead it seemed as if she had paled even more than before.

'It was your father. It was Jack Blackshaw.' Mother whispered the words so softly that Frederick could hardly believe he had heard them. He felt his blood run cold as their import came to him. He could not speak for a moment. He stood, stupefied.

At last he said with bitterness, 'Are all the men in this family depraved? Does it run in the blood, do you think?'

Then he wished he had bitten his tongue as he saw the hurt and fear in his mother's eyes again.

'Do nothing. Do nothing, Freddie,' she pleaded. 'Do nothing until I am gone. But don't let him – don't let him – Mary – Maggie – poor little Therese—' She had fallen back, exhausted, on to the pillows.

He was white to the lips with anger. 'He'll not harm anyone again,' he told her as he made her comfortable. Rage was burning in him. 'He won't be here. I'm going to get rid of him.'

Tears had come to her eyes. 'Take care,' she pleaded. 'He's a devil.'

'I'll cast him out. It will be easy. I owe him nothing.'

He looked down at his mother and gave a sorrowful smile. 'Don't imagine I'll wait, Mother,' he said. 'Don't ask any more forbearance from me. I'm going to avenge you both. Now.'

Frederick threw his weight against the door of the study and heard the crash of heavy oak behind him as he faced the man he used to be ashamed of hating.

Sir Jack Blackshaw stood with his back to the window. 'What brings you?' His voice was deliberately bluff. 'What's all this about?' Then his bushy eyebrows rose in alarm at Frederick's advance across the room. 'You've seen your mother?'

Frederick's fists were clenched in readiness. 'You know why I'm here,' he snarled. 'I don't know why you are.'

'Stop!' Blackshaw ordered. 'Control yourself.' The veins on his temple bulged.

But Frederick was upon him, hands grabbing for his neck.

The older man struck out with unexpected power, catching him under the solar plexus, making him drop his hands and retch for his breath for precious moments until he was able to gather his strength again. Then he straightened as he clenched and raised his right hand.

'Wait, man!' Jack Blackshaw stepped backwards to avoid the fist that was raised against him. 'Listen!'

Frederick went for him again, this time aiming for the face he wanted to smash to a red, lifeless pulp.

His bare knuckles connected with Blackshaw's jaw. There was a satisfying roar of pain, then his father reeled back, awkwardly, to fall against the narrow table at the window, sending books and a marble bust hurtling on to the parquet floor, almost smashing his prized Chinese jar which toppled sideways on to the carpet.

'Get up!' Frederick said. 'Come on! Fight! You loved

nothing better than a fight when I was smaller than you.'
He waited for his father to pull himself to his feet, unable
to hit a man – not even Sir Jack Blackshaw whom he still
thought of as his father – when that man was on the floor.

His father lay there, snorting for breath, blood oozing
from the corner of his mouth. He pulled from his pocket
a handkerchief and wiped the corner of his mouth before
turning a look of venom on to Frederick.

'Bloody fool,' he said. 'You can't do anything now.'

'Get up!'

'Put your fists down. In Hell's name! What will it
benefit you to kill me?'

Frederick stepped across the litter of books and
dragged his father to his feet. 'I don't give a damn about
benefiting myself,' he roared. 'I've had all I'm going to
take from you. You'll pay for this!' He tried to set him
on to his feet but the old man would not stand. He was
forced to push him backwards into one of the leather
armchairs.

'Pay for what?' his father sneered. 'Every bloody thing
has been paid for by me.'

'You've feathered your nest,' Frederick answered. 'But
you'll do no more of it. I'm taking over.'

'How do you think you'll live?' Rage was in every line
of his father's face.

'Don't waste a minute asking questions,' Frederick said
savagely. 'Get off my land! Get out of here. You've no
time to lose.'

'There'll be nothing left if I go,' Blackshaw said in a
voice that was an uneasy mixture of bravado and defiance.
'No money. Nothing.'

'The estate is mine.' Frederick was having to make an
effort to keep his hands off his father.

'What's left of it. Your mother has signed away most
of your inheritance.'

'So! We're getting to the truth are we? Your scheme
won't stand up. You can't do a thing to dispossess me.
The estate is mine.'

Jack Blackshaw tried to pull himself upright in the armchair. 'You'll discover, my fine soldier, that the estate is entailed. Mortgaged. Borrowed against,' he said.

Frederick pushed him back into the chair. 'Stay there. It's much safer,' he warned. He leaned forward until his face was only inches from the face of the man he detested. The urge to smash the leer off his father's face was almost unendurable. 'You are vicious. You have no principles. Why are you still here?' he demanded. 'What do you hope to gain?'

Jack Blackshaw, who had the same ruthless set to his face that Frederick knew well from his childhood, said, 'Take you hands off me and I'll tell you.'

Frederick drew back. 'Coward! Stand up.'

Blackshaw struggled to stand and went to sit behind his desk. He had a look of fear for all his bravado. He put the handkerchief to his mouth again and spat into it roughly.

Then, apparently satisfied that he could speak, he said slowly, 'I've borrowed against Hetherington. Your mother has signed a loan.' His bushy eyebrows were raised and his lip, swelling from the blow to his jaw, was lifted in derision as he said, 'Everything but my house is yours. The estate. The land. All two thousand unprofitable acres of it, farms and forest, village and wasteland. All of it yours. And a millstone around your stupid neck.' He drew a deep breath. 'I will never, never leave the house I built.'

Frederick could hold back no longer. He reached across the desk and, taking his father's shoulders in his strong hands, pulled him from behind the desk only to thrust him against the back of a leather armchair and hold him there.

'You'll be lucky to get out of here alive. Don't tempt me to finish you off.'

Blackshaw fell back against the desk as Frederick loosed him and, after struggling to stand, gasped in pain before he said, 'There's nothing you can do. It's signed and sealed. I shall live in this house.'

Frederick knew nothing of the law. He'd have to study the marriage settlement before he was sure of his ground. 'You've not answered my question. Why are you here? In your shoes I'd have gone. I'd have gone years ago.'

'When your mother dies I shall install a woman at Hetherington.'

Frederick fought back the desire to strike him. He took a sharp breath and said with controlled sarcasm, 'And who, in God's name, do you expect to favour with the title of second Lady Blackshaw?'

'Therese.' Blackshaw said her name sharply. 'We can't marry. She's my niece. And she won't come to me whilst your mother's alive. But afterwards . . . Therese and the boy . . . and your sisters . . . Will all live here, with me.'

'I don't believe it.' Frederick would not let Blackshaw see his shock. He clenched his fist and gritted his teeth. 'You are mad. Therese? Impossible.'

'She's mine,' Blackshaw said furiously.

Blackshaw was blind. Therese must loathe the man who had ruined her. Therese would not be here on the estate if she had been properly provided for – as she would be when he took charge. Heavy sarcasm was in his voice. 'Does Therese know about it?' he asked. 'Or are you planning to surprise her?'

'She knows.'

The air of mockery left Frederick. He felt anger surge in him again. 'Why hasn't Therese come into her inheritance? There's property and an income in trust for her.'

'It's still intact.'

'So you have only defrauded my mother and me?'

A weak smile crossed Blackshaw's face at this point, then, seeming to hold himself back, he drew the bushy eyebrows together and said in a matter-of-fact tone, 'No. Your mother has signed a loan document. The money raised by mortgage is mine. I'm within my rights to use such money as I will.'

'Then take your ill-gotten gains and go!' Frederick was tempted to hit him again but, with an effort, held himself in check as he spoke. 'Go whilst you can.'

Sir Jack Blackshaw, growing red-faced again, said, 'I am entitled, both under common law and the terms of my lease, to live in the family home until I die.'

Frederick gave a laugh of derision that helped him to stifle the urge to make an end of his father. 'Do that!' he said. 'Try it! Stay on if you wish. Your dying day may come sooner than you think!'

# Chapter Eleven

The house was bustling with activity when the doctor came to see Aunt Harriet. Alice had meant to tell her aunt that she had sent for him but with all the excitement it had gone right out of her head. She and Aunt Harriet were in the drawing room, polishing the furniture and washing the tiled hearth. The rugs had been beaten yesterday so there were only the pleasant jobs to do. Alice enjoyed polishing. She could rub away fiercely whilst inside her heart was as light as a feather.

She was holding her success to herself as if in a little golden box that she could open every few minutes. Her future on the stage was such a dazzling prospect that she dared not look at it; dared not think about it for too long at a time or she was sure she would start to scream and run and jump for joy. She put all her effort and concentration into buffing the round table in the window and almost leaped out of her skin when Polly came into the room.

'Doctor Williamson,' Polly said. 'He's askin' for you, ma'am.'

Aunt Harriet turned to Alice. 'You haven't . . . ?' she asked. Her face had gone pale again.

'Yes. Yes, Aunt Harriet.' Alice was going pink and apologetic. 'I thought it best . . .'

Aunt Harriet put down the yellow duster and removed her little waist-apron. 'Very well,' she said. 'Tell him I shall see him upstairs, in my room.'

Polly said, 'Yes, ma'am,' and went from the room to the hall where the doctor was waiting.

Alice heard her aunt greet the doctor and then heard their footsteps going up the stairs. She went on with her polishing. It was all for the best that Aunt Harriet saw the doctor. Papa would think she had failed in her duty if he came to hear about Aunt Harriet's 'turn' yesterday. Then she stood for a moment savouring the thought of Papa's homecoming before returning to her vigorous polishing.

Fifteen minutes later there was a tap at the drawing room door. Who on earth would knock at the door?

'Come in,' she said.

The door opened and Dr Williamson entered and closed the door firmly behind him. He was a tall, thin, elderly man with a goatee beard and small moustaches. He wore gold-rimmed glasses and behind them keen brown eyes missed nothing.

'Miss Davenport?'

'How d'you do.' Alice then put out her hand quickly. Once he had shaken it she asked, 'There's nothing the matter with Aunt Harriet, is there? Nothing serious?'

He was stroking his chin and looking steadily into her face. 'Indeed, there is,' he said.

Alice felt the colour drain from her face. 'What?'

'How long have you – there are five of you I understand. How long has Miss Walker had responsibility for you all?' he said with great solemnity.

Alice's voice was hardly more than a whisper. 'We have been here for two and a half years,' she said. 'But why?'

'My patient was told, four years ago, that she should live a quiet life,' he said. 'Your aunt has a heart murmur. A condition of the heart we call angina.'

'She's going to be all right, isn't she?' Alice asked, anxiety pitching her voice high. 'What's the cause of angina?'

The doctor was stroking his beard slowly and once again he looked keenly at her. 'You are the eldest?'

'Yes.'

'Then you should know that your aunt has narrowly escaped death. An attack can be fatal.'

Alice dropped down on to one of the high-backed, velvet chairs. She could not say a word. All she could do was listen whilst the doctor told her everything. He went to stand at the window as he said very solemnly, 'The most frequent causes of an attack are physical exercise, especially going uphill or against the wind and, secondly, emotional excitement, whether depressing or exhilarating.'

He looked at her for a moment without speaking. 'Is your aunt under any great emotional strain? Anything out of the ordinary?'

Alice heard herself answering him in a high, nervous voice, 'Yes. Oh, yes. She is.'

'How much longer will your aunt have responsibility for you all?' he asked.

'Papa—' Alice began. She started again. 'My father will be home today,' she said.

She could not tell this doctor that they all, and Aunt Harriet most of all, expected Papa to marry Aunt Harriet.

'Then I hope that you will not stay for much longer,' he said. 'My patient needs rest. Absolute rest. There must be no excitement. No anxieties.'

Alice saw in an instant that Dr Williamson was right, though she thought he was exceeding his duties by making her feel that they alone were responsible for poor Aunt Harriet's ill-health. And yet a doctor must put his patient's welfare before other considerations.

'What treatment is she to have? In the meantime,' she asked.

'I shall give you some glass capsules of nitrate of amyl which she can crush in a handkerchief and inhale,' he answered. 'That is for the angina pain.'

'And will she recover? Completely? If she can lead a more tranquil life?'

'Nobody can say. She should lead a quiet life.

Preferably in a warm climate. She must never go out in the wind. Sea air is not beneficial.' He frowned and tugged at the goatee beard again. 'But your aunt must have peace of mind.'

Alice saw him to the door and felt the terrible weight of responsibility descend upon her again. The two and a half years they had been here had almost killed her poor aunt. Papa must help her to make Aunt Harriet well again.

George and Leopold were brushing the garden path when the postboy came back at five o'clock with a telegram.

'Telegram!' The boy swung open the gate and handed the yellow envelope to George. 'It's addressed to you and Miss Alice!'

'All right. Off you go,' George said. The telegram boy always knew more than was good for him. It would not have surprised George if the cheeky lad had reported the message before they had time to read it themselves. He took the envelope and went inside in search of Alice.

He found her, dressed in her blue Ninon dress for Papa's homecoming, in the dining room helping Aunt Harriet lay the table. The best Wedgwood dinner service and the lead crystal water glasses were being laid out over Aunt Harriet's lace tablecloth.

He handed the telegram to her.

'You read it, George,' she said and her face was bright with excitement for they knew it was from Papa. 'I can't bear to open a telegram.'

George tore the envelope and took out the sheet of paper. He began to read, stopping halfway through to look at them as the message became clear.

Arrived Hetherington Cheshire. Here until Sunday. George and Alice to attend victory celebrations here Friday. Will be met Knutsford station 3 o'clock. Evening dress for grand ball. Papa

Alice felt as if she had been struck. Her voice went down to a whisper, 'Read it again, George. Read it slowly,' she said. Had she understood? Papa? Not coming? After all this time away from them? Why not? Wasn't he as eager to see them as they were for their first sight of him?

George was dumbstruck as well.

'What can it mean?' Alice snatched the telegram from George's hand and read it for herself before turning with a horrified expression towards Aunt Harriet.

But Aunt Harriet had gone pale. She looked as if she might faint and, when she spoke, the light and girlish tone that had been hers all day had gone. 'Your Papa is bound to attend these – these victory celebrations, I expect,' she said flatly. 'He has asked that you join him. You and George.'

Alice felt cold and all at once drained. It took her a moment or two to collect her thoughts whilst she was aware of George and Aunt Harriet's eyes upon her. 'I'm not going,' she said.

Aunt Harriet appeared to be making a great effort not to let her own disappointment show. She spoke with slow deliberation. 'Run down to the kitchen, Alice. Tell Mrs Brock we'll eat dinner when she's ready. There's no need for her to stay longer than necessary.' After she had spoken, looking all at once old, she gave Alice and George a tight-lipped smile and hurried from the room.

The door closed behind her.

'We'll have to go.' George's voice was firm. 'We can't say "No". We can't ignore orders.'

'Poor Aunt Harriet.' Alice was close to tears. She had seen the shock in her aunt's eyes. 'Doesn't he care?'

George put an arm around her shoulder before saying quietly, 'I don't think Papa is going to marry her.' His face revealed the sympathy he felt for Aunt Harriet even as he added with a note of finality, 'I never thought he would.'

Alice's spirit was evaporating. Everything depended

on Aunt Harriet and Papa marrying – their home – and Aunt Harriet's health, for Papa would cure her of angina. He had been wonderful when Mama was ill. And it seemed that just as she had her future within her grasp it was snatched a little further away. 'I don't know what to think,' she said. 'I can't take it in.'

George's warm hand on her shoulder was comforting. 'He may not be allowed leave,' he said. 'Until Sunday.'

Hot tears of disappointment were pricking behind her eyes. 'But he could surely fit in a flying visit. Why doesn't he want to see us?'

George pulled a large white handkerchief from his pocket and handed it to her. 'Here,' he said. 'Blow your nose. We'll know soon. Run down to the kitchen and tell cook, will you?'

Alice dabbed at her eyes, blew into the handkerchief and gave George a painful little smile before leaving him there in the dining room and going to the kitchen to pass on the message. In the kitchen, Mrs Brock and Polly were arranging salads in large china bowls. There was an air of excitement even in here. Alice was the bringer of bad news. 'Papa is not returning tonight,' she announced. 'Please serve dinner as soon as you can.' Then, before she could find herself bursting into tears of frustration and hurt in front of Mrs Brock, she fled to the safety of her bedroom and sank down on to the bed.

Now her future was in doubt. What of the Manchester Theatre company? She had only a few days in which to accept. They had told her to reply within a week and the date on the letter was yesterday's. She had meant to speak to Papa tonight after supper. She wanted him to release her from her duties to the family. She'd expected him to shoulder her burden and give her his blessing.

Again she felt tears scorching behind her eyes. Then she reminded herself how selfish and wicked it was to think only of oneself when Aunt Harriet had been dealt such a dreadful blow. She went in search of Aunt Harriet and found her, seated in one of the tall velvet-backed armchairs in the drawing room. 'Are you all right, Aunt Harriet?' she asked.

'Yes, child.' Aunt Harriet turned to look at her and Alice saw that colour had returned to her face.

'I'm terribly disappointed,' Alice told her. 'I was so sure Papa would be with us tonight.'

'You will have to start preparing for your stay at Hetherington,' Aunt Harriet said quietly. 'After supper we'll look through your wardrobe. George has got evening clothes.'

Alice knew then that she would have to go. She also knew that she would hate the ball. All the other guests would know what they were about and she and George would look foolish and gauche. They would probably be the youngest ones there. They had never been anywhere – never mixed socially with other army people. They would be afraid of letting Papa down. There might be lords and ladies there – snobbish women like Lady Cranston-Bartlett who looked down their noses.

Would they be obliged to sit at a banqueting table and eat their way through the ten or twelve courses she had heard were usual? How would they know which knives and forks to use if there was a great array of cutlery at every place? Would the yellow silk dress be good enough? 'What will a grand ball be like?' she said. 'It's you who should be going, Aunt Harriet. George and I have never been anywhere important. I won't be expected to curtsey, will I?'

Aunt Harriet indicated with a sharp movement of her hands that Alice was to be seated. Alice felt the quick stirrings of consternation and to her own annoyance found that it was tinged with a growing feeling of excitement. She had never been to a ball; only to social evenings at church. 'You'll have to tell me what to do,' she said. 'What shall I wear? Is the yellow silk all right?'

Aunt Harriet smiled. 'It's very flattering, Alice. And there's a fine scarlet jacket in Boothroyd's on Lord Street. I intended to buy it for you for your birthday.'

Alice said, 'But my birthday's not until October . . . '

'And I saw a scarlet Robin Hood hat in Mrs Moly-neaux's' Aunt Harriet said. 'I'll buy them in advance of your birthday. You can wear them with your best grey skirt.'

'Oh! Aunt Harriet, thank you.' Alice went to take her aunt's hands in her own but her aunt was on her feet, squaring her shoulders as if for battle. 'I'll tell you all you need to know about the etiquette, Alice,' she said as she went towards the door. 'You already have charming manners. I am sure that, being so like Clara, you will manage very well without grovelling at anyone's feet.'

By the time they were all seated at the supper table, the mood of uncertainty had lifted a little. Alice had managed to persuade herself, encouraged by Aunt Harriet, that of course Papa would have to attend the celebrations. He would have no choice. And, as for their own invitations, hers and George's, well, Papa could not have invited the whole family. Someone had to be at home with baby Arthur.

It was whilst they were eating the dessert of rice moulds with stewed rhubarb – Mrs Brock must have put away into tins the meringues she had made for Papa – that the sound of the front door knocker came echoing down the hall and they all stopped speaking to listen as Polly Gosling went in answer.

At last they heard the sound of a man's feet. He was being shown to the drawing room. Polly returned to the dining room.

'Well, Gosling?' Aunt Harriet said.

'It's that young man, ma'am. Him as came yesterday. An' I can't mekk out a word he says,' Polly announced before, red with suppressed laughter, she added, 'I can mekk out as he wants to speak to Meez Aleez.'

'Very well.'

Aunt Harriet turned to Alice when Polly had gone. 'Do you know who it might be, Alice?' she asked.

Alice, all eyes upon her, leaped to her feet. There was

only one person in the world who had ever addressed her as Meez Aleez.

'Karl Reinhardt,' she said. 'I'll go and speak to him.'

She almost ran from the room, then, exercising great self-control, slowed down her movements as she turned the handle of the drawing-room door to find Karl Reinhardt standing, stiff, formal and very handsome in a dark English-style suit with a waistcoat and white wing-collared shirt.

'You wanted to see me?' she asked.

His face with its expression of severity and aloofness softened a little when he looked at her. Once again he gave her the strained smile he had shown in the railway carriage. 'I want to see you. Yes,' he said.

'What for?' She found she could not be annoyed with him although she was going to tick him off for presuming to visit her without even asking her permission. He really was a strange and intense young man. But she seemed to feel a lifting of her spirits, almost a sensation of relief, whenever she was near him. He had come to her aid twice in as many days. It was uncanny that he'd been on hand on both occasions. However, that did not give him the right to come to the house and knock at the door.

'Sit down,' she said as she first closed the door then came to sit opposite to him.

He had the same proud look that she had first noticed when they met in the railway carriage. It was something to do with his being foreign of course, the way he would hold her gaze a little longer than was polite.

'Why are you here?' she asked. 'You should not come uninvited to a house.'

He was not in the least put out by her sharp words. He had not even blushed for shame. Rather he was holding himself cool and aloof, looking down his long nose at her as with head held well back he said, 'You have met my mother and my father. I want you shall marry me.'

Had he not looked so deadly serious Alice might have wanted to laugh. But Karl was not making an ass of himself. He was bold and there was challenge in his eyes. She would have to humour him.

'Karl,' she said. 'You can't go around proposing to girls you have only just met.'

'I do not. I do not propose marriage to other girls.'

She said with studied patience, 'We do not even know one another.'

'I take chance. With you,' he answered.

Alice leaned forward a little and looked into his eyes; they were the bluest, keenest eyes she had ever seen. 'It is not done. Not in England, Karl. Not with girls of good family. Like your sisters are.' She sat back, and to lighten the tension between them, she smiled. 'There.'

Still in the arrogant, demanding tone of voice he asked, 'Is your father home from war? I ask him for hand in marriage.'

'Papa is not home from the war.'

Karl was looking at her all this time, with proud eyes that were full of determination. She had to make him see that it was ridiculous that he should presume to approach Papa with a proposal of marriage to her.

She stood up and put out her hand so that he'd know she was dismissing him. 'My Papa will be here soon,' she said. 'I will ask him to see you since you have been so kind to me. But you will be turned away very sharply if there is any more talk of marriage.'

He stood up, looking not crestfallen but rather as if it were only a small setback he had been asked to bear. 'You like me?' he asked.

At this she could not stop the smile. She did like him. She had been drawn to him when first she had seen him. She was grateful to him for acting as her protector – and the same feeling was coming to her as she looked at his clear-cut features and into his bright, blue eyes.

But he must understand that she would not allow this kind of pursuit. Besides, she had no intention of allowing

189

any young man to contemplate marriage to her. 'I like you, Karl,' she said. 'But I do not intend to marry.'

'I can meet your Papa?'

'Yes. When he comes back.'

'I shall not come until one week. First I have to go to see family. We shall all go to – to *Schloss*. We all shall stay in *Schloss*.' He looked cross with himself as he added, 'I do not know these words.'

'I'll show you to the door, Karl.' Alice again offered her hand. 'And invite you to come again in a week's time.'

He stood, snapped his heels together, bowed and then, smiling, went towards the door. 'Good night.'

At six o'clock when he entered the Green Saloon where the reception was being held, Charles saw that about fifty people were there already. More were arriving and being announced as he went forward. Sir Jack Blackshaw, who seemed to have a swelling on his face that Charles had not spotted on arrival, welcomed him and made some introductions before Frederick took over. In their presence Charles could sense the enmity between father and son. It was almost tangible, the barely-concealed anger in Frederick until he moved away from his father's side.

Charles found himself shaking a hand, saying a few words here and there to more people than he was ever likely to remember.

At the moment of introduction to Frederick's cousin, Charles saw that Therese was even more beautiful than her photograph had suggested. He had a quick impression of an enchanting girl in a dress of turquoise satin and then she had spoken and the low husky voice and the eyes of bluish-green had captivated him for the few moments before they were interrupted by James and two more unattached young officers.

'If I were Frederick,' he thought as he moved on, 'I should waste no time at all in claiming her. She is a girl who will entice every red-blooded man she ever meets.'

He left their group and went to a quieter corner of the room to stand and observe. Drinks were being handed round by uniformed servants. No sooner was a glass emptied than it was refilled and the sounds, the talk, the laughter, the sweet lightness of the women's voices were a delight after the years of violence the regiment had lived through.

He found himself standing by one of the marble pillars supporting the balcony which ran around the large room. In front of him a long window gave a view of the wide sweep of carriage-drive and forecourt and he went forward to stand at the window and watch the people who were still arriving for the reception and dinner. Carriages halted, guests were being ushered inside by footmen and announced by the butler at the door of the saloon. A Daimler drew up as he watched and the occupants, a middle-aged couple and their son and daughter, alighted at the door.

He left the window and returned his attention to the saloon. Indoors it was a splendid house. Portraits, of ancestors he supposed, were hung here. On the panels between finely wrought silver sconces were oil paintings of the women of the family and he went slowly from one to the other admiring their remote ancient beauty.

At the far side of the saloon a small orchestra was playing a selection from *The Mikado* and all at once Charles found that his mood had changed to one of quick anxiety. Suddenly he found himself longing, with a feeling that had left him at Clara's death, for a woman's love.

'Good Lord,' he thought to himself. 'What is the matter with me? My moods are swinging from elation to despair in a moment.'

A wave of intense regret came over him. Why had he come here to Hetherington where he must witness other, younger men's happiness in sweet new romances. He could have stayed in the barracks. Or he could have gone straight to Southport and been reunited with the children

– spent at least a couple of hours with them before returning. He left his scrutiny of the portraits and went in search of diverting company.

To his great delight he found it a few moments later when Frederick introduced him to one of the most talented men in the world of textile engineering, the man he had seen arriving in the Daimler, an Austrian of his own age, Johann Reinhardt and his charming wife, Ekaterina.

Therese, seated on one of the gilt sofas under a large Reynolds of Lady Margaret, could not remember ever having been as happy. The orchestra was halfway through 'Tit Willow', one of her favourite songs from the operetta and she was surrounded by young officers.

The air was heady with scents of the hundreds of flowers; orange blossom, gardenia and freesia from the glasshouses and gardens. Her head too was spinning with excitement. She so loved the company of men.

'It was a delight, seeing you at last,' James Horden, one of these officers said as he seated himself beside the sofa.

'And it is no longer?' Therese teased.

'Oh! No – I did not mean to say . . .' James, face reddening above the scarlet dress jacket, looked embarrassed.

Therese touched his arm lightly with a gloved hand. Her emerald and diamond bracelet sparkled prettily against the white lace.

'Then you must tell me exactly what you mean to say,' Therese chided. But she knew she spoke with such vivacious charm that James would think himself favoured.

'Your picture – your photograph went with us throughout the campaigns,' James said earnestly.

'Then I too have been to South Africa?' Therese laughed the soft, low gurgling laugh that always seemed to attract attention.

'Yes. Latterly we – er – Miss Blackshaw? It is Miss Blackshaw?' James asked.

'Yes. Miss,' Therese said firmly. 'I was widowed. I have reverted to my maiden name. Miss Blackshaw.'

'Latterly,' James went on, 'your portrait hung in the field hospital.'

'Good Heavens!' She laughed again. 'On whose prescription did I hang there?'

'Captain Davenport's.'

'The Captain Davenport I have just met?'

'Indeed, Miss Blackshaw.' James looked pleased with himself, as if he were delighted to have amused her.

'Then I must ask him if I effected any cures,' Therese said.

James laughed at this. 'Captain Davenport said that the sight of a pretty young woman would do more for a man's recovery than all the medication he could prescribe.'

'So,' she laughed again. 'I have not only been to South Africa but I have been a ministering angel?'

Therese looked beyond James to where Freddie stood, introducing Captain Davenport to Johann Reinhardt and the *Gnadige Frau*. Captain Davenport was an interesting man. She had placed him at her left at dinner she remembered. Now that she knew all about his field-hospital treatments she would tease him a little.

'Will there be many at the ball on Friday?' Another officer was speaking to her.

'There will be more than a hundred guests,' she answered. 'A lot of them are here today. As many again are coming on Friday.' She smiled sweetly at James again. 'I believe Captain Davenport's son and daughter are coming.'

Freddie was coming towards them. Poor Freddie seemed to be the only person who was not enjoying the reception. His face wore the expression she knew so well – controlled anger, which she knew would be the result of seeing his mother so very ill. She would go to him.

'Excuse me,' she said to the men as she stood. James leaped to his feet as she excused herself. 'I believe dinner is soon to be served,' she explained as she left them and crossed the floor towards Freddie.

Freddie's expression did not soften as it normally did in her presence. 'Stay by my side, Therese,' he said in a low voice. 'We're seated together, aren't we?'

'Yes. We are at the foot of the table. Your father, Mary and Maggie are at the head.'

Freddie had gripped her arm above the elbow where the gloves ended. He did not know his strength. 'Darling?' Therese said. 'Please! Loosen your grip.'

Freddie let her elbow go but held on to her upper arm as he bent down to say in a low voice that grated with anger, 'I know, Therese. I know who fathered your son.'

She felt faint. She must not let anything show in her face. 'Try not to think about it,' she whispered, all the time smiling and nodding at the people who were looking their way. 'There's nothing you can do.'

Freddie turned a look of fury upon her. Thankfully, his voice when he spoke was not much more than a harsh whisper. 'There's everything I can do. And I mean to.'

Therese looked up at him with eyes a blazing show of confidence. 'We have to lead the guests in to dine, Frederick,' she said. 'Please? Are you ready?'

Freddie drew in his breath sharply and composed his features into a mask of neutrality which she knew concealed a simmering anger. He held out his arm to her as Leigh announced that the supper was ready to serve.

Once they were seated, she slipped her hand under the table and held on to Freddie's for a few seconds. He squeezed hers in return and gave a strained smile. Therese bowed her head, still holding Freddie's hand, as grace was said.

There were two tables which seen from above would make the shape of the letter 'T'. She and Freddie were seated at the end of the stalk. Sir Jack Blackshaw, flanked by Mary and Maggie, was in the centre of the top table.

The long tables were a picture; silver and crystal glittered under the chandeliers. Candelabra, placed every three places along the damask cloths, were surrounded at their bases with wreaths of mock-orange. Silver epergnes trailed ivy. At every place was a menu card in a silver holder. She had written them herself.

She turned to speak to Captain Davenport as artichoke soup, the first of the seven courses, was being served.

'I understand that I was prescribed as a comfort to the troops, Captain,' she said.

His blue eyes which she saw were full of humour, crinkled slightly at the corners with great charm as he answered, 'How much more effective the genuine medicine might have been, Miss Blackshaw.'

He had the most marvellous voice, deep and musical. She wanted to keep him talking but knew it would be a breach of good manners were she to ignore Freddie or keep Captain Davenport from conversation with Ekaterina Reinhardt who sat on his left.

She lowered the heavy lids slightly. 'You are flirting with me, Captain,' she teased.

He said nothing for a few moments as she and then he were served with their soup but she had seen that her remark had amused him. He had chuckled as soon as she had spoken.

She glanced sideways at him as they were served. He had clear-cut features which seemed to Therese the most interesting she had ever seen. Then, as the footman moved to his left, his magnetic eyes met and held hers as in his exciting voice he rebuked her.

'On the contrary, Miss Blackshaw. It is you who is flirting with me.'

He was smiling as he said this and he added, probably in response to the delight in her own face, 'Please allow me to return the compliment.'

He lifted his wine, looked her full in the face as if she were the only woman in the world and there were no-one else to see and hear them, raised the glass to his lips and said in an undertone, 'To the most beautiful woman in the room.'

Therese found herself going pink, but it was the flush of pleasure, not embarrassment. She looked about her and saw that Captain Davenport's compliment had gone unnoticed. Freddie was talking to young Irmgard Reinhardt and the captain himself had turned his attention to the *Gnadige Frau*. Only when she looked away from the immediate group did she find herself looking into the livid brown eyes of her uncle who had obviously missed nothing.

She did not care tuppence for her uncle and his fury. All at once she felt as if the room were filled with half-people; people with only half the wit, intelligence and beauty of herself and the man at her side. It was a wonderful feeling of freedom that she felt in the presence of the older man. She would console Freddie later, when the supper was over and the evening guests had departed. For this evening she would enjoy the delights of light flirtation and good company.

After the last guest had gone and she and Freddie had shaken the last hands and waved the last wave into the soft silvery light of a Cheshire night, Therese took Freddie by the arm.

'Let us walk, Freddie,' she said. 'I want to stay out here, do you?'

'Are you warm enough?' Freddie placed a hand on her bare neck. 'Shall I get something for you?'

'All right. A shawl. Anything.' She smiled up at him. 'Don't be long.'

He left her and went indoors again as she began to walk across the fine gravel of the forecourt at this, the west entrance, until Freddie re-appeared carrying a fringed woollen shawl. 'Will this be all right?' he asked.

It was hideous, an old woman's shawl. Heaven knew where he had found it but she smiled and allowed him to place it across her shoulders. 'It was a marvellous reception and supper party,' she said as together they went, dress trailing, feet crunching on the gravel around the west side of the Hall. 'Did you think so?'

'I don't know how you can enjoy yourself,' he answered in the low angry voice he had used before supper. 'After all that has happened.'

'Freddie darling! Please don't.' He had gone a few paces ahead and she had to hurry to catch up with him. When she reached his side she took hold of his arm and held it tightly. 'I feel so ashamed, Freddie,' she said in a tight little whisper.

He whirled round, his brown eyes blazing with fury. 'I don't blame you, you fool,' he said. 'You were an innocent child.'

They had reached the front of Hetherington where the two towers and the bedrooms, with Sir Jack Blackshaw's study below, were situated. The Green Saloon and the billiards and cards rooms faced west. There was no need to lower their voices here. The study was unoccupied. They went to stand by the stone sundial which was set in the centre of one of the lawn circles under the west tower.

'I ought to have known better,' Therese said, taking his hand again and trying to calm him. 'Don't dwell on it, darling. It's all being taken care of.'

Freddie spoke harshly. 'You are not going to live with him, Therese. I'll kill him before I'd see you—'

'What?' She snatched her hand away from Freddie's. It was she who spoke angrily. 'What are you talking about?'

'My father says you and he are going to live as man and wife. As soon as Mother dies.'

'My God! How can he think that? He knows I hate him.' How could Freddie have thought she would ever contemplate any kind of arrangement with his father? Her uncle would have said that to taunt Freddie. Sir Jack Blackshaw could not possibly entertain any hope of her.

She said, 'How could you think that?'

'He said so.'

'And you believed him?'

Freddie pulled her roughly towards himself. 'I can look after you,' he said. 'I'll make it up to you.'

'Freddie!' She pushed him back until he was at arms' length. 'Listen to me. I confronted your father. I insisted that he provide for Peter and me. There is nothing you can do. I'm content now.'

'You can't be.'

'I have got the deeds of a house. In Macclesfield. There is property in the town which has been put in my name. I'll have the rents to live on and he . . .' She hesitated and looked up again into Freddie's face to see his reaction. It was impossible to read his expression in this half-light. 'Your father is going to settle an annuity on us of £2,000 a year.'

'He'll not get away with this.'

Freddie was almost at the point of explosion, she could tell. Therese changed her own tone and spoke in a sharper voice than she had been using.

'He must,' she said quickly. 'Don't you see? I cannot have any scandal. I cannot allow gossip and lies to follow us. I'm going to make a new life for myself and Peter.'

'Therese! Therese!' Freddie's voice was raised again. 'The property was yours. It was yours after your parents died. The income from that property was what they lived on—'

'Stop!' she came back at him angrily. 'I have to accept it. And I don't want you to talk about it. Not to anyone! Not ever!'

'When I take over—' Freddie began.

Therese had to make him understand. 'Stop it! When you take over I'll be gone. Tomorrow I'm going to Macclesfield. To look at the houses.'

She shivered, with agitation not cold. She pulled the shawl more closely around herself, holding it at her throat with her left hand whilst she put her right hand on to Freddie's arm.

Freddie wrapped his arms around her shoulders, placed his dark head against hers, pulled her close to himself and said in a voice that was harsh with violence, 'If he stays here any longer I'm going to kill him.'

'You are not going to do anything – anything to him, my darling,' she ended softly. 'He is your father. So please. Please don't. For your sake – and for mine and Peter's.'

Charles had decided not to play billiards with the men after the supper guests had left. He was not in the mood either for a game of bridge or poker as some of the younger ones were. Since he had left the supper table, since that most delightful of women had left his side, he had felt bereft. She had a light, deliciously sharp wit, a husky voice that made one afraid to miss a word or an inflection of its spell-binding quality and, to his surprise and delight, was an expert on natural medicines and herbal treatments.

He had asked her to show him around her workplace, which she had modestly referred to as her kitchen, refusing, she said, to give it so grand a name as a laboratory. She had smiled at his request but had not invited him to call on her at the Dower House. Once she left, his light-hearted mood had gone and he found he was tired and unaccountably sad. He went straight to his room in the west tower without bidding 'good night' to the rest of the company.

It was as he was drawing the curtains that he saw her again. Therese and Frederick were standing beside a stone sundial. She looked small and vulnerable, wrapped in a shawl that reached to the ground. The night was not very dark and as he watched her he felt within himself an agonizing wave of desire for her; desire such as he had not felt for any woman since his wife had died.

Then Frederick took her in his arms and he could bear to watch no more. He turned from the window and went to lie on the bed.

He would leave Hetherington after the parade on Sunday. He wished with all his heart that he had not come to this place; that he had not met her – for he was being drawn, as he had been with Clara, into a headlong rush of passionate love such as he had never expected to know again; a love which he had always thought belonged to youth alone.

This time he could not hope, much less demand, that the girl he loved would ever be his. He made a supreme effort and at last succeeded in forcing his thoughts from desire for another man's girl to his need for sleep and his longing to see his children again.

# *Chapter Twelve*

Thursday was hot and the town noisy and gay, with soldiers everywhere. Aunt Harriet had asked them not to go near the Promenade and the funfair for fear of being accosted so, when evening came, Alice and George walked down to the tree-shaded municipal gardens of Lord Street to listen to the band of the Volunteer Artillery. Tomorrow they were going to Hetherington.

They bought tickets and followed the crowd into the enclosure. They were early, right at the front of the queue, and when the gates opened they found seats directly in front of the raised octagonal bandstand.

Alice leaned back against the painted slats of a folding metal seat, glad of the cool evening air playing about her shoulders and feet. She had hardly had a minute to think about the Manchester Repertory Company all day, for the morning had been taken up with shopping for her new clothes.

Aunt Harriet had been pale but very excitable and Alice had watched her carefully, afraid that she might have another attack of angina. Aunt Harriet had sworn her to secrecy about the doctor's diagnosis, saying the doctor was a fool and that she had never had a thing wrong with her heart. The other day, she said, she'd had an attack of indigestion.

Alice knew that the doctor was right. Two and a half years of looking after five children had been too much for her aunt. In the beginning, when they all thought Papa would be gone for only a few months, it had been an adventure. The adventurous months must have become oppressive years to her aunt and as they, the children, had flourished so her aunt had become fatigued.

With the optimism of youth Alice believed that when her aunt married Papa her life would improve. She opened her eyes. Soon the daylight would be gone. The sky to westward was already streaked purple and gold, orange and pink as the sun went down into the sea. Above their heads the night sky was dark blue with bright little points of starry light beginning to appear.

'Chester is the finest example of a medieval city in the whole country,' George started to say. 'If we set off early, tomorrow, we can—'

Tomorrow – tomorrow. She'd tell Papa about the stage career tomorrow. She'd written out her acceptance. She could post it in Chester tomorrow.

'Can you smell the flowers?' Alice said. She could imagine she was in a garden. When she closed her eyes she could ignore the noise; the soldiers and girls' laughter, the chatter of the men and women, the swishing skirts and footfalls as other spectators passed in front of them to their places. Geraniums and roses were in full bloom in the flower borders. Their perfume seemed all the stronger when the sun was not on them. 'I love to be out here at night under the trees.'

She spoke fast for there were times when, instead of the feeling of release that came to her away from the house and her responsibilities, she felt she had experienced a premonition. She shivered. Tonight she had the irrational, silly idea that she would never sit here again.

The municipal gardens in the evening was the place where all the young and fashionable people of the town congregated. It was here that young men strolled to catch the eyes of the girls who paraded in their fine clothes. To the left of Alice three terra cotta fountains played, splashing cascades of water into the ornamental pool.

The seats were all taken and people were standing,

looking down on the gardens from the steps of the pillared and porticoed Cambridge Hall. The feeling of unease passed and Alice turned to George. 'What was it you said about tomorrow?'

George repeated it.

'All right. We'll set off first thing.' She raised her eyebrows anxiously as she added, 'I'll be glad when it's all over.' She adjusted her straw hat and smoothed down the muslin dress. 'I'm afraid we'll make fools of ourselves.'

'You'll have to act,' George answered. 'It'll be easy. You can act hoity-toity.'

She wanted to smile at the look on George's face but somehow the prospect of tomorrow did not seem funny. 'Have you heard all we have to do?'

'All what?'

She answered with an edge of worry in her voice. 'We have to remember when to take our hats off and all that . . . keep our hats on at afternoon tea if we're invited out and all that . . . ?'

George laughed. 'Do I have to keep my bowler on?'

'No, you idiot!' said Alice as she too began to smile at the thought.

The musicians were tuning up. It always gave her a thrill hearing the orchestra in a theatre. It was the same here as the cornets' silvery arpeggios slid up and down the scale. 'Are you ready? Have you packed?' she asked.

George nodded. 'Yes. I won't be taking a lot.'

'I will. Aunt Harriet insists. I've to take just about everything. "Just in case", she says.'

George gave her one of his comical looks. He could lift one eyebrow and wag his ears. She didn't want to start to laugh so she closed her eyes and left George to his sizing-up of all the pretty girls who were sitting near them. She thought for a few minutes about last night when Aunt Harriet had spoken for an hour and a half, telling her everything she might want to know about how to behave at Hetherington.

At the sound of clapping, Alice turned her attention back to the bandstand. The conductor was going up the steps. She whispered across the little space between George's seat and hers. 'Did you know that Polly Gosling's going with us?'

'Polly?' George asked. 'Won't she be needed at home?'

'I'm to have—' Alice could not keep the ridiculous smile off her face at the thought of it. 'I'm to have – Polly has to pretend to be – a lady's maid!'

'I'll bet Polly's looking forward to that.'

Alice gave a sigh. Polly had asked her how she should conduct herself. 'She is. She can't stop going on about it. She said to me, "Eeh! I've always wanted to be a lady's maid and see how the toffs live." '

The band was starting to play 'Dolly Grey'.

'Sh. Sh!' George whispered. 'The concert's started.' He gave her one of his cheerful grins before leaning over to her and adding quietly, 'Polly's too pretty to be in service much longer. She'll be wedded and bedded before she's much older.'

'Will she?' Alice raised her eyebrows and looked askance at George. He must be joking. His expression was one of intense concentration on the music.

For the journey to Hetherington Alice wore the scarlet jacket and hat. The jacket had a tight waistline, narrow sleeves, wide shoulders and it fitted her exactly. Beneath it a white silk blouse with lacy jabot was worn tucked into a pale grey skirt. The red Robin Hood hat was pinned over the piled-up hair Polly had arranged for her. Aunt Harriet said that she looked very ladylike.

The day had already been too busy for them to follow George's suggestion and start early. It had been ten o'clock in the morning before they boarded the train for Manchester where they made a connection for Knutsford. The Roman city of Chester would not be on their itinerary today.

After they had changed trains and were steaming away from Manchester into Cheshire, Alice went nervously over everything again. She was not afraid of putting a foot wrong, for Aunt Harriet's talk had been quite explicit. But she felt she could no more give herself airs than she could bow to anyone. Aunt Harriet's talk had simply confirmed her belief in the unpleasantness of snobbery and pretence. But she didn't want to let Papa down by doing anything wrong.

She looked out of the window at the flat Cheshire countryside, yet saw nothing. Papa's face was as clear in her mind as if he had only left them yesterday. She could hardly believe that she'd not seen him for all this time and yet soon they would all be together again. And she was acutely conscious of the fact that Papa would see a change in them. She and George were grown up and Papa would expect them to behave as adults.

She would have to convince Papa that she was an adult too, for she needed his permission to accept the place at the Manchester Repertory Company. She was only seventeen. The law of the land stated that a girl could not make her own decisions until she was twenty-one. Someone had told her that it was not true but Aunt Harriet said it was the case. But Aunt Harriet did not want her to go on the stage – and had assured her that Papa would not allow it either.

She glanced at George across the compartment, glad he was with them. Nothing upset him. He was never in the least put out and when he wasn't airing his knowledge he had them all in fits of laughter. He looked more and more like Papa every day. He was looking out of the window, smiling, nudging Polly and pointing out things of interest in the lush green country they were steaming through.

'Nearly there, Polly,' George was saying to the happily smiling little housemaid. 'What do you know about Knutsford?'

'Wasn't it where Mrs Cranford lived?' Polly ventured.

'Or were it Mrs Gaskell? I prefer Marie Corelli myself. Have you read *The Sorrows of Satan*?'

Alice smiled at Polly's serious face. Polly, so keen to 'better herself' as she called it, had taken to walking down the street in what she called a refined manner, keeping her eyes on the pavement. She borrowed books from Southport's Atkinson library. Polly read everything she could lay hands on; fairy stories and encyclopedias, Latin grammars and *Home Chat*. She scuttled up to her attic room with a book tucked under her apron every night.

'Knutsford is said to derive from Knut's Ford,' George was saying. 'King Canute is supposed to have crossed a stream here after a battle.'

Alice watched Polly go pinker by the minute, so impressed was she with George's rather childish habit of telling everyone all he knew about anything.

Polly sighed. 'Well, I never.'

George got to his feet a few minutes later. 'We're here,' he said. The train slowed, pulled in at the station and George leaped out ahead of them. 'I'll look for a porter,' he called over his shoulder. 'I'll ask him to get our baggage off the train.'

Alice stepped down on to the sunny platform and waited while people pushed ahead of them until George came to their side and they all went towards the gate, George in front, looking over the heads of the other passengers to see who was there to meet them.

'There's Papa,' he said at last, excitement making his voice hoarse. 'Over by the gate.'

Alice saw him at the same moment. He looked so tall, so dignified and handsome in his tweed suit as, with head held high, he searched the faces of the crowd for them. She felt her heart stand still as it always used to do when Papa looked at her.

They were almost upon him before he saw them and, as he recognized her, Alice saw the fleeting look of shock in Papa's eyes as she went to him. Then the lovely smile and the beautiful voice seemed to enfold her as he took her hands in his and kissed her warmly and soundly on each cheek and held her close.

'Oh, Alice, my sweet girl. How like your mother you are. I have missed you all so much.' He turned to George, placed an arm around his shoulder and squeezed his hand. 'And you George. You are as tall as I am. I had not expected that.'

Polly, standing behind them, was introduced and then Papa led them out on to the street to where the green lacquered carriage with its liveried coachman waited to drive them to Hetherington.

Less than an hour later, while Polly was calmly and efficiently putting away her clothes in the most luxurious bedroom Alice had ever seen, Alice found herself being escorted around the grounds of Hetherington by Papa.

It was odd, being escorted by Papa. It had never happened before. Papa had gone away leaving a child behind and had returned to find a young woman. It must seem even more strange to him. She wondered if he saw her as a young woman with her own life ahead of her or did he think she was still 'Papa's right-hand girl' and 'the responsible child'?

But she was so enjoying this walking about the parterre on the arm of her handsome father. She stopped to admire the flower beds and looked up towards the house. 'I never knew such places existed,' she said. 'What a house. It's a sort of old brick palace, isn't it?'

'It's not old,' Papa answered. 'It was built in an old, Jacobean and Gothic-revival style.'

'I don't like the outside. To me it looks like an angry old man.' She turned her back on the house and felt its presence looming behind her. Then she smiled at Papa. 'But my room, Papa! It's full of – things. I've never seen anything like the inside of the house.'

Papa was smiling at her and, pleased that she had amused him, she continued, chattering blithely about this and that, waiting for her moment – the moment when she'd tell him about the stage.

Then she realized that Papa had gone quiet. She stopped walking and looked at him. 'Is anything the matter?' she asked.

He smiled again, the warm understanding smile she had never forgotten. 'Walk with me to the rose garden,' he said. 'Hetherington Hall may be ugly but the gardens are marvellous.'

They walked, Alice proud to be seen by the other guests as she took Papa's arm along the brick walkways and raked gravel paths of the parterre until they came to the sunken rose garden where the air was still and sweet with the scent of the hundreds of roses. Roses, massed in beds of reds and pinks, yellows and white, were separated by low granite walls and green gravel paths. On each of the side walks in the geometric garden were pretty pergolas and rustic seats.

'Sit here,' Papa said when they reached the seat at the far side of the garden. 'I want to talk to you.'

They sat on a rustic seat under the arched lattice of the pergola, facing the rose beds. There was nobody else about in the rose garden. Papa took her hand in his and held it there for a moment before he spoke.

'Alice,' he said. 'I have been giving a lot of thought to the future.'

'And I, Papa,' she replied. This was her moment to speak. She must talk about the Manchester Repertory Company. She had been rehearsing the very words she would use and suddenly she was filled with a quick nervousness – a feeling that she had to tell him, this minute.

But Papa had lifted a hand to silence her and she looked into his serious face. His blue eyes had a kind of sadness in them that made her want to put her arms around him to give comfort. But Papa would never allow demonstrations of affection in public and his voice when he spoke was serious, not sad. He spoke as seriously as he had done before he went to war.

'I am going to ask you once again to put the family before everything else, Alice,' he said quietly.

All at once the day that was warm and scented, chilled and clouded as Papa spoke. A cold shiver went through her. 'What do you mean?' Her voice had dropped to a mere whisper. 'How can I do more?'

'I am not going back with you.'

His voice seemed to come to her from a distance. And as she looked into his eyes – not sad or crinkled with amusement but full of serious intent – Alice knew that Papa was going to ask that more of her life be given to them all. She heard the words, through a haze of unreality.

'. . . Look for a practice . . . Not in Southport.'

She must tell him quickly about her first acting part in Manchester. 'I'm—' she began.

Papa was not listening. His orders were being given, 'Your Aunt Harriet has done enough . . . My responsibility to take care of you all . . .' he was saying.

She made to interrupt him again but he lifted his hand to indicate that he had not finished. The sweet sickly smell of roses was making her head light as Papa outlined her future for her, '. . . your duty to Papa and your sister and brothers . . . Until the baby is old enough to go away to school . . .'

Arthur would not be able to go away to school for nearly five years. She would be old. She would be nearly twenty-three in five years' time. 'Papa!' she said. 'I have to tell you—'

Her voice trailed away as she listened to Papa, the officer, giving his orders. 'You and George can return to Southport on Monday. I want you to remain here for the Cathedral service on Sunday but afterwards you will go back and start to assemble our belongings. It will not take Papa more than a few weeks. I shall come for you when I have found us a new home . . .'

At last she managed to speak. 'But Papa! I want to earn my living. You said! You said we were all to prepare—'

Papa's face was stern now that he had come to the end. It was as if he were not prepared to listen to any argument. And Alice knew that he would not. He never had asked what they might want. Papa had always made the decisions. And Papa's decisions, once made, were not to be questioned.

'There is no question of your earning a living, Alice. You will receive an allowance so that you have independent means. You have never let the side down. I have always relied upon you. The family needs you.'

Alice lifted her eyes from the rose bed and turned a white face to Papa. 'Oh, Papa,' she said. 'Is there no other way?'

'There is no other way,' Papa said.

Alice could not bear to let Papa down. Papa had only just returned from fighting a war. If she were to refuse? She screwed up her courage. 'When Arthur goes to school, Papa?'

Papa said, 'Well?'

'I want to be an actress.'

Papa smiled, took her hands in his and began almost absent-mindedly to pat them. He looked at her for a few seconds with the expression she remembered so well, benign and loving. 'You are so like your mother,' he said.

'I have been offered a part. I've been offered a paid job. With the Manchester Repertory Company, Papa.' The words came out in a rush. 'I have to give them my reply—'

The benign look went in a second. 'You will write immediately and tell them you cannot take it. You must be prompt and honourable in these matters, Alice.'

'Perhaps—? If the responsibility were shared between Beatrice and me—?'

'I need both of you,' Papa said firmly. 'A general practitioner ordinarily needs a wife. He needs a wife to love and support him and he needs help. I have no wife.

I have no-one to love and support me. I need you and Beatrice. Until I am established there will be no money for servants.'

Alice, seeing her last chance slip away, said with a boldness she did not know she had, 'If Beatrice and I shared the responsibility I could travel to Manchester every day—'

'No!' Papa was not accustomed to having his orders questioned. 'I will have to buy into a practice. I don't know where I will find a vacancy. You will do as I tell you. You will return to Southport on Monday and prepare for your departure.'

Alice was near to tears as she answered. 'I'm going back tomorrow.'

Papa seemed to be paying attention to her at last. His face looked less stern. His eyebrows lifted as he told her, 'There is to be a medal ceremony and a service of thanksgiving at Chester Cathedral on Sunday. The regiment and the whole county will be there.'

Alice took a deep breath, bit her lip, fought back her tears but insisted. 'I have to take my Sunday School class. I gave my word. I can't not do it.'

There was a pause. For the first time since they had been reunited he was listening to her. After a few moments he smiled and said, 'I am very proud of you, Alice. I will arrange the travelling for you.'

Alice dropped her eyes. 'Shall I be allowed to go on the stage when Arthur goes to school?'

'Of course you will.' She heard Papa sigh with relief then draw in his breath sharply as footsteps were heard, crunching on the gravel in front of them.

Alice looked up at the same moment that Papa got to his feet. Approaching them across the rose garden path was the young officer she had last seen on the day Papa embarked. At his side was the mother of the baby. It was Captain Freddie Blackshaw and, dressed in palest grey silk and pink chiffon, his wife – the girl with the beautiful eyes.

Papa slipped a hand under her elbow. 'My daughter, Alice Davenport. Miss Therese Blackshaw.'

Alice smiled and held out her hand to Therese. Therese hesitated for a moment, then she gave an embarrassed laugh before proffering her own hand. Alice had the awful feeling that she had made a mistake in shaking Therese's hand but by then Papa was introducing the officer to her.

'Major Blackshaw. My daughter, Alice Davenport.'

Alice found herself looking into the most wonderful warm brown eyes she had ever seen. The tall young major with rugged features and silky black moustache took a step towards her and took her hand in his own.

'Delighted to meet you, Miss Davenport,' he said. His voice was as brown and warm as his eyes and when he smiled at her and their eyes met then it seemed to Alice that the sun shone brighter. Something magnetic was passing between them. His teeth were straight and square, white against his sunbrowned face as he smiled, and the feel of his firm hand clasping her own sent a tingling sensation through her body.

She felt again the same wave of longing that had coursed through her when she had first set eyes on him. What was it? What was happening to her? She must try to control herself.

'Thank you,' she said and heard the girl – had Papa said Miss Blackshaw instead of Mrs? – heard the girl smothering a little husky laugh again. Was it impolite to thank someone for a compliment?

'We're on our way to the Dower House for afternoon tea,' the girl was saying. 'Won't you come with us?'

Alice saw Papa grow suddenly cold and somehow scrupulous; there was no other way to describe the way he said, 'I think not, thank you. But I'm sure that Alice will be delighted.'

Major Blackshaw was speaking again in his deep, warm voice. 'I'll be at the Dower House later, Therese. I won't join the ladies for tea. I'll go up to see Mother.' He looked at Papa and said, 'I should like you to look at her, Charles. If you would.'

'I'd be delighted to meet Lady Blackshaw,' Papa answered.

Major Blackshaw had turned to her again. 'I look forward to seeing you at the ball tonight, Alice.' His eyes appeared to light up as he spoke. 'I may call you Alice, may I?'

'Oh. Oh yes!' Alice stammered in reply. 'Please do.'

Then he looked at her in the way that Alice would always remember. It was for only a moment but their eyes met and it was almost as if the rest of the world ceased to exist. Brown eyes, lively and challenging, met the cool grey of her own and deep inside herself something sprang, something exploded, into life.

'Until then, ladies,' Frederick said as he turned and went swiftly away from them.

Therese inclined her head and spoke to Papa. 'Captain Davenport,' she said in a teasing, rather pleading voice, 'won't you change your mind and take tea with us?'

'No thank you. I leave my daughter in your care, Miss Blackshaw. I'm sure Alice will be pleased to join you.'

Then Papa too turned and was gone.

Alice was left facing Major Blackshaw's wife. Therese was looking at her with the long greenish-bluish eyes that seemed to be assessing her. And in those few moments when neither girl spoke Alice knew that in Therese Blackshaw she had made an enemy.

Was she going mad? How could two such opposite emotions spring into life in one person in one minute? Sexual awareness she knew had sprung into being when Major Blackshaw had looked at her.

And naked dislike, jealousy and fear were in every nerve and fibre of the woman who was facing her. Yet she was quite the prettiest woman Alice had ever seen; prettier than she had looked the last time Alice saw her. Today her dark hair was dressed in the full, upswept style that Alice thought of as resembling a fat round pin cushion. Therese did not appear to need the false hair that so many women used to achieve the same full, wide effect. On top of the luxuriant hair she wore a confection of pink chiffon, straw and pink silk carnations.

And the long green eyes with thick black lashes were aloof as they made an appraisal of her. The voice when she spoke had lost the husky inviting quality and now had an icy politeness. 'You have had a pleasant journey, Miss Davenport?' she asked. 'When did you get here?'

'I have been here for an hour – Mrs Blackshaw,' Alice answered.

'Miss.'

'I beg your pardon?' Alice said, flustered in case she had made a second gaffe.

'Miss Blackshaw.' Therese's pretty mouth closed firmly after she had spoken. She brushed an imaginary piece of dust from the grey silk of her dress before shaking her head quickly as she looked again into Alice's face. 'I am a widow, Miss Davenport. My husband died soon after we were married.'

'Oh dear. I am sorry . . .'

'Not at all. I prefer not to talk about it.' She gave Alice a dimpling smile that only accentuated the coldness in her eyes. 'You are coming to the Dower House for afternoon tea?'

'I'd like to. Very much,' Alice said hastily, feeling awkward and gauche again. Had she trodden on the young widow's finer feelings? 'Perhaps I should go back to my room,' she said. 'Should I change for tea?'

Therese's eyes went swiftly over her in a top-to-toe evaluation. 'You look perfectly charming.'

Therese had an offhand, insincere manner. But they had only just met. Perhaps she was mistaken. The unfriendly manner of Miss Blackshaw could be the fashion of the circles she moved in.

Alice made another gauche remark. 'Do I look all right?'

'You'll do nicely,' the husky voice came back. 'I don't expect there will be many people there.'

And Alice knew that she looked all wrong. Her clothes were not made to measure as Therese's were. Her shoes were of poorer, heavy leather instead of the fine kid of Therese's. Even the hat, which had looked so smart in Mrs Molyneux's, was nothing like the hats she had seen here this afternoon.

Then she felt herself to be wicked and ungrateful to poor Aunt Harriet who had wanted her to look 'ladylike' and had made her look a fool in wool and felt and strong leather when all the girls and women she had seen this afternoon were wearing lawn, foulard and georgette.

Alice walked along beside Therese and knew herself to be completely out of her depth. Yet they had only exchanged a few words. Alice had never made an enemy before but the aversion, the animosity, that was coming to her from Therese was almost palpable. It made her wary as she walked and made conversation for the half-mile that seemed to take for ever until they reached the gates of the Dower House.

No sooner had the door been opened to them by a tail-coated butler than Therese, apparently glad to be relieved of her company, left with a quick nod and a few words to the manservant. 'Show Miss Davenport the offices, Hodge.'

Alice followed Hodge, who looked a kindlier man than the terrifying Leigh at Hetherington, down a stone-floored corridor to a little room that had been reserved for the ladies' use. She closed the door, went towards the marble washstand and looked at herself in the gilt-framed looking-glass above it.

Her hat was straight. She fixed the pin more securely. Her hair was in place. Then she looked at her eyes. The wide grey eyes seemed to be so large that they dominated her smooth oval face. The pupils were dilated with nervous excitement. During the last half-hour in the garden she had felt intensely every strong emotion the human heart was capable of feeling – sympathy and a daughter's loyalty to Papa – the anger and hatred from Therese had produced fear in herself – and love. For blind passionate love-at-first-sight she knew had struck her – and it's object was a man who was not hers to love.

She undid the tiny buttons at the wrist band of her lacy gloves, peeled them back and took a handkerchief from the tiny purse that dangled from her wrist.

Rubbing hard with a corner of the handkerchief at her soft full mouth to redden her lips she gave a quick smile into the glass, revealing the little expanse of rosy-red gum and her square white teeth. Her smile made her look friendly and she had always thought a little childish, but she tried to laugh at herself and her reflection. It helped. It helped to dispel the nervous feeling that the thought of meeting Therese again was bringing.

She took a deep breath. She would have to act as if she were older and wiser than her seventeen years.

As if it mattered two hoots whether Therese liked her or not, she tried to tell herself. Just as long as she didn't drop her plate or her cup of tea, nobody would even notice her.

In thinking this Alice was quite wrong. Therese was very interested indeed in the daughter of Captain Davenport.

# Chapter Thirteen

Therese had never seen anyone so statuesque, so much the cool Nordic beauty, as Captain Davenport's daughter. She had also known, at the moment of introduction to Alice Davenport, that Freddie – her own dear, darling Freddie – was captivated.

Before they had met Alice and her father in the rose garden, Freddie had been dark and brooding, threatening revenge upon his father, saying that he would not attend the ball if his father were there. It had taken her an hour to persuade him that it was his duty to attend; to persuade him to come to the ball at least until supper was over.

All the guests would be told, if they did not already know, that Freddie's mother was an invalid. They would not expect to meet her. Therese had told Freddie that he could absent himself with impunity after supper and sit with his mother since that was all he seemed to want to do.

Freddie had the habit of placing his hand round her arm, just above the elbow, whenever they stood together. At the very moment he had set eyes upon Alice Davenport Therese had felt his hand loosen and then, as if gripped by some other force, tighten until she almost jumped.

A knife had gone into her heart. It was the end of everything. The only man who had ever loved her had in her presence fallen headlong under the spell of another. She had never really wanted any other love from Freddie than the brotherly affection and protection he had always shown to her. But she could not bear to see him – her own, dearest and best Freddie – wanting love of any kind from any other woman. She would not be supplanted.

Captain Davenport had reawakened her own fires with no more than a look, a compliment, and an instant recognition of mutual need. She had not seen him since last night's dinner until they met this afternoon but she knew that he had cooled towards her. She had seen Captain Davenport and Alice clasping hands under the pergola, seen the looks of devotion that had passed between father and daughter. His daughter's presence must have been the reason for his frosty greeting.

Alice Davenport already had the love of her father. How many men did she need? And the wretch, not content to have frozen her, Therese, out of her father's affections had conquered Freddie with her blushing, hesitant beauty.

As soon as she handed Alice over to Hodge she went up to her room. There she changed her grey silk for a tea gown of pale pink musette before going down to the conservatory to put Alice Davenport in her place.

The hexagonal dining table had been removed and small tables, cane and basket chairs were set, spaced out between earthware jardinieres of ferns and high wooden plant stands which held trailing purple fuchsias and scarlet geraniums.

There was a hum of conversation punctuated by little bursts of high-pitched laughter and the click of silver on china as Therese entered the conservatory. Mary and Maggie were pouring tea and offering tiny sandwich triangles of cucumber and ham to the several ladies who had already arrived.

None of the men had come and Therese felt peevishly disappointed to see so many unaccompanied ladies, preferring as she did the undercurrents of flirtation that were possible with men. Alice Davenport and a young married woman were standing by the door, exchanging polite nothings as Therese termed the small talk that passed between women.

Therese went immediately to speak to the handsome Ekaterina Reinhardt and her daughter Irmgard who, since it would be impolite for them to converse with one another in their native German tongue, were silent. They sat stiffly side by side; the mother small, erect and proud wearing her thick black hair tightly coiled and pinned about her square head. Irmgard, tall and exuberant, wore hers in the same style, less severely pinned.

The *Gnadige Frau*, the dear madam, as Therese still thought of her, had not become fluent in English despite her years of residence.

'Dear Frau Reinhardt—' Therese came to their table, smiling sweetly, 'Have you met Miss Davenport?'

'*Ja*,' Ekaterina Reinhardt answered, unsmiling.

Therese had not altered her original impression of the wife of Johann Reinhardt. She found her stern and unfriendly, disapproving of any sign of impropriety. The *Gnadige Frau* ruled her household with high autocracy. Her husband was fiery and clever but it was Frau Reinhardt who held the reins. Johann Reinhardt normally did not accept invitations to Hetherington and Frau Reinhardt did not invite anyone to their splendid country house in the lower slopes of the Pennine Hills above Macclesfield.

She kept the sweet smile on her face. 'Then allow me,' she said as she turned to face the girl she now thought of as her foremost rival. 'Alice?'

Alice stopped talking to the young wife and looked in her direction. She had an unnerving expression of determination that made Therese hesitate for a moment before, holding out a lace-mittened hand in invitation she said, 'Do come and speak to Frau Reinhardt.'

Alice came across the tiled floor. Therese made the introductions, 'Frau Reinhardt. May I present Miss Alice Davenport to you?' Then to Alice she said, 'Frau Reinhardt and her daughter Irmgard.'

They were all laughing as if they shared a joke and the silly, vigorous girl was shaking hands again Therese noticed. Why hadn't she been taught to incline her head and smile prettily when presented? Hearty behaviour was not attractive in a lady and hand-shaking at afternoon tea was quite unnecessary. Who did she think she was? A cavalry officer?

Therese did not let her annoyance show. 'Alice is the daughter of Captain Davenport,' she said. 'I hope she didn't crush your hand.' Here she gave a throaty little laugh as if to imply that, of course, she was speaking in jest.

'I know. I know Miss Davenport.' Ekaterina Reinhardt's smile vanished when she looked at Therese. She was a stern and forbidding woman and she turned a glowering look upon her hostess. '*Ja*,' she said.

'Your husband and Captain Davenport have become friends, I hear,' Therese said. 'I was told that Alice's father and Herr Reinhardt were driven to Macclesfield this morning in your horseless carriage.'

Then seeing that the *Gnadige Frau* sat, expressionless, Therese turned to Irmgard. 'Perhaps you can translate?'

'*Mutti*? Mother?' Irmgard Reinhardt said something to her mother who responded in rapid German before she turned with a little smile of apology to Alice. 'My mother does not speak very much English. She asked me to say how glad she is to meet you once again, Miss Davenport. Is your aunt recovered?'

'Yes,' Alice said. 'She is. Thank you.'

Irmgard Reinhardt pulled forward a rattan chair and smiled more broadly. 'Please sit with us.'

Alice sat. 'Call me Alice,' she said.

'And you will use my name? Irmgard.'

'I have asked Frau Reinhardt's son to be your partner at supper tonight, Alice.' Therese was still standing at the table. 'I'm sure you will enjoy his company.'

Alice turned to her. 'Which son, Miss Blackshaw?' she asked. 'I think I have already met one of them.'

Irmgard Reinhardt gave a delighted laugh. 'Karl – my brother Karl and I have been invited to the ball. We are all staying at Hetherington.'

'Then I shall be delighted to be his supper partner,' Alice answered. 'We've met. In Southport. Two or three times.'

'And your brother George is to partner Irmgard,' said Therese. She had hoped to disconcert Alice but the girl was enjoying herself, smiling and chatting with the Reinhardts.

By this time two ladies at the table next to theirs had joined in the conversation and Mary and Maggie, their main duties done, had joined the group.

'Is your mother well?' one of the ladies asked Mary.

Mary said, 'Lady Blackshaw is in fine spirits today. Now that Frederick is home Mother's happiness is complete.'

'The regiment's return must have given happiness to many families,' Alice was saying as if she were trying to make conversation, Therese thought. 'We have all looked forward to Papa's homecoming.'

Therese interrupted her. 'Lady Blackshaw has particular reason to rejoice,' she said. 'My aunt has been an invalid for some years. Freddie is all she lives for.'

Here Maggie's frosty demeanour began to dissolve. 'But Mother is not possessive of him, Therese,' she said, a rare smile crossing her face. 'Nothing would please her more than if Freddie were to marry.'

Therese laughed. 'There is not a girl in the country who could come anywhere near Lady Blackshaw's expectations for Freddie. I shall have to marry him myself.' She knew they were all listening. Alice Davenport's eyes were round, like great big saucers as she continued. 'After all, whoever marries Freddie will be the next Lady Blackshaw.'

'That's enough of that kind of talk, Therese,' Mary said in her gentle way. 'You are Frederick's cousin you know.'

Therese was determined to have her say, even if it did upset Mary and Maggie. They could all pretend she was being flippant and making jokes in bad taste if they wished. She meant it to upset Alice Davenport, not her cousins.

'Oh!' she said with a quick little husky laugh. 'It is commonplace amongst the aristocracy for cousins to marry. It happens all the time.'

Maggie gave her a stern look. 'Enough!' she said. 'That's quite enough. We're not aristocracy.'

With a sigh of pleasure Therese saw the look of distaste on Alice Davenport's face.

'I was having a little fun, Maggie,' she said with an air of pained apology. 'And we've had precious little of that these last few years.'

She felt a little wave of inward satisfaction when she saw Alice's face grow paler. She hoped the girl understood her message, her warning. Alice Davenport must never aspire to be the next Lady Blackshaw. The fact that she had taken Freddie's fancy did not mean a thing.

Maggie clearly wanted to make the other ladies see that it was simply a family joke to speak in this way about such trifles as marriage proposals. 'I'm sure Mother would think anyone a good catch for Mary and me,' she said and made a few of the ladies giggle.

'I am not so sure,' Mary said. 'There was an occasion some years ago when our medical practitioner . . .' She smiled at the memory '. . . made so bold as to express an interest in me—'

'—And Mother practically had him struck off the register,' Maggie said with an air of finality that raised a gale of laughter.

It seemed that everyone but Alice Davenport saw the funny side of Maggie's little joke. Mary had deliberately not told them all that the man who had 'made so bold' to her had been at least seventy-five years old. It was a joke between the girls to refer so to Mary's only offer of marriage.

Therese saw that Alice was not laughing. She was tapping her toe quickly against the tiled floor.

To Therese's critical eye, Captain Davenport's daughter was awkward and had a total absence of social graces. She had probably never been in so grand a house. She did not even know what to do when introduced, much less make a good impression when presented to her superiors.

One of the Knutsford ladies was asking, 'And you three – the three Misses Blackshaw – have made all the celebration arrangements?'

Mary said, 'We have done most of it. We ordered the menus and the preparations for the ball. Therese ordered the band and has supervised everything.'

'Then you are to be congratulated,' another guest said. 'What a feat of organization.'

'We can't take all the credit,' Maggie protested. 'After all Hetherington has a large staff.'

Even Maggie's strident voice did not daunt Alice, Therese saw. Her blonde head was held high, the determined chin had risen. 'How many?' Alice asked in her clear, unmistakable voice. 'Exactly how many servants do you have working for you?'

There was a shocked little silence whilst Alice, who it appeared did not know that she had been impertinent, waited for one of the Misses Blackshaw to reply.

Therese was the first to speak. 'Heavens!' she cried, waving her little gloved hands about in a gesture of alarm. 'I have never counted them. They cost so little! Half a crown a week buys a housemaid. One simply ensures that there are plenty of them about.'

Alice's expression showed that she had taken Therese's flippant answer literally. Disapproval was written all over her face.

In Therese's opinion Alice was tasting sour grapes. She determined to have a little fun at the younger girl's expense. 'You manage without servants, do you?' she asked.

'Not entirely,' Alice answered. 'We have a maid and a cook. But then we pay them a lot more than half a crown a week. And we all treat them with respect.'

'All? How many of you are there?' Therese asked, to show Alice that she too could be impertinent. 'You manage without servants and yet you are the eldest of a large family aren't you?'

'Oh, yes.' Alice answered her with a smile. 'There's me, George and Beatrice, Leopold and Arthur.'

'How frightfully amusing.' Therese clapped her hands in delight. 'I've never heard of a whole family being named after the Old Queen's children.' She lifted her pretty hands in a gesture of surprise. 'How terribly – er – terribly—' Here she let the smile drop and lowered her deep eyelids. 'Patriotic!' she ended.

'Papa chose them,' Alice said with quiet and innocent dignity. Then, remembering something significant only to herself, the radiant smile that had enchanted Freddie lit up her calm face. 'Mama used to choose really remarkable names. She always used to say that Papa registered our births before she could have her own way.'

Alice looked Therese straight in the face at this point and said, 'Your mother, Miss Blackshaw? Does she live here?'

'My mother is dead. She was the daughter of an Austrian countess,' Therese answered. She found herself feeling obliged to explain, to impress this girl. 'My name is Theresa Alexandra von Heilbronn Blackshaw. You may call me Therese.'

Therese was disconcerted now. The remark that had confounded her was Alice's reference to her mother in the past tense. Was Captain Davenport a widower? She had assumed, Heaven knew why, when she had copied out the guest list given by Freddie, that he was married.

Before she met him she had wondered if Captain Davenport were the sort of man who would invite his children here as a back-door entrée into society. Of course he was not. She had been much too quick in her assumptions.

The blood rushed to her head, making her feel light-headed as it sang around her consciousness. That handsome, cultured, exciting man was not married.

'Your mother—?' she said to Alice. 'She is—?'

'My mother died the year before Papa went to Africa,' Alice replied. 'She was an actress.'

'An actress?' Therese could not keep the shock out of her voice. Her eyebrows had flown up in horror at this revelation. Actresses were not accepted in polite society. 'Your mother was an actress?'

Alice had coloured to the roots of her hair. But it was not shame that made her get to her feet, pick up her bag and prepare to leave. Her cheeks were pink with defensive anger.

'Yes. My mama was an actress,' she flared. 'And before you can say a hateful word about Mama, Therese, I want you to know that she was the most beloved of women. And we and our Papa will never, never recover from the loss of her.'

Therese saw that Alice's eyes were brimming with unshed tears and at last she began to feel ashamed of herself for hurting the girl's feelings. 'I'm sure . . .' she began with a note of apology.

But Alice was smiling a controlled smile of polite good nature towards the Reinhardt women, and holding out her hand in that friendly, schoolgirl manner which no longer seemed so gauche.

'I'll go back to Hetherington Hall,' she was saying, 'and dress for dinner. Good afternoon, ladies.'

She left the Dower House and walked quickly the half-mile to Hetherington where she went immediately up to her room and found Polly in a high state of excitement.

'There's your things,' Polly said. 'On the bed.'

On the four-poster bed were spread out her clothes;

the pale lemon silk ball gown, trimmed with little gold-ribbon bows that followed the swooping lines of the skirt where it was held at the back in a tumbling series of pleats. The gown, which was lined in white silk to make a chemise unnecessary, was hook-fastened down the back. It had tiny off-the-shoulder sleeves which joined the low curving line of the neck and were trimmed with the same ribbon and bows. It was a little too large for her and she had worked for hours on the new trimming at the neckline to make it less revealing. Her starched white petticoat, freshly ironed, was spread about the pillow with her silk stockings and ruched elastic garters beside it.

She would have liked to be left alone, to lie on the bed thinking about the puzzling events of the day but she couldn't ask Polly to go away for an hour and anyway Polly was beaming with importance. Her cheeks were pink and she was almost at bursting-point in her eager-ness to talk.

'In five minutes, after I've rung this 'ere bell,' Polly pointed to the long embroidered silk of the bell-pull, 'a housemaid will fetch the water. Look!'

She almost ran across the carpeted floor to push aside a four-sectioned screen and reveal the hip bath she had set before the fireplace. On a rail in front of the empty grate three soft towels and two small washcloths were laid.

'Oh, Polly!' Alice dropped down on to a chair at the fireside. 'You seem to be enjoying it all.'

'I am.' Polly stood in front of her, head quizzically on one side. 'What's up?'

'I . . . Oh!' All at once Alice felt tears spring hot to her eyes and run down her cheeks. It should have been the best day of her life; Papa was back and she was going to a real ball and all she could think about was her dis-appointment. She had fallen in love. She had made an enemy and she would have to wait for years until she could become an actress. 'Oh, Polly!'

'Don't tekk on.' Polly was on her knees before her, pulling at the ties on her laced shoes, easing her feet out of the pointed leather. 'Blow your nose and shurrup. I want to practise on you.'

Alice had to smile a little at Polly. 'Whatever for?' she asked through her tears. 'Practise what?'

'Lady's maid,' Polly answered. 'I want to be one.' She sat back on her heels and grinned. 'You should see what goes on in a place like this.'

'What?' Alice pressed her lips together to control herself, took a deep breath and sighed. 'Tell me, Polly. Talk and talk. Keep talking. I don't want to think about everything that has gone wrong today.'

Polly began to pull the laces from the leather shoes Alice had worn. 'Well, now. Us "visiting ladies' maids" are treated right well. I was tekken to the steward's room – that's the butler's parlour – and waited on.' She looked up at Alice to see what kind of impression she'd made.

Seeing nothing to make her stop she said, 'Me! Being waited on by the hall boy!' She gave a little frown of concentration as she recited, 'The hall boy valets the butler. His job – the hallboy's job – is to wake the butler, lay out his clothes, brush his shoes, make his tea, fetch his hot shaving water, and look after the "visiting ladies' maids"—'

It sounded to Alice as if the butler were pretending to be as grand as the master of the house. 'And what do the ladies' maids do?' she asked, since she knew this was what Polly wanted to tell her.

Polly rocked back on her heels. 'The ladies' maids do for their mistresses.' She went into a reverie for a second then came to and tapped Alice on the ankle to get her attention.

'There's Maisie. She's Miss Therese's maid and she has a lot to do.' She looked sideways at Alice, perhaps expecting to be silenced. Alice would not show that she was interested. She kept her face a mask of unconcern.

'They say Miss Therese were a proper little devil when

she were little. She used to ride astride a pony, dressed up as a stable-lad,' Polly announced in a rush.

Alice noticed with a little surge of superior feeling, Polly had pronounced the name Miss Treez. She would not correct her though Polly would wish her to.

'The servants told you this, did they?' she said. 'What else do they say about Miss Treez, then?'

'You're not supposed to ask. We're meant to listen and never give our opinions.' Polly smiled here and added, 'That's what yer aunt says an' all.'

As soon as she had spoken Polly got to her feet and went to the door, opened it and closed it again after looking up and down the landing. She came back to the fireside and whispered.

'They say Therese's cousin Frederick – that's Major Blackshaw – is the father of her baby!'

Alice could not speak.

Polly's round face went even pinker as she went on, 'They said he was in India with the army and she was in India with her parents. He gets her in the family way. She comes home and cracks on she was married for a bit, but her husband died.'

'No!' A wave of revulsion swept through Alice at this piece of gossip. 'You shouldn't listen to such lies, Polly,' she said. 'Much less believe them.' But even as she said this Alice asked herself if the servants were speaking the truth. She had seen Therese and the baby at the embarkation parade. Why, otherwise, would Therese have stood there on a freezing morning to wave and cry out words of love to Frederick Blackshaw? 'If it were true, Polly,' she said, 'they'd have married at once.'

'Sir Jack Blackshaw was her guardian. Miss Therese was only eighteen,' Polly answered, looking hurt. 'I'm only telling you what they say.'

'I know you are,' Alice said.

'Young Frederick – that's what the older ones call him – is going to take over the estate now he's back. It will all go to him when his mother dies.' Polly spoke gravely. 'And he's going to marry Miss Therese.'

But if it were true, Alice reasoned, Therese would not have spoken with such carelessness about Freddie's marrying her. She had clearly annoyed Mary and Maggie by her talk. Then she felt an unaccountable, slow sinking at her heart. 'And all this – all this talk goes on in the servants' quarters?'

'The servants' hall,' Polly corrected. 'Maisie told me. Miss Therese's maid. She's from Liverpool like I am. I knew her as soon as I saw her. She's a right one. Her real name's Madeleine – only Miss Therese said it was too posh – to grand for a servant so she made her answer to Maisie.'

Polly took a deep breath and added, 'Maisie hates her.'

'Then why doesn't Maisie leave?' Alice asked. 'Why does she stay? She's not a bond-maid.' It had always seemed amazing that little Polly was able to draw confidences and confessions from people as easily as drawing breath.

'She stays because—' Polly looked serious. 'I can't tell you.'

'Go on!' Alice couldn't stop herself from trying to draw information. She didn't care one whit she assured herself, not one whit did she care about Therese. But it gave her a shameful little thrill knowing that the girl who had tried to embarrass her, who so obviously hated her, was blind to the duplicity of her own maid. 'What is it? Why does she stay?'

'It's Sir Jack Blackshaw. Maisie has fallen in love with him. The old master takes her to his room – and he does, you know – and she has to tell him everything about Miss Therese first because he wants to know what she's up to. Maisie says she's going to make him marry her when his wife dies. Then she'll show 'em a thing or two.'

Polly, Alice saw, did have the grace to look doubtful about all this. Polly's face was pink with embarrassment as she finished. To Alice it sounded as if this Maisie were an over-imaginative young fool. Maisie was probably making the whole thing up to impress Polly.

Polly looked reflective again. 'I feel sorry for Maisie, somehow. I think she's going a bit mad. That's why she told me. She can't tell anyone here, see. If she did they, the butler and them, they'd give her the sack.'

'Fancy saying such things,' Alice said. 'When his wife is an invalid.' She tried not to let Polly see that all this talk was upsetting her. 'Take it with a pinch of salt, Polly. Maisie could be making it up.'

She went to the window and looked out over the wide Cheshire acres. How could it be that rich and powerful people such as the Blackshaws didn't know that their servants were betraying them and destroying their reputations? She would know at once if someone bore her ill-will. Therese's hostility had been blatant. Therese need not have tried to belittle her. The snobbish condescension she'd seen this afternoon had upset her but she didn't need it spelling out to her. She had made an enemy of Therese the moment Frederick Blackshaw had touched her hand.

She left the window and, trying to forget the feel of Frederick Blackshaw's hand on hers, said to Polly, 'Ring for the hot water. I'll have my bath.'

# Chapter Fourteen

After he left Alice, Charles walked through the grounds
alone for a time until, nearing the Island Pool, he found
Johann Reinhardt, deep in thought walking along the
same woodland path.

'Captain Davenport.' The Austrian nodded his head
in a little formal bow. 'We walk together?'

It would be good to walk and talk with Reinhardt.
'Thank you, Herr Reinhardt,' Charles said.

Since he had left Therese and Frederick, he had spent
the last half-hour dwelling on his misplaced fascination
with the girl he believed would soon be Frederick's wife.
In fact, since he'd met her, his every moment had been
spent thinking about her, looking for her or castigating
himself for the foolishness of an older man's attraction
to a young girl.

Johann Reinhardt gave a first impression of being an
impulsive man. Closer acquaintance such as Charles had
already made with him had revealed the Austrian as a
man of great scientific intelligence. And it had been a
revelation to Charles to discover that the Austrian, when
English words failed him and his native German would
not be understood, could drop with ease into fluent Latin.

By Reinhardt's account educated men in Middle
Europe always spoke in Latin as well as German and
their native tongue, be it Hungarian, Czech or Serbian.
This had made for easy communication between them
and, although their acquaintance was only of hours'
standing, already they had a strong rapport.

This morning, after he had reported for duty and spent an hour at the barracks, Herr Reinhardt had taken him in the Daimler to Macclesfield and driven him around the town where, Charles knew, a medical practice had a vacancy. He'd had an enjoyable morning, being shown over the surgery and later looking over the Blackshaw textile-engineering works. The old town and the parkland areas where the big hospitals were situated had impressed him. The prospect of the Pennine Hills rising beyond the town gave splendid inviting views from almost every angle, promising days of walking and climbing.

And with all that to see Charles had found himself looking for Therese, half-expecting to see her at every turn since she had mentioned her Macclesfield property last evening. The town was almost deserted and the engineering works closed but it was explained to him that the town's annual holiday, Barnaby, named for St Barnabas, was in progress.

The factory, Herr Reinhardt said, was going to be renamed Blackshaw and Rinehart. Herr Reinhardt would soon apply for papers of naturalization for himself and the family. His only sorrow was his eldest son's obstinate refusal to become British. The Reinhardts would adopt the Anglicized spelling of the family name when they became British subjects.

Even now, as he and Herr Reinhardt strode out towards the pool, talking of the wide issues of nationality and allegiance, Charles found he was only concentrating with half of his mind. In his thoughts he asked himself again and again why Therese and Frederick had not announced their intention to marry.

The evidence of his eyes pointed to Frederick's being her child's father. She could have conceived Frederick's child in India on a visit to her parents. Their fondness for one another was plain to see. The only mystery was why they had not married before he left for South Africa.

Yet he found himself puzzling over the different stories; Therese's claim to have been married and widowed in Vienna and Frederick's shipboard declaration of love. Frederick had not once said, 'My widowed cousin' or 'My married cousin'. He scolded himself silently and yet he could not put thoughts of her out of his mind.

'Have your children arrived?' Johann Reinhardt asked.

'Yes. I left my daughter in the care of young Miss Blackshaw,' Charles said.

He had done it again. He had mentioned her name, brought Therese into a conversation. He was beginning to annoy himself with what appeared to be his obsessive behaviour. Reinhardt would not expect him to talk about a ladies' tea-party.

He was mistaken. His companion, striding quickly and purposefully around the Island Pool, looked up at him and said, 'Miss Blackshaw? The Miss Blackshaw we escorted from Vienna?'

'The young Miss Blackshaw,' Charles said. 'I didn't know that you knew her in Vienna. It must have been some years ago.'

'Yes. We lived in Prague. We went to Vienna for her. Her guardian, Sir Jack Blackshaw, asked us to be her chaperones. That was in '98 when we first came to England.'

'Then it could not have been the same girl,' Charles said. 'For I understand that the young Therese Blackshaw was married and widowed in Vienna. The Miss Blackshaw I speak of returned to her relatives, this Blackshaw family here in Cheshire, to have her baby after the death of her husband.'

'It is the same.' Johann Reinhardt stopped, frowned and gave a wry smile. 'The girl we brought from Austria was not married. She was not a widow. She was an orphan. Her parents had died in India. We went to school for her.'

'She was expecting a child?' Charles stopped in his tracks. A puzzled frown crossed his brow. This story did not make sense. It did not tie in with what he knew of

Therese and Frederick's circumstances. Frederick was with the regiment in India at the time the Reinhardts came to Cheshire. Then, not wishing to make too much of it in front of Reinhardt, he smiled and started to walk alongside him again.

Reinhardt said, 'She was not expecting a child. The child was born a little over nine months after she came back to England. We took good care of her on the journey. Ekaterina would not have let her come to harm when she was entrusted to her. Ekaterina is very strict with the children.'

'Then who—'

Johann Reinhardt shrugged. 'I do not know,' he said as he began to walk swiftly again. 'I can suppose, but I do not repeat what I suppose. It is not our concern now. Not mine and Ekaterina's.'

'Of course not.' A wave of relief swept through Charles. Frederick, then, could not be the father of Therese's baby. He reproved himself for thinking Frederick might have behaved shamefully. He had served with Frederick for two and a half years. Frederick was a valiant and true comrade. Dishonourable behaviour was beneath Frederick. To protect Therese, her family had put about the story of brief, early marriage and widowhood.

Therese's pregnancy must have been the result of an indiscretion. And indiscretions were understandable and forgivable in a girl who had no protector. He felt a sudden wave of elation lifting his spirits as he strode around the lake talking mechanics in Latin with Johann Reinhardt.

Tomorrow he would rise early and come out here for a swim. All at once he felt ten years younger.

If she was having a miserable time, Alice thought as she sat for a few moments alone in her room, how much worse it must be for Papa. All that had happened to her was the supercilious treatment of her that Therese had shown.

The dark cloud of disappointment that had descended

on her after Papa's talk in the rose garden had not lifted but Alice was a little ashamed of herself. She must have sounded reluctant when he told her she was to continue to serve the family.

After all she told herself, she was young, she had a lifetime ahead of her and poor Papa must be worried sick as to how he would provide for them all. He had little enough money left; certainly not enough to set up house, pay a housekeeper and find a nursemaid or nanny for baby Arthur. He needed her now as never before. What kind of a daughter would he think he had? Certainly not the dutiful, responsible girl he'd left behind.

Then half an hour before she was due to go downstairs Papa came to her room. She was relieved to see him again for she felt jumpy and nervous. The nervousness was due to the ordeal of afternoon tea but the jumpiness had come upon her soon after Polly told of the servants' hall gossip.

Papa seemed in better spirits and he looked straight and slim, like a knight she thought, as he came into the room in all the regalia of his dress uniform. He was so very handsome. Papa was so very much more handsome than all the young officers put together. There was not a man in the world to compare with him. He spoke to her in that marvellous, hypnotic voice. Alice had known people fall silent, one by one, when he spoke.

'You know that Herr Reinhardt's wife has offered to be your chaperone this evening?' he said.

'Yes, Papa.' Alice laughed. 'I don't think I will give Frau Reinhardt too much trouble.' She had already been told that she was to sit with the Reinhardt family.

'Then . . .' he said, 'Your young man . . . Your supper partner is the son of Herr Reinhardt. He will be waiting at the foot of the staircase for you when you are ready.'

He said nothing more though Alice waited for a moment. Surely this was not all Papa had come to tell her? 'I know that Karl will be waiting for me,' she answered. 'And we have met. In Southport.'

'Ah.' Papa stood for a moment as if waiting for her to

say more. Then he gave a little smile and said, with a certain hesitation, 'That is all. That is all I came to say.'

For the first time since she had arrived at Hetherington, Alice felt the stirrings of merriment. She looked at Papa's crestfallen face. 'You look very handsome in your uniform, Papa.'

He laughed, throwing back his fine head, showing the straight white teeth and the crinkling lines at his eyes. 'You are growing up to be exactly like your mother, Alice,' he said at last. 'Clara always saw through my vanities and my fears.'

'You need not have looked to me, Papa,' she said. 'You'll have all the ladies swooning at your feet.'

Papa was irresistible to women. She was sure he knew it.

Alice was sick with nerves as she left her room to go downstairs to the ball. She had been introduced to Sir Jack Blackshaw by Papa when they arrived this afternoon.

Frederick had not been there but his father had stared into her face and gripped her hand so hard that the big diamond ring he wore on his little finger hurt her through her gloves. She had almost winced. It had been a brief handshake and he had soon turned to shake hands with another of the house guests but her first impression of him had been an alarming one. She had felt herself to be in danger. There was an air of menace about him; the same sense of threat she had met with at the audition with Mr Squibb.

She looked about as she reached the top of the staircase but he was not there and, relieved, she came down the wide staircase, willow slim and graceful in the yellow gown. Mama's ivory fan dangled from her wrist and her hair had been dressed and threaded through with silk roses by Polly in the high-crowned style that made a golden halo around her head. She glanced down, over the mahogany and cast-iron balustrade, at the faces below. Half a dozen men were waiting; some in uniform, others in evening dress.

Karl Reinhardt, looking immaculate in black with white tie and tails, was amongst them. Thank goodness Karl was to be her supper partner. He appeared completely at ease in this company. She would never be able to live like these people did. Every word exchanged with a servant could be twisted. She had not heard one kind word uttered, not seen one kind action offered since her arrival here this afternoon.

Karl's blue eyes in his long serious face lit up with pleasure as she reached the bottom of the stairs. She held out a hand to him. 'Karl,' she said with relief when she found she had negotiated both gown and stairs without mishap. 'I'm glad to see you here.'

'My father bought mechanic factory from this family Blackshaw.'

'I know. I met your mother again and met your sister this afternoon.' Her voice had gone high and wavering. She tried to swallow the lump in her throat as she went with Karl towards the ballroom.

Music was coming to them as they passed along the Rose Gallery towards the Great Hall where the ball was being held. There was an exciting mixture of scents in the air. In the ill-lit gallery, lamps were burning on scented colsa-oil and this, mingling with the sweet scent from the bowls of rose-petals set under the gallery portraits, made Alice dizzy with nervous anticipation.

'Ah!' Karl said. 'There they are. My family is waiting for us.'

'Papa is with them,' said Alice as she saw Papa rise to his feet at their approach.

The Reinhardt family were sitting on gilt chaise-longues at the far end of the Rose Gallery where it opened out into an anteroom of the Great Hall. Major Frederick Blackshaw, also wearing the scarlet and blue dress uniform, waited with a crowd of officers and girls who, laughing and talking, scribbled names on dance cards to everyone's evident pleasure.

Johann Reinhardt and Papa got to their feet as she approached.

'Alice. Herr Reinhardt,' Papa said.

'We've met,' said Alice but again found herself shaking hands and smiling like a clockwork doll. Concentration was impossible for she was aware of another pair of eyes upon her. To her dismay she had felt her heart stand still the moment she set eyes on Frederick Blackshaw. Every nerve in her body seemed to be straining towards him.

He had come to stand beside them and, as soon as the introduction to Karl's father had been made, Frederick placed a hand on her arm, just above the elbow where her lace glove ended. The gesture was proprietary, the sensation like an electric shock. 'May I be the first to claim some dances, Alice,' he asked.

His touch was like fire on her flesh and, as she looked into his brown eyes, Alice felt as if her limbs were not under the control of her will. 'Of course,' she agreed, astonished that her voice sounded normal for she could not forget Polly's gossip. Was Frederick the father of Therese's baby? And why, if they were going to marry, was he looking at her with eyes brilliant with interest?

'I also,' Karl snapped. He had come to stand in front of her. He put out his hand for her dance card at the same time giving Frederick a sharp nod of acknowledgement.

Alice was amused to see the masculine rivalry she had so often witnessed between her brothers here being displayed by grown men. She relaxed a little. 'I shall put both of your names on the card,' she said. 'And Papa's, and George's.' She smiled quickly from one to the other. 'And I shall leave a few free after supper.'

Together the families Davenport and Reinhardt went into the ballroom where Sir Jack Blackshaw, Mary, Maggie and Therese waited to greet them. By some miracle Frederick had appeared on the end of the receiving line.

And by another miracle it appeared that she would not have to shake hands with anybody she had already met. So she went along the line, nodding and smiling to Mary and Maggie, receiving a condescending nod from Therese until all at once she was there, in front of Frederick Blackshaw. He held her hand firmly and looked deep into her eyes and again she felt the shock of contact and the sense that he was as reluctant to unclasp her hand as she was to remove it.

How could his touch have this effect? He belonged to Therese. If the rumours had any truth in them then very soon he would be married to her. And yet she knew, when she looked into his eyes, that something vital had passed between them.

The two families moved to a place by one of the windows, under the gallery where older guests were seated. Up there she saw Polly and the girl Maisie at the servants' end, keeping the spare pairs of white gloves the men wore to protect the girls' gowns. Alice smiled up at her, knowing that Polly would be watching everything, storing up impressions to relive later. And Alice would have given anything at that moment, seeing Polly's beaming face, to wipe out the snobbery and pretence and divisions that made it impossible for her little friend to join in the fun.

The evening then began for Alice in a whirl of music, laughter and dance.

Here in the Great Hall the windows were open to the cool summer air and the misty evening view of carriage-drive, lawns and the distant oak wood. Small tables and gilt chairs had been placed between the carved oak pillars which supported the gallery that swept around three sides of the hall. Garlands and leaves hung from the balcony rail above the heads of the guests. The great brass chandeliers on gilded chains sent a myriad of lights leaping from point to shining point above the dancers.

239

It was quite the grandest room she had ever been in. Although Hetherington from the outside was ugly, inside every room, gallery and reception area was magnificent.

Her card, up to supper, was almost filled and she was swept on to the floor at once by Karl, her first partner in the quadrille, and at every turn, every movement of the dance she knew that the brown eyes of Frederick Blackshaw were following her.

She danced next with Karl's father, and he – Frederick Blackshaw – seemed never to be more than a few yards away. Wherever she looked she was aware of the flash of his scarlet jacket, the laughing mouth, the dark moustache, his handsome face, of hot brown eyes following her progress around the floor. She was being swept along as if in a magical trance, knowing he was watching her.

The military band was perfect and so delighted was she to dance – the old-fashioned polka with James Horden, a barn dance with George as partner and a Dashing White Sergeant with Karl – that she barely noticed that Papa and Therese were almost always together.

Irmgard Reinhardt was fun and Frau Reinhardt seemed softer than she had appeared to be at afternoon tea. With Irmgard as translator, Karl's mother asked Alice to spend a weekend as Irmgard's guest at their Macclesfield home. And for all their attention, for all their bright amusing conversation, hardly a word registered. His eyes were still upon her, every time she looked up she saw him watching her.

She barely noticed that Papa's laugh, Papa's look of love was absent when he danced with Mary and Maggie Blackshaw; that it only lit up his face when he had Therese in his arms. All she was conscious of was that she and Frederick Blackshaw were being irresistibly drawn together, for she could not keep her eyes from his now.

Half an hour before supper, when she and Karl's father took to the floor in a veleta, Alice, seeing a gentler Therese smiling up into her father's face, only noticed with pleasure that Papa looked happy at last. She had not seen that look in his eyes since Mama had died. She had not heard his delighted laugh for years.

But Karl's father was offering the Daimler to herself and Karl for the journey to Southport tomorrow and she heard her own voice, as if it came from a stranger asking, 'My brother? And our . . . Our maid?'

'Yes. Yes. All,' Herr Reinhardt said. 'My chauffeur will be waiting for you all after breakfast tomorrow.'

Alice had been counting the dances. She had been ticking them off in her mind until he should come to her and suddenly he was there, standing before her, tall and strong and dazzling in scarlet, silver and blue. Frederick Blackshaw had come to claim his waltz before the supper dance and Alice knew it again, just as she had when their eyes first met, the still, breathless minute that could make the rest of her world fade about her and all her senses crystallize into one.

'Our dance, I believe,' he said as he took her hand and escorted her to the floor. His brown eyes held hers steady as she went, light-hearted with magic, into his arms. She felt the pressure of his white-gloved hand in the small of her back, the caress of his fingers on her raised hand as they danced, without speaking.

And she was certain he had felt it too for they were close and the touch of him was sending fire pulsing through her. It was as if they were both entranced. Everybody in the room must surely see it in her face, that she had eyes for nobody but him. Did she look bewitched?

The music and his touch alike were inflaming her senses and yet all about them other dancers, talking, flirtatious and laughing, appeared unaware of them. His brown, glowing eyes were challenging hers. He drew her closer.

'After supper,' he said, 'I want to see you alone. Will you walk in the garden with me?'

If they were missed then her good name was ruined. Alice hesitated.

He gave a low laugh as he held her gaze. 'The supper is going to be served outside, Alice,' he said. 'On the terrace. It is too warm to eat indoors.'

Then he must have seen the blush that had risen to her cheeks and he pressed her hand to his heart very quickly when nobody was looking at them. 'Let me have a little time alone with you. Nobody will be counting the guests for the supper-hour.'

He had tightened his hold, drawing her even nearer to him until she could feel the velour-smooth jacket of scarlet pressing hard into her bare upper arm, feel the iron strength of his hand hard on her back. He spoke again. 'The rose-garden, at nine-thirty?'

It was as if she were acting a part for, even as she blushed, she had begun to think of the excuses she could give to Frau Reinhardt who had watched her like a hawk all night. Her heart was knocking against her ribs, a metallic taste was in her mouth and the pupils of her eyes were dilated with the enormity of what she was about to do and yet she could not draw back. She looked up into his fiery brown eyes. 'Yes,' she said.

He loosened his hands a little and smiled as they assumed the proper distance between dancing partners.

The night was warm and honeysuckle scented as Alice retraced her steps of the afternoon to where Frederick waited for her at the pergola. Her yellow dress shimmered in the moonlight as she went towards him. There was no sound save that of her slippered feet treading the crisp gravel and her heart's noisy beating which sounded like a drum in her ears, beating time to the words in her head.

She must be bewitched – all her life she had been 'the responsible child', the dutiful girl. And now? She had slipped out of her bedroom where Frau Reinhardt had escorted her when she said that she was faint and overcome with the heat. It was dreadful behaviour.

But she saw him standing there – the tall, dark and handsome soldier in his dress uniform waiting for his lady – and she knew that the midsummer night had worked its magic on her. Tonight she was a different girl from the old dutiful Alice. The two glasses of champagne had not gone to her head. This was real. For the next hour she was going to live – careless of reputation, for already she had lied to Papa, Frau Reinhardt, Karl and Polly – she would live as Mama had lived, without a thought for tomorrow.

'Alice?'

'It's me,' she answered softly so that nobody else should hear, though there was nobody but themselves in the moonlit garden. The moon, high above the gardens, cast silvery light on the granite coping stones of the walks. The beds of pale roses looked ghostly white. Moonlight shone on crimson flowers and turned their petals to dark magenta.

He put out both hands to her and she took hold of them and looked into his dark eyes that were youthful and playful and brilliant with desire. The eagerness that was in him went strangely with the tight-fitting uniform, his major's rank and the once-proud name of Blackshaw. His voice sounded slower and deeper than it had done before when he said, 'Will they send out a search party for you?'

She laughed softly. 'No,' she answered. 'I told everyone that the heat was too much for me. I said I needed to rest for an hour.'

And she knew in her heart that one part of herself was acting, for her own voice sounded normal whilst inside her head the words were going, *Oh, talk not to me of a name great in story. The days of our youth are the days of our glory.*

He pulled her closer. 'So. You deceived them all for me?' He too was laughing, gently, as if pleased by

243

her frankness. 'Do you know why I wanted to see you alone?'

Of course she knew why he wanted to see her alone. He wanted to take her in his arms and kiss her. A tremor was going through his hands even as she answered him, 'Because you wanted to—' Then she stopped in case he thought her bold.

He let her hands go. 'Walk in the garden with me, Alice,' he said. 'I want to talk to you.'

She slipped her hand into his and went where he led her; through the rose garden and on to the Deer Park Walk and all the time they walked she knew that they both were holding themselves back from stopping and falling into one another's arms.

And as they went he told her that he had never found it easy to make small talk nor to speak of his hopes and fears, even to those nearest to him, yet he found himself talking easily and naturally with her; as if they had known one another for ever.

But she was burning inside as he talked. Every word he spoke seemed to be increasing her love for him. His hand about hers was different from any hand she had ever held before. She was conscious of the body of the man whose hand joined her to him. Yet she talked as they went. In a nervous voice, for she hardly trusted herself to speak, she spoke about her wish to become an actress.

'You will have all the stage-door Johnnies in the kingdom waiting outside your door,' he teased as they went slowly along the walk towards the Hollin Gate.

'I'm going to be a Shakespearian actress,' she told him. 'Not variety.' She glanced sideways at him and the look made him stop and take both her hands in his again.

He looked at her without speaking for a moment and it was as if he were making a great effort to stop himself from embracing her there. Then, 'Recite something for me,' he said. 'Shakespeare.'

She was mesmerized by his eyes, his mouth which was only inches from her own. She wanted him to kiss her.

She wanted to feel the strong arms about her, wanted to feel his hands caressing her. 'I could recite a poem by Lord Byron, if you'd like,' she heard herself saying.

'Please,' he said and pulled her away from the path to sit on a seat beneath one of the oak trees.

She would never forget this night. She had never known such agonizing pleasure, such a longing to be kissed, as she felt when she was saying these words of love written so long ago by a nobleman who loved a girl.

His hand slid along the back of the seat to rest upon her bare shoulder and his touch on her bare skin was like a flame that might burn her. Still she went on with the poem, looking into his eyes until on the very last verse he joined in and spoke them with her, his voice low and intense, his eyes never leaving her face.

'There chiefly I sought thee, there only I found thee;
Her glance was the best of the rays that surround thee;
When it sparkled o'er aught that was bright in my story, I knew it was love, and I felt it was glory.'

There was stillness between them for a few moments.

'I think I am in love with you,' he said quietly so that she only just heard him.

Had it not been for the fact that they were startled by seeing the shadowy figure of a girl in maid's dress dart from behind the trees near the gate and run through them on to the road and away, she knew that Frederick would have kissed her then.

The spell seemed to have been broken. He took his hand off her shoulder. 'One of our maids must have an assignation,' he said. 'I wonder who it was?'

Then he laughed with her and put a hand out to help her to her feet, turning her away from the gate and back towards the garden.

And, even though the magic of the poetry and the moment when he might have kissed her were lost, fire was raging inside her. His hand in hers was tightening and loosening, he was almost pulling her, making her feet go faster until they were nearly running back to their trysting place.

Once he stopped, looked at her with the burning light of passion in his eyes and said, 'You said you wanted to be an actress. But what about marriage? Supposing you lost your heart? What then?'

She said nothing for a few moments. She held his hands tight. 'Has my father ever told you about how he and Mama met and fell in love?' she asked.

'Tell me.' He began to pull her again, towards the rose garden as she told him the story of her father's courtship of her mother.

They were back in the garden by the time she had ended the tale and she was not sure he had ever heard it all. All she knew was that she was talking and talking, nervously talking because once he did take her in his arms, she knew she would be lost. She would be hopelessly and irretrievably lost in love for him when he kissed her.

They stopped. His arms about her. Her voice was no more than a whisper. 'It happened on a midsummer night,' she ended her story. She looked into his eyes. 'I've talked too much, haven't I?'

He held her close and his mouth was almost upon hers. 'It is midsummer night, tonight, Alice,' he said. 'Do you think you could love me a little?'

She could not answer him.

His voice was faster, hoarse as he grasped her shoulders where they were uncovered. 'I want to kiss you.'

'Do you?' she whispered. Then his hands were sliding down her upper arms, pinning them to her body as he looked deep into her eyes for a moment before his mouth came down on hers.

And in the moment that their mouths found one another all restraint was gone. All the passion and need and love that was in her leaped into life. Her long slender arms went up about his neck as she tasted the sweetness that their hungry mouths were making, moving against one another. Her fingers were sliding around in his hair, holding his head close.

He stopped, held her away from himself whilst his hands tightened around her shoulders. 'Alice?' he said.

She did not want him to stop kissing her. She went closer to him, pressing, pushing her body against his, not knowing that every movement of hers was exciting him beyond endurance.

'How old are you?'

'Seventeen.'

He loosened his grip a little, then said softly, his mouth close to her hair. 'You ought not to have come into the garden. You ought not to have come here with a man who has never had anyone as lovely as you in his arms before.'

She did not answer. She smiled up at him and her heart was thudding under the thin yellow silk of her bodice. Her head was reeling with the sight and the scent and the touch of him as she swayed, slim, pliant and willing against his chest.

He kissed her again, deep, passionate kisses that made her breath come fast, made a flush come to her cheeks as he kissed her in the hollow of her neck and the roughness of his chin on her satin-like throat made her quake with desire for him.

'Alice – oh God – Alice—' He stopped, still holding her close as he spoke. 'You are so beautiful. You are everything I ever wanted in a woman.'

She was seeking his mouth again and, shamelessly, she let the shoulders of her dress drop low so that his hands might fall on her breasts which were growing tense and full, waiting for his touch.

Behind the rose garden was a tree-shaded little hollow, where the grass was long and lush and he had an arm about her waist and was taking her towards it. And her feet were following his over the little granite wall and into the secret shady place.

He let go of her hands and she stood, shaking, quaking with love for him whilst he unbuttoned his scarlet jacket and laid it on the grass for her to lie upon. He wore only a white singlet beneath the jacket and he took that off and his brown strong shoulders and arms were hard and muscular and fine in the glancing moonlight that shone between the trees. Neither of them spoke as he gently pulled her down to the ground but their eyes were dark and neither could tear their eyes from the other.

And it seemed natural for her to do what she did, for, kneeling on his jacket, with his help she unfastened the hooks of her dress and untied her ribbons until the yellow bodice fell to her waist. She was aching with love for him and a wild and desperate need to have his bare chest next to hers. She would not listen to the voice of caution that faintly and distantly told her that she was behaving like a wanton.

He gazed at her for a few moments then slowly he placed his hands behind her waist and dropped his head and as his mouth closed over her firm warm breast she gave a little cry, for inside she was melting, dissolving.

He pulled her down until they lay on his things on the ground; she on her back and he leaning on one elbow, touching her face tenderly and gazing into her eyes with a look of wonder.

'I can't believe that I've found you,' he said softly. 'I can't believe it. After all these years of war . . . I should find a girl . . .'

She pulled him down towards herself, seeking his kisses until his mouth was on hers again and her tongue was searching for his. She let her long slim body mould itself against the length of him so that he must feel the fire that was growing and melting and liquefying in her. Tomorrow – tomorrow – she didn't care if she died tomorrow – she could not stop herself – only let this thing happen to her – now.

He pulled her up and turned her around so that she lay back against his chest and she felt the hard pressure of him against her back whilst his hands were holding her full round breasts, teasing them, making her weak with desire.

Then she turned quickly in his arms, looked at him with eyes wide with unfulfilled passion so that he knew she wanted more. He could not resist her. His warm open mouth was hungry against her throat and moving down on to the soft pale fullness until she cried out and called his name and let her fingers seek for him under the tight cloth that was all that separated him from her.

And he could not stop himself either for he was urgent with need; repeating her name, over and over and over again.

'Alice. Alice. Alice . . .' He pushed her flat on to the ground with his mouth still on hers, his hand holding her breast as she twisted in pleasure under him, moaning softly. She wanted his love as much as he wanted her. He began to kiss her more fiercely and still every kiss, every movement, met an instant response in her.

Nothing mattered now except the night, the love, the need of their bodies.

The soft grasses were cool and silky against her white skin as he slipped his hands under the skirt and pulled it and her cotton petticoat up, rumpling the clothes about her waist, gazing down at her buttermilk skin and golden body hair.

And she was pulling him down, pressing her lips against his scarred shoulder, calling his name softly, telling him to be quick – to love her now, now, now.

It was too much. He wanted her; wanted to feel the hot, secret body closing around him.

Hastily he removed the last of his clothing. His hands were on her thighs where the stockings ended and her skin was soft and silky warm.

'Freddie . . . Oh . . . Now . . . Oh . . . Freddie . . .' she was crying.

'I won't hurt you,' he whispered and saw her eyes close, heard her draw in her breath quickly. He wanted to watch

249

her face and hear her sweet words of love as he went into her . . .

And it was at that moment that he heard it . . .

. . . Charles Davenport's laughter. The unmistakable sound of his laugh was coming across the rose garden as his footsteps sounded on the gravel walk. The sound was punctuated by Therese's husky, teasing voice.

He must not let Alice hear their voices.

Instantly he rolled away from her, pressed his hands over her ears as he brought his mouth down on hers again, cold, without passion, keeping her still, shocked and quietening until he was sure that the voices were fading and the intruders were going away; until their voices receded as the distance lengthened.

The urgency left him and it came to him, in the few seconds of cool reasoning that followed, that he was behaving like a seducer.

He was angry with himself. He had allowed desire for the daughter to make him come close to forgetting his bond, the bond of honour that he shared with Charles Davenport.

With terrible haste he got to his feet and stood, pulling on his clothes, fastening buttons and hooks and all the time looking away from her. 'I am sorry,' he said in a hoarse voice which must have sounded to Alice to be full of anger. He was not accustomed to interpreting nuances, signs and signals of distress. He heard his voice sounding harsh and authoritative. And it must have seemed, when he thought about it later, to have sounded a note of scorn. 'I'm behaving like my father. Making playthings of women—' He was rambling in his self-disgust.

He turned and looked down upon her dishevelled figure where she lay; cold and shamed now that he had turned his back upon her. 'Fasten your clothes!' he ordered in a quick, hard voice. 'Before I forget myself.'

Tears of embarrassment and panic were falling on to her hands as, with fumbling fingers, she tried to cover herself, pulling the yellow silk dress about her shoulders to hide her nakedness.

He made no move to help or console her but stood looking down at her with a face tight and grim. Then he spoke, again in the harsh voice. 'How much does Karl Reinhardt mean to you?'

She seemed to be trying to collect her thoughts, to appear calm. But she was leaning forward with arms twisted behind her, fastening the hooks of her dress with shaking fingers as tears streamed down her face. 'Karl is a friend,' she wept.

He was angry. But he was angry with himself. He could not bear to see her cry and it seemed that whatever he said only added to her distress. He meant to tell her that he was jealous of another man's attentions to her. What he heard himself say was, 'You must be more naive than I supposed. Karl Reinhardt is in love with you.'

At his words her tears subsided. She began to collect the strands of loose hair. Then she stood up and faced him. He saw her swallow hard before she answered him, struggling to gain composure. 'Did you bring me here because of Karl? Because he wants to marry me?'

'No,' he said. 'I'm sorry.' He took her hands in his and held them. He felt a tremor run through her arms.

Her eyes were wide and dark centred as she looked into his face. 'Then why did you?'

'I'm being clumsy,' he said. But he did not release her hands. 'I don't know how else to behave. It has never happened to me before.'

'What has never happened before?' she whispered.

He looked long and hard into her eyes before saying, in a voice that must have sounded to her to be full of remorse and regret, 'I'm sorry. I've fallen in love with you.'

Now it seemed she thought nothing of him. 'Why tell me if it causes you regret?' she asked, quick and cutting in her pain. 'I don't think you are free to speak of love.'

'Not free?'

'If you are going to marry Therese, then why . . . ?'

'Marry Therese? Who told you that I am going to marry Therese?'

She did not answer. She looked pale and afraid of him.

'I want to know.' He shooks her hands in his own and his voice was rough. 'Who said I am going to marry my cousin?'

She had begun to cry again. 'I watched the embarkation parade.' Her shoulders were shaking with sobs as she whispered, 'And just as your regiment was passing, Therese and her baby came to stand beside us.'

She could have been no older than fifteen when she had first seen him. How could she remember what she had seen at fifteen? She was almost choking on her tears. He could only just make out her words as she went on, 'Therese was calling out to you. She was calling to her darling to come back to her. I thought that she was – I thought she was – your wife.'

'And when you came here you were shocked to find that she was not my wife?' he asked. Even to himself he sounded cold and distant.

She did not reply for a moment. She was making a great effort to control herself. The tears ceased and she said in a whispering voice of resignation, 'Something like that.'

He let go of her hands. He did not know how to comfort her. His face was tight and strained. He said, 'I want my mother to see you.'

Whenever he would think about the events of the night afterwards, he would remember that it was at this point that she became colder and as tight-faced and strained as himself. 'I am going home tomorrow,' she said.

'Tomorrow?'

'I play the piano for the Sunday School. I never break my word.' Her eyes were fixed upon his face.

He said, 'Not tomorrow. Now.'

'I can't.'

He was offended, horribly offended at her refusal to

252

meet his dying mother. 'Why?' he demanded. 'Why do you refuse to be presented to my mother?'

Tears came bright to her eyes again. She was trying not to let him see them. She had a sudden upsurge of pride. She squared her shoulders and made a mask of her face before she spoke. 'I could not bear to be "presented" to your mother,' she said at last in an awful, chilling voice.

There was a terrible, shocked silence between them as soon as she had spoken. Frederick felt himself grow white with anger and disbelief.

He would like to strike her. His hands were clenched at his sides and his breath was being drawn in very quickly.

Instead of giving in to this impulse he made a polite mask of his face. He put his shoulders back and with soldierly dignity said, 'Then good night, Miss Davenport. I apologize for my behaviour. I'll not waste your time again.'

He turned quickly and walked away from her.

She wished she had not said it. She hadn't even meant it. If she could take back the words she would. If she could bring herself to apologize, to apologize for the effect they'd had, she would. But she found herself only able to stand there, as shocked into silence as he had been by the apparent venom of her answer.

She watched his retreating figure and asked herself why she had spoken so callously. What had she done? If anyone had refused to meet her own mother she would have felt just as Freddie did.

She loved him. It was just as Mama had said it would be. She felt as if she belonged to him since she had invited him to seduce, to ravish her. And she had wanted his love just as much as he had wanted hers. Then she asked herself in heaviness of heart had she made a Jezebel of herself, like Therese's deceitful little maid, with a man who would henceforward hold her cheap?

Had she let Papa down? Would Frederick and all the

Blackshaw family despise them all? Papa, George and herself?

All at once she was plunged into the depths of self-loathing. She had let them all down. What had possessed her? She could not bear to think that any of them, George or Polly or Karl and his family, would guess at her shameful behaviour, learn of her guilty secret. She was cold. She began to shake, with fright at what might have happened had he not stopped her from making a wicked wanton of herself. She could have found herself with child and she would have had to kill herself to save Papa's good name.

She had yet to experience the terrible longing for Frederick that would come to torment her when she remembered his kisses.

She could not go back into the ballroom and face them all. She could not bear to see Frederick again. Suddenly, sickeningly, an image came into her mind. She saw him, with Therese in his arms, dancing in the happy crowd in the Great Hall, under chandeliers and banners of greenery, to the music that had started up again – the Strauss waltz she could hear floating across the gardens from the brightly lit ballroom.

'No. No,' she cried as she ran blindly beside the rose beds towards the garden entrance of Hetherington and the safety of her room in the West Tower.

She hoped at that moment she might never see any of them again.

# Chapter Fifteen

Therese lay naked on her bed. She had been there for two hours, restless, hot and unable to sleep. She could not keep at bay the impulses and visions in her head that came together, then fragmented into a hundred impressions and unanswered questions.

She went over them again in her mind, the happenings of last night, still asking herself if he was as drawn to her as she was to him. He had danced with Mary and Maggie twice. Mary and Maggie, instead of behaving like the staid sisters they were, had been vying with one another for his attention. He had encouraged them, she was sure.

She couldn't bear to see him smile at any woman but her. Every time he had smiled and danced with anyone but herself she had been sick to her jealous heart.

For she and Charles danced together so well. Their feet fitted perfectly. She had whirled in the Schottische with him, been gracious and light as they danced the veleta, waltzed until her head was spinning with the thrill of his closeness. And he had been charming and amusing, delighting her with his company and the feel of his arm around her.

Had he noticed her own increasing passion for him? For she had paraded her charms shamelessly. She wanted his eye to fall upon her every time he turned his head. He must never so much as look at another woman.

Freddie had spent the entire night making sheep's eyes at Alice Davenport and talking about the wretched girl; fishing for information about her from Charles. He must have known how devastating it was, to any woman, to have to sit there smiling through a litany of praise to her rival. Finally she had refused to go to the supper table with him and had taken Charles's arm instead of Freddie's at supper.

She had been forced to have a duty dance with her uncle and he had been in a fury, glowering and scowling at her at every turn, even being rude to her maid when she had asked him to go to the balcony for clean gloves before he touched her. She knew that her uncle was jealous when he saw her enjoying herself with Captain Davenport.

But was Charles at this moment suffering the torments, the cravings of unfulfilled desires, that she was?

It seemed incredible to her that only days ago she had spoken to Sir Jack Blackshaw and made threats about marrying Freddie; incredible that she could ever have allowed any intimacy at all with her uncle; incredible to think of the nights when she could not sleep for the sexual imaginings she had no hope of satisfying, since in those distant nights she had had no lover to dream of, as she now had.

For only now – only in Charles's company – did she know the madness, the magic of love.

She closed her eyes, the better to remember.

After they had returned to the ballroom after supper and danced a few dances he suddenly left her presence and she had known a moment of panic before, looking through the Great Hall windows, she saw him standing on the lawn by the sundial. His back was to the house, his hands were clasped behind his scarlet tunic and his feet were apart. His bearing was of a man waiting for someone.

She had gone outside, crossed the grass to his side and then, foolishly, pretended that she was surprised to see him there.

'Oh, Captain Davenport!' she said. 'I did not think to find you here.'

He looked down at her with the quiet, thoughtful expression on his face that gave nothing of his own feelings away. It could be a fatherly interest he was showing. She went on, babbling away like a love-sick ninny, 'Upon my word,' she said as she rapidly waved her silver filigree fan in front of her face, 'it is so hot in the house. I need ten minutes in the cool air.'

He was still looking at her. For a moment she thought he could see right through into her fibbing soul.

Then slowly he put out a hand to her. 'I was waiting for you.'

He had known that she would follow him. She saw that he had taken off the white gloves the men wore for dancing, so she peeled down her own lace ones and put her hand in his.

'Walk in the garden with me,' he said.

They walked for a while in silence then, 'Tell me about yourself,' he said when they had put a distance between the house and themselves. They were approaching the rose garden. 'I want to hear all about you. Tell me what you are doing with your life. What gives you happiness?'

'When I am not dancing, or walking in the night with the most dashing of soldiers, do you mean, Captain?'

He had laughed then. His laughter was a lovely resounding sound that carried across the parterre and rose garden they were crossing on their way to the orangery.

'Dear girl,' he said. 'You flatter me.' But he had held her hand a little tighter and she felt the side of his thumb sliding along her wrist in a most sensual way.

'When I am not engaged in such risky adventures,' she had teased, 'I concoct things.'

He laughed again and said, 'Tell me again. Tell me all about these things. Tell me about your concoctions.'

She began to tell him then in detail of her interest, her obsession almost with her lotions and potions and cures and creams. She found him interested and knowledge-able, asking her about the effects of certain plants, about

257

the waxes and oils she used as bases, how she stabilized her creams. He told her about his own medical discoveries; though he would not give them so elevated a name, he said.

They were still talking, earnestly and in a very down-to-earth manner, as they approached the Orangery. 'When I was a little girl I used to try to make magic,' she told him then; to make him laugh again. 'In my witch's kitchen I'd mix all sorts of things – spiders' webs and cuckoo-spit.'

'What did you discover? Did any of your spells work?' he asked, in a gently funny manner, pleased it appeared at the thought of her fiendishness.

She stood still and looked into his face with a boldness she thought might shock him. 'I wanted to play Cupid,' she said. 'I wanted to make a love-philtre – or a magic powder to sprinkle on to a sleeper's eyes . . . So that when he awoke and saw me he would fall madly in love with me.'

He stood still, no longer jocular. They were beside the Orangery, away from the trees where the moonlight was falling full upon her face.

'One such as Oberon ordered to be used in *A Midsummer Night's Dream*?' he asked in a much lower voice, though there was no risk of their being overheard here.

'Yes.'

'And did you think it possible to make this magic?' he said quietly. 'Do you think it happens that way? Do you believe that a man and a woman can fall in love at first sight?'

She wanted to see if he were still teasing but he had turned his head away and was looking into the distance as if recalling some past time.

'I believe it completely,' she said. 'It has happened to me. I knew in an instant.' She wanted to tell him. She wanted to say that it was he whom she loved. But she could not – not yet. He must know. And if he knew then he should speak first.

He was still looking into space, listening to her, but in a terrible way was holding himself back from her advances.

'Young women should take into account more than the power of love when they marry,' he said.

'But if a young girl should fall so completely in love,' she said, 'it would be impossible to ignore it. It could only happen to the young. And it cannot happen more than once in a lifetime.'

Here he turned his face to hers as if he were tempted to contradict her; but she carried on, determined to let him see that what she was saying was irrefutable. 'It would be a betrayal of magic, of belief, of love itself, if any such girl were to turn her back upon it.'

He looked down into her eyes and she, all at once afraid she was throwing herself at his feet, looked away up into the night sky which was starless save for one brilliant ball of light, larger than any star and brighter even than the moon.

'What is that?' She pointed to the star. She was sure he would know. He seemed to her to know everything in the world that was worth the knowing.

'Venus,' he answered with a trace again of amusement in his voice. 'Venus; the largest object in the sky.'

'Venus is the goddess of love.' She spoke in the low husky voice that was almost a whisper as she turned her face from the Heavens to look into his eyes. 'She is also the mother of Cupid. Don't you acknowledge her power?'

He took both her hands in his and held them steady as he looked at her face for what seemed an eternity. She held her breath, willing him to speak of love. He did not speak but slowly he drew her into his arms.

It was a long, restrained kiss that he gave and she knew that he was holding himself back. But she felt, behind the restraint, the iron strength in every muscle of him and knew that for him it had a greater significance than a mere stolen kiss in the dark. There had been a feeling of reverence in his embrace that had moved her almost to tears.

When he released her she had taken his hand and together they had gone back to the Great Hall in silence.

After the dancing was finished and the guests gathered in the anteroom for champagne and breakfast, she had left the company without taking leave of any of them and had come back here to the Dower House, to lie on her bed, think of him and long with every nerve in her body for his touch.

Sleep was impossible.

Oh, it was hot. She stretched her arms out to cool her sides. Dawn was breaking. There was so little darkness. She could not sleep.

She half sat against the pillows, watching a glistening line of sweat between her heavy, dark-tipped breasts that had always seemed too voluptuous for the size of her. She watched it trickle down towards her almost-flat stomach.

Maisie had not been here when she'd come in and, finding the maid absent and her nightclothes not laid out, she had undressed herself and stretched out on top of the silk counterpane. The dress, of palest green satin, lay in a crumpled heap on the floor.

She raised her knees, felt cooler air like a blessing on her hot sticky thighs.

'Damnation!' She whispered the words. 'I'm lying here like a love-starved old spinster and every inch of me is crawling for the feel of his hands. How much longer can I endure it?'

She put her feet down on to the cool boards, stood and reached for her silk kimono which was draped across a low Hepplewhite chair. She pulled it tight around herself and went to the window, drew back the curtains and watched the sky lightening in the east.

'I'll go to the pool,' she said, 'for marsh marigolds and celandines. It will take my mind off Charles Davenport.'

She kept an Austrian peasant blouse and a black,

colour-banded dirndl skirt in the wardrobe for her dawn forays to the pool and woods. It was worn with a cambric half-petticoat with a drawstring waist.

Quickly she tied the embroidered blouse and fastened the hooks of the skirt. Then she slipped her bare feet into short ankle boots of soft black leather. Around her shoulders she hung a fringed silk shawl. Her hair was loose.

Early mornings were her favourite hours. There was nobody about at five o'clock; servants perhaps at Hetherington and a hallboy and scullery-maid here at the Dower House, but she never saw any of them when she went out into the silvery grey dawn that was hanging heavy with dew all about her.

Nobody, not even estate workers coming in from the tenanted farms, would take the route she followed to the Island Pool.

She reached the pool in fifteen minutes and at last felt the long grasses brushing wetly against the bare skin of her legs as, with skirts lifted, she pushed her way to the water's edge. There she began to search in the close green growth for the saucer-faced flowers of the lesser celandine.

The Island Pool, here shaded by willows, was a natural covert for the water-bugs whose collection she had long since relinquished. But waterfowl and ducks, gliding, feeding on the duckweeds a yard or more from the water's edge, were disturbed by her movements and set up a chorus of protest, fluttering, rising into the morning air. Beyond the reeds, just out of reach, waving its bright yellow flowers above the water was a yellow flag iris, a plant she had been hoping to find.

She would have to wade out to gather it. She took off the boots and laid them on the grass then pulled up her skirts and tucked their hems inside the waistband. She went to the water and looked up, just after she put her right foot into the soft, slippery weed and felt the muddy lake bottom squelching between her toes.

Someone was on the island, diving into the glassy water from the little wooden platform they used to tie up the boat. The boat, however, was not there at the island jetty and the man's long tanned body flashed, naked, into the water as she looked.

What did it matter? Whoever it was would not have seen her. She put her left foot in and began to inch her way gingerly to the plants, for she was afraid of deep water and the lake shelved quickly here. She went slowly and carefully towards the thick green mass of sword-like leaves. The water came up to her knees here and quickly she started to pull. She wanted the long acrid roots for her cure for toothache, as well as the flowers for a face-cream and the stem and leaves for black dye.

The swimmer was approaching. He was only yards away when she recognized him.

Charles Davenport, standing in deep water which reached up to his smooth chest, called out, 'Who is that?'

She had been working with her face averted but she turned, shook back the cloud of dark hair that was obscuring her face and, laughing softly, answered him.

'It is I. Therese.' She put her head on one side in the flirtatious way she knew he liked. 'I had no idea that you were an early bird, Captain.' She saw that he was smiling back at her and added, 'Perhaps I should say, "an early fish", Charles.'

He was laughing at her, wading towards her as she went back to the grass verge, the irises safely caught up in the looped apron she had made of her clothes. She placed them on the ground, released her skirts and faced him again.

'Are you a health and fitness man, Charles?' she asked as she began to walk alongside the water towards the little wooden jetty where the boat was tied. 'It is quite the fashion to be so, isn't it?'

'The fashion?' he called to her as he waded out towards the boat. 'What fashion?'

'Yes,' she said. She felt the wetness of the cambric

underskirt flapping around her ankles as she walked carefully over the grassy, weedy pathway towards the boat. She wanted to get there first. 'Everyone is doing it. Taking an hour of good, healthy exercise before breakfast.'

She was going to be a devil this morning. He should pay for his stirring her into a froth of passion last night. She would row away with his clothes. She could see them, lying across the flat seat of the little row-boat. 'Are you one of the new breed of outdoor man, Charles?'

He answered her in the same light-hearted manner she had used, chuckling the low amused laugh she loved as he said, 'I am not one of the – one of the "Under the spreading chestnut tree, Sunday cycling club" type of athlete if that's what you're looking for.'

The water was a little shallower where the boat was. He came, wading and full of laughter out towards the boat. He was almost upon her when she stepped off the jetty into the boat and slammed the oar into the rotting wood of the pier support. She cast away and began to row towards the island.

His laughter ceased and he stood, waist deep, watching her. Then he plunged head first into the water and began to swim fast and noisily towards the island. He must have guessed what she meant to do.

She reached the island platform first and, heart thumping with excitement, climbed out with his clothes, tied the boat to the iron ring and, stumbling a little, went along the boards. There she stopped and stood, hand on hips, waiting for him to come alongside. As soon as he reached her she was going to run on to the little island and hide the clothes she had put down beside her.

He was only feet away from her, standing in the deep water which reached almost to his armpits. He did not seem to be amused at her antics but was looking at her in a challenging way. 'I asked you. What kind of a man are you looking for, Therese?' he demanded.

She caught her breath at the look – the look of raw

masculine need on his handsome face. She found her voice, heard with surprise that it sounded normal and to provoke him even more she said, 'If I say that I am not looking for any sort of man?'

Suddenly she saw that her behaviour had maddened him. She saw his expression harden.

'Then you should take yourself home. At once,' he said in a voice that was authoritative and final.

She felt herself begin to quake, there was no other way to describe the strange inward shaking that came to her as, standing above him, she looked into those keen blue eyes. She would not back down. Not now. Not when she was so near to having her heart's desire. 'And if I refuse?'

'I won't be responsible for what will happen.'

She did not reply; she merely looked at him from under the heavy eyelids.

He made no move to pull himself out of the water. He was waiting for her answer but, at last, in a warning voice that left her in no doubt of his intent, he said, 'Don't play games Therese! I am flesh and blood, like any other man.'

Then in her lowest, slowest voice she said to him, 'And if I say that I am? If I say that I am looking for a flesh and blood man? What then?'

There was a silence between them; no sound but the gentle lapping of water against the boat. The sun had just risen above the tree tops and lit the water further back, towards the reeds at the far side of the lake and Therese noticed every detail . . . the silence . . . his face with the brows drawing together . . . the feel of the rough wooden planks under her bare feet.

He raised his hands out of the water towards her, 'Leap into my arms.'

There was no more doubt in her. She knew that he knew it too. It had happened to him as well. Her limbs did not seem to belong to her as she slowly unhooked the black skirt and the under garments, letting them slide to the wet planks beside his clothes. She untied the neck strings of the blouse and pulled it off over her head, then she stood there for a second, heavy-breasted and narrow-waisted, her black hair in a cloud that reached below her shoulders – cold morning air on her warm flesh – before with a little cry she leaped into the arms that were reaching up for her.

Water swirled around her waist, shocking her with its sharp coldness, making her gasp as she felt his strong arms tighten around her. Then her hands were clasped behind his neck and the hot fiery strength of his mouth was upon hers, her tongue against his, her head full of exploding stars of wild sensations following one upon another as his kisses went deeper and searching into her.

With feet planted firmly in the lake bed, one strong arm around her back, crushing her breasts against his chest, his other pulling her hips in against the hardness of himself they swayed in the buoyant water. At last he stopped the deep kisses and released her a little so that his blue eyes were looking deep into the green of her own.

'Marry me?' he said.

All around her shoulders her wet hair floated. He would not see the brightening in her eyes, she was sure, although his face was blurring in her sight. 'Yes. Oh, yes,' she said. 'Please.'

Then he held her out from his body for a moment, to look at her – at the bouncing breasts that filled the space between their bodies, her nipples dark and tense breaking the surface of the water. He buried his face into her neck, then he lifted her until his mouth fastened upon her breast, making her cry out as sweet, sweet longings spun and radiated inside her.

She moved in towards him and slowly she wound her legs around his waist, pressed her inside legs and her thighs hard around his body, as when she rode a horse astride, and as she did so she let her hips move sinuously in a circular motion to please him and tease him, knowing that he wanted nothing so much as the hardness of himself inside her slippery, narrow little depths.

And while he was growing more urgent with need of her she dropped her right hand down under the water until her slim fingers held him and she lowered herself on to the long firmness of him and caught her breath at the sensation of his going inside her.

She began to call out softly with the delight of the feel of him moving in her, filling her gently and easily and slowly until she could sink no deeper and she began to move in a quickening closing rhythm that was making her back bend, her breasts harden as she felt his mouth come down fast on to her own.

His hands were clenched tight around her tiny waist, pushing her hips down and he was gritting his teeth and making harsh sounds in his throat as he thrust hard, far and high inside her, until she cried out with the sweet agony of his lovemaking.

And all the time she was singing with joy inside, knowing that this would be her response for ever to this man and his love and need and the slaking that was coming to them both as, breast high in green water, they cried out in release.

She clung to him, her arms tight about his neck, her face pressed into the space below his chin when they had loved.

He made to put her down and she cried out again, begging him not to do so, telling him that she could not swim. At her words he held her so hard to himself, brushed kisses all over her wet face and, in a voice full of wonder and disbelief at her recklessness he said, over and over again, 'Oh, Therese! Therese! I love you.'

And he carried her in his arms on to the island and slowly and carefully laid her down upon the grass and there they made love again and again.

And lying in the long grass on the island, before he rowed her back, he said that she was to think very seriously before she agreed to marry him. He would not hold her to it if she changed her mind.

For if she took him as her husband then her life would

be very different from the one she was leading. She would have few of the extravagances she was used to. She would have a part to play as the wife of a doctor – a man too old for her – a man who had five children she must be prepared to be mother to. She would have to be especially kind to Alice, who had mothered the children since her own mother died and who was the living image of her mother.

'I have a child myself,' she reminded him. Then very sincerely she said, 'And I shall never tell you the name of his father.'

'I will never ask,' he said slowly. 'I don't want to know anything about your other loves.'

He rowed across the lake, fastened the boat to the wooden jetty and helped her on to the bank. Then he held her close and kissed her before they parted as he promised, 'I will be a faithful husband. There will never be another woman in my life and I shall love you without reserve, wholly and completely, until the day I die.'

Waves of happiness swept over her as she told him that her mind was made up. But he insisted that she think it over and give him his answer after the Cathedral service on Sunday.

He was troubled about the great difference in their ages. She was not in the least bothered about age. Already she felt herself older and wiser than he.

Two hours later, at eight o'clock, Therese sat in the day nursery, crooning to the baby in her arms as she gazed, without seeing, towards the ornate plaster ceiling.

Peter loved her fine contralto voice. He lay against her bosom, contentedly sucking his thumb to the songs that made him rock to and fro.

Inside her chemise, next to her heart she had put the note that Charles had sent to her, only half an hour after they had parted. He had gone to his room, written out such beautiful words of love and given the note to one of the Hetherington servants. It had come up with her breakfast tray and was written in a strong, sloping hand.

My beloved,
I am thinking of you and the sacred love I have for you. You are gone from my sight only one half-hour and already I am disconsolate.

With every minute that passes, you become more necessary to me. Therese, love of my life, I am counting the hours until I know my fate.

Your devoted Charles

She looked down at the child in her arms. Peter had that adorable, sleepy-dreamy expression on his sweet face as she held him on her knee in the old rocking chair and sang the little lullabies that delighted him.

She always put her own words to the tunes, making them up as she went; telling him about the world he lived in, about Mama and what she would do that day. Today her head was filled with such delights, such thoughts that she went over the morning's happiness as she sang.

'Lulla, lulla, lulla-lulla bye-by,' she sang. 'Mama's going to marry, marry, marry—'

'Marry marry marry,' Peter echoed happily.

'Mama's going to marry. Marry Charley,' she sang, pleasing herself with the use of a nickname she had not as yet used.

'Marry-marry-Charlee,' Peter joined in.

She laughed softly at the innocent words and shushed him as she hummed and thought about Charles and their future.

She would be a wonderful wife. There was nothing she would not do for him. She would help him in his work, dispense his prescriptions for him, engage staff and keep house for him, entertain their friends, bear his children . . . or rather she would bear their children for he had already five and she one.

His children might present a problem. No! The eldest

two she had met. The son George who was so like his father would be another man in her entourage. The younger girl and boy would be a help to her. The baby would be a companion for Peter.

Alice Davenport was the only cloud on her horizon. It was clear that she was a reminder to Charles of his first wife. She could not tolerate competition. A husband must be found for Alice. Not, of course, Freddie. A suitable young man must be found for her. Once she and Charles were man and wife she would speak to him about it.

Alice tossed and turned all night and fell asleep only an hour before being roused by Polly who placed a tray on her bedside table.

'Here's your tea,' Polly said before going to the tall windows to pull back the curtains.

Sunlight streamed across the bedroom. Alice sat up and, as she did so, recollections of last night came flooding back. She could blush, merely in remembering, she discovered as a dull heat came spreading across her face and neck. 'What time is it?'

'Eight o'clock.' Polly was all brisk efficiency this morning. 'We have to be at the coach house at half past.'

'Just us?'

'No. Karl Reinhardt has to be back at work. Five of us are going – the chauffeur, Karl Reinhardt, you, George and me,' Polly said.

Alice, her tangled hair falling about the crumpled lawn nightdress, sipped at the tea. 'Have you ever been for a ride in a horseless carriage?' she asked mechanically.

'No.' Polly told her. 'I've seen plenty. In Southport.'

'I can't go down to breakfast.' Embarrassment and fear at the prospect of seeing Frederick came washing over Alice. 'Will you get something to eat for me?' If she were to go downstairs she might see him again. And she could not bear it.

She had fallen in love with him. It had happened to her; love at first sight, just as it had to Mama – just as

269

in the words of the poem, 'I knew it was love, And I felt it was glory.'

As she drank the tea she recalled the night in all its detail and wondered how it was that she had agreed to go into the garden with a man she was so hopelessly attracted to. He was almost a stranger and he belonged to Therese. What had come over her? She could only suppose that in her vanity and self-delusion she had been acting; acting Mama's part, the part of Helena in *A Midsummer Night's Dream*, that strange and beautiful play of youth and magic and fancy.

Now she regretted it bitterly. For, unlike in Mama and Papa's love story, Frederick had not asked her to forsake everything for him. Frederick had turned his back on her and her offering of herself.

'I'll go down and bring some toast and coffee to you,' Polly was saying. 'Will that be enough?'

'Yes,' Alice answered. And, as well as tears of shame for her abandoned behaviour, she wanted to cry with regret for the cruel words she had spoken. Now she could reflect on it she knew she had been wrong to go into the garden at all, or having gone, to allow so much as a kiss.

'I'll get dressed and we can put as much distance as possible between ourselves and Hetherington,' Alice said, forcing herself to stop these useless recriminations; telling herself that she hoped she might never see him again – never experience again the violent, convulsive emotions that being near to him brought.

'Don't be like that,' Polly said. 'I know you left early. You enjoyed the first half, didn't you?'

'I did.' Alice took another few sips of tea and tried to sound sensible so as not to arouse Polly's suspicions. 'Far too much.'

Polly put her hand out for the cup and saucer. 'You missed a lot of it, you know,' she said. 'It were good fun after supper. Sir Jack Blackshaw didn't come back afterwards and everyone seemed happier somehow with him gone. Major Blackshaw came back late and bad-tempered and Maisie disappeared but I don't think anyone except me noticed it all. They were all having a wonderful time, dancing and . . . chattering . . . and . . . Oh! I don't know . . .'

Alice didn't even answer but Polly had not noticed.

'I came back here to look for you. But you wasn't in . . .' Polly said.

'I walked in the garden for a little . . .'

'I thought that's what it was,' Polly chattered on. 'So I came back and I was all alone up there for a bit until George took pity on me and came and sat with me.'

'Don't talk about it,' Alice said. 'Please, Polly.'

'Sorry!' Polly said. 'You are in a state this morning.' She went to the door. 'I'll be back up as soon as I can get your breakfast.'

She would not give Frederick another thought, Alice told herself. She put her feet to the floor, pulled on her wrap and went to the window. Her room was at the corner of the West Tower. It had two windows; one overlooking the front, the other the west entrance of Hetherington.

She looked out of this front window. On the gravel drive the Reinhardt's Daimler rolled towards the coach-yard gates. She turned away from the window and started to dress for the journey home.

Within the half hour she had eaten her toast, made herself ready and gone down to the sunny yard, dressed in the scarlet jacket again and the Robin Hood hat secured to her head by a chiffon scarf.

They were all there: Papa in his uniform laughing and talking with Herr Reinhardt as if he hadn't a care in the world, George and Polly laughing with two grooms who were working on the motor-car. Karl was standing at the arched entrance to the coach house, watching the preparations.

A chauffeur, wearing grey uniform and black shiny-peaked hat with as much gold braid and as many crested buttons as an admiral might wear, supervised the grooms. He had long leather gauntlets and black knee-high boots and he stood a little apart from them all, aloof as he regarded the men who were vigorously polishing the glossy black lacquer of the Daimler.

Alice went to stand by George and Polly, watching the grooms who hissed and hummed as they swept their chamois leathers along the flanks of the Daimler. It was Polly who asked the impertinent question, 'What are you making those funny noises for?'

'Why, miss,' said one of the lads as he raised his cap to her, 'it's a habit. We always do it. It calms the horses.'

Everyone laughed and Alice felt a slight lifting of her spirits as the picnic hamper was stowed aboard and Karl called out to them, 'Come over here. I show you the map.'

She walked ahead of the others into the vast, stone coach house where gleaming ranks of carriages were kept: broughams, Landaus, bogies, box carts and governess carts. Karl had spread a big linen-paper map across the floor of a governess cart.

Alice thought of Karl as her closest friend and felt a grateful rush of affection towards him as he described the route for the benefit of herself and Polly.

'We take road from Knutsford to Warrington,' Karl said. 'We shall go on swinging bridge over grand canal.'

'The Manchester Ship Canal?' Alice asked.

'Yes.'

'Eeh!' said Polly.

'It has only been opened for eight years,' George put in with a great display of knowing. 'They have not quite finished the new Salford dock.'

'Eeh!' said Polly. 'Well, I never.'

Alice smiled to herself as she listened to George showing off to Polly again. 'Shall you drive?' she asked Karl.

'My father not permit,' Karl said quietly. 'When Father is not there, I drive.'

'I thought you disliked engines,' she whispered back. 'You told me so.'

Karl smiled at her fondly. 'I like engines for travel. I

like Daimler engines. Machines for making textiles I dislike.'

'How long will the journey take?' Alice asked, anxious to get going, to leave Hetherington behind them, not to chance seeing Frederick again.

Karl folded the map and they followed him as he went to the Daimler and placed it in one of the leather pockets inside the front passenger door. He looked very self-assured. 'The journey take five hours. More than sixty miles to travel,' he announced. 'We shall stop one hour for picnic.'

Then the chauffeur swung the handle and the great horseless carriage jumped and began to shake as the engine jerked into life. The chromium plate on the door handles and windscreen caught the sunlight and sent it splintering into their eyes as they were helped aloft by the grooms. Alice felt excitement begin to stir in her as the doors were fastened and they settled into the deep leather upholstery under the high canvas canopy which Karl promised to take down after the picnic.

It was then, just seconds before they were to move forward, that Frederick came into the yard. He wore his other uniform, his khaki with riding breeches and long boots. Then she remembered that, of course, he and Papa had to report in an hour's time. Colour rose hot in her cheeks as she felt the familiar force of his presence. Her breath was being suffocated out of her as he approached.

But it seemed he did not want to speak to her. He gave a quick glance and nod in her direction then went to Papa's side. She saw him speak to Papa but the engine noise drowned their talking. A few words came to her over the throttling sound of the engine. 'When . . . ?' she heard Papa say. There was a look of worried surprise and alarm on Papa's face.

'Come with me . . .' Frederick was saying, '. . . confirm it.'

She heard Papa answer, 'I'll be there directly. Send for your own doctor and your lawyer.'

Papa turned his attention back to the departing Daimler as they rattled over the cobblestones away from him. She returned his wave and saw that the smile had gone from his face. Then as they rolled through the coach-yard gates she saw him following Frederick.

They passed the Dower House before they went through the Italian Gates. All the windows in the great sandstone mansion were curtained.

'Eeh,' said Polly. 'She's gone then.'

'Who? Who's gone?' said Alice.

'Her Ladyship must be dead.' Polly's face had lost its fresh, happy expression. 'They all – all the staff – said she was a proper lady. She was only waiting for her son, for Major Blackshaw to come back to her, so she could die in peace.'

Alice felt herself grow cold and light-headed as Polly spoke. 'I didn't know . . . I didn't know,' she heard herself repeating. 'We were told she was an invalid.'

'Major Blackshaw's hardly left her side since he came back,' Polly was saying.

'Don't! Don't Polly!' Tears started to roll down Alice's cheeks as she realized what she had done. 'Why did nobody tell me?'

'Don't take on, love,' Polly said. 'Them sort, them kind of people never tell anyone anything.' She placed a comforting hand on Alice's arm. 'We wasn't to know.'

# Chapter Sixteen

Within two days of their return from Hetherington, Aunt Harriet was taken into hospital after another, milder, attack of angina. Papa's decision not to practise in Southport had been a great blow to her, Alice knew. Her face had gone white, her very stature seemed to shrink and yet she had managed to hold on to the shreds of her pride even as they took her in the horse-ambulance to hospital.

Dr Williamson said she was to have complete rest for a month. One visitor only would be allowed, on a Sunday afternoon. Lady Cranston-Bartlett had claimed the privilege of visiting and had left them with only the bulletin-board at the hospital gates for news of Aunt Harriet's progress.

Two weeks later Alice was almost at the end of her tether. She stood by the deep white sink in the kitchen at Duke Street at seven o'clock in the morning, up to her elbows in black, gritty water. She had been trying for half an hour to wash the plate covers of the Eagle range where fallen soot had clogged the stove so that it could not be lit.

Mrs Brock had left, to work for Lady Cranston-Bartlett until Aunt Harriet came home, she said. Alice suspected that the only condition under which Mrs Brock might return would be when the Davenport family had left the house.

She was in a fury of desperation as she tried to prevent the cold filthy water from splashing on to the Holland apron she wore over one of Polly's calico dresses. Polly was late down this morning and the kitchen fire had not been started. Without a kitchen fire the water was cold and there would be no cup of tea until either the fire or the stove could be lit.

She looked up at the sound of Polly coming into the kitchen and spoke with quick irritation. 'Thank Heaven you're here,' she said. 'Help me light the range, will you?'

Polly, guilty about her late appearance, said, 'I slept in. I'm usually up at six.' She came towards the sink and gave Alice an apologetic smile before saying, 'Leave over. Get yourself cleaned up. They'll have to have summat – I mean "something" – cold for breakfast.'

Alice began to fill a bowl with clean water to soap her hands and arms. 'I'll move to the table,' she said. 'If you think you can do it.'

Polly, for all her air of apology, seemed to recover her good cheer quickly and Alice was glad that she never took umbrage. Unlike herself, the young maid didn't seem to be flagging under the load of work. Without Polly's help the last two weeks would have been impossible. She herself had lost weight, grown pale from lack of exercise and fresh air and had been tearful and restless when she should have been sleeping.

Night after night she tossed and turned, thinking of Papa – praying that he would soon find a practice. And when she did close her eyes a picture of Frederick came as clear as if he were there, holding her in his arms, loving her. She would burn with heat or shame, she knew not which and be unable to lie another moment with the sweet longings tormenting her. She had given hardly a thought to the Manchester Repertory Company since she had written and turned down their offer. She never had the time to think about acting.

In contrast to herself Polly appeared to thrive. Polly's face and figure had lost their full roundness. Pert prettiness, pointed chin and a slimmer, more curvaceous body had replaced the chubby figure of a month ago. 'How much longer before we hear from your father?' Polly stuck her square little hands in the black water.

'Soon, I hope.' Alice scrubbed furiously. Her arms were ringed with dirt to the elbows.

Polly began to lift the heavy flue covers out of the pail of water and put them down on the folded newspapers Alice had placed on the floor. 'We'll manage,' she said.

Alice reached for the rough towel behind the kitchen door then came back to the table and sat down on a chair as she dried her arms. She must tell Polly that the money Papa left had almost gone. She had forgotten to ask Papa for more and with Aunt Harriet gone she hadn't enough to pay Polly's wages. It was unfair not to give Polly warning.

Taking a deep breath she said firmly, 'There's no money, Polly. I've paid the sweep and the gardener and the windowcleaner from the money I take from the bank each week. There's not enough to pay for everything.'

Polly looked almost defiant but did not answer. It made Alice even more determined to make things clear to the maid. 'It's serious, Polly. Financial straits—'

Polly still did not answer.

'I have to give notice.' Her hands were crushing the calico of the dress into a crumpled mess as she tried to emphasize her statement. 'I can't pay your wages after next week.'

'I'm not going!' Polly set her mouth in the obstinate line that meant business. She continued working as if she wanted no more talk on the matter, upending the bucket of water into the sink, running the tap, scrubbing at the blackened sides with an enormous brush as the water ran away. 'So there!'

She grabbed a handful of scouring powder from a tin under the draining board and threw it into the sink, quickly getting to work on the bucket, brush flying under and round it as if by punishing the galvanized iron she could rid both herself and Alice of all that irked them.

And Alice heard every word Polly muttered to herself as she scrubbed.

'It's only been two weeks . . . It's not a lifetime . . . Your father's worried sick, that's what . . . If we can't keep going without daily orders . . . What sort of a family are we . . . ?' Then as if to apologize for placing herself with the family, 'How could you run this house alone?'

'There's Beattie. And George,' Alice said.

'Aye. But you're in charge.' Polly took the bucket to the back door and placed it on the step before returning to tackle the stove. 'And you've never had a minute to yourself since we got back,' she said. 'Your young man . . .' Here she stopped at the expression on Alice's face but soon went on to say, 'Karl Reinhardt comes round here every evening and sits here talking to you. You shouldn't let him in. If your father or your aunt knew about it there'd soon be something said.'

There might be something said, but Karl's attention was like a lifeline. She said with a quick show of defensiveness, 'There's no impropriety. You and everyone are always here too.'

Every day since their return he had seen her. Every morning flowers, with a polite and odd-sounding message, were delivered to the house. He must have told the florist what to say. "To Miss Alice Davenport and My love" had been the first. "My heart wishes you. Alice Davenport" which was a strange way of putting his heartfelt wishes and just yesterday, "Please accept Karl Reinhardt." He would be going through his savings like water but would not be told to stop.

But she had come to look forward to his supper-time visits to the house. They talked. She recited her favourite poetry. Sometimes Beattie played the piano. And they laughed together; she and Karl, George, Beattie and Polly. The evenings of laughter were all that she looked forward to.

George had a delicious, dry sense of humour, Polly a cheeky irreverence and Karl it turned out, though he lacked completely any sense of humour such as she and George shared, was a practical joker. Only last night he had brought them chocolates he had made himself in the kitchen of the Victoria Hotel . . . and the centres were filled with forcemeat stuffing. They had laughed till they cried at the expressions on one another's faces when they bit into them.

Polly was smiling back at her, 'I feel sorry for you and Karl. You can't go anywhere together and it's not as if you can go to the bandstand with George like you used to do. With Arthur to look after an' all.' She took off the cover to the soot-door with the small iron handle and said as she did so, 'They all look to you to make decisions. The house'd go to pot if you wasn't here.'

'Weren't here,' Alice corrected her automatically. She began to collect a pile of plates and cups and saucers and stack them on the heavy oak trolley. 'Will we have the stove alight soon?'

'In five minutes,' Polly answered. 'I'll put t' kettle on soon as—' She peered under the flue cover. 'It's full o' soot. Fetch paper and sticks over will yer?' Then she laughed and said, 'I mean – "would you be so good as to parse me the paper?"'

Alice brought them and, smiling, she watched, fascinated by Polly's capable movements. Polly was taking the soot from under the stove top, raking, clattering with the long-handled scraper of angled iron, letting the heavy black soot tumble through the tiny slot of an opening on to the shovel. 'Doesn't the sweep do this?' she asked.

'No,' Polly laughed. 'Sweeps do chimneys. The stove gets done every week.'

'Oh, Lord,' Alice said as soon as Polly had put the cover back and been handed the paper and sticks, 'I wonder if Papa's found anything? I wish he'd write. I wish I knew where he was. If we had a telephone he could have told us how things were.'

'He'll find summat,' Polly said as she bent to the fire

door and started to stuff the crumpled paper in. 'He'll soon send for you. Have you finished your packing?'

Alice had spent the last two weeks packing into the three trunks which filled the hall the clothes and books and accumulation of belongings that five young people collect in two and a half years.

'There's not a lot left to do,' she said. 'But it's the money that worries me.' There was so much to pay for with Aunt Harriet gone. Alice had had no idea that so much of her aunt's money had been poured into caring for them all. 'We could go on for weeks if I didn't have to pay the wages. But I have to pay the gardener and you. If Papa doesn't come to rescue us soon we'll all be in Queer Street.'

'He won't leave you short,' Polly said. 'Not if I know Doctor Davenport.'

Alice smiled. 'But you don't know Papa,' she said. 'You only saw him for a day.'

'It were enough,' Polly said emphatically. 'He's the sort you'd work your fingers to the bone for.'

Alice was pleased that Polly too was already full of admiration for Papa. She remembered how she used to look up to him – how a "Well done!" from Papa was the greatest accolade a child could want. She remembered that she used to think Papa was God when she was little. She still adored him and was glad Polly did too.

Polly put a match to the paper and the fire flared, caught the sticks and spread up to the little pieces of coal. She closed the door and pulled out a damper. 'I can hear the postman,' she said. 'Go and see if there's a letter.'

'You used to meet the postboy,' Alice said, now trying to tease a little. 'On the back steps.'

'Not now. He puts them through the door,' Polly answered.

'Then I'll go.' Alice went out of the kitchen, along the passageway and the narrow little space she had left between the trunks. And here they were. Papa's letters, a thick and bulky one for her, a thinner one for Aunt

Harriet, the strong handwriting bold across the vellum envelope. She felt a great wave of relief and pleasure as she went to the stairs and called up, 'Beattie! George! Leo! Come down. A letter from Papa!'

Overhead, doors banged and footsteps thundered. Then they were all downstairs, following her into the dining room where, smiling with anticipation, Alice slit the letter open.

It was two pages long but there were two large, folded five pound notes inside. Alice took the money and flattened it carefully upon the table top before she began to read.

Dear children,

I expect that you have carried out my instructions and are prepared to leave Southport and join me in our new home. Papa has purchased a medical practice in Macclesfield, a town which will suit us admirably.

You cannot have anticipated the other great improvement in our circumstances which will enrich all our lives.

You have a new Mama.

The shock at this point made Alice stop reading and look at the others who appeared to have been struck dumb. She read.

She is more lovely, more gentle than any other woman alive and I am the most fortunate of men.

We were married by special licence a week ago. For family reasons it had to be a quiet affair and your new Mama has asked me not to mention her name until she meets you all in person. So secrecy is the order of the day.

I am sorry to have deprived you of the chance to share in our happiness. Please reserve a suite for us at the best hotel in Southport. We will arrive at Duke Street on Saturday in time for dinner when you will all prepare to meet and welcome the woman you are going to love as much as does your fond,

Papa


Underneath he had written, 'I have written to your aunt separately, thanking her for all her caring help during the war. Soon we will thank her in person.'

They stared from one to the other for a few moments. Beattie spoke first. 'I wonder who . . . ?'

Beattie put her hand out for the letter. 'It must be someone he's met in this, this place we're going to move to. This Macclesfield place.'

George spoke quietly. 'Or at Hetherington Hall.'

Alice said, 'Papa was leaving Hetherington on the Monday. We'd have known.'

George obviously had some idea he would not give voice to. He shrugged slowly and asked, 'Would we?'

Alice snapped, 'There was nobody there as old as Papa.'

'They're arriving tomorrow. Papa will expect us to have dinner and a room reserved for them at a hotel.' Beattie's was the practical voice. 'Where will we book them in?'

'They'll sleep here, in Aunt Harriet's bed!' Foreboding as well as anger had descended upon Alice. 'Where else?'

'Do you think it's right?' Beattie said. 'Perhaps he doesn't mean to stay very long. Perhaps he means us all to go to Macclesfield when . . .'

Fury was rising in Alice. 'If he can bring her to Aunt Harriet's house – he doesn't know Aunt Harriet is ill – if he can bring her here—! A New Mama, he expects us to call her—! If he can come here with her he can – damned well sleep here!'

She was plain, old-fashioned angry. She could rage and scream out loud at Papa's outrageous behaviour. Didn't he know that everyone thought he'd marry Aunt Harriet? Why was he being so coy? He had not even mentioned the woman's name? A new Mama? It was incredible. It was unbelievable!

Yet – useless to say unbelievable. The unbelievable had happened. Papa would not play a joke like this upon them. She had to believe it. Papa was married.

She got up from the table and hurried from the room, outrage rising in her at every step of the way, down the passage and into the kitchen to Polly.

'We're going to live in Macclesfield, Polly,' she almost shouted. 'With Papa and his new bride!'

'Eeh,' said Polly. 'Well I never.' She flopped down on to the kitchen chair. 'They'll not be wanting me, then.'

'You'll go where I go,' she said. 'If you want to come with me then you shall. I've taken my very last orders from Papa!'

She was seething. How could he? How could Papa have done this? He had asked her, begged her, to give up all of her own plans; to give up the stage for him. And he was so insensitive, so crass, as to write and tell her that he was married! Married! Who on earth could he have married?

She was still simmering with rage when she gave them all her orders. George and Leopold were to tidy the front garden, sweep the path and swill out the outhouse and lavatory. Beattie was to look after Arthur, clean the silver and dust. Polly was to beeswax the furniture and the stair sides, scrub the tiled kitchen floor and prepare vegetables. For herself she would have to make the beds, tidy the bedrooms and then go to the indoor market in Eastbank Street for food. She could also pay Polly her seven and sixpence, pay the grocer from Papa's money and give him another order for delivery in the afternoon.

She went upstairs and found Beattie there, dressing Arthur who was excitedly chattering as Beattie fastened his buttons.

'A Mama,' he chattered. 'Arthur's got a Mama. Has

you got a Mama, Beattie? Has Georgie got a Mama, Beattie?'

'Yes, darling,' Beattie was assuring him. 'Stand still while Beattie – ' She caught sight of Alice in the doorway. 'Are you going to write to the theatre, Alice?' she asked.

'The Manchester one?'

'Yes. They may not have filled the place.'

'I can't,' Alice said.

'Why not?'

'I've already told them I'm not going. I promised Papa.'

Alice stood stock-still. Why was she afraid to break her word to Papa? Papa had acted in an outrageous way, riding roughshod over them all, imposing a new regime, a new mother, a new way and place of life on them. He ought not to expect her loyalty. And yet she knew that he would expect her to carry out his orders until he countermanded them.

'I'm not sure.' Alice stood in the doorway, watching Beattie for a moment. She couldn't tell all to her sister. Beattie was too young to understand. She said, 'I'm not sure I want to be an actress any longer.' Then she said quietly, 'Something happened, Beattie. At the victory ball.'

'Whatever was it?' said Beattie as if she were humouring a younger person.

'I can't tell you,' Alice said.

Beatrice went on placidly fastening Arthur's buttons and Alice blurted out, 'Mama said we could change our natures by acting a part. I tried to act like a . . . like . . .' She paused for breath and looked at Beattie with huge grey eyes full of worry and remorse. 'I couldn't do it.'

'I don't understand you at all.' Beattie straightened up and began to brush Arthur's curls with a little silver-backed brush.

'Oh, Beattie,' Alice said. 'What changed in me wasn't my nature. I acted like a . . . Oh! No. I can't tell you.'

284

Beattie looked up from her brushing. 'Did you make a fool of yourself?' she said.

Alice was longing to talk about Frederick. She wanted to hear words of comfort, wanted to think that all was not lost. But she could not tell Beattie. She said, 'I wish there was someone to tell. I've never needed my Mama as much as I do now. Mama would have known what I ought to do – apologize or something.'

'Apologize? What for?'

What for? It would be impossible to tell Beattie that she wanted to beg his forgiveness for refusing to meet his mother. If nothing else she should have done that.

A few days after they returned to Southport, Karl had told her that his father had telephoned the Victoria Hotel as he did every day, pleading with him to return. Herr Reinhardt had told Karl that Frederick's father had died suddenly. Karl must have got it wrong. Everyone knew that it was Frederick's mother who had died.

Beattie was asking, 'What do you need to apologize for?'

'What I did afterwards,' Alice told her. 'Said things I shouldn't. Made it worse.'

'You got your come-uppance, did you?' Beattie said.

'Yes,' Alice replied. 'And I don't want it to happen again. Now I'm more determined than ever to be in charge of my own life, earn my own money, make decisions.'

'Arthur's got a Mama. Arthur's got a Mama—' At that point Polly came on to the landing. 'There's a messenger boy from the Victoria Hotel downstairs,' she said, puffing after her dash up the stairs.

Alice, harassed, ran down to the kitchen where she found one of the Victoria Hotel's new messenger boys. He stood in the open doorway, a young lad wearing the maroon and grey monkey-jacket and round cap; the uniform of Karl's hotel.

Only last week Karl had sent one of the new boys round to every department in the hundred-bedroom hotel, telling him to ask the various managers for a long stand. The poor lad had been repeatedly told, 'Just wait there,' until after several such episodes it had occurred to him that Karl was having a practical joke at his expense.

This new boy was holding out an envelope addressed to herself. Alice took and opened it as the boy said, 'It's from someone called Blackshaw.'

It was a printed invitation card which someone had filled in with her name and that of Blackshaw, Hetherington.

'Miss Alice Davenport and companion are cordially invited to the Victoria Hotel, Promenade, Southport. Luncheon.' This was followed by today's date and a signature which looked like "Blackshaw, Hetherington".

Karl must be fooling her again. He'd know that she wouldn't take it seriously if he'd asked her to go alone, and knowing Aunt Harriet was in hospital he'd put 'and companion' where her aunt's name should have been. Also, Karl didn't know that she loved Freddie. He would never have played such a trick if he'd known.

She looked at the boy. 'Are you a new boy?'

'I started today,' he said, blushing furiously.

'Who gave you the letter?'

The boy looked doubtful and hung his head.

'Was it a young or an old man?' Alice persisted.

'A young man, miss.'

'A tall, dark-haired young man?'

'Yes.'

A devilish urge to get her own back on Karl blazed into life in her. 'Then tell him that I shall be delighted to accept. I'll be there at twelve thirty,' she said. 'I'll go directly to the dining room.'

She sent him back, without a tip, for her purse was empty.

Upstairs again she said to Beattie, 'It's Karl. He's either making a fool of the new boy or trying to make one of me.'

Beattie laughed when Alice showed her the card. 'Who will you take if you go?'

'I'll go myself! I'll barge straight in. I'll go up to the hall porter and give him the card. I'll get my own back on Karl Reinhardt this time, Beattie.' She was going to enjoy turning the tables on Karl for once.

'What will you wear?' Beattie asked.

'The blue ninon. I've got nothing else,' Alice smiled. 'Though I'll look an idiot in the Victoria Hotel in blue ninon.'

'Aren't you afraid?' Beattie asked. 'I mean – going alone? No young girl goes to luncheon with anybody – alone!'

Alice laughed at Beattie's shocked face. Suddenly she'd had enough of rules and regulations and proprieties that only she was expected to follow. Papa ignored them. So would she. 'I shall enjoy it!' she declared. 'I've never been inside the Victoria Hotel.'

'Or any other hotel,' Beattie reminded her. 'Don't forget to go to the market will you?'

'I'll go on the way back. I'll buy a brace of chickens,' Alice said.

Alice prepared for her luncheon appointment with no inkling that she was doing any other then getting ready to give Karl a taste of his own medicine. His last week's practical joke had been a morning delivery to the house of one of the Victoria Hotel's invitation cards, written in Karl's own Gothic-script handwriting, requesting the presence of the entire Davenport family at a state banquet for His Catholic and Apostolic Majesty, Emperor Franz Joseph of Austria. Naturally, today she could not take Karl's clowning about seriously.

At eleven o'clock in the morning, after she had done her work and seen to everyone else, she stood in the kitchen curling her hair with tongs which she was heating over the range.

'The card made me laugh for the first time today,

Polly,' she said. 'It will be funny to see Karl abashed for once. I wonder what he'll do when I arrive?'

'You'll mebbe feel abashed yourself when you walk through them doors,' Polly answered. 'All the toffs will be there.'

Alice answered, 'Karl will be in the foyer. He's in charge of the restaurant from breakfast until afternoon.' She wrapped a cloth around the handles of the curler, picked it up carefully and began to wind another strand of straight blonde hair around the tongs. 'He's maître d'hôtel – in the mornings.' She smiled, anticipating Karl's confusion when the tables were turned upon him. 'He'll never expect me to turn up.'

'No,' said Polly. 'I'll bet he won't!'

'Why did you say it like that, Polly?'

'Suppose—' Polly gave one of her old-fashioned looks, paused then said in a rush, 'Suppose it is him – suppose it's Sir Jack Blackshaw?'

Alice laughed. 'Don't be ridiculous. What on earth would he want with me?'

'You could have asked Maisie that!' Polly's cheeks had gone bright pink.

If she had not looked so embarrassed Alice would have told Polly off for being facetious. As it was she pulled a face and tut-tutted to make Polly laugh. 'Is there anything we want?' Alice asked before she left the kitchen. 'I'll buy two chickens for tomorrow's dinner. Anything else?'

'We'll have to think up something for the pudding,' Polly said. 'Something special. See if there's anything; anything like pineapples or suchlike in the market.'

At noon Alice left the house. It was a glorious day and once she had turned into Lord Street she stopped to read the boards outside the Opera House and Winter Gardens. Maybe Papa would take them all to see *Don Giovanni* at the Opera House if his bride's tastes ran to such pleasures. The woman, she would never think of her as a new Mama, would obviously be far too old, and too like Papa in her preferences, to enjoy the circus or the variety show at the Winter Gardens.

With a little sinking feeling in her heart, Alice admitted to herself that what she most dreaded was a lengthy family gathering in the drawing room whilst they all got to know one another. She would try not to think about it for the moment.

The tree-lined boulevard of Lord Street was at its fashionable best, dappled with sunlight and thronged both sides with people. On the west side of the street the well-dressed shopped, walking along the red-tiled pavements under the glass canopies which fronted and shaded the shops. Over their heads baskets of scarlet geraniums hung from painted cast-iron brackets.

The eastern side was lined with lime, plane and chestnut trees but there, on the opposite side to the one where Alice walked, ornamental gardens fronted the bandstand, the library, town hall and banks. It always seemed to her that everywhere was prosperous bustle in her pretty adopted home town.

She turned left into Neville Street a few minutes before half past twelve, past the Parisian Cafe and Hobbs the Hatter, past the bazaars and ice-cream parlours and, exactly on time, reached the Promenade and the steps of the Victoria Hotel. She stood for a second or two before she ascended them, breathing in the clean, salty air. Today the air was filled with its exciting mixture of scents from sand and sea and the little oyster, shrimp and mussel stalls which lined the underpass that led to the beach.

She had never before been inside the Victoria Hotel, never gone up the six wide steps that led to the great revolving doors of mahogany and glass.

It was busy, thronged in the airy foyer with fashionable women whose dresses alone would have cost more than Alice's yearly clothes allowance. She had never seen so many beautiful women, so many elegant, wealthy men gathered together before. Even at Hetherington, the smartest place she had ever seen, there had been a lot of uniformed soldiers and their wives.

This clientele made her feel, all of a sudden, foolish, badly dressed and insignificant. There was no sign of Karl. But she could not change her mind and leave, for a forbidding commissionaire in his maroon and grey uniform, with a look of condescension on his florid face, was coming towards her.

'Madam?' he asked. 'Is madam looking for someone?'

Alice reminded herself that this was all Karl's doing. She took a deep breath and nervously handed him the invitation card. 'I have a luncheon appointment,' came the true, clear voice.

The commissionaire appeared not to be in upon the joke for the air of disdain had left him. He looked at the card and became obsequious.

'Of course, ma'am,' he said. 'Follow me, please.'

Her instinct all at once was to say 'No', to escape. It was too late. Every eye she thought was upon her as they threaded their way through the groups, across the marble-floored hall and through one of the four sets of glass doors which led into a vast dining room.

They went down the blue carpet of the centre aisle to the far side, by the windows. Most of the tables were taken. The room was lively with chatter, the sound of silver lids being lifted, laughter, the hearty talk of morning-suited men, the hurrying waiters with their laden trays.

She looked straight ahead, following the commissionaire, belief that this was a practical joke fading with every step. Then she thanked God. There was Karl, standing by a table, with a startled look on his face. It was too late to turn and flee and she set her face into an expression of smiling politeness. The commissionaire stood aside.

And Alice felt the blood drain from her face, wished the ground would swallow her up as she found herself looking straight into the face of Frederick Blackshaw.

Frederick rose to his feet. Through a hazy feeling of unreality she heard the commissionaire say, 'Sir Frederick. Your guest.'

Her legs seemed to be giving way. Her knees turned to water, a metallic taste was in her mouth. She was hypnotized. She could not tear her eyes away from the strong jawline, the fiery brown eyes, the black, too-long and too-wavy hair that curled into the nape of Frederick's neck.

Her eyes were enormous in her pale face as she stood before him and put out her hand. 'Sir Frederick Blackshaw?' She was surprised that her voice sounded assured and clear when inside she was in a ferment.

Karl's face was thunderous.

Frederick, darkly handsome in mourning black, took her hand and held it for a moment. 'Please be seated, Alice,' he said. 'It's good of you to come.'

She tried to appear calm whilst he gave his order to Karl. 'Two dry sherries,' he said. 'And bring the menu.'

When Karl had gone she leaned across the big circular table. 'That was Karl,' she said.

'Karl Reinhardt?' Frederick asked. 'The Karl who came to Hetherington as my guest? I didn't know he was a waiter.'

'Karl won't accept money or support from his family,' Alice explained, wondering why on earth they were talking about Karl. 'He quarrelled with his father, you see,' she ended lamely.

Frederick smiled at her. 'It's not important.' His voice was deep and warm and the eyes fixed on hers seemed to be showing something quite the opposite of his formal manner.

'Why are you here?' She was nervous but as she spoke she went through the everyday motions of normal behaviour, placing her gloves at the side of her place, giving a shaky smile. 'Why have you come here?' she said. 'And why – Sir Frederick?'

He looked puzzled but still his eyes were fond upon her face. 'You don't know?'

The wine waiter had brought their sherries and he leaned back whilst the glass was placed before him.

'No. Why?' she repeated when the man had gone.

He did not take his eyes away from hers as he spoke. 'My father was found dead on the morning you left Hetherington. I inherited the title as well as the estate. I'm Sir Frederick Blackshaw.'

# Chapter Seventeen

'There should have been a paragraph in the Lancashire papers,' Frederick said. 'My father's death rated two columns in the *Chester Chronicle*.'

'We've cancelled the newspapers,' Alice said in an apologetic voice. Her eyes were wide. 'What happened?'

She was more beautiful than she had been on the night of the ball – the night of his father's death. Frederick's heart contracted with love for her. He wanted to lean across and touch her hand but two waiters were here at the table and Karl Reinhardt, his face a study in suppressed anger, was standing behind her chair.

He couldn't tell her about his father's death until they had gone. And he couldn't correct a lifetime's habit for he still referred to Sir Jack Blackshaw as Father – and would continue to do so to protect his mother's honour and the reputation of the family whose good name he was determined to restore.

He kept stealing glances at Alice as she bent her head over the menu. Twice she looked up at him with entreating eyes but her voice was clear and normal. 'I'll have the brown Windsor soup, please,' she said. 'And then, if I may, the lemon sole.'

'I'll have the same,' he said to the waiter at his side. 'And a bottle of Chablis.'

As soon as the waiters and Karl Reinhardt had moved away she leaned forward and repeated her question. 'What happened?'

He looked at her lovely face, wanting to feast his eyes upon her, and found he could not ask her to imagine the events of the morning after they had been in one another's arms.

He said, bleakly, 'He was found in his study. Shot through the heart.'

How could he describe the awful scene that his father's valet had discovered? Sir Jack Blackshaw had been lying face down in a pool of blood that was sticky-brown about the Persian carpet. The valet had called him and he, obeying his first instincts, had lifted the body and carried it to the bedroom, though as soon as he touched him he'd known his father was beyond help.

He couldn't tell Alice all this.

'I don't understand,' she said. 'Was it suicide?'

'I don't think so. But there is no reason for anyone to want to kill him.' Then, 'Most people merely disliked him. But all who knew him know that he'd never take his own life.'

The waiters were back, ladling the glutinous soup on to their plates and, as they served them, Frederick's mind went back to the later events of that morning.

Sir Jack Blackshaw's gun lay on the study carpet. There was no sign of foul play, the police had said, but a new system was in operation at Scotland Yard, of identifying criminals from fingerprints. They lifted the gun carefully and wrapped it in a cloth, to send it to London.

He watched the waiters finish serving the soup, then he nodded to them briskly, a signal for them to leave.

'So you are Sir Frederick Blackshaw?' Alice was taking her soup slowly as if she were not tasting it but willing it to grow less in the deep, blue-banded plate.

'The reason I asked you here—' He spoke in a dry, flat way and yet found himself looking at her in exactly the same way he had done in the garden, with eyes on fire for her.

'Why?' she asked quickly.

He made his face impassive. 'I know you regret what so nearly happened between us Alice,' he said quietly.

'I . . . I don't . . .' She was blushing.

He watched her face as she looked down at the plate she had pushed away from her. He put his spoon down too. He didn't want it. This was going to be the hardest, the cruellest thing he had ever done. Every instinct in him was telling him to take her in his arms, to ask her forgiveness for his clumsy behaviour, to beg her to return his love. But he had to deny it. She looked up and her lovely face was trusting as he said, 'You must be ashamed. As I am. I'm sorry it happened.'

Once again the waiters came back to the table, taking away their soup plates, bringing warmed ones and serving fish and sauces and spoonfuls of petits pois and creamy potato.

And whilst the waiters worked and she, with natural grace, smiled at them and pretended pleasure in the food they were serving, Frederick kept the conversation going with a succession of trite little banalities. The meaningless small talk lessened the tension between them, made them appear unremarkable to other diners and gave him the chance to reflect again on the aftermath of his father's death.

The guests had all gone after being interviewed by the police; all except Charles who had nowhere to go and who had taken Mother's treatment under his care.

On the Sunday after the Cathedral service he had gone to his father's study and there had discovered the truth about the financial mess that had been the Blackshaw fortune.

He discovered with a shock that, far from having untold wealth, his father's was an empire of failed business deals and loans at exorbitant rates of interest. It had all been a show, a sham. Even his army commission was supported by borrowed money and this was one of the worst humiliations. When he had gone into the army not only had a candidate officer to pass the stiff examination at Sandhurst and be recommended by senior men, he also had to have a guaranteed independent income, to play polo, hunt and keep up his social obligations to the regiment. All this had been based on mortgaged property and he wondered if he could support it any longer.

He had been at the desk for three hours, realizing with the evidence of every ledger, every balance sheet, that the Blackshaws were almost ruined. He had been facing this fact when Therese came to him to tell him of her marriage plans.

'I'll postpone the wedding for a few weeks,' she said. 'But Charles won't wait until all this – all this dreadful investigation is over.'

'Of course he can't,' Frederick said. 'Neither should you wait. You must marry at once. It can be arranged in a few days' time, by special licence.'

'I've something else to tell you, Freddie.' She sat down on the leather chair at the far side of the desk. The death of her uncle had given her barely a moment's concern. She was radiant with happiness. Her dark hair was shining with health and life. Her blue-green eyes which missed nothing, not a look, not a blink, not a moth or speck of dust, were shining in an expression of challenge.

'What is it?'

'I have a legal document granting me a sum of two thousand pounds per annum from the estate.'

The pleasure with which he had greeted her news left him. 'There's no money. Only debt.' He looked straight into her eyes. 'You can't have two thousand pounds.'

'Your father said we should be provided for,' Therese said.

Frederick interrupted, 'You are entitled to your own father's estate – the Macclesfield house and the cottage rents. My father left that intact. I'll give you five hundred a year. That's all.' He said again, 'There's no more to be had. And I'm under suspicion.'

'Suspicion? Who suspects you?'

'The police are not convinced that he killed himself.' His face was set into hard lines. 'Apparently a servant, your personal maid in fact, told the inspector that she had heard us fighting. She heard me threaten to kill him.'

'Maisie said this?' Therese had paled and gripped the edge of the desk. 'Maisie has gone. She's done this for spite.'

'I threatened. But I didn't do it. I couldn't even bring myself to do him a proper injury when I had the chance.'

'The police won't take her word against yours. Why should you want to kill him? What do they think?'

Frederick had not wanted to tell her all. He thought for a moment but finally he knew that it had to be said.

'Apparently, servant gossip has it that I am the father of your son. They believe that you and I planned to marry but my father refused consent. They said that as soon as I returned from the war I would marry you. My father stood in our way.'

She had gone paler. 'Who – who are they? Who are these servants who gossip?'

'Does it matter who says it?' Frederick demanded. 'It's one of the stories – one of the fables they invent and then pass on as fact.'

Therese said, 'They passed that on as fact to the police? And you ask if it matters? The servants here told the police all that nonsense?'

'Gossip is nasty,' he answered. He indicated the papers. 'But there's no money. Nothing but debt and disgrace.' He got up, looked through the window then turned and slammed his hand hard down on the table top. 'Financial ruin is enough without being under suspicion of murder! Without these damned police investigations. I can hardly believe I'm a suspect.'

'I'll make no claim,' Therese said. 'We'll manage, Charles and I. We'll have my Macclesfield property and Charles's earnings.'

'You'll have your five hundred a year,' he said to her,

determined not to let the name of Blackshaw sink any lower by sending her into marriage without a settlement.

He looked up at that moment, still thinking about his worries and for a second he was startled, seeing Alice across the table from him.

He was here in Southport with Alice, not with Therese at Hetherington.

Alice broke in upon his thoughts. 'Aunt Harriet has gone into hospital,' she was saying. 'We've been running things ourselves. It will be a relief when Papa comes back . . .'

He must be giving Alice the impression that she was talking to an imbecile. He smiled and poured a glass of wine for her, watched her lift and sip it and, as he drank his and made reply to little confidences, he found that his mind was back again, in the study, with Therese on the day he had talked with her.

Before she had left him, Therese had shown one of her sudden changes of mood. 'There's one more thing—'

'What?'

She spoke the word slowly. 'Alice.'

He did not let her see that he was disconcerted. He knew all about Therese's antipathy to women. 'What about Alice?'

'You cannot have her.'

He was startled by her outburst. 'What makes you think that I—'

But she came back at him swift and decisively. 'I know, Freddie. You've done nothing but talk about her since you met her. It's out of the question. You shall not have her.'

Had it really been so obvious? 'Why not?' he said.

'It would be dreadful. Incestuous almost, if you were to marry my daughter.'

At last he laughed. 'Alice is not your daughter!'

'She will be. She is my future husband's daughter. And I am afraid that Charles would call off our marriage if he thought . . .'

298

The laughter died on his lips. He stared in astonishment. 'Charles would never do that.'

But he knew Therese in this mood. Nobody would convince her that she was wrong. Her eyes were flashing. 'Charles will have heard the servants' talk. Even amongst the men in your own regiment it was suspected that you and I—' She stopped here, squared her shoulders and said with an air of finality, 'I've told Charles that I can't reveal the name of Peter's father . . .'

He interrupted her sharply. 'Charles doesn't think that you and I are lovers – or ever were, does he?'

'No. But Charles respects my decision not to tell. He knows I'm protecting Peter.' Here she had softened her voice. 'But Freddie, you must realize that no scandal can ever be attached to Charles's name. He'd never forgive us if his daughter were implicated in what has happened.'

'So I am to keep away from you, Charles and Alice once you are married. Is that what you want?'

A little smile came to the corners of Therese's mouth. 'No. Just at first. Give us six months until all is forgotten.'

He didn't reply and she went on, eagerly, 'Freddie, believe me, you can do nothing. Not yet. Alice is only seventeen. You can't think of marriage until you've put your financial affairs in order!' She gave him a sorrowing look. 'And until you are no longer under suspicion.'

She was exaggerating but there was truth in what she said. 'And Alice?' he cut in. 'Alice must never suspect that it is you who stands in our way. Is that it?'

'Freddie, darling! I know! I just know she'd agree to wait until this investigation business is over before taking your – your pursuit of her seriously. Say nothing for at least six months. Promise me that you won't speak to her yet! Please, Freddie!'

Her eyes were filling with tears. 'Heaven knows what a girl of that age might do if she thought you were encouraging her.'

He went quiet for a moment, then, 'I'll ask Alice to wait,' he said.

But Therese would not accept even that. 'Alice is like her mother! Charles said his first wife was reckless. She ran away to him the moment she set eyes on Charles. Think, Freddie! Think of Alice's reputation. Charles thinks she's a sensible, responsible girl. What would he think if she did anything rash as a result of a lark? A schoolgirl crush?'

He asked himself if Therese was right and he saw that, at only seventeen, Alice was too young. 'I won't wait for ever,' he said. 'I can't deal with all this . . .' He looked down at the paper-strewn desk. 'I feel like chucking it all in . . . going to India . . . if I can't . . .' His fingers drummed on the desk top. 'Karl Reinhardt wants her.'

Her face was pink with haughty indignation. 'Do you think that Charles would allow her to marry a foreigner?' she asked. 'What has Karl Reinhardt to offer?'

Her words struck a note of truth. If Karl Reinhardt were not a serious rival perhaps he should wait until he was no longer under suspicion. God knows he had nothing to offer. And he could not expect a girl as young and innocent as Alice to share the cloud of debt and disgrace he was under.

But he did not want to promise too much to this new, demanding Therese. 'And you, Therese?' he asked, 'Would you like to see Alice married to me?'

She had given an embarrassed laugh. Therese would hate it if Alice were ever set above her as the next Lady Blackshaw. But he believed now that for all their sakes, especially Alice's, he must for the moment control his passion for her. He must not speak of love until their lives had returned to normal and until Alice was old enough to make her own decisions. But he would have to keep away from Alice for the time being. Being near to her would be asking too much of his promise to exert self-control.

And it was proving easier to make promises to oneself in privacy and solitude, than it was to keep them. It was a different thing entirely when the girl you loved was sitting opposite to you, dressed to the nines in sky-blue silk, looking at you with wide, clear eyes as Alice herself was doing across the dining table.

'My sister Beatrice wants to train for a nurse,' she was saying, since their conversation had taken a turn into the shallow waters of talk of sisterly affection. 'But it is not for me, I'm afraid.'

'No. I'm sure you are right.' Frederick spoke quickly and a little impatiently, tired of the meaningless chatter they had been exchanging whilst waiters hovered. He waved away the waiter who was standing at the table.

She had sensed his mood, for her face became serious when he leaned across and said in a more urgent voice, 'It seems suspicion has fallen on me. I've been questioned by the police.'

She put down her knife and fork and stared at him. And again a wine waiter was at the table, filling his glass, pouring for them both. She was not able to say anything until he had left them then, 'Why should anyone suspect you?'

'A servant – Therese's maid – overheard an argument that developed between my father and me.' He felt his mouth tighten. 'The girl went to the police. The police want to know my movements on the night of the ball.'

Alice looked around and when she spoke her voice was a whisper. 'You were with me until . . .'

He too put down his knife and fork and, speaking in an undertone, said, 'I had to tell the police about our being in the garden together. They questioned everyone, wanting to know where everyone was. The body was found in the morning but it was evident to the police surgeon that he died soon after supper.'

She pushed her plate away but he continued, 'If the police come to Southport and question you, you must tell them the truth.'

She had gone white. Her eyes were large and yet they held his steadily. 'Of course I will,' she said. 'Do you expect them to come?'

'I don't know. I hope not.'

'Are you being watched?' she asked.

He leaned across the table again. 'No. Nothing like that. Eventually, I think they will believe that my father took his own life. They'll say that his mind was disturbed by my mother's illness.'

Alice took a gulp of the wine. 'Then why did you—?'

He spoke quickly, trying to get everything said before the waiters returned. 'The girl who went to the police must have had her reasons. She has left the estate, so I hope her word will be discounted.'

The wine seemed to be giving her courage. Alice took another drink before asking again, 'I meant, why did you ask me to have luncheon with you, in the Victoria Hotel, of all places?'

He stared for a moment or two, thinking out his answer. Then he said, 'I didn't want you upset by a visit from the police which might never come. Or to think you had to tell lies – about an episode that you thought of as no more than a lark.'

'I see.'

'And if you had come with your aunt – I didn't know her name by the way – I was hoping we might have a few minutes alone.'

Whilst their uneaten food was being taken away, Alice gazed into the distance beyond the windows he had his back to. It was as if a curtain had come down between them. The only memory he must have of their love must seem like a lapse of good manners to him. 'An episode no more than a lark,' he had said.

'If we had not been together,' she said quietly, 'you wouldn't be under suspicion.'

'Don't think about that,' he said. 'I have put it from my mind.'

She stared at him, across the table, across the silence that had followed his words. His words and gestures still seemed to her to be at odds with his facial expression.

But he did not speak again and she turned her head as she heard the approach of a waiter.

'Would ma'am like to see the menu?'

Karl was standing to her right, holding out the leather-backed binder. He put a hand over hers and pressed it as he handed the thing to her. Karl's attention did not help. It made her annoyed and she pulled her hand away sharply and placed it on her lap.

'Nothing else, thank you.' She almost snapped at him, so upset was she.

Frederick too wanted nothing more. When Karl had gone he poured the last of the wine from their bottle. And again she saw the look of love on his face and could believe that all was not lost. It was all confusion. Frederick's expression was telling her one thing, his words something entirely the opposite.

She took another sip of the wine that was making her a little light-headed, to steel her nerve for the apology that she owed to him. Even if he never spoke to her again, if all feeling for her was truly gone, she would not want him to think her cold and heartless.

She raised her eyes to his over the top of the crystal goblet. 'I'm sorry,' she said.

It was not what he had expected to hear for his eyebrows lifted in questioning. 'Sorry?'

'I'm sorry about your mother.'

He looked puzzled. 'Why?' he asked.

She'd hoped he would accept her apology without question, yet he seemed not to have understood. 'I'm sorry she's dead,' she explained.

His eyebrows flew up in surprise. 'My mother's not dead.'

'Not—'

She imagined she saw annoyance in him as he said, 'My mother has started to improve. We're beginning to think the last diagnosis was wrong and your father has changed her treatment. What made you think she was dead?'

Her voice did not come for a moment then, 'When we left Hetherington,' she said, 'the curtains at the Dower House were drawn.'

'What time was that?' He drank the last of his wine in a quick draught.

'Half past eight.'

'Why shouldn't you expect curtains to be drawn at half past eight?'

He seemed distant, he seemed to be years, aeons older than herself. She felt awful. 'In Lancashire,' she said, 'when someone dies . . . they draw the curtains.'

He was puzzled, unsmiling. 'Who does?'

Alice felt sickness rise in her throat. She wished herself gone from here. She was self-conscious, growing red with embarrassment as she said, 'Everyone in the street. They all pull their curtains.'

'Whatever for?' He was smiling a little. Perhaps he was humouring her.

'I don't know,' she said miserably. She did know. It was something to do with spirits of the dead but she was not going to say that now.

He seemed remote again. He too must wish himself gone. He had put down his empty glass and pushed back his chair. 'What a strange – what a very odd thing to do. It's a Lancashire street custom you say?'

'It must be. If you've never heard of it. I thought it was universal. I didn't know.' She put down her glass and picked up her gloves. She would try to get out of here without letting Frederick or anyone see that she was on the brink of breaking down in tears.

She stood and he too got to his feet, letting the waiter signal to the commissionaire. Frederick nodded to the man who went ahead of them, through the restaurant, towards the foyer.

When they were there in the now empty foyer, he seemed to want to tell her something. He took her hands in his own and looked long and quietly into her face.

'Wait for me.' He spoke the words earnestly; again it

appeared that he was trying to say something more than the simple words conveyed. 'Will you wait, Alice?'

She was bewildered. Was she being fanciful? Was she trying to read the unspoken behind his words? She held on to his hands, not knowing what to say, what he might want her to say.

She said nothing and after a moment or two he went to the desk to pay his bill and she stood rooted to the spot, aware of the coolness out here where the door, revolving, let the salty-clean air come wafting around with every turn. Then he was at her side again asking, 'Shall I call a cab for you?'

'No.' She looked into his face as she spoke. 'I'm going to the market. What time is your train?'

'I have twenty minutes. I'll walk to the station,' he said. He ushered her out on to the steps of the hotel.

Alice drew deeply of the fresh, clean air. She could not let him go like this. There were things she wanted to know. 'Why did you ask me here?' she said, surprised that her voice was clear and normal, all trace of nerves had gone. 'You could have told me all this at the house.'

'If I'd gone to your house you'd have had to explain something you'd rather forget. You'd have to explain to your father and Therese.'

'Therese? What has she to do with it?'

'Now that Therese is married.'

'You have married Therese?'

'Me? Of course not.' He was looking at her as if she were an idiot. Then he paused for a few moments before saying in an astonished voice, 'You don't know?'

She could not speak. Her eyes were wide with alarm.

'Your father and Therese were married last week.'

She stared at him, unable to believe her ears. She said, 'Therese? And Papa?'

'Yes. Of course.' He had simply stated a fact and suddenly was impatient to be gone for he placed his hands on her shoulders, touched her cheek with his own in a gentle gesture of farewell. 'So I expect we're in some way related to one another. Therese will no doubt explain it all to you.'

Then he looked hard and long at her and he was not impersonal any longer. He said in a quiet voice, 'Alice? When all this is over . . .' And she thought, in that dreadful moment that was filled with shock and hope, that he was going to say what she longed to hear.

But he stopped there and it seemed as if he were holding himself back, checking himself against saying something he might regret, so that her heart sank like a stone when after a moment he held her at arms' length and said sadly, 'Goodbye, Alice.'

She watched him walking away from her and, within seconds, disappear into the crowd and she was left, shocked and shaking with either hurt or anger; she could no longer tell.

She felt the touch of Karl's hand upon her arm, drawing her back into the hotel foyer. 'I take you to my room,' he said firmly. 'After, we go to your home together.' He led her towards the new electric lift and numbly she watched him clash the lattice iron doors. Her head was faint with disbelief as they were carried to the top floor of the hotel. Then Karl led her to his little room, closed the door behind them and took her hands in his. 'You are in love with this man,' he said calmly.

She did not answer and he said, 'I see it for myself. I see your face when you talk with him.'

'Do my secrets show in my face? Is it really so obvious?'

'To me,' he answered. 'But I don't play poker every night – and not know what a look means.'

'Oh, Karl! What can I do?' It was as if floodgates had opened. Tears ran down her face as he kissed her with great tenderness. And it felt as if she were returning to a safe place, feeling his arms holding her, his rather prim mouth warm against hers.

He released her. 'I change my clothes,' he said. 'You tell me what he said. Then we go to your house.'

And she found herself, sitting by the window high

above the Promenade, tearfully pouring her heart out to Karl whilst he took off his suit of tails, hung it carefully and then, standing there in his long cotton combinations without a shred of self-consciousness, just as one of her brothers might have done, he washed his hands and face.

He dressed himself in a fresh white shirt and starched collar whilst she cried. He put on his immaculate, foreign-looking clothes whilst she told him he'd been right about Sir Jack Blackshaw's death. And he frowned thoughtfully and washed his hands again whilst she told him that the police were investigating, questioning everyone who had been at the celebrations.

She did not tell him that she and Frederick had been together in the garden. She didn't tell him that her memory of Frederick's love was an enchanted one; that even if Frederick saw it as no more than a lark, she held it dear. And last she told him about Papa; about Papa's new practice in Macclesfield and about the woman he had married.

Karl had finished dressing by the time she was through with her tale of woe and her tears had subsided. He stood above her, looking into her face with fierce protectiveness. 'You can never be happy in house with this woman,' he said.

'I think Papa expects us to be loving towards her,' she answered him. 'But I know that she hates me.'

'Therese will make slaves of you all,' Karl pronounced seriously. 'She try to make my mother her servant on the journey from Vienna.' He smiled as if remembering something amusing before saying, 'She did not know that nobody – not nobody – can – what is word?' He frowned, then in triumph said, 'Nobody can compel my mother!'

'I didn't know that you had met Therese in Vienna,' Alice said wearily. 'Was she married to her first husband then?'

Karl looked deep into her eyes as he replied slowly and emphatically. 'No. She was never married. It is big lie that she was married. She had baby after she come back from Vienna. Some man at Hetherington made her baby.'

'Who?' Alice asked softly. 'Who was it do you think?'

Karl's lips were pressed tightly together, reminding Alice of a child in his determination not to speak. But his eyes were alight and full of hope when at last he spoke.

'I ask again,' he said. 'I want you shall marry me.'

A great feeling of weariness came to her. Her shoulders sagged as she glanced down at her hands where they lay, loose in her lap. She did not want to hurt Karl. He was always dependable and attentive. Her feelings for him were warm and affectionate. They were nothing like those of a girl for the man she loves.

'It is very sweet of you, Karl,' she whispered. Then she got to her feet and taking his hands in her own she said very simply, 'But you know that I love Freddie Blackshaw.'

'You will forget him. I shall make you so happy that you will love me.' He was almost in tears as he pleaded with her. 'You shall become famous actress. There is school in Vienna for actresses. I asked my mother. She tell me so. You shall become actress like Sarah Berhardt. You shall be anything you want to be. Marry me. Only marry me! Please!'

She could not bear this. The sight of poor Karl, poor proud Karl, humbling himself before her was more than she could stand. Her own tears were coming again. She took him by the arm and shook him. 'Karl! Karl!' she cried. 'Please don't!'

He stopped. His face was white as if shocked by his own outburst. 'You like me?'

'You know that I like you. Very much. But soon I shall leave Southport. And you will forget me.'

'Never!'

He spoke with such vehemence that Alice was startled out of her tearful state. She could not stay here. Someone might hear them. All at once she became cool and practical. She picked up her handbag and began to pull on her gloves.

'I'll go,' she said. 'I have to go to the market. Don't come round to the house this evening. I'll have no time to talk.'

'Why not?'

'I must spend the evening plucking chickens and preparing a meal for Papa and – I can hardly bear to say her name – Therese.'

He too had quietened. The familiar look of arrogant authority had returned to his face. 'That is all right,' he said. 'I bring special chocolate to house. Make dessert for you.'

Alice could not refuse him. He was looking into her face with bold foreign eyes as he said, 'I want my wife shall be able to cook.'

'Karl!' Alice felt some of her fighting spirit return. 'It is manners to wait until you are asked!' Then realizing what she had said she began to laugh hysterically at her own remark.

Karl had seen the joke. He snapped his heels together, bent his head over her hands and looked into her face as he said with a smile, 'Always, the man ask. In Bohemia it is the custom.'

# Chapter Eighteen

Afterwards Alice would remember the arrival of Papa and Therese with feelings of anger and despair. As soon as she saw Therese, clinging proudly to Papa's arm, Alice had wanted to give in to the first wild instinct for flight. She had wanted to get away – to give in to the irresponsible side of her nature, that which was Mama's nature in her – and take the next train to Manchester and to beg the Manchester Repertory Company to take her on.

Papa had taken her aside soon after they arrived at Duke Street. He told her that she was needed at their new home in Macclesfield. He wanted her by his side and he said, 'Baby Arthur needs you, Alice. Arthur will need you until he becomes used to his new Mama.'

Then the responsible, dutiful side of herself surfaced and she knew that she could not break her word, could not leave baby Arthur, would not abandon her sister and brothers into the care of Therese. If she had, she would never have been able to live with herself.

But five months later, in Macclesfield, she knew that Karl had been right. She could not live any longer under the same roof as Therese.

Five months it had been since they came to Macclesfield and only George appeared to have settled, going daily to the Macclesfield Technical School to study textile mechanics. Papa had accepted that his eldest son would not follow in his footsteps but still he had high expectations of George.

But this new, married-to-Therese, family-doctor Papa was very different from the officer who had gone to South Africa. The soldier Papa was no more. The fond Papa who enjoyed family evenings of recitations and song around the piano was no more.

All that had gone. Therese did not care for what she called 'precocious behaviour in children'. Therese would not allow what she called 'showing off'. Therese did not care for tricks, recitations and acting. Therese said they were all too old for such silliness.

Family evenings were centred around Therese. Therese wanted Papa to pay court to her, to indulge her and behave like a man half his age. Alice had to bite her tongue every time Therese spoke.

On the late afternoon of a clear winter's day Alice and Karl were walking along a moorland road in the Pennine hills high above the town, returning from the ten-mile Sunday walk that was a feature of every weekend in Karl's family. The rest of Karl's family had gone ahead, making for Beaufort Lodge, their home in the lower slopes of the hills.

Alice reminded herself that all but Karl were hoping to be naturalized British subjects and were known as the Rinehart family. She could see them through the trees in the distance, a mile below where she and Karl had stopped; three pairs, the mother and father in front of the tall figures of Irmgard and Heinz, little Renate and Anna following.

Karl had left Southport and returned to live with his family at the same time as the Davenports came to Macclesfield. And Karl was the only person whom Therese allowed to call at their new home freely. He made good use of this open invitation, coming to see the Davenports at least twice a week; telephoning on one pretext or another on the evenings he did not come. For both Karl's family and their own were connected to the telephone system.

This was the third weekend that Alice had been invited

to Karl's home. On the first occasion it was as Irmgard's friend she had come. On the second visit Frau Reinhardt herself had sent the letter of invitation to her, through Papa. This time the letter had been addressed to herself.

Alice had been looking forward to this visit for the last two weeks. She'd hoped to be able to spend a few hours walking alone. The hills drew her, as they did Papa whose pleasure was to come here when there was no morning surgery, to walk for hours in splendid solitude.

Behind them the road ran upward, snaking its way across the moors to Buxton. Ahead were spectacular views at every bend: peaceful farms, a cluster of pretty cottages, a glimpse of a kinder way of life away from the battleground Therese had made of their home in Macclesfield.

They stood, she and Karl, about six miles from the market town's centre. Macclesfield could be seen clearly from here. Alice placed her elbows on the drystone wall to take a look at the vista below. Peewits were calling plaintively, breaking the silence of the wild moorland at their backs, as Karl came to lean on the wall beside her.

'There's Lancashire,' Alice said, looking down over the trees at a patchwork of greens and browns and yellowing fields with their miles of rambling, grey-stone walls, towards the distant city of Manchester. 'We're standing in Cheshire and behind us is Derbyshire.' She indicated left with a wide sweep of her arm, 'That way, Staffordshire.'

Karl caught her wrist as her arm descended, held it fast and pulled her round to face him. 'Which way lies Prague?' he said.

'Karl!' She shook her hand free. 'Stop it! We have to be back at your house soon. Don't let's quarrel.' She stamped her feet to warm them. The lined, calfskin boots and the thick coat of blue wool she was wearing had been purchased with these weekends of walking in mind.

'Shall we catch the others up?' she said, smiling at

Karl's serious expression as she pulled the brim of her soft felt hat down firmly so that it covered her ears.

She had hoped to be alone for a little time so that she could come to a decision about her future. For, though she knew that she could not spend another month under her stepmother's roof, she had to be sure that Beattie and George were all right. Leopold, to everyone's surprise, had insisted on staying at his Liverpool school. He would come to Macclesfield only in the longer holidays he said and Papa had agreed. Leopold's short school holidays would be spent in Southport with Aunt Harriet who was back in Duke Street.

But Karl stood resolute with shoulders back, blocking her path, hands in the pockets of his long tweed coat, the proud head tilted as he looked down at her from under the peak of his checked hat. 'We walk in a minute,' he said. 'It will not be dark for an hour. I ask you again. When will you marry me?'

Alice studied his serious face before she said, 'You know that I'm not going to stay in Macclesfield?'

'My family—' Here he hesitated for a second. She saw his mouth tighten. 'They want you shall marry me. My father, he said you must give answer.'

'Your father said this?'

He looked not one whit abashed, Alice saw. There were great differences between the way of life of Karl's family and her own. Karl's parents were of the old world; courteous, formal and old-fashioned. They had been surprised that she'd been allowed to visit them unaccompanied, since Karl's sisters were chaperoned everywhere. The younger girls curtsied to their mother and, until Alice had asked them not to, to herself. And Karl's father ceremoniously kissed her hand each time she arrived at Beaufort Lodge.

'My father and mother say it is time. They say good girl will give answer.' He was not smiling. 'My father speak to me about it,' he explained. 'He say I must ask today. They want you for daughter, not friend.'

He made no move towards her as he spoke. He was too proud to make her feel responsible for his own unhappiness yet Alice had always suspected that it was because of her that he had left Southport. He worked for his father now, doing work that he hated.

'I didn't think I was misleading you, Karl,' she said. Had she encouraged him? Did the fact that he liked her give him the right to pursue her? Should she have been firm from the start? Ought she to have accepted the invitations to Beaufort Lodge when his parents saw them as a courtship ritual? And last of all, she asked herself, was she sure that she could not love Karl, since she had eagerly accepted the invitations?

She said, 'I thought I'd go to Manchester. Apply again to the Repertory Company.'

He was silent for a moment, then he said, 'You are using it as an escape? When you refused in first place?'

'I . . . I don't think so.' She was not really sure any more. All she knew for certain was that she had to get away from Therese and Papa.

'I don't care if you become actress. If you are my wife.'

Alice put out her hands to him. He came closer and placed his hands upon her shoulders. 'I can't wait for ever,' he said. 'If you refuse me – I shall not ask again – I am going back to my country.'

'But what will you do, if you go back?' she asked him. 'How will you make a living?'

He answered slowly, as if he had been rehearsing what he should say to her, as if he wanted to say the thing that would please her the most, as if he dared not say what was really on his mind. 'I make hotel of my grandmother's house. It is very big. She lives in one part of it only. It will make splendid hotel. But I want you beside me.'

Alice leaned her head against his strong right arm and took a deep breath. 'I don't want you to go back to Prague. I know that you want to marry me but . . .' She hesitated before saying, with great sincerity, 'I don't love you.'

'You will.' His arm tightened around her. 'If you marry me we shall do anything you want to do. You can be actress. I shall have money from my grandmother when I marry. I shall pay for acting school for you.'

He pressed his cold lips against the side of her temple. 'I ask you to think about it. For one week only.'

She wished she could love him. His great fondness for her was plain. But she did not believe that Karl loved her in the way a lover should. He was proud and he had set his heart on having her, but there was a cold, distant quality about Karl that no true lover would have.

But she answered him with a sinking heart for she knew that her friendship with the Reinhardts would have to end if she turned Karl down. 'All right. I'll give you my answer a week from today. Let's walk down the hill before they come searching for us.'

The Beeches, Therese's house in Victoria Road, was half-hidden from the road behind a dense quarter acre of trees. In summer the rambling, early-Victorian house could not be seen either from the road or the gates. Rhododendrons bordered the winding drive that curved around the wood and branched, one wider path going towards the front of the house and a narrow one leading to the back where the stables, staff accommodation, coach and coal houses faced the kitchen window across a cobbled yard.

It was late November, the leaves had fallen and, when Alice was set down at the gates the following morning by the Rineharts' chauffeur, she could see the front of the house through the trees. The cab Papa took to the surgery was waiting outside the front door.

Therese insisted that Papa use a cab every day though Papa could have walked and the twelve pounds a year the cab cost could, if added to the miserable amount Polly and the cook received, have made for a happier kitchen staff.

She went in at the back door and made her way at once

down the corridor into the high, gloomy front hall where she found Papa. Therese was helping him into his coat.

Papa's surgery was in Park Green, an attractive square at the lower end of town, and the practice was partly funded by charity. On Monday mornings he was on duty in the free surgery and this charity work was much resented by Therese who couldn't bear to think that the people who came from far and wide to be treated by Papa were not paying patients.

The Beeches cost more in upkeep than Papa earned but then Papa had always left financial matters to her. Nowadays, of course, all the responsibility was Therese's and when Alice was trying to think fairly she allowed that this was the reason for Therese's fury.

For it infuriated Therese to see Papa giving his services free every Monday morning to the poor who flocked to him from the Dams. The Dams, where Therese owned property, was the slum area of the town. In the Dams, the river Bollin was dammed to give power to the mills. There, when the river was in spate, it overflowed its steep fortified banks or, underground, swilled into the cellars and yards of her neglected cottages.

'There you are,' Therese said briskly as Alice came in. 'You should have been here at eight o'clock.'

'You knew I shouldn't be,' Alice replied quickly. 'I said that Karl's father would send me home in the motor-car.'

She gave Therese a cold glance and went towards Papa. 'Can I speak to you, Papa?' she asked. 'Before you leave?'

Papa made to put down his bag but before he could do so Therese moved quickly to stop him. She threw a look of fury at Alice before presenting her sweet and loving face to Papa. 'You have no time, Charles. The cab is waiting, dear,' she said in the husky voice from which all sign of irritation was absent. 'I can talk to Alice.'

'I'll speak to you this afternoon, Alice.' Papa seemed relieved that Therese had spoken and spared him an interruption of his morning schedule. 'Before my patients arrive.'

Papa had a consulting room here at the house where he saw his wealthy patients between two and four o'clock. He bent to hold and kiss Therese, lingering over the pleasure with closed eyes before he released her and let her open the door for him.

Alice knew again the sick-at-heart feeling it gave her, watching Papa kiss Therese so passionately. And she asked herself why it should upset her. She certainly didn't want to deny Papa's need for affection but it seemed that now he was in love – and no longer an army officer – he had lost all his reserve. He used to take Mama in his arms and kiss her when he came home but he had never made such open displays of his feelings for her.

Then Alice felt ashamed of herself for not delighting in Papa's happiness. Was she simply jealous that Therese had taken over her own responsibilities and her role as right-hand-girl? For Papa let Therese do everything for him. None of his children could have him to themselves for a second but Therese was there, handling him, ushering him hither and thither as if he were incapable of independent action. And it was quite plain that Papa loved it; he basked in her attention.

Therese stood on the step, smart in her morning black and white clothes which still fitted her though they had been told in confidence, for it was not to be announced publicly yet, that a new baby would be born to them in the summer. She was watching Papa depart in the trap. The driver let the reins out and they were gone, trundling over the gravel drive towards the broad Victoria Road.

Then she turned, fiery and quick on to Alice. 'Make yourself useful. You have had a weekend of pleasure with those – the "Parvenu" Reinhardts.'

Alice saw that Therese was in one of her worst moods, insulting Karl's family by implying that they were what she called 'newly rich foreign upstarts'.

317

'Take off your coat,' she said. 'I want you to clean and air the dispensary before Charles returns home.'

The blood rose hot into Alice's face. 'I won't be spoken to like this,' she answered back. 'Do it yourself.'

'Are you defying me?' Therese's eyes were flashing.

Then, as if she were thinking of something other than her spitefulness, she appeared to make a great effort to calm down. Alice saw her draw in a long breath and say, 'I want to make up my lavender salve. Your Papa has started to prescribe it.'

Alice took off her coat and hung it in the hall cupboard with an air of indifference to Therese's rantings, though inside her stomach twisted into knots. She weighed in her mind the prospect of more verbal battle with Therese if she refused against the fact that the dispensary would be a welcome change from her daily work.

Therese had detailed her daily work as 'dining-room responsibilities'. The title covered everything; pastry and bread-making, preserving, ordering and buying food, taking complete charge of the pantry and silver and being answerable to Therese should anything be wrong at meal times.

Alice decided to do the dispensary. If she refused there were many thoroughly nasty jobs she would feel obliged to do. And, though she would never admit it to Therese herself, she actually enjoyed watching the making and mixing of Therese's creams and cures. And Papa had told her that it was her duty to help run the house for the thirty-shilling allowance that was always left at her place at the breakfast table on the first day of the month.

'I'll start on the dispensary when I've been to see the boys in the nursery,' she said. She had no worries about the little ones. Arthur was the only one of Papa's children whom Therese loved. Arthur and Peter were soulmates, the sunniest members of the household and loved by all.

Beattie came into the hall at that moment. 'The boys are being given breakfast by Polly,' she said to Therese. 'Is that all right?'

'Where's Cosgrove?' Therese's eyes were cold and hard.

'She's gone. You remember. She went yesterday in the afternoon.' Beattie spoke in her lovely soothing voice but Alice saw in the expression on her sister's face that she, too, was under strain. Beattie was tied to the house by Therese, weighed down with duties, allowed out once a week to Christian Endeavour meetings.

Therese had put a framed text over the double bed Alice and Beattie shared. 'Bear your Cross with Patience and Loyalty,' it read.

Beattie, pale yet quietly insistent, said to Therese, 'Cosgrove went into the room when you and Papa were – were resting.'

Alice knew instantly what must have happened. It was sickening to herself and to Beattie that, after luncheon, every day at one o'clock Papa would be ushered upstairs by Therese to the bedroom where a fire had been lit all morning, though the downstairs rooms were cold until afternoon. Always, after the meal was over, Therese said, 'I want to massage your back and neck, Charles.' She believed that her creams and potions would prevent 'cheloid' which she said was a fibrous condition at the back of the neck. Papa always laughed when she said it and when she turned to them and said, 'Don't trouble your Papa for an hour. Answer the telephone. Charles must have time to recover from all the thankless work he does for the poor.'

Then, like a lamb, Papa followed her to the bedroom. He went willingly though he used to forbid anyone to have a heated bedroom and had never been a man who needed daytime rests. And from the room would come the sounds of Papa's laughter, of the creaking bed, of Therese's cries of pleasure until blessed silence befell the house for the hour that was sacrosanct.

And Alice and Beattie waited in the sitting room below Papa's bedroom, not speaking above a whisper, watching the clock until the hands approached two and their duty was to take tea upstairs and summon the sleeping pair. Papa and Therese never left this task to the servants.

Yesterday, Alice realized, Cosgrove had either misread the time or mistaken their door for that of the nursery where the boys had their afternoon rest. The nanny would have gone into the room and found Papa and the pregnant Therese lying naked in their bed.

Alice looked from Beattie to Therese. What would Therese do next?

Therese laughed. She laughed the low gurgling laugh that Papa loved to hear. 'Good riddance!' she said. 'I never liked the woman. Beatrice will do very nicely as Nanny.'

Beatrice was already 'in charge of household linen', which in practice meant that Beattie had responsibility for supervising the washing, doing the ironing, mending and making for the house and keeping the babies' clothes in order.

Beattie said, 'Perhaps you should do some of the work yourself. You could give the boys their afternoon walk.'

Alice looked from one to the other swiftly. Therese would be furious that Beattie had spoken back.

'Why?' Therese said. Her eyelids were lower- ing in the way that normally warned of trouble. Then, quickly, she smiled. 'Should I keep a dog and bark myself?'

Beattie went even paler. She bit her lip to prevent herself from crying.

Therese pretended not to see Beattie's white face. She went towards the stairs, smiling as if delighted with the morning so far and saying casually as she placed a tiny hand on the carved newel post, 'Don't waste time, girls. Devil's work means idle hands!'

Alice turned to comfort Beattie. 'Don't upset yourself,' she said quietly. 'She really has gone too far. She treats us as servants—'

Beattie was crying quietly. 'She treats us as dogs,' she said. 'You heard her.'

'Well I'm not going to let her.' Alice pulled Beattie towards herself, put an arm around her and kissed her sister's cheek. 'I'll make things better for you, Beattie. Leave it to me.'

Beattie gave a watery smile, fumbled for a handkerchief in her apron pocket and blew her nose. 'I don't want you to get into bother for my sake, Alice,' she said. 'As soon as I'm old enough I'm going to leave here. I'll train for a nurse.'

When Beattie left the hallway, Alice put on the white coat she had to wear for her task and opened the door to the dark passageway leading to the side wing. The dispensary adjoined Papa's consulting room and she stood for a moment before starting to collect for cleaning the familiar things that reminded her of their home in Chester.

She had always loved to be amongst Papa's things; the tall glasses, lidded jars in plain and coloured glass, clear glass globes, brass weights and the little sealed packets of pills that filled the shelves.

In the middle of the morning, Therese went to the dispensary, wearing her white coat over the morning clothes. She went to the bench and watched Alice for a few minutes. Her green eyes narrowed as she watched the girl, graceful and calm, finishing her work, replacing the last of the jars on the shelves.

'Would you like to help me?' she asked in as simple a tone of voice as she could manage. She must not put Alice on her guard.

Alice, surprised by the friendly overture, smiled and said, 'Shall I make the waxed boxes?'

'Yes.' Therese lit the burner and placed the iron pan of candle wax above it. She opened a drawer and took out the marked card Alice would use as a template, a scalpel and the thick paper for the boxes. 'You know how to do it. I want to mix the salve.'

Therese was nervous as well as angry. She must not

let any of her feelings show. What she had to do today must ever afterwards be seen to have been done for Alice's own good. Charles must never suspect that she was capable of meanness and scheming. Last week, on her visit to Hetherington to see Aunt Augusta, Freddie had let slip the fact that he had spent the critical last hours of his father's life in Alice's arms. He had been explaining, in confidence to her, that there was no need to ask Alice to verify his movements. He believed that the investigation had taken a different turn.

She pretended to be intent upon her task of measuring the distilled essence of lavender into a marked glass phial as she said casually, 'You know that Freddie . . .' She stopped and then said, 'You know that Sir Frederick Blackshaw has been questioned by the police, do you Alice?'

She saw a blush rise in the girl's cheeks.

'Has he?' Alice said.

'He has.' Therese looked at her steadily. 'And he asked me to tell you that it would be best if you were to make a statement. A voluntary statement you understand—'

Alice turned wide grey eyes that were filled with alarm on to her. But she would see nothing, no expression in hers.

'What do you mean?' Alice asked.

'I mean, my dear Alice, that you must write down exactly what happened betwen you and Freddie. Where you were and for how long. Say exactly what took place even if it embarrasses you to do so. If Freddie proposed marriage to you then you must say so. If you accepted him you must say so.'

'Oh, no!' Alice said. 'All we did was—'

'Well?' Therese raised her eyebrows.

'Nothing.'

'Then you will make the declaration? I shall take it to Hetherington next week if you do. You have to do this, you realize?'

'I will.' Alice looked down at the bench before she

spoke again. This time her voice was no more than a whisper. 'Do you think that Freddie is really under suspicion?' she asked. 'I was told that his commanding officer stepped in.'

'What did you hear? And how?'

Alice seemed to be stumbling a little over her reply. 'It was Polly. Polly told me. But she often gets things wrong.'

She appeared to have lost her normal quiet calm. Therese saw a little tremor go through Alice's hands. 'What did Polly tell you?' she asked.

'She said . . . She said that the commanding officer went to the police. Told them about Freddie – about Freddie's being decorated for gallantry.'

Then Therese saw Alice swallow a lump in her throat, saw her anguished look as, in a tone of voice that told almost all she wanted to know, Alice pleaded with her. 'If the officer said Freddie could not behave dishonourably . . .' Alice's eyes were bright with tears. 'Therese! Tell me! Why are they still questioning him?'

'They have no proof. The fingerprints on the gun did not match Freddie's,' Therese answered. Her own voice was cold and unemotional. 'His marks were all over the room of course. Money was stolen. And Sir Jack Blackshaw's diamond ring was taken. The police know that Freddie has not stolen them.'

She saw Alice grow pale. Alice would get no favours, no sympathy from her. 'But Freddie has no acceptable alibi,' she said. 'You are the one who can provide it.'

Alice turned her head aside. She said nothing.

Therese waited for a response but Alice seemed to have taken control of herself and worked on, cutting, folding and dipping the shapes into the melted wax; quickly folding the corner pieces to make the little boxes, pinching and holding the corners with the long tweezers Therese kept for the purpose.

Therese had to know all that had taken place. Freddie had not asked for the declaration. It was she who wanted to know more. Freddie, realizing his mistake as soon as he had spoken, had tried to make his and Alice's rendezvous in the garden seem unimportant. She had not been fooled. She must make Alice see that any hopes she might have of Freddie . . .

'So what will you do?' Therese demanded.

Still the wretched girl would not answer. Anger rose in Therese again. She began noisily and quickly to open drawers, assembling the ingredients for her salve; lanolin, lavender oil, witch hazel, orris root. All Freddie's worries, all her own worries she believed, would be ended if Freddie were to marry money. Freddie would see to it that she didn't suffer the indignities of poverty she and Charles were suffering.

Lately Freddie had been enquiring too often about Alice, asking if she were well, if she appeared happy, saying that soon enough time would have elapsed, the risk of scandal diminished, to make his feelings known. He was going to speak to Charles at Christmas, to ask his permission to court her.

'Do you expect Freddie to propose marriage, Alice?' she asked sharply.

Since Freddie had told her about the time he'd spent with Alice in the garden Therese had done nothing but fret about it. She had barely been able to concentrate on anything. And in three months' time they were to be visited by her friend from the Vienna days. Xanthe Madison and her banker father were coming to London for the season. It was her intention to engineer a meeting between Freddie and the wealthy heiress.

'I don't—' Alice turned to look at Therese. But Therese's eyes were hooded, clever and watchful. Then it appeared that the intemperance of speech Charles was always warning Alice of surfaced. All at once she answered in a breezy, nonchalant manner.

'What should I say? If Freddie proposes to me how do you think I should answer?'

Therese stopped what she was doing. 'You say "No".'

'Supposing I accept?'

There was silence between them. Therese had planned her next move. It was the move she'd hoped not to make. She had hoped to find Alice of a different turn of mind; hoped that Alice saw the tryst with Freddie as no more than an evening's fun. She'd hoped that the visits to Beaufort Lodge would have resulted in Alice's betrothal to Karl.

She had not expected to see, to hear, what she had just seen in Alice. The girl was in love.

Therese would not allow her any hope. She looked over her shoulder, pretending fear that they might be overheard. Then, slowly she said, 'You will have heard the gossip that was put about by the servants at Hetherington?' Alice did not answer and she went on, slowly as before. 'Did you never question it? Did you never suspect that I was not a widow? That my darling Peter was conceived out of wedlock?'

'I heard the talk,' Alice answered, softly and fearfully.

'What did you hear? Servant talk! Who do the servants say was responsible?' With every word Therese felt her voice rising from its low throaty purr until Alice must surely sense the hysteria behind her outward appearance of control.

'I have no idea,' Alice said. 'And I don't want to know.'

'Peter is every inch a Blackshaw.' Therese banged her pretty little hand hard against the bench. 'And if I were not protecting the family's good name . . . The world would know him as one!'

Alice felt a surge of sickness and disgust rise up in her. Did Papa know about this? Could Papa have married Therese and remained a friend of Frederick's if he had known? Was this the reason that there had been no word from Frederick? For all communication between Frederick and the Davenports had ceased since Papa and Therese had married.

And why had Frederick told Therese about their night in the garden? It was as if he had betrayed her. Alice could do nothing but stare into the cold eyes of her stepmother.

'Don't think for a minute that your Papa or I will ever give consent to a marriage between you and Freddie!' Therese flung the words down before, clearly overcome with anger, she turned and stalked out of the dispensary.

Alice heard the sound of Therese's footsteps on the tiled passageway fade into silence before, once more sick at heart, she closed the dispensary door and went to the hall for her coat. She would go to see Papa. This morning. She would not tell him what she knew. She had to speak privately to Papa again.

She left the house a few minutes later, without a word to Beattie or anyone.

Victoria Road where the Beeches stood was a mile long. It curved gently from the walled park and grounds of the lunatic asylum at the far end to the Infirmary and West Park at the other. It was the Infirmary route that Alice took, thinking to go the quickest way, to distance herself from Therese and the sick, ugly thoughts that her stepmother had put into her mind.

She walked along the main street, Chestergate. She went past the now-familiar shops that seemed small and ill-stocked compared with the grand Southport ones she had left behind. The shops themselves were interspersed every few yards with public houses. Alice had never seen a town with so many taverns; the Crown, the Anchor, the George, the Bate Hall, the Macclesfield Arms, the Bull's Head, the Angel, the Feathers and now she was passing the Swan With Two Necks in the middle of Chestergate.

'Hey! You!'

Alice stopped and looked across the road.

It was Maisie, Therese's former maid, dressed in a gaudy red suit and feathered hat. She was hanging on to the arm of a portly old man who looked almost as tipsy as herself.

'Tell yer bloody stepmother, from me . . . !' The girl

was shouting as she went, almost staggering with drink as the man pulled her upright.

'That's enough!' the old man said. 'You don't have to tell the whole world.'

'Stuck-up bitch!' Maisie hurled the insult across the narrow, cobbled street and waved a grubby hand that sported a fine diamond ring in Alice's direction.

Polly had told Alice that Maisie had come to Macclesfield and was a 'kept woman'. She was apparently 'kept', Alice saw, by a fat old man with more money than sense. Alice pretended not to see them though Maisie must know that she had been shocked by the girl's coarse, drunken behaviour and blowsy looks.

At the Market Place she turned right at Parr's Penny Bank and made her way down the steep incline of Mill Street where in her haste she almost slipped on the frosty cobbles as she crossed the road.

The waiting room was packed and she had to stand in a corner. A young woman made room for Alice, snatching up a child whose face was covered in sores. Alice, fighting back her own misery, to her shame pretended not to see them and knew that one of Papa's charity cases, as well as Maisie, would think her stuck up. She did not set herself above anyone. She was at times afraid of Papa's patients.

She tried to take her mind off her own problems which ought to seem as nothing compared with those of the women here. These women, she knew, were forced to live in foul conditions. In the Dams, where so many of them lived, beetles as big as a child's fist, rats and mice infested the houses. And there was row upon row of Therese's houses. She ought to feel shame, ought to wish to alleviate their suffering, as Papa did. Yet, looking at these faces in the waiting room, they did not seem to Alice to be cowed by their circumstances. They could be aggressive, threatening and unfriendly.

She had only once been in the Dams. It was on the day the clerk had fallen ill and Therese had asked Alice to collect the rents. She had been almost dragged inside the cottages, to see and report back on the dampness. They had insulted her. She had listened to stories of hardship from men with beer on their breath, until she had no sympathy left. She had been followed by jeering children and spat upon by a coarse woman who stood, lazing, at the open door of her filthy hovel.

Looking at them, Alice could not help but believe that if life had dealt her a rotten deal such as they had been dealt, she would fight her way upwards, out of it.

At last the waiting room was empty and she went towards the door of Papa's little room.

'Come in.'

Papa looked surprised and pleased when she sat down at his desk. 'What is it, Alice? Couldn't you wait until I came home?'

'No. I must speak to you.'

'Well?'

'It's Therese,' she said baldly. 'I can't live with her any longer.'

Papa's eyes were kindly but he let out a long-drawn sigh, leaned across the desk and touched her hand. 'I knew you were unhappy, my darling. But why?'

'I can't live this way. Do you know that we . . . that Beattie and I . . . are treated like servants.'

Papa looked thoughtful for a few moments before he said, 'You must try to remember, Alice, that your mother—' He stopped here and, seeing the look of protest on her face, smiled and corrected himself. 'That, until she married me, your step-Mama had never needed so much as to tie her own shoelace. She is not accustomed to domestic responsibility. We must allow for it. It will take her some time to—'

'Nonsense!' Alice stood up, her face pink and angry. 'Therese knows exactly what she's doing! She is slamming every door in our faces. She tries to make life so unpleasant for us that we will have to go.'

'Alice! The Beeches is your home.'

There was another silence between them. Then Alice saw little worry lines she had not noticed before draw his brows together. 'Where could you and Beattie go?' he asked.

Alice stared at him. He would never have asked such a question in the old days. Why had she come here? It was clear that Papa was so besotted he could see nobody's point of view but Therese's. 'I could go on the stage. If you will let me—'

Papa sighed. 'No. It's out of the question. Your . . . Therese would not like it.' He began to gather his papers together and place them in a neat pile in front of him before he looked up to where she was standing, struck silent for a moment by Papa's change of heart.

He had told her, at Hetherington, that she would be allowed to act.

The loving and indulgent expression was upon his face, the expression he only nowadays showed to Therese. 'I never dreamed I'd be so fortunate,' he said. 'I have a beautiful, gentle girl for a wife.' He stood up and the loving look was gone. 'And my children, the children who will soon lead their own adult lives, are not content to see their father blessed.'

'Papa! You know we don't begrudge you your happiness. But we have to be able to see a little way ahead for ourselves. We're young and impatient. We want independence. Doors should be opening for us—'

Papa put up his hand in the warning gesture he always used when he wanted to bring a conversation to an end. He never listened. He never had.

'I hoped, Alice, that you would have found a young man to love and marry,' he said. 'How old are you?'

'Eighteen last month, Papa.'

'Your own dear mother was married at your age.'

'But? But you and Mama—' she began to say before she saw Papa's face grow stern again. He did not want to be reminded of Mama.

'Then if you have not found love you should consider

working for your living,' he said in the old officer-voice she used to know so well. 'There are many opportunities for young women these days.'

'But you said, Papa! You said I should.'

'I've changed my mind. Beatrice will be allowed to train as a nurse. You will be placed as a pupil-teacher.'

Then it was as if he had saddened. He came around the side of the desk and put a hand upon her shoulder. And his voice was filled with a kind of weariness. 'I had a visit from George this morning. Here. First thing. He was waiting on the step for me.'

Alice was taken by surprise. 'What did George want?' It had to be something serious or George would never have come to Papa's surgery.

Papa looked as if he had been disillusioned. 'George asked me for help. He has taken advantage of our maid. Polly Gosling is expecting a baby.'

A chill went through her. 'Oh, no,' she whispered. 'What did you say to him?'

Papa still had his hand on her shoulder. He looked into her face with eyes full of sadness. 'What did he think I would say, Alice?' he asked. 'I wonder – did he think I could remove the inconvenience? Compound his dishonour?'

There was a moment when neither of them spoke, then Papa said, 'I told George that he must make an honest woman of her. They are to be married as soon as it can be arranged. It will be a quiet business. No celebration. Nothing like that.'

'But George has no money. No work. No home.'

'George will be found work. I am going directly to speak to Johann, to John Rinehart about it.'

There was nothing to be gained by staying longer. Alice left the surgery in near despair. Her heart was going out to George and Polly who had sunk low in Papa's estimation. How had George thought Papa would arrange for an illegal operation to be performed on Polly? Papa? Papa, who thought a mother and baby the most beautiful

330

sight in the world? Papa was a man of honour and principle. Papa would never countenance anything so despicable.

Then back came the thoughts of Therese's confession this morning. Had Papa believed Therese's story of a young marriage and early widowhood? Would he have married her if he'd suspected that she and Frederick . . . that she and Frederick had had what everyone called intimate relations.

She could not think clearly. She found herself walking the long way home, holding her skirts above her boots as she climbed the Hundred-and-Eight steps from the Waters Green to the Market Place; stopping at the top to gaze at the hills she had walked on yesterday.

She couldn't return to the house yet. She would walk, alone, through the town to the big West Park where she could think without interruption. She would try to find rational answers to the questions that were whirling around in her head.

In the icy cold she went, circling the park, once, twice, around the crown bowling green. She stood for a while in silence, looking at the great cannon that had been brought back from the Crimea. She went towards the bandstand. There were no children swinging. The park was deserted but for herself and some grounds-men.

'What can I do?' she asked herself. And there was no answer. 'Do I still want to be an actress?' And every time the answer to that question was, 'No. I don't want it any longer.'

She looked around the hushed museum, staring without seeing at the stuffed panda, at ivory carved into Chinese pagodas, at specimen cases of bright blue butterflies, at the stuffed tiger with shining eyes that appeared to follow her about the little room. 'Shall I marry Karl?' she asked herself.

Frederick would never come back to her. Why had he told Therese about their lovemaking in the garden? And why had he not come to her for the letter that might prove his innocence? Why did he stay away?

'Should I marry Karl?' she asked herself. Should she marry Karl and go to Bohemia – never come back here? What was there for her if she stayed here?

'Can I bear it if Karl leaves me?' For, once Karl left the country, he would never return.

She walked about the pathways, around the pond, over the ornamental bridge until afternoon came and then faded into a grey misty dusk. She looked at her wrist-watch. It was after four o'clock. Her feet were like ice, the trees were shaking in their topmost branches as a wind began to blow from the east.

But she had come to a decision. The keeper's bell was clanging in the distance as she made her way towards the gates and set her feet in the direction of Commercial Road and the Blackshaw and Rinehart Textile Engineering works where she would find Karl.

One question still persisted, one question coloured all the others.

'Does it matter what I do, where I go, who I marry, when I shall always carry in my heart this agonizing, unrequited love for Frederick Blackshaw?'

# Chapter Nineteen

Charles and John Rinehart had made all the church arrangements with great speed and with enormous difficulty. Special licenses and the bishop's dispensation had to be obtained since weddings were never celebrated in church during Advent. Only the formalities were being observed and the short service was to be held in the vestry, not at the altar.

But, given the urgency of George and Polly's need and the haste demanded by Karl, everything was going according to plan. The banns had been called over the past three weeks at the parish church of St Michael and All Angels in the town centre and on the Thursday, a week before Christmas at ten o'clock in the morning, the double ceremony was about to be held.

The two fathers had not consulted her about the service though Therese would have enjoyed overseeing the weddings. She would have done it willingly, just as willingly as she had gathered together a beautiful trousseau for Alice.

A large wooden chest stood in the house, containing a dozen of everything from linen sheets down to facecloths, all monogrammed with Alice's new initials. It would be sent on when Alice and Karl had a home. Sewing women had worked from morning until night on Alice's new underwear, nightwear, daywear and the simple wedding dress. And throughout all Therese's hard work the wretched girl had barely spoken a civil word to her.

The morning was sunny and bitterly cold. Outside in

the Market Place all was noise and bustle but they could hear nothing in here in the vestry, nothing but devotional organ music for Charles had engaged the organist who was playing to an empty church. The tune was un-recognizable.

Wearing a high-crowned blue hat and a silver fox coat that came down almost to the ground Therese sat next to the end on the second row of the cold and gloomy little vestry, waiting for the family to arrive. Being so young she could hardly look the part of proud stepmother she thought, but she knew that she cut a good figure.

The Daimler had come to the Beeches and taken her, Aunt Harriet, Leopold and Beatrice to church. It had picked up Heinz who was to give Polly away and had gone back for Charles, Alice and Polly. Polly Gosling, who had contacted her family for permission to marry, had nobody present.

'I'm so glad you came,' Therese whispered to the children's Aunt Harriet. She had been surprised to discover that she actually liked Harriet Walker. She felt completely at ease with her. She added, leaning a little towards Harriet, 'A pity it had to be held in here.'

The vestry was small; a few lines of chairs had been placed in rows before the high wooden cabinet that, with an embroidered cloth and two candelabra, was having to serve as an altar.

Aunt Harriet, towering above her even when seated, whispered back, 'Where's the reception to be held?'

'Beaufort Lodge.' Therese spoke softly and nodded in the direction of the Rinehart family. The Rineharts were giving the cake and champagne reception and were also paying for the honeymoon in Austria for Alice and Karl. The young couple had two train connections to make before catching the night sailing from Hull to Hamburg, for the honeymoon would be spent in Bohemia.

Charles had given fifty pounds each to Alice and George.

Under Austrian conventions, Therese knew, a girl

without a good dowry had little chance of finding a husband so it was extremely generous of the Rineharts to do so much for Alice. Alice was eighteen, for Heavens' sake. Lots of girls of her age and younger were married.

She glanced across the two feet of space separating the Davenports from the Reinhardts, or Rineharts as they were to be called. Ekaterina, as stiff-backed as ever, was wearing a tightly fitted coat of grey cashmere wool which had a deep band of dark brown fur, Therese could not name it, which touched the floor. Hems were worn shorter and ought to reveal the shoe.

The organist was playing a little louder, so that the music could be heard through the open door, 'Behold I Bring You Glad Tidings'. She would never have chosen it had the choice been hers and not Alice's. Alice knew about Polly's condition. Therese would not have termed the news of Polly's pregnancy 'glad tidings'.

The *Gnadige Frau* gave a nod in her direction. Therese inclined her head and smiled. After the service, two hired carriages would take the guests and the wedding parties to Beaufort Lodge. Despite the nervousness which she believed was due to the haste, the occasion, and Charles's anxieties for his children, Therese was looking forward to the reception.

Frau Rinehart had never invited her to their home. Charles often suggested that they ask the Austrians to dine at the Beeches, but she had so far managed to find excuses not to. She simply hated to share Charles's company though she had made up her mind in future, if she liked Beaufort Lodge, to think of the *Gnadige Frau* simply as Mrs Rinehart.

The Rinehart family made an impressive gathering, filling the row across the little divide, whereas their party barely filled half a row. There was Leopold, Beatrice, Harriet and herself on the second row. George, in front of her, sat opposite Karl.

Therese had not issued invitations. Last night Charles had asked why the Blackshaws were not coming. 'Lady

Blackshaw is quite well enough to travel, Therese,' he had said.

'I haven't even told them about the weddings, darling,' she answered him. 'I thought it best to keep the numbers down.'

They had been in their room, warming themselves at the fire before getting into bed. She had begun to explain. 'The Rineharts are holding the reception, remember. It really falls to the parents of the bride and I didn't want to foist a crowd on them. Under the circumstances . . . George and Polly . . . I assumed that Alice wanted no fuss.'

'I hope they don't feel slighted,' he said, 'when we tell them at Christmas.'

'Who?' she asked.

'Lady Blackshaw, Frederick and his sisters, of course.'

She was surprised at his concern. 'I don't think George and Alice mean much to them,' she said.

He bent towards the fire and rubbed his hands together in the glow but he looked at her with hurt eyes. 'Don't you?' he asked. 'I thought that Frederick, in particular, asked after George and Alice a great deal since he met them.'

'Oh, darling. I'm sorry.' She put her arms around his waist and knew the comfort of his love for her as he pulled her close.

'Do you know, Therese, I once harboured a hope—' He looked into her face. 'At Hetherington, Frederick showed such an interest in Alice that I had this silly feeling they might—'

His voice tailed off a little at this point, then he turned to gaze at the flames and lightly kiss the top of her head. 'Oh, it was nonsense, really. All that matters is that she marries the man she loves.' Then he pulled her close again. 'You do believe she is marrying the right man, don't you?' he asked. 'It came as a shock. We'd spoken only hours before Karl came to ask for her hand.'

'What did she talk about when she saw you?' Therese

had a sudden fear that Alice might have told Charles about their confrontation. She wished she hadn't implied that Frederick was Peter's father. There had been no need to demand a written statement. Alice must already have been planning to marry Karl. 'What did she talk about when she saw you?'

'She asked permission to go on the stage,' Charles said.

'And you refused her?'

'Yes.' He was speaking quietly. 'She is so very like Clara. Acting wouldn't make her happy.'

'Then you did right,' she said.

'Do you think Karl is the right man for her?' His eyes were clouded with worry about his daughter. 'There is a remoteness, an arrogance, about him that troubles me though he seems obsessed with Alice. He can't bear to be apart from her for longer than a day. His father told me so.'

'I can't bear to be apart from you for an hour, my darling,' she told him in a soft, pleading voice. 'I am only alive, only sure of you – when we are making love.'

Charles was not listening. 'I couldn't bear it if Alice were unhappily married.'

'Of course Karl Rinehart is the man for her. I knew it the moment I saw them together,' she lied. But she had a tremor of fear even as she spoke, for between Alice and Karl she had seen not a whisper of the sexual desire she had seen explode into life at the moment of Alice and Frederick's first meeting.

And she had broken her promise. She had promised to be a mother to Charles's children and no mother would behave as she had done. Charles believed her to be gentle and good. Charles would despise her if he knew of her duplicity, of the ill-will she bore Alice. Charles was devoted to Alice, who reminded him of his first wife.

'You see,' he was saying, 'I believe that marriages are only happy when the couple share . . .' He looked down at her now, 'The kind of passionate love you and I will always know.'

337

She had begun to cry. Huge hot tears had poured down her face. She had never loved anyone as she loved this husband of hers. He was loving and good and honest. He had every quality she lacked. 'I love you, Charles,' she had wept as he held her in his arms. 'Never stop loving me, will you?'

'My darling,' he had said. 'I hadn't meant to upset you. What did I say?'

But he had carried her to the bed and kissed her gently. And only when he was holding her, loving her, was she sure that he was hers; that there was no woman on earth he preferred to herself; nothing he needed but her, her soul and her body.

Now she returned her attention to the church for Charles would be here in a moment, taking his place beside her.

Then, exactly on time, she heard in the distance the outer oak doors being pulled back. The organist began to play 'The Trumpet Shall Sound' from *The Messiah* and the notes floated around the empty church.

Therese turned her head to watch as the little procession came into the vestry. First came Charles with Alice, who looked too pale in her dress of turquoise foulard. She carried a posy of white carnations and held her Papa's arm tightly. Therese thought that Charles, so tall and fair, looked much too young to be Alice's father. He was very serious.

Karl, handsome in his dark morning suit, came forward to meet her and the three stepped aside as Polly, on Heinz's arm, looking pretty in dusky pink, came to stand beside them.

George, very like his father, but nervous, took his place at Polly's side and the ceremony began with those wonderful words, 'Dearly beloved. We are gathered together here . . .'

It made her want to cry. She and Charles had made do with a registry office wedding. How she would have loved to make her vows in church, 'In the Sight of

God and in the face of this Congregation . . .'

Then, before she could control the welling pain in her throat, Charles was beside her, his eyes bright with love for her and for his children who were solemnly promising in the hushed, stuffy little vestry, 'To love, cherish and obey . . .'

She held tight on to the ivory prayer book as the Solemnisation of Matrimony was said, as those trusting children of Charles's declared so much, so young.

The priest now intoned the final words, 'I pronounce that they be man and wife together.'

The lump was still in her throat when she opened the book at hymn number two hundred and twenty.

The organist had come into the room, to play for them on the upright piano that was used at choir practice. She could only just manage to sing, in a voice that was a shadow of her normal fine contralto, 'Jesus Shall Reign Where'er the Sun'.

What was the thinking behind the choice? Therese asked herself as she read the words in advance of singing them. They were on the second verse.

'People and Realms of Every tongue—' That was evidently it. The hymn was chosen because she was marrying a foreigner.

'Blessings abound where'er He reigns; The prisoner leaps to lose his chains;'

She wondered if there were any significance in the image of leaping and losing of chains.

She slipped her hand into Charles's and felt the pressure of his thumb against hers. It would be all right.


Three days after the wedding they went to Hetherington to celebrate Christmas; Charles and herself, Beatrice and the boys. There would be servants a-plenty at the house Therese assured Beatrice. They would be glad to help with the children and, when the children were settled, Beatrice would be allowed to join the adults for an hour or so every evening.

339

The two train journeys were behind them, they had been collected at the station, their boxes unpacked in their bedroom in the West Tower and at last she and Charles were alone. The servant made good the fire and left the room. They undressed and Therese lay on the counterpane, watching Charles. He stood, hands in the pockets of his dressing-gown, looking over the gardens in the almost-dark bedroom where the scent of burning pine logs was filling the air.

And his deep, beautiful voice was warming her soul. 'This is the room I had when I came back from South Africa,' he said and turned, smiled and held out his arms. 'Come here.'

Therese wrapped the velvet dressing-gown more firmly round her thickened waist and went to him.

The lines at the corners of his blue eyes fanned out as he smiled down at her. 'Happy, my darling?' he asked.

She slid her hands under his gown, holding him, hard and muscular against her own swelling body. 'I'm so afraid of it, Charles,' she answered, her voice husky and muffled as she pressed her face against his chest. 'Frightened it won't last. Sometimes I wake in the night and I'm afraid that it was all a dream. Then I reach out my hands and find you there.'

'You need have no fear that I'll be gone,' he said. 'I shall always be beside you.'

She looked up at him. 'What would you do if you found out that I am not gentle? That I am not good – as you think I am?' she said. 'Would you abandon me?'

'No.' He gave a mock-serious frown of disapproval. 'I'd probably be disillusioned and should become dictatorial and autocratic. Just as my children think I am already.' Then he smiled at her anxious face and kissed her. 'But I love you. I need you too much ever to live without you.'

He folded his arms around her and led her gently to the bed. The fire threw shadows that leaped and sprawled across the high ceiling, light and shade reflecting, dancing about them as he put her down and lay beside her. He looked at her for a long, long time, deep into her eyes as he removed her gown and his own.

So matched were they in desire, so much had they grown towards one another, that a look, a touch was all that was needed before she responded to the man who was everything to her. Charles was her husband, her God . . . she was filling again with love for him.

Afterwards she heard Charles get up and stand beside the bed in the firelight, looking at her. 'Can you be ready? Can you adorn yourself, my dear, in ten minutes?' he asked when she opened her eyes.

'Yes. Oh, darling! There's no hurry.'

'I want to speak to Frederick,' he answered her. 'Do you realize that I've not seen him since we were married?'

'I told you why,' she said hastily. 'He has been trying to sort out his father's affairs. Then there was the month in London—'

He laughed. 'It's all right. You need not make excuses for Frederick.' He leaned across the bed and tugged gently at her hair. 'I shall go down and have five minutes' talk before we all meet for drinks. How's that? Do you give me leave?'

'You make me sound like an ogress.' She smiled and levered herself up into a sitting position. 'Help me with my dress before you go, will you? I'll allow you ten minutes then I'll follow you down.'

He dressed himself quickly and she, languid in her new found serenity, went to the wardrobe and looked into the long glass at her naked body. Pregnancy suited her. The bony edges of her hips and ribs were gone. Not only was her body rounding, filling and slowing but, since Alice had married Karl, all the fears and threats in her daily life had lifted.

She took out her clothes, stepped into her drawers, pulled the chemise over her head and fastened it, then slid her arms into the satin dress of emerald green which had been enlarged to accommodate the bulge that would soon be impossible to disguise.

'Shall we tell them tonight, Charles?' she said as he helped her, fastening her hooks. Charles was practised at fastening hooks now that she had no personal maid. 'Shall I tell Aunt Augusta first about the baby? Or will you simply announce it?'

He kissed the nape of her neck. 'They'll know, goose!' he said. 'One look at your face will tell them. You're more beautiful. Your skin . . . Your hair—'

He planted a kiss on the top of her head as she sat at the dressing-table. In their lovemaking her thick, dark hair had fallen about her shoulders and she began to brush, to lift, to pile it up on top of her head. Her milky-white arms flashed in the firelight.

'Pass my emeralds,' she said, indicating with a swift pass of her hand the square jewel case which lay on the sofa-table in the window. She had not worn jewellery for months.

She watched through the looking glass as Charles went to the table and opened her box, a small leather case that was lined with purple velvet.

Then she felt her heart turn over. To her horror she saw the shocked, questioning look on Charles's face as he withdrew a long envelope, sealed in red wax with her own seal. It was addressed in Alice's round hand-writing to Sir Frederick Blackshaw of Hetherington Hall.

'What's this?' He came to stand beside her, saw her face from which all the colour had drained.

She could not speak.

He had seen, in her eyes and in her very posture, that she was riven with fear. His expression was stern. He said in a voice that to her ears was cold and frightening, 'You must tell me. What possible reason can my daughter have for writing to Frederick?'

Therese felt as if her life blood were draining from her head to the soles of her feet. She could not answer. She could only stare from the letter to the eyes of the man she loved.

Her head was light, white, spinning as he put the letter in the inner pocket of his evening coat and, in a voice in which intimacy had turned to ice, said, 'I will take this letter to Frederick. And demand an explanation.'

He found him in his father's old study, sitting by the fire with a glass of whisky in his hand.

'Come in, Charles.' Frederick stood up as soon as he opened the door. 'Join me in a glass.'

Charles closed the door and went to stand at the fire. Slowly he took the letter from his inner pocket and handed it to the man, the colleague-at-arms with whom he had shared nearly three years of his life. He'd imagined that he knew Frederick. 'Can you tell me why my daughter should have written to you?' he asked.

Frederick looked startled. He held the envelope, turned it over, saw Therese's seal and looked at Charles who instantly saw the loss of colour, saw the tension in the muscles of Frederick's jaw. It was a reaction a patient who had something to hide might show. Therese had revealed the same symptoms.

'Open it,' Charles said firmly. 'I will help myself to a drink whilst you do so.'

'Do you want me to read it now?'

'Yes. It is addressed to you. I want an explanation.'

Frederick took the letter to the desk and placed it on the blotter. He moved the lamp closer and looked up at Charles before he slit the envelope carefully and lifted out two sheets of paper, one of which was closely written in Alice's hand.

Charles took a sip of the spirit which seemed tasteless in his mouth as Frederick read. It took him three minutes and, as Charles watched, he saw Frederick's face grow pale, then saw a look of anger, then, as he read the last page, Charles saw hurt and finally tears in the brown eyes of his friend.

He saw Frederick's shoulders lift, heard the sound of a man in distress, watched him place his arms on the desk before him. Then Frederick dropped his head into his hands and in a voice of despair said, 'Read it, Charles.'

Charles went slowly to the desk and took up the letter. The belief that he had a right to know what his daughter had written was gone. The letter must reveal the duplicity of someone close to him. He stifled the feeling that he was an intruder, the sudden impulse to put down the pages. One sheet bore only a few words. They were:

My Statement.

This is to verify that I, Alice Davenport, was in the garden of Hetherington Hall with Major Frederick Blackshaw on the night of the Victory Ball, from nine thirty until ten forty-five p.m. I am sure of the time because after we had spent the hour together I returned to my bedroom and looked at the clock.

Major Blackshaw went to see his mother at the Dower House. I saw him go.

Alice Davenport

Charles put the page down and looked at Frederick who was still sitting, elbows on the table, head in his hands, staring down at the desk with eyes from which all the warmth had gone.

'Read the letter, Charles,' Frederick said.

Charles read:

Dear, dear Freddie,

It is the eve of my wedding to Karl and, before I put my youth behind me, I have to put everything in my life in order.

Therese told me that to clear you of suspicion I must make a confession, telling all that we had done in the garden on the night of the ball. I could not put all that into words but I hope the statement I have made will be enough.

Therese also told me that she was not married and widowed in Vienna but that Peter is your child. I cannot believe her but I wonder why she wants me to think ill of you.

Also I must apologize for my rudeness in refusing to meet your mother. It was not because she was ill. My reason was one I am sure you would not have liked me for if you had known. Long before I was invited to Hetherington I made a vow to myself, that I would never pay court to anyone. I have not changed my mind about that but I am sorry that I refused to be presented to your mother. I should have liked to meet her.

Most of all I am sorry that I will never see you again.

I know that you regret our loving because you told me so. But if you ever think of me, please think of that night, of the hour we spent together in the garden. Think of the poem. It was the one my mother used to recite when I asked how I should know it, if I fell in love.

I knew. It was my moment of glory. It was midsummer night when I fell in love with you. It was the happiest night of my whole life.

Alice

# Chapter Twenty

**Bohemia, 1903**

The crossing from Hull to Hamburg had been rough;
three days of ceaseless tossing and pitching. They had
spent the first two nights of their honeymoon in their
cabin, prostrated with seasickness which was worse than
any illness Alice had ever experienced. Added to the
homesickness that had increased with every mile they
travelled from Macclesfield, she felt weak and disoriented
when they disembarked, still unsteady on her feet. Then
train connections had to be made and the loading and
unloading of their cases and boxes had to be supervised.

The rough sea crossing had been followed by four train
journeys; Hamburg to Leipzig, Leipzig to Dresden,
Dresden to Prague. Now, five days after their wedding
in Macclesfield, at half past eleven in the morning they
were on the final stretch. Alice was weary, crumpled and
aching from the hard benches of the third-class carriages
and longing for the end of all the travelling.

She had been sitting for the last hour by the window,
staring out at the white world of snow; but now railway
embankments rose up on both sides and all she could see
was the seemingly endless lines of wires that drooped,
snow laden between high poles. Karl was deep in conversation with the couple opposite, a soldier and a
blowsy-looking woman whose appearance reminded
Alice of Maisie, drunk and aggressive in Macclesfield.

A hazy mist seemed to be spreading across her eyes
and her mind. She was glad not to have to pretend
interest in their conversation, for the soldier spoke

German and the woman only Czech. She recognized a few words in German and could tell by their cadences which language was being spoken for the German sounds were strong and guttural and the Czech harsher, more repetitive.

The marriage was five days old and unconsummated. The last two nights had been spent sleeping on separate wooden bunks, in company with strangers, hurtling across the dark German plain.

They hadn't needed to travel this way for Karl's father had been generous, giving them enough for first-class travel via Paris and Vienna in *wagons-lits*. Karl had saved half, telling her that they must go by the cheaper rail and sea route. With Alice's money from Papa they had enough to maintain them for a few months whilst Karl looked for work. He had explained to her that it would be years before he could realize his dreams of making a hotel. It could not happen until his grandmother's house became his. He was going to work and save.

Alice felt as if she had spent weary weeks, not hours, watching and listening as Karl conversed with their various travelling companions, mostly men who enjoyed talking politics or military matters, but the train was slowing and Karl had turned from speaking to the couple opposite to speak to her.

'They are leaving the train at Koniggratz,' he said as he tapped her arm as if to wake her from a sleep.

That was the next stop. Alice looked at the soldier and his girl and gave a weak smile.

'Pavel here,' Karl nodded towards the smiling soldier. 'He is telling me that the government bring in conscription. I shall join the army.' He said it with a careless air that was totally false.

Alice stared at him for a few seconds to see if he were making a joke. Then she wondered if she had perhaps lost her concentration again. Had she mis-heard him? 'What?' she said.

'I tell you I shall join army. I shall be conscripted for two years.'

She was wide awake now. She stared at him. He was not joking. 'Did you know this already?'

'I think I read somewhere,' he said. 'In English papers.'

'You knew.' She was hot with anger now and frustrated with the need not to show it, not to embarrass him before the strangers. How dare he conceal from her something so important?

His voice was short, curt. 'We speak later.' He did not look directly at her but smiled at the soldier and his girl who had risen to their feet and were pulling on coats and gathering their belongings.

The furious feeling inside Alice would not die down. She would not be treated as anything less than an equal partner in marriage. Karl was not going to make decisions that affected them both without consulting her. What did he think would happen to her when he was in the army? He had told her that he would easily find work when he came home to Bohemia. How much did the Austrian army pay to their conscripts?

But now she had to make a show of politeness, had to smile at the couple as the train slowed down for the approach to the station. And all at once it was brought home to her – the fact that it was she who was the foreigner here.

Koniggratz, the sign on the station building said in giant Gothic script. Underneath, in plain lettering that was half the size of the German, Hradec Kralove, the Czech name of the Sudeten town where a decisive battle had been fought at nearby Sadowa. Koniggratz, the cathedral city on the Elbe, had been wrested by Prussia from Austria-Hungary thirty-five years ago.

This dual-monarchy – Emperor Franz Josef ruled both Austria and Hungary – was an empire encompassing many races and languages. Now Alice saw that even the towns in this foreign land had a dual identity. Was it an ominous sign?

When the couple left the train she turned on Karl. 'You knew! You knew all along. All the time you were telling me of your hotel – your grandmother's house we're going to make into an hotel when we've saved the money – all the time you were talking about our future, you knew!'

He evidently did not want to discuss it. Did he think she should not concern herself about what he'd see as men's affairs? 'We cannot make hotel immediately. You know this.' He stood up and began to assemble their belongings.

'What do you imagine I'm going to do whilst you are in the army?'

He did not answer her but began to push his arms into the sleeves of the long overcoat that reached almost to his ankles, making him look tall and more foreign than he had done in England.

Had he known her better he would have expected to come up against her determination. She was angry. 'I said, "What shall I do?" '

'You come with me. Live near army camp. Like soldiers' wives do in my country.' He had told her once about the traditions of the Germanic and Slavonic races who liked to take their womenfolk with them when they fought. Wives and families would find a good vantage-point and watch the battles, cheering on their soldiers.

Alice knew a sudden impulse to strike him across his smug face. She fought it down and, white-faced, said in a cold, controlled voice, 'You're under a mis-apprehension, Karl. I shall do no such thing.'

But he was looking at her as if he were not aware that she meant it. And once again the hazy, dreamlike feeling came over her, as if all this was happening to somebody else, not herself.

'We speak about it later.' Karl reached up to the wooden rack for the grey squirrel coat and beaver hat that were his wedding gift to her. 'It may happen that I have to do my army service in Prague. We can find apartment there.' He held out her coat. 'Nearly there,' he said. 'Next stop – ours!'

They were going to spend their honeymoon in the house that would be Karl's inheritance, his grandmother's house in the Sudeten mountains of Western Silesia.

Karl began to fasten the buckles on her high winter boots then they stood by the window, fastening their outdoor things as the train pulled into the station and stopped. He jumped down ahead of her and held out his hands. She took a deep breath of the icy-cold, fresh mountain air and, used now to lowering herself to the ground from the high iron steps of the trains, she reached for his hand as she went down the last step. Finally she stood on the snow-packed station, wrapped to the ears in fur.

'Here comes welcome party.' Karl took her arm and hurried, almost pulled her, towards a small family group who were approaching them. She stood by as Karl was kissed on both cheeks and embraced by a large bear-like man.

'Uncle Max Bauer,' Karl said to Alice. His Uncle Max had an engineering works outside Prague. Alice was given a bear-hug by the big man.

Karl introduced her to the rest of the family. 'Olga – Max's wife. Sister of my mother.'

A little dark-haired woman dressed in furs, a little younger but very like Ekaterina Reinhardt, held out her hand. Alice was not sure whether to hug, kiss or shake hands and she stood for a few seconds until Olga laughed and put out both her arms to embrace her, chattering in incomprehensible, rapid German.

Two adolescent boys came forward. 'My cousins, Hans and Josef – we call him Seppie,' Karl said.

The tall, dark-haired boys, who were learning English, managed a few formal words of welcome before once again the conversation was beyond her understanding and Alice followed as they made their way outside.

She stood for a few moments, her breath almost knocked out of her by the beauty of the scene before her, whilst all about her were speaking in foreign tongues. In the far distance, high mountains disappeared at their summits into fleecy white cloud. On the slopes of the lower hills a forest of snow-laden fir trees swept down to the road. The air was crystal-clear and, overhead, the sky was a high, pale blue with a giant yellow sun lighting the sparkling frost on the tops of the trees.

Their cases and boxes were being loaded onto a horse-drawn open sledge. Ahead of the luggage sledge, two covered carriages on runners were being drawn by three horses abreast. Shiny harness glittered in the sunlight, bells were jingling on the decorated arch of bent wood above the horses' heads. The centre horse, between the shafts, was trampling the snow as if eager to be off as their drivers shouted and called.

At last the luggage was lashed down and they were settled into the first of the two carriage sledges; Karl, Olga and herself. Fur rugs were wrapped around their legs and tucked in, shawls and blankets were placed about their shoulders before they moved forward for the drive to Ilyinka, the home of Karl's grandmother.

'You like?' Karl asked. 'You like troika?'

Alice said, 'I thought the troika was a Russian cart.'

Karl laughed at her, translated for Olga, then turned his attention back to her. 'My grandmother – Babushka – was born in Russia. She lived in Ukraine. She has kept Russian customs.'

'And she has kept her troikas?'

Karl laughed again. 'Troika means three horses pulling. Pulling sledge, or cart or carriage.'

They crossed a wide frozen river shortly after they left the station area and the horses slowed their pace as the road began to climb a little, into the hills. Alice was seated by the open side and watched the second troika carrying Uncle Max and his sons go skimming, the steel runners singing, across the blue- white ice of the river. The sturdy

centre horse between the shafts appeared to do most of
the work. He trotted with head high, looking straight
ahead. The outer two cantered, each on a single rein,
their heads turned outwards.

Karl's grandmother was more than eighty years old.
'What name do I use for your grandmother?' she asked
Karl in a whisper.

The whisper was not necessary. Olga spoke only
German and Czech.

'Babushka. The same,' Karl replied. 'Babushka is head
of family.'

'Your grandmother?'

'Yes. Always. The grandmother is the first.' It took
time to conduct a conversation since everything had to
be translated for Olga whenever a few words had been
exchanged. Alice sat in her corner, comfortably warm
and cosy in the rugs, enjoying the cold, pine-scented
breeze that came rushing by the open window-space and
made her feel alive again. The sledge must have some
kind of springing for the ride was smoother than any
she had experienced in a cab. Then it seemed to her
ridiculous that she should compare this with a ride in a
cab.

And all at once she felt happier. It had come to her
that she was on the brink of a great adventure. Laughter
bubbled up inside her as she turned a smiling face to
Karl. 'What about the grandfather? Isn't he the head of
the family?'

'No. Grandfather is dead. But in my family always the
man earn the money. Man is most important outside
house. In the house, the woman rule. The oldest woman
rule and all obey her.'

He seemed to have caught her mood of gaiety for he
held her gloved hand tightly under the fur rug, gave it a
quick squeeze and said, 'Babushka – she is like Queen.
You make curtsey to her.'

Alice stopped laughing. 'Really? Are you joking?'

'No.' His face became serious for a moment. 'I too am

respectful. Everybody do it all the time in my country –
bow and curtsey.'

Then Alice saw that she must respect the customs of
her husband's country. She must curtsey to Karl's
grandmother. Babushka was a frail old lady and she,
Alice, would not offend the head of her new family.

She knew that Karl's grandparents had been Russians
from the Ukraine whose wealth had come from the
iron works his grandfather owned. They were proud of
their two soldier sons who had commissions in the
army of the Little Father in far-off St Petersburg. When
war came they had followed their sons to the Crimea to
watch the Russian army defeat the British and French
invaders.

What they had seen was carnage.

Their Russian side was ill-prepared for battle and,
when the bombardment started, waggons, carts and their
own private carriage were used to draw loads to the
batteries from dawn to sunset.

Two days into the battle they had seen their own young
soldier sons put to the sword by the British. And since
they had lost their sons and witnessed the defeat of the
Russian army they had not been able to face returning
to their home in Alexandrovsk in the Ukraine; they had
wanted a new start and had abandoned their home and
their iron works. They had nothing when they arrived in
Silesia in '56 but a few heirlooms and Babushka's jewels,
some of which they had sold. And here, under Prussian
rule, they had prospered and made a second business in
engineering and had been blessed with two daughters
when they were over forty years old. They bought land
and built the house they called Ilyinka to remind them
of the Ilyin estate on the Dnieper where Babushka had
been born. Then, only eleven years after their flight from
Russia, war came again to threaten their survival. This
time, with the triumph of the Prussian needle-gun, the
Habsburgs had been turned out of Germany at the battle
of Koniggratz. This time Elena Pavlovna and Fyodor

Ivanovich Voroshilov found themselves living on the right side – on the victor's side.

Alice remembered being told all this by her mother-in-law, Babushka's daughter, Ekaterina, and a little shiver went through her now as she thought about the Russian woman she was soon to meet. The Russian woman who had lost everything, half a century ago when her soldier sons were killed at Sevastopol, was having to accept Alice, granddaughter of a man who fought at Balaclava, into her family.

Now she tried to give all her attention to the glimpses of scenery she could see between the trees. The troika was taking them upwards and at every bend and curve a new sight of the mountains or deep shadowed valleys was revealed to her.

She was beginning to feel like a character in one of Grimm's fairy tales or an actress who had been asked to play a part in a great Russian drama. The whole experience, marriage, the journey and being here, rushing through the deep Silesian forest by troika, seemed like a fable. Perhaps if she pinched herself she would wake up at any moment and find herself in bed with Beattie beside her and a ridiculous framed text over her head.

Karl had finished translating for Olga.

Alice looked at this man who was her husband and resumed their earlier conversation. 'In England it is the man – the Papa – who has to be obeyed,' she said.

'I know. That is why I ask your father to marry you.'

'What about you?' She smiled at Karl's mistake but would not correct him here. Karl had asked Papa for her hand on the day she had wandered about Macclesfield trying to make up her mind. Again the strange hazy feeling passed through her, as if she were trying to remember something. She did not try to catch the thought but said, 'Did you have to ask your Babushka?'

'I ask my mother,' Karl said. 'She gave her blessing. But she say that Babushka will think we are not properly

354

married until we have been married in Russian Orthodox church.'

There was a moment when neither of them spoke, then he said solemnly, 'The one I was baptized in.'

Alice felt his hand go still in hers. She could not believe her ears. She pulled hers out of his hold and turned to face him. It was the second time today that he had told her something he'd been concealing quite deliberately. She stared at him. 'You are a Catholic? But we were married in my church.'

Karl said, 'Russian Orthodox is not Catholic.'

'I thought it was . . .' Alice said. She was almost . . . but not quite . . . sure.

Karl said quickly, 'I was baptized in Orthodox faith. To please Babushka. I have never practised it. Church of England is the same as Church of Russia. My parents are married in Orthodox church in village near to Ilyinka. For Babushka, we must have ceremony there also. It is not proper wedding. It is blessing of marriage only. For Babushka.'

She couldn't be sure that Karl was telling the truth any more. She was nearly sure that the Russian Church was Catholic. But if that were so and the priest knew that Karl's wife was a Protestant then she was nearly sure that they would not be allowed to have a ceremony of blessing in a Catholic church. Surely Karl would not lie to his church? Or lie to his grandmother? Surely he wouldn't lie about something so serious.

Suddenly she had the urge to strike Karl. 'Why didn't you tell me?'

'In case you refuse. We have ceremony. Babushka says we are in sin together if we – if I make marriage with you until it is done.'

'I see.'

'You agree?'

'I'm shocked.' She turned her head, to look out again, not wanting him to see that his words had brought her to the point of tears – tears of outrage at the enormity of his deception.

She spoke harshly. 'I'm shocked that you didn't tell me before – that we can't – that we're not properly married yet.'

'I tell Babushka we shall not do it. We can go to Prague tomorrow.'

Alice did not speak. It mattered not one jot to her that they had to go through another ceremony but the knowledge that Karl would lie as he had done in order to have her was a terrible revelation.

Anger, impotent anger for there was nothing she could do about it now, was making her head spin. 'It wasn't necessary,' she said. 'You should have told me. I would have agreed.'

'You agree? You will go to church? Tomorrow?'

'Yes.' The feeling of unreality continued.

Karl spoke to Olga. Alice heard the word 'Babushka' several times, heard 'kirche' repeated between them, saw Olga's friendly face smiling encouragement at her when she looked across at Karl.

Alice tried to smile back out of politeness. She must try to hide her true feelings for she knew now that she and this husband of hers had a great divide to cross. She would not be treated as if she had no opinions, no will of her own. She returned her attention to the passing scene.

The path through the trees was steeper and the troika was slowing, lurching a little as they rounded tight corners. The horses' breath, white vapour, came snorting from their flaring red nostrils as they were urged onwards and upwards, deeper into the forest.

At one o'clock they halted for a picnic in a hunting lodge. The horses were tethered whilst the drivers, with all of them following, carried the baskets through the trees, along a narrow winding path until they came to a wooden house that appeared to be made from rough logs. Inside, the cabin had an air of homeliness even though the fire was not lighted. Rugs and skins hung from the walls. There were long benches around three sides of the living room and these too were covered with cushions and gaily patterned rugs. In the centre of the room was a long table and seating for ten.

The Bauer family had brought baskets with linen-wrapped parcels of sweet soft bread, cheeses and sliced, spiced meats. There was schnapps, vodka and beer for the men and, for Olga and herself, red wine and crystal drinking glasses.

Within minutes Olga had put a match to the fire and they were seated at the table, eating their picnic lunch, with the three young men making a great display of good-natured bantering and enjoyment.

They descended to the track again; the horses were harnessed and the last lap of their journey began. They travelled for at least two miles, Alice estimated, by the time the sun began to sink behind the mountains in the west and from the open side Alice could see nothing but dense, dark greenness.

And still they went forward, sliding along the level stretches, hurling about in the rough parts where the forest road turned sharply, their ears filled with the shouts of the driver.

Then suddenly they were out of the trees, into the fading light of late afternoon and skimming along a broad drive that swept round a formal circular garden. The horses came to halt with a great noise of jingling bells, crunching runners cutting into the deep snow and the driver yelling as at last they drew up in front of the house.

No, Alice thought, not a house. It was a mansion. It was a slightly neglected mansion with a broad shallow roof of yellow tiles. She had a swift impression of three storeys, each with eight tall windows glowing orange in the setting sun, of wide, shallow steps that stretched across the front, of great carved oaken doors that were being thrown back in welcome to them.

They were helped out by an old manservant and stood

for a moment or two whilst the second troika pulled up and Olga went to stand beside it as the Bauer family got out.

Karl took her hand and they went inside, through the wide and shabby entrance hall, up a polished stairway, following the same old manservant until at length double doors of maple wood were thrown back.

A long, formally arranged room was revealed. Down each side high-backed chairs with ornate carvings were set between small oak tables with thick carved legs. On each table was a lighted lamp.

At the far end of the room where three tall candelabra of gilt cast flickering shadows on her proud, erect form, stood a tiny white-haired figure, dressed in gold brocade. Beside Karl's grandmother, for it must be she, was a small table holding two boxes.

Not a word was uttered as Alice and Karl handed their outer wear to the bent old man. Alice ran nervous fingers over the skirt of her grey travelling dress before slipping her hand into Karl's as they walked down the narrow runner of Persian carpet to stand in front of Babushka.

Alice had a quick impression of an imperious old lady, stately and severe, whose very presence was magisterial and awesome. Then Karl let go of her hand, dropped to his knees in front of his grandmother, bowed his head and rose, kissing her outstretched bony hand. And Alice nervously made a very graceful curtsey and took and kissed the hand which was held out to her.

Immediately the ritual was completed Babushka embraced them, first Karl and then herself and still without speaking took the two inlaid ebony boxes from the side table and handed one each to them.

Alice looked at her to see if she should open it, and a silly great feeling – like falling gently and affectionately in love – came over her. She found herself looking into the wizened face of the old lady whose bright little blue eyes were twinkling in merriment. Babushka nodded.

Alice opened her box. Inside was a necklace; a choker

of diamonds and sapphires suspended in elaborate filigree cascades from seven flat, linked bands of gold. It would be a perfect fit. Alice had never seen anything so beautiful, not in any of the shops in Southport, not in Therese's jewellery box, not even on portraits of beautiful and famous women. She glanced at Karl. 'For me?'

'It is custom.' Karl was looking over her shoulder at the necklace. 'Wife of heir is given jewels.'

'They are magnificent.' She looked at him with glistening eyes. 'I'm overcome, Karl,' she whispered. 'I don't know what to say. How can I thank her?'

'Take her arm. Kiss her on face,' he whispered back. 'I too. She gave me money. Enough gulden to last one year.'

Alice did as he said and was immediately embraced by the old lady who alternated between holding her close and at arms' length as she took in every little detail, punctuating her display of affection with what sounded to Alice like, 'Bravo Karl' and '*Liebchen*, Alicia.'

When they had finished kissing, Karl took her hand again and, just as Alice thought they would be taken to their separate rooms, in answer to a signal from Babushka, a door was thrown back and a little party of welcoming village people in the pretty national costume came into the hall and surrounded them.

An hour later, when the greeting of guests was over, Alice was taken on a tour of the house by the same old manservant who seemed always to be in attendance. He seemed to be the only man in attendance though Karl said that there was a girl in the kitchen and a woman who cleaned for Babushka.

The house was big and rambling and most of the rooms were not being used. Dust covers had been placed over the good furniture, and walls and ceiling in almost every room were in need of paint and varnish. It would take a fortune to make this house into an hotel. And where would the guests come from? And why should guests come at all to an hotel that was hours by horse-transport from the nearest railway station? It was an impossible idea. Karl must be mad to think of it.

Last of all Alice was taken to the bedroom she and Karl would share tomorrow.

The large room with a warm oak floor had white-painted walls and was heated very efficiently by a lighted porcelain stove. Goat skin rugs were scattered here and there but the room was dominated by the enormous bed. It stood in the centre of the right-hand wall, facing the door to a dressing-room. The bed had four corner posts, supported by life-sized, carved figures of bears, a feature of much of the ornamentation of the house. The back of the bed, branches and leaves carved by craftsmen, reached to a great height; Alice guessed it to be about ten feet, only about four feet below a beamed ceiling.

Upon the bed and its solid hair mattress were laid deep cambric bags of goose-down. The one she would lie on had a plain linen cover, the over-down and pillows were covered with embroidered cases of fine lawn. She had seen the same things at Beaufort Lodge.

She went to the dressing-room and found that her clothes had been hung in a wall-length wardrobe of mahogany and mirrors. A long marble-topped table, with an inset washbasin of white china, held two huge ewers, one of cold and one of hot water, dishes of soap, sponges and towels.

Already she had been shown the little room next door where, against a tiled wall, ran a long varnished seat, fronted with a carved panel and with two lidded places. Enamelled water pitchers stood ready-filled for pouring down the chute after use.

Alice looked at herself in the glass above the washstand. Her hair was dishevelled, her lace collar crumpled, she needed a wash and a rest before she should start on her hair and dressing. There were two hours to go until supper-time – and all at once, instead of the bone-weariness she had expected to feel, she found herself extraordinarily happy.

'I have never been so free in my whole life, until now,' she said to her reflection. 'At last my life is my own. I feel as if I can do anything I want to do.'

She grinned at herself in the mirror and, seeing the slightly gummy smile, the curled-back top lip that was as red as if she had rouged it, laughed softly to herself. 'If I laugh out loud someone will think I am mad,' she said. 'Perhaps I am. Instead of feeling that I have given up my life into Karl's keeping, I just know that I have come into my own.'

After washing she put on her dressing-gown, knotted the cord around her waist and, still full of unexpected energy, this surge of well-being, went to the high, white-draped window where a desk was set with writing paper, envelopes, pens and ink. She pulled back the curtains and unfastened the wooden shutters. She could not open a frame for air. They were double, with a foot of space between the inner and outer glass panes.

She was looking over a courtyard at the back of the house. Facing her was a high wall at the far side of what must be a kitchen garden and, beyond the wall, a road. There were glasshouses under this wall; evidently one was heated since it was the only one of a line of outhouses without a roof laden with snow.

The moon was not visible from where Alice stood but she could see clearly, against the white of the snow, the silent landscape before her, the swept cobbled yard, the garden, wall and the road beyond. The road went in a series of gentle curves from the hill the house stood upon to where in the distance she could see the twinkling lights of a village and the spire of the church. Tomorrow morning the ceremony of blessing would be held in the sacristy of that church.

Everything was becoming dreamlike again. She looked back at the bed and tried not to be nervous about her wedding night. Karl was almost obsessive in his need to have her at his side and yet she knew, as she turned her face to the window and looked back at the night scene before her, that Karl had never given any hint that either romantic tenderness or burning desire was a part of his need for her. And she wondered if the sharing of married love would coax them into life in Karl for both tender feelings and strong and passionate desire were part of her nature.

After church tomorrow the proper Christmas festivities would begin. The true feast in old Catholic Europe was Christmas Eve.

Tomorrow's dinner, a traditional meal – wine soup and fried carp with potato salad – would be shared by the family; Olga, Max, Hans and Seppie as well as Babushka and themselves. It would be followed by another, midnight visit to the church. Then would come the *Bescherung*; the giving and receiving of presents. They had brought with them gifts for Babushka and the Bauer family. She had a gold hunter watch for Karl, inscribed with their names and the date of the wedding.

After the *Bescherung*, she would come up here with Karl to lie in bed with a man for the first time. On Christmas Day she would be a wife, not a virgin or a bride. She would be properly married at last.

And again she felt this strange excitement as if she had been freed and she wondered why it should be. 'Why am I not fretful? Why no longer homesick?' she asked herself. 'Why am I not afraid that this hasty marriage will bring regrets?'

She looked down the hill towards the church. At nine o'clock in the morning they would be taken together by troika. She was to wear the jewelled necklace which Babushka had given to her and Babushka's white and gold wedding dress, carefully preserved and surviving their trek from the Ukraine to Silesia, a richly embroidered over-gown in a straight, split-sided classical style that was worn over a plain white skirt, so that it would always fit the wearer. Her name had already been stitched into the hem next to those of Ekaterina and Olga.

She had given her wedding ring to Uncle Max who

was keeping both hers and Karl's. He would hand each of them the other's ring and the high point of the little ceremony would be when the rings were exchanged and they became man and wife.

And, as she stood there and looked down at her left hand without its ring, she found connections between her elusive, troubling thoughts of today and her life in England where the man she had loved in her moment of glory still lived under a cloud of doubt and suspicion.

She pulled the curtains quickly, brought one of the lamps to the desk and sat down to write a letter to Frederick.

# Chapter Twenty-one

Frederick's office overlooked the formal gardens at Hetherington. Outside, the sky was pale, the parterre frost-rimed and the road and the pathways white with trodden snow. In the distance he could see Mary and Maggie each with a small boy by the hand. Peter Blackshaw and Arthur Davenport, muffled in woollen scarves, overcoats and oversized tweed caps were being taken for a sedate little walk. By the time they reached the oak woods the boys would be running rings around their devoted aunts who liked to get their hands on the little boys at every opportunity.

They had many such opportunities, for Therese's son and stepson were brought to Hetherington every week by their new nanny. For himself, he had avoided Therese since he had read Alice's first letter, the one in which she told him she loved him and had made her sad little confession. Now he held in his hand the one he had received that morning.

He turned away from the window as the boys vanished from sight into the trees, went to the desk and slammed his fist down on the desk bell. Whilst he waited for Grieve to answer his call he read the letter again.

Dear Frederick,

You may not welcome a letter from me but in case it helps I must tell you that I have been trying to make sense of the events surrounding your father's death.

Before her marriage to Papa, Therese had a maid, Maisie, who was known to George's wife, Polly. (Polly was our maid at the time of the victory celebrations. We brought her with us to Hetherington.) This is all going to sound very sordid and I don't want you to think I take pleasure in repeating servants' gossip, but so many little incidents keep coming to mind that I cannot explain or justify.

The servant girl we saw running away on the night of the ball could have been Maisie, for Maisie did not come back on to the balcony after supper.

Maisie has been seen by Therese, Polly and by me in Macclesfield. She dresses in fine style and apparently has no need to work. It is rumoured that she is 'kept' by two wealthy men of the town, so this might account for the upturn in her fortunes.

What it does not explain is why Maisie was wearing your father's diamond ring when I last saw her. I noticed the identical ring on your father's hand when I was introduced to him.

If she left the estate when we were in the garden then how did Maisie know your father was dead? He was not found until the morning and yet apparently Maisie went to the police in Macclesfield on the same day.

But most puzzling of all is the reason behind Maisie's going to the police to tell them about your quarrel. What did she gain from talking unless she feared that suspicion might fall on her?

I think Maisie knows a lot more than she has told.

My very best wishes to you,
Alice.


It had taken two months to reach here. He turned quickly as the office door opened. 'I want the trap ready in half an hour,' he said to Grieve. 'I'm going to Macclesfield after I've seen Lady Blackshaw.'

'Yes, sir,' the man answered. 'Back for dinner, sir?'

'I'm not sure. Have someone meet the six o'clock train. If I'm not on it I won't be back today.'

'Very good, sir.'

Grieve was proving to be an excellent manservant. Leigh had been poached from Hetherington last year and Hodge promoted to butler. The loss of Leigh had not been a grievous one. The Dower House was closed and Mother and his sisters had moved to the Hetherington Hall to save expense. The house staff had been cut by half, outside staff had been reduced and only one carriage and the pony trap were being driven and maintained.

Frederick tidied his office and went upstairs to the Green Salon to see Mother. He found her sitting, writing by the fire. 'You look marvellous, Mother,' he said as he kissed her on the cheek. 'I believe you're getting fat!'

'Freddie!' She managed to smile and look cross at the same time. 'How impertinent! A gentleman never comments on a lady's shape, especially in such vulgar language. You must stop making these remarks.'

'I can't,' he said. 'Every day I see an improvement in you.' Then he asked a little anxiously, 'You're better aren't you? No signs of the old complaint, whatever it was?'

She smiled. 'I can hardly believe it. I am restored to life, by Charles.'

Charles, at the time of the victory celebrations, had examined his mother. After spending an hour listening to every detail of her illness and after examining her minutely he had said that he could find no evidence of a tumour.

'In fact, Lady Blackshaw,' he'd said, 'my opinion is that in the beginning you had biliary colic, complicated with a peptic ulcer. Digestive diseases are notoriously difficult to diagnose, of course.' He had asked Frederick to come into the room then and said, 'I believe that your mother is presently suffering from starvation and laudanum poisoning. I propose that her bed is moved into the fresh air and that treatment starts immediately.

She must take a little milk, beaten eggs and fruit every two hours until her appetite returns. All medication must cease.'

There had been a week when Mother had suffered a lot of pain and Charles said that this was because her body had come to depend on the poison but she had suffered bravely and after that her recovery had been rapid. Frederick kissed her on her smooth cheek and said, 'You look wonderful, sitting here under your portrait, lovelier than you were at twenty.'

She said, 'Flatterer!'

He knew that she loved him to talk like this. He grinned at her. 'Who are you writing to?'

'I'm making a guest list. The Madisons are due in at Liverpool on Monday.'

'The American people you've invited? Who are they? When are they coming?' He was asking to please her, for he had no interest in the social side of life at Hetherington.

Mother smiled mysteriously and said, 'I'm doing it for Therese. She can't have them stay at the Beeches. It's far too small.'

'I said, "Who are they?" ' Frederick asked again, trying to make a show of impatience.

'The girl Xanthe was at school in Vienna with Therese. Her father's a wealthy banker.' She looked up at him with eyes full of the naughty humour that had always delighted him. 'The father's name is Warner Madison, Senior,' she said in a droll American accent, rolling the words slowly. 'Therese says that the girl is very plain but has hopes of marrying into the upper crust.'

He roared with laughter. 'Then why on Earth are they coming here?'

'For a rest, Therese says. But we're not quite beyond the pale, socially!' She did the American accent again as she added, 'And my. I do declare that you're a bit of a swell y'rself, Sir Frederick. Therese wrote me about your lovely little place here – and your lovely little old title—'

Frederick was chuckling. 'I'm sure Therese has

someone else in mind if she's seeking a titled husband for her rich and ugly friend. I'm feeling sorry for the American girl now. Her friend, Therese, is hardly singing her praises.'

Mother ignored his criticism of Therese. 'Therese has asked me if I will invite every eligible bachelor we know to meet her Xanthe.' She gave him a quick glance of assessment. 'I can only think of one or two . . . But there's not one who could hold a candle to you, my darling. I predict that Miss Madison will fall madly in love with you.'

Frederick raised his eyebrows. 'I hope you are joking,' he said. 'When will they be here? How long are they staying?'

'Monday – for three weeks,' Mother answered. 'Therese can't entertain them, in her condition. But she's going to stay here at Hetherington, with the boys, whilst they are here.'

Then a more serious expression crossed her face as she said, 'I want to talk to you about Therese.'

'I don't want to talk about her.'

'You must. I can't go on like this. I don't know what has caused the trouble but it must be ended.'

'I don't know myself!' The memory of Therese's treachery made him almost shout the words. He had never learned to hide his true feelings, especially from his mother.

She was not fooled. 'I repeat. It must be ended. It's upsetting your sisters. And poor Therese must be calm. It's harmful to an unborn child for the mother to be fretful and unhappy.'

'Can we talk about something else?'

'The estate?'

He went to the fireplace and placed his hand against the cool marble. 'We're only just surviving. I've sold one of the farms and increased the rents on the tenanted land to repay the loans.'

'And?'

'I can reduce the mortgages if I can sell another parcel of land and . . .'

'And what?'

He hated to tell her this but could see no other way out. 'The Dower House,' he said slowly. 'It will have to go.'

'When?'

'Don't you mind?' He hated the idea of selling her old childhood home almost as much as she would. But if he did not reduce the estate's commitments then not only the Dower House, but possibly Hetherington itself, would have to be sold.

'Is there nothing else we can sell?' she asked. 'What about the works in Macclesfield. Can't we take more out?'

'No. We're lucky to have Reinhardt. He's turned the old business into profit. We have orders for machinery from all over the world. The profits are shared in a partnership.' He paused for a moment before saying, 'Reinhardt is a brilliant engineer and a clever business-man. Everything he touches turns to gold. But every penny we get from Blackshaw and Rinehart is swallowed up in keeping Hetherington afloat.'

'So we have to sell my house?' Mother said.

He couldn't bear to see the look of loss in her eyes. He said, 'Look, Mother. I'm no good at this. I'm a soldier, not an accountant.'

Command had been sympathetic about his absences but there were limits to their understanding. And he doubted his ability to settle to civilian life. If he sold more land, ran the home farm at a profit and found a good and honest man for estate factor he would be able to give most of his time to the army. He pulled out the gold half-hunter and flipped open the lid.

The trap and driver would be at the front entrance in ten minutes.

Mother turned from him, picked up her writing case and said, 'If you don't patch up your difference with Therese I'm going to make Therese tell me everything.'

He knew that the time had come to end hostilities. At last he said, 'I'll see her today. Bury the hatchet.' He pecked her cheek, left the salon and went downstairs to the cloakroom where he put on a tweed greatcoat and rammed a matching deerstalker hat on his head. Then he stood for a few moments in the entrance hall, tapping his fingers impatiently against an ancient Greek urn.

Whilst he waited for the trap he let his thoughts go back to the break with Charles and Therese at Christmas. He had watched the shock on Charles's face when they'd discovered Therese's treachery, but Charles, protective of her and loyal to the last, had taken her home to Macclesfield instead of making her explain her despicable behaviour.

In any case, by the time he had read Alice's confession of love for him it had been too late. He had had to accept the fact that, like most of the people in the world he believed, he had been disappointed in love. He'd get over it. Eventually.

When Alice ran off with young Rinehart and married him in secret, for that was how he saw it, his first inclination had been to return to barracks and request an overseas posting. It was common practice. One or two of the men who had fought in South Africa had done that very thing. James Horden, jilted soon after they returned, had gone to America on a shooting exercise. But, for himself, he had been pleaded with by Mother, his sisters and, through Charles, by a desperate Therese, to stay; to give all his energies to managing the estate.

He saw the trap approach and stop. 'Knutsford Station,' he ordered the driver as he seated himself in the back. The trap swished along the Roman Road, spraying grey slushy water as they went. He thought about his future actions and he warned himself not to let the hopes Alice's letter had raised rise too high.

It had become clear that the police were not satisfied with what they had learned so far. Every month or so they questioned him until he wondered if they were trying to make him forget his earlier statement or contradict a previous reply to the same question. He was also afraid that if such was their intention then sooner or later he might inadvertently play into their hands by 'tripping over himself'.

He had heard about a man who would act as a kind of private inspector. He would go first to George's, for Alice had given him the address, then he would see the investigator, show him Alice's letter and hope for a quick end to the affair.

There were delays all along the way and it was twelve o'clock before he got off the train in the old cattle market in Macclesfield's Waters Green where a Thursday cattle market was in progress and the iron-railed sheep pens were surrounded by red-faced farmers.

Opposite the station a straggling line of stalls ascended the steep hill up to the Market Place itself. There, amongst the multitude of stalls in the crowded square, he tried to find someone who could give him directions.

At last he found a young boy who said cheekily, 'The Dams is what yer want. Ah'll tekk yer fer a shillin.'

Frederick followed the lad down a maze of back streets that were slippery with melting snow, descending at every step of the route until finally he stopped in front of a house in the shabbiest, dampest street in town which sloped down to the River Bollin and the mills. Here the smell of damp cotton and the rattling and clattering of the machinery filled every corner of the streets and houses.

Lower down the street, women were baling out water from their open doors, throwing it into the street.

He paid the boy and knocked at George's door, trying not to see the little knot of ill-clothed, dirty children who were standing, staring at him from a few yards' distance.

A woman at the bottom of the hill was shouting, 'Them culverts under London Road mun be full!'

Her neighbour opposite the narrow street called back, 'Aye. Drains here are made up wi' muck, an' all.'

371

He tried not to see the faces of women who, not working in the mills, peered furtively from behind skimpy curtains and bare windows as he waited.

Then his knock was answered by a young woman with a grey shawl about her shoulders and Frederick saw that the front door opened straight into a tiny room which was at least a foot lower than the level of the street. She seemed to recognize him though he did not remember ever having seen her before as he asked, 'Mrs Davenport?'

'It's – Major Blackshaw . . . I mean Sir Frederick Blackshaw – isn't it?' She smiled timidly. 'Come in, sir. Please do.'

Frederick ducked his head to get through the low doorway. He had to step over a high, cement sill that was clearly there to hold back flooding from the river. He stepped down into a small room that smelled of mildew, stone-dampness and the stomach-turning odour of the undrained yard outside. How could anyone live like this? Was Charles Davenport's son trying to make a life for himself and his wife in the Dams?

The room itself was almost bare of furnishings and was only a little larger than the toy house he and Therese had played in when they were children. The house was dark and it took him a few seconds to get used to the gloom. Two Windsor chairs, a scrubbed table and a wooden chest were all the furnishings. A thick rag mat was laid upon the cheap linoleum square that only covered half of the stone floor. There were three doors; the front door, a door to a narrow funnel of space where a steep, twisting staircase led to the room above and a door opposite the one he'd entered by. This door now opened, revealing another step down into a small lean-to of rough, lime-washed brick that was only big enough to hold a table and a brown, shallow slopstone.

Charles's son, shirt-sleeves rolled back, heavy boots on his feet, came into the room. 'Were you looking for us?' he asked in a voice completely at odds with these surroundings. George had the looks and the speech of his father.

'Yes. I wanted to ask your wife—'

'Polly.' Polly said. 'Call me Polly. Sit down, sir, won't you? You're lucky to catch him, sir. My George only has a half-hour for his dinner.' She beamed at George. 'And he's been helping out with the flooding down the way.'

'Thank you.' Frederick sat opposite George, where a good fire burned in the little iron range, whilst Polly stood almost to attention beside her husband. He said, 'Look. I'd rather we cut out the formalities. Don't call me "Sir". I'd like to think of you as family now that Therese is married to your father.'

'That's very nice of you.' Polly smiled and patted George on the shoulder. 'Isn't it George?'

George grinned and reached up to clasp his wife's hand and Frederick wondered where to begin. After a few seconds he withdrew the envelope from his pocket and handed it to Polly. 'I think the letter will be self-explanatory,' he said. 'I wonder if you can add anything to it.'

George had come to stand beside her and look with a questioning expression. 'Go ahead,' Frederick said. 'Read it.'

'Eeh,' Polly handed the letter to George. 'I wouldn't put it past her.'

'Who?' Frederick said.

'Maisie.'

George, unsmiling, handed the letter back. 'So Alice and you were together in the garden,' he said. 'Did all this happen on the night of the ball?'

'Can we talk? Do you have to go back to the factory? Will you lose your job or your pay?' Frederick said.

George looked quickly at his wife. 'Not at all. I can put in an extra few hours on Saturday . . .'

'Can we go somewhere? Where Polly won't be offended,' Frederick turned to Polly. 'I'm not saying

373

anything George can't tell you afterwards, but I think it might be better if—'

Polly's cheery little round face broke into a beaming smile, 'Take George somewhere where you can talk man to man, like. I shan't mind. Honest.'

They went in single file since it was crowded, up the steep cobbled incline of Mill Street, unable to hear one another speak for the noises of rattling carts and the shouts of drivers. Frederick quickened his pace as they approached the Market Place. Seeing the living conditions of Charles's son had upset him. Now the crowded street was adding to his irritation. He would never be able to live or work in close proximity to the mass of civilians who seemed to him to be trying to edge him off the pavement into the gutter that was running with mud and water.

He asked George when they reached the square, 'Which one?' They were in front of an ancient, black-and-white timbered tavern. 'This?' He jerked his head towards the nearest building. 'The Angel?'

'Turn left,' George said. 'We'll talk at the Bate Hall. There's a small room upstairs where they have a fire.'

They went quickly through the slithering wetness along the narrow, cobbled street of Chestergate to the old coaching inn where they were shown to the quiet room George asked for. When the door closed behind them they drew chairs up to the fire and sat, awkward and self-conscious, until a serving girl set tankards and a tall pewter jug of hot punch in front of them.

Frederick said, 'What do you do for a living?'

'I'm training to be an engineer,' George said. 'A machine engineer – with Blackshaw and Rinehart.'

'Like the work?'

'Not much.' George's smile faded. He took a deep draught of the hot punch and put the tankard back on the table.

'Does your father know how you and your wife are living?' said Frederick.

374

'You mean the house? The neighbourhood?'

'Of course. Has Charles seen it?'

George grinned and looked to Frederick for permission to help himself to another fill of punch.

'Go ahead. I'll ring for more.' Frederick went to the door and jangled the little hand bell.

A girl came to the foot of the stairs and Frederick called down to her and ordered another jug before returning to the fireside and repeating his question.

George looked troubled. 'My father and I are not on speaking terms at the moment,' he said.

'Why not?'

'I refused his offer – a rent-free flat over the surgery. I didn't want to start married life under any obligations.'

Frederick nearly exploded with annoyance. 'But this is ridiculous!' he said.

George said wryly, 'My father told us often enough that his own suffering in his early years did him no harm.'

'Your father wasn't married when life was hard for him. His struggles were all in his childhood. Before he had a family to support.'

George grinned. 'We won't be there much longer. I'm going to Southport next week to see my rich old aunt and throw myself on her mercy.'

Frederick looked at him closely, unable to guess whether or not George meant it. 'Who owns your house?' he demanded.

'Therese,' George said. 'She let us have it. It's only a shilling a week.'

Frederick tried to hide his disgust. 'I see.'

The girl had come into the room and replaced the empty jug. Frederick thought fast and as soon as the door was closed asked sharply, 'You don't think I seduced Alice, do you?'

George laughed. It was the same deep, hearty laugh as his father's. 'Not unless she cooperated,' he said. 'I can't imagine Alice allowing anyone to seduce her unless she wished it. My sister has always been decisive.'

Frederick found himself smiling back. 'I didn't seduce her,' he said. 'I wanted to—'

'All right!' The smile had gone from George's face. 'I'm worried though, by the date on the letter.'

'Why? What's significant about the date?'

George said, 'She must have written it only hours after she arrived in Bohemia, in the first few days of her honeymoon. What does that say about her marriage?'

Frederick felt the surge of longing for Alice that came over him too often for his peace of mind. He made a stronger effort to put thoughts of her from him. 'I didn't notice . . .'

'I don't expect you've come all this way to justify your flirtation,' George said quietly.

Frederick agreed. 'Will you see this – this Maisie? Try to get at the truth?'

'Why me?'

'She knows I'm a suspect.' Frederick took a deep draught from his tankard before explaining more. 'It was she who went to the police and accused me.'

George was considering his answer. Then, 'Yes,' he said. 'I'll do it.'

Frederick topped up his tankard with the warming drink that was making him feel relaxed and very much at ease with George. 'How much?' he asked.

George looked puzzled. 'How much what?'

'Money,' Frederick said. 'For your services.'

'Don't be a fool. Anyway I don't expect she'll tell me anything. Polly can do the groundwork.'

They sat, staring into the fire for a few minutes. An idea had been forming in Frederick's mind during the short time they had spent together and, though he normally thought things through a lot more carefully, he decided to act upon it at once. 'Do you enjoy engineering?' he asked.

'No. But Polly's expecting—'

Frederick interrupted him. 'What would you say if I offered you a job as my factor?'

'Factor? What's that?'

'A factor is a man employed as a kind of agent to manage heritable estates.'

'What does it entail?'

'Look.' Frederick leaned forward. He had made his mind up that George was the man he wanted. 'I need a man I can trust. I'm going back into the army as soon as I've found someone to manage Hetherington.'

George asked, 'Will you be away from Cheshire for long?'

'I'll probably remain at headquarters in Chester. But I could be sent off at a moment's notice. I need someone to look after Hetherington. Will you do it?'

'I've never done anything like that . . .' George said. He drew his brows together and raised a hand to stop Frederick from saying more whilst he thought.

Frederick could only judge by the passing expressions on George's face that the more George considered it the better he liked the idea for after a few moments he asked, 'Where would I live? What would I do?'

'Live in the Lodge House at the Hollin Gate. It's a good house and it's empty at present.'

'And—'

'Manage. Look after the staff. Engage temporary workers for the manager of the home farm and for maintenance work on the house and gardens. Supervise them. Pay the wages. Collect the rents. Keep the books. Factoring is the profitable running of an estate. Not much chance of that. You might be better than I am at keeping it on an even keel. You'd have instruction. I wouldn't expect a lot at first.'

'It's a good offer. I don't know what to say.'

Frederick warned him, 'It wouldn't be enough for a very ambitious man. You won't rise to the top of the tree – as you might in engineering. But you'll be secure and comfortable. Your wife could find work in the house, if she wanted it, once the children are old enough—'

'I'll take it!' George stood and leaned back casually against the fireplace. Then he straightened up and said, 'Do you know how old I am?'

Frederick had not even thought about it. 'Older than Alice?' he guessed.

George said nothing.

'Don't answer,' Frederick said quickly. 'You look older than me. I'm acting on a hunch and I'm not usually wrong. Can you give orders? Command respect and obedience from men older than yourself?'

'I said I'll take it!'

Frederick relaxed, smiled and held out his hand.

George shook hands. 'I'll see this Maisie woman for you. Report back.'

'Right.' Frederick took out his watch and flipped open the lid. 'I have an appointment in Manchester.'

George gave an embarrassed cough. 'When do I start?'

Frederick said, 'How long do you need?'

'A week.'

'Very well. Hetherington a week on Monday.'

Frederick wanted to leave. If he were to see this man and be back in Macclesfield later, to see Therese, he'd have to get a move on. 'Anything else?' he asked.

'Is the house furnished?'

It came to Frederick in a flash that George and Polly would have nothing to set up house with. George would be too proud to ask for help. 'Look here,' he said. 'Bring your wife over next week. She can have a look at the place. The house is furnished but it may not be to her taste. There's a storehouse of furniture that's not in use. She can rummage around there if she wants to change things about.' He pulled out his wallet. 'And take this,' he said. He took out three five-pound notes. 'The wages are ten pounds a month with a rent-free house and fuel. I'll pay you a month in advance and your removal expenses. If you have to spend any of this on talking to the girl, Maisie—'

'That's all right,' George said. He took the notes and

378

folded them, his air of importance growing visibly as Frederick watched him. 'It's a very good wage, ten pounds a month.' He looked quickly at Frederick. 'You know what you are doing, do you? Twenty shillings a week is considered a fair wage for a working man—'

'Yes,' Frederick said sharply. 'Today I saw how he lives on it.'

George put the notes in his pocket, smiled and held out his hand again. 'You'd best be off then,' he said. 'Don't miss your train.'

Leaving the public house a few minutes later Frederick made straight for the station and the train to Manchester.

There, in a neat villa a short distance from Deansgate, he found the investigator, Tom Lees, who had been recommended to him by a fellow officer recently named in a divorce case.

Frederick felt instant mistrust for the little, fawning man who ushered him into the small stuffy back-parlour of the house. He felt inclined not to ask him to handle the case. But he realized as the man offered him tea and biscuits in the dingy room that he knew of nobody else and would have to trust him.

'So, Sir Frederick,' the man squeaked after he had read Alice's letter, 'it seems that the police are hoping for a confession of guilt, in the absence of real evidence.'

'It would appear so.'

'I'll make my enquiries of this Maisie girl and I'll write to your – your—' Here he waved the letter at Frederick. 'Your lady-love, is it Sir Frederick?'

All at once Frederick had had enough. He looked in disgust at Tom Lees. 'No. It bloody well isn't!'

He'd have no more to do with this. He would not have a shifty character like this man even speaking Alice's name. If he never got to the truth he'd suffer the damned consequences rather than have Alice involved.

'Then er . . .' Lees enquired. 'What shall I . . . ?'

But Frederick had slammed down the cup and saucer

379

and was making his way to the door and out into the cold, fresh air of Manchester. One way or another he'd satisfy himself about the death. He'd not 'crack'. Eventually the police would close the file.

# Chapter Twenty-two

On Thursday afternoons Charles took a skin clinic at the Infirmary instead of seeing his private patients. It was late and he was sitting at the desk, making notes on the scourge of skin disease that was sweeping through the town. He had almost finished when Beatrice came into the consulting room.

Beattie looked very serious and efficient in her long grey uniform dress and black boots. A starched white apron with straps firmly crossed behind her back fitted her tall, slim figure well and on her upswept blonde hair she wore the formidable cap, high and lacy with long, under-chin ties of the first-year cadet-student.

'Hello, darling.' Charles got up, took her arm and led her to the chair next to the desk. 'Well?'

'I've just been told, Papa,' she said in her quiet, unruffled way. 'The patient you sent in yesterday—'

'The girl from the Dams?'

'Yes. She died this morning. It was typhoid.'

Charles felt the sinking heaviness that came when he lost a patient. He had visited the fourteen-year-old girl yesterday and he'd had no choice but to have her admitted here. There were six younger children in the family and all lived in a two-roomed cottage. Her symptoms, especially the headache, had led him to suspect the worst but he had hoped, prayed for anything other than typhoid. It would spread like forest fire through the Dams. He'd have to persuade George to take the flat over the surgery.

'Are they sure?'

'Certain, Papa.'

'Then you'll have to remain here, Beatrice.'

'I know. They're isolating the ward. I'm going over to the Nurses' Home, to collect my spare uniforms and personal things. Then I go back to the ward.'

'Poor Beatrice. I'll be kept informed of course.'

'Papa?' Beatrice spoke softly now.

'Well?'

'I was in the house. This morning. I saw Therese—' She was gripping the edge of his desk and had turned worried eyes on to his face. 'You don't think I could have passed it on to anyone, do you?'

'Were you in close contact with the girl who died, Beatrice?'

'Yes.'

The likelihood was that Beatrice had not passed on the infection. But he would have to take precautions at home. The boys would have to remain at Hetherington for the next three weeks until all danger was past. Therese must remain at home. Her American friend would not be allowed to be in her company. She must bathe daily and walk in the fresh air every afternoon.

'Thank you for telling me, darling,' he said. 'I'll telegraph Southport. Aunt Harriet must not let Leopold come for the weekend until everyone's clear. Go back to your duties.'

When she had gone and before he could collect his notes together, there was another knock at the door. It was the sanitary inspector, here to talk about the conditions in the Dams.

It was another hour before he was able to leave for home.

Therese, large and ungainly in one of the loose robes she wore to conceal her condition, opened the door of the study. Opposite was the dispensary where Charles had been closeted for an hour. He had been looking stern and

382

had replied brusquely when she suggested that they sit in the drawing room, by the fire.

'I have urgent work to do,' he'd said. 'And then you and I must have a serious talk.'

She'd flounced off into the study. He knew she had only one more day at home before she left him for three whole weeks to be at Hetherington with the Madisons. She'd simmered with annoyance whilst she worked on the accounts.

At the closed dispensary door she took a deep breath. 'Charles, darling?' She spoke in her sweetest voice although she was quietly furious. She had just finished and it appeared that dozens of his patients had not paid anything for months.

There was no reply. She opened the door and saw Charles leaning over the bench, intently writing. He looked up and saw her. 'I said we'll talk later, Therese,' he said.

'I've been doing the accounts,' she said. Charles always wanted to have 'serious little talks' lately. 'Are you ready to sign them?'

Unsmiling, he straightened up and followed her into the study. 'Where are they?'

Therese showed him the stack of accounts rendered on the desk. 'Sign them and I'll address the envelopes,' she said.

He put an arm around her shoulders and absent-mindedly kissed the top of her head. 'You do too much,' he said. 'Why give yourself all this trouble. I'd have done them.'

'Charles,' she said, 'they have to be posted tomorrow.' She pointed to the chair next to her own. 'Sit down. Sign them.'

He smiled gently at her and her heart, as always, almost melted. But she frowned. It was vital he signed the accounts. Charles had no inkling of how much it cost to run the house.

He picked up the first bill, scrutinized it and sighed.

Then, as she watched, he screwed it up into a ball and dropped it in the waste-paper basket. Therese stared in horror as he did the same with the second. He signed the third one and handed it to her.

She was so shocked that she said nothing until he was halfway through and the waste-paper basket was filling with crumpled accounts rendered. He had made it plain that she was to leave all decisions about his work to him. Since the time she had asked him to cut back on his charity work and he had refused her, she had made it a rule to say nothing but this time she would not stay silent. 'You must send them out,' she ordered. Her voice was rising with anger. 'These people must pay. Why should they have their treatment free?'

He put the pen down on the blotting paper, looked into her narrowed green eyes, and placing a hand comfortingly over her own said, 'You can't get blood from a stone, Therese.'

'But . . .'

He held on to her hand firmly. 'I never refuse treatment to my patients.'

'If they can't pay they shouldn't receive treatment!' Therese pulled her hand away sharply. 'How do you think we can live, if you behave as if – as if you were Almighty God?' she blazed.

As soon as the words were out she knew she had gone too far. He would not allow her to speak like this. He could turn, become severe and autocratic in the face of her temper.

She took a handkerchief from the pocket of the velvet robe, dashed it to her eyes and sat down again. 'I'm sorry, Charles,' she whispered. 'But I'm so very worried about money.'

He would not be soft-soaped. He ignored her tears. 'You should be,' he answered. 'If you saw the people I treat you would be too worried to take it from them.'

'I? Take it from them?'

'My poorest patients live in your houses. It costs them

384

a shilling a week in rent for property that should be pulled down.'

'I can do nothing. A shilling? What do you think I can buy with a shilling?' she cried.

He sat for a moment or two without speaking. Then, 'You receive the rents from fifty houses. You can do a lot with fifty shillings.'

'Charles!' she protested. 'Are you trying to intimidate me? You know that my houses – my rents – are an essential part of my income.'

'I mean it.' He went to the fireplace and looked gravely at her. 'We have a case of typhoid. The sanitary inspector is investigating.'

'It has nothing to do with me,' she said. 'If they won't look after themselves properly what can I do?'

'The first thing you have to do, Therese, is live in isolation for the next three weeks. You have been in contact with typhoid. All precautions will be taken.'

Surely he couldn't mean it? But she saw nothing in his face but gravity. 'I have to go – the Madisons are expecting me at Hetherington . . .'

Charles's face was severe. 'I'll call them by telephone.'

'But . . . ?'

He frowned in annoyance. 'Frederick and Lady Black-shaw will understand. They will see that your friends are well looked after.' Then he went quiet, waiting until he was sure she had nothing more to say. 'There is the other matter we have to talk about.'

'What?'

'Your houses.'

'I've said to you, Charles, already. If they won't look after themselves – as we do . . .' Her voice trailed away when she saw the look on his face. She knew when it was fruitless to argue with him.

He began, 'Every sanitary authority has power under the Public Health Act of 1875 to take summary proceedings for the closing of homes unsuitable for human habitation—'

'My houses are . . .'

'I had to agree with him. They should be condemned.'

'Charles!'

He lifted his fingers to indicate that he had not finished and it was as if the very room had stilled and was listening. 'The Macclesfield inspector is going to look at your houses, to ascertain if a nuisance exists.'

'Nuisance?'

'Under the Act "nuisance" means injurious to health.'

'Oh, really, Charles!' she said. He could not possibly understand how much trouble the wretched houses were. If she could wash her hands of them she would. But the income was essential.

He strode now to the window where he stood looking out over the garden whilst she was almost in tears. Outrage that Charles and this horrible man dared to speak about her behind her back rose and stuck in her throat. Charles would not be disloyal, she knew. The dreadful sanitary inspector must have threatened her, through her own husband. 'They can't do this to me!' she cried.

He turned and looked at her. 'Come here,' he said. All the love he had for her was shining in his eyes and she felt her anger dissolve in a wave of love for him as she went to stand beside him and watch the last rays of wintry sun slanting across the trunks of the still-bare beech trees. He took her hand in his and without looking at her he said, 'I can't protect you from the consequences of all your actions, my darling.'

He said, 'It is their duty to institute proceedings. If judgment goes against you – if you disobey an abatement order – you are liable for a penalty of ten shillings a day for each of the houses.' He took both of her hands in his and led her back to the seat by the desk. 'Defects include lack of air space, darkness, dampness, lack of water supply and sanitary arrangements.'

Every one of those applied to the houses in the Dams.

'There has to be adequate paving or drainage of courts,

yards and passages. If you go in contempt of an order for clearance, which might be the result of the inspector's visit, the penalty is twenty shillings a day, for each house.'

'What do you propose? That I forgo the rents?' she asked, almost in tears again.

'No. What I demand – what the law demands, Therese, is that you improve that property. You must put in sanitation with water closets in the yards. You must put running water in every house.'

'How do you think we will live?'

He must have seen her face grow white and frightened, for now he smiled, the fond, protective smile she loved and he pulled her again to her feet and placed an arm about her shoulders. 'There is your income, my darling. Five hundred pounds a year is not inconsiderable. There are my earnings from the private practice and there are the royalties – the commission on the paregoric.' He pulled her close. 'And soon I shall have another ointment – a white precipitate – to sell.'

'Oh, Charles.' She knew that Charles was right. He always was right. She put her tear-stained face up to his. 'You are good. I will. I will repair the houses.'

'You have no choice but to repair and improve them. There will be no return for years on your property.'

'We're poor, Charles, aren't we?' she whispered.

He looked into her face. 'If you would allow it, I could have your creams made up. I could sell them, as patent cures. They would bring a good sum of money . . .' He stopped when he saw the tears vanish, saw the look of horror on her face.

She would never contemplate selling her own inventions. 'Don't be ridiculous!' she said. 'They are mine. I could not bear it if any old crone could buy my preparations.'

'Yet you allow me to prescribe the lavender salve, the almond hand cream . . .'

'But I only make them for the family, my dearest friends and your private patients!'

He would not try to dissuade her. He put his arms tight around her and kissed her but before he could say anything more they were interrupted by the sound of the front-door knocker being struck.

After a few moments the new housemaid tapped at the study door. 'There's a man in the hall. He says he's Sir Frederick Blackshaw.'

Charles laughed his great resounding laugh. 'Then if he says so, he is.' He went eagerly to the hallway to welcome Frederick.

Therese, who had remained in the study, heard Freddie's voice as Charles greeted him. Her heart was skipping beats again. She ran into the hall. 'Freddie. Oh, darling Freddie.'

He put out a hand. 'Therese,' he said in an awful, formal voice that Charles would never recognize, as she did, for the coldness it conveyed.

'I want to speak to Therese,' Freddie said as soon as they had gone into the drawing room.

'Shall I leave you to your talk?' Charles asked.

'No, darling.' Therese began nervously to usher them about. 'Sit here, Freddie. Charles will get you a drink. You will dine with us of course . . .'

Freddie sat. 'I'll have a brandy, Charles,' he said. 'I ought to return to Hetherington this evening so perhaps I won't dine . . .'

Charles gave Frederick the glass and went to the door. He must have seen what was wanted of him. 'I'll finish the work on the formula I'm writing. I'm sure you have plenty to say to one another.'

Therese closed the door and, with a dramatic sigh, leaned her back against it. Frederick was as bold and dashing as ever but instead of the warm conspiracy that had always existed between them she felt his mistrust of her like an accusation.

'I'm sorry.' She hoped to sound regretful and endearing but heard her own empty-sounding words fall flat. She had wanted to take the bull by the horns –

apologize – have done with it so that they could resume their old relationship.

He stood with his back to the fire, brown eyes flashing with anger. She had never seen him so angry. 'I can't help thinking that you and Charles made too much fuss about—'

Frederick's hand came up swiftly to warn her to stop. 'That's enough!' His face was thunderous. 'You know exactly what you've done. But there's no going back.' He quickly drained the glass. Then he held it out to her. 'Give me another. A large one.'

She pushed the flat of her hands against the door in a nonchalant manner and, obediently, went to take his glass and refill it. And as she took the glass and held it out to him she tried again. 'I said I'm sorry. You won't believe me, will you?' She looked up at him under the heavy lids in the way that used to charm him. 'Truly I didn't know that Alice cared for you, Frederick.'

'Liar!'

'Freddie! Please!'

He banged down the glass on the high wooden mantel-shelf making her start at his fury. 'Don't be submissive, Therese,' he said. 'It doesn't suit you.'

She had never known Freddie like this. She didn't know how to deal with him so she stood, shocked into silence, as he continued to rail at her. 'I've not come here to listen to your excuses. You know what you've done. You've ruined my life. You've ruined Alice's. And now you are going to make amends!'

She bit her lip. 'Very well. What shall I do?'

'Write to Alice. Tell her everything. Ask her forgiveness – and by God, you'll wish her well, and mean it! I want to see the letter.'

'I can't do that!' She took a step away, dropped on to the chaise longue. Then she glanced up at Freddie from under the thick black lashes, to see if he were showing any concern for her.

389

'Why not?' He seemed to be sneering at her. Her darling Freddie hated her.

'I don't suppose she'll even reply,' she said.

'Good! Then she's not burdened with any false sentiment about you, Therese,' he said. 'As I was.'

It was true. Freddie hated her. Tears of self-pity came prickling under her eyelids. 'She writes to Charles every week. She never mentions my name. Never asks how I am or how near to giving birth—'

'I'm sure Charles gives a bulletin on your progress,' he said. 'You can cease this "Little Misunderstood" nonsense. You are a big girl. There's no-one but yourself to blame for this. And nobody but you can put it right.' He took another gulp of the brandy and, this time, said nothing.

She wondered if, under the effects of all the alcohol, the heat was going out of his anger. She dabbed at her eyes and cast a glance down, at the pattern on the oriental rug at her feet. She hoped to give the impression of contrition, of broken-hearted regret, as she whispered, 'If only I knew how to put it right, Freddie, I would. If I thought that Alice could love me, I'd do anything – anything at all . . .'

He did not answer. There was a long silence between them and she was afraid to break it; afraid to look up in case she saw contempt on his face again. Then he spoke. In the soft and gentle voice he used to use to her she heard him say, 'Does Charles tell you how she is? Do you read her letters?'

And she knew, Therese knew Freddie so well. He was still in love with Alice. He had come here, not to hear her apology, but to hear news of her, to get information about Alice. 'Yes,' she answered firmly. 'She's well.'

'How is she living?' he demanded.

'She has lessons in German and Czech every day. She and Karl have a large apartment above a restaurant in Vaclavske Namesti. It's the square where the Wenceslas statue—'

390

'I know where it is!' he replied sharply. 'I meant to ask how she is being supported.'

'They live on Karl's army pay and an allowance from his grandmother,' Therese saw that he was giving attention to her. 'The Austrian government has brought in conscription.'

He drew in his breath sharply. 'Of course!' he said. 'Conscription!' His face was flushed from the brandy and he was gripping his almost-empty glass as if he would snap the short stem into two.

She continued, 'Karl will be in the army for two years.'

He said, 'Longer than that, if he's gone for Officer Training.'

'Karl was at a military academy before they came to England. He need only do his two years' service, Alice said, and still have a rank.'

He did not reply to this but a soft look came into his eyes. 'So she's not at the same address?'

'The same? You know her address?'

He put a hand into his inside pocket and carefully, as if it were precious, brought out a letter and handed it across. 'She wrote to me. What do you make of it?'

She read it, taking her time. Freddie must not guess that her mind was racing. The content of the letter was immaterial. She was certain that Freddie need have no worry. She didn't care whether her uncle shot himself or Maisie did it for him. But she wanted Freddie to think her sincere and repentant. 'She is very clever,' she said. 'Alice has an analytical mind. She'll be an asset to Karl and the Reinhardt family.'

She reminded him again that Alice now belonged to another man, another family, another country. 'I hope you use the information wisely. Don't contact her again. The Reinhardts are very formal, very strict about these matters.'

He drank down the last of the brandy so fast that she wondered if he might fall, drunk, at her feet. 'Don't take any more, Freddie,' she said. 'You'll be ill.'

He did not answer for a moment. Then, when she thought he was about to tell her to hold her tongue, mind her own affairs, he said, 'I don't like it. I don't like to think of Alice married to a Prussian or whatever Reinhardt is. There's going to be a hell of a fight over the Balkans before long.'

Then he lapsed into silence again and stood there, soldierly and straight. She put out her hands. 'All right?' she whispered. 'Is everything all right again? Can we be friends? After all, we're still cousins.'

He looked at her, his features relaxing as he shook his head gently and took her outstretched hands in his own and held them for a few moments. He had forgiven her. She would tell him that she would not be coming to Hetherington. He would go to Liverpool for her – meet the Madisons off the White Star liner that was bringing Xanthe and her father to Cheshire.

She would show him the studio portrait of Xanthe. It flattered her, made her look slimmer and more *soignée* than she had been when they were at the lyceum in Vienna. But they had been young innocent virgins in Vienna. In Xanthe's delicately coloured photograph there was an inviting, almost sensuous look in her friend's big amber eyes. Xanthe had clearly been living life to the full.

'What are you going to do?' she asked. 'Leave the army? Or demand a posting? India?'

'I'm staying in. I'll remain at Chester. There's to be a volunteer force – a Territorial Army. I want to be involved. There's bound to be trouble soon.'

'I hope you are wrong, darling,' she said. 'From where do you see trouble coming?'

'The Balkan situation grows more dangerous every day.'

'Karl's with the Austrian army,' she said. 'Their army is run by professionals. None of those little Balkan countries would be so foolish as to challenge the might of Austria.'

He looked at her as if she couldn't possibly understand. 'Austria is ruled by an old man who thinks more of the uniforms than he does of fighting. Germany is turning out armaments faster than any other country.' He added, 'Germany and Austria are not re-arming for nothing. I want to talk to Charles about it after dinner. I'm invited to stay, am I?'

'Of course, darling. Of course you are.'

'And you will write to Alice? You will apologize to her? Be a friend to her?'

'Yes,' she said. 'I'll do anything for you.' But it was to be two years before she began to think fondly of Alice. It was to be two years before her dislike of women shifted its focus from Alice and became fixed upon her friend, Xanthe Madison.

# Chapter Twenty-three

**Prague, Spring, 1905**

For two years, whilst Karl had been at the Prague barracks, Alice had scrimped and scraped to make ends meet. Their apartment above a *Kaffeehaus* in Wenceslas Square – Vaclavske Namesti or Rossmarkt in Czech and German – she kept spotlessly clean. Only occasionally did she have to call on the services of the black-eyed little Elsa Prochaska, the Czech serving girl who helped in the apartments, cleaned the communal stairs and served in the *Kaffeehaus*.

She had vowed never to live in poverty, dirt and disorder once her childhood was over and, though it was a challenge to her to manage on the little Karl could spare from his army pay, she would be glad when the years of penny-pinching were over. The objectives she set for herself – to keep the flat clean, to have good food on the table, and to be a good officer's wife to Karl – were difficult to meet.

Since his conscription, Karl had become particular about his food and clothes. His uniform had to be exactly right – immaculately pressed without a speck or spot upon it, his boots polished to a glittering shine, his sword sharp and keen. His batman saw to this but when he was off duty, and the Austrian army were not allowed to wear mufti off duty, if a stranger should touch him he'd step back quickly and afterwards brush the area with his hand as if his jacket had been made dusty or contaminated. Alice would tell him not to go to extremes but he paid no heed.

He was finicky about his food; the table must be set precisely and there must be neither too much nor too little food; no fat on his meat, no stalks or skins on his vegetables, no burnt bits. In the matter of his food, Alice found Karl very hard to please. She had never seen this side of Karl before they were married but then, in England, she'd hardly ever seen him in domestic surroundings. She wondered if he had been tyrannical with his mother; wondered if all foreign men were like this.

His behaviour was odd but, Alice had told herself, there had always been the knowledge that his service would be over in two years' time and they could begin to lead the normal family life she wanted so much.

Her habit was to rise at six, make breakfast for Karl before he went to the castle barracks, and then go out early to make her purchases at market stalls before the city became lively and noisy.

This morning she left Wenceslas Square where the statue of the saint, mounted on his horse, dominated the wide, tree-lined, cobbled boulevard, and went through the narrow streets down to the river.

She loved this city. Prague, like Rome, was built on seven hills and filled with palaces and churches, domes and spires. There were warrens of narrow, roofed-in passages, arcades, twisting streets; houses where doors opened into one lane and it was possible to go down a passageway and out, unobserved, into another street.

Best of all she liked to stand by the river early on amber-coloured mornings such as today's when the sun was lost in a mist, flooding the town with warm golden light. On the banks of the River Moldau, the Vltava to Prague's Czech citizens, acacia and lime trees were in bloom and today as she looked out across the river she saw that the hillside gardens of the Lesser Town, the Kleinseite, were a mass of blossoming trees.

The Prague scents were magical; on a spring morning the air was fresh and soft and full like new bread.

She stood and looked and breathed deeply and the sights and scents of the city began to work their magic upon her, calming her, helping her recover her sense of proportion. For last night they had quarrelled, furiously and violently for the first time.

The foundations for the explosion of tempers had been laid a week before, on the night they were to celebrate the end of his army service. Karl was going to take up work in the offices of Max Bauer's Engineering Works in a month's time and Alice had asked their friends, the Mannersmanns, to supper.

She had prepared a meal of stew with liver dumplings, potatoes and salad. She had made a chocolate cake to a recipe of Babushka's that she had perfected. Two bottles of white wine were cooling in a container of crushed ice in the kitchen and she and Elsa Prochaska had spent the morning scrubbing and polishing the apartment for the occasion.

Karl had come home from the castle barracks a little earlier than usual and, without warning, without once having discussed the possibility with her, had announced that he was not going to leave the army.

'I shall stay in army for one more year,' he had said. 'I cannot leave the Imperial Uhlanen. I shall be promoted to full Leutnant.'

Bitterly disappointed and upset, Alice had cancelled the celebration supper and had given the cake to Elsa, in part-payment for her work. She had tried not to let Karl see how upset she was because he was so proud of his promotion which he said would mean that they would have more money. But she had been hurt and a little tearful at the prospect of another year's hardship and another year's wait to try to have the baby she wanted.

And whilst Alice was upstairs in the apartment trying to see everything from Karl's point of view, downstairs the seventeen-year-old Elsa Prochaska, who had no use for a whole cake, sold the *Schokolade Kuchen* to Herr Ferleitner, the proprietor of the *Kaffeehaus* in the square.

The following day, Herr Ferleitner had knocked at the apartment door to ask Alice if she would make him a *Schokolade Kuchen* each day. She could use the premises of the *Kaffeehaus*, he said. There was a small room off his kitchen where she would not be seen from the restaurant. He would provide the ingredients and would also pay for the *Schokolade Kuchen*.

Alice saw at once that an opportunity to make a little money for herself had fallen right into her lap. She said, 'May I give you my answer tomorrow?' and, when Herr Ferleitner had reluctantly agreed to wait, she'd spent the rest of the day in a fever of excitement, wondering what to charge him.

She counted the cost of the ingredients over and over and they did not come to a great amount of money. She walked about the city, looking at the prices of *Kuchen* in the shops and knew that she would not want so little for her efforts. And finally she had decided – If they wanted her cakes they should not have them cheap. She'd demand four crowns for her *Schokolade Kuchen*, to include the price of the ingredients. She gave her price to Herr Ferleitner. He accepted it. He gave her the use of the small kitchen, the use of the steel moulds she needed and asked for not one but two *Kuchen* each day.

She had rewarded herself by buying a new green blouse and had then started to save the money she made.

Then, last night, Alice had been standing at the window in her floral skirt and the new green blouse, waiting for Karl. The apartment's big sitting-room window overlooked Wenceslas Square. From this vantage point she always watched for his return and last night she had been in a happy, excited mood for she was going to tell him about her little success.

She looked down from her window. In the square below the apartment, customers were seated at the pavement tables of the *Kaffeehaus*. The square was noisy with electric trams, the sounds of carts and horses and shouted orders and conversations in Czech and German.

She saw Karl striding across the square, erect and proud in his green and silver uniform. Men, ordinary working men, were leaping aside. In Prague, as elsewhere in Austria-Hungary, a uniform had to be obeyed. A soldier took precedence over a civilian in the street. Everyone got out of Karl's way.

He stopped to speak to Herr Ferleitner down below and Alice saw the man nodding rapidly as if apologizing for giving Karl some inconvenience.

A few moments later she opened the door of the apartment to him and saw that his face was like thunder. 'What is this I hear? You are working at the *Kaffeehaus*? My wife? The wife of an Uhlan officer works for a living?'

'What do you mean?' she began. 'I only . . .'

He held up his hand imperiously. 'I saw your cakes being served to customers out in the street. I was told you had made them. Explain!'

Anger rose in her. How dare he speak like this to her? She felt her face going white as she slammed the front door so that they should not be heard on the stairs.

She heard herself, icy-voiced, saying, 'You dare tell me what I can do when I have no money to call my own?' Karl had never told her what his army pay was but she had assumed it was very little indeed and that he was ashamed to earn such a paltry sum.

He pushed past her into the sitting room. He stood with his back to the window and said in a voice blazing with anger, 'A Leutnant is paid two hundred crowns on the first day of the month.'

It was a terrible shock to hear that he earned so much. Two hundred crowns seemed to her to be a great deal of money, especially as Babushka allowed them a hundred crowns a month on top of his pay.

'Where does it go?' she demanded. 'You spend as much as that? You spend two hundred crowns – and the hundred crowns Babushka allows you.'

'I can only afford to give you fifty crowns each month,'

he shouted angrily. 'You know that an officer is expected to live up to his station in life.'

'Your station in life?' She would not shout as he was doing but her voice was heavy with sarcasm and contempt. 'What station in life does a wife have? What station for the poor wife of this splendid officer of the Imperial Army?'

He lurched forward and took hold of her arm, holding it tightly, his fingers marking her as, with a face flaming red, he began to list his financial obligations to the army. 'Out of this pittance,' he yelled, 'I have to pay mess bills, rent, tailor's bills, shoemaker and buy all the little luxuries incidental to my rank. And I also must pay out for anything that may happen to my horse!'

Alice snatched her arm out of his grasp and fought back the rage that was urging her to slap him across the face. She would not allow him to rant at her like this. Nor would she put up with living as they were, on the brink of poverty, when Karl had so much money to spend. She put her shoulders back and faced him bravely. 'You think three hundred crowns is a pittance? And you want to stay in the army? You are mad!'

She stepped backwards. Her cheeks were flaming red and her hand came up to smack his face. Then slowly she let it drop to her side. He should not make her lose her temper. But he must know that she meant every word. 'I shall not stay here and go mad with you.'

He had never seen such determination. His hands went slack. The high colour went from his face. 'What do you mean?' he said, clearly shocked by her show of temper. She had never even raised her voice to him before.

'I mean, that unless you either leave the army or allow me to earn my own money, I shall go home to England.' She took a deep breath and coolly she said, 'And if I go I will never come back.'

Now it seemed he wanted to try a different approach. He tried to appeal to her sense of his dignity.

'You cannot do these things, Alice,' he said. 'You

399

cannot earn money. And you must stay here. If you leave me – or if you earn money – you will make me into a laughing stock. And anyone who is a laughing stock in the eyes of the regiment remains so for ever. There is no forgiving, no forgetting in the army. An officer must always act *standesgemäss* – in accordance with the code.'

He said then, 'If your behaviour came to the ears of my fellow officers I should have to resign.'

She stood her ground. He should not try to make her feel guilty. 'Are you telling me to leave you?'

She knew that he would not want her to leave him. In what she now knew was an infantile way he loved her. Karl, like a child, needed her approval of him. And he used this need, his dependence on her good opinion of him, as a form of blackmail.

'No,' he answered. 'You are my wife. You make promise to obey me. And I say that you shall never work for your living.'

'You dare to tell me that I have broken my promises to you? You who promised me that you would let me do anything I wished? That I should become an actress?' She had no wish to become an actress. Not here. But that did not alter the fact that he had deceived her from the start. 'You promised me that I should have a good home and children! What have I got? Nothing!'

He said that they should not have children until his army service was over and she had agreed to that. But he behaved as if she had no right to anything but the little he felt he might spare her from his 'pittance'.

There was a cold finality in her as she looked at his white, angry face and said, 'I tell you that I shall do exactly as I please! There is no reason why anyone but you and I should know that I am earning money. But if they find out – and if you are expected to resign – then you have a big choice to make Karl. I have made mine.'

All this had happened last night and now, as she stood on the banks of the Vltava in the early morning, she knew that she had been right not to give in to Karl's threats and pleas. Later he had accepted her ultimatum. Now she had a chance to earn money, a challenge, a purpose in life.

And to cheer herself she took out of her handbag Aunt Harriet's letter that had come by the early post. She had been saving it. Karl showed no interest in the letters she received from England; one each week from Papa and one each month from Aunt Harriet. She leaned on the iron railings and tore open the envelope.

Dear Alice,
    You will have heard that Lady Cranston-Bartlett died recently and that my dear friend left to me the house on Lord Street and a little money . . .

Alice could not resist a smile when she read this, for Papa, no doubt poking sly fun, had told her that Aunt Harriet had been left a colossal fortune in Lady Cranston-Bartlett's will.

    I have given each of you children three hundred pounds. Yours I have deposited in an account I opened in your name at Parr's Bank on Lord Street. I like to think that when you and Karl come home for a holiday you will have no need to bring your Austrian savings out of the country.

Three hundred pounds would buy a small house in England. Alice stopped reading for a moment and gazed across the river. A holiday in England would be wonderful. But Karl said he would never go back.

    I shall visit Prague as soon as everything is in order here but that may not be for two years as Leopold is only sixteen. Leopold is having private tuition at the house after that dreadful business at the school. It was monstrous that he should have been accused of dishonesty. I wanted to bring an action to clear his name but your Papa thought it wiser to accept the expulsion, saying it would be impossible to prove that Leopold was blameless. I disagreed but your Papa had the last word.

Alice had only been given the briefest of outlines by Papa of the trouble. It seemed that Leopold had got into a scrape after collecting money from the senior boys and not putting it on the horses. It all sounded childish – and since betting was not allowed it seemed to her that many more boys than Leopold ought to have been disciplined. But then there was some earlier trouble she remembered; something about Leopold's having taken time off school to play in a billiards tournament for money.

Your two baby half-sisters are delightful. Charles is so proud of them. Edith, the elder, is tall and the image of her father with her flaxen curls and huge blue eyes. Baby Constance is tiny with Therese's turquoise eyes and straight blonde hair. I expect you have a family photograph.

The photograph, of Papa and Therese with the two girls, Edith standing, Constance on Therese's knee, had pride of place in her bedroom. Every night, before she put out the lamp, Alice looked at it and longed to see her new sisters whom she did not consider to be as Aunt Harriet called them, half-sisters. And every night Alice longed, sick and empty inside, for the child of her own that Karl denied her.

George is proving to be very competent as estate factor at Hetherington and Beatrice is a tower of strength. She works hard at the infirmary. When she is not there she is at home, helping your Papa or taking the babies to the park in the perambulator. I am sure she tells you all about it in her letters.

In fact Beattie had only written three letters and their content was spare, the style laboured. Writing letters was clearly a travail to Beattie.

To Alice's great surprise she had received more letters from Therese than she had from her sister. The first one from Therese had been the longest, full of cryptic references to past misunderstandings. These caged references to their quarrel were plainly an attempt to patch up differences and Alice had made no mention of it in her replies. After about a year nothing was said about misunderstandings. Later letters from Therese, particularly the most recent ones, showed a softening towards her. Alice looked down at the letter in her hand again.

> I think of you often. When I go to Macclesfield with Leopold I feel your absence keenly. It is such a pity that Karl did not want to join his father in the factory. You could be enjoying a good life together with all your family round you in Macclesfield where you are so much missed.

Alice felt the tears come prickling but knew that letters from home always did this to her. She was not sorry to be living here in Prague. She felt she had been destined to come. If she had not married Karl then she would never have known Babushka. She could not imagine life without the wonderful old lady she visited every few weeks. Babushka was her adviser, her dearest friend and had become through marriage her honoured grandmother.

She folded the letter, put it in her handbag and looked out again over the river. The river that ran sparkling and clear through the very heart of Europe was hundreds of miles from the coast and yet she saw seagulls wheeling and crying high above the water, bringing back memories of her morning walks beside the sea in Southport.

There had not been time in the last two years to do any more than run the apartment, learn the two languages of the city and visit her beloved Babushka whenever Karl gave her the train fare. Soon, of course, she would be able to afford the fare at any time if the demand for the *Schokolade Kuchen* grew.

It was astonishing that only yesterday one of the hotels in the square had asked if she would make four. If more were wanted she would decide whether to engage a kitchen girl or pay Elsa Prochaska's wages and keep her as an assistant. She'd find a box-maker if the orders increased . . . She already had plans for supplying the whole of Prague . . . But maybe she would look further afield – make smaller *Kuchen* she could send long distances . . .

A laugh began to bubble inside her as she turned away from the river to walk back to the square. She scolded herself for being fanciful. After all, she had only been making the cakes for a week. The novelty of her creations might be a few days' wonder Surely businesses didn't grow at the speed of her imagination?

Before she began to make the *Kuchen* today, she wanted to buy violets with unblemished petals for crystallizing and storing as cake decorations.

Ahead of her was the Graben at the other side of Wenceslas Square. Flower-sellers with carts piled high with bunches and baskets of scented blooms were calling their wares in Czech and Hungarian, the Slavonic languages that with Polish, Hungarian, Serbian and Russian could be understood from here in Prague to outermost Siberia.

'You're out early, Frau Reinhardt!'

Alice wheeled round to find her friend and German tutor standing behind her. Frau Mannersmann was the American wife of a German-speaking professor of English at the university. Margaret Mannersmann was ten years older than herself but a strong friendship had sprung up between them.

As well as teaching her the German and Czech languages, Margaret had enlightened her on the intricacies and intrigues of this city where rioting between German and Czech students was frequent and often violent. Margaret it was who had told her that German-speaking and Czech-speaking people had been enemies since the medieval monarchs, with their treacheries and alliances, invited German settlers into Czech Bohemia to colonize and develop the country.

Alice smiled at Margaret Mannersmann and put out her hand. 'You are out early,' she said.

Margaret shook her hand. 'I saw Karl. He said you'd be here. He asked when you two are next coming to have supper with me and Rudolf.'

Rudolf Mannersmann, Karl's friend, concerned himself with politics. The last time they had met, Rudolf had told Alice that a recent law had given both the Czech and the German languages equal status so that a citizen could now demand to be dealt with and have his children taught in his own tongue.

Margaret, whose interests were languages and history, liked to tease her husband. She had replied that the Germans believe themselves to be the *Herrenvolk*, the master race, with a God-given right to rule and that German was still the language of the army, the law and the Emperor's court.

Her remarks had annoyed Karl who could not bear to have his country's problems made light of. Yet Margaret's observations were fair, Alice knew. Czechs outnumbered the Germans in Prague by a huge majority and had fought through the centuries for every advance they had made. Separate schools were part of the problem but jobs were the root of it since German-speaking peoples owned the land, mines, factories and houses. A Czech man could lose his livelihood and his home if he spoke out against German dominance.

To Alice it seemed an insuperable problem and she'd been determined to learn to speak both languages. At last she could make herself understood in both German and Czech, though to Karl's annoyance she found she spoke

Czech more comfortably; perhaps because she spoke more to little Elsa Prochaska than anyone.

'You look very *chic* this morning, Alice,' Margaret was saying.

'Thank you.' Alice was wearing her best; the ankle-length suit of deep violet woollen cloth. The jacket buttoned high and the collar and hem were trimmed in black astrakhan. On her hair, which she wore in a loose chignon, sat a little pill-box of black velvet.

She said, 'Why are you looking for me?'

Margaret shrugged her shoulders though the lively smile never left her face. 'Perhaps this isn't the time to ask you . . .' she said.

'What?'

'We need someone to produce *The Merchant of Venice*,' Margaret said, adding quickly, 'For the Drama Festival. You're fluent in German and Czech.'

'I couldn't possibly translate Shakespeare!'

Margaret answered her eagerly. 'We want to produce it in English and get both Czechs and Germans into the theatre. You know what they're like for only supporting their own cultures. The Germans regard Czech as the servants' language.'

Alice, as an officer's wife, could not embroil herself in anything that could be construed as political. Last week there had been another riot, with Czech students throwing rotten eggs at the German street inscriptions. It had not been serious this time but spontaneous mass rioting was violent and frightening. Often the mobs got out of control and turned to looting, arson and shooting. The violence had spread all over the monarchy and every day brought news of trouble somewhere in the dual realm.

'I know you've done some acting—' Margaret was saying. 'And it will be fun to do it in English. We get little enough opportunity to speak our own language—'

Alice could not imagine how one could act in or produce a Shakespeare play for an audience which at best would only be able to appreciate the plot. She took her friend's arm and started to walk towards the flower-sellers. 'Can I let you know? When I've spoken to Karl about it?'

'All right. You are coming to us on Friday. I can wait until then.'

When Karl was not on duty they went out, alternating between Olga and Max Bauer's modern flat on the outskirts of Prague and the Mannersmanns' apartment near to the Clementinum, the city within a city in the Old Town.

There the American girl cooked the dishes of her homeland – Brunswick stew or chicken gumbo. Rudolf Mannersmann and Karl talked politics and she and Margaret read the English and American poets to one another.

She said goodbye to Margaret, bought violets, a big shallow basket of them, and started to walk back to the apartment, thinking, worrying a little as she went – about the quarrel, her threat to leave Karl and the state of the marriage itself, for it was a nagging, constantly worrying area of her life.

Their marriage had not improved during the two years of Karl's army service. Karl seemed content with it and assured her of his continued love for her but it seemed to her that they had never had a period of tenderness or romantic affection.

Their few short weeks of honeymoon had been a time of clumsy but eager attempts to please one another. Then had come the summons to arms. Karl had spent two months in Officer Training Camp on the Hungarian border and, afterwards, when he came home on leave everything was different.

They had agreed that there were to be no children until he had left the army. And Karl never made the mistake of making love to her properly during the time of the month when she might conceive. Later he would say that he was busy, or tired and they made love less and less.

Then he began to turn away from her affectionate advances in case she might expect more.

Sometimes he did not make love to her for weeks on end and eventually she would ask, 'Do you love me? Have you found another?' though she was sure he never looked at another woman in that way. And he would reassure her and make love to her that very night. And she would imagine that he did not want to make love to her but was doing a kind of duty which he carried out with speed and efficiency . . . and without a spark of passion.

About a fortnight after their quarrel, Alice went out in the middle of the morning to buy sugar and nuts and butter for her *Schokolade Kuchen*. That morning a note had been left in her kitchen asking for four extra *Kuchen* from the hotel across the square. She had to buy more ingredients, for last night she had gone down in the evening to make six cakes; two for the *Kaffeehaus* and four for the hotel.

Now that he saw that she was earning more money from her hobby than he earned from his army pay, and now that not one of his fellow officers had discovered their guilty secret, Karl had started to take an interest in her enterprise. He had made sheets of praline last night and had assembled everything for the caramel and the shortbread she would make today. And she had enjoyed having him work with her. They had laughed together for the first time in many months.

She bought the ingredients and came into the square at the lower end where the Old and New Town met, passed the bank and made her way to the top. The *Kaffeehaus* was almost opposite the great statue.

Karl, immaculate in uniform, was off-duty this morning and sitting at an outside table in the shade of a tree, deep in heated conversation with a dark-haired young man. He did not even see her as she threaded her way between the tables and went through the outside door and into her small kitchen behind the restaurant.

Elsa Prochaska who lived with Jan, her handsome student-brother on the top floor of the building, was making salads at the scrubbed table near to the deep white sink.

'Ach!' Elsa was muttering as Alice waited for Karl to follow her into the kitchen. 'The *Leutnant*! He spend much time *sprechen-politik*.'

'That's enough, Elsa,' Alice spoke sharply to her in Czech. 'The *Leutnant* is my husband.'

The girl flushed and then slowly a smile lit the black-button eyes in her wide Slavonic face. 'We make *Kuchen*?'

'Soon.'

At that moment Karl came pushing through the door from the cafe.

'Who were you talking to, Karl?' she asked.

'Seppie.' Karl spoke hastily. 'Come into the *Kaffeehaus* with me. Seppie has gone to the bank but he'll be back. He wants to talk to you. I don't want him to see you here . . .'

'Was that Seppie?' Alice asked. Olga and Max's son was an eighteen-year-old law student at Charles University. 'He's grown since I saw him last. I didn't know him.'

Karl began to speak in English. 'He's going to give up his studies. Join the army.'

Alice's eyebrows lifted. 'Has Seppie enlisted? They don't conscript students.'

'He's—' Karl jerked his head in the direction of the cafe. 'We'll talk in there.' He turned to Elsa and said in German, 'Bring coffee.'

Alice followed him into the almost-empty restaurant where Karl chose a table far away from the occupied ones.

'Why can't you talk in front of Elsa?' she said. 'She doesn't understand English.'

'Elsa may speak German but she's Czech. Her brother's a Young Czech, a supporter of Doctor Kramar, the Evil Genius of Central Europe.'

There were two factions within the Czech nationalist movement, Alice knew. Kramar's faction embraced negative, obstructive policies; Masaryk, who opposed Kramar, advocated democracy and universal male suffrage. The German minority were afraid of votes for all men since it would lead to Czechs outnumbering them in the Reichsrat.

And Alice could not bear to hear all these old arguments. 'Karl!' she protested. 'Jan Prochaska's a nice young man. He's a student of history. Elsa is helping him through university. They live quietly on the top floor here. You can't think of Jan Prochaska as dangerous. Really!'

'You don't understand, Alice,' Karl said. 'You are not born Bohemian. You are only married to one.'

'Oh, Karl!' Now Alice couldn't keep her voice down. She saw the warning look on Karl's face and lowered her voice as Elsa came towards them. 'I wish you wouldn't get involved with all these factions – Austrians versus Hungarians – Germans versus Czechs and Slovaks—'

'I'm not. Not with the Czechs. My sympathies are with the emperor.'

Alice turned now to Elsa who had placed the little demitasses of black coffee on the table before them. 'Will you break up the chocolate ready to melt, Elsa?'

'*Ja!*' A broad smile broke over the girl's normally expressionless face.

'When I've finished my coffee we can make the *Kuchen.*'

'*Ja.*' Elsa, still smiling, went into the kitchen to prepare the ingredients for the cakes.

'Have you more to make?' Karl asked. 'I thought you did six last night.'

'I did. And they were all ordered. I have to make four more for the restaurant and the hotel.'

Karl said, now with a puzzled look on his face, 'But the owner of the hotel was in this morning. He has given an order – for ten more.'

A great shiver of excitement went through her. She wasn't being fanciful then. 'Oh, Karl!' She leaned across the table and put her hand over his. 'It looks as though I've found it!'

'What?'

'The thing that will make our fortune.' Excitement was growing in her with every thought that came to her. She looked at him with eyes sparkling. 'I shall open a shop. There are two empty rooms next door to the *Kaffeehaus*. One with a window on to the street . . . I can make the cakes, lots of them if we take on workers . . . I can employ people to sell them over the counter. Take orders. I think this is my chance!'

But he was staring at the wall above her head. He had not listened to a word she'd spoken. His mind, she knew, would be upon Seppie, the army and the political intrigues of the city.

'Are you listening?' she asked.

He looked into her face now and smiled the old proud and arrogant smile she knew. 'Do as you wish, Alice,' he said. 'I'll help you establish your factory.'

She laughed. 'Not a factory! Idiot! A shop.'

'Very well. A shop.' He drank down the last of his coffee and stood up. 'We talk later,' he said.

Alice went into the kitchen where Elsa had set up the table against the far wall.

She put on her white cover-all and lit the flame under the large double boiler that held enough broken pieces of chocolate couverture to make the moulds for four cakes. As soon as these were set they could be turned out and the moulds made ready again. She had already enough crumbled shortbread and cold soft caramel to do the four *Kuchen*. Sheets of praline, nut and sugar-toffee brittle, were waiting to be crushed and rolled. She would do the extra ten cakes tonight.

Elsa was watching her closely. Alice began to stir the melting chocolate, all the while talking to the young girl in a mixture of Czech and German that the girl understood perfectly, so that she would understand the importance of every step.

'I stir gently, Elsa. Look.' Alice glanced at Elsa. 'Pass the thermometer.'

Elsa handed over the long glass and brass tube.

'Is it warm? And perfectly dry?' Alice asked.

'*Ja.*'

'It is vital that the chocolate be properly tempered,' she said, concentrating hard as she stirred and dipped and read the heat. 'Cocoa-butter contains very complex fats.'

She told Elsa, repeating Babushka's explanations, 'No water or steam must touch the melting chocolate. And as soon as it reaches forty-six degrees—' Here she read, stirred and waited.

'It's ready.' She lifted the porcelain bowl, wiped it carefully with a cloth and nodded to Elsa to push along the marble tempering-slab. And as soon as it was poured she began to work the chocolate with a large palette knife then, as quickly as she could, returned it to the bowl before it set.

'I'm taking great care,' she explained. 'It must be taken to thirty-one degrees only.' She dipped the thermometer in again and stirred slowly. 'I want to keep a smooth surface. I must not introduce air.'

Elsa, anticipating her next command, brought the dry, polished metal moulds that would shape the chocolate shells for the cakes. Then Alice began to run the warm, melted chocolate into the shiny steel moulds, lifting, turning and tapping until they were all coated evenly.

'There!' She smiled at Elsa when it was done.

The girl took them, carrying them as carefully as if they contained molten gold, to place them on a shelf in the pantry. Then, whilst the cases were hardening, Alice ran upstairs to the apartment where she knew Karl and Seppie would be talking.

They were in the sitting room and got to their feet when she entered.

'Seppie.' Alice put out her hand fondly to the young man who stood stiffly before her. She was very fond of both Seppie and Hans.

Seppie, tall and dark like Karl but broader in stature and in nature more reserved, took her hand in his and raised it to his lips. 'I leave Prague,' he said.

Karl said, as if he expected her to know why he was explaining, 'Russia has lost half a million men. Soon she will lose the war with Japan. Then her interest will return to the Near and Middle East.'

Seppie was looking at Karl with eyes full of admiration and Alice was all at once sick of all this fighting talk.

'Fighting – fighting!' she said in exasperation. 'Why do men always talk about fighting? There's revolution in Russia! They are fighting inside their country and they are fighting a war with Japan. Hasn't Russia had enough of fighting?'

'The Russians are not fighting men,' Karl said calmly. 'They will throw down their guns and run away.'

Alice remembered Babushka's words. 'When the distance between the rich and poor becomes too great, the poor rise up against their masters.'

'Are the Russian peasants rising against their masters?' she asked. Only two months ago on what had become known as Bloody Sunday the Czar's troops had been ordered to fire upon five hundred striking men. The men were marching peacefully to the Winter Palace in Petersburg to petition the Czar for better conditions. And afterwards? Afterwards, the Czar said he knew nothing about it.

'Is it possible that the Czar knows nothing of what goes on, on his palace doorstep?' she demanded. 'Or is the distance between him and his subjects already too wide?'

Seppie now began in a quiet and rational way to explain it. 'Two years ago King Alexander and Queen Draga of Serbia were murdered,' he said. 'Russia is now the protector of Serbia.'

'What has this to do with us?' she said. 'What bearing can it have for us? For you, Seppie?'

'Germany wants to build a railway line all the way from Berlin to Baghdad,' Seppie said patiently. 'The Balkan states are in the way. Serbia, Bosnia and Herzegovina are the countries of Slavonic peoples. They do not want an alliance with Austria-Hungary. If Bosnia and Herzegovina are annexed then Serbia will look to friendly Russia to protect her. And Russia will become the enemy of Germany.'

Then Seppie took a deep breath and said, 'I come today to tell you that I am going to join the army.'

There was silence from both Karl and Seppie. They seemed to be waiting for her reaction though Alice knew that what they wanted was her approval.

She looked at young Seppie's serious face. 'Which army?' she asked him mischievously. 'You have a Russian grandmother and a German father. Do you know which side you should take, Seppie?'

There was a dreadful silence. Both men, Karl and Seppie, looked at her with faces white with horror. She had thought to make light of all this fighting talk. She had tried to make a joke and had given offence. She seldom made intemperate remarks these days, since she only spoke in Czech and German.

'Seppie has joined the kaiser's army.' Karl's voice was cold. He spoke again to Seppie. 'I am sorry,' he said quietly. 'Alice will not try to understand.'

But Seppie had taken her hand again and held it firmly in his own. 'I must go now,' he said. 'I will see you again, very soon.'

Karl too was going to go down to the square again. A cold feeling came over Alice as she watched him go. How could all this constant talk and argument about politics and wars help anyone? Why couldn't people just get on with one another in this beautiful city that had everything a normal person could want of life?

They had been gone only a few minutes before

Karl was back, his annoyance with her evidently forgotten.

'Telegram message!' he announced. 'For you.'

With shaking hands, for she still hated the new system of delivering news, Alice opened the envelope and read.

Therese's grandmother dead. Therese asks Alice to join her at once. Von Heilbronn residence. Gloriettegasse. Vienna. Please help. Papa.

She stared at the paper. Why should Therese want her to go to Vienna? Surely she was the last person Therese would ask. But Papa would not send such a message and plea unless he meant it.

She handed it to Karl. 'What do you think?' she said.

'You shall go.' He became at once authoritative. 'I make enquiry about train.'

'What about the *Schokolade Kuchen*?' was all she could think to say.

'Elsa and I can make.' Karl put a hand on her shoulder. 'You go. If you wish to do so then you take your stepmother to Ilyinka after Vienna. She shall see that we are not savages in Bohemia.'

'Karl! Therese will do what has to be done and hurry back home to Papa. I'm not being asked to join her for a holiday, you know.'

But even as she spoke she wondered why Therese should have asked Papa to send for her. Surely she was the last person on earth Therese would want beside her at a time like this?

And for the second time in her life Alice was mistaken in her judgement of Therese and her motives.

# Chapter Twenty-four

## Vienna

Alice was still puzzled as to why she in particular had been asked for help. She arrived in Vienna on the afternoon of the following day, dressed in sombre clothes of dark grey in recognition of Therese's loss. She had never known the old Countess Isabella Theresa von Heilbronn and Therese would not expect her to wear black.

At the station she was met by a bent, grizzle-haired old manservant who seemed tired of life and impatient to be done with her. In a crotchety voice he ordered that her cases be sent to the house. Then he went ahead of her to the line of *fiakers* that waited in the spring sunshine outside the station.

'Gloriettegasse!' he grunted to the carriage driver before sitting stiffly in the seat beside her.

The Gloriettegasse was a quiet street adjacent to the gardens of the emperor's palace of Schonbrunn. Alice had always wanted to see this city on the Danube; the splendid imperial city that was the creation of the Habsburgs. The Hungarian border was only a few miles away from Vienna and the city itself had, through the ages, gathered into its melting-pot all the nationalities under the Habsburgs' rule. There were no national rivalries here, yet Prague was bedevilled with them.

She had asked Karl to bring her here but there had never been any money for holidays. And she'd read about the heart of the Habsburgs' empire that encompassed and absorbed settlers from Burgundy and the

Franche-Comte, from Flanders and Spain. With the partition of Poland had come Poles and White Russians; from Lombardy had come Italians; from Bohemia had come Czechs. And all these nations had melded to become a civilized, gifted and handsome people, known throughout the world for their tolerance.

Would she be able to see anything of Vienna whilst she was here or would she be entombed with a grieving Therese in some dark and dismal corner of the city? She was eager to catch a glimpse of the glittering city of the court, the theatre and music and as she craned her neck forward she saw monuments rising through clouds of blossoming trees.

The old man sat silent, head held stiffly, staring into the distance as the carriage rolled along. They passed the emperor's palace and then St Stephen's Cathedral. They sped on the Karntnerstrasse in a line of elegant carriages and, within an hour, drew up in the quiet street which ran alongside the palace gardens, in front of a green-shuttered town house with elaborate cast-iron balconies. The manservant gave his orders to the carriage driver and rang the door bell.

Therese answered the door. She was dressed from head to toe in deep mourning-black. Alice had never seen Therese in anything other than clear pastels or silks of jewel-bright richness.

'Thank you for coming, Alice,' Therese said, taking her hands in her own and on tiptoe kissing her on the cheek in the disdainful manner she had always shown.

Alice returned her embrace coolly and her heart sank at the prospect of spending time alone with Therese. But then Therese held on to her hand with cold fingers for a few moments longer than was necessary as if she needed the warm touch of Alice's and Alice knew in that moment that this was a changed Therese. She saw that her stepmother's eyes were dark-shadowed and her skin was pale and dull and that her hands were shaking.

'I hope I can help you,' she said and heard her own

417

voice, clear and confident, ringing around the great gloomy hall that was crammed almost to capacity with dark, heavy furniture of a past era; armoires, sideboards and show cases filled with porcelain figures. The walls were hung with brooding portraits of men in the wigs and ruffles of their day.

The old man closed the door behind her.

'Follow me, Alice, will you?' Therese said, ignoring the manservant's presence as if he had not been there. 'I'm so glad you are here.'

She went ahead into a second hallway and then on into a drawing room that overlooked the Gloriettegasse. This too was so full of furniture that there was barely room to move. An involuntary shiver went through Alice and Therese must have sensed it for she said quickly, 'I only want to stay here for two or three days. My grandmother left the house – left the last of the lease – to her old servants. I'm to have the contents. I want to go through my grandmother's papers and have the furniture taken away and sold.'

It was all said in a quick, anxious voice. Alice knew that words of condolence and sympathy would be out of place. It was plain that Therese was not grieving. 'Don't you want to keep anything?'

'I'll keep my grandmother's recipes. She was something of a herbalist,' Therese said without enthusiasm. 'I'll keep the family portraits. Perhaps I'll take the porcelain.'

It was going to be a miserable two or three days, Alice saw. She took off her coat and unpinned her hat. 'Where do I put these?'

'I'll show you to your room.' Therese went ahead again, through a long and overfull dining room, down a corridor and into a bedroom where the great oak bed was prepared for her and her cases had been placed on the floor.

Therese said from the doorway, 'You'll have seen how unpleasant the old man is. Do you think we will be able

418

to manage without these ghastly servants if we take our meals in the restaurant? I will give them leave to go. There is a bathroom. And a kitchen.'

'I'm sure we'll manage.' Alice plonked her coat and hat on the bed and made an effort at giving an air of good cheer. It was no use Therese moping for longer than necessary. She knew why Papa had wanted her to come. Therese would be hopeless if left to do all this herself. She picked up her case, opened it and began to take things out.

Therese stood watching her in the doorway, a tiny, slight figure. In every line of her body, in the expression on her face, was fear and for the first time Alice knew pity for her. Therese was terrified of being alone in the house that must hold so many memories.

Therese came into the room, closed the door and spoke with low urgency. 'I'll be glad when we leave here,' she said. 'I hate this house. I want no reminders.'

The air of false cheerfulness quickly fell away from Alice. 'You lived here with your grandmother did you?'

Therese's eyes filled with tears. 'Yes. My grandmother had an evil influence on everyone she had dealings with. Including me.'

Alice could think of nothing to say in reply. She wished she had not asked.

Therese continued, 'She was a disappointed woman. A mere countess in Vienna where everyone has a title and where rank and social connections mean more than life itself.'

Alice recalled the time when Therese had set such things high. Therese, her eyes still full of tears, said, 'I was never allowed to speak to my grandmother except in the third person.'

Alice did not understand this. 'What do you mean?'

'I had to say, "Did my grandmother, the countess, enjoy her drive?" and "May I ask a favour of the countess?" And she would not look into my face when

419

she'd turn to that manservant and say, "No. Take the creature out of my sight." '

Alice's horrified expression must have prompted Therese to explain. 'She detested me,' she said. 'You cannot know what it means to a child, to be detested.'

'Surely you were mistaken?' Alice said. A grandmother could not detest her own child's child, could she?

Therese's mouth was being pulled down at the corners and she was trying to hold it firm by clenching her teeth. 'Nobody ever wanted me. I was packed off – to Cheshire – to Vienna – to India.'

'Alone?'

'I had nannies. Later a governess. Later still a maid. I had servants and clothes. I was never hungry or cold,' she said. 'Perhaps that's enough.'

Alice shook her head. 'It's not. It's not enough.'

Then, in a voice that was choking with suppressed anger and pain, Therese said, 'My grandmother was wicked, cold and snobbish. Her life was spent scheming and planning. She was capable of anything; any evil. I'm afraid of finding evidence of all she did when I go through her papers.' She took a black-bordered handkerchief from a pocket and began to blow her nose with ferocity. 'Don't be shocked. You've been very lucky. You have always been surrounded by love and affection.' She closed her lips tightly together for a moment before adding quietly, 'I never knew anything but fear. Until I met Charles.'

'I'm sorry,' Alice said in quiet voice. She didn't know what else to say. She had to hold herself back from giving in to the sudden urge to comfort Therese. She wanted to go up and put her arms about her stepmother's shoulder but she knew that Therese would shrink from any gesture of affection.

'So,' Therese said at last. 'Don't expect me to show grief.' She had pulled herself together. 'If there is anything you want, anything you would like for your home in Prague, please – take it,' she said.

There followed the most extraordinary two days with Therese almost always at Alice's side as they listed the glass, china, porcelain and the pieces of furniture for removal by the auctioneers. There was no sign from Therese that she had uncovered any dreadful secrets of the countess's and Alice was pleased to see the strain that Therese was under begin to lessen as first one then another box and document case revealed nothing of significance.

Alice sent out for food which she cooked in the cold and gloomy kitchen in the basement. Therese ate these offerings with enjoyment and Alice felt oddly touched that she should.

And in the evenings Alice lit the stove in the big room and brought a tray of hot food and drinks for them to share and they sat together, eating and reading, in silence. And it seemed to Alice that inside this silence understanding was growing; a little centre of affectionate feeling that, had the circumstances been right, might have gathered around itself something solid and good.

On the third day the work was almost finished. They had been out to a restaurant for their midday meal where they had eaten boiled beef, *Tafelspitz*, and a heavy, filling pudding of dumplings with apricots. They had drunk bitter, fig-flavoured coffee that was only found in Vienna and afterwards when they returned to the drawing room for the first time since she had arrived Alice felt satisfied, very comfortable and relaxed.

She was to say which furniture she would have sent to Prague and had already decided upon a French desk in rosewood, with inlays of mother-of-pearl and ebony and a galleried and gilded top.

'You have good taste, Alice,' Therese said when she chose it. 'It is probably the most valuable piece in the house.'

'Are you sure you wouldn't rather have the money?' Alice asked. 'If you sold it you'd have more . . .'

Therese smiled. 'No. The money this furniture raises

is going to be spent on my property. I won't benefit from it.'

'Then can I have the Chinese cabinet as well?' The glossy black cabinet, tall and lacquered, had dozens of drawers and hidey-holes and had quite taken Alice's fancy. There were secret drawers and cupboards-behind-cupboards and all cleverly painted with golden dragons and stylized flowers and not an inch unadorned. She had always had a taste for the over-ornate that had fallen from fashion.

'Yes. It won't become valuable in your lifetime though.' Therese laughed now. It was the low gurgling laugh Alice had not heard since she had arrived in Vienna.

'How do you know it won't,' Alice asked. She was thrilled with her gifts and sure that they must be the most sought-after pieces. 'One can never be sure of the fashion.'

'I'm not talking about fashion,' Therese said. 'I'm talking about age and beauty.' She was smiling broadly as she spoke.

'Then how do you know what will age well?' Alice smiled back at her.

'I'm learning,' Therese said. 'I buy things; I collect paintings and Japanese vases as an investment.' Then she smiled more deeply. 'And when Charles and I are poor and old I shall sell my little Degas pictures and Renoir drawings. Charles believes they will never amount to much.'

Alice smiled back at her. 'Papa's the sort who would never have a picture on the wall or an ornament on a table,' she agreed. 'He'd say they only gather dust.'

Therese laughed. She seemed to want to hang on to the closeness that had sprung up between them in the last three days. 'Have you something more colourful to wear, Alice?' she asked.

'Yes. My violet suit . . .' Alice answered. 'Why?'

Therese's eyes were shining. 'We are going to go out,' she said. 'I couldn't buy tickets for the Burgtheater. I know you like the theatre. But I have ordered a *fiaker* to come for us in an hour.'

'Where to?' Alice felt a great lightening of her spirits at the prospect. Therese's face was alight with eagerness and frivolity.

'We are going to be driven round Vienna. I shall show you the sights . . .'

'Ooh. Thank you!' Alice was smiling, relaxing into laughter. Therese's enthusiasm was infectious.

'We shall drive in an open carriage, just as if we were two great empresses,' Therese said. 'I will show you the Danube and point out the Vienna Woods. We'll drive to the Hofburg down the Augustinerstrasse. We'll see the Spanish Riding School.'

She was laughing, head thrown back. She had begun to lift her skirts and to twirl them a little and in those moments Alice saw beneath the hard surface of Therese – saw the joyful girl, the gaiety that Papa loved in her.

Therese continued, 'We will go to the Wurstelprater – the Prater gardens and we will wish we had the children with us. It is the biggest funfair in the world and everyone goes there, young and old – to the circus and the Punch and Judy shows.'

She laughed again and her laughter was so infectious that Alice joined in as Therese finished, 'And if they will allow us in, since we have no titles and we are not accompanied by Herren Grafs – earls to you, Alice.'

This remark seemed to delight her even more. They both began to laugh, tears of laughter at Therese's silly expression – 'Earls to you, Alice!' – which would probably become a family catchphrase. Therese was mopping her eyes as she finished the sentence . . . 'If we had Herren Grafs to accompany us we could end the day at Frau Sacher's in a room full of plush and – and – chandeliers – in company with the most elegant and gracious people in Europe.'

It was not until four days later, after a visit to the

apartment in Prague, that they went to Ilyinka and it was there in Babushka's house that Alice knew how much closer they had drawn to one another. She would be disappointed to see Therese go home. This time she would be losing a friend.

They were sitting in the salon after supper and darling little Babushka had joined them at the table under the window that looked on to the sweep of gravel at the front of the house.

The four trees nearest the entrance to the house had been hung with coloured lamps on Babushka's orders to welcome Therese, who was gazing out on to the scene with a faraway look in her eyes.

'It reminds me a little of Hetherington,' Therese said softly, almost to herself.

Babushka brought in a silver samovar and placed it on the table. The little spirit heater made a gentle, hissing sound, soothing and pleasing. Tea cups were being placed in front of them by Babushka who had dressed for the occasion in the gold robe Alice had only seen once before, on her arrival here two years ago.

Alice smiled at Babushka, who would have scorned an offer of help. Alice knew better than to volunteer to do the honours for her. The first serving from the samovar was a ceremony that was always performed by the head of the household in this old Russian family.

Babushka was eighty-five. Alice watched her steady hands as she placed small china cups before them. She must have let her anxiety for the old lady's health show in overconcern at some time, for Babushka had promised, with great sincerity, that she had no intention of dying for a long time.

She had told Alice that she wanted to see the great-grandchild who would inherit Ilyinka. And Alice prayed that Babushka would not have to wait too long, that she might watch the growing up of the as yet not-conceived great-grandchild she so wanted.

But tonight Alice would not think about the lack of

love in her marriage or the marriage act itself which, if it were not completed, would never lead to conception. Tonight she wanted simply to watch Babushka and Therese.

Babushka's bright eyes twinkled merrily in the dear old wrinkled face that was the only outward sign of her great age. Her brain was quick, her memory sharp; for all that she only used a quarter of Ilyinka she ran the place with the competence of a woman thirty years younger. She walked daily around her gardens and glasshouses, for these were kept tended by a few women from the village who could take their share of the produce.

And Alice was idiotically pleased when Therese had instantly seen all this. She had seen with delight that the impression Therese had made upon Babushka was a good one. She did not ask herself why it pleased her, when it would not have done before.

Therese had spoken about her life in India, Vienna and England. She had talked a little but with pride of Papa and the four little children. She had shown the old lady photographs of Papa and the children. In return Babushka had spoken of her two daughters. Nobody had ever heard Elena Pavlovna speak about her two sons who were dead. She had shown Therese over Ilyinka and twinkled with pleasure when Therese admired the carvings and the ikons.

Therese was relaxed, sipping her tea, making the most charming of light conversations in German with Babushka whilst Alice looked on.

Babushka excused herself at nine o'clock after lighted lamps and another samovar were brought into the room.

When Babushka had gone and they were seated, facing one another over the table, Therese began to talk with unusual animation.

'Did I ever tell you about my American friend, Xanthe Madison?' she asked. 'The one who travels all over the world.'

425

'I knew you wrote to someone in Boston.'

Therese was speaking fast and needed little encouragement to continue. 'She visited England just before Edith was born. She and her father.'

Alice said, 'And?'

'I was in quarantine at the time. We had an outbreak of typhoid in Macclesfield so I asked Freddie to . . .' She had begun to wave her right hand as she spoke.

'To what?'

'To be my stand-in. My understudy. To escort Xanthe.'

Why was Therese telling her all this? Alice tried to look unconcerned. Why was her heart missing beats? Why had her knees turned to water at the mere sound of his name? Surely she couldn't still be in love with Freddie.

'Xanthe's father bought the Dower House for her.'

Alice put down her cup. Her hands had begun to tremble and she did not want Therese to see her agitation. 'I didn't know it was for sale,' she managed to say and was surprised that her voice sounded normal.

'Yes. Freddie's father left a lot of debt, you know.'

'I didn't know,' she said. She knew that Therese would be watching her face for any sign of agitation.

'Freddie did wonders of course.' Therese was looking at Alice from under the heavy lids. Her face, no longer white and frightened as it had been in Vienna, was flushed and her eyes were bright. 'He did his very best to avoid having to sell anything.'

Alice hoped she was showing a look of polite detachment. Some response was expected of her. She said, 'But he had to sell the Dower House?'

'Freddie was never a good businessman,' Therese went on, talking fast again. 'He loves the army, his sport and his horses more than . . .' She glanced at Alice. 'More than anything else.'

'So your friend lives on the estate?' Alice knew she was acting again She knew that Therese for some reason wanted to be sure that she felt nothing for Freddie.

'Yes,' Therese replied. 'She spends more time in Cheshire than anywhere else.'

'Then why didn't you ask her to come with you to Vienna?' Alice asked sharply. She was tired of all this doubletalk. Why didn't Therese come to the point?

'Charles wouldn't allow it. He has forbidden her to come to the Beeches.'

Alice opened her eyes wide in surprise. 'Papa? I can't imagine Papa denying you anything, Therese.'

'Charles says that Xanthe is the only woman he has ever known who is utterly depraved.'

'Good Heavens.' Alice could not imagine Papa speaking about a woman in that way. 'She must have done something truly awful for Papa to forbid her the house. What on Earth can she have done?'

'I don't know for certain.' Therese spoke softly and when Alice looked closely she saw that there was a steely look in her eyes. 'But I think . . .'

'What?'

'She plays fast and loose with men,' Therese said. 'Do you know what I mean by that?'

'Of course I do.'

'Xanthe cannot resist men, Alice. She is one of those women who changes completely whenever a man comes into the room.'

'In what way does she change?'

'Have you never met the type of woman . . .' Therese waited for a second before continuing. 'You think she is your friend. You tell her all your secrets. And suddenly a man comes into the room and you find that she has made you into her rival for his affections.'

'I don't think I've ever met such a woman,' Alice laughed.

Therese said, 'It's not funny, Alice. Not funny at all when your best friend goes behind your back and tries to make fast and loose with your own husband.'

'But Papa wouldn't . . .' Alice could not stop smiling. 'You just said that he thinks her depraved.'

Therese said, 'Men do strange things. You don't know.' She spoke in a fast, angry little voice. 'Xanthe used to go to Charles's surgery. She was always pestering him. She fell in love with him. And now he forbids her to come to the house . . .'

'Is she still his patient? What's wrong with her?'

'Charles says there's nothing wrong with her. He says she makes mischief. He says that she'll be trouble wherever she goes.' Therese looked hard at Alice. 'There are things . . . things a woman will tell her best friend . . . that she would never tell to her own husband.'

Alice said nothing then and Therese, after a moment, asked, 'Do you know what I mean? Are there things you have not told Karl?'

Alice felt colour come rising into her face but the lamps were not bright enough for Therese to see it so she answered, 'Oh, I suppose there are . . .'

'Xanthe suggested to Charles that I was not married and widowed in Vienna. I'm afraid she might have put a lot of nasty ideas in your father's head.'

'You are imagining intrigue where none exists,' Alice said with a show of impatience. The conversation was getting nowhere. 'If your friend is rich and flighty then I'm sure Papa will see right through her.'

'I wish she'd go back to America,' Therese said. 'I wish she'd set off on her travels again. Leave us alone. What she wants with us I can't imagine.'

Alice did not want to talk about this Xanthe but whilst Therese was so indiscreet she would ask her what she did want to know. 'What happened about the police enquiries? Into the old Sir Jack Blackshaw's death?'

Therese's face lost the mournful look at once. 'You'll hardly believe this,' she said eagerly as she leaned forward, took another cup of tea and began to relate the story with evident pleasure.

'Xanthe's father, Warner Madison, took a great liking to Freddie when he was negotiating to buy the Dower

House. Xanthe wanted it badly you see. Her father is completely in the palm of her hand.'

'And?'

'Maybe Freddie confided in him. Maybe George had become involved. The upshot was that Warner Madison, not wanting Xanthe to live where there was any hint of scandal I suppose, went to Macclesfield and spoke to Maisie. She was my maid if you remember.'

'I remember,' Alice said.

'Maisie told him the most astonishing story. She claimed that my uncle was her lover and had fathered a baby born to her in Macclesfield. She went to see him on the night of the ball to tell him that she was expecting his child and that he must provide for them. By her account, Sir Jack Blackshaw gave her money and told her to go away. When she refused, he took out a gun and threatened her. There was a struggle and the gun went off. Maisie ran away.'

Alice felt a great lump come into her throat. 'What do you think?'

'It is exactly what one would have expected of my uncle. Maisie certainly had a child. A boy. She brought him round to the Beeches after Warner Madison had spoken to her. She was in a frightful state. But when I saw the baby I knew at once. He was every inch a Blackshaw. There was no mistaking it. I told Warner Madison I thought Maisie was telling the truth. And Warner Madison gave her a lot of money to go to the police and make a statement.'

Alice swallowed hard. 'Did the police accept her story?'

'Warner Madison paid for the best lawyer in the country to represent Maisie. He promised to bring the child up himself if the case went against her. He also promised money to Maisie to help her make a new life in America when the case was over.'

'And?'

'The police accepted her confession. An inquest was

held and the verdict was accidental death. Maisie is in New York.'

The lump was there again. Her voice sounded faint. 'And Freddie?'

There was a long silence whilst Therese looked from the window to Alice and back again. 'Freddie was very upset when he heard about the child. He wanted to call a halt to the whole business. It was too late for that.' She stared into space for a moment, deep in thought, then she said, 'After that Freddie took no interest in any of it. He left everything to Warner Madison and spent the entire time in sporting activities.' She turned to Alice. 'You know Captain Sir Philip de Grey Egerton of "D" squadron, of course?'

'No.'

'Of Oulton Park, near Chester?'

'Never heard of him.'

'I can hardly believe that. Your Aunt Harriet has heard of him. Your father knows him.'

'Nevertheless,' said Alice patiently, 'I don't know these people.' All she wanted to hear was Freddie's news. Now. Before Therese left she wanted every last scrap of news about him . . .

She should not be so interested but she couldn't hold herself back from asking. 'You were saying . . . about Freddie.'

'Oh, yes. Freddie seemed to throw himself into sport. When he wasn't hunting or racing in point-to-point he was on the polo field. He could have asked for a posting to India, of course. You know that the Cheshire regiment has always had a presence in India?'

'Yes. I know,' said Alice again, impatiently this time. 'But what about Freddie?'

'He wouldn't budge until all the enquiries were over.'

'And when they were?'

'He went a bit wild. His mother has always said that unless Freddie settles down to marriage he'll be no use to anyone! And that's exactly what's happening. He's going wild. There's no other way to explain it.'

A great wave of nostalgia and love swept over Alice. 'What does he do?' she asked. 'In what way is he going wild?'

'When it was all over and Maisie had gone he began to start enjoying himself again. He started to drink more than he should. He accepts every invitation that comes his way . . . goes to weekend parties . . . entertains a lot . . . does things he used to hate. He went to London . . . as a guest of the Madisons who have a town house in Eaton Square. In their gratitude for being allowed to buy the Dower House they invited him to spend the summer with them on the Riviera. They have a villa in Nice.'

## Prague, 1905

She came down here every morning – winter and summer alike. Unless she did so her day felt wrong. Alice was standing by the bank of the Vltava at seven o'clock on an October morning. She needed the exercise and she needed to be alone for a little time each day. Six months had passed since she and Therese had been together and now the letters from Therese came more frequently and were more intimate than before but today she had only one to read – from Aunt Harriet.

It was colder this morning. The paths were not swept as yet and the scent of trodden leaves hung in the air, reminding her most strangely of autumn in Duke Street, even though the view from here was nothing like Duke Street. She gazed out across the river that soon would freeze over for the winter months.

Soon the seagulls would go away and leave the Vltava to the skaters and carriage drivers and the occasional daring driver of a motor-car making a short cut from bank to bank.

She turned from her gazing and opened Aunt Harriet's letter.

Dear Alice,

A lot has happened since I last wrote to you. Leopold has obtained a position and given up his studies. He was invited to join a Liverpool Property Company. They have premises in Southport and were looking for a trustworthy and presentable young man to look after the office.

It has all caused quite a lot of upset in the family as your Papa does not approve because the offices are near an amusement arcade.

I believe the property is presently being used as a gentlemen's club where billiards are played. It is very respectable I am told, though I have not been invited to see inside. Ladies are not allowed, Leopold tells me.

Sometimes, Alice thought, Leopold makes an ass of Aunt Harriet. It was too bad of him to behave in this way. He had always been a clever boy and ought to have stayed at school. She turned to the second page of the letter.

I have become quite adventurous myself since Leopold is occupied almost day and night with his work. You will hardly believe this but your old Aunt Harriet has taken up cards! I go three times a week to different church halls to play whist and am becoming quite expert. I don't consider whist to be gambling although there are prizes to be won. It is very entertaining and I have made friends with all classes of people through this interest. It has broadened my outlook, Leopold says.

Alice could not help but laugh at this. She simply could not picture Aunt Harriet, severe in her black dresses, doing anything as – infra dig she would once have called it – as playing cards in public.

*I hear that Karl's family are coming to visit you in the autumn . . .*

They were arriving this very day, at three o'clock in the afternoon.

*. . . I am sure you will be happy to see them and hear of their success. Blackshaw and Rinehart has expanded. The factory is twice the size it was when you left Macclesfield.*

Alice wished she could show Aunt Harriet her own business which was becoming very profitable since she had leased the little shop next to the *Kaffeehaus*. Working behind the scenes, for the sake of Karl's standing with his fellow officers, Alice employed four people to help make the *Schokolade Kuchen* and still they could not keep pace with the orders.

The cakes were known locally as Alicia Kuchen which she thought very funny. She sold nothing but the confection in her shop and the cakes were made in all sizes from the smallest, which could be eaten by one person with their coffee, to the largest which cut into twelve big pieces and was sold in a box almost the size of a hat box.

She came to the last page of Aunt Harriet's letter and had to look back to see if she had missed anything, it seemed so disjointed; so apropos of nothing . . .

*I was not invited to the wedding, of course, but I read about it in the newspapers and have seen the photo- graphs. The Society Wedding of the Year, from the account in Cheshire Life and Therese and your Papa looked splendid.*

Alice shook her head in bewilderment. She had not been told about any wedding Papa and Therese had attended. If it had really been a grand occasion she was sure Papa or Therese would have mentioned it. Aunt

433

Harriet was simply interesting herself as usual with the lives of others.

Alice smiled to herself as she folded the letter and put it back in the envelope. That kind of sycophancy used to annoy her she recalled as she went back to Vaclavske Namesti. It had little relevance to her life in Bohemia.

At three o'clock Karl, in his splendid uniform, and Alice, in her furs, stood on the platform on the main Prague station, a grand opulent place in the Art Nouveau style that had only recently been built. Beside them, Olga and Max with Hans and a uniformed Seppie waited to greet the family that the Bauers and Babushka had not seen for seven years.

Alice dared not take Karl's hand though she would have liked to do so as the train pulled in. She was so excited at the prospect of seeing them again that she needed to steady herself. Behind her, three porters stood ready to carry the baggage to one of the three carriages that waited outside.

Then they were here, coming down the platform with arms outstretched in greeting and Alice was being hugged by a tearful Irmgard, kissed on the cheek by her mother-in-law and having her arm taken and fingers pressed to the lips of Karl's father.

From then on the rest of the day passed in talk and laughter, congratulations, admiration for her little shop and the four-roomed flat above the restaurant that Alice had furnished so lovingly.

She had made ready the two spare bedrooms and placed bowls of flowers on the tables. She had prepared tea, English afternoon tea with sandwiches and scones, bread and butter, raspberry jam and one of the *Schoko-lade Kuchen*.

And Ekaterina, whom she was allowed to call *Mutti* and Johann, whom she called *Vater*, were full of praise for her and full of chatter in German and English. Vater no longer expected Karl to speak English with him. He had forgiven his wayward son for returning to Bohemia and Alice saw bright tears in Karl's blue eyes when his father took him in his arms.

It was a wonderful day. And in two days' time they would all, all but Karl who had been refused leave by the new colonel, travel by train and wheel-carriage troika to Ilyinka and their beloved Babushka.

After tea and before supper, Irmgard, who simply would not leave Alice's side, came down to the bakehouse kitchen to help make the chocolate moulds for *Kuchen*.

'Irmgard,' Alice said as she lit the flame below the double boiler, 'talk to me in English. I want to hear news of England, in English.'

Irmgard laughed in delight. 'I think in English,' she said. 'Sometimes in my dreams I talk in a strange mixture of German and English . . .'

'Me too,' Alice said and was about to tell Irmgard all about Margaret Mannersmann and their poetry readings and play-production but her sister-in-law was unstoppable.

Irmgard's blue eyes were sparkling with pleasure as she chattered away.

'Vater plays chess with your Papa,' she said. 'Every Tuesday evening . . .'

'And sometimes I go with him, to see the babies and talk to Beattie, if she's there . . .

'And Mutti and Vater won't allow me to work . . .

'And I want to be a nurse, like Beattie . . .

'I am only allowed to go to the Chadwick Free Library by myself . . .

'In fact I've been nowhere. Since the wedding . . .'

Alice interrupted her here. 'Calm down, Irmgard,' she said. 'Not so fast. Whose wedding?'

Irmgard was silent for a moment or two so that Alice turned from stirring the couverture, to look at her.

'Sir Frederick Blackshaw's wedding,' Irmgard said. 'Didn't you hear about it? Your father and stepmother were there . . .'

Alice felt faint. Her head had gone light and dizzy. She leaned on the edge of the table. Irmgard must not see her reaction. Waves of hot embarrassment followed and a terrible feeling of sick disappointment. And all the time Irmgard heedlessly went on chattering.

'An American girl. Miss Xanthe Madison from Boston . . .'

Why should she feel this way? Why did her hands shake? Why should she be shocked that Freddie had married?

'So much money, you wouldn't believe it . . .'

Had Papa and Therese known she'd be upset at the news? Was that why they hadn't told her? And why – why did she care?

'I heard that she chased Sir Frederick Blackshaw like fury . . .'

'Her father bought the Dower House for her long before she married Sir Frederick . . . And her father did some kind of a deal to get the terrible suspicion lifted from Sir Frederick . . . It was something to do with his father's death . . .'

Alice took a deep breath and looked at Irmgard steadily. 'Do you think it's a love-match, Irmgard?' she said. 'Does he love her – or her money?'

'Ooh! I don't know about that,' said Irmgard vaguely. 'She is not really pretty. She has round yellow eyes that are a bit blank. Only they come to life whenever a man comes near.'

Alice said nothing and Irmgard looked at her and asked, 'Have you ever met women like that, Alice?'

'I don't know. I don't think I have.'

Irmgard gave a little laugh and said, 'You'd know if you had. Xanthe's most peculiar. She seems to lose interest in you at once, whatever you are talking about, and just fixes her eyes on a man. Then she sidles about him until he notices her. It's very odd.'

Why, again why did she care? Why had her stomach turned over, her knees turned to water at the sound of his name? Why couldn't she bear to think of him making love to the blank-faced, rich, sidling-around, American who was Lady Blackshaw?

Alice had no recollection afterwards of finishing the chocolate shells, of drinking coffee in the kitchen with Irmgard and Elsa Prochaska when she was done. She did not remember that Elsa's brother, Jan Prochaska, had joined them. She had no recollection of leaving Irmgard there, falling head-over-heels in love with a handsome Czech student of history.

She felt she did not come down to reality until she and Karl were alone in their bedroom.

Karl liked to darken the room and then pull back the curtains so that they could see one another in the moonlight that fell slanting across their bed.

The room looked ghostly with the pale beam lighting upon the lace-trimmed linen on her dressing-table. The red roses had become deep purple in the almost-darkness.

Tonight there was no need to ask if he still loved her for he turned to her as soon as the curtains were drawn back.

'Take off nightdress,' he said as he began to remove his own nightshirt.

He did not mean to sound brusque, Alice knew. In his usual efficient way he was trying to rouse her expectations of pleasure in his arms. Tonight though, for the first time, she would not make excuses for his manner.

She lay still underneath her goose-down quilt and found that she was shaking. And her trembling did not come from unfulfilled desire as it so often did. 'Karl?' she whispered.

'What is matter?' He stood, looking down at her face.

'I don't want . . .' she began to explain.

He stared at her for a moment in surprise, before at last smiling. 'I understand,' he said. 'When Vater and my mother are in next room . . .'

'Thank you,' Alice said.

It was the first time she had refused him but tonight she did not want his clenched-teeth kisses. She did not want to feel the hard probings of his fingers, hurting her until she called out and he took her cries of hurt for those of need.

She did not want him to make love as he always did, lifting himself on to his elbows so that they barely touched, averting his eyes from her face as, with great force and speed, he brought himself to the high point of his desire. She did not want him to pull away sharply and spill himself outside her body and turn away from her at once to fall into a deep, satisfied sleep.

And she would be left, shaking and wakeful, her womb denied and her body clamouring until sleep came to blot out the misery of what should be married love.

And she would dream, as she was certain she would this very night, of a midsummer night under the stars, the scent of roses, the whispered words of Lord Byron's poetry and the sweet caresses of a dark-haired tempestuous lover.

# Chapter Twenty-five

Three years were to pass before any other member of either family came to see them in Prague and during those years success in her business, hard unceasing work to secure her success, and modest riches came to Alice. And with the riches, though she had little enough time to spend the money, came confidence.

A year before they were visited by Beatrice, Alice and Karl had another quarrel, this time about everything; about Karl's not wanting children, about the fact that now she earned a lot of money and he had only his army pittance and about Karl's jealous and possessive behaviour, for he seldom left her side when he was not on duty.

In the early days when she was the stranger in a foreign land she looked to him for advice and support. Now that she was established and successful she believed that he looked to her. And she would ask herself, 'Why not? Surely that is what marriage means – supporting one another through good and bad.' And it had come about, perhaps through her neglect of these matters, that Karl made all the decisions about their daily life; the banking, the bills and their purchases for the apartment. Alice was always too busy working to take these responsibilities on herself.

But she could not help but see how little actual work Karl did. She knew that when he was on duty he worked hard; he told her so. An officer's life was not all drill, riding and order-giving. When he was off duty he liked to give orders. He also liked to pay the wages . . . and he talked . . . and talked . . . and talked politics until she thought she would go mad.

And as well as this he followed her about. If she were working in the kitchen, he sat in the kitchen. If she were upstairs in the apartment then he would sit at a pavement table outside the *Kaffeehaus* down below, talking politics with anyone who would listen.

But Alice was never to know what had preceded Karl's volte-face about the army.

Their own quarrel was not as severe as their first and had ended quickly, with Karl saying, 'I have heard enough. I shall leave the army.' She would suspect for ever that his fellow-officers had discovered that one of their number had a wife who was neither Austrian nor high-born but an Englishwoman who earned her own money. And, instead of feeling guilty as he no doubt expected her to, Alice was quietly pleased that at last her opinion counted.

In fact it was not Alice's working which had caused Karl's trouble nor was it simply the matter of promotion which had led to his disillusionment with the army.

On the day after their quarrel Karl was sitting outside the *Kaffeehaus* in the morning. He had been to the tobacconist's and bought two 'chancery doubles' – the official form of the Austrian civil and military administration – on which he would write his resignation. He folded it neatly with the aid of a knife – ultra-correct in his last act as a soldier.

Colonel Hawliczek had once again blocked his promotion. Hawliczek – who had ponderously worked his way up through the ranks – who betrayed his peasant origins with his stocky body and ox-like head and his crude abusiveness – had been transferred from one provincial garrison to another over the years until finally he'd been posted to Prague and had taken an instant dislike to Karl.

Yesterday Colonel Hawliczek had 'wiped the floor'

with Leutnant Reinhardt on the parade ground. Karl had given a wrong order and sent horses shying and whinnying and sent soldiers charging in the wrong direction. It had been an error. No doubt about that. He knew he had only himself to blame.

But the colonel, squat on his chestnut gelding, waited only thirty paces from the regiment once they were in lines again and Karl had reined in before him to a deathly silence from the parade ground.

True, Hawliczek had lowered his normal grating voice when in coarse language he had derided him but to the last man, to the last peasant at the back, they all had seen the colonel's crimson face, heard the shrilling 'damn-fool order' and 'bloody stupid order' that he had let fly at him. And once an officer had been humiliated, in the mess the ragging and sneering would go on for ever. Every asinine act was immortalized amongst the officers.

And not content with making an ass of Leutnant Reinhardt on the parade ground, Colonel Hawliczek had called him before him to tell him that he would not be considered for promotion – and he hoped that it was not the case that Karl had been seen, off duty, without uniform at a political meeting.

Colonel Hawliczek was a dedicated officer, his life was the service. He had no time for women, he read nothing but army regulations. Nothing existed for him but the army: and, of the army, nothing but the cavalry, and, of the cavalry, nothing but the Uhlan and, of the Uhlan, nothing but Karl's regiment.

Colonel Hawliczek, though out of place amongst the company of officers in the barracks, knew his army regulations. They were the word of God to him. He knew every line. 'An officer and a soldier does not involve himself in political activity,' he had screamed at Karl. 'What have you to say for yourself?'

This is what Karl would have to say for himself . . . He squared his shoulders as he prepared to lend to his handwriting a melodramatic flourish . . .

## Prague, October 1908

Last night they had celebrated Alice's twenty-fourth birthday and tomorrow Beatrice was going home.

Beatrice was twenty-two. She had finished her probation and training and before starting her new job she was taking a long holiday. And as Beatrice's holiday drew to a close, a dread of parting from her sister seemed to overtake Alice.

It was October. Prague was enjoying a spell of warm summery weather that was most unusual, Alice told Beattie. This was the first year she could remember when the leaves were still on the treees and no frost had come to her city.

She and Beatrice had returned last Sunday evening from a weekend at Ilyinka where Beattie had met Olga and Max Bauer and their son, Hans. Hans was eighteen and his conscription papers had come. He was leaving the following week for service in the imperial army and had been saying his farewells to his old Babushka before he went.

They still lived above the *Kaffeehaus* in Wenceslas Square but they had moved one storey higher into a larger apartment which also had a top floor of small rooms for the house and shop staff and on Beattie's last day they had left the flat early in the morning to go on a round of the five shops in Prague which were Alice's business. The shops sold quality chocolates from Switzerland and Alicia Kuchen.

Alice tucked her arm into her sister's as they walked back across the Charles Bridge after collecting the weekend's takings from the smallest of the shops, in the Kleinseite. The sisters looked very much like twins today – both of them so blonde and tall and slim. They had come out of their bedrooms this morning wearing blue coats and hats and had looked at one another and laughed at the coincidence.

'I wish you'd come and live here for a few years,' Alice said.

'I can't.' Beatrice was squeezing her arm tight. 'I don't want to leave Macclesfield.'

Alice stopped, halting Beatrice with her as she pointed ahead. 'You can't prefer Macclesfield to Prague, Beattie. Look at that.'

Ahead, across the bridge, was the Old Town, an uprush of painted houses stacked one above the other up the hill. There were palaces and domes, gilded pinnacles and copper spires. Higher, looking as if they were sitting on the shoulders of all beneath them, St Vitus's Cathedral and the castle seemed to be shining against the sky.

It was a splendid sight and she knew that Beatrice had fallen in love with the city too, with its innumerable cobbled slopes, the squares and steps. She loved the scented breezes and the city sounds; the limpid notes of chapel bells hanging in the air, carillons and peals ringing out over the rooftops.

'The sights and sounds of Prague are wonderful,' Beattie said. 'And the music. But the tensions are a different matter.'

Alice said, 'You'd soon learn to ignore all that. There will always be little skirmishes. Europe is vast, Babushka says . . .'

'No,' Beatrice cut in. 'I'm not worried about trouble in Prague. Austria's a friend of Britain's but we read every day in the papers about the German ship-building programme.'

'They exaggerate, Beattie,' Alice answered. 'There's nothing like that in our papers. And there would be if it were true.' She held Beattie's hand a little tighter. 'Anyway, what difference can it make if we are all friends?'

'Papa says that Austria has to have an alliance with a maritime power.'

'King Edward is always visiting the kaiser,' Alice said. 'They are blood relations. Britain and Germany are staunch allies.' She hated to think that in England there was the same political talk, the same rivalries and fears that she had learned to live with. Nowadays she paid no attention at all. They were a part of life here and she was used to it.

Beatrice smiled and tucked her hand deeper into Alice's. 'Papa says if there's a war it will be in the Balkans.' She paused for a moment then, 'But I'm sure there won't be any trouble,' she said.

Alice felt a great surge of love and affection for her sister. 'I wish you'd come here.' She held Beattie's arm tight. 'You wouldn't have to work so hard, Beattie. This is the first holiday you've ever had. You wouldn't have to work at all until you could speak a little German.'

Beattie stopped and looked at her. 'I have never seen anyone work as hard as you do, Alice,' she said. 'I have my hours off. You never stop. You should have a bit of fun.'

'You wouldn't be sponging or anything, if that's what—'

Beatrice tapped her arm quickly before Alice could promise more.

'I'm sorry, Beattie.' Alice tugged at her arm and began to walk on again, her eyes very bright. 'It's just that – that I don't want you to go,' she said. They had reached the far side of the bridge and begun to make their way to Wenceslas Square. She stopped again. 'Sometimes I get these terrible longings – to go home – to see everyone.'

'It's been the best four weeks I can remember,' Beatrice said. 'Seeing you, meeting the Mannersmanns and seeing Irmgard and Jan Prochaska so happy together.'

Irmgard had returned to Prague after her first visit three years ago when she had fallen in love with the young Czech student. Jan and Irmgard had married and were living not far from Alice and Karl. Jan was now a civil servant who was posted about quite a lot. Irmgard was expecting a baby in the spring.

They reached the *Kaffeehaus* and found Karl at the pavement cafe, 'holding forth' as Alice called it, in the group of men who came every morning to talk politics. Alice went straight past them without speaking.

Sometimes it seemed Alice couldn't refrain from bitter comment on Karl's activities. Sometimes she wanted to go up to him, there in the street – ask why wasn't he doing something useful? Why was he always *sprechen politik* as Elsa Prochaska always called it. Why did he never stop talking and do some real, hard work? It was years since she had seen Karl soil his hands with work. She wanted to ask him this in front of everyone. She would never do it, of course. She would never embarrass him, never let him down, make an ass of him in front of friends – but the temptation to do so was something she constantly fought.

At the start of her holiday Beatrice had asked if Karl still played his practical jokes. They had all had such fun in the old days, she reminded Alice. Alice had looked startled, as if she had forgotten those funny times when Karl would play his daft pranks. Then she'd said sharply to Beatrice, 'Karl doesn't know the difference between a fool and a fraud.' And Beattie had not asked her to explain.

Now, upstairs in the apartment, Alice took off her hat and went to the sitting room. Beatrice followed her and they stood there at the window for a few minutes watching the bustling crowds below in the square; the sparking of the overhead tram wires as the coupled trams tugged up the wide cobbled incline.

Beatrice said, 'Will you come to Macclesfield next year?'

Alice, feeling a bit tearful again, shook her head. 'I don't want to miss a minute of Babushka's life, Beattie,' she said. 'She's eighty-nine. She can't go on for ever.'

Last weekend Alice had hired a chauffeur-driven Renault and they had been driven to the vineyards on the hillside below the village. Babushka had talked knowledgeably to the workers who were cutting bunches of grapes with sharp little knives. And Beatrice had told her Babushka was easily the healthiest old lady she had ever seen.

'She'd still be here, Alice, if you had a week or so back home. And there's Irmgard and Karl, Olga and Max to look after her.'

'I know,' Alice pulled herself up and made herself say brightly, 'but I enjoy being with her. She tells me about her young life in Russia and I talk about all of you, and Papa, and our old life in Cheshire.'

She turned from the window and went to the Chinese lacquered cabinet. 'I'll look for some photographs for you to take home,' she said. 'You can show them to Papa and Therese.'

'Thank you. They'll love them. Papa's much softer now, you know.'

'In what way?' Alice asked.

Beatrice smiled. 'You remember how strict he was with us? He was a real Victorian wasn't he? Being seen and not heard and keeping up appearances – and soldierly behaviour!'

'I suppose he was.' Alice was standing, one hand on the Chinese cabinet, watching her. 'He wasn't unkind. We all adored him. We'd do anything to please him. If Papa said "well done" our happiness was complete, wasn't it?'

'Yes,' Beatrice answered. 'But you should see him with the four young ones. They are allowed much more leeway than we were.' She looked up at Alice. 'They're well-behaved. Their manners are irreproachable outside the house. But they can say anything they like to Papa and Therese.'

'Oh,' Alice said sadly.

And all at once it came over her, how poor she was in the things that mattered. She had worked so hard and all she had to show for it was – money. It was years since she'd had anything to do with children. She wanted a

446

child. She wanted to be a mother. Irmgard was so large she might be having twins. How had she come to agree to Karl's demands that they wait longer?

She took a deep breath to control the great wave of sadness that had come over her and turned to listen to Beattie who was still talking.

'Have you forgiven Therese?' Beattie was asking. 'I never quite knew what she'd done to you, you know.'

'I don't suppose you did,' Alice answered. Then she gave Beatrice one of her puzzling looks and asked, for reasons she knew would be beyond Beattie's understanding, 'How are they fairing? Sir Frederick Blackshaw and his wife? Aunt Harriet said it had been the wedding of nineteen-four.'

'I hear that it was the disaster of the century, never mind the wedding of the year,' Beattie said. 'Lady Blackshaw, junior, is the talk of the county, according to Therese. She's "fast" and "unspeakable" in Papa's eyes.'

Beattie gave Alice one of her sweet smiles. She wouldn't want Alice to think she had become spiteful. She explained, 'Xanthe is the only woman Papa thoroughly dislikes.'

'Why? Why do you think that is?' Alice asked.

'She's "pathologically unfaithful" Papa says,' Beatrice answered. 'I think she's had a love affair with every man she's ever taken a shine to.'

'Surely not?' Alice was shocked. Surely no woman – no woman in her right mind – would be unfaithful to Freddie. And as she thought about him all the old longings started up in her, the weak-kneed sensations that merely thinking about him brought to trouble her.

'Ooh. Not with Papa!' Beatrice was saying. 'Papa is not the kind of man who'd . . .'

'I know!' Alice said hurriedly. 'Don't let's talk about them any more.'

She became reflective for a few monents before she gave Beatrice a dazzling smile. 'I've forgiven Therese for what she did,' she said. 'We came to understand one

447

another in Vienna. She gave me this cabinet.' Here she tapped her hand on the Chinese furniture.

'I've seen one of these in Matron's room,' Beatrice said. 'They are very clever, the Chinese, aren't they?' Then she added, 'Therese has another hobby now. Besides her creams and herbal cures. She collects . . .' Beatrice smiled, remembering Papa's remarks. 'Papa calls it old junk.'

Alice said, 'I wonder she didn't keep this one. It came from her grandmother's house.'

Beatrice went to look. 'May I open it? See if it's the same inside?'

' "Open it?" ' What do you mean? It's all separate little drawers and cupboards.'

'Matron's comes open,' Beatrice said, 'like this.' She pulled out the third drawer from the top. Her hand slid inside. 'I'm feeling for the knob. Here it is.' She put her forefinger in and pressed. 'It's just the same as Matron's.' The front of the cabinet, from the centre upwards, swung out towards her.

'Heavens! I didn't know.' Alice put her hand on to the out-swung front and drew it open. 'Look!'

In the space inside, where in matron's cabinet the patients' rings and watches were kept, here were documents tied with faded brown ribbon. 'What on earth?' Alice took out the first package, untied the ribbon and opened a letter.

Then Beatrice must have seen her face grow pale, her hands tighten as she read. Quickly she put the sheet of paper back in the parchment envelope and tied it. 'I'll look at it later.' Alice's face was white and shocked. 'Don't say anything . . . to Therese . . . back home . . . about this, will you Beattie?'

'Of course not.'

Alice, her heart knocking against her ribs, now turned her back on the Chinese cabinet. 'Come into the bedroom with me. I want to give you something out of my wardrobe.'

'Are you sure?'

Alice had a wardrobe full of expensive clothes, dresses, costumes, shoes and jackets; any one outfit she knew would cost three months' of Beatrice's wages.

'You can have anything that takes your fancy,' Alice said now, head tilted back. 'We're the same size, aren't we?'

Beatrice looked at her. 'I think we are,' she answered. 'I'm glad we are. I'm taller and slimmer than when you last saw me, aren't I?'

'Prettier, too,' Alice said and saw the pink flush of pleasure on her sister's face.

'I love the silver-grey suit,' Beattie said. 'Have you finished with it?'

'Try it on. Take it,' Alice said gaily.

Then Karl came up to the apartment and for the rest of Beattie's stay they were all happy together. Karl was 'up to his old tricks' as Alice, laughing at his expression, called it. Karl passed round a plate of tiny chocolates which they bit into with care in case they contained something awful. Smiling and joking he offered them cognac in the middle of the morning, telling them that the Emperor Francis Joseph had just annexed two little Balkan countries called Bosnia and Herzegovina and that consequently they were going out that very evening to celebrate.

The Bosnia and Herzegovina part of Karl's story turned out to be true but they had all enjoyed a wonderful day. They had gone in the evening to a Beethoven concert, held inside the Thun Palace. Afterwards, when their heads were still sounding with the music, Karl had taken them home to the flat above the *Kaffeehaus* with Beattie on one arm and herself on the other.

And later that night Alice lay in bed, wide awake. Beattie would be asleep, probably dreaming about the delightful prospect of going home to Papa and Therese and the children.

Alice, lying in bed next to a sleeping Karl, came all at once to a decision. She watched Karl for a moment or two where he lay deep in contented slumber. Then, quickly, before she could change her mind, she took hold of his shoulder and shook him out of sleep.

'Karl?' Her voice was clear and steady.

He turned over and smiled, half in sleep. 'Well?'

'If it were not for Babushka and the shops and my workers I should go back with Beattie. And if I did . . .'

He was wide awake now but his face registered only hurt as he asked, 'Why? Why do you torment me?'

'You know why. I want a baby.'

He said, 'But we have agreed. We wait until there is enough money.'

She must make him see. If he failed her now then there was no chance for their marriage. This was the moment for demanding, not discussion. If he would not agree then she would leave him. 'We did not agree! It was your decision! And now I tell you—'

He sat bolt upright and tried to make her see his point of view, 'Wait until we have enough money.'

'There is plenty of money. I will not wait any longer.'

There was silence between them but he knew her well enough, after five years of marriage, to know that she did not make idle threats. She kept her grey eyes fixed upon his face.

He put his hands gently on her face and kissed her full on the soft red mouth. Then he said in the voice she knew as his most sincere, 'Very well. Tomorrow night. After we have been to Mannersmanns' apartment, when we come home. We make baby.'

She could see, by the light of the moon that was falling across his face, that he meant it.

He said, 'You must promise – as you did at our wedding – you gave your word. Never, never speak about leaving me again, will you?'

'I will. I promise,' she answered. Then she touched his face and pulled his mouth down onto hers.

'Kiss me very, very passionately, Karl. Make love to me. I want to make the baby. Now.'

A little over a week after she had said goodbye to Alice in Prague, Beatrice, dressed in the silver-grey suit which Alice had given to her left the Infirmary and walked along Victoria Road towards the Beeches. In her hand she carried a small suitcase. She was going to spend the last week of her holiday travelling with Papa, first to the Lodge to see George and Polly and then on to Southport to drop the boys off at school and visit Leopold and Aunt Harriet.

It was nine o'clock in the morning. Papa had sent a message last night that she was to be at the Beeches at half past nine, for today, for the first time in his life, he was going to drive his motor-car. She walked up the driveway to the front of the house and there it stood in all its splendour – the Argyll. Papa said it had been especially designed for doctors.

She walked around it, admiring the high black body, the blue leather upholstery that was deep-buttoned exactly like a coach. The long bonnet gleamed shiny black. The wheel spokes shone silvery bright. At the rear, behind the coach body, was a wooden seat where a footman or driver would have ridden had it been the carriage it resembled. A long running board either side made it easy to climb into.

It was going to be exciting. She had only ridden in a motor-car twice before; once to Alice's wedding and last week with Alice in a chauffeur-driven Renault to Ilyinka. She wondered if she would be relegated to the little wooden seat, or if the boys might share it and she and Papa could sit inside. Therese did not want to go, Papa said.

She opened the front door herself, put her case in the hall and went down the passageway to the back door and out into the garden. She could hear the shouts of laughter from Arthur and Peter, both nine years old now, who were playing a last game of tennis on the court behind the shrubbery.

She stood on the garden path, feeling the sun beating warmly down on the back of her neck as she watched them for a few minutes. The boys had not seen her nor had Therese who, dressed plainly in a bottle-green jacket and black and green striped skirt had the five-year-old Edith by one hand and Constance, who was four, by the other.

Therese was laughing at something one of the children had said and was shooing them towards the far side of the grass where Nanny Redfern was sitting. The girls ran, blonde hair streaming, white pinafores billowing about them as they went helter-skelter over the lawn and Therese stood, hands on hips, watching them go.

Whilst Beatrice was watching the scene from the garden Charles stood at the morning-room window of the Beeches. The lawn and path were carpeted with leaves which Slater, the gardener, had not cleared. It was Therese's twenty-eighth birthday and she had declared herself depressed and the day a day of mourning. But she was laughing at something one of the girls had said and Charles knew the familiar rush of desire that the sound of her laughter and the very sight of her still brought.

Beyond the shrubbery Peter and Arthur were making wild swings with their rackets over the net on the tennis court. It was the perfect family scene and he stood with his hands in his pockets, filled with paternal pride.

The door opened. The housemaid was bringing in a tray with coffee and biscuits and setting it down on the dark oak table that was placed near to the fire.

'Thank you,' he said. 'Has Beatrice arrived yet?'

'I think so, sir,' the girl answered. 'Her case is in the 'all, sir.'

Charles tapped on the French window. Therese turned to smile at him and he pointed towards the table. She nodded and smiled and he opened the glass door for her and kissed her soundly as soon as she was inside.

'Come with us?' he said when they moved apart. 'I can send the boys back to school on the train. Please come – with Beatrice and me.'

'No.' Therese pulled away and went to the table. 'I'm going to enjoy a week to myself. There are two auction sales this week. And, much as I like Harriet, I don't want to go to Southport. I shall make my almond balm and I'm going to try to fix a new rose scent. The attar of roses has arrived.'

She began to pour the coffee, holding one silver jug in each hand, pouring coffee and milk simultaneously and glancing at him with the sea-green inviting eyes as she did so.

He took the cup and saucer and went to sit in a chintz-covered armchair by the window. Therese had exquisite taste; a flair for choosing exactly the right and yet the unusual pieces of furniture. His home had been furnished on a shoe-string and there wasn't a palace to compare with it.

He was the most fortunate man in the world and never happier than when she was at his side. And today, when he had a week of leisure stretching ahead of him, Therese had made up her mind to stay in Macclesfield. She would have some happy hours in the salerooms of the auction houses.

'You do realize, Therese, that this is the first time I shall have driven the motor-car.'

'You will be perfectly all right, Charles.' She made a tutting noise as if impatient with him but her eyes were full of mischief. 'It was you who insisted we sold the horse and trap. I knew you would not like to drive yourself. We can't afford a chauffeur.'

'There is only seating for two inside, three at a pinch, and one outside. If I had a chauffeur I should not be able to take anyone with me.' He smiled. 'And if you buy anything large this week as you did last . . .' This was a reference to the William and Mary bureau which stood in an alcove of the drawing-room. '. . . you will not have your willing slave at hand to bring it home for you with all the assorted ironmongery . . .'

'Silver!' she corrected him. 'Ironmongery. Indeed!'

At that moment Beatrice came into the room, dressed in a long grey outfit and wide hat tied down with chiffon against the motoring-wind that would ruffle the elaborate coiffure she adopted when not on duty.

'My case is in the hall, Papa,' she said.

'I hope it's small.' He indicated that she help herself to coffee. 'The boys' boxes will have to be strapped on to the back and . . .'

'It's small.' Beatrice smiled her sweet, slow smile.

'There will be four boxes, mind,' Charles reminded her.

'I'm sitting with you, am I?'

'Yes. You, one boy and I will sit inside. The other can sit at the back. They can change over after Hetherington.'

'I didn't know you were going to Hetherington,' Therese said. 'I thought you wanted to "deal with" Leopold and try to talk sense into Harriet.'

'What's all this?' Beatrice asked. 'Aunt Harriet?'

'Haven't you heard?' Therese said.

'No.'

Papa said, 'Your Aunt Harriet is being courted – squired about Southport – by a man nobody knows.'

'How exciting. Who said?' Beatrice was smiling, sipping her coffee and looking at him over the rim of her cup.

'Leopold told us.'

'What does Leopold think of it all?'

He said severely, 'Leopold has been dismissed again.'

'I didn't think you could be dismissed,' Beatrice said. 'When you were an articled clerk. You got him the post, Papa. Surely they would have to tell you . . .'

'You can be dismissed. Leopold was. He is once again in charge of a gambling hall.' Charles felt the pangs of worry that Leopold's behaviour always brought. So he tried to make light of Harriet's behaviour. 'I suspect that it is through the good offices of Leopold that Harriet has become involved with Captain Cork.'

'Oh, Papa!' Beatrice was laughing. 'Captain who?'

Charles tried to hide his own amusement. 'Cork. Captain Cork. He claims to have been in the artillery. That is all that your aunt can tell us about his military career.'

But before he could give the problems of Harriet and Leopold any more thought the door flew open again and the boys almost fell into the room.

'Mama! Papa!' Arthur called as if determined to speak before Peter did.

'The horseless – the motor-car . . .' Peter interrupted him eagerly. 'Can we help Slater with the boxes?' Peter had dark hair, the pointed hairline of the Blackshaws and the brown eyes, large and round, that all the Blackshaw family, except Therese, had.

'Can we both sit on the back seat, Papa?' Arthur was the quieter boy. He had thick fair hair, a serious face and a complexion that went bright pink when he was excited.

They were all smiling as the youngsters carried on at great speed, interrupting one another, nudging and pushing in their shared excitement.

'There's plenty of room.'

'True, Papa. We've tried it. We fit!' Peter said.

'What are you going to do? Sitting out there?' Beatrice asked them in her severest voice.

'Well, it's a new game . . .' Peter began.

'I'll tell it . . .' Arthur said. 'If you do, they'll say "No" to it.'

'He has a rifle and I have a pistol . . .'

'Not real ones . . .'

'Enough,' Therese said.

'And shoot the legs off the horses . . .'

'Not in real life . . .'

'Course not. Fool!' Peter was laughing so hard there were tears running down his face.

Therese clapped her hands together to quieten them. 'As long as you promise Mama—'

'What?' they chorused.

'There's to be no loud shrieking. No shouting.'

'Then we can sit outside?'

Charles put a hand up to silence them. 'That's enough! Go outside. Help Slater with the trunks. Beatrice's and my cases can be stowed under the front seat.'

The boys ran from the room and Charles picked up his motoring coat, gauntlets and checked hat. Therese stood and helped him into the coat and, after kissing her quickly, they went together round to the front of the Beeches where the shining Argyll waited; brass lamps gleaming at either side of the windscreen, the black bonnet polished, the tyres pumped and Slater, the gardener, waited, starting handle at the ready, until they climbed aboard.

Thirty minutes later they were on the open road. Charles had managed to turn the tight corner at the village of Broken Cross without mishap and they were rolling along at twenty-five miles an hour, past the Cock Inn at Henbury and heading for Chelford.

He relaxed and smiled at Beatrice. 'Tell me about your holiday,' he said. 'How was Alice?'

'Oh. Papa. You should see it. Prague is the most beautiful city on earth.' Beatrice's eyes were shining as she began to tell the story of her holiday.

All Charles had to do was to keep the motor-car steady and give the odd word of encouragement to her.

'Alice is rich, Papa. Her business, her chocolate cake business, is so busy. She has five shops in Prague. At the back of her shop in Wenceslas Square they have an enormous room where ten people do nothing but make the cakes, day in day out. And Alice is looking for bigger premises – a small factory – so she can make more and send them by train to Vienna.' Beattie gave a big sigh. 'Have you eaten the one I brought home for you? They're delicious aren't they?'

'Magnificent. I've never tasted anything better,' Charles moved the hand throttle down a notch and the noise of the engine rose. It was most satisfying. He was beginning to enjoy driving a motor-car. When the noise settled and he could talk above it again he said, 'I was worried about your being there when Bosnia and Herzegovina were annexed. Were there riots? Demonstrations?'

'No. Nothing.'

'It will be the start of things, I fear.'

John Rinehart had been shocked at Austria's action. So, it appeared, had the kaiser, although the German ruler had said he was standing by his ally 'like a knight in shining armour'.

Charles squeezed the horn bulb, to warn a cart that he was about to pass. And when the cart was safely behind them he asked Beatrice, 'Alice? How does she look?'

'She looks wonderful. She seems to thrive on all that hard work. She's thinner and paler . . . and she never stops working day and night.'

He turned his head to smile at her. 'Not too bumpy a ride, is it?'

'Perfect. I've never been in anything so comfortable.' Beatrice looked behind, through the small window at the back of the seat. 'Peter and Arthur are all right,' she said.

It was marvellous weather for driving, Charles decided. And the right time of the year. The fallen leaves on the road were saving his tyres from the punctures that he'd heard were a motoring hazard. The leaves were also keeping the dust down.

He said, 'And Karl? You haven't mentioned Karl.'

Beatrice didn't reply for a moment and Charles turned to look at her. 'Well? Karl?'

'I don't know what to say, Papa.' Beatrice did not say anything for some time. They bowled along in silence for a mile or so with Beatrice pretending a great interest in the familiar countryside, declaring that everything looked so much better from her new vantage point.

Charles would not expect her to break any confidence she and Alice shared so he too was quiet. Then it all came out in a rush.

'He spends most of his time talking politics. Alice is busy with her shops.'

'What do you mean? "Talking politics?" ' he asked.

Beatrice was looking at him as if trying to sort out her thoughts. She said, 'They have universal suffrage. They are more advanced than we are, Papa. All men over the age of twenty-four have to be inscribed in the voting lists according to nationality.'

Charles began to tell Beatrice the facts behind the problems the Austrian Empire had with nationality. He and John Rinehart discussed it endlessly. He said, 'There are too many languages, peoples and cultures. It's been impossible to legislate for them all. One nation's gain will always be another's loss.'

Beatrice listened intently then, 'Alice said that the official language was to be decided locally. In a town where a fifth or more were the minority they could demand to be dealt with in their own language.'

It was a long, smooth stretch of road they were driving upon. Charles felt himself growing in driving ability by the minute. 'And what has been the effect? Did Alice say?'

'If a man works for a German and if what is known as his *Umgangssprache* – his everyday language – is German, then he'd best register German or lose his job.'

So Beatrice had found Prague just as John Rinehart had said she would. 'The divisions remain then?' he said.

'Yes. Families are split. One brother will opt for the father's, the other the mother's and yet another for the language in which he was educated.'

They were approaching Chelford and, though the village comprised only a few houses on either side of the road, there was an almost hump-backed railway bridge to negotiate. And Beatrice was still chattering.

'You'll think I'm imagining it,' she said. 'But I did talk

to people when Alice was busy – Jan Prochaska and Irmgard, and Margaret Mannersmann. There isn't the same easy-going, say-anything atmosphere in Prague that there is here. Alice must have grown used to it.'

'Just a minute, darling,' Charles said. 'Don't speak until we're safely over.' He pulled in at the side of the road and then started again in the first gear, swaying backwards and forwards as if urging on the horses, trying not to heed the sounds of Beatrice's stifled laughter and the cries of encouragement from the boys as he drove the car up, up and over the bridge.

There. It was done. He smiled again.

'We have one more sharp bend, at Lower Peover, then it's a clear straight road until we approach Hetherington,' he said. 'When we reach Hetherington I think I'll park it outside the first gate. George can put it in the shed for me.'

He looked at Beatrice's serious face and returned to their earlier conversation.

'How has all this affected Karl and Alice?'

Beatrice said, 'Irmgard's husband is Czech. So Karl avoids him. Karl has two cousins. Seppie is in the kaiser's army. He's twenty. Hans is eighteen and has just been called up. He was a law student with Czech sympathies. He used to go on the rampage with the student riots.'

He didn't like to think of Alice and Karl being divided in opinion. Young couples should try to act as one. He looked at Beatrice. 'And do you think it has caused a problem between Alice and Karl?'

'Alice says Karl never heeds her advice. She tells him not to lose sight of ordinary life. He sees everything from the standpoint of military ascendancy.'

'Oh, dear.' There didn't seem much else he could say. Karl had always seemed such an honest, earnest young man. They were almost there. 'Shall I attempt the gates, Beatrice?' he asked.

'Yes.' She was laughing at him openly. 'The boys are dying to drive up to the door. They love to show off.'

'Right. Hold tight.' He stopped the Argyll again, started it in first gear, squared up for the turn and the run through the gates. And did it.

Driving a motor-car really was the most remarkable business.

# Chapter Twenty-six

Shortly after the Argyll was safely parked in the yard of the Lodge, Frederick's motor cycle roared through the Hollin Gate. He was in a foul temper. The summons to Hetherington had come in the middle of a meeting with his senior officer.

He pulled off his goggles and helmet and slung them over the handlebars for the slower manoeuvring of the Humber along the bridle path towards the Tenants' Hall at the northern corner of the estate.

He was unconcerned that he cut a handsome figure in his khaki uniform and leather motoring boots. He was only proud of his new promotion. Major, the Duke of Westminster, had become Lord Lieutenant of the County on the resignation of Earl Egerton of Tatton and he, Major Frederick Blackshaw, had been appointed third-in-command. He went bumping over the stony path alongside the boundary wall, not even asking himself what all the alarm could be about. George had proved an excellent factor, steering the estate into solvency if not profit, and normally George attended to any of the few disputes amongst the tenant farmers.

The Territorial Army had recently come into being and there were a hundred and one decisions to be made. He was furious that he had been called away from making the final arrangements for their last camp at Plovers Moss in Oulton.

He drew up at the Tenants' Hall which was used both as a meeting place for the farmers and estate workers and as an elementary school for the village and estate children. It was a long brick building with a wooden roof and veranda; spacious inside with four classrooms and a meeting room.

Inside, George was sitting at a table surrounded by angry men, all shouting at once.

'All right!' Frederick went to the table to sit beside George. The shouting eased. 'What's it all about?'

The men began again but he raised his hand in the quick military way that silenced men. Their voices died away again.

George said, 'It's about the new road. It's going to cut through the woodland and the boundary wall and slice a five-mile stretch through the farms.'

'What road?' He'd been told nothing about any proposed new road.

George took the plan from the chair beside him and spread it across the table. Frederick scrutinized it and his face reddened with outrage and anger. The plan detailed the carving out of a new road from the existing old highway to Manchester to connect with the old Roman road to Chester. According to the drawings the estate would be split into two halves with Hetherington Hall one side, the oak forest on the other and the Dower House and the Italian gates demolished to make a connection with the Chester road.

'Whose plan is this? Who drew it up? On whose orders?' he demanded.

There was a chorus of answers from the hall. He could hear shouts of 'The costs of boundary fencing', 'Spoiling an estate that's been here for centuries', several of 'Your wife', 'the new Lady Blackshaw' and one of 'That Bloody American'.

Xanthe was behind it. Anger was growing and bursting in him. He stood and banged his hand on the table. 'There will be no bloody road through my estate,' he roared. 'You have my word. Go back to your farms.'

They began to disperse, grumbling loudly, the floor

creaking under their heavy boots. When they had gone he turned to George. 'How long have you known about it?'

George folded the plans. 'I thought you'd commissioned it.'

'Well, I hadn't.'

George, in his unperturbable way, said, 'I was told that the road will provide what the young Lady Blackshaw calls, "access for motor vehicles". Her chauffeur says nobody will risk their Daimlers and Silver Ghosts on Hetherington Roads.'

'Nobody?'

George grinned. 'I think there are plans to do more ambitious entertaining, sir,' he said.

'Never mind the "sir" nonsense,' Frederick said sharply. 'You only need use it when subordinates are present. Otherwise I'll start calling you Factor.' He felt the anger crystallize and focus. 'I thought she was in London. She said she'd be in Eaton Square for a month.'

'They are arriving this afternoon,' George answered.

'They?'

'Lady Blackshaw and your weekend guests.' George looked at him with eyebrows raised. 'Had you forgotten?'

Of course he hadn't forgotten. Xanthe made no pretence even of telling him what she was about. She knew he'd have been at the barracks. She'd jotted down the dates of his absences before she went to London. He looked evenly at George. 'I must have forgotten,' he said. 'Foolish of me.'

'Shall we go?' George went ahead and held open the door.

Outside on the veranda, still fuming, Frederick said, 'It makes a lot of extra work for the staff. This entertaining. What about your wife?'

To George's little wife, Polly, had fallen the duty of engaging extra hands for the kitchens when Xanthe filled the place with her friends and the guests whose return invitations she coveted. And if she persisted in trying to

463

lure every man she met into a liaison with her then there was nothing more certain than that the invitations would not come her way. He was scowling now at the prospect of another weekend of her antics.

'Polly has called in the extra staff. She won't be at the Hall tonight as we're entertaining at the Lodge,' George said. 'My father and sister and the boys have arrived.'

'Sister?'

'Beatrice,' George said. 'Papa, Beatrice and the boys are here. I wonder you didn't see his motor-car.'

'You say Charles has driven over?' The weekend would be a better prospect with Charles here. He could also ask Therese to talk some sense into Xanthe.

'Papa has bought an Argyll. With the money from his latest medicine,' George replied.

Frederick went down the veranda steps. 'Is Therese with him?'

'No.'

By this time he was standing beside the Humber, ready to run alongside it and jump into the saddle when the engine started. He was disappointed that Therese wasn't here. His anger was returning. 'I don't know what's come between Therese and my wife,' he said. 'They were close friends. I haven't seen Therese for months.' Then he started the run. 'I'll be along tonight,' he called over his shoulder. 'I want to talk to your father.'

He throttled hard as soon as he was in the saddle and felt the machine leap forward on the stony road that would bring him to the west entrance of Hetherington in five minutes' time. This track would certainly not suffice for any of the guests' Silver Ghosts but the broad driveway, gravelled and raked every day as it was should not need any improving. What was Xanthe thinking of? He was still angry when he reached the Hall, left the Humber on the gravel and went quickly and noisily in at the quiet west entrance.

There was no sign of life. She may not have returned yet. When she was 'in residence', as Xanthe so

464

pretentiously called her infrequent stays under her husband's roof, there was usually plenty of evidence. She travelled everywhere with a huge staff and he'd have expected to see her butler and lady's maid about as well as motor-cars and carriages filling the driveway and coach yard, excited voices, people piling out of their vehicles into the house for a weekend of pleasure.

He had been going along with Xanthe's wild excesses for years now. But she was proving more than a match for him. He made his way through the house to their rooms and as he went he remembered her impact the first time he had seen her. He'd been at a low ebb. He'd lost the girl he loved and was struggling to keep the estate together. The police had been constantly questioning him about his father's death.

And then Xanthe, exotic and different, had come into his life. She'd been larger than life, had no inhibitions, no reserve, no false modesty he'd thought. And she had wanted him. She had made it plain that she wanted him. There was nothing she would not do for him – buy the Dower House – pay off the last of the mortgage on Hetherington – pay off Maisie.

He smiled grimly to himself. For now he knew that Xanthe would – and did – do the same for every man who caught her eye. He opened the door of his bedroom and heard her, in the bathroom which connected their rooms. The Hall had fewer bedrooms since she had installed modern bathrooms, one to every floor, one in each of the towers.

She was singing in the thin little voice that contrasted ill with her full, well covered body. Frederick tried the door. It opened and he went inside. She was in the bath in a room cloudy with steam and the pungent smell of gardenia. Her hair had been dyed since last he'd seen her. Today it was the colour of dried apricots. She had wound a pink chiffon scarf around the elaborate arrangement of curls and artificial 'frizzettes' she used to bolster out its proportions. There was, thankfully, no sign of her maid.

It was impossible to guess at her mood. Xanthe's blank expression did not give anything away. In the early days he had found slowness mysterious and sultry but the truth had come early. Now he thought them inane. There was in Xanthe a lack of true vitality, despite her restless seeking of stimulation.

She gazed at him over the high side of the tub. 'Why are you back so soon?' she drawled. 'Pass the towel to me, please.'

He picked up the towel, went to the side of the deep white bathtub and held it open for her. 'I've been brought back from Chester. To put paid to your crazy plans to carve my estate up,' he said. He watched her as she hauled herself out, pink and dripping. Her smooth face was vapid and irritating to him.

'You don't have the right to do that, Frederick, my dear,' she drawled as she gathered the towel around herself. 'My Daddy said I must have everything just right. No expense will be spared.'

She was speaking the truth. Warner Madison was a friend of his and a good man. Xanthe's mother was dead and Warner could deny his only daughter nothing. 'Then you will tell your Daddy,' he said with all the control he could find in himself, 'that there are things he can't buy. My estate is one of them. The road stays as it is.'

She went slowly to stand by a marble-topped washstand and began to caress herself with the big towel, looking at him to see if he were responding to the suggestive movements.

He stood, hands in pockets, feet apart, looking at the high ceiling, forcing himself to control the rush of anger and excitement that was filling him. 'Why are you back?' he snapped. 'You knew I'd be away.'

She drew the towel slowly along her arm and let it fall away, exposing one full heavy breast. 'I have invited my own very special friends here,' she said. 'Since you refuse to ask all those nice dukes and earls from your regiment . . .'

He turned upon her a look that anyone but she would have known for one of contempt. His title was one of the lowest ranking. He said, 'The Duke of Westminster wouldn't come to one of your silly soirées, woman! Who do you think we are? Royalty?'

She narrowed her eyes. She let the towel fall and she pulled it into a loose knot at her narrow waist. 'I have news for you, my boy,' she drawled. 'A man is coming to Hetherington tonight and he is higher than any old duke you know.'

'Don't talk nonsense.'

She began to pour lotion from a large bottle into the palm of her hand; she spread it on her neck and then stroked it into her breasts. 'This is a foreign man of noble birth, Freddie. He says I am the most exciting woman he has ever met.' She wiped her hands on the towel, looked up at him and said, 'I have never had a man who could satisfy my needs, Freddie dear.'

He felt himself responding to the insolent invitation. He would not do it this time. 'Don't make a bloody fool of yourself!'

She came towards him slowly. 'I want to be asked to everything, Frederick. And I want to go everywhere and do everything. You sure stand in my way.'

She was goading him into taking her by force. He knew it and so did she.

'I always have my own way.' She turned the amber eyes on to him. 'I sure like to see you when you're good and mad.' He felt the familiar rage come quick and hot through his body. He may as well not be married to her for all the love she had ever given him. And yet she taunted him like this, saying that other men, other lovers could give her what she wanted.

He pulled her round and held her, saw the challenge in the yellow animal eyes and, grasping her bare arm, he pushed her towards the door, kicking it closed behind them as she stumbled through it. Then he picked her up and threw her on to the bed and stood for a moment watching her as she lay, the towel abandoned about her, her legs spread apart in an attitude as inviting as a harlot's, smiling at him as he drew the bolt on the door and began to take off his uniform.

'You'd best be quick, Frederick,' she drawled. 'We have not got too much time.'

And within seconds she was writhing under him, gasping as he pushed himself into her and, without a word of love, without a kiss, without even looking into her face, he found the quick urgent relief that was all that the marriage act had come to mean to either of them.

She got up immediately it was over and, trailing the towel behind her, went to the bathroom and closed the door. And he lay on his back, desire and fury spent, listening to the sounds from the room next door. Water was running. Rubber tubes were being used to wash out her insides. He could hear it all. He knew what she was about. There were to be no children. She would not entertain the prospect.

He felt shame as well as returning anger. That was all he ever knew after the experience of lovemaking with his wife. And at that moment he made up his mind that this was the last time he would know shame and anger for her. He got off the bed, went to the dividing door and locked it against her. From this moment on he would seek his pleasures outside marriage. It was over.

It was seven o'clock when he reached the Lodge. He had timed his arrival to coincide with George and Polly's suppertime, for he enjoyed visiting them. George's sons and Therese's followed him about whenever they were allowed to. The boys saw him as their hero, he knew. He enjoyed the boys' adulation and played up to them shamelessly.

The Davenport family had given him his first taste of normal, family life and he found himself being increasingly drawn to it; wishing he had a happy marriage; wishing with all his heart that he had children. Polly was not only an excellent housekeeper and a good cook but she was also even-tempered and happy. He had never seen George's wife upset. Nor was she given to moods. Her ready smile always made him feel welcome and tonight she beamed at him as she answered his knock.

'Eeh. Come in,' she said.

Polly had never once used his name. She evidently thought that to use his Christian name would be overly familiar, yet to use his title too formal. Frederick had no idea how to help her overcome the problem and had decided that his best course was to pretend he didn't notice.

'Thank you, Polly. Is Charles here?' He went into the square, panelled hall and gave her his coat.

Charles came out of the sitting room to greet him and moments later they were seated at the side of a roaring log fire, glasses of mulled wine to hand, with the sounds of children, George's three little boys and his two 'followers', Arthur and Peter, running up the stairs outside the room.

'How is the Territorial Army?' Charles asked.

'Good. It's good, Charles.' Frederick's face was alight. 'A lot of changes. Next year's camp will be at Salisbury Plain.'

Charles nodded approvingly.

'We'll be with the Welsh Border Mounted Brigade, the Shropshire Yeomanry, the Denbighshires and East Lancashires.'

'What about the Balkans then?' Charles asked him.

'It's not over. By a long way,' he answered gravely. 'I don't think we'll be drawn into anything this time. It's the kaiser who worries me.'

'Did you go to Germany?' Charles said.

'Yes. The Krupps works are going non-stop on armaments.'

George came into the room at this point, filled his own glass and drew up beside them.

Frederick, relaxed into the comfortable chair, said to

him, 'Have you told your father about your latest adventure?'

'What's this?' Charles asked. 'What are you keeping to yourself, George?'

George said, 'I've joined the Territorials.'

'Good.' Charles looked pleased. 'Why didn't you say?'

'Oh,' George shrugged in his deprecating manner. 'It's not like er . . . nothing like your service, Papa. Fighting. Joining up when there's someone to fight, you know.'

'Are you in already?' Charles asked.

'Yep. Done the training. Learned to ride,' George said.

Frederick said, 'He'll be useful to me, Charles. A factor who can't ride is a bit of a liability. We'll have him out with the hunt, yet.' He grinned, seeing the expression on George's face.

'Your father is becoming more daring,' he said to George in an aside. 'The motor-car,' he explained. Then to Charles, 'Where are you going from here?'

'To Southport. My son Leopold can't be contained. He's nineteen and has charge of a gambling hall.'

George chuckled. 'They call him "Chips Davenport" in Southport. He's quite a character.'

'And then there's his aunt—' Charles said with a worried frown creasing his brow. 'I think Harriet must have taken leave of her senses . . . At her age!'

George laughed out loud. 'Aunt Harriet's your age. She can't be too old to think of marriage.'

Charles had not lost the worried look and Frederick looked from one to the other of them; father and son so alike. He asked, 'Who is marrying? And when? Tell me.'

George stood and refilled their glasses. 'My aunt is going to marry one Captain Cork of the Artillery,' he told them with his eyes full of laughter.

'The Artillery? You mean the Royal Artillery?' Frederick said. 'What's so funny about the Gunners, George?'

'I met him last week,' George said, clearly trying to keep a straight face. 'He's a dapper little chap. Wears

470

spats. And a monocle. Plays whist on Wednesday and Friday afternoons at the Liberal Club. Fond of the ladies, I'd say.'

'Good Lord,' Charles groaned. 'She's not just "courting" then? She going to tie the knot?'

George handed the filled glass to his father. 'Let us raise our glasses,' he said. 'To Captain Reginald Brassington-Cork. Ladies' man and Liberal. Artillery, retired.'

George's voice was slow, deep and humorous. He had a wonderful, dry way of reporting the goings-on around him. Only the merriment in his eyes revealed his enjoyment of them. He said, 'Leopold took him to the races at Haydock. And says that our retired captain doesn't know a howitzer from a starting pistol.'

Frederick could not keep a straight face when George went into one of his monologues.

'How did they meet?' Charles interrupted him.

'He partners her at whist, Papa,' George said solemnly. 'And as the good man told Leopold, "The only way I'll ever stop dear old Hatters from trumping my aces is to marry her!" '

They went in to supper where, at George's table, Frederick had spent some of the most entertaining and relaxing hours he could remember. Young Arthur and Peter were allowed to join Beatrice and the men and Polly served them with what she modestly called a brown stew but was a delicious casserole of steak and onions with heaped oval plates of crisp roasted potatoes and dishes of fresh garden carrots, parsnips and chopped greens.

George was generous with the wine and was good company. He'd be a great asset to an officers' mess if ever he joined the regulars, Frederick thought. Talk and laughter sparked around the candle-lit table. Polly's pretty face was pink with pleasure at their compliments and at last, when they had eaten all they could, she said, 'Now for the big treat!'

She hurried from the room and returned carrying a

large silver-plated tray with a chocolate confection upon it. 'One of Alice's,' she said.

Frederick asked, 'Alice?'

Polly took a long silver knife and serving slicer and began to divide the cake. 'Yes. Our Alice sent this all the way from Prague.' She began to pass the plates along. 'She's a rich young woman. She has a factory, Beatrice says. Sends them all over the city. People working for her.'

She handed a plate to Frederick. 'What do you think of that then?'

'I'm flabbergasted,' he said. 'I'd no idea Alice was so enterprising.'

Beatrice, like yet unlike the girl Frederick had never for a moment forgotten, said, 'She showed me all round her shops and her factory last week.'

'You went to Prague?' Frederick asked. 'You were with Alice? Is she going to return the visit? Come home?'

Charles was looking at him keenly. Frederick returned the look with a careless smile and saw relief cross Charles's face.

'No,' said Beatrice. 'She won't come home. But I expect she'll make it to Aunt Harriet's wedding.' She looked at her father's disconcerted face and added quickly, 'If it comes to pass, of course.'

Frederick pretended interest now in the slice of cake. If it 'came to pass', as Beatrice had suggested, then he knew that he would have to see her. He need only hint that an invitation might be accepted should Sir Frederick Blackshaw receive one, for one to be sent, he knew.

And tonight, when he had to return to the Hall, to pay false respects to the people Xanthe had invited to his home, he would dance with the women who danced, flirt with the women who flirted and dream of the girl who had wound herself around his heart with her kisses and her poetry and her offer of love in her moment of glory.

Alice tried to live with the knowledge that she would be

childless. And she could not. She knew that she would hope, until hope had gone, that the doctors were wrong. Sometimes a terrible fear would paralyse her, as if her blood really had run cold, when she contemplated life without a child. And she knew that these were not simply dark moods, as Mama's had been, but a deep, deep anguished longing that overcame her. These moods never swung to optimism. There was nothing on the other side of this coin.

She had not sought medical advice for the first year and then, as disappointments followed one another with monthly regularity, she made an appointment with one of the best specialists in Vienna.

There, after four days of investigations, she was given the verdict.

The procedures had been uncomfortable and embarrassing but they were as nothing to the final interview with three doctors who faced her across a table and began to question her.

'Did Frau Reinhardt allow her husband his full conjugal rights?' asked the first of the white-coated doctors, who, this being Vienna, had to be addressed as Dozent, a professor.

'Yes,' she replied, blushing at the cold manner of the questioning.

'Has Frau Reinhardt ever used herbal preparations as pessaries?' This from the second doctor, older and with a small goatee beard and spectacles.

'No,' was her answer.

The first doctor spoke again. 'Has Frau Reinhardt ever attempted to rid herself of . . .'

'Of course not!' She was no longer embarrassed. This was becoming more like an interrogation than a consultation.

The youngest, a man not much older than herself, spoke now. 'Has Frau Reinhardt used the new rubber devices? This morbid and unnatural practice weakens the faculties of the mind and violates the . . .'

'No!' At this point she could take no more. She was crying and yet she stood up and slammed her hand down hard on the table in front of her questioners.

'No!' she cried. 'And if I had, what on Earth has it to do with you? And if I had, then why would I be here?'

She had wanted to scream at them, to ask if they were doctors or moral-inquisitors. They sat, embarrassed and silent, as she made an effort to clam herself. They would have made up their minds already. She would be classed as another hysterical woman.

'You are waiting for me to answer one of your questions in the way you expect, gentlemen,' she said in a frightened voice. 'So that you can say that I have brought my misfortune upon myself.'

The old man came around to her side of the table and put a hand upon her shoulder.

'You are a poor woman,' he said.

And she had mistaken his meaning and with the little pride she had left she had replied that, indeed, she was not a poor woman.

'You are. You are a poor woman indeed,' he assured her. 'Everything except your ovaries is functioning properly. Your ovaries are not active. You are barren.'

When she returned to Prague with the terrible knowledge of her deficiency there was no-one to console her. Karl had not been upset. Margaret Mannersmann was not the one to tell for she had never confided in Alice about her own childlessness. Only Babushka, her darling honoured grandmother, had comforted her.

Babushka had thrown up her tiny little hands and cried out, 'Aie, Aie, Aie. They know nothing! Fyodor and I we have two sons. And, after, for eighteen years. Nothing. Then we make new life. New place. New air. New children.'

And for a little time Alice had taken heart but, at length, one month's disappointment became next month's resignation and she had instead put all her energies into the ever-profitable and rewarding business that had to be her only consolation.

It was to be another three years before Aunt Harriet married Captain Cork. The first postponement came as a result of the captain's needing an operation. Aunt Harriet didn't disclose the nature of his illness but wrote to Alice all the time. She told of her fears for her husband-to-be whom she had taken into her home and, after engaging night and day nursing for him, she had seen him through the long months of his recovery. Alice was delighted when, after a long, worrying illness Aunt Harriet's devotion was rewarded and Captain Cork made a splendid recovery.

The second postponement occurred only a month before the wedding day. The King died suddenly. Aunt Harriet and Captain Cork cancelled all the arrangements and put back the wedding until the following summer. Evidently the captain shared Aunt Harriet's respect for tradition and privilege. So it was in 1911, three years after announcing their intention, that Aunt Harriet and Captain Cork had finally set the date.

The day of Alice's departure for England was almost here. She was nearly sick with excitement. After all these years – after nine years in Bohemia – she was going to see England and her family again. She had hardly slept for days. New clothes from top to toe had been bought. The orders were going to be taken care of, by Karl and the ever-faithful Elsa Prochaska. Babushka would not miss her as Karl's parents were coming over and going straight to Ilyinka. Irmgard, Jan and the twins were coming to Prague from their home in Bratislava. They would stay here in the flat with Karl. Karl would not go with her to England. He would never go back. She was going alone.

Her trunk was packed. She was as fluttery as a child who is going to a birthday party.

The embossed invitation card was wedged between the carved fruit and flowers that adorned the back of their sideboard in the apartment.

Captain Reginald B. Cork and Miss Harriet A. Walker request the pleasure of the company of Karl and Alice on the occasion of their wedding.

Saturday 17th June at St Paul's Church, Duke Street, Southport. 11 a.m.

Reception. Victoria Hotel, Promenade, at noon.

A note was enclosed, telling Alice that a suite of rooms had been reserved at the Victoria Hotel for herself and Karl.

Alice took down the invitation and placed it in the inner pocket of her small travelling bag. The big box had been taken down to the main station this afternoon to be loaded on to the Prague to Paris train she was catching in the morning.

In an hour's time she and Karl were going to a concert in the Bertramska, the gardens of Mozart's Bertram Villa. It was their favourite way of spending a summer evening in the city; sitting on folding seats in the open air, the scent of the lilac trees all about them as they listened to the Prague Symphony Orchestra. Mozart's Haffner and Jupiter symphonies were being performed tonight.

Alice picked up her hat, a pale green straw with a wide brim and ruched band of white silk. Her dress, high at the neck and inset with fine Bohemian lace, was the identical shade of green. She took two pearl-tipped hatpins and fastened the hat over the blonde hair she now wore swept up to fall in a cascade of curls at the back of her head.

She looked at her reflection and saw that her cheeks were flushed pink, her grey eyes were large and lustrous and her mouth fuller, redder than usual. Would they see a difference in her, her family? She was twenty-seven years old. She peered hard into the glass to see if there were any signs of ageing, then laughed softly to herself, seeing none.

There was a hollow feeling of excitement in the pit of her stomach at the prospect of tomorrow's journey. And she had again the same sense of unreality she had experienced on her journey to Bohemia eight years ago; a silly feeling that when she went home her life was going to be changed. Forever.

She had tried to put these feelings aside. They were irrational and fanciful and to still them she had kept Karl awake for half of last night, talking; making him listen as she repeated her last-minute instructions.

'Will you go to see Babushka? Every weekend?'

'Yes. Mutti and Vater will be here as well,' Karl said.

'I won't see your mother and father this year.'

'You have not seen yours since we married.' He turned away from her and tried to get to sleep.

'I'll visit Heinz at the Macclesfield works.' She felt she was chattering away to herself.

'All right,' he said sleepily.

She poked him in the shoulder. 'And I'll stay for a few days with Anna and Renate. We are going to watch the coronation procession.'

Karl's two youngest sisters were recently married, Anna to a doctor and Renate to a school teacher. They lived close to one another in a village near London, called Hampstead.

He was falling asleep again.

'Karl! I've thought about something else.'

He made no reply. She shook his shoulder. 'Don't you dare open the shops, Karl. You know I've given the staff a holiday.'

He turned back to her and grinned. 'You are trying to ruin us. Giving paid holidays to shop workers.'

'Promise you won't?'

'Promise.' He had rolled over then and within seconds was snoring.

She had finally slept in spite of her excitement and

once this day dawned she was able to tick off the hours as they flew by in her last-minute preparations and packing.

Now she heard him come into the dining room and saw through the glass that he was standing behind her. He never normally showed affection. In fact if they passed in a doorway and there was a chance they might accidentally touch he would stand back, flatten himself against the post and apologize. But tonight he came close and put his hands around her small waist. 'I will miss you,' he said. 'I am afraid you won't come back to me.'

She twisted in his arms and faced him. 'Don't be silly, Karl.' She laughed at the mournful look on his face. 'I shall never leave you and Babushka.'

'Perhaps when you see them all again . . . Perhaps when you see everyone . . . Perhaps you will think it is better, there.'

'You know me better than that,' she said. 'I give you my word. I will come back.'

# Chapter Twenty-seven

Alice had not known how tired and overworked she'd been until she'd set off on the journey. Deliberately, she had not made conversation with strangers and it had taken two days to cross Austria and France, so that when she'd not been sleeping in the *wagon-lit* she'd done nothing but sit, look, think and be lulled by the movements of the trains into a soporific trance.

It was not until Dover that she experienced the quick lightness of heart a returned exile must know. She was hearing her own language being spoken again. She had forgotten how wonderful it was to know you were 'at home' – that you were a part of all this. That it was yours.

Four hours later she was heading north with clouds of white steam rushing past the carriage window in a dense white stream, obscuring the green fields of Staffordshire from view as the train sped onwards to Macclesfield. The last fellow-travellers had left the Pullman car at Stafford and, all alone now, she closed her eyes. There was nothing to do but try and still the elation that was expanding inside her at the prospect of seeing the family again.

And, as she closed her eyes and thought about them and tried to picture their faces, her mind went back to Beattie's visit and the discovery of Therese's family letters in the Chinese cabinet.

She was sure Therese had never known all the secrets she had uncovered.

The first shock had come with the letters; the crude,

suggestive love-letters from Sir Jack Blackshaw to Therese's grandmother. It was immediately clear that he had been her lover when he was a young man and she a middle-aged woman with a marriageable daughter. The second shock had come in the form of books of receipts and the realization that Frederick's father had been sending money to the old countess for years.

Alice had put them all in date order before starting to read them and from one of the first, dated March 1868, she discovered that a marriage had been arranged by the countess between her lover, Jack Blackshaw, and the countess's only daughter, Hildegard. A price had been agreed and the date set.

The cold and clever bargaining between a woman and her daughter's future husband was handled like an agreement to supply coal. This was followed by a letter dated only weeks after the marriage contract had been drawn up. It was from Blackshaw to the countess telling her that he had married another girl. He had married a young girl. It was done. The promise to marry the countess's daughter was cancelled.

This one must have been followed by threats of breach-of-promise actions in the courts by the old countess, such was the tone of Blackshaw's reply.

After this he had paid her irregular sums of money but had promised to find a husband for the slighted Hildegard. And it was plain that the old countess still saw him over these years for the suggestive letters still came – with their references to 'recent delights in your arms'.

Then had come *the* letter – a marriage agreement between Jack's brother Edward and Hildegard, the countess's daughter. This letter told of how Edward had been the secret lover of Jack's wife, Augusta. Jack had been made a cuckold. Jack's third child – Frederick – had been fathered by Edward.

The words he had used were, 'You wanted me to marry Hildegard so that she would have money and an English title, since your Austrian title cannot be passed down to her. Now, Isabella Theresa, you must be content with a *husband* for her.' There followed an agreement, a commitment to bring up Edward's children at Hetherington since Edward was being sent to India and the Indian climate was unsuitable for children. There were agreements about property, the income from which would be used to finance the lease and the upkeep of the countess's house for the next thirty-five years.

Perhaps thirty-five years was the length the lease had to run, Alice thought, for there would have been only a few years left on the lease when the countess died and this would explain the surly attitude of the old woman's servants in Vienna.

The last letter was also the last one Sir Jack Blackshaw had written to the countess. It had been written only days before he died. Alice read it with horrified disbelief.

To The Countess Isabella Theresa von Heilbronn.
From Sir Jack Blackshaw, Hetherington Hall, Cheshire.

Dear Isabella Theresa,

Your granddaughter came to see me yesterday. She demanded money and the property which belonged to her father and mother. The Macclesfield property is that which has provided your income.

A sum of thirty thousand gulden has been deposited in your bank account. This is in final settlement of any monies you might have expected to receive in the coming years.

I am forced to bring our association to an end, my dear countess. There must be no further contact between us.

When first we met you were widowed and a mere countess in Vienna with a daughter of marriageable age. You wanted security for yourself and a title for Hildegard. And you have always known that I had no fond feelings either for Hildegard or my wife, Augusta. It was for the Cheshire lands and the estate that I broke

481

my promise to marry your daughter. It was not, as you have always thought, that her dowry was insufficient.

I must now make clear to you the English principles of inheritance through the male line since you do not appear to understand them.

As the elder son of a titled man, the title came to me on the death of my father. Under our system the eldest legitimate son gets everything. When I die the title will go to Frederick Blackshaw.

Although my brother Edward fathered Frederick out of wedlock and Therese within marriage to your daughter, Edward would have needed a son *by his marriage* for there to be any disputing Frederick's right to the family name when I die.

Had Therese been a boy then your threats to "tell all" might have some weight.

It could be argued that Peter Blackshaw as my only son is my illegitimate heir. If Therese knew the facts of Frederick's real parentage then perhaps she might try to establish his claim to the title. This could only be of relevance to young Peter Blackshaw if Frederick Blackshaw were to die, since by not renouncing Frederick when he was born, by default I acknowledged Edward's son as my own.

Over the years I have financed you, your daughter and Therese. You and I were lovers for many years and your daughter Hildegard welcomed my advances on more than one occasion. But it is your granddaughter, Therese, whom I love.

She is mine. I "know" her. I fathered her son. I know that when Lady Blackshaw is dead she will come to me willingly.

At the moment she believes that I raped her. No doubt she has told you as much. But we know, my dear Isabella, don't we, that when a lady protests too much . . . !

There can be few men who can boast that they have

"known" grandmother, mother and daughter in one family . . .

Alice had stopped reading at this point. The letter had continued in the explicit and suggestive manner of the others. The letters had explained everything that had puzzled her and it gave her no satisfaction at all to realize that she now knew more, probably, than either Therese or Frederick did.

She had burned the letters. There was nothing that would benefit anyone in them. And she had promised herself that she would never so much as think about them again.

And here she was, sitting in a train, almost at her destination and remembering all those terrible old secrets. She scolded herself for thinking about it. All the Blackshaw business was in the past. A shiver ran through her as she fastened her little check jacket, adjusted her hat and looked out of the window.

Even if she were to see Frederick again she would not see the young handsome soldier who had captured her heart when she was little more than a child. Would she?

He would be thirty-four years old. He was married to a rich American woman. He wouldn't remember little Miss Alice Davenport. Would he?

And again she scolded herself for even thinking such things. She had freedom and liberty, money and position. What more could any woman want from life? The only blessings she did not have were a loving marriage and a child.

Why was she afraid of so much as seeing Freddie Blackshaw again? She must control herself. She must not allow herself the weak indulgence of such imaginings.

The train was slowing. It was pulling into Macclesfield Station and a porter was running alongside, opening the carriage door.

And there on the sunny platform, with the two twelve-year-old boys beside him, was Papa. He did not look the least bit different and he had seen her and was running along the platform, like a man half his age. He opened wide the door for her and, as she stepped down, he took her into his arms and hugged and held her until they almost had to be prised apart by Arthur and Peter.

Papa, bright-eyed and for the first time in his life, speechless, could only look at her and hold her tight and clench his teeth so that he wouldn't cry. Then he left her with the boys whilst he went to start the car and order a porter to have her box sent to the Beeches immediately.

Alice blinked to clear her eyes of the misty tears of happiness before she looked at Arthur – the baby she had held in her arms like a Mama until he was three years old.

'Mama said to tell you that she and Beatrice are waiting at the house for you,' Arthur said solemnly. He looked like Papa and was the taller boy and plainly the leader since he had spoken first and Peter was hanging back.

He was so much the younger version of Frederick that a shock of recognition had gone through her.

'There isn't room for us – and Mama and Aunt Beattie – in the car,' Peter said eagerly. 'We asked for a day off school.'

'For me? Oh, thank you,' Alice said. She held out her hands in a gesture of invitation and smiled at the serious youngsters. 'Let's get into the motor-car and ask our Papa to take us for a drive around Macclesfield, shall we?' It was the right thing to say. The boys, one either side, escorted her up the tunnel slope to the station entrance in Hibel Road where Papa waited for them in the Argyll which today had the roof and windows taken down.

'Can we do a tour, Papa?' she said. 'I want Arthur and Peter to show me the town and their school.'

'Right. First to Commercial Road. You can see your father-in-law's new factory,' Papa said as he let in the gear.

They had reached Blackshaw and Rinehart and were

484

flying past the factory at thirty miles an hour. 'Will it go a little slower?' Alice asked nervously.

'No.' Papa laughed at the groans they could hear coming from the back. 'Hold tight. I'm going to take her up Wallgate in a minute. I have to go fast. I'm always afraid we won't make it and I'll find myself rolling backwards into the cattle pens.'

'Go on, Papa! Have a crash. Just a little one. Please?' The boys were urging him on and Alice found herself clinging tightly to the edge of the seat as the great vehicle began to chug slowly up the steep cobbled incline that twisted narrowly from the Waters Green to the Market Place.

Then they bowled along again, down Jordangate to King Edward Street and past the boys' school and along Prestbury Road and at last turned into Victoria Road for the ride to the Beeches.

Therese was standing at the front door with the two girls standing one either side of her and the girls were hopping excitedly from one foot to another as the Argyll jerked to a stop on the gravel. Then almost at once they were clamouring for her attention whilst Alice exclaimed over them, kissing and lifting them.

'Nanny is taking them to the park this afternoon,' Therese said as, laughing at their exuberance, she unfastened their quick little fingers before they could pull Alice to the ground.

Therese, looking pleased to see her and pretty in a dress of deep rose silk, kissed her warmly and led her inside.

She had transformed the big, gloomy house that Alice remembered. Walls were done with pale-coloured wallpapers that made a perfect background to the framed drawings and paintings she had collected. Curtains too were in light velvets and cretonnes. The dark polished floorboards were covered with carpets from India and China.

There were vases of flowers in every corner and on

485

every little table. Every alcove and turn of a stair or corridor had a small table or a low Hepplewhite chair and every one was lit by means of electric lights inside coloured glass sconces.

Alice's old bedroom had been repainted and furnished for her and here a high bed with tall slatted ends was draped with a lace-edged, snow-white counterpane which Therese had bunched up in the middle so that it looked like a huge butterfly and the jewel-bright cushions like markings on the wings.

'It's beautiful,' she said when they had finally all come to a halt at her bedroom doorway. 'I have been so looking forward to all this.' She waved her arms to include them all in the sweep of her hands, then with a bump she dropped down on to the bed and sighed. 'I can't believe I'm really here with you all,' she said.

Therese was beaming with pleasure. 'We've asked George and Polly and their four children to come over on Friday, the day before the wedding,' she said. 'And Frederick and Xanthe.'

At the mention of his name Alice felt as if her heart had come up into her mouth. She looked wide-eyed at Therese and was afraid her stepmother might see her alarm. But it had become obvious, from Therese's letters and since her visit to Vienna, that the whole episode of the romantic attachment between herself and Frederick was firmly in the past as far as everyone was concerned.

And if Frederick and Xanthe were coming to the Beeches to see her then the old night of romance must be firmly in the past as far as Frederick was concerned. Alice was cross with herself for responding so visibly to the mention of his name.

Unless she could control these silly, automatic responses she'd have to act as she had never acted before when she found herself in the company of Freddie and his wife.

And as she was thinking these thoughts Beatrice

stepped inside the doorway and said, 'They can't come. Frederick and Xanthe.'

'Who said not?' Therese turned quickly to ask Beattie.

'There was a telephone call,' Beattie told them all. 'Xanthe's butler. She's leaving tomorrow. They are going to Boston and on to Newport. Her summer visit to the States.'

Therese's face lost all its animation at Beattie's words. 'Well! The selfish creature! When Xanthe says, "We are going to the States" she means that she and her retinue are going. Not Frederick,' she said. 'Xanthe is the most dreadful wife. It makes me ill the way she chops and changes – the way she lets Freddie down all the time.'

She turned to the boys. 'Go and get your things ready,' she said before explaining to Alice, 'They're Boy Scouts. They aren't going to the wedding. The camp starts on Friday. Harriet doesn't mind.'

The boys ran down the stairs, followed by Beatrice who had to return to the Infirmary. When they had gone Therese came into the room and closed the door. 'May I sit and talk to you whilst you unpack?' she asked.

'Of course.'

The box had been placed under the window by Slater who seemed to be the only manservant Papa and Therese kept. Alice opened it and began to take out her clothes.

'I'm sorry you have to unpack for yourself. We only have Slater and his wife here,' Therese said. 'He works outside and Mrs Slater cooks. The laundry's sent out these days. Our only other help is a daily woman.' There was resignation in her voice as she said, 'I really feel we are doing very badly.'

'You can't be poor. With Papa's earnings, your property and the medicines,' Alice answered quickly. Then she smiled to take away any note of criticism her words might be having. 'If you really wanted to, you could make a lot of money.'

Therese didn't reply so Alice added cheerfully, 'You appear to manage very well without a staff.'

Therese shrugged her shoulders. 'What do you have? How many?'

'I have ten in the bakery, two in each of the shops. Mostly men. And two women who come into the apartment daily; one cleans and washes, the other cooks.'

Therese had been sitting on the bed, watching as Alice put her clothes on hangers and into the tallboy drawers. She went to the window and looked out over the garden.

'When you've done that would you like me to show you the dispensary?' she asked in a high, false voice. Then she added with an air of indifference that would fool nobody, 'Are you . . . ? . . . Are you at all interested?'

'Very.' Alice pulled the last few items from the box and let the lid fall with a thud. She stood up. 'Let's go,' she said and followed, smiling as Therese led the way down the stairs to the room next to Papa's consulting room.

The dispensary too had been improved. There were large windows to let in more light and a new workbench with inset bunsen burners and sinks. At the back of the room in a floor-to-ceiling cupboard that was fronted in glass were Therese's jars and bottles; her creams and cures, potions and medicines, all beautifully labelled and boxed.

Alice was fascinated by it all. She had always loved the dispensary; loved to watch Therese mixing, measuring, stirring and pouring. She had always been fascinated by the precise nature of Therese's artistry. She often thought it was this fascination that had led her to master her skills, led her to her success with the chocolate confections.

'You could become very rich indeed,' Alice said. 'If you sold some of your preparations. I daren't give any of the "Cream of Violets" to my other friends in Prague. Only to Margaret Mannersmann. And Margaret begs me all the time for a steady supply.'

Therese looked pleased. The cream was one of her own favourites, Alice knew. The violet scent was derived from orris root and not from the flowers that grew under the mossy banks of Cheshire. The secret of the pale violet colour was one of Therese's own.

'I'd like to be rich, Alice,' she said. 'But I couldn't sell all these at a price anyone could afford.' She opened a drawer under the bench and brought out a small book. 'I write down all I spend on the ingredients,' she explained. 'Look!' She handed the book to Alice. 'See how much they cost.'

Alice was fascinated. There were records of purchases going back years. Therese bought attar of roses from the Balkans and Persia. She bought amber resins from America and France; rare oils and musk from India, China and Ceylon; flower essences from the Italian Alps, and sandalwood from West Africa.

'Do you use a lot of these?' Alice asked in wonderment.

'Oh, yes. I won't use substitutes, you see.' Therese's face was animated. 'Cheaper oils go rancid. The only thing I don't make is cold cream. I buy that from Monsieur Eugene Rimmel of Paris.'

'You could be a very rich woman,' Alice told her. 'If you made and sold them.'

'Oh!' Therese waved her hands about in a dismissive gesture. 'Nobody would pay it.'

'They would!' Alice was excited by the ideas that were coming faster than she could put them into words. 'My cakes aren't cheap. You wouldn't be selling to the poor. Rich people pay high prices. I could sell my cakes at half the price if I used cheap ingredients. But they wouldn't be the same.'

Therese lifted a hand in a quick little signal for her to stop. 'I'll consider it,' she said. 'When we are in even more dire straits.'

'Oh! Surely?' Alice said. Therese exaggerated. Alice herself had managed on far less, when Papa was in the army.

'I'm sorry. It's dreadfully rude of me, talking about money.' Therese looked embarrassed. She gave a little smile to cover up her faux pas and said, 'But you are family, after all. It's just that everyone I know is much richer than we are. We seem poor in comparison.'

'You are not poor. Surely not?' Alice could see that there was no shortage of money for a comfortable living at the Beeches. She wondered if Therese were disappointed in the life Papa had provided for them. 'Whom do you envy?'

'I don't envy. There's nobody I'd change places with. But there's Ekaterina . . .' Therese's voice trailed off here.

Alice came to the Reinhardts' defence. 'There's a great deal of entertaining to do at Beaufort Lodge.'

'We don't entertain much. We're not society.' Therese had a slightly mournful expression. 'And there's Xanthe and Frederick.'

Alice turned her head away so that Therese should not see her expression. 'She's rich, is she?' She looked at the little book again, trying to appear nonchalant. But now that she was here, in England, in Cheshire, not far from him, she found it hard to control her reactions. It was hard to conceal her eagerness to hear about him since the same old twist of excitement came at the sound of his name, knotting her insides as she waited for Therese to answer. She knew perfectly well that Xanthe was rich. Something was driving her on. She tried to tell herself that all she wanted was to see how deep were the differences between Therese and her old schoolfriend.

Why was she behaving like this? Why, after all this time, should she be acting like a lovesick schoolgirl? Oh, it was more than that. Her very heartbeat was faster at the mention of his name.

Therese was giving the impression of wanting to talk, to get off her chest all that had been irritating her about Xanthe. Her voice was faster, more like the Therese of old, as she protested, 'I'm not envious. She's too vulgar. She's never in one place for long. She does everything, goes everywhere.'

It came to Alice again, the quick eager excitement, the sense of being under a compulsion. 'Tell me. Tell me about their lives.'

'Their lives? Hers and Frederick's? You're mistaken if

you think Frederick shares it.' Therese's lip had curled in scorn. 'It's not a marriage. She travels about the world with a great retinue; butler, ladies' maids, footmen, chauffeurs. She has to have everything new and fashionable.'

'Why?' Alice asked, feigning only a mild interest. 'Where does she go to?'

Therese obviously wanted to talk about her. 'In January she goes to the Palace in St Moritz, then, when she's bored with there, to the Ritz in Paris. Spring is spent at her villa in Nice then she goes back to London for the season. After that she goes to Hetherington for about a week.'

She looked at Alice with eyes bright with annoyance. Alice nodded encouragingly.

'Then off to the States she goes, on the latest Cunard liner. She and the lady's maid go first class, the entourage third. And always with about sixty pieces of luggage, clothes for all seasons and all occasions, everything numbered and catalogued.'

It was Alice's turn to show her scorn. Her lip curled in genuine disgust as she said emphatically, 'I should hate it.' She gave Therese one of her most decided answers. 'I should absolutely hate it. Truly. I could think of nothing worse than sleeping in a different bed, eating different food, meeting new people all the year round.'

Therese made no reply and Alice said, 'You'd hate it too. You know you would.'

Therese reached out and put a hand on top of hers. 'Oh, Alice you are so sensible,' she said wistfully. 'I wish you lived here.'

Alice decided to make Therese talk about something else. Thinking about Frederick and Xanthe was doing her no good at all. 'Well, I'm here,' she said cheerily. 'And I shall be here until the wedding. How are we going to fill the days?'

At that, Papa came and joined them in the dispensary.

He stood with an arm around Therese's shoulders, protective and warm and loving.

And, looking at such real closeness that was the love of Papa and Therese, a lump came into Alice's throat. She had forgotten that a loving man behaves in this way in his own home; that a man need not be formal and correct with his wife as Karl was with her. And she knew a desperate feeling of loss. All at once she was sharply, painfully aware of what was missing in her marriage.

Papa, his arm still around Therese and looking with deep affection into her face, said, 'Show Alice your latest . . . er . . .'

Therese laughed at him. 'Don't be silly, Charles.'

'What is it?' Alice asked. 'Tell me. Do.'

Papa, pretending for the sake of good manners that he was acting in jest, was stroking Therese's eyelid and pulling a funny, teasing face. 'If you'd let me prescribe it for my bald patients, darling . . . ' he began to say before she tapped his hand away in fun.

'It's an eyelash restorer, Alice,' she said. 'And it works . . . Look!'

Alice came closer and admired the thick, lustrous lashes.

'Very good,' she said.

'I dye them,' Therese said. 'With chloride of gold.'

'She restores them with poison and paints them with gold!' Papa teased.

'Sulphate of quinine, my darling. And sweet almond oil,' Therese corrected him.

But Papa laughed again. 'Have it your own way,' he said.

Then Alice suddenly could not bear to see such an open show of love and find herself outside its warmth. She changed the subject to one Papa would treat seriously. 'Are you still as busy, Papa?'

He dropped his arm from Therese's shoulder. 'Yes. And if all goes well I soon will be busier.'

'If what goes well?'

'David Lloyd George's medical scheme,' he said, smiling a little as if he approved of it all. 'Everyone will be able to join a doctor's panel. It will only cost a few pence each week. The government will pay a retainer to the doctors.'

'It sounds good,' Alice said.

'Who will collect the money from the patients?' said Therese in the arch tones of old. 'That's what I want to know.'

'The employers,' Papa told her. 'It will be marvellous for everyone.'

He looked at Alice. 'You've heard about our old age pensions?'

'No,' she said. They did receive English newspapers in Prague but she must have missed it. 'Really? How much?'

'Five shillings a week for a single man, seven and sixpence for a married couple,' Papa said. 'I can't wait to draw mine.'

Therese said, 'Alice doesn't want to hear all this socialist stuff, Charles. We were wondering how best to fill her days here.'

But the days flew by so fast that it was not until Friday, the day before the wedding, that Alice went to the factory to see Karl's brother, Heinz. Directly after luncheon George and Polly were to arrive in Macclesfield.

She had dressed in her most sombre dress, a navy-blue poplin with gigot sleeves and three deep bands of tucking above the ankle-length hem which held the skirt firmly down in an almost straight line. The dress's severity was only relieved by the high, choker-style neckband in crisp white lace. She wore, in defiance of all the advice to the contrary, a white straw hat with navy ribbons.

Heinz was the complete opposite of Karl in every way and as Alice followed him around the works she found herself wondering at the difference between the two men;

Heinz, an oil-stained dedicated worker, and Karl so well turned out and fastidious.

The factory was a terrifying place. Iron shafting, revolving at speed above the heads of the men who worked at the benches, ran the length of the machine-rooms. The noise was dreadful; the screaming and squealing of metal-on-metal, the thundering of the pulleys and belts at every position where dangerous operations were carried out.

Showers and streams of sparks were all about the benches where metal was being cut, curls of steel were flying, there was the smell of hot oil, sweaty men and the air was thick with fumes of the great gas engines in the basement.

And Heinz, who was wedded to his factory and had neither time nor inclination for social life, had not stopped talking and shouting in her ears about cutting and grinding and cast-iron flywheels and filling her ears with all those mechanical-sounding words that could be Swahili for all they meant to her.

Then out of the blue, when she was wondering how soon she might leave the works without offending him, she heard Heinz shout across the bench to a man who had appeared, from nowhere, to stand opposite to her.

'Here's my partner.'

Alice lifted her head and at once her knees turned to water. It was Frederick. She was looking into the face of the man she had thought and dreamed about for seven years.

He was exactly the same: tall and broad, with such dark curling hair. Hot brown eyes that were looking with admiration into her own, his strong athletic body in the dark business suit, all were just as she remembered. Waves of heat alternated with a cold, light-headed sensation and when he said her name it was in the same warm, deep voice that sent a tremor running along her spine.

'Alice!' he said above the din that was all around them.

He looked at Heinz. 'Shall I take your sister-in-law to the office, Rinehart?'

'By all means. I have to go up to the tool-shop,' Heinz said, glad not to have to spend any more time with her.

Then Heinz was gone and she was following Freddie, her feet going of their own accord, for nothing seemed to be under her control any more.

She went behind him to the little office inside the big outer doors that opened on to Commercial Road. And as she went, every nerve, every bone sprang painfully into life. She was conscious of every last inch of her body.

And the moment she was through the door he closed it quietly behind her and filled every inch of space with his presence. She could hear, see, smell and even taste the man in the air about him as in the semi-darkness of that cubby-hole of a place he stood before her and silently held out his arms to her.

Her hands reached out to him, but he was drawing her to him, his strong, straight mouth was crushing down on her open lips and her head was spinning as she answered his kisses with the desperation of need and the years of wanting his touch.

Never, never had she known such a burning, melting longing that could drown out all other feeling as he pulled away for a moment and with his face pressed close to hers he said, 'I've waited so long for you . . .'

She slid her hands around his back, beneath the serge so that her fingers were sliding inside to the silky white cloth of his shirt and she could feel his hard, muscular body pressing into hers, smell the leathery, spicy smell of him. He put his hands upon her shoulders and looked directly into her eyes as the deep, warm voice demanded, 'Stay with me in Southport?'

'Are you going . . . ?' But his mouth was upon hers again and she was responding to the deep kisses and the touch of his hands. She was falling down, down, fathoms and fathoms deep in love with him again and all the time knowing that she would never, never surface.

# Chapter Twenty-eight

The Silver Ghost, outside in Commercial Road, had a small crowd of men around it when they left Black-shaw and Rinehart. The men fell back, silent and respectful as Frederick opened the door and helped her aboard.

It would be very different in Prague where a Rolls Royce, if it drew attention, would be surrounded by as many mutinous men as admirers. But she could not think of Prague when she had the taste of his mouth on her tongue; when she was sitting here beside the man she loved, still on fire from his kisses.

Frederick had put one hand on the windscreen and, playful as a young animal, had leaped into the driving seat as if he had not a care in the world. He looked at her, smiling broadly as they began to glide away from the works. 'I told Therese I'd bring you back. George and Polly and the children are there already.'

Her heart was thumping like a sledgehammer whilst he looked as if nothing perturbed him. She glanced sideways at him. His moustache had been shaved away but his hair was as dark, his chin as aggressive, mouth as strong and as sensual and eyes as fiery as she remembered them. And his hands, sure and sensitive when in contact with reins and bit, were hard and brown and steady on the wheel.

She knew an unbearable agony of love and newly-awakened desire when she looked at him. But, as if to keep up the pretence of normal polite conversation, she said, 'Beattie told me that you and your wife weren't coming . . .'

As soon as the words were out he lost the carefree air. His brow creased in annoyance as he said tersely, 'My wife has gone to America. On the *Mauretania*. She travels a great deal.'

She'd known she must mention his wife, right at the start. There was no use pretending that either of them was free but she was relieved that he had responded this way; glad that he didn't want to talk about Xanthe.

She did not know how she should be . . . what she should say. Perhaps this was the time to act. So, to restore his good humour though she was shaking with nervous tension, she said in her calmest manner, 'Will you drive through Park Green so that everyone will see me? I have never been in such a car before.'

Silently he did as she asked and when they had almost completed the tour of the cobbled square she made another attempt to lighten the excitement that was like a tight-strung nerve between them. This time she heard her own voice, high and unnatural in her ears. 'Your coming over to Macclesfield would be a lovely surprise for Papa and Therese.'

He did not look at her. 'Don't play-act with me. Please, Alice.' He was looking straight ahead as he spoke, his expression proud and serious, his voice the officer voice of command. 'You must have known I'd want to see you.'

Colour came hot to her face. Did he expect an admission of love? She said softly, 'How could I have known?'

He was turning the car for the run up to Park Lane. He did not speak for a moment until, with the serious look still on his face, he said, 'You haven't forgotten. You've not forgotten any of it. I knew the moment I looked at you.'

She didn't know how to behave for, here in the open air with people watching them, shyness had come over her and idiotically she began to pretend to an interest in the route they were travelling. They had passed the park

497

and were rolling on towards Ivy Lane where fields and woods stretched out about them.

He turned to look at her and his face was dark and fierce and the expression in his eyes made her look away from him, over the fields. He said, 'You must have known what would happen if we met. There has never been a day when I haven't thought about you.'

The soft agony inside her made her unable to look into his face. For if she did, her eyes would betray the longing for him that was devouring her. Her voice was low and gentle as she answered, 'I was very young then, Freddie. You were a brave, proud soldier, the son of a proud family, returned from a war . . .'

He drew the car in near to a hedge at the side of the lane, disconnected the gear handle and pulled on the brake. The engine was a low, throaty purring background sound as he took her in his arms again.

There was a field of waving green wheat beyond the hedge, flooded with scarlet poppies. She would always remember the scene, the waving wheat, the peppery scent of hawthorn hedging, the moment and Freddie pulling her to himself and holding her close with iron strong arms and, as if the years of her marriage had never been, saying, 'You shouldn't need all this, Alice Davenport. Why do you need convincing?'

He was searching her face and his brown eyes were on fire, burning with need for her. 'I love you. And I know that you love me.'

The scent of grasses and sweet warm earth was all around them as his kisses rained down upon her face and her fingers were threading in and out of his brown hair and touching his face. Her body under the severe navy-blue dress was alive and waiting for his touch.

She was drowning again in love for him, and desire for him was growing and blossoming deep inside her.

Once they arrived at the Beeches, Frederick let her go inside to greet her family whilst he parked the motor car in the old stable-yard.

He had spoken with regret of the childless marriage he was trapped into, in talk with Therese some months ago and Therese, whom he knew thoroughly disliked Xanthe, had in an indiscreet and confidential moment told him that Alice was unable to have children. When he went inside the house his heart filled with love and pity for his darling Alice for every time he caught sight of her she had Polly and George's latest baby son in her arms and was gazing at the infant with such a look of devotion that his heart turned over inside himself with love for her.

It was difficult not to show his interest in Alice but he was sure he had managed to hide it, for when finally he left the Beeches before nightfall they were all outside on the gravel path waving to him and telling him that they would see him the following day in Southport.

And as he drove on almost deserted roads his mind went back, recalling the last few hours in the company of the Davenport family and the wonder that nobody but he and Alice had sensed the electric shock waves that had passed between them with every word that was spoken, every charged look he exchanged with the girl he loved.

He began to sing as he drove on the empty roads. He sang songs about abiding love that could never change. He sang to himself all the love songs he knew. He sang joyously, mixing the words from one song into another, holding close to himself the exultant knowledge that he loved her; that she loved him; that love was a fever that could never leave the bloodstream and that soon – tomorrow – she would be his.

At dinner he had been seated opposite her at the circular table and every time their eyes met across the table he felt waves of desire for her. And he was astonished that Therese missed it all. It was not like Therese to miss so much as a meaningful glance but, having only a housemaid to help her, she had been fully occupied in serving and refilling dishes and had noticed nothing.

After the supper they went to the drawing room where

Charles, evidently delighted to have almost all of his family under his roof again, brought in brandies for the men and port wine for the ladies and when everyone was settled, said, 'Shall we do our party-pieces?'

There were cries of 'No. Papa!' and 'You first, then,' and Charles put down his glass and held out his hand toward Therese. 'Shall we start?' he said. 'What shall I play for you, Therese?'

'We've been practising for weeks,' Therese laughed.

'Ah. Then perhaps we should go last. So as not to . . .'

'Just play, Papa,' Beattie said in her practical voice. 'Never mind the overture. Get on with the show.'

Charles and Therese sang two songs; first came the amusing 'Oh, No John! No John! No John! No!' which had broken the ice beautifully. Then Charles played again and Therese sang 'Early One Morning' and after all the applause had died away Beatrice went to the piano and did a wonderful, faultless rendering of 'Robin's Return'.

George was next. He was a marvellous raconteur and knew some funny monologues. They had all held their sides when he came to the end of the one about the man who took his girl out to do a bit of train-spotting. It wasn't really very funny, Frederick remembered, but when George did a broad Lancashire accent and put on the gormless expression – and when he came to the last line which he delivered very slowly, 'And after we wotched all the trains – coom in – We wotched all the trains – go owt' nobody could speak for laughing.

Polly told a funny story in an odd, self-conscious way. She was pink with embarrassment and though everyone clapped Polly looked glad to sit down afterwards.

Then, 'Recitation! Alice!' they all called out.

He wanted to sit, looking at her. He wanted to keep his eyes on the slender ankles so loosely crossed. He wanted to admire her long white neck with the black ribbon band and cameo that set off her taffeta silk dress of striped blue and black.

She rose to her feet and went to stand with her back

to the white stone fireplace. Her eyes were sparkling, the soft full mouth was moving in merriment and her hair was a cloud of gold around her lovely face as she asked, 'What shall I do? Has anyone any preferences?'

He was unable to stop himself. 'Do the Lord Byron poem.'

'Which one?' somebody asked.

Alice made no reply. Her eyes were huge as she waited for him to speak.

'It always reminds me of my homecoming from the war,' he said. 'Where Byron's theme is that the glories of youth and love are worth more than the glories of name and fame . . .'

'Oh, yes,' she had said, and it seemed to him that the rest of the company faded into nothingness as she began to speak again the lines he had last heard seven years ago, when she was in his arms, on a midsummer night.

> Oh, talk not to me of a name great in story;
> The days of our youth are the days of our glory;
> And the myrtle and ivy of sweet two-and-twenty
> Are worth all your laurels though ever so plenty.
>
> What are garlands and crowns to the brow that is wrinkled?
> 'Tis but as a dead-flower with May-dew besprinkled.
> Then away with all such from the head that is hoary!
> What care I for wreaths that can only give glory!
>
> Oh, Fame! if I e'er took delight in thy praises,
> 'Twas less for the sake of thy high-sounding phrases,
> Than to see the bright eyes of the dear one discover,
> She thought that I was not unworthy to love her.
>
> There chiefly I sought thee, there only I found thee;
> Her glance was the best of the rays that surround thee;
> When it sparkled o'er aught that was bright in my story,
> I knew it was love, and I felt it was glory.

There was applause and she went to sit down, across the room from where he sat. Charles passed more brandies and port wine around and then turned to him and said, 'Talking about war, Frederick, reminds me to ask you . . .'

He took the glass from Charles's hand. 'Thank you.'

'What do you think about German rearmament,' Charles finished.

'Dangerous,' he answered. But tonight he didn't want to talk to Charles. He looked at Alice, 'What about Prague, Alice? Do you hear more than we do?'

'Only *Tratsch*!' she said. '*Tratsch* – gossip you know. The *Kaffeehaus* seems to be a meeting place for Prague's gossipmongers. Nobody likes the kaiser much.'

Therese went off at a tangent at this point. 'Will the regiment have a presence at the coronation, Freddie?'

'Yes,' he said. 'The Yeomanry's sending twenty men. There's myself, a sergeant trumpeter and a cook. We're going to line the streets at Hyde Park Corner, dismounted; officers in full dress, men in khaki.

'I wish I could go,' said Therese. 'They say it's going to be the most splendid coronation ever with delegations from fifty-eight countries. I adore a spectacle.'

'You can't really think there's going to be a war, Papa,' Beatrice said. 'Not with all these monarchs and princes coming to attend the coronation.'

Frederick said with a kind of weary conviction, 'There will be a war. In the Balkans.'

'You don't think Germany and Austria-Hungary would be involved – and Britain – do you?' asked Alice.

He told them then exactly what his worst fears were. 'If it spread so far,' he said, 'it could bring down every European dynasty and empire; the Romanovs, Hohenzollerns, Habsburgs and the whole of the Ottoman Empire.'

Arriving late, Frederick went straight to his suite of rooms at the Palace Hotel in Birkdale. And he was pleased with them. It was perfect. There was a bathroom with a deep bath and marble panels and mirrors about the walls. They would drink champagne in the bath together.

The windows of the bedroom and sitting room looked out to sea. They would go, unobserved, for midnight walks along the sand and he would love her, fill every moment with delight in her and demand that she stay here until he divorced Xanthe.

And although he thought he would spend a sleepless night in an agony of longing it was morning and time to go to the Victoria Hotel and have her boxes sent as quickly as possible to the Palace. The sun shone and the blood was singing in his veins as he drove back to his hotel where he ate breakfast and called for a motor-taxi to take him to Southport. Then he joined the guests in the church of St Paul's, for the wedding of Miss Harriet Walker and Brassington-Cork, the dapper little private soldier who, Frederick had discovered, pretended to have held the rank of captain.

They had seated him on the right-hand side of the aisle, with the groom's contingent, to even up the numbers he supposed, for the groom's side was barely represented. On the left of the church was the Davenport family. Alice was sitting, not an arm's length from him, across the aisle.

She was wearing blue; a dusky, shady blue he would describe it as, silky and clinging about her hips and her wrists, full about the bodice and creamy and lacy up to her throat where she wore a necklace of flat gold bands linked together with falls of diamonds and sapphires settling against the whiteness of her neck.

His insides tightened as he looked at her and watched a pink flush come spreading across her cheekbones, knowing his eyes were upon her. He could not tear them away for she had a high smooth brow and a long straight nose and the full soft mouth he could taste in merely watching looked sweet and vulnerable above her determined chin.

She turned her head to smile at him, as if she were idly looking round the church and he discovered that he felt as a young boy would, lost in wonder at being the object of her smile. He smiled back and saw a glory of blonde hair cascading from under the layers of blue velvet and lace and fronds and diaphanous stuff that looked as if it could float of its own accord up to the vaulted roof of the church.

Therese and Charles nodded and smiled at him and he was amazed that they didn't see his love in his face. He had not even noticed that the service had started. He glanced at the bridal couple. The woman, who wore blue, was tall, serene and graceful with thick dark-blonde and silver hair. The bridegroom Charles disapproved of seemed ideally suited to his bride. The natty little man, a few inches shorter than his bride, was almost overcome with tears when he heard his wife promising to love and obey him.

Outside, afterwards, when the photographer was lining up the wedding party, disappearing under his black cloth and appearing again only to bark out orders for stillness and holding everything for a few moments, Alice came up to him.

'I'm booked in at the Victoria,' she said softly whilst at the same time dazzling all about her with her infectious happiness.

Ridiculously, he couldn't bear to see her smiling for anyone but himself. He reached for her hand, held it for a moment and said, 'I've had your boxes moved to my suite at the Palace Hotel.'

The blush spread quickly across her face. She bit her lip in a quick, nervous action before she turned the shining grey eyes upon him and, barely whispering again, said, 'I hope we don't regret this, Freddie.'

The photographer was finished and they were taken by open landaus to the Victoria Hotel. There, in the same dining room as before, Frederick found himself seated beside Alice at the wedding breakfast. And, exactly like the last time, they were having to conceal from all around them the magnetism that was making every presence but the presence of the other meaningless and peripheral.

Therese looked fetching in maroon silk and a gigantic hat that appeared to Frederick to have half a grouse moor about its crown. She came up to him afterwards, when the speeches were over and the tables cleared. 'Are you returning to Hetherington tonight, Freddie?' she said. 'You mustn't let Xanthe's erratic behaviour spoil everything for—'

'No. I'm going to Manchester,' he lied. 'Why?'

'What a pity. I thought you might have looked after dear Alice,' she said.

He looked at her sharply to see if she meant anything by it but decided she didn't since she was her usual social self as she added, 'Alice is staying here for a few days, to visit her old haunts, then she's going on to London, to spend a few days with her Rinehart sisters-in-law before going back to Prague.'

'Will you miss her?' he asked slyly. 'I thought that you and she . . . ?'

'Oh, Heavens!' she cried. 'That is all in the past. Alice is my only true friend.'

Alice was at his side as they saw Charles, Therese and Beatrice off from the steps of the Victoria Hotel and, after them, George and Polly said their farewells. The younger brother Leopold, whom Frederick easily recognized as the black sheep of the family with his slicked back, shiny hair and affected speech, waved his silver and ebony cigarette holder, said his languid 'goodbyes' and left the wedding party, to return to his roulette tables. And last of all the bridal couple were seen off at the pier head by the two remaining guests, himself and Alice. The newlyweds were to catch a late afternoon steamer to the Isle of Man.

And when all of them had departed he found that they were at last standing together, side by side on the pier, waving to a boat whose passengers would not be able to distinguish them from the crush of people around them.

She was his. He took her hand firmly in his own. 'Come,' he said. 'I can't wait any longer.'

'Nor I,' she replied.

And afterwards they would have no recollection of the going there, of the tram journey along the pier and the second tram ride from Lord Street to Birkdale or the unspoken decision between them not to waste time on decorous travel but to hurry, to run like the wind along the sandy road to the palatial hotel where they could be alone.

Then the door was closed behind them. Frederick slid the bolt. Her box had been brought, her clothes unpacked and their night clothes laid, side by side, on the padded silk quilt of the bed.

But that was all she noticed of her surroundings before she was in his arms, her hot mouth moving sweetly under the pressure of his whilst her hands unpinned the ridiculous hat and threw it aside.

Her hair was down about her shoulders and he was burying his face in her silky scented tresses whilst his fingers unfastened the hooks and little covered buttons that held her blue silk gown about her.

His fingers were clumsy and she helped him until her clothes were gone and she stood before him, tall and slender with milky-white skin that was ice and fire under his hands as she searched with her fingers inside his shirt, releasing it, pulling aside the cloth until his bare chest was hard up against her soft pale body and her firm little nipples were pressing into his flesh as he held her close.

Then the last of their clothing was off, heaped on the floor beside them and in his strong, hard arms he lifted her and laid her on top of the quilted bed and slowly and lovingly began to touch, to stroke her body.

'You are the most beautiful . . .' he started to say but she did not want to hear him talk for she pulled his face down until their open mouths found and tasted the sweetness that was the other's.

And he had stopped kissing her and had taken her breast into his mouth, making the nervous pathways to the deepest part of her a tangling web of silvery, slippery tightness.

'Freddie. Love me,' she whispered.

He caressed her and held her and slid his hands inside her thighs where her softness made him so full and urgent that she knew he must stop himself until she was ready.

He sat back on his heels and saw her eyes open wide as she reached out and stroked her hands down the brown, muscular body until she had him in her hand and gently and easily she held him and lifted her head and moved her legs apart so that she might watch as he went into her.

He looked into her beautiful face where she lay beneath him, her skin as soft and white as buttermilk, pink nipples rigid and pointing, a triangle of pale blonde hair . . .

And he could not delay any longer. He pushed her hips flat on to the bed and bent his head so that her firm breast was filling his mouth . . . and she was moving under him in pleasure, crying out to him, holding his head and giving a little gasp as gently he slid his fingers inside her to widen her so that she could take him easily.

Then he kissed her half-closed eyes and heard his own voice, strange and hoarse, repeating her name; 'Alice . . . Alice . . . Alice,' as with long expert hands he felt inside the hot slippery narrowness and firmly went into her.

She was calling, 'Freddie, Freddie, quickly, Freddie.'

And, as he sank into her divine body, she cried out until his mouth came down on hers to quieten her whilst he went further, deeper and higher into her and she melted and liquefied and held him in time to the slow rhythmic movements. And she wound her long white legs about his body as he gently took his mouth from hers so that he could watch her face and taste the saltiness of her neck as she cried again, softly, that she loved him, loved and loved him.

He thrust himself faster and harder until their movements and their cries and their bodies were as one, rising, falling in perfect union and her scent, heady and floral, ran like his blood, hot through him; he tasted her skin, heard quickening cries; felt the tightening and closing depths that were moving around him.

Her hair was damp and spread about the quilt and her breath was catching and sobbing as he reached deeper and faster into her.

And she had always known that it would be like this for he was touching something inside her that was a part of him and a part of her . . . and it was opening and holding, drawing this man into her . . . and she cried out that the force of him was lighting a fire in her that had never burned before . . . something was flaring into life that she had not known before . . . pleasure that was the sweetest softest pain as he came streaming into her and she abandoned herself to him and wave after wave of release.

And as their joy subsided, and whilst he was still in her and his weight was on her and he was whispering words of love and thanks into the creases of her neck and putting soft kisses on her eyes, something else was happening in the depths of her body where her barren womb had waited so long for his seed.

He held her fast; his hands were holding her hips hard against him until their bodies stilled and left them weak and languorous and suffused with wonder and peace at the harmony of their lovemaking.

She lay, relaxed and warm, whilst he planted kisses all over her body, laughing as he kissed each inch of her, saying, joyfully, 'You are all mine. All mine.'

Then he stopped and raised himself and looked into her face. 'You belong to me now, Alice.'

'I know,' she answered.

'You were never loved like that before, were you, Alice Davenport?' he laughed. 'Never.'

'No. Never.'

'Tell me when you are ready for more, because I won't be able to stop myself now . . .'

'Freddie—!' She pulled him close and tears of love and happiness and a terrible agonizing longing filled her. 'Never, never stop loving me . . .'

Later they had supper sent up to them in the suite and with it they drank champagne so that they were merry and light-headed when the time came for the moonlight walk along the sands of Birkdale and Ainsdale.

The shallow tide lapped at their bare feet as they went along the water's edge; they sunk to their ankle bones in soft cool sands above the water mark and last of all they climbed the sand dunes where the sound of the sea was a slow shoosh-shooshing sound as they lay in one another's arms. There they rested against the grassy clumps, watching the velvet, starry sky above their heads in a night scented with marram grass and the close salt sea.

Alice moved in a little closer to Frederick's side. 'How long will you stay?' she asked, all at once afraid that he would leave her.

'As long as you want to stay.' He tightened his arm around her shoulder. 'We can go to London whenever you wish.'

'I have to see my sisters-in-law.' She rolled on to her side and looked into the dark passionate eyes that could burn into her.

'I can allow you half a day,' he said. 'But that is all.'

His features were strong and dark and when he spoke his teeth glinted square and brilliant white in the moonlight. It made her heart stand still to think that they would have to part. 'I can't bear to think about leaving,' she said.

He sat up and took her hands in his. 'You are not going back to Prague,' he said.

It sounded like an order, not a question. She could not bring herself to tell him, here, that she must return. She would put it from her mind for the few remaining days they would have together. She leaned forward and lifted the hands that he still held and placed them against her breasts, saw his features soften, his eyes fill with desire again as he began to slide his hand inside the dress and feel her body's response to his touch.

And in the days that followed he did not refer again to her leaving him but spoke instead of his love for her, his need of her and the bitter regrets he had that he had not fled with her, that very first night in Cheshire.

He said, in the middle of the night when he had held her close against his naked body until his movements, his need roused her from sleep, 'I knew the moment I saw you that there would be no other girl for me.'

She turned to him, awake and alive at his touch. 'It was my fault,' she said. 'I refused to meet your mother. It seems petty and trivial now.'

He sat up and began to stroke her face. 'You thought you would have to defer to her, didn't you?'

She placed her hands on the broad shoulders that were above her. 'I thought . . . I still think,' she said, 'that it is demeaning. I don't know why I should.'

'And you – a soldier's daughter?' he said playfully as he kissed her in the hollow space between her breasts. 'Hierarchy and order are the biggest part of a soldier's life.'

'I had so much responsibility . . . so much work, even as a child . . . I think I was making a kind of protest. Why should I be a slave . . . and defer?' She was being aroused by him even as she tried to give him an answer. His hands were upon her hips and sliding into her waist. 'Perhaps that is why I . . .' she tried to say.

He was laughing softly at her. 'I think my mother would agree with you,' he said. But he was holding her breast, gentle and playful, making her respond, making her dissolve in a whirlpool of need and longing and desire.

Then he stopped. His dark face was stern as he said, 'I want everyone to defer to you.'

She smiled at the serious face next to hers. 'I don't.'

'Don't you mind it when nobody even speaks your name?'

'What do you mean?' she asked, though she knew. They had walked about Southport's parks and Promenade shamelessly, arm-in-arm, and it was as though she were reliving the night when she cared not a jot for tomorrow, for she could not feel shame at being seen with him. They had not walked down Lord Street or Duke Street, or anywhere that they might see old friends or Leopold but although she had seen nobody who remembered her from her two years' living here, heads had turned when occasionally somebody recognized Freddie and wondered who the woman was.

He said, 'I mean here. In the hotel. The staff will say, "Sir Frederick Blackshaw and – er – er—" They know we're not married. I want to say when I introduce you, "This is Lady Blackshaw." '

'Then am I an embarrassment?' she teased as she slid her fingers smoothly along the length of his leg and saw love for herself burning in his eyes.

He did not answer her.

And as the next days went by they drew ever closer for they discovered that they shared not only love but a deep affinity in character and tastes and attitude. They could talk easily and lead one another in with their thoughts and responses in a way that neither had known before.

Alice would say, 'When will the men . . .' And he'd say, 'They will be in London on . . .' And then hours later she might say, 'If Papa asks you . . .' And he'd say, 'I'll say I was in London . . .'

But on the last night of their stay in Southport he said gravely, 'We have to talk.'

She answered, 'I have to go back, Freddie.'

They had driven to Kew Gardens where they were to spend this, their second, midsummer night together, dining and dancing in the pavilion and watching the illuminated carnival on the lake. It was nine o'clock, not yet dark and they were walking in the little throng of people who strolled at the lakeside.

Her arm was in his and she felt a tightening in the muscle under her hand as he said, 'Stay here with me, Alice. We'll face it together.'

She had to make him see that it was impossible for her to stay. 'How can we?' she said. 'What we have to do is face our own . . . Your wife . . . Karl . . . with what we've done. It has to be that way. Surely you see that.'

His voice was hard and grating. 'I said, don't go!'

'Freddie!' she was speaking softly so that nobody would hear them. 'What are you asking? That I simply stay on? That I don't tell them? That I leave Karl and Babushka? Break my word?'

He was holding her hand hard against himself, as if he wanted to fasten her to his side. 'I can't let you go back.' His dark features were strained and tense.

But she would not do it this way. She had given her word to Karl that she would return. It was going to be a terrible thing for him to bear, her desertion. She could not make it easy but she could do it with courage and honesty. She looked at Freddie's taut face and said, 'Give me two weeks.'

He stopped walking, turned and faced her. 'I am afraid of what Karl might do.' He had both of her hands in his and she cared nothing for the fact that anyone might overhear them.

Freddie was trying to talk her into remaining. 'He's jealous and possessive. He may not let you go.'

'Karl is jealous. And possessive,' she said. 'But he is proud. Karl would never keep me by force.' She lowered her voice. 'I have to break it to them, my darling,' she said.

'He could lock you up.'

She smiled back into his hurt and anxious face. 'No. Karl wouldn't do that.'

512

'I would!' But, as he said it, even he had to smile at his own vehemence.

She smiled back. 'Darling. Be rational. You'll never be given a divorce if there's any suspicion that you want to marry again.' She stopped speaking for a moment and held faster on to his hands. 'When I come back I shall have to tell everyone – Papa, Therese, Mutti, Vater – that I am leaving Karl. It is going to be a terrible thing for them to live down.'

His features had softened. 'This is our very last night together?'

'Yes,' she answered. 'And it's midsummer night.'

He was smiling at her again. 'Let's not waste it,' he said as he drew her to him and kissed her face.

And she would always believe that it was the most magical night of her life. It was everything that the night of their first meeting was and more, for they knew that this night could not possibly end in lovers' disappointment and sadness.

They dined in the pavilion with a hundred other people whom they did not know. Then they strolled for ten minutes by the lake and when they returned, as if by magic, the tables were cleared away and chairs placed around the walls and the parquet floor was a smooth brown shining mirror for the waltz, the two-step and the new, exciting tango.

And Frederick danced as well as he rode and sported. Their bodies interlocked. They floated in the waltz and they soared in the tango. And last of all, with a crowd of gay strangers, they did the cake-walk and kicked their feet to the ragtime music of Irving Berlin.

When they drove back to the Palace afterwards, like overexcited schoolchildren they were singing, 'Alexander's Ragtime Band' and laughing as they tried to remember the words and music of 'Everybody's Doin' It'.

But Frederick had to be at Kensington barracks on

Thursday for the coronation day rehearsals and Alice could not bear to remember last night for, with every mile that passed on the road to London, the silences between them lengthened as the hour when they would part drew nearer.

He would not believe that she would come back to him if she returned to Prague. He had become silent and brooding and when he spoke it was in few words, and those with a quick cutting edge.

Finally he drew to a halt in front of Renate's house in Hampstead. Their 'alibi' was ready; Sir Frederick Blackshaw had been at the same wedding as she and, hearing that she was coming to London when he was there for the parade, had offered to bring her from the station.

'You'd think it was simple, wouldn't you?' Alice said in a quiet, toneless voice now that the moment of parting was here. 'You'd think it simple enough to tell a little fib or two.'

His eyes were bright as he reached for her hand and they sat in silence in the quiet street for a few moments. Then he appeared to be making a great effort to be rational. 'You know that I want to tell everyone,' he said, without looking at her. 'I want it over and done with. Brought out into the open.'

'We can't—' Her face she knew was white and strained. 'I have to go back, Freddie. I gave my word.'

He turned his head to look at her. 'You think he's going to make it easy for you, don't you?'

That was not what she thought. Frederick was trying to hurt her, to lessen his own hurt. 'No, I don't think it will be easy, going back.'

'You want him to "throw you out on to the street". Then you can lay half of the blame on Karl.' He simply could not see it from any viewpoint but his own.

'Frederick?' she spoke softly.

He was not listening. 'If you go back,' he said, 'I shall leave the country.'

'Don't. Please don't . . .' She was on the point of tears.

He turned, angrily. 'If you are not back here before the end of July . . . I shall ask for a tour of duty in India. That will take care of the next couple of years.'

'Hold me, Freddie. Give me courage.'

'No.' His face became a mask. He let go of her hand and opened the door on his side of the motor-car.

Then he strode across the pavement and up the steps of Renate's house.

And she sat, fighting back the great lump of pain in her throat, praying that God would give her the courage to leave him; that she would not cry – out here on the street where everyone would know what had happened; praying that she would not make an exhibition of herself and of him in front of Renate and Anna.

A maid had answered his knock and a manservant was coming up the area steps to carry her box indoors.

And Renate and Anna were approaching her, hugging her and welcoming her, over the doorstep and into the house.

She turned a white face on to Frederick as he, refusing their invitation to stay, turned to her and said, 'If you change your mind Alice, be at Kensington barracks at nine o'clock on Saturday morning.'

Then he bowed and was gone.

# Chapter Twenty-nine

They had to be colourful, Renate said, so that the kings and queens and princes should have a spectacle to look out upon from their carriages. She insisted that they dress in bright, patriotic colours and, early the next morning, Alice, in scarlet, Renate in white and Anna in blue took up positions on Constitution Hill. Here they would be able to see everything. Alice dared not ask the girls that they all stand at Hyde Park Corner. And had they stood there she was sure that Freddie would not be able to pick her out from the massing crowds that were lining the roads.

They had brought a cardboard box full of sandwiches and three corked bottles of lemonade, to see them through the day, and Renate and Anna, who made a point of watching every state occasion, were as excited as children on a school treat. And afterwards Alice would never know how they lived through the day for she was aware of a desperate, gnawing emptiness that was like a slow death when she was separated from Freddie. And she knew that she would have to quell all her longings for, in four days' time, she would be back in Prague, facing Karl with the fact that she could no longer be his wife.

'Look!' Renate was shouting. 'Here they come!'

The marching and mounted soldiers were coming towards them, regalia was glittering in the sunlight, the horses' hooves and jingling harness were a steady clattering background to shrill trumpeters' notes and further distant, the military bands.

Anna said, 'Can you see the Cheshires, Alice? Your Papa was a captain, wasn't he?'

But Anna's words went unheard. Alice was digging her fingernails into the palms of her hands for she had seen him, long before Anna spoke. 'They are coming,' she whispered too quietly for Anna and Renate to hear. The voices in the crowd – every known language of two hemispheres, faded into silence as she saw him.

It was joy and pride and physical pain to her, to watch him, as she had twelve years ago, wearing the blue and silver uniform; this time mounted on a bay horse at the head of his troop as he passed, head held high, eyes straight ahead.

Enthusiasm and patriotism had taken hold of everybody around them. The pavements and windows were a riot of waving flags and the crowd was shouting, cheering louder and louder as coaches and carriages came rolling behind the lines of marching men and the triumphant music of the bands.

Cries of recognition were going up and all at once in a voice high and wild with excitement Renate called out, 'There's Austria's future king!'

Now Alice caught the mood of the others. 'Archduke Karl?' she asked as the carriage passed them. 'Is that him?'

'Which one?' Anna was hopping up and down in her excitement.

They saw a young handsome man, sitting with the German crown prince and princess and the crown prince of Egypt in a carriage placed immediately in front of the British royal family's procession. Then followed the coaches carrying kings and queens, princes and monarchs, all the crowned and uncrowned heads of Europe, until at last the royal coach passed and they glimpsed their own king and his stately, beautiful queen.

After the procession had passed they ran to the Mall where in two hours' time, Alice knew, at the sight of soldiers marching all the old feelings of fear and foreboding would pass over her again as the great parade returned from the Abbey.

She had telegraphed to the apartment from Paris and as the train drew in to Prague station she could barely stand steadily on her feet. She was sick and shaken. She had never been a good traveller but there was a slow sinking in the pit of her stomach, as if she were dropping very fast in a lift. It was a new sensation altogether which she could only put down to fear.

Karl was waiting on the platform for her and, to her dismay, he threw his arms around her in the most demonstrative welcome he had ever made, though in this country, even more than at home, displays of affection were thought of as highly improper. She let him kiss her cheek in front of everyone.

'I miss you so much,' he said. 'I am afraid you will stay in England.' He looked hard into her pale face, searching it for a sign that she was happy to be back. 'I am very happy you are home.'

Her heart was sinking. If he had been his normal aloof self it would have made everything easier for she knew, as soon as he had spoken, that once he had been told about herself and Frederick he would see even these little familiarities as an act of betrayal.

Later, after she had been welcomed home by Elsa Prochaska, the sick feeling returned. Words were coming to her from a far distance as if she were about to faint. Perhaps it was due to having to concentrate hard to speak in German and Czech after two weeks of speaking nothing but English.

Karl was still acting like the devoted lover, fussing about her. She must tell him, and tell him quickly, before he said or did anything else he might later see as compromising the officer code he still lived by.

Military regulations in Austria prescribed that an officer must act *standesgemass* even in his private life and Karl, though no longer an officer, could never forget that his moral code was not that of society in general but the special, proud code of his caste, where to be dishonoured was worse than death.

A celebration supper was laid out on the dining-room table: cold beef and dill salad, cold, spiced potatoes, *apfelpitta* – an apple pastry, fruit and a bottle of champagne chilling in an ice-bucket.

And she had to tell him. Before she took a bite to eat in her own home, she had to tell him.

He had closed the door behind Elsa and the porter who had brought her trunk. And he had come to stand with her in front of the big, carved sideboard.

'Karl?' There was a hollow, sinking feeling inside her as she looked up into his blue, proud eyes. 'I have to tell you something.'

Instantly his face changed and became a mask of pride as if he sensed something different in her at last. 'Don't tell me,' he said quickly.

She would have given anything not to, but it must be so. 'You have to know. I must tell you. I have been . . .'

'Don't say it!' He moved swiftly towards her. 'You saw him again? Frederick Blackshaw?'

Her face was chalk-white. 'Yes.'

'You are still in love with this man.' It was a demand, not a question.

'Yes.'

Karl held fast on to her hands until she almost cried out. Then with a quick action he let them go. 'Say nothing more. You have come back to me. It is enough.'

She could not cry though she needed the relief of tears. 'I'm sorry. I didn't want to hurt you.'

'I said, enough! You say you love him. You are mistaken. You have come home to me.'

'You don't understand.' She bent her head and drew a handkerchief from the handbag she had placed on a dining chair. She clutched it tightly and, before she lost the last shred of her courage in the face of his stoicism, she said, 'Our marriage is over, Karl. I am going to leave you. I am going home to England.'

He did not speak for a moment then, with growing fear for him, Alice saw Karl's shoulders pull backwards and the blood came rushing to his pale cheeks. His lips were pressed firmly together and his eyes were staring at her fixedly, with an expression of horror. 'You know that I cannot live without you,' he said.

A shudder passed through her as she saw him begin to tremble, to quiver and she dared not make a move towards him. She could only hold on to the furniture, rooted to the spot, as he raised his head and stared at her with a wild, awful look in his eyes.

She put a hand to her mouth in fear. Karl was making wild noises that were half scream and half roar and she could only look on helplessly as with violent, jerking strides he went to the door and out across the hall to the bedroom as the door slammed behind him.

The room was reeling. Her throat was constricted and suddenly she could take no more, but dropped into one of the carved, high-back chairs that stood next to the sideboard, cold and empty and hating herself for what she had done to him.

She was frightened by the dreadful convulsions she had seen as faintly she heard him in the bedroom across the hall. He must have gathered his senses for he was noisily moving things, a box was scraping across the floor, a cupboard door was opening. She could only shake and hold her breath and stay quiet until she knew what he intended to do.

Then she heard the bedroom door opening. She heard him crossing the hall. She saw the door handle turn, watched the door being flung wide.

And then she screamed . . . a long high scream as she watched in horror as Karl came into the room, holding the sharp, keen-bladed sabre . . .

She screamed as he held it before him, his hands about

the blade, halfway between the point and the handle. It was pointing not at her but at his own stomach . . .

She screamed, 'No! No! Karl!' as with both hands wrapped about the blade and with the handle pointing to the floor, and uttering a shriek he threw himself forward on to the sword.

Alice put both of her hands to her mouth to prevent herself from being violently sick and passing out on to the floor in a dead faint as the blade plunged into him and he rolled slowly to the floor at her feet.

She stood for a moment only then she flew, like the wind, to the door of the apartment and she screamed up the stairs for help.

'Help! Anybody please help! Hurry!' until with unbounded relief she saw the little, Slavonic-faced Elsa come running down the stairs.

'A doctor! Quickly, Elsa!' she shouted. 'There has been an accident! The *meister*! My husband! He has injured himself.' And she saw litle Elsa running like a gazelle down the two flights of steps and out into the square to bring help whilst she turned and ran back into the apartment, terrified at what might await her, her heart hot with shame that she could be the cause of her husband's wish for death.

Karl was alive. He was grey faced, groaning and half-conscious and blood was oozing, purple, thick and sticky around the blade which had entered his body below the heart. She tried to remember all she had read in Papa's medical books but all that came to her was that she must not move him; that the doctor must be the one to move him.

'Alice, Alice—' he was saying her name in a soft, sighing voice that was an indication of loss of blood.

'Sh! Sh!' She lay beside him and put her face close to his and with tears pouring down her cheeks, she repeated, whispering the words so that he should understand and not be alarmed, 'Karl, my dearest . . . Don't talk . . . Save your strength . . .' She was shaking, taking his cold hand in hers, trying to pass some of her warmth into him. 'Oh, please Karl. Don't die. Please don't die.'

Then afterwards she would hardly remember how they had pulled her away from him – the doctors and Elsa Prochaska. She did not recall, though it happened, that she cleared the dining table so that they could lift him on to it; that she assured the doctors that Karl had been cleaning his sword when the accident happened. It was not until they cut his clothes away and began to withdraw the blade that she fainted and was put to bed by Elsa Prochaska. They gave her chloral for sedation whilst they took Karl to hospital in the city's new motor-ambulance.

It was four days before, at his bedside in the little room near to the public ward, the specialist told her that the blade had punctured his diaphragm, collapsed his lung and severed his spleen. Luckily the thin blade had missed his heart, stomach and liver. His recovery would be complete in three months. It was a miracle.

Now she could never leave him. Karl knew she would not.

A week after she had left England promising to return, with a breaking heart Alice had to make Frederick believe that she had deceived him. She wrote, 'Dear Freddie, I can never return to England. It is my duty to stay in Prague where Karl needs me. I cannot turn my back on everything. Alice.'

News of Karl's accident had been broken to Babushka by Alice so that the old lady had not been shocked or distressed by his slow recovery but more concerned, she said, for Alice.

'Alicia *liebchen*!' Babushka said. 'You are fatigued.'

'I'm all right.' It was a warm, early September evening and they had returned from church. 'I'm tired. That is all. My shops are busy. And I walk each day to the hospital to see Karl.

The light was like liquid gold falling through the rusty leaves of the trees around Ilyinka and they were seated outside the house on a garden bench, sipping pale golden wine. It was peaceful and quiet and Alice should have been at peace but she knew that inside herself a struggle was being waged.

Her heart was breaking and, even so, every time a vision of Frederick came to her she had to make a tremendous effort of will and force her thoughts into other channels. She would recite some silly rhyme to herself again and again whenever she thought about him. She seemed to know instinctively that she must do this. She must not allow herself to think – not a single second's thought must she give to her sorrowing heart – until it was numb and dead and all the pain had gone. She had to make these efforts to save her sanity. She had to fasten her thoughts, to concentrate on something, no matter how trivial, to take her mind off the terrible gaping void that his absence had brought to her.

She turned to smile at Babushka again. 'I am only tired, Babushka. I will recover.'

'Aie! Aie!' Babushka said. 'You cannot be tired. You are too young, child. How old are you?'

'Soon I shall be twenty-eight,' she answered.

'And when did you last have a . . .' Babushka paused for a moment and looked hard at Alice. 'When did you last have a season?'

'My period?' Alice could not help but smile at her little grandmother. It amused her to think that the old lady even remembered such things. But Babushka's face was straight, not amused and she replied, 'It was some months ago. My last one came about two weeks before I went to my aunt's wedding.'

Then her eyes flew wide as she remembered how long it was. She had seldom been more than a week late. Could it really be almost three months? She had put it down to worry and overwork – and maybe even anaemia for she was pale and tired nowadays. She wanted to sleep. Sometimes if she sat in a chair for a few moments she would fall into a deep sleep.

'You don't think . . . ?' she said, to Babushka.

Babushka's little wrinkled face was twinkling, bright with eagerness. 'I call doctor. Today.'

And it was there, at Ilyinka, that the news was given to her. The doctor's examination was quick and painless and definite. 'Frau Reinhardt is three months into her first pregnancy. All is well. The baby will be born in March.'

That night she could not sleep for excitement. She was going to have a baby. And it was Frederick's baby, there was no question about it. What would she have done if she had gone back? What would have happened if she had found out that she was expecting Fredericks's baby when she was back in England, without Karl? All of them would have been in an impossible situation; herself, Papa, the Rineharts and Frederick . . .

No! She would not think about Frederick . . . She would tell Karl tomorrow. And if she thought he would not have a relapse she would tell him tomorrow that the child was not his. He was almost fit to come home and spent the daytime hours outdoors, recuperating.

For the visiting hour she dressed carefully, in a costume of yellow and brown check with a high, feathered hat in the same colours. She found him sitting on a wooden seat under an elm tree in the hospital gardens. He had not seen her approach and he jumped and gave a surprised little cry as she spoke. 'Karl?'

'Alice! You are early.'

She sat down beside him on the bench. 'Prepare yourself for a shock, Karl.'

He paled and reached for her hand quickly and searching her face for signs asked anxiously, 'What is matter?'

She would have to tell him at once. He was not well enough to be given suspenseful hints. She patted his hand slowly and said, 'A baby, Karl. I am expecting a baby. In March.' She had deliberately said 'I' not 'we' and she knew, instantly, from his expression that he had understood.

He was silent, as if he were shocked for a moment.

'Then I am the one who is – what did they say? Deficient? Barren?'

She held on to his hand tightly, without answering.

'You will stay with me, Alice,' he said quietly. 'You cannot return to England.'

'Can you accept another man's child as your own?'

He was quiet for a second or two then turned to her with eyes filled with tears. He couldn't speak for a moment for the constriction in his throat but she saw that he wanted to tell her something that went too deep for words. Karl had never been able to speak about emotions and feelings.

She waited for his answer and, at last, with tears now flowing he took her hands in his own, held them tightly and said, 'I am sorry, Alice. I am sorry I have been bad husband for you.'

'No, Karl.' She was crying too, silent great tears were falling, pouring down her face. 'You have done nothing to deserve this. I am the one. I could not be a good wife to you.'

He took a large white handkerchief from his pocket and began to mop her face tenderly. 'I shall be very, very good father,' he said. 'Baby will be mine. You cannot go back.'

'Thank you,' she said through her tears.

Karl stood up now and lifted her to her feet and kept hold of her hand. 'I come home tomorrow,' he said. 'I shall do the work. You must rest and make strong baby.'

Her mind's trickery was working for she could think about Frederick without pain – without feeling – without a reaction of any kind. She had hypnotized herself; made herself cold and numb in the part of her heart where love for Frederick had been.

And never did a woman take to pregnancy so well. Her passions might be numb and dead inside her but her body grew rounder and rosier, fat like a cat in contentment. Her eyes were large and sparkling, her hair grew thicker and more glossy, her step was, incongruously, lighter and quicker.

And letters flew between Macclesfield and Prague, between Southport and Prague. Papa and Therese were delighted with her news and promised to visit her, in spring. If it could be arranged then they would come in time for her baby's birth. It would not be ethical, Papa wrote, for him to do the delivery but he wanted to be near at hand, in case she needed him. And Therese would be the best person in the world, he said, to advise her on nursing and feeding a baby.

Alice spent two months in training Elsa Prochaska, not only in the making of *Schokolade Kuchen*, for Elsa was already an expert like herself, but in the supervising of the shops.

She made ready a day and a night nursery in the spare bedrooms of the apartment, for the baby and the nurse-maid, so that she could watch the running of the business once her child was born. For she intended to work.

And darling Babushka, superstitious Babushka who had always told her that as one little light went out another came into the world to replace it, said that the news had made her young again. She did not care, she said, that her own light would soon go out. Continuity was assured. Babushka was going to find a good girl from the village as nursemaid.

And Karl was kindness and gentleness itself. She had been watching him closely for any sign that he would not accept the child as his own but he had become protective of her and proud of her swelling figure. He told her that he was glad it had happened, for how else would he ever have a son? And she had begun to laugh again and to relax with him and point out that she might have a daughter.

And though she could think of him without pain she dared not, not for a second, think about Frederick's own longing for a child of his own.

They visited Olga and Max in their smart apartment

that was filled with modern furniture of the Art Nouveau school. And Karl was boastful about the baby and declaimed on the merits of this one or that other method of child-rearing.

On their visits to the Mannersmanns he became self-important and full of opinions on the upbringing of children. And in Prague, when he sat at the pavement cafe or inside the *Kaffeehaus*, he talked less about politics and more about family life. And he would call her by funny, affectionate names before the other customers so that they should see how it was with them; that he had a beautiful English girl for a wife and would soon be a father.

Winter approached and the Vltava froze. Alice would not skate on the river this winter, nor take a short cut across the ice. The land grew iron hard before the first snow came. But her preparations were all made.

The baby was to be born at Ilyinka and at last, at the end of November, she made her journey to Babushka's home to await the arrival of her child.

Papa and Therese were arriving today. It was the very end of February; it was Thursday the twenty-ninth for this was a leap year. Babushka said leap years always brought changes into the family. Babushka had married in a leap year and one of her children had been born on the twenty-ninth of February.

Alice felt that she might even follow this pattern. It seemed to her likely that the baby might be born today, though it was not due until the middle of March. She could not possibly grow any larger, wait any longer.

Papa and Therese were to travel up to Ilyinka by troika, just as Alice had done, and the drivers of the troika and the luggage sledge had set off at dawn.

Babushka still kept her horses and the sledges and sledge-carriage. Karl told his grandmother that if the forest road were improved then, with chains around the wheels of a motor-car, the journey could be accomplished in a quarter the time horses took. The forest road to Ilyinka was hardly more than a track and the route which could bring visitors to Ilyinka by the better road from the village was a roundabout route through the mountains that could take days.

Everything was ready. Alice checked Papa and Therese's bedroom, the very one where she and Karl had spent their honeymoon. There were several bowls of scented petals. The great bed with the bear-carved posts was polished, the bed was made with her monogrammed fine linen and loaded with goose-down quilts.

Babushka, tinier than before, wizened and shrunken though still as alert, was dressed in her gold ceremonial dress an hour before they were to arrive and Alice herself looked like a galleon in full sail; tall and billowing in a pale-velvet gown and enormous embroidered cape that Babushka liked her to wear. It was another of Babushka's old customs, that her daughters and granddaughter wear the waiting-in cape she had embroidered for her own confinements.

Karl was here. He had left the shops in the care of the staff for a week.

'I hear them,' Babushka said when neither she nor Karl could hear anything but the faint crackling of the logs in the blue-tiled stove at the far end of the big entrance hall where they waited.

'Yes. I too,' Karl said after a few more seconds and then Alice herself heard them, the drivers' calls, horses' hooves on the packed snow and, at last, the flurry and shouting outside the big oak doors as the sledge-carriage came to a stop.

The doors were flung open and they were here and Babushka was stepping forward to greet them, in her formal Russian manner and Papa was bowing over the tiny little figure, kissing her fingers and Therese, overflowing in furs to her feet, was curtseying to the dear little Russian grandmother.

It was the most perfect time, Alice was to think later,

the first and last time that she would have them all around her.

Later in the evening, after they had eaten and were seated about the samovar in the room that overlooked the white garden and the lantern-lit trees, Karl asked Papa to put on snow boots and fur hat and overcoat and take a tour of the house and grounds with him so that they could talk, man to man. Papa was delighted to go with him and left the ladies drinking tea and talking as they had done on Therese's last visit.

Then Babushka excused herself and went to bed early.

At last Alice was alone with Therese. 'Thank you for all the things you've brought, Therese,' she said. In her room were boxes and jars, bottles and packets of Therese's creams and lotions, ointments and oils.

'I've written the instructions on the outside wrappings for you,' Therese said. 'I hope you find them useful.'

'How are my brothers?' Alice asked. 'Arthur and Peter.'

'I can scarcely believe it. They'll be fourteen in October. They are big. Still full of fun. Arthur is the serious one but still the leader. Peter is a bit wild. Like Freddie when he was small . . .' She tailed away here as if unsure whether or not to say more about Peter's resembling Frederick.

But Alice did not want there to be any unanswered questions in Therese's mind, any reminders of the time Therese had implied that Peter was Frederick's son. Alice knew the truth but she would never let Therese know what she had discovered.

She said quickly, to save Therese's having to say more, 'How is Leopold? Aunt Harriet will do nothing but sing his praises. I can't find out anything.'

Therese sipped at her tea before replying. 'He is the manager of a large restaurant and dancing palais. Charles disapproves, of course. But I think Leopold will do well for himself.'

'Palais?' Alice asked. 'Dancing palais? What's that?'

'They have them all over the country nowadays; ballrooms. The young people go there. To dance and to meet one another informally. You can even pay sixpence and choose one of the men if nobody asks you to dance. It's all very different. Much better.'

'Does Beattie go to one?'

Therese laughed. 'No. There isn't one in Macclesfield. And your Papa would not allow her to go if there were. Beatrice is such a serious girl. Balls or no balls – palais balls or grand balls, I despair of Beatrice finding a husband.'

Alice poured herself a second cup. She had only just taken to drinking it again, after almost nine months of finding herself sickened by tea. 'I don't think Beattie sees marriage as her aim,' she said.

'Hm!' Therese said. She passed her cup to Alice. 'What a pity Xanthe ever did.'

'Why? What has Xanthe done?'

'She's going to divorce Freddie.' Therese looked at Alice across the table and spoke in confidential tone of voice, friend to friend when speaking of an absent friend, 'Poor Freddie has done nothing to deserve it. Freddie is totally innocent of any wrongdoing. He has been patient with her. He has put up with so much. Freddie is in India for two years and she has refused to go. She has refused to be a good army wife. Xanthe says she is finished with him.'

'Oh.' Alice could think of nothing else to say.

Therese continued, 'She says that the only thing that has stopped her before is her father. Warner Madison thinks Freddie is wonderful. It will break his heart when Xanthe gets back to Boston and tells him that the marriage is over.'

Alice didn't speak for a few moments. Then she asked quietly, 'She hasn't gone yet? Xanthe? Do you really think she will divorce him?'

Therese pressed her lips tightly together, to stop herself from saying more than she should about her erstwhile friend. 'If she doesn't kill herself first. She has bought a very fast motor-car. She drives it herself at tremendous speed, taking terrible risks when she has had too much to drink.'

On the following day, the first of March, traditionally, baskets and bunches of violets were given and the house was filled with flowers and the sense that spring was here though it was the hardest winter anyone could remember and the snows still deep everywhere.

The whole of northern Europe had been in winter's icy grip for months. The Vltava was still frozen. Papa said that in England they had never known such severe weather. Icebergs had been seen far south of the Arctic circle, floating free in the Atlantic.

But at Ilyinka they were used to severe cold. The windows all had their extra frames in position. Wood for the stoves was piled to the roof of the log stores and the rooms they used were kept warm and comfortable.

And at midnight as the first day of March became the second day, and eight days before her expected date, Alice had to go into the bedroom adjoining her own and wake Karl.

'I think you must bring the doctor,' she whispered in a voice thrilling with excitement for she knew that it was time and that the pains gathering and cramping around her were strengthening with every contraction.

The nurse was in residence and was called to the bedside. A driver harnessed a single horse to the sledge-carriage and went to the village to call the doctor. Papa and Therese were wakened with the news for they had asked to be told when her labour started. And Babushka stationed herself in the room next to Alice's.

She had been afraid that when the time came she would cry and scream, for she believed herself highly susceptible to pain, feeling intensely the twinges that others appeared to tolerate with ease.

But she amazed herself throughout that night. She had to hold tight on to the hands of her nurse towards the end of her labour. She moaned a little and gripped the hands, the pains were so prolonged, then sighed with relief when they passed, then moaned again, they were coming so fast, barely giving her time to catch her breath before another was upon her and she was striving upwards out of the deep troughs of pain that all but overwhelmed her.

Then it changed and she snatched at hands as it felt as if a train were rushing through her. She was panting and making strange grunting sounds alternately, gripping the arms that were propping her up, pushing with her bare feet into the shoulders of the nurse who encouraged her onwards, her baby forwards into the light.

The doctor offered her chloroform and she gritted her teeth and shook her head violently as the last tremendous pain and effort took her into the moment, when she felt the head, in a round easing movement come through.

She heard the cry of her child before her last effort brought the shoulders and body out in a slippery, sliding, slithering moment of wonder. Then she reached down between her legs and lifted the wet, blood-streaked little body and held it to her face, to her breast, kissing and crying over the baby daughter that was the most beautiful being she had ever seen in her life.

She was sitting up in bed, washed and brushed, brimming with excitement, love and wonder when they came in to see her; Babushka and Papa, Therese and Karl. She had the oddest sense that everything had changed. They all looked different to her. They seemed hesitant and respectful and she . . . ?

She felt like an empress sitting there, high in her bed, her baby in her arms, her courtiers paying their respects around her.

Babushka was helped to hold the baby for she was too frail and afraid she might drop her.

'Aie! Aie! Aie!' she repeated and her little eyes brightened and shone in her wrinkled face. '*Schon, schon,*' she said softly. '*Liebchen, liebchen. Schon. Liebchen.*'

Papa held his granddaughter. His eyes were soft with love for her and he looked into Alice's eyes and said, 'I am so happy. This is the proudest moment of my life, darling.' He kissed the little face and handed the baby with great love and tenderness to Therese.

'Isn't she beautiful?' he said as Therese took the infant in her arms. 'The dark hair,' Papa said. 'The shape of the nose. So like Karl don't you think?'

Therese cradled the baby in the crook of her arm, bent her head over, the better to see her, and drew back the lacy shawl that was shading the infant face.

Then her eyes lifted with a quick little shock from the child to Alice. 'Oh!' she said softly. 'She's the living image of her father. The likeness is unmistakable. Every inch her father's child.'

Alice gazed serenely back at Therese. Therese knew. But Therese would keep her knowledge to herself. Alice smiled her stubborn smile and knew that another secret little bond had come into being between herself and Therese.

Then Karl held the baby, holding her to him closely, looking with wonder into the tiny face.

'What are you going to call her?' Papa asked.

'I am going to choose the name,' Karl announced. 'I am following in Davenport family tradition. Not ours.'

They all looked at Alice and she nodded. 'We agreed. The baby was to be Karl if she had been a boy. Tell them, Karl.'

Karl announced very carefully and solemnly. 'Her first name is to be Zita. Named for the princess who will one day be Empress of Austria. She is wife of Karl, heir-apparent after Franz Ferdinand.'

'And her second name is Helena,' Alice told them. 'Babushka's name is Elena, mine Helena so the baby is to be christened Zita Helena.'

'If she has to have a pet name you are all to call her Tzitelina . . . pronounced "Zeet-ell-eena".'

★　　★　　★

533

A light went out, just as Babushka had said it would. But it was not Babushka's light. Babushka's light appeared to be shining just as brightly though she was ninety-three years old. It was in the September of the year Zita was born, in 1912, that the news came through to Alice at Ilyinka, that Irmgard's husband, Jan Prochaska had been killed.

A telegram had been sent by Karl. 'Jan Prochaska shot dead. Street riot in Bratislava. Irmgard here. We need you.'

'Karl wants me to go to Prague,' she told Babushka. 'I don't want to leave you and Zita but I have to go.' It was ten o'clock in the morning and Babushka was in the salon with her.

Babushka's eyes were as bright as ever. Her mind was as sharp and she said in a decided little voice, 'You shall go. Take Zita and the nurse. You should be with Karl. It is wrong that you are here.'

'I shall come back as soon as I've done what has to be . . .'

'No!' Babushka put up her little hand. 'You will stay in Prague. With your husband. You have been too long away from him. And your business.'

Alice knew that she had been indulging herself since Zita's birth. She had begun to see herself as having found her 'niche' in life and to think she would never want any other. For she had taken to motherhood completely. She had not been away from her child for more than an hour or two, and that when Zita was sleeping. She said, 'The business is all right. Elsa can supervise the bakery as well as I can. Karl is looking after the shops.'

'Aie! Aie!' Babushka seemed to be annoyed at Alice's defence of her absence from Prague since the birth. 'Men do not see what has to be done. You will see. When you go back. You see what is happening. Go.'

Babushka meant what she said. She still made all the decisions at Ilyinka. But she would miss the little one for she took Zita on to her lap every morning and afternoon, humming old Russian songs to her until the baby fell asleep in her frail old arms and had to be laid in her nursery crib.

'I'll go,' Alice said and saw Babushka's old face relax into a smile. 'I shall take Franziska, Babushka?'

'Yes. Yes. She is good nursemaid.'

Franziska was a good little nursemaid, fair and plump and happy. Alice knew that once they were settled into the apartment she would be able to leave Zita in Franziska's care for hours at a time, returning only to feed the baby for her daughter was not weaned.

Six hours later she was on the train to Prague, pacing the length of the train's corridor, whilst in their compartment Zita slept and Franziska watched.

There was nothing to distract her out here; no view, for the banks were high and the flashing past of the telegraph poles the only indication that the train was rushing onwards at great speed and Alice could do nothing but watch and wonder if she had been too much in her honoured grandmother's company.

Was she becoming superstitious like Babushka? Babushka waited for events to follow one another in a pre-ordained pattern. Now Alice herself was asking which would be the next death. Babushka said that births, deaths, fortunes and misfortunes came in threes. She had pointed out to Alice that Irmgard had twins and she had Zita. That was three great-grandchildren, Babushka said, as if it proved the old wives' tale. But there had been more, minor events and occurrences, that seemed to follow in this superstitious manner.

Jan Prochaska's was the second violent and unexpected death this year. Therese had written to say that Freddie's wife was dead. There had been a dreadful accident at Mere Corner near Knutsford. Xanthe had been killed instantly.

When at last they reached the apartment, Alice found everything in chaos. There was a stack of unopened letters on the hall table. Irmgard, inconsolable, was in bed and the three-year-old twin boys, unwashed and hungry, were toddling in and out of all the rooms, wailing and fractious. Karl was in the bakehouse, keeping out of the way, and the housemaid had locked herself in the kitchen so that she could prepare the supper.

It took two hours before all was running smoothly again and Alice and Franziska had fed the children, made beds ready for them and had the three little ones tucked up and asleep.

Then later, around the supper table with Irmgard and Elsa Prochaska, Jan's sister, they discussed what had to be done.

Irmgard had eaten nothing and was sitting, slumped in her chair, her normally vivacious face dull, white and beaten. 'I can't stay in Bohemia,' she said. 'There's nothing to keep me here.'

'Don't you think the twins . . .' Alice began to ask.

'No! No!' Irmgard moaned. 'The boys will be better if we get away.'

Little black-eyed Elsa, impassive throughout Irmgard's hysteria, said, 'My mother wishes you to go to her.' She waited for a reaction but Irmgard was past reacting. 'She is poor. She lives for the twins. She will look after you.'

Karl said, 'Have you money, Irmgard?'

'No. Nothing.'

'I have savings,' Elsa said. 'I give you money.'

'No need,' said Karl, who must have known that Elsa could have very little in the way of savings. But there was no arguing with Karl when he used that voice. Karl had decided. 'I provide. You shall have money. How much do you want?'

'Enough to get home to Macclesfield,' Irmgard said. 'To pay my way for a month or two. I can't go home to Mutti and Vater as a pauper. I will pay you back when I can.'

'No need,' Karl said again. 'You keep it.'

'I go too,' Elsa said. 'And my mother.'

And so it was decided. Elsa would not be budged; not by wheedling or reason. The twins were Jan's children and Irmgard was Elsa's sister-in-law. They could not leave the old mother behind. They would all go to Macclesfield.

It would cost Karl a fortune to send them home and to provide enough money for six months' living expenses in Macclesfield. But family honour had to be satisfied. Karl had to provide for his sister. Alice would be left without Elsa, the girl who had been running her business for her for almost a year.

When the decision had been agreed and Irmgard had gone to bed and Elsa to her flat on the top floor Alice kissed Karl 'good night' and told him that she would be with him in bed in an hour's time and she smiled to herself to see the look of pleasure on Karl's face, that she would be a wife to him again.

First she had to deal with the letters.

And so that she should enjoy her solitude for a little while she poured herself a glass of wine and picked up the letter from Therese.

From the postmark she saw that it had been sent three weeks ago. She would not scold Karl for not sending it on to her at Ilyinka. The post was sometimes slow.

Dear Alice,

I have more bad news for you. Only four months after Xanthe's death my aunt, Lady Blackshaw, had a sudden recurrence of biliary colic and peptic ulcer. Within four days of its diagnosis she died. I can't tell you what a shock it has been. Aunt Augusta made a dramatic recovery nine years ago and we thought her cure was complete.

Charles says it often happens that the condition recurs and that she was very lucky to have the extra years granted her. But that is no consolation to Frederick, Mary, Maggie and me. We all miss her dreadfully.

I know you won't be able to come home for the funeral. It is not expected but I wonder if you might drop a note of sympathy to Frederick. He is only just back from India and is bitter and unapproachable. He has come home to Cheshire for good, and though he will remain in the regiment he also has to take charge of Hetherington. He is not very good at managing the estate.

The other news is that Harriet and Reggie are going to live in Cannes. I expect you know that Southport is too damp for Reggie. He has persuaded your aunt that she will enjoy the French climate. I shall be sorry to see them go. Leopold is going to keep on the Lord Street house for your aunt. Your Papa thinks it all very dire news and suspects Reggie of ulterior motives. But Reggie has made Harriet very happy. What does money matter?

I came into a little money when my aunt died. I had no idea she was going to do such a kindness for me. It has been a Godsend. Everything is terribly expensive nowadays.

Love, Therese.


So the superstition was fulfilled again. Lady Blackshaw's was the third death. She could not possibly write to Frederick. Therese must have known it was out of the question. A great heavy, oppressive cloud seemed to be descending.

She opened the bills next and found that everything in Prague, too, was nowadays very expensive. She knew how much she had taken in from the shops. There would be nothing like as much profit this year. She would have to put up the price of the *Schokolade Kuchen* or keep a stricter watch on the bakery and kitchen.

It was time to start working again.

# Chapter Thirty

Frederick had been home from India for twelve months and had put behind himself the troubles of the last two and a half years. Today he felt he could look to the future with hope. Soon he would set about finding a new role in life for himself – leave the army – marry again and settle down to the running of the estate. He was thirty-six, in the peak of physical condition, still had his dark good looks and was, he supposed, still attractive enough to women to be able to exercise some choice in the matter of finding a second wife. But for the moment he was going to enjoy every day as it came to him.

And today life was good enough. It was good enough to be out at dawn on a cold Cheshire morning with the cobbles of the stable-yard ringing under twelve sets of iron shoes as he led the troopers out for the early morning ride to the parade ground. The troop ambled at a jog-trot on the road once the yard was behind them and Frederick turned his head and saw the men, some stiff as if they were drunk with sleep, swaying in their saddles.

He was passionately fond of riding. There was no need to think further than the head of his cross-bred bay gelding – no worries this morning. Hetherington would be there when he came in from the morning's drill but there were no regrets when mounted on a horse for the losses of the last years.

A pale mist was hanging over the land as he broke into a faster trot and turned right to cross the open fields.

'Hup! Canter!' he called to the troop behind him, to

surprise men and horses out of their stupor. The horses had recognized the springy turf under their hooves and within twenty paces Major Blackshaw gave the order to gallop. That would waken the men at his back he knew.

There was no need to urge the horses on for at the first pressure from strong legs they were off like the wind with the reins hanging slack. The blood was coursing through his limbs. His head was forward over the animal's neck and the cold air whistled across his brow and cheeks. His mouth was wide open to drink in the rushing air and behind him he heard the even thud of hooves, horses' snorting and the rhythmic creaking of saddles.

He was thrilled afresh every day by the morning gallop that chased away thoughts of Balkan wars, Serbian victories and a rearming Russia.

He felt his every sense quicken; he could taste the dew of the night as they rode, like one single body, horses and men, carried along by a single impetus. Not a second was there to think about a dead, faithless wife, the loss of his mother or the girl he loved who had played him false.

He turned and glanced behind him. The troopers had lost their lethargy. They drew themselves up in the saddle, smiling, exhilarated by speed and the animal joy of flight. He looked ahead again. It was good to be alive, to be strong and virile, to ride through the cold morning with the sounds behind you of twelve horses, and men whose breath was turning to vapour streams behind them. They all felt as he did that they could ride on for ever – to the ends of the earth.

Suddenly he gave the order, 'Trot!' and heard behind the astonished gasp, the jerks as they tugged reins and, like a great machine, the column resumed a lumbering trot. He had remembered that he had to be back at Hetherington for luncheon for a meeting with Rinehart whom he'd not seen for months. George would be there as they had business to discuss. There was no way of avoiding the duties that running the estate laid upon him.

Mary and Maggie were proving every bit as capable of

running the house as Mother had been. This morning they were entertaining a group of ladies – regimental wives and charity workers – at a luncheon which was to be served in the Great Hall.

He looked back again at the men who were casting furtive glances in his direction. Normally, knowing his passion for riding, they galloped full tilt to the regimental parade ground. This slow pace was giving him time to think about the problems of the estate.

Xanthe had not put any money into Hetherington. Warner Madison had bought the Dower House and that had reverted to the estate when she died but Warner had been an astute banking man whose legendary generosity to his daughter had been in allowing her unlimited funds. Xanthe's living expenses had been met by her father. She had not cost Freddie a penny piece. And by the same rule, though she had made improvements to the house, she had brought no money to the marriage. All he was left with was a bigger staff, the Silver Ghost and several wardrobes full of ladies' clothes.

Hell! He'd have all that to think about in three hours' time when he was back at Hetherington. Frederick, smiling to himself to imagine the murderous thoughts of the troopers behind him, at his caprice, gave them the order again, 'Hup! Canter! And Go!'

He had returned to Hetherington, bathed and changed his uniform for a dark business suit by the time the luncheon guests started to arrive. He could hear the women's chatter and laughter outside his office door as they greeted one another and were shown by the butler, Hodge, into the anteroom of the hall.

He was in his office with George, trying to make sense of the accounts. To his inexpert eye the outgoings of the estate were going to be much greater than the income this year.

'How many staff have we?' he asked George. 'And how much is left in the kitty?' Xanthe had engaged a bigger house-staff for Hetherington than they used to keep.

Many were still here and the extra servants had to be paid, housed and fed.

George looked resigned. 'Not a lot. You're not in debt. And you've done well, considering you inherited debt, to put everything into the black again. But there are heavy outgoings. You need some steady income. The rents don't bring in enough.'

'How many staff?' Frederick repeated.

George asked, 'Including me and Polly?'

'Not including you and Polly,' he said. 'How many? Give me the indoor staff first.'

George recited them. 'Butler, valet, two footmen, an odd man and pantry boy. That's all the men.'

'And outdoors?' Frederick asked.

'Five gardeners. Coachman-chauffeur. And a groom.'

'How many women do we have?' He laughed as he saw the look on George's face, and added, 'In service I mean.'

'One housekeeper, two ladies' maids, three house-maids, sewing maid, still-room maid, scullery maid, cook. And two daily women.'

'Thanks.' Frederick put his head into his hands, then he lifted his face towards George and smiled. 'We can keep going for another year,' he said.

George began to stack the sheets of paper, ready to start his calculations. 'I'll take a cut,' he said. 'You can do without me. If I can keep my house I'll pay rent. I could become a regular soldier.' He smiled wryly. 'Or find work.'

'Don't think of it. You'll be the last to go, George. If we end up on the parish, we'll go together.' He was laughing. 'I'm joking, old man,' he said. 'Don't worry. I'll marry for money. Add those figures up, will you.'

Frederick went to the window. The parterre was trim with low hedges and shrubs cut-back for winter. Gravel paths were raked and in the distance the oak woods were bare of leaves. He could see the great sweep of carriage-way he had learned to call a driveway curving round towards the distant boundary wall. The Hollin Gate was less than a mile away and a car, late-comers to the luncheon party he supposed, was coming swiftly towards the house.

No, it wasn't more ladies. 'It's Rinehart's Daimler,' Frederick said.

Ten minutes later John Rinehart was in the office and Hodge was bringing in a tray with decanters and glasses.

'What will you have, gentlemen?' asked Frederick. He nodded to dismiss Hodge. 'I'll do it.'

John Rinehart asked for brandy, George for whisky.

'We'll join the ladies afterwards,' Frederick said.

John Rinehart spoke up. 'I want your opinion on the new contract.' John Rinehart's English was perfect now. A faint trace of German was all that remained and that only when he was excited as he appeared to be this morning. He had taken his brandy and seated himself in Frederick's leather chair by the log fire.

'Contract?' Frederick pulled up chairs for George and himself. The works' profits had been slipping for almost a year and Rinehart had been travelling abroad a good deal, trying to find orders.

'Government contract,' Rinehart said. 'I spent six months in Europe for nothing. I get back and I'm called to London. The government wants us to switch to armaments.'

Frederick asked, 'Not a foreign contract, is it?'

'Machine-gun parts. It's a good deal. We could expand the works into the empty cotton mill next door.'

'What's the problem then?' George spoke up. 'Does it have anything to do with me? Should I go?'

Frederick said, 'I'll want to know if we can raise the money, George. How are the coffers?' He laughed. Hetherington was constantly facing insolvency.

'Can you afford not to?' George said. 'You'll lose anyway if Blackshaw and Rinehart doesn't break even.'

Rinehart looked doubtful and Frederick asked, 'Why are you hesitating?'

Rinehart passed his glass over for another brandy. 'I

don't want to make armaments,' he said. 'I don't want
to believe there'll be war.'

'Why?' George asked. 'Friends and family on the other
side?'

'No,' Rinehart said. 'I'm Austrian, not German.
Austria can't afford to go to war. The kaiser wants war.
He's well prepared. But Austria? Austria's army is out
of date. It is an infantry force. Franz Joseph won't even
have armoured cars. He thinks they'll frighten the
horses.'

They all laughed but Rinehart said, 'I'm serious. Their
artillery is obsolete and the emperor is old and moribund.
He won't have typewriters in the palaces, or electric lifts.
He certainly won't allow the soldiers to use machine-guns
instead of sabres.'

'If Austria-Hungary challenges Serbia would we be
drawn in?' George asked Frederick.

'We couldn't stay out,' Frederick retorted sharply. 'We
will need arms. You're British now, Rinehart.'

'Yes. But I have nephews. One in the kaiser's army.
The other with the emperor's. And my son Karl . . . He
has recovered from his injuries . . . He would be called
up again.'

'Injuries?' Frederick said. 'Was your son injured?'

'Yes.' Rinehart looked worried. 'It was some time ago,
on the very night Alice returned from her holiday here.
Karl was cleaning his sword. His hands slipped and he
fell on to it.'

'Good God!' George said. 'Alice didn't write and tell
us this. Are you sure?'

'Certain,' Rinehart answered.

Frederick felt a cold shiver run through him. Surely a
soldier – an officer – would not do something as half-
witted . . . As foolish a thing . . . He refused to follow
that train of thought. He had put all that behind him.

George was asking Rinehart, 'Did you see Alice and
Karl when you were in Prague?'

Rinehart had a wistful look as he said quietly, 'I came

back last week. I saw them all. They are all very well. My only granddaughter. She is beautiful.'

Frederick asked, as much from politeness as curiosity for he had trained himself not to think about Alice, 'How old is your granddaughter?'

'One year, nine months.'

Frederick frowned at this. 'I thought she was younger.'

Therese had written to him when he was in India with the news that Karl and Alice had had a daughter. But Therese had told him that the baby was born ten months after Alice had gone back to Bohemia. If that were so the baby should only be one year and seven months . . . Therese had implied that the husband and wife reunion had been so joyful that . . . Therese would not tell lies to him would she? Why should she? If it were true that the child had been born . . . No. He would not imagine it. Would not for a second consider the explanations that were coming to him – that Karl had attempted to kill himself when Alice told him that she was . . . That she was what? Expecting another man's child? No!

He became angry with himself. Rinehart must have got it wrong. He must stop these ridiculous thoughts.

'Someone has to make the machine-guns, Rinehart. We'll do it.' He put down his own empty glass. 'Shall we go in to the luncheon?'

Zita was two years old, a beautiful, affectionate child with dark curls and great brown eyes that she rolled in a most beguiling manner, making willing slaves of them all.

Karl was besotted with her and would run up to the apartment several times a day merely to watch her at play or else he would put her upon his shoulders and take her down to the *Kaffeehaus* for his acquaintances to exclaim over.

Alice, who was the most protective of mothers, would not allow the child out of sight for more than a few hours at a time, so it was not until there had been months of indecisive discussion that she agreed to have

545

a few days' holiday in Vienna with Karl during June of 1914.

Every contingency had been covered. Franziska and Zita would spend the week with Babushka at Ilyinka. Franziska was to go to the village every morning at eight to telephone the hotel on the Karntnerstrasse and report on Zita's well being. If Zita should appear to be in the least fretful, if she cried for her Mama and Papa, if she would not take her *suppe* or should she refuse her *milch* then Alice would return at once. The shops would remain open, Alice had decided. They had competent staff and the business was making good profits again.

'Do you think we should have brought Zita and Franziska?' she said when they were on the train for Vienna. It felt so strange not to have the child near her and this was the third time she had asked the question though they had only travelled a few miles.

'No,' Karl said firmly. 'Tzitelina will be happier at Ilyinka than she would be in Vienna. Don't talk about it.'

Alice was wearing a navy-blue suit for travelling. It had a gently flared skirt to her ankles and a jacket with a deep peplum. Her white blouse was high at the neck and the hat, a forward-tipping navy straw, had a short eye-veil of white net. As they had the compartment to themselves and the train would not stop for an hour or more, she unpinned the hat and placed it on the seat beside her and looked across at Karl.

He was as handsome as ever, slim and straight, his hair as dark at thirty-four as it had been twelve years ago, his narrow face deeply furrowed at each side of his long nose. He had a natural elegance in the way he sat and held his head high and proud.

They must look to outsiders like the ideal couple, she thought as she settled back against the red velvet cushions and closed her eyes for a moment. It was odd that sometimes, out of the blue, she could be disturbed by the sort of premonition that was coming to her, a dreamlike feeling of impending change.

'I think you should sell the business.' Karl's voice startled her out of her reverie. 'Babushka is very old. She can't live much longer. It is better if you are at Ilyinka.'

She had been thinking about it lately. It had taken a great deal of hard work to get the shops into profit again after her absence and she had known that her heart was no longer in it.

'Did you know I'd lost interest?' she asked him.

He was silent for a moment and, as she waited for his answer, she asked herself how it was that between herself and Karl so many things over the years had gone unsaid . . . his reluctance to have children . . . her love for Frederick . . . his complete acceptance of Zita as his own child. They had never thrashed out the big differences between them. He had never once spoken about the time he had tried to kill himself but referred to it as his 'accident'. Should she have made him face himself? Was she as much of a mystery to him as he was to her?

He answered her question. 'You've changed since Tzitelina was born.'

She smiled. 'For the better?'

He looked at her keenly. 'You have lost the sparkle you used to have,' he said.

She wondered why she should feel annoyed with him for saying such a thing. 'Me? Sparkle?' she said.

'Yes. Since you became a mother you are always dutiful and responsible.' He was smiling. 'You always were these things but sometimes I ask myself "Where is the other Alice?"'

'What do you mean?' she asked, though she knew exactly what was now missing in her.

'You used to change,' he said. 'You would be serious and responsible, then all at once you would change. You would become unreasonable – reckless with no thought for the consequences. You would have your own way if

547

you had to blow up a bridge or take everything apart to get it. It was magnificent watching you!'

He was grinning happily as if full of happy memories; the time when she told him that she would work, the night she demanded a baby, and the day she agreed to marry him. He said again, 'Where is the other Alice? Has she gone for ever?'

'No,' Alice said. 'Not for ever.' But she wanted to cry out, 'Oh! No! Karl. She is here, facing her responsibilities, sorrowing for what might have been – much, much too late – and longing to go home with her child.'

She pulled herself up sharply. She never allowed herself to think that way. She made a determined effort to return her thoughts to here and now and said, 'I've not changed all that much. I've lost interest in the business though. You were right.'

'Because of Zita?'

'No,' she said. 'It's not Zita. It started when I heard that Irmgard and Elsa Prochaska had set up in Macclesfield. Making my cakes.'

'How can that affect you?' Karl smiled at her. 'They are not in competition with you. You can't patent a recipe.'

'It's silly I suppose.' She turned her head to look out of the window. 'Perhaps it's childish. But I don't feel the same about it any more.'

'Their cakes are not nearly as good as yours,' Karl said.

'I know. But it was a shock to hear what Irmgard and Elsa were doing. It was my idea. My recipe. I feel as if they've cheated me.'

Perhaps it was irrational and mean to feel this way. But Alice knew that she would never have done anything like that. Between herself and Therese there was an unspoken code; there was regard for the other's individuality. She would no more make and sell as her own one of Therese's creams than would Therese do as Irmgard had done.

Karl was still smiling at her. 'What about selling, then? What about putting the money into stocks?'

'I'll think about it,' she said. 'I'll make up my mind whilst we're away from Prague.' She closed her eyes and let the dreamlike feeling that was descending on her have sway.

Vienna was wonderful. She was glad Franziska and Zita were not here once she began to enjoy herself. She and Karl walked in the Vienna woods and went to the Prater on the first day. On the second evening Karl took her to the Burgtheater. On the last day they would be able to watch the Corpus Christi parades.

And it was the last day and it seemed that the whole of Vienna was out early. Bells were pealing at five o'clock in the morning. Girls, wearing cotton dresses and hats trimmed with fresh flowers, thronged the streets. In every window, lighted candles flickered below saintly pictures or portraits of the emperor. Bands were playing on street corners as they made their way to the Lobkowitz Palace from where they would be able to see everything.

First came the Uhlanen, cascades of gold braid tumbling down their backs. The lancers were followed by the infantry in tight red trousers, and guards' officers in snow-white tunics with great gushes of green or white feathers in their tall toque hats.

Karl was excited. He was almost in tears of pride as the military passed them and the long line of pedestrians and carriages followed. And all the old feelings came simmering to a boil in Alice as she watched. All her fears and premonitions seemed to crystallize as she focused on the parade.

First came the state coach, pulled by six horses, with the mayor of Vienna inside, wearing his gold chain of office. The coach was followed by more soldiers and then, as a hush descended on the crowd about them, came the magnificent gold coach of the emperor, pulled by eight white horses. Alice stood to attention from respect but all around her the people were bowing and curtseying; some women were crying as the tall old man, sitting erect and remote in a uniform covered in sashes, ribbons and medals, went by.

Then came the princes, the archdukes, dukes and lesser aristocracy. It was like a page from a story book.

'Archduke Karl!' Karl nudged her elbow. 'And the Princess Zita.'

And although Alice was glad she had witnessed it all, she could not tell anybody, least of all Karl, about the sense of impending disaster the spectacle had brought to her.

The feeling did not leave her until almost three weeks after they had returned to Prague and word came through on 28 June, an hour after it had happened to Franz Ferdinand, the heir of the Austrian Empire, and his morganatic wife, Sophie; word of the assassin's shots that rang out in Sarajevo.

It was just as Frederick had said it would be.

In the wake of those shots would topple every king, every prince, every heir and every heir-apparent they had seen in the processions of Vienna.

By midnight on 4 August, Karl was in uniform and stationed at the Hradcin castle in Prague. His cousin, Hans Bauer was in Eastern Galicia at Kolomea where the empires of the Romanovs and Habsburgs rubbed shoulders. His other cousin, Seppie Bauer, and his regiment were on their way to Mons.

Europe was at war.


## Macclesfield, 1915

On the Monday before Christmas in the second year of the war, at the Macclesfield Infirmary, the hospital almoner was the first to hear the news from an ambulance driver. She ran out of the office in the main corridor and passed it on to a Red Cross nurse who went in search of Sister Beatrice Davenport of Westminster Ward, Men's Medical.

'Do you know where Doctor Davenport is?' Beatrice asked. She never said Papa at the hospital.

'He's operating this morning. Amputating a foot. Some poor devil from the trenches at Loos.'

'He'll think he's a lucky man,' Beatrice said sadly, 'if all he loses is a foot. I've men in my ward with their lungs all but gone.' She looked grim for a moment. 'Damned gas!' she muttered. Then, 'Sorry,' she said to the shocked Red Cross volunteer.

She left a senior nurse in charge of the ward and went as fast as dignity and regulations allowed along the green-tiled corridor to the operating suite. She rapped at the door and someone came.

'You'd better mask and gown,' the theatre sister said stiffly, 'if you want to speak to him. I hope it's urgent. Doctor Davenport doesn't allow any interruptions . . .'

'No. I won't come in.' Beattie liked Sister Potts, the theatre sister whose severe manner was tempered by a generous heart. Sister Potts knew that Beatrice was Dr Davenport's daughter and that she would not breach regulations for nothing. Beatrice said, 'Tell him will you . . . Tell him the War Office has just announced that "The Gallipoli expedition has been abandoned. The men have all been safely evacuated." '

Sister Potts nodded and repeated it.

Beattie smiled. 'His son Leopold went out a year ago with the Lancashire Fusiliers.'

'Right,' Sister said. 'Anything else?'

'Tell him I'm going to the Beeches this afternoon. I'll pass the news on,' Beatrice said.

She had the afternoon free. Normally she did not take all her time off but there was a temporary lull in the ward today. Four men had been discharged and they were not expecting the next batch until tomorrow.

It was cold and lashing with rain when she walked to the Beeches. It would not be a white Christmas this year she was sure but now that they knew Leopold was safe it would be a better one for them all. If only they had

551

news of George. The Territorials had been mobilized the day after war was declared and George had gone to France almost immediately with one of the Cheshire infantry regiments.

George was in Flanders, just like the poor boy whom Papa had operated on this morning. If it was as wet in France as here it would be Hell for the men.

George had become a different man since he'd been out there. He'd had one spell of leave and had told Polly, though Polly of course had passed it on, of the horrors of the trenches. Polly said George never slept for more than two hours at a time and he'd wake, sweating with relief, when he found he was in his bed.

The casualties they had to deal with in Macclesfield were men who could travel from the battlefields; not the worst cases but those whose injuries were considered minor. The military hospitals were full and the Macclesfield Infirmary did the less severe operations; foot amputations where wounds had turned gangrenous, sometimes an arm at the elbow or a leg at the knee. But in Beatrice's ward were the men who'd fallen victim to chlorine and mustard gases, men whose lungs were bubbling with fluid, men who were shell-shocked and would have to be sent to the asylum when their visible wounds had healed.

Beatrice hadn't told the family yet that she'd put her name down to be sent to France. She was waiting to be called into service. It wouldn't be long.

When she got to the Beeches she found Therese, in red velvet with a long white overall, in the dispensary, working at frantic speed, shaking jars like a whirling dervish.

Therese didn't speak for a moment then, 'I'll have these healing lotions ready for you to take back this afternoon,' she said. 'Charles says it's better than anything you've got on the wards.'

'Leopold's on his way home,' Beatrice said.

Therese put down the jar and leaned her forehead

552

against the glass-fronted cupboard. 'Thank God,' she said.

'Any word from George?'

'No. But Frederick's home. A week's leave. Now that they are using Hetherington as a training camp he'll have a few days there before he comes here on Christmas Eve.'

Frederick commanded a cavalry unit in France. Beatrice said quietly, 'I'm going to join up.'

'What's that you say?' Therese said.

'Queen Alexandra's Nurses,' Beatrice answered. 'I've asked to be posted out there.' She crossed the cold dispensary to Therese's side. 'Let me help.'

'Thank you.' Therese passed two of the jars along the bench and they both began to shake furiously.

'That's it.' Therese put down her jar. The contents had 'done' and had turned from a loose watery mixture with several dissimilar elements in it, into a creamy, pink lotion.

'You ought to ask Mr Rinehart to make you a machine to mix them with,' Beatrice said. 'You'd be able to make bigger quantities then, and faster.'

Therese began to shake the next jar hard. She had to keep working. She couldn't stop. She dared not think too much, worry too hard about them all.

All the jars were done within the next few minutes and she began carefully to pour the smooth, slow-running lotion into tall glass bottles in a steady stream. When she had done she said, 'Put the corks in, Beatrice. The labels are in the box. I'll go to the kitchen and make a cup of tea.'

She left Beatrice in the dispensary and went along to the kitchen. She had to keep working.

A few minutes later Beatrice joined her there. 'You seem to manage, Therese,' she said, 'and you only have . . .'

'A cook and a cleaner. Nobody can get servants even if they can afford them. Bigger wages in the factories.

553

But they'll have nothing like these home comforts, of course.'

It was a touch of her old, defiant self and Beatrice smiled. 'Will they come back when it's over?'

Therese stood stock still. 'I hope it's over soon, Beatrice. Oh, God, how I pray for it to be ended.'

Beatrice would know what she meant, without asking. The boys, Arthur and Peter, were sixteen. Next year they'd be seventeen and the papers were full of irate letters demanding that conscription be brought in. The last one she and Beatrice had read was written by a high-ranking, serving officer, home on leave;

There is nothing in London to suggest that sixty miles away a life and death struggle is being fought. Any number of unmarried men meander the streets. Thousands are killed for lack of ammunition; men in the trenches, day after day, night after night because there is nobody to relieve them. It is Hell Let Loose in the trenches and our men at the front read of fellows striking here for another halfpenny an hour.

Thinking about it again Therese felt a cold rush of fear. Charles had said it was only a matter of weeks before the government would have to bring in conscription.

'If they conscript,' Beatrice was asking, 'at what age will they want them to go?'

'Eighteen,' Therese whispered. 'I hope they forget all about it.'

'Let's hope Arthur and Peter don't do anything foolish,' Beatrice said sternly. 'There's many a patient in the Infirmary who signed up at sixteen, some at fifteen. They don't ask too many questions you know.'

Therese stopped in her tracks and, speaking fast and urgently, said, 'I've got to do something, Beatrice. I feel such a – a parasite!'

'What can you do?' Beatrice asked in her practical way.

'Isn't it enough that you're here? The girls have to be looked after.'

Edith and Constance, self-sufficient children who were eleven and twelve years old, were at a small day school and would be home in time for tea. Therese always felt that her two daughters had little need of their Mama. They were Daddy's girls and looked to Charles for affection and approval.

She must make Beatrice understand. 'I want to do a bit more than Red Cross work, Beatrice,' she said. 'All I do is give tea-parties where we roll bandages and knit comforters. And I keep thinking of Alice . . .'

Beatrice didn't answer and Therese looked closely at her. Two slow tears were rolling down the calm sweet face. 'What is it Beatrice?' she asked.

'I wish she'd come home,' Beatrice whispered. 'She could have come home . . . Before all this happened . . .'

Therese felt the cold fear run down her back again as it did every time she thought about Alice and the baby. Beatrice was no fool. Words of comfort were not what was wanted.

'She couldn't have left Karl,' Therese whispered. 'Or her Babushka. Alice isn't the sort of girl who'd run away . . .'

'Did you read the article in yesterday's paper, Beattie?' she asked.

Only last month it seemed, Thomas Masaryk, the exiled hard-headed Czech nationalist, had issued a manifesto in Paris, calling for the Czech Legionnaires to fight on the side of the allies. The Czechs had always been deterred from making careers in an army whose motto seemed to be, 'No weak pandering to the Slavs.' It had been a terrible shock to the Czech people when Austria-Hungary went to war against Serbia and Russia.

'Yes. I read it.' Beatrice made a choking sound and her shoulders heaved as she tried to control the tears. 'It can only make things worse for Alice if there's internal fighting. I'm frightened for her. There was such an

atmosphere when I was there . . . Hostility to foreigners
. . . When I think that Alice and Zita might be suffering
. . .'

'Dry your eyes,' Therese said, fumbling in the pocket
of her overall for a handkerchief. 'Here.'

Beatrice took the handkerchief gratefully. 'Thanks,'
she said. 'I'm sorry I made a fool of myself. I just hope
Alice is safe.'

'Let's hope they are at Ilyinka,' Therese said quietly,
'with Babushka.'

# Chapter Thirty-one

## Bohemia, 1917

The air of decadent gloom and political intrigue had lifted in Prague right at the start of the war. There had been calls for action and young men were seized with impatience to draw their sabres. In the cobbled squares and the castle fortress slender young soldiers in splendid uniforms had been seen every day, vaulting into saddles, parading on prancing horses and marching bravely off to war to the sounds of drums and clarions and fifes.

Alice had not seen Karl since he was sent to Galicia at the end of 1914.

The Alicia Kuchen shops had gone – closed down, right at the beginning. There had been no need to do any soul-searching about whether or not her heart was still in it. Within weeks of the outbreak of war there was nothing to be had. Chocolate had been an early shortage but before the chocolate couverture disappeared the working men had gone. There had been ten men in the bakery and two in each of the shops and nothing for it but to close the business.

And very soon after that the money began to run out. Karl had decided early on to put their savings into war loans. He'd said that since they could not think of making Ilyinka into a hotel until victory went to the emperor, then the emperor and his government should have their savings on loan until he returned from the war which would be over by Christmas.

Alice had been terrified at the prospect of putting their money behind the war effort but there had been nothing else for it. On the day that war was declared share values had sunk in Vienna and had been dropping ever since. The only place they could hope for a return on their money was in war loans.

Ilyinka had been requisitioned by the authorities. There was nothing of comparable size in the village and stationed here were a few of the senior military and many, many civilian officials. But the men were behaving impeccably and kept to their own quarters so that most of the time they had hardly been aware of their presence.

Now the war was three years old. Nobody believed it would ever end and as Alice looked around her she wished she had used their savings to buy goods. Goods could be exchanged in the country villages for butter and eggs and milk and flour. The money she had in her cash tin was little enough and Karl's army pay was not sufficient to pay the inflated prices for basic foods.

In the village below Ilyinka the only flours obtainable were made from barley and maize, and these were on ration. Constantly they were exhorted to eat less and less. Government officials supervised the operation of the flour mills to ensure that nothing was sold; wheat flour had to go to feed the army. Alice was thin and pale. She ate one meal a day, though she gave Zita three. And she prayed that she would always be able to buy milk, an egg every week and a little meat, flour and vegetables every day so that Zita would grow straight, strong and healthy. All they had in store at Ilyinka were potatoes and many bottles of wine in a cellar.

Then on the night of 5 December, the Eve of St Nicholas, Babushka died.

Alice found her in the morning, looking as if she were sleeping peacefully.

The little grandmother had gone early to bed last night and her last words were that she wanted Tzitelina to enjoy the Saint's Day. The nuts and apples and sweets she had put aside were laid out on the carved chest in her bedroom. Alice took them away. She would give them to Zita a little at a time. Such treats were like gold and she went to her room and placed the tiny bags of poor quality chocolate and the hazelnuts in the top drawer of her own dressing-table.

It was almost midday, the priest had gone and had promised to send a message from the village to Olga in Prague. Alice was going to try to explain everything, very gently, to Zita.

She was in the salon at the front of the house, the only public room they had to themselves. It was also the only warm room. Since the men were all gone to war the log sheds were low, down to one month's supply. Every afternoon they went into the forest, gathering kindling and branches. But Zita was only five and couldn't go far in the arctic conditions outside. And there were deserters hiding in the forest and army scouts searching them out; shots cracking into the still air, making them run for home.

Zita, in her brown dress and white, starched pinafore, had come into the salon and was standing in front of her, her eyes wide and dark, her glossy, dark curls framing the little round face.

'Zita?' Alice picked the child up and held her close. 'Do you remember what Mama told you? About Heaven?'

'Yes, Mama.'

This was going to be so hard. 'What did Mama say?'

Zita looked solemn and thoughtful. 'Heaven is where good people go when they die.'

'Oh, darling.' Tears were coming hot to her eyes. She held the child tighter. There was no easy way to break such news gently. 'Babushka! Babushka!' she wept. 'Oh, my little one, our Babushka is dead.'

Zita's eyes were sad and large and, it seemed to Alice, too wise for one so young. She stroked Alice's face, as if she knew that it would give comfort. Then, 'Is Papa dead? Did Papa go to Heaven?' Zita asked.

The child had asked again; she asked every day about the Papa she had never forgotten. Alice put Zita on the floor, dried her eyes and tried to control her tears as she said quietly, 'We don't know, Zita. Your Papa is a soldier. Mama doesn't know where he is.'

There was a moment's silence whilst Zita thought about it, looking with the great brown eyes into Alice's own. 'Can Zita see Babushka? Before she goes to Heaven?'

'Don't make a noise.' Alice took her daughter's hand and together they left the room and climbed the stairs until they reached Babushka's door.

They stood by the bed in the darkened room for a moment before Alice lifted Zita high so that she should see and, if God were good to the child, remember this moment.

'Babushka sleeping?' Zita turned her big brown eyes on to Alice's face.

'Yes. A kind of sleeping.'

Then Zita slid out of Alice's arms to the floor and took her hand. 'Don't wake Babushka, Mama,' she said softly, her finger to her lips. 'Babushka will cry if she wakes up here, instead of Heaven.'

And it was such a childlike observation yet so profound that Alice took Zita in her arms again and smiled and kissed her and comforted her gently in a voice soaked with tears. Then she took her back to the salon and waited by the window for Franziska to come up from the kitchen.

Later she would go to the village to see if there was any food to be had. She would read the notices pinned to the church door and hope and pray that Karl's would not be amongst the names of the fallen for the church-door notices were the hardest of all to face. For she knew that for every victory the Austrian army celebrated many of her own countrymen lay dead.

In the early days there had been victories for the village to celebrate. This or that place on the eastern front would be taken and eventually an official notice would be posted on the church door but before the official news came exaggeration was the rule. A message would come in the morning, '500 prisoners taken at Lemberg' and, by lunchtime, rumour would have it that a whole city and five thousand men had been captured. Flags would be hung from windows, trees and posts – and the village people would look away, not speaking when Alice went to the village. After a time, though there were fewer and fewer victories to celebrate, she did not often go to the village alone. The village people knew as well as she did that for every Austrian soldier killed one or more British soldiers lived. She could feel their hostility, without their saying a word, when the name of one of the villagers was posted.

Now, without Babushka she would be here at Ilyinka alone and friendless – the enemy in the camp: her only protection her position as the wife of a fighting soldier.

'I take Zita?' Franziska had come into the salon and put out her hands for the child.

Zita ran to her eagerly. '*Suppe, Suppe,*' she cried.

Franziska laughed and scooped her up. '*Ja! Suppe!*' she said. It was poor-man's soup and today's would be as it was on most days, a watery broth made from bone stock with barley flour mixed to a paste and rapidly stirred in so that it formed doughy lumps in the bubbling, salty liquid. Zita loved it.

Later, when Franziska had taken Zita to the kitchen, Alice placed a few more logs on the stove and sat for a little time.

Olga would not be here today. It would take her at least two days to come from Prague since there was no troika and driver. And Alice dreaded the arrival of Olga and Max. Olga's mind had been turned by the news of Seppie's death right at the beginning of the war. Olga had been behaving badly towards herself and Zita long before she had announced that Hans had been captured by the Russians.

There was a letter from Karl on the table. Alice had read it every day since she had received it a week ago. It was dated a fortnight earlier. She picked it up again.

November, 1917
Eastern Front

My darling wife and baby Tzitelina,

I am not allowed to tell you where I am. Or how I
am except I am alive and well. The fighting has been
very strong. We have lost many good men. War is not
the brave and splendid act I thought it was. But I fight
like the true soldier. If I am spared I will be enough
happy to be with you again.

If I am not spared, Alice, you take the child back to
England. Tzitelina will have a future. I made my will
before I left Prague, to leave Ilyinka to Tzitelina after
I die. She can do with it what she wish when she is
grown up. She can grow up in England please.

You are the best happening in my life. I love you
very badly.

Karl

It made her cry every time she read it. Karl had written
it in English for her, daring the censors to do as they
wished.

Three days later Olga was at Ilyinka. Babushka's coffin
had been taken down to the churchyard in the village and
a mass was to be said for her at ten o'clock in the morning
before the burial at twelve.

Olga had hardly spoken a word since she had arrived
last night. Uncle Max Bauer and she had driven to Ilyinka
on the circuitous valley route, leaving their car in the
village and walking up the hill. Uncle Max, too, seemed
to be resentful of Alice's presence in the house.

Yesterday she had gone out alone. She had taken some
more of her own table-linen to a farmer who lived two
miles beyond the village. He wanted to provide a dowry
for his daughter and was willing to exchange good linen
for milk, eggs, butter and cheese. With them she had
prepared a small feast for Olga and Max.

On the table in the salon were cheese kromeskies,

sauerkraut, pickled cucumbers, hard-boiled eggs and, using some prunes given to her by one of the billeted officers at Ilyinka, she had made an acceptable, ersatz fruit-cake. There was blackberry-leaf tea and barley-bean coffee, for the real items had long since disappeared from the shops. And, of course, there was good Bohemian wine from the cellars.

Olga and Max had said not a word in thanks or praise to her and as they all walked down the hill to the church, booted and clad in heavy furs over their black mourning clothes, the silence was only broken by Zita's piping voice.

'Will we walk all the way back, Mama?'

'No, darling. The *Wagen* – the farmer's *Wagen* will wait for us outside the churchyard.' Alice held tight on to Zita's mittened hand to prevent her from slipping. The sun was shining this morning and the air as cold and clear as chilled white wine. The new snow was crunching underfoot and down below in the village the church bell was tolling slowly for Babushka.

Why didn't Olga speak? Or Max? What had she done? She turned to smile at them but both looked away.

'Soldiers, Mama!' Zita said excitedly.

Alice saw them coming up the hill. One of them was an officer wearing the great fur cape that was fastened with the silver braid of Karl's regiment. But it was not Karl. This officer was tall and fair. The soldiers passed the group without acknowledging them and went on their way upwards, towards Ilyinka. Perhaps there was going to be a change over of officers at the house.

There was no notice on the church door. Alice helped Zita off with her coat in the porch. She handed both hers and the child's to a nun who took them away and then they went, down the centre of the crowded church, to their reserved seats at the front. She loved this church, the masses, flickering candles, the heavy scent of the incense and the beautiful painted ikons. She had not taken instruction but as Karl's wife and Babushka's

563

granddaughter she had been allowed to come every Sunday, to listen to a mass. Zita had been christened here.

And she felt it again, the strange stillness that sent the old shiverings down her spine. Something was going to happen, to change. It was the passing of Babushka's soul, she believed. She let herself be carried away as the priest intoned the mass for the dead:

*Requiem aeternam dona eis, Domine: et lux perpetua luceat eis.*

She was thankful that the church was full, thankful that afterwards the churchyard was packed with villagers who were paying respects to a woman they had all loved. It made it easier to bear, knowing others felt it too.

And the strange stillness of heart persisted. And again Olga and Max did not speak to her. In fact, they seemed even more hostile once the church was behind them and they returned by cart to Ilyinka.

It was not until their coats had been taken, this time by little Franziska, and they had assembled in the salon that Alice saw what Olga and Max were wearing.

On the lapel of Max's jacket and on the left breast of Olga's black dress they wore large cardboard badges, on which they had inked the words, 'GOTT STRAFE ENGLAND' – God Punish England.

Alice felt all her control go. She stood, with tears pouring down her face, and crying and sobbing she shouted at them. 'I never want to see you again. Why are you here? Why are you doing this to me? Get out of this house! Go! Go!'

Max made a move towards her. 'You are not entitled to this house,' he said. 'If anything happens to Karl then Ilyinka will be ours.'

'Ilyinka belongs to Karl. It belongs to Zita.' She heard her voice, screaming at them like a fishwife. 'Leave us!'

She was shaking with anger as she watched them, huffing and puffing in indignation, calling for their furs, fastening them. She had not wanted to claim Ilyinka for

564

herself. It was Babushka she had loved. Not what Babushka owned. How could they be so cruel?

As soon as she had conquered her rage she heard her own voice, intemperate perhaps, but more than that – she heard her own self sounding as snobbish and scathing as ever Therese had been in her most haughty moments.

'I shall have legal documents drawn up by a good Prague lawyer,' she said. 'I shall have them witnessed at the church and placed in the priest's safekeeping. If Karl does not return then you will have to fight – like the gutter-sweepings of Europe that you are – to contest Babushka's will.'

She had really enjoyed saying that. She stood at the bedroom window and watched them go, slipping and stumbling in their haste to be gone from her as they descended the hill to the village again. Then wearily and without any malice left in her she pulled the shutters against the fading light and went downstairs to the salon.

As soon as she entered and closed the door behind her and before she reached the stove, she heard someone knocking.

'Come in,' she said.

It was the officer she had seen on her walk to the church, the tall fair-haired officer.

'I am sorry, Frau Reinhardt,' he said. He came to stand in front of her and bowed his head quickly in the military fashion. 'Leutnant Bergner. I am afraid I have bad news.'

And she knew. The coldness, the sadness was all-pervasive now. She knew why he was here. 'It's Karl? My husband? He's . . .'

'Yes, Frau Reinhardt.' The man was trying to keep his face impassive but Alice saw a muscle tightening under his bottom lip. 'Leutnant Karl Reinhardt was killed in action. Last week. I wanted to tell you myself.'

She could not take much more of sorrow and death and loss. She was afraid too, for anything poor Karl had suffered, afraid for herself, afraid for Zita, but even though she was sick with fear she fought back her tears bravely. Grief and pain would come to her later, when she was alone. Her voice was thin and high. 'You were his friend?'

'Yes.'

He put his hand into his inner pocket and brought out a small envelope. 'This is all I was allowed to bring . . .'

Her hand shook a little as she took the envelope. She knew what it contained. The wedding ring she had exchanged for his. And the tiny framed photographs of herself and Zita.

'Thank you,' she whispered. 'Can you stay? I want to hear everything. Please stay and talk to me about Karl.'

'I must return to the garrison tomorrow, Frau Reinhardt,' he said. 'Soon we are leaving for France.' He smiled politely. 'One of the officers here at Ilyinka says I may share his quarters tonight. I would like to talk to you. Thank you.'

Alice said, 'Please sit down. We will share the wine and the . . .' She indicated the food, '. . . the little supper I made.'

'It is a feast, Frau Reinhardt.'

She found the tears come springing to her eyes again and again she fought them back. She must not cry, not until later. The poor Leutnant Bergner would not know what to do if she were to break down in front of him. 'Karl's grandmother died,' she began to explain in a halting voice. 'We were to gather here for a meal . . .' She couldn't speak for a moment, then she squared her shoulders and said, 'Karl's relatives have gone, without sharing the food with me.'

'I heard it all,' he said gently. 'Karl was afraid that something like this might happen.' He helped her pull up one of the small tables to the stove and then, as he put more logs into the flames, Alice set glasses and the wine upon the table.

'Did Karl tell you that I'm an Englishwoman?'

'He did. He always was afraid you might find yourself in danger.'

She indicated the food. 'Please . . . Eat.' And she watched him go to put food on his plate, saw that he was hungry.

'What do you think?' she asked him.

He looked back at her from the table. 'I think you will be safe until the war ends.' He asked, 'Shall I bring food for you?'

'No, thank you. Later I will.'

He had returned to the table with his laden plate and begun to eat. 'You know that the Russians are going to pull out of the war?'

The Russians had forced the Czar to abdicate in March. They were having yet another revolution in Russia. She said, 'The Russians are war-weary. As we are.'

The Leutnant shrugged his shoulders. 'All of us are tired of fighting. But the Czechs will continue until they achieve their own victory. Until they have their country back.' He began to eat again, very quickly, as if he had not seen good food for years.

Alice knew that he was embarrassed by his appetite and pretended not to notice. She said, 'What do you think will happen to me and Zita? Did Karl say?'

He looked at her with eyes filled with sorrow. 'I believe that no matter who wins, for you and your daughter life will be impossible.' He paused then, 'This Sudetenland, this Silesia, may be a part of Germany or it may be part of a Czechoslovak state. You will be an outsider. Karl would want me to tell you this.'

'Do you really think I am in danger?'

He gave a pale smile as he continued to eat. 'No. Not in danger of your life. But in parts of the old empire . . . Romania and Hungary are already making laws in readiness . . . It will be the same here.'

Alice sipped a little of the wine, trying to appear still and calm though inside she was afraid. 'Please don't be afraid to tell me,' she said. 'What will be the same here?'

'The first thing they will do is to devalue the currency.

567

What you have saved will be worth nothing. Everyone has to start again, you can see.'

She didn't answer him. He stopped eating and said solemnly, 'The next thing they do is to forbid the holding of land or property by a foreigner.'

If that were to happen there would be nothing for them here. She must go home as soon as the war was over.

She looked up at the Leutnant who had put down his plate and was leaning back in his chair. 'Have you friends in Bohemia?' he asked. 'English friends?'

'No.' She had no-one. The Mannersmanns had gone home to America when war was declared.

'Have you anybody in Europe?'

'I expect my brothers will be fighting at the front.'

Then, thinking about her home, her brothers and her family, knowing they would be as sick at heart for her as she was for them, she could hold back her tears no more. A great gulping cry seemed to be tearing from her. She could not help herself. This good, kind man would have to face her own brothers across the mud and wretchedness of Flanders' fields.

He put a hand out to her but she could not take it. She was so afraid of letting the last of her defences go. She had to be strong for Zita. She made an enormous effort to calm down, to stop the terrible cries that were shaking her. She reached into the side-pocket of her black skirt and withdrew a great handkerchief. She blew her nose furiously and pressed the handkerchief to her eyes. Her throat was hurting as she forced the muscles to tighten so that she could speak again.

Then she raised a white, tear-streaked face to him and said, 'Leutnant. May I ask something more of you?'

'Of course.'

She was in control again. Her hands were trembling but her voice was quiet as she said, 'I have an aunt. She lives in the South of France. If I give you a letter . . . will you be able to post it? If there is a postal service in France then . . .' She broke off here and took a deep breath. 'She could tell my family at least, that we are still alive and well.'

'Please. Write it,' he said. 'I shall not be able to post it in France but there is a small chance I may send it by Vienna, through Switzerland.'

Alice went to the table by the window and took paper and ink and a pen and, having invited Leutnant Bergner to take what he wanted of the food again, she began to write.

Dear Aunt Harriet,

Babushka is dead. Karl is dead. He was killed by the Russians on the Eastern Front. Zita and I are safe and well but we have nothing. No money. We are at Ilyinka, in the Sudeten mountains of Western Silesia. Papa and Therese know where it is. Please tell them that you have heard from me and ask if they can help me when this awful war is over.

Alice

## Chapter Thirty-two

**France, 1918**

A messenger came up to Frederick's dug-out with the orders. 'Go forward at first light. No retreat. Whatever happens, no retreat.' The paper was unsigned and the company was wrongly addressed.

In the dug-out he heard rats scurrying and fighting under the ammunition-case table where a map and the orders from headquarters lay. Above the noise of roaring artillery he could hear the vermin, tussling over something they had brought in from the forward trench. The Gunners were putting up an intense bombardment that was to be followed by forty minutes' discharge of gas, concentrating on the German front line.

'Captain Thomas!' He had to shout though the officer was barely a yard away.

'Sir?'

'Go to the line trenches. Three platoons in readiness! Tell the officers and platoon sergeants what's happened. I'll query this bloody order. It says we're going over in the first wave. I'm going back to H.Q. to check. This looks as if it ought to be for "B" company. Not us.'

'Shall I tell the men, sir?' the captain shouted back.

'No. I'll break it to them when I get back. We go over at dawn either way. First wave or second. There's another hour to go.'

The dug-out was ankle deep in wet clay. One of the three platoons was made up of forty new boys, most of them barely eighteen. They were in a front-line trench, knee deep in slimy mud that stank of blood, cordite,

570

latrines and the decomposing corpses that lay above ground.

Frederick had not met the new boys yet; young soldiers who had arrived less than an hour ago after a five-hour march from the railway station. He felt intense pity for these new lads, fresh from the training fields of England and about to be plunged straight into the first wave of battle if the orders were correct.

The Big Push. A Highland regiment on the Cheshires' left and the Middlesex on their right. And the orders he had in his hand were for 'B' company, higher up the line. It would be as big a balls-up as the '15 offensive had been. And command had had longer to prepare for this one.

Why the Hell wasn't it over? Everyone on both sides of the line was waiting for the generals and the politicians to call a halt to the slaughter. The people were calling for an armistice. A few days ago even the *Frankfurter Zeitung*, the newspaper that was recognized as Europe's only democratic and influential one, had demanded that Kaiser Wilhelm abdicate.

The field telephone had been hit by a shell. He started back along the communications trench. His feet were numb with the autumn cold and wet. He had not taken his boots off for four days. He'd fought with one or other of his platoons at every battle for the last four days and they had moved no further though they'd lost three quarters of the men of the three platoons he commanded.

In his pocket was the letter he'd written a few days ago. It was addressed to Charles. He'd drop it at H.Q. They would let it go without censoring if he 'caught it' this time. Nobody would censor or even open a dead comrade's last letter home.

Dear Charles, (he'd written)

Thanks for the letter and all your news. Let's hope Arthur and Peter aren't sent out here. They could be kept in England as they are only just eighteen. Glad to hear George has recovered from the operation and is in good heart again. One and a half legs is plenty, tell him. I hear that Leopold has been promoted again and that he has been awarded the M.M. Well done.

I saw Beatrice. She's at the army hospital, one of the better ones, at A—s. On my last two days' leave I took her to Paris. Her fiancé, Captain Whitmore, is a fine fellow I'm sure you will take to. Tom Whitmore couldn't get leave to join us but we had a splendid time, wining and dining, walking and talking. She told me about the mess the army has made of Hetherington now it's being used for training – lawns churned up under tyres, wooden huts all over the parkland. My sisters don't mention it in their letters. It doesn't matter. All that matters is that we win this fight.

Tomorrow starts the Big Push. The Germans are falling back now we have the Doughboys (Americans) with us. It can't last much longer.

We are no longer fighting like cavalrymen. Remember how it was, Charles? There's hardly a decent horse to be had and the cavalry regiments are front-line troops. Most of the horses were massacred. Most of the men I came out with are dead and their fate comes to me as hearsay.

We've generals on the staff who can't read a map. They march the troops off their feet, leave supplies behind and send boys who've never seen a trench before, much less fired a shot in anger, straight into battle.

I seem to have acquired a reputation merely for surviving – four years and I haven't 'got it' yet. I'm superstitious. I have not been hit for almost a week and feel compelled to write in case this is 'it'.

Before I go, if it is 'it' I want to thank you for the experience of a loving family I would never have known but for your valued and true friendship. You have been a powerful influence for good on me though you may not have known it. I've had enough of the soldier's life. If I see this lot out I shall settle down.

Do you remember the *Tintagel Castle*? Our talk on deck? You said that you saw no other reason to marry than to fulfil the passionate feelings you had for your wife. I often think about it. I think you are right but I'll have to settle for less. Alice was the only girl I loved in that way.

I fear I am becoming sentimental and unsoldierly. There is a big job still to be done here.

Frederick.

He had reached the H.Q., a large cluster of dug-outs in the reserve line. He put his letter in the postbox and went to the colonel's dug-out. The colonel with his adjutant were seated at a table that was laid with linen, silver and glass. A whisky bottle, half empty, sat on the table before them. They were eating some kind of pie with mashed potatoes and sliced carrots.

Frederick went to the table and saluted.

'Well, Major?' The Colonel looked up.

'The orders, sir.' Frederick put the order paper on the tablecloth beside the colonel's plate. 'For us or "B" Company?'

The colonel glanced at the orders dully. He looked up. 'Pencil?'

Frederick handed him a stub of pencil and watched as the old boy scrawled his name across the page. He then wrote, laboriously and large, the letter 'A' at the top. Frederick took the order paper and pencil, folded the order and put it in his pocket. He stepped back smartly and saluted.

'By the way, Major . . .' the colonel said, 'I noticed some of the men in your platoons had their shoulder buttons undone. See that it doesn't happen again.'

After he got back to the dug-out, Frederick went to visit the new platoon to give them courage, more confidence, more fighting spirit than he had himself.

The noise was deafening; flashes of fire, Very lights

and flares lit the white, frightened faces of the lads who turned their heads to look at him, like schoolboys when a master enters the classroom. He raised his hand to signal that they were to gather at the end of the trench and they came, pulling themselves slowly through the stinking mess that dragged them down at every pace. He heard his own voice, shouting the orders, the same orders he'd been giving for too long. 'You'll receive a double tot of rum before the attack. Wait in silence for the order to charge. Bayonets fixed.'

One of the boys at the front called up, 'Do we go over the top here, sir?'

'No,' he yelled. 'Move up the line. Forward position.'

'Sir?'

Frederick knew that voice. Even under the thundering guns he knew. Startled, he looked in the direction the voice had come from. It was Peter Blackshaw. And next to him, Arthur Davenport.

His stomach turned over. 'Arthur? Peter?'

'Sir?'

'Sir?'

Frederick took a deep breath and looked around the group. Sniper fire, a hail of bullets, whistled overhead. The boards underneath the mud were vibrating with the pounding that the ground beyond the trench was taking.

'I expect you all know that these soldiers are my nephews?' he said. There was a cheer which was being drowned by the noise of the artillery bombardment. 'We'll be all right, lads!' he shouted at the top of his voice. 'We'll have a celebration when we get back.'

'Listen!' He shouted again. 'Your objective is the enemy trenches. Men who lose touch, join up with the nearest company and push on!'

'Will the wires be cut, sir?'

His ears were almost bursting with noise. 'The Gunners will have punched holes through our wire. The barrage will have brought the enemy wire down!'

'Do we stay in the captured trenches, sir?'

'No. Push on.'

'What if we're injured, sir?'

'You'll find No Man's Land full of shell craters. Crawl into one. Don't lose your rifle. Snipe as long as you can at the enemy. We'll come for you at dusk.'

Afterwards, Frederick would have to struggle to recall it all.

Watery, pale dawn light; the German positions outlined little more than two hundred yards ahead in the east; a cheer going up as he signalled and blew the whistle for the charge; the new lads scrambling, with himself beside them, heart hammering, metallic taste in the mouth, over the parapet towards the German trenches into a hail of enemy fire.

And they were rushing in a zig-zagging, crouching run amidst the noise, screams, yells and shouts towards the barbed wire entanglements on the German side of the three-hundred-yard stretch of No Man's land.

The barbed wire had not been cut. It needed bombs, not bloody shrapnel. The Highland regiment had attempted it and they were hanging, dead on the wires.

To their right the Middlesex regiment were being mown down like a swathe of corn.

'Down!' he screamed as German machine-guns opened fire.

Beatrice had been on duty for twelve hours when they brought the boys in.

'Make them comfortable,' the doctor said after a quick examination. 'There's no help for them.'

It was the death sentence. Nothing was to be done for them. Nothing could be done. She had known it was hopeless as soon as she'd seen their grey faces, felt the thready pulses.

Arthur had been shot through the chest and lungs. Already his lungs were filling with fluid and when he spoke his speech was rambling and theatrical. The bullets had missed all the heart's great arteries and veins. If they had not he would have been killed outright. At least she would have him to herself for a few hours.

'Beattie,' he whispered and reached for her hand.

Peter's spine had been broken so that he didn't know his legs were gone. He had lost so much blood he'd not regain consciousness but lay in the bed next to Arthur's, a beautiful boy. She had washed him and he lay, pale and dark-haired against the sheet. There was little clean linen but she had found the sheets, two for each of them so that they should imagine that they were home, in safe hands, if they felt the comforting clean smoothness under their bodies.

The military hospital was a commandeered monastery and she had given the boys one of the monks' cells. Their iron cribs were cramped close together in a room meant for one and there was less than six inches between them for her to go on weary, swollen feet. High above their heads a tiny stained-glass window cast coloured rainbows of light over the beds where her brothers lay.

'Are you coming?' Her friend Mary popped her head round the cell door. 'It's time you knocked off. We'll be back on duty in eight hours' time.'

'Go without me, Mary,' Beattie whispered.

'Who . . . ?' Mary looked over the sleeping forms.

'My brothers.' Beatrice turned her pale tearful face to her friend. She dared not let Arthur see her tears. She did not want him to know that he'd never walk, talk, laugh or love after tonight. 'My darling brothers, Mary. I'm going to stay with them.'

'My God!' Mary whispered back. 'Will you send for your mother and father? It's been done before.'

'No.' Beatrice put her finger to lips. 'Too late,' she mouthed.

And Mary, her dear friend, nodded quickly. 'I'll bring you something to eat and drink, later. I'll get someone to do your next duty,' she said softly before she closed the door quietly.

And when Beatrice turned back to the beds she saw that Peter was going, slipping silently away from her. And she had nursed men and women, soldiers and civilians and never had she seen anyone go so peacefully and quietly. She kissed his closed eyes and thought she saw a faint, slight smile cross the young dark face before a long-drawn sigh was the last breath he took and his features closed and withdrew into the mask of death.

It was dark before Arthur died. They had brought him in at two in the afternoon and he died at eight, quietly rambling about the great visions he was having; of journeys, of girls dancing around his bed; of running through flowering orchards and flying on saffron-yellow wings.

And when they were both gone Beatrice washed them and laid them out in white monks' shrouds she had found in a cupboard months before. Then softly she left them in peace, side by side as they had always been.

The nurses' quarters were in the old laundry building a little way from the monastery. There were worse conditions she knew, in some of the other hospitals, but tonight she longed for privacy and solitude instead of the chatter, the cheer or the complaints of the twenty nurses who were her sleeping companions in the dormitory.

'They broke through,' one of the girls was saying as she entered the long low room. 'The Germans are on the run.'

'When do you think it'll be over?' an older nurse said.

Then a hush came over them as Beattie came into the room.

'We're so sorry, Davenport,' one of the girls said.

There was a little chorus of 'Yes,' and 'Sorry about it all . . .' from the girls. Beatrice wearily threw herself down on her bed and pressed her face into the pillow and her friend, Mary, came to sit on her bed and comfort her.

A tea pot was produced and Beattie was cosseted and put to bed. Tea and calvados brandy was brought to her and though she protested, 'No, I promise, I'll not crack up or anything,' they sat with her until at last she fell into bone-weary sleep.

In the morning she didn't go down to the cell. She knew that the boys would be gone and others would be in their place. Arthur and Peter would be on their way to the military cemetery. She went to the ward and, pale faced, sick at heart and weary, she had to start again for the sake of the men who needed her.

Beds were crammed close together in the old refectory, round the walls and in two double rows back to back in the centre. In the chapel next door the theatre was going full tilt. The theatre staff looked as if they had been going all night.

Yet she knew that conditions here were not as bad as most. At least here they had washing water from a pump in the yard and boiled, sterilized water for the men to drink, from the kitchens below. The nurses' quarters were kept clean and there was a laundry, run by a religious order. Linen was always short but what they had was clean and well-mended. Men in the corridor were sitting, lying and propped up against the walls. They had called to her as she went in and she'd sent two of the VADs out to them to give first aid.

Here in the ward four nurses and three VADs were trying to attend all the patients.

She went to the top of the ward and spoke to the staff nurse. 'What's happened overnight?' She picked up the night-duty log from the monks' bench. Every morning she made a point of checking the log, though the nurses had often not had time to write it up. This hospital was run so differently from the Infirmary where strict discipline was always observed but Beatrice tried to have some kind of order and a record of her patients' progress.

'Fourteen deaths, Sister Davenport. Three amputations at the femur. Six stomach wounds. They've been stitched. They're in the side ward. Nothing more can be done for them . . .'

'Don't ever say that, Nurse!' Beatrice rebuked her. 'You have seen recoveries. You've seen miracles. We all have.'

'Sorry, Sister Davenport,' the nurse said. She looked a little shamefaced. 'Oh. And a head injury. An officer in one of the cells. A baronet or something.'

Beatrice ran her finger down the list of names. It stopped moving at Major F. Blackshaw.

'When did they bring Major Blackshaw in?' she asked.

'Last night. He went over with the lot we had yesterday. They pulled him out of No Man's Land when it was dark.'

So Frederick had gone over with the boys. Beatrice felt sick to her soul. Soon there would be nobody left. The boys dead. George shot to pieces. She felt like screaming, shouting to the Heavens, 'Stop fighting. In the name of God, stop it!'

Instead she spoke calmly to the nurse. 'Has he been seen?'

'Yes. But there's not much . . .' Here she stopped and corrected herself when she saw the expression on Beatrice's face. 'The doctor says there's not a lot can be done. He was shot through the left shoulder and at the ulnar-radial . . .'

'Yes. Yes. His elbow,' Beatrice said.

'His wounds have been dressed. His arm's in plaster,' the nurse finished. 'He's in the cell . . .' Here she looked at Beatrice's stern face and seemed to take courage. 'The surgeon says there's brain damage. He'll be dead before nightfall!'

At her words Beatrice felt all the fight that was in her rise up in one enormous protest at what was being done. 'Like Hell he will!' she stormed. 'He'll not die! Not while I'm in charge here.' She slammed the log book into the startled nurse's hands. 'I'm going to take a look at Major Blackshaw,' she said. 'See that everything is done here, Nurse. I'll leave you in charge.'

'Yes, Sister Davenport.'

Beatrice picked up her own bag of equipment and went down to the cells. In the one the boys had been in yesterday she found Frederick. He was unconscious and, from the waist down, covered in mud. Nobody had found the time to clean him. She'd make her observations whilst she washed and changed her patient.

She went for water, towels and soap herself. Nobody else should touch him. He had become her talisman. If she could save Frederick then she'd know that everything would be all right. She took off his clothes and his boots and, so that he should not chill, she covered him with blankets whilst she worked. She washed him all over then started at his feet, bathing, massaging and warming them for she had always had the notion that if the feet were clean and warm some kind of signal went to the brain. It was quite unscientific she knew and old-fashioned, but Therese had taught her that and she'd seen it work.

His colour was becoming normal as she worked and when she had finished with his feet and lower body she began to oil and massage his chest and to ease the stiffening she could feel in his neck.

He was starting to make the heavy snorting sounds that a patient with a cerebral haemorrhage makes but, as she worked on, she became convinced that he'd recover consciousness, that his condition was improving. When she had done he was clean and warm and his circulation had been stimulated. She opened her bag again and propped him into a sitting position.

Therese had given her some of her cures and she selected a bottle that was labelled, 'Sloe and Bryony. Dutch Myrtle and Wood Sorrel. Two teaspoonfuls in water as required. To restore mental balance following injury.'

She put the dose into a warm honey and water solution and slowly and patiently began to administer it, feeding him from the teaspoon, little by little, drop by drop at first until she saw the throat begin to work and he had taken half a cupful.

Throughout the day she returned to the cell every fifteen minutes. At tea-time she brought tea and her sandwiches to the cell and she saw, with every visit, that his colour was better, his breathing deeper and slower. And at eight o'clock at night at last his temperature came down to normal and he opened his eyes.

'Frederick?'

'Who is it?' he said.

'Beatrice.'

'What happened?'

She smiled a great satisfied smile of contentment. 'I will tell you in the morning. Just sleep for now.'

She left him, telling the night staff to continue her treatment. Then she did what had to be done to help her patients in the wards until at last, at ten o'clock, she went off duty.

Outside, Captain Whitmore was waiting for her. 'I heard about your brothers, Beatrice,' he said, taking her arm in the pitch black quietness of the monastery garden. 'I'm sorry.'

'Don't talk about it, Tom.' Beatrice answered the pressure of his hand in hers.

'Do you want to walk for a little?' he asked. 'I've got a torch.'

'Yes.' He was a dear, dear man. Tom Whitmore was forty-three, more than ten years older than herself. He had been a reservist who had volunteered at the beginning. He had never been fighting fit but, a solicitor by profession, had been given a rank and was in charge of three units in France, run by serving women of the WAAC Clerical. From these units the awful notices about the deaths of soldiers were sent, relatives were traced and contacted, property returned and last effects were gathered together for sending home. From here also the Red Cross was informed about enemy prisoners who had died. Their effects too were dealt with.

As they went slowly down the path towards the road to the village, the torchlight bouncing in front of them,

Tom held her close. 'I've had the most extraordinary decision to make today,' he said. 'I had to go through the effects of a captured Austrian lieutenant.'

'Oh.'

'And in his wallet he had a letter from an English girl who is a widow of one of his comrades.'

'Is that so unusual?' Beatrice asked.

'Well. It sounds a bit far-fetched, Bea. But I think the girl is your sister.'

'Alice?' Beatrice stopped still. 'Surely not?'

'It was Alice. The husband's name was Karl.'

'And Karl's dead?'

He took both her hands in his. 'She must have asked this lieutenant to post the letter for her if he could. He, quite clearly, couldn't do it. Have you an aunt who lives in Cannes?'

'Yes.'

'Then it is the one.'

Beatrice asked quietly, 'Where is the letter?'

'I posted it.'

# Chapter Thirty-three

**France, 1918**

The military hospital near Abbeville had an attractive convalescent ward at the back of the building. French windows gave on to a tiled veranda that had an elaborate iron and glass roof and wooden, slatted shutters you could raise and lower.

Frederick was alone there, standing by one of the wicker chairs, looking out towards the road beyond the leafless hedge that bordered the grass. It was good to see the horses and carts and the occasional motor-car go by. For weeks he'd seen nothing but the bare walls of his cell whilst he'd made a slow recovery from the injuries. The shoulder wound had festered and an abscess had formed deep under the broken clavicle.

The sun was shining though it was mid-November. The armistice had been signed.

The others must prefer the noise of the ward for he had the veranda to himself. He was glad of the quiet; in the ward were eight men, all officers like himself and all waiting for the transport that would take them to Boulogne and home.

He saw a staff car arriving, turning in at the gates and following the drive towards the front of the hospital.

'Are you all right, sir?' One of the nurses came out to speak to him.

'Yes. Leave me alone,' he said. Then, 'Sorry, Nurse. But I don't want to talk at the moment.'

He really would have to pull himself together. He was edgy and rough. The nurse was doing her duty, not trying to annoy him.

His plastered arm was supported by a sling. His wounds were dressed and padded.

'Have your dressings been changed?' The nurse asked. There was a great hole in his shoulder that had to be packed every day.

'Yes. Yes. Be a good nurse. Run along.' This time he did not smile or apologize and she went.

He sat down in the wicker chair, stretched out his long legs and watched the road for a little time.

When first he had come to in the monastery hospital he'd been aggressive, demanding to be sent back to the line. He had fought with doctors and nurses; anger and fever had been boiling in him. He'd wanted to kill – to avenge the deaths of Arthur and Peter – though he'd long since lost all hatred for an enemy who had lain in the mud only yards away from him.

And Beatrice, through all his weeks of fever and madness, like an angel of mercy had soothed him and explained to him that he couldn't even stand, let alone fight; that they were not even able to move him.

It was strange to realize that after all that time he'd not been there when the bugles blew the 'cease fire'. He had not witnessed the German soldiers tearing off their uniforms, drinking beer with the British Tommies, saying happily 'There goes the old Pomp and Glory' as they wheeled barrow-loads of swords on to the scrap heap the day after the war was ended.

This morning he'd been visited by an officer from his regiment, one of the men who had first reached the Rhineland. The officer had been horrified at what they found there; famine and starvation throughout the land. British troops had given their rations to the hungry children. General Plumer had asked for food to be sent urgently. Winston Churchill had given orders for the mercy despatch of food to the people who had so recently been the enemy. And all the time, whilst the soldiers wanted to give help, the great powers were insisting on a hunger blockade of Germany for twelve months after the war.

Knowing all this, the anger he'd felt in the monastery hospital was gone and his moods swung hourly from irritability to despair. A dreadful black depression seemed to have come upon him. He dared not look back. He'd seen too many good men reduced to trembling, twitching wrecks, unable to sleep, for with sleep they relived the nightmares of battle.

He could sleep only for two hours at a time and was ridiculously thankful to wake and find himself alive and sane. Then he'd try to look forward and his future looked bleak. He no longer felt optimistic, no longer said to himself, 'When this is over . . .'

It was over.

A motor-car, a white Benz, rolled slowly through the gates and on to the front entrance.

The nurse was back. 'There's a lady to see you, sir.'

'A lady? For me?' He stood up. He could only imagine it might be Beatrice.

'Yes, sir,' the nurse said. 'Shall I show her in?'

'Of course.'

But there was no need for the nurse to open the door to his visitor for the door was opening from the other side.

'Therese!'

'Freddie. Darling!'

Dressed in black, she was standing timidly in front of him, not daring to touch him for fear she'd hurt him. Then she stood on tiptoe and with closed eyes she kissed his face.

He took her hand in his good one and held tight. 'Oh, I am so glad to see you. I – I don't know what to say, Therese.'

'Please say nothing.' She was fighting back tears as she drew up a wicker chair and sat beside him. Then she turned to the nurse and, with a touch of the old imperious girl he knew, said, 'You may go.'

When the nurse had gone she took his hand in hers and he saw that her eyes were brimming with tears. 'I came to see where they'd been buried, Freddie. We got your letter. I was brought here in a staff car. By one of the colonels.'

'How are you?' he asked gently.

'How are you?' she asked. 'You look awful.'

'Do I?' He managed a weak smile here. 'I'm numb, Therese. I've no feeling. Nothing.'

'Do you remember anything of it?'

'I remember everything until I was hit.'

'Did you see them?'

'I was with them. They were . . .' He was going to say that they were brave, but a brave boy who died implies a suffering that a mother would not want to imagine. 'They wouldn't know a thing. They were hit in the first moments.'

He looked into her troubled, beautiful eyes. 'You don't want to know more than that, Therese,' he said gently. 'They died soldiers' deaths. That is enough.'

'And you? You saw it?'

'I remember nothing after I was hit. Blackness. Silence. That's all.'

She took out a handkerchief and dabbed at her eyes. 'It's all over.'

'Yes,' he said. 'All over. How's Charles?'

She blew her nose violently. 'He's crushed.'

'What do you mean? Crushed?'

She appeared to have taken hold of herself again. 'He can't get over it. His hair went white overnight. He can't believe that they are gone. He's lost three of his children. Arthur, Peter whom he always treated as his own, and Alice. We've had no word since the war started. Rinehart has heard nothing. We can only suppose they're dead.'

She turned her pale face towards him again. 'Charles can hardly bear to treat his patients. He thinks the boys would have survived if he'd been there when . . .'

'That's not true!' Frederick said. 'Everything that could be done was.'

'There's nothing I can say or do to console him.' She put her hand in his. 'Charles will have to give up his practice and his hospital work. I can't bear to see him suffer.'

'I'm sorry.' He held on to her hand. 'What will you do?'

'I can't even grieve, Freddie,' she said quietly. 'I try to feel and all that happens is that I shed a few tears. Maybe I am being strong for Charles's sake. I don't know.'

He squeezed her hand gently. She said, 'I shall throw myself into some activity. I'm used to it now. I've done a lot of Red Cross work.' She gave a watery smile. 'But that will have to stop. I think I shall do as Alice suggested . . .' She stopped here for a moment as if deep in some almost-forgotten thoughts before she went on, 'Alice said I should market my cures. I wish she were here. I'll encourage Charles to put all his energies into it as well. He can make his pharmacological things. I'll do what I can with mine.'

'You could move back to the Dower House. All of you.' He did not think that she'd want to return to the Hetherington estate but he must offer.

'I'm not at all sure . . .'

They were interrupted again by the nurse who had come on to the veranda.

'There's a gentleman to see you, sir,' she said.

'You mean an officer?' It might be news of his passage home.

'A captain sir. Captain Brassington-Cork he said, sir.'

Therese had jumped to her feet. 'Reggie?' she said. 'It must be Reggie.'

The door was open and they heard him, the dapper man whom Frederick had last seen on the little fellow's wedding day.

587

'Brassington-Cork,' they heard. 'Captain Cork, tell the Major.'

There was a pause and then, 'Of course I know him. Last time we met was at my wedding.'

Then he came in, suited entirely in pale grey, with a red spotted bow-tie glaring under his white wing collar. His monocle bounced on a gold chain at his lapel.

'Therese, my dear,' he said as he took her hand and kissed it. 'I had no idea I'd find you.'

He turned to Frederick. 'Tremendous spot of luck really. Finding Therese here,' he said. 'Beatrice wrote. Told us about everything. The boys. Terribly sorry, old thing.'

Frederick found himself smiling. Poor old Reginald was so obviously a fraud. But he'd driven all the way from Cannes to see him. He was touched by the little chap's doing so much. He indicated a seat. 'And you've come all this way to see me . . . ?' he asked.

But Reginald had taken a letter from his pocket. 'The truth is,' he said, 'we had this letter from Alice. It arrived a week ago. It's a plea for help . . .'

Therese took the letter from his hand, opened it and began to read out loud, ' "Dear Aunt Harriet, Babushka is dead. Karl is dead. He was killed by the Russians on the Eastern Front. Zita and I are safe and well but we have nothing. No money. We are at Ilyinka, in the Sudeten mountains of Western Silesia. Papa and Therese know where it is. Please tell them that you have heard from me and ask if they can help me when this awful war is over. Alice." '

She looked up from the page. 'It was written last year,' she said.

'Yes,' said Reginald. 'It came to us with a note from Captain Whitmore. Alice had given the letter to Karl's comrade to post. It was in his wallet when he died.'

'Then how? Why . . . ?' Therese began.

Reginald Brassington-Cork, full of importance, said,

'We knew where Beatrice was. Knew she'd nursed you, Major Blackshaw . . . Frederick if I may . . .'

As soon as Frederick heard her name – the moment Therese read Alice's words – all his senses came to life again; love for her came shuddering through him like a hundred of the uncontrollable fevers he'd lived through.

Reginald was still explaining. 'God alone knows how long the post might take. Or if the letter would ever get to Macclesfield.'

'So you decided to come to me . . .' Frederick interrupted him.

Reginald continued in his most pompous voice. 'So I said to Hatters, I said, "Listen old girl, I'll deliver it myself. If anyone can get a message through to Charles, it will be Frederick." '

'Have you tried to contact Alice?' Therese asked anxiously. 'Did you try?'

'No luck, I'm afraid,' Reginald said. 'Hatters tried to have money sent to her. You can't get money in or out.'

Reginald stood up at this point and said, 'I said to Hatters, "If there's anything we can do, Hattie. Anything at all. It will be done." '

He put out a hand to Frederick. 'So. Er . . . Frederick, I'm at a little place in Abbeville. Small hotel. Nothing showy. If they let you out this evening . . . When you two have had a little tête-à-tête . . .'

He smiled and shook Frederick's hand. 'Come down and dine with me. We'll thrash something out between us, eh? Maybe get some of your army chaps to help, eh? They'll be sending an occupying doo-dah I expect.'

Then he kissed Therese's hand, put the monocle into his eye and strutted away.

The moment the door closed behind Captain Brassington-Cork, Therese gave a great sigh of relief. 'Thank God she's safe.' She then looked at him and tears began to pour down her face, free hot tears that she could not control.

'She'll still be all right, won't she, Freddie?' she said. 'It couldn't happen that she's gone as well . . .'

Frederick felt his insides curl into a knot. 'I hope so. Give me a little time to think, Therese. I've got to think of a way of getting them out; Alice and . . . And what did she say was the name of Karl's daughter?'

Therese made no reply. She was sitting, tears gone, her head in her hands, motionless.

Frederick looked hard at her to see if she were still overcome. But he could not see her face. And she was as still as death and silent. He waited a few moments – waited for a word from her, but she had not moved an inch. She seemed to be holding her breath, so deathly quiet was she. What was this? Therese had never been a good liar.

In a controlled and careful voice, for inside it was as if every thought and word hung on her answer, he said, 'I asked you, Therese. What is the name of the child? What is the name of Karl's daughter?'

Then, and it was as if all the old stuff that was Therese rose up in her again, she stood up and her white face was tear-streaked as she looked down at him.

'Don't be a fool, Freddie,' she said. 'You know perfectly well that Zita is not Karl's daughter.'

He had to believe it. The knot in his stomach grew tighter. Therese would not lie to him about this.

'Not Karl's?' he whispered. 'Then what are you saying, Therese?'

Her eyes were blazing with conviction. 'I knew the moment I saw her,' she said. 'Alice's child is every inch a Blackshaw! Zita is your daughter, Freddie!'

# Chapter Thirty-four

**Czechoslovakia, 1918**

Winter had set in early this year. Silently the snow came in mid-October; great drifting falls, night after night until Alice was afraid the very house would suffocate. She was afraid she would wake one morning to find that they were living underneath a white mountain, buried alive.

But these fears were as nothing to the fear of violence which she lived with; deserters from the army, anarchists and vengeful mobs were roaming the country, breaking down doors, demanding to be let in to steal, to loot the houses of the rich. It was their turn, they said, to take.

Alice made sure that they were always safely locked in at night. She felt that the government officials who were still in residence at Ilyinka were a protection during the hours of daylight. And she had guns; she had brought them from the hunting lodge and hoped that the mobs knew there were arms at Ilyinka.

Soon she would use the guns for their old purpose. She had never fired a shot in her life but once there was no food to be had from the village or the farms, she was prepared to hunt.

Not until December did the snow stop falling. The government men who showed no sign of leaving Ilyinka had shovelled out a deep, narrow cutting through to the entrance of the house. When she opened the door sheer white cliffs rose either side of a neat white trodden path that went, following the curve of the old drive, to the road to the village.

'Mama! Mama! Where are you going?' Zita came flying

down the staircase to stand, arms outstretched, in front of the great oak doors.

'Mama is going to the village, Zita.' Alice fastened the ties of her fur coat – a sable that touched the ground when it had been Babushka's. On Alice it stopped six inches above the ankle – the now-fashionable length.

'I come, Mama?'

'No.' Alice began to pull the big fur hat over her hair. She wore her hair in a plait that she wound round and round her head like the Finnish women did.

She could not take the child with her. Last night she'd had the strangest dream in which she had seen Papa, white-haired and old, weeping. And when she awoke she found herself with one of her moods of agitation, of premonition. Besides, Zita's boots would not last the winter. Already they needed the stitching reinforced.

'Stay with Franziska, Zita,' she said. 'Mama is going to look for food.'

'Buy oranges.'

The child had not forgotten the fruit they had stored in the summer. There were six oranges in the dark cellar; two for Christmas Day, two for St Stephen's Day and two for New Year.

'Find a Papa for me, Mama.' Zita had dropped her hands and was looking at her feet. She looked up. 'I don't have a Papa, do I?'

'No.'

She had to explain it to Zita every day. Men, soldiers, were returning to the village all the time but there were many, many children who had no Papa. Zita was six years old and still she remembered being held shoulder-high when she was only two. She remembered a tall soldier-Papa who would never return.

'There is no Papa, darling,' she said. She bent to kiss Zita on her upturned face before she fastened the straps on her leather boots and pulled on long, fur-lined gloves. 'I'll be back soon,' she said.

Zita turned and ran, like a cat on skinny legs, up

the stairs to Franziska who stood, laughing, waiting for her.

'What you take?' Franziska asked.

'The last of the towels,' Alice said. 'After this . . . I don't know!'

She picked up her bag. Inside were four hand towels, monogrammed with her initials.

She went outside. She had wrapped a scarf around her nose and mouth so that the icy air would not freeze her lungs and she went, muffled everywhere but for the few inches where her eyes were, down the hill towards the village where her first stop would be the church.

It had become part of her daily routine to stop at the church and read the notices. On the day after the Armistice there had been a jostling crowd around the church, exclaiming over the paper pinned to the door.

We are no longer an Empire. We are a republic.
Emperor Karl has left the country.
Czesko-Slovenska-Republika

It had been followed a few days later by a notice demanding that all foreigners register.

Then the Austrian banknotes had been overstamped and devalued.

And it did not matter any more. As long as she could find enough food for Zita, herself and Franziska for the next few months until the thaws came, it was all she asked.

She had reached the church and went through the gate and the churchyard to see the notice pinned to the door.

Foreigners to register before January 31st.
Your registry centre:
Ilyinka

The priest, an Austrian and a sympathetic friend of Alice's, was standing behind her. 'I want to speak to you, Frau Reinhardt,' he said. 'Please come into the church.'

Alice followed him into the dark church and sat in one of the pews at the back.

'You saw the notice,' the priest said. 'How will you register?'

'I shall not register,' she answered him.

'You are going to leave us?'

Alice looked into his kindly face. 'Father,' she said, 'I have spent the weeks since the peace in securing everything for Zita. I want to be sure that if she ever comes back, her claim to her property is recognized. You have a copy of all the documents. I posted a copy to a lawyer in Prague. The property belongs to Zita. The papers are in safekeeping. The deeds of Ilyinka – the wills – Karl's and Babushka's – I mean Elena Petrovna Voroshilov . . .'

'Yes, yes.' He spoke urgently. 'You have done all you can. But if the property is wanted they will confiscate it – take it from you. Zita was born in Czechoslovakia as we must call our land. Zita is a Czechoslovak national. You are not.'

'I know,' she said. 'And I am going home to England with Zita. As soon as we can escape.'

'This country is not a prison, Frau Reinhardt.'

He spoke gently and Alice knew that he was trying to help her. He had been a support to her since Babushka had died and she had always been frank with him.

'You know what happened in Prague, don't you?' she said quietly.

In Prague, as soon as the peace was declared, mobs of Czechs had stormed into the main squares, pulling down monuments, smashing shops owned by people of German origin. She had been told that the *Kaffeehaus* of Herr Ferleitner was now occupied by a Czech and renamed *Kavarny Nove Mesto* and there was nothing to be done about it.

'Mass hatred – sparked off by a few innocent remarks, Father?' she said. 'You may say that the country is not a

594

prison but for me and other German-speaking people it is as frightening as a prison. I have been afraid since the peace. I shall go to Prague again, when we leave the country.'

'Do you need money?' he asked.

'Yes. I need money for the journey to Prague, that is all.'

'I shall give you money. The church will give you money. You can return it when it is possible.'

'Thank you, Father.'

Babushka had left money but it was not a fortune and, since the laws of the country forbade it, Alice was not allowed to draw on it for herself and Zita. It would eventually come to Zita, but by then would be worth little enough if koruna were to be devalued again.

The priest asked, 'What will you do when you get to Prague?'

'I have some jewels left. As soon as it is safe to go, I shall travel to Prague. Get what I can for the jewels. Buy train tickets to Vienna, to Paris, to my home in Macclesfield.'

She smiled at him. 'I have a little money in England. I shall use it until I find some way to earn a living for Zita and me.'

He said, in a kind and concerned voice, 'Frau Reinhardt, do you have food?'

'I sold some jewellery in Prague before the peace,' she said. 'I bought condensed milk and tinned beef. I have potatoes in my cellar. Some beans. A little pig fat and a little salted butter. I dried some onions and mushrooms and in the autumn I stored nuts. All are safe.'

He stood up. 'And today?'

'Today I am going to exchange the last of my trousseau, Father. For milk and eggs.' She got to her feet.

The priest laughed. 'It must be quite worn, by now,' he said. 'Your trousseau linen.'

Alice found herself laughing too. 'Father! Really!' Then she went quiet and said, 'It is sixteen years since

I married Karl. Imagine, still having a trousseau at the age of thirty-four!'

He was silent for a few moments, then he said, 'I know you are not of the faith, Frau Reinhardt, but I should like to say a few prayers for you. Please come to the altar rail.'

She followed him to the front of the church and knelt quietly whilst he placed a hand on her shoulder and spoke first the words of the Old Testament: 'My thoughts are thoughts of peace and not punishment; you shall call upon me and I will hear you and will bring you back from all the places of captivity.'

And when he had spoken the words of the prophet he touched her head and blessed her: '*Dominus vobiscum.*'

'*Et cum spiritu tuo,*' she answered.

She left the church and walked up the hill at the other side of the village, towards the farm. The old farmer, since his daughter was married, was not so eager to exchange his precious food for linen and she felt nervous, anxious, as she went across the cobbled yard and knocked.

There was no reply and yet she knew that they were there and found that her feeling of agitation had returned. She knocked again. She called through the closed door, 'It is I. Frau Reinhardt. I am come for milk and food for my child.'

Still they did not come. She had to buy milk and eggs. There would be no feast, no Christmas in three weeks' time if she could not buy.

She knocked again. The door opened a little way and she saw the farmer, scowling, push his wife behind him.

'Go away. There is no food.'

'Oh, please,' she begged. 'Open the door. I need milk for my child . . .'

He slammed the door in her face.

There was no help in tears though she was very close to crying. She pulled the scarf close about her mouth and nose and started to trudge further on, another two miles up the hill to the next farm. It would be dark before she arrived home. She hoped that Franziska had the sense to lock the big doors after the government men had gone.

Two hours later, the precious can of milk clutched to her chest, a cleaned and plucked chicken dangling by its string-tied feet from her elbow, she climbed the hill to Ilyinka again.

She was pleased with her day's bargaining but inside there was a hopeless feeling; for it would be the last time anyone from the farms would have food for her.

They had changed towards her, become resentful. They asked in a pointed way if Frau Reinhardt, being a foreigner, intended to remain amongst them for much longer. They would recall, in a pointed manner, the days when all who could sought employment at Ilyinka. They were speaking of Babushka as if she had been a tyrant.

Alice knew that she had contributed nothing to the life of Ilyinka and the village but it hurt her dreadfully to think that Babushka, who had been so good to them all, was maligned after her death.

Perhaps she should gather their belongings, hers, Zita's and Franziska's if she wished, and they should leave after Christmas. They could not last another three months without fresh food. Perhaps she should ask the government officials at Ilyinka to help them get to Prague, to see that they had safe passage out of the country.

There was a big white motor-car grinding up the hill, chains around the wheels. She kept close to the wall, away from the churned-up road so that she would be in no danger if the motor-car should skid. The car must have been driven by a foreigner who had lost his way for it passed the end of the road where Ilyinka was, and continued up the hill a little way and there was nothing up there but the forest track.

She went quickly through the narrow way that had been cut. At either side walls of snow rose sheer – to a height of eight feet. The sky was dark above her head but she saw her way very well through the white-walled cutting.

Franziska let her in. They had been watching for her from her bedroom window.

'Mama! Mama!' Zita threw herself into Alice's arms as soon as she had put down the can of milk and the chicken. 'We saw a big white motor-car. It has stopped. Two men are coming to see us.'

Alice did not take off her coat and hat. 'Run upstairs!' she ordered. She turned and slid the bolts across the great oaken doors. 'Go quickly Zita! Hide in your bedroom. Don't open the door unless I tell you it is safe! Franziska. Stay with me.'

Zita, frightened, ran whilst she, all at once calm and resolute, went to the cupboard and reached on top for the loaded rifle.

Then she went up the stairs and stood on the top step and nodded to Franziska. They had rehearsed this, in case they were ever attacked. Franziska was to stand near the door, so that she could slip out and run to the priest if need be. Alice was quite prepared to shoot as many men as she needed to, to guard Zita.

They could hear footsteps outside. Alice held her breath. Franziska took up her position. There was a banging on the door. Not an aggressive banging such as a mob might make.

Alice waited in silence.

There was another knock. Alice waited for a few moments then she called, 'Who is it? Speak!'

She heard a man coughing. Then he spoke. In English.

'Alice?'

'Yes.'

'It's Reginald. Captain Brassington-Cork. Open up, Alice. There's a girl.'

Alice felt her knees grow boneless with relief. She held the gun loosely in front of herself as she nodded to Franziska.

Franziska slid the bolt and stepped back as she pulled open the oaken door.

It was Captain Cork. And standing beside him, tall and broad and strong in an army greatcoat that had one sleeve dangling loose, Frederick.

The gun slid from her hands to the carpet. She went down the steps as if in a trance. She could not believe her own eyes.

'Freddie!' she cried, running into his arms.

And his arm was around her and he was holding her close and she had tears streaming down her face as, laughing and crying at the same time she put her hands up on to his dear, dear face and whispered and said his name, over and over again.

He was crying too. She had never seen a man in tears. Only Papa in her dream last night. And here was her darling Freddie, eyes filled with tears of happiness as he held her tight and kissed her.

She heard Captain Cork, behind them, pick up the gun and unload it. Heard him saying with an air of nonchalance, 'On the safe side, eh?'

Frederick was still holding and kissing her when Zita, freed by Franziska, came down the stairs and threw herself against her Mama's coat.

'Mama! Mama!' she cried. 'Is this my Papa. My Papa?'

Then Frederick stopped kissing Alice but held her a little away from himself as he looked for the first time into the face of his daughter.

'Zita?' he said. 'Can this be Zita?'

Zita put her arms up to him and he scooped her up in his good, right arm and held her where he could look into her face; the face that was so like his own. One pair of big, beguiling brown eyes looked directly into Freddie's. And his older and wiser brown eyes fastened themselves joyfully on the child's face.

'Are you my Papa?' Zita repeated.

It sounded to Alice like a plea. Frederick looked at her over Zita's shoulder. And she could say nothing. She looked at him with great shining grey eyes that were glimmering with happiness.

'Yes. Yes, my darling,' Freddie said, pulling their little one in, holding her close against his face and pressing kisses on her round little round cheeks. 'Oh, yes, angel-child. I am your Papa.'

It had taken them a week to cross Europe, driving every day from after breakfast until late afternoon when Captain Cork or Uncle Reggie as he insisted they call him, would sail into the grandest hotel in the area and find rooms for them; one for himself, one for Zita and the best bedroom in the hotel for herself and Freddie.

Every day, every little challenge, revealed another aspect of this resourceful character who was Aunt Harriet's husband.

He'd told them they could have half a day free in Paris and still, he promised, they would be home in Macclesfield on Christmas Eve. Alice had been persuaded, by Freddie and Zita, to have her hair bobbed and water-waved in Paris and now, as they bowled along the last miles of the journey, through Staffordshire towards Cheshire, she felt a happiness and contentment such as she'd never known in her life before.

She was seated at the side of Uncle Reggie, since Zita could not bear to be parted from her Papa, nor he from her. Alice listened to them, as they sat in the back of the Benz, singing and laughing and playing silly little guessing games. Whenever there was silence in the back of the car Alice would turn to see Frederick asleep with his arm around Zita and the child awake, her face a picture of contentment.

She pulled the fur coat a little tighter around herself and rested her head on the upholstery whilst she closed her eyes and thought about the spilling happiness this last week had brought to her.

On the evening that Freddie and Captain Cork had

arrived at Ilyinka she had been in a high state of nervous excitement.

It was ridiculous to remember it as it had happened but no sooner had Freddie put Zita down than she'd said, 'I will make beds up for you . . . I'll try to find something to eat . . . You must be hungry . . .'

Freddie took her hand and led her up the stairs to the maple doors of the salon.

'In here?' he asked in a deep, serious voice.

'Yes,' she had babbled, 'I'll just take off my coat . . . Give me yours . . . Where is Captain Cork . . . ?'

He pulled her inside, closed the door behind them and slowly he said, 'Don't let us go through all that again, Alice.'

She could not answer. She gazed into his eyes, waiting for him to say more.

He smiled at her and said, 'You wouldn't have leaped, would you? If I'd asked you to leap into my arms, as your mother did, you would have said "Who? Me?"'

But even as she nodded to please him, inside herself her heart was singing, 'I would, Freddie. I was head over heels in love with you. Nothing would have been too rash for me.'

Then he kissed her, deep kisses that made her head reel, made her insides melt until she was faint with love for him.

He held her at arms' length, studied her face and said, 'We sleep in the same bed. No more silly nonsense. No more acting. We are getting married as soon as we get home. Therese and your father are making all the arrangements.'

Later she cooked the chicken for them, for they were all hungry. They had brought chocolates and fruit cake and cheeses from France and Alice found the best wines from the cellar and they laughed and talked and were deliciously light-headed when they went up to bed.

And dear little Franziska had cried when she knew they would be leaving. She would go home to her Czech family in the village, she said. She begged Alice to return one day, for the rioting and mayhem and anger of the people would soon be over. It was normal, in the middle of a revolution, for people to have no clear purpose. The new people, the real Czechoslovakian people, would make a civilized country they would be proud of.

And dear little Franzisca had lighted the stove in the main bedroom where the bear-post bed was piled with goose-down quilts and feather mattress and pillows, and precious candles had been found and placed in the pretty Bohemian glass holders all about the room.

When the house was asleep they lay together, awake and aroused, side by side. And Alice was afraid that she would hurt him if she touched his naked body, for the shoulder wound went deep and the skin around the dressing she had changed for him was puckered and red.

He slipped his good arm around her shoulder and held her. 'What are we going to tell Zita?' he said.

'We're going to tell the truth. But not until she is old enough.'

'Are we going to let everyone think she is Karl's child?' he asked.

'Oh, Freddie,' she turned to face him. 'Zita is the only child Karl could ever have. He knew she was yours. Had it not been for Zita, Karl would have died without trace. He left nothing else to mark his living. All he had to leave, he left to her. This house. Everything . . . will be Zita's one day.'

He was quiet for a moment then he said, in the serious, thoughtful voice, 'Don't be deceived, Alice. There will be nothing here for Zita. They are confiscating property, they have devalued the currency. Zita won't want to come back.'

'But we can't tell her yet, Freddie. There's Mutti and Vater – the Rineharts believe she's Karl's child.'

He smiled at her. 'We'll come to the best decision', he said, 'when we've had time to talk it through.' Then he slid his hand down from her shoulder until he was caressing her breast, teasing her, making her soften inside.

'Alice?'

'Yes.'

'Don't you want to make love to me?' he teased as he pulled her over to lie on top of him.

'I'm afraid of hurting you . . .'

But he was holding her to him, looking into her face with eyes blazing with love and need of her as she lowered herself close, close into him. Her hair was falling in a curtain around their faces as she sought his mouth and let their close hot bodies move as one, holding, giving, taking in one another's arms.

And afterwards, as they lay, warm and contented, he reached out and held her hand in the almost darkness and he whispered the words of the poem to her:

Oh, talk not to me of a name great in story;
The days of our youth are the days of our glory;
And the myrtle and ivy of sweet two-and-twenty
Are worth all your laurels though ever so plenty.

What are garlands and crowns to the brow that is wrinkled?
'Tis but as a dead-flower with May-dew besprinkled.
Then away with all such from the head that is hoary!
What care I for wreaths that can only give glory!

Oh, Fame! if I e'er took delight in thy praises,
'Twas less for the sake of thy high-sounding phrases,
Than to see the bright eyes of the dear one discover,
She thought that I was not unworthy to love her.

There chiefly I sought thee, there only I found thee;
Her glance was the best of the rays that surround thee;
When it sparkled o'er aught that was bright in my story,
I knew it was love, and I felt it was glory.

By the flickering light of the candles she saw the look

603

of love for her in his brown, glowing eyes and she lay for a moment with her hand in his before she turned to kiss his beloved face and whisper, 'I knew, Freddie. Right from the start I knew it was love.'

'And I,' he answered. Then in a warm, teasing voice he said, 'When you marry me, Alice, when you are mine for ever will you allow yourself to be called Lady Blackshaw?'

She didn't answer and he said softly, 'If you'd rather not, I won't use my title in future.'

She had a little tight lump in her throat as she heard him say those words to her. Then she whispered back, 'I will accept the title, Freddie. We can't let it drop, for if we have a son he may want to follow in his father's footsteps.'

She felt his hand warm and secure in hers in the darkness and she lifted it to her lips and said, 'And he may want to look back and be told about you . . . and me . . . and how it was when we were young. He may even be proud of us, as we were in the days of our glory.'


THE END

## PRAISE FOR THE MORNING
by Audrey Reimann

Caroline Shrigley always thought of herself as an old maid, even though she was only twenty-five years old. Her parents had died when she was young, leaving her to raise her small sister, and run the Temperance Hotel in Middlesfield, the northern town where respectability was everything. The only man who had ever courted her had been killed in the Great War, and her life had settled into a rigid routine of work, chapel, and making sure that Jane had all the advantages she had never had. And then Patrick Kennedy exploded into her life.

He was a wild, handsome, passionate Irishman. He released all the suppressed emotion and longings that Carrie had always managed to subdue. It seemed as though happiness was within her grasp – until the day she discovered that Patrick had betrayed her.

From then on she devoted herself to revenge, the pursuit of money and success, and a denial of love, even for her own daughter. But she never forgot Patrick Kennedy – and he never stopped loving her.

0 552 13670 0

# THE MOSES CHILD
by Audrey Reimann

Oliver Wainwright was sixteen when he first set eyes on Florence Mawdesley. He was hiding in the water of the lake on Sir Philip Oldfield's land – taking refuge after stealing a mallard duck.

She was standing at the water's edge, silk-gowned, sheltered by her parasol, the privileged, aristocratic granddaughter of Sir Philip Oldfield. Oliver thought he had never seen anyone so lovely.

That same day he ran away – left the estate and the life of servitude that had killed his father – and took the first steps towards his future – as a self-made cotton king, a mill owner, a man of property. It was in the mill that he met Rosie, dark, warm, beautiful, who began to cast her spell over him, even though she was a married woman.

But even as he rose to power – fighting Sir Philip Oldfield's vicious and vindictive revenge every inch of the way – he never forgot the vision of the beautiful girl at the water's edge.

0 552 13521 6

# THE SHOEMAKER'S DAUGHTER
by Iris Gower

When Hari Morgan's father died, he left her nothing but an ailing mother and the tools of his shoemaking business. But what he also passed on to his daughter was a rare and unusual gift – that of designing and making shoes that were stylish and different. One of the first to realize this was Emily Grenfell, spoilt, pettish daughter of Thomas Grenfell, one of the richest men in Swansea. Emily, who resented the beauty and courage of Hari Morgan, nonetheless was delighted with the dancing slippers she made for her debut at the Race Ball, one of the grandest events of the year. It was to be the beginning of a lifetime of friendship, hatred and rivalry between the two girls for, as Hari's business and fame began to grow, so Emily's fortune began to decline.

And between the two girls lay an even deeper tension, for Emily was about to be betrothed to her cousin, Craig Grenfell, a man who Hari could not help loving and wanting for herself, a man who finally betrayed her. From then on, Hari was determined that nothing and no-one would prevent her rise to a triumphant success.

0 552 13686 7

# A SELECTION OF FINE TITLES
# AVAILABLE FROM CORGI BOOKS

THE PRICES SHOWN BELOW WERE CORRECT AT THE TIME OF GOING TO PRESS.
HOWEVER TRANSWORLD PUBLISHERS RESERVE THE RIGHT TO SHOW NEW
RETAIL PRICES ON COVERS WHICH MAY DIFFER FROM THOSE PREVIOUSLY
ADVERTISED IN THE TEXT OR ELSEWHERE.

| | | | | |
|---|---|---|---|---|
| ☐ | 13855 X | ELLAN VANNIN | *Lyn Andrews* | £3.99 |
| ☐ | 13933 5 | THE LEAVING OF LIVERPOOL | *Lyn Andrews* | £3.99 |
| ☐ | 13718 9 | LIVERPOOL LOU | *Lyn Andrews* | £3.99 |
| ☐ | 13600 X | THE SISTERS O'DONNELL | *Lyn Andrews* | £3.99 |
| ☐ | 13482 1 | THE WHITE EMPRESS | *Lyn Andrews* | £3.99 |
| ☐ | 13289 6 | MOVING AWAY | *Louise Brindley* | £2.99 |
| ☐ | 13449 6 | THE INCONSTANT MOON | *Louise Brindley* | £3.99 |
| ☐ | 13829 0 | THE SMOKE SCREEN | *Louise Brindley* | £3.99 |
| ☐ | 13230 6 | AN EQUAL CHANCE | *Brenda Clark* | £3.99 |
| ☐ | 13690 5 | BEYOND THE WORLD | *Brenda Clark* | £4.99 |
| ☐ | 13686 7 | THE SHOEMAKER'S DAUGHTER | *Iris Gower* | £4.99 |
| ☐ | 13521 6 | THE MOSES CHILD | *Audrey Reimann* | £3.99 |
| ☐ | 13670 0 | PRAISE FOR THE MORNING | *Audrey Reimann* | £3.99 |
| ☐ | 13636 0 | CARA'S LAND | *Elvi Rhodes* | £4.99 |
| ☐ | 12607 1 | DOCTOR ROSE | *Elvi Rhodes* | £3.50 |
| ☐ | 13185 7 | THE GOLDEN GIRLS | *Elvi Rhodes* | £4.99 |
| ☐ | 13481 3 | THE HOUSE OF BONNEAU | *Elvi Rhodes* | £3.99 |
| ☐ | 13309 4 | MADELEINE | *Elvi Rhodes* | £4.99 |
| ☐ | 12367 6 | OPAL | *Elvi Rhodes* | £3.99 |
| ☐ | 12803 1 | RUTH APPLEBY | *Elvi Rhodes* | £4.99 |
| ☐ | 13738 3 | SUMMER PROMISE AND OTHER STORIES | *Elvi Rhodes* | £3.99 |
| ☐ | 13413 9 | THE QUIET WAR OF REBECCA SHELDON | *Kathleen Rowntree* | £3.99 |
| ☐ | 13557 8 | BRIEF SHINING | *Kathleen Rowntree* | £3.99 |
| ☐ | 12357 7 | A SCATTERING OF DAISIES | *Susan Sallis* | £3.99 |
| ☐ | 12579 2 | THE DAFFODILS OF NEWENT | *Susan Sallis* | £3.99 |
| ☐ | 12880 5 | BLUEBELL WINDOWS | *Susan Sallis* | £3.99 |
| ☐ | 13756 1 | AN ORDINARY WOMAN | *Susan Sallis* | £4.99 |
| ☐ | 13136 9 | ROSEMARY FOR REMEMBRANCE | *Susan Sallis* | £3.99 |
| ☐ | 13346 9 | SUMMER VISITORS | *Susan Sallis* | £3.99 |
| ☐ | 13545 3 | BY SUN AND CANDLELIGHT | *Susan Sallis* | £3.99 |
| ☐ | 13850 9 | THE BIRD OF HAPPINESS | *Sally Stewart* | £3.99 |
| ☐ | 13938 6 | A ROSE FOR EVERY MONTH | *Sally Stewart* | £3.99 |
| ☐ | 13850 9 | THE WOMEN OF PROVIDENCE | *Sally Stewart* | £3.99 |

All Corgi/Bantam Books are available at your bookshop or newsagent, or can be
ordered from the following address:
Corgi/Bantam Books,
Cash Sales Department,
P.O. Box 11, Falmouth, Cornwall TR10 9EN

UK and B.F.P.O. customers please send a cheque or postal order (no currency) and
allow £1.00 for postage and packing for the first book plus 50p for the second book
and 30p for each additional book to a maximum charge of £3.00 (7 books plus).

Overseas customers, including Eire, please allow £2.00 for postage and packing for
the first book plus £1.00 for the second book and 50p for each subsequent title
ordered.

NAME (Block Letters) ...............................................................................

ADDRESS ...............................................................................................

............................................................................................................